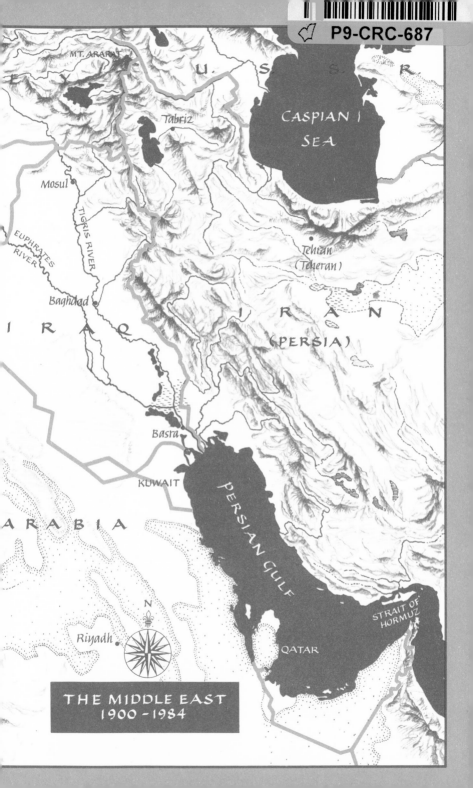

P9-CRC-687

MT. ARARAT

Tabriz

CASPIAN
SEA

U. S. S. R.

Mosul

TIGRIS RIVER

EUPHRATES
RIVER

Baghdad

Tehran
(Teheran)

I R A N
(PERSIA)

I R A Q

Basra

KUWAIT

A R A B I A

PERSIAN GULF

Riyadh

N

STRAIT OF
HORMUZ

QATAR

THE MIDDLE EAST
1900-1984

THE HAJ

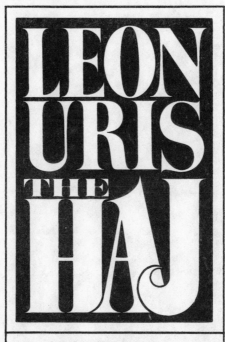

LEON URIS
THE HAJ

Doubleday & Company, Inc.
GARDEN CITY, NEW YORK
1984

DESIGNED BY LAURENCE ALEXANDER

Library of Congress Cataloging in Publication Data

Uris, Leon, 1924–
The Haj.

Sequel to: Exodus.
I. Title.
PS3541.R46H3 1984   813'.54   83–20765
ISBN 0-385-3459-8

For
MARK

In order to spend the years necessary to travel, research, and write a novel such as *The Haj*, the writer must necessarily become a self-centered creator and is apt to test the strength of his relationships. My wife, Jill, embraced this project with no less devotion than myself. She unselfishly gave everything: compassion, loyalty, love. She took care of me, often in dark and dangerous places. And importantly, she made a major contribution by her astute and wise advice during the writing. These pages could scarcely have been written without such a partner at my side.

I was already aware from writing *Trinity* that my research associate, Diane Eagle, possessed a mystical quality of understanding what I was trying to say and what the story required. *The Haj* was a ponderous challenge for any researcher. She answered by pulling a thousand and one brilliant reports. Each day when I went into battle at the typewriter, the facts in these reports were close at hand and immediate assistance was only an office away. She not only added considerably to the background and authenticity of the novel, she lightened my work load immensely. Mostly, I want to thank Diane as a buddy for her unfaltering friendship to Jill and me.

Many of the events in The Haj are a matter of history and public record. Many of the scenes were created around historical incidents and used as a backdrop for the purpose of fiction.

There may be persons alive who took part in events similar to those described in this book. It is possible, therefore, that some may be mistaken for characters in the novel.

Let me emphasize that all the characters in The Haj are the complete creation of the author, and entirely fictional.

The exceptions, of course, are the recognizable public figures who were associated historically with this period, such as David Ben-Gurion, the Mufti of Jerusalem, Abdullah, Yigal Allon, and others.

Arabic and Hebrew words often have many different spellings when translated. I have settled on the easiest and most recognizable spelling for the reader.

Young Ibrahim quietly took his place at his father's bedside, watching the old man wheeze out his final scene.

The glazed eyes of the sheik gave his son an inkling of recognition and he rallied his remaining strength. Reaching beneath the pillow, he withdrew the jeweled dagger and, trembling, handed it to Ibrahim, enacting the ancient rite of the passage of power.

"This belongs to Farouk," Ibrahim said. "He is my elder."

"Your brother is a dog with no teeth," the father rasped. "Already the others are conspiring to select a new muktar. The power must remain with us, the Soukoris," he said and thrust the dagger into his son's hand. "It is small, as weapons go," the sheik said, "but it is the weapon by which we rule our people. They know the meaning of the dagger and the courage of the man who can drive it in to the hilt."

The old sheik died and the village wailed, and true to his dying thoughts, the four other clans had selected a new muktar for Tabah, breaking the Soukori hold of a century. An hour after his father was buried, Ibrahim invited eight of the leading members of the other clans to his home. In the center of the room stood a crude wooden table. Ibrahim suddenly produced eight knives and stabbed them in a line into the planking, then pulled back his robes, revealing the jeweled dagger.

"I believe," he said, "it is time that we hold an election for the new muktar. If anyone disagrees with the continuity of the Soukori rule . . ." He left the sentence unfinished and waved an open hand at the array of knives. Ordinarily the election of a new muktar would take a thousand hours of haggling before coming to the conclusion that Ibrahim had now presented to them. This election was over within a minute, with each of the eight adversaries stopping before him one at a time, bowing, kissing his hand, and declaring his loyalty.

Ibrahim al Soukori was in his mid twenties and Muktar of Tabah, and he knew the power of the dagger in Arab life.

Part One

The Valley of Ayalon

Chapter One

I am Ishmael. I was born in Palestine during the riots of 1936. Since many things written here took place before my birth, you ask, "How could Ishmael know of them?" Take the case of my father, Ibrahim, becoming the Muktar of Tabah. In our world the repetition of stories is a way of life. Everyone eventually knows all of the tales of the past.

Other events happened here when I was not present. Aha! How could I know of these? Do not forget, my esteemed reader, that we Arabs are unusually gifted in matters of fantasy and magic. Did we not give the world *A Thousand and One Nights?*

There are times I will speak to you in my own voice. Others will speak in theirs. Our tale comes from a million suns and moons and comets and all that I cannot possibly know will reach these pages with the help of Allah and our special magic.

As a male child I was entitled to my mother's breasts for as long as I demanded them and was not weaned until my fifth birthday. Usually this signaled the boy was coming out of the kitchen, but I was small and still able to hide among the women. My mother, Hagar, was a large woman with great breasts. Not only were they filled with milk, but they gave me a place where I could nestle and feel an enormous comfort. I managed to hide from the world of men until 1944, when I was eight years of age.

One day my father, Ibrahim, sent my mother away to her own village many miles to the south. She was rarely given time off, so her sudden departure was both traumatic and ominous for me. As an infant and a young child, I lived with women who sheltered and protected me. My grandmother had raised me part of the time because my mother not only had the duties of the kitchen, the house, and the family, but she worked in the big fields and attended the plot beside the house as well. It was a few days after my grandmother died that my mother was sent away.

Fetching water had been my only chore. I had gone to the village well with my mother every day. Now she was gone. I was

greeted with taunts. The women all cackled and laughed at me.
They told me my father was going to take a second wife. That
was why my father had sent her out of the village, to spare himself her anger and humiliation. Soon my playmates joined in the
chorus of taunts and some threw stones at me.

I saw my father taking his morning stroll to the coffeehouse,
which was owned by him and my Uncle Farouk and which was
where he spent most of his day. I ran up to him and cried about
what was happening. As usual, he brushed me aside harshly,
walking on. I ran after him and tugged at his coat, a tug barely
strong enough to demand his attention. As he turned I threw my
little fist at him and said I hated him.

My father grabbed me by the arm and shook me so violently I
thought I would faint. Then he tossed me like garbage, so that I
landed in the open sewer that ran down from the top of the
village.

There I was, dressed as a girl, shrieking at the top of my lungs.
I could feel salt from my tears and snot from my nose dripping
into my mouth. I shrieked in desperation, for even at that age I
realized there was nothing I could do about my situation. There
was no way to either rebel or protest.

I have seen that little boy over and over again in refugee camps
playing in garbage dumps, being hit and shaken and taunted by
adults and family and playmates. All screaming to an unhearing
Allah.

Our Village of Tabah sat near the road to Jerusalem. My family
was of the Soukori clan, which had once belonged to the Wahhabi
Bedouin tribe. The Wahhabi were great warriors who came from
the Arabian Peninsula about two hundred and fifty years ago and
purified the region for Islam through sword and fire.

Eventually the power of the Wahhabi was broken by invading
Turkish and Egyptian armies. Many of the clans split off from the
main tribe and some migrated to Palestine. Our branch of the
tribe roamed an area between Gaza and Beersheba, crossing back
and forth from the Negev to the Sinai deserts.

Several clans, numbering over a hundred and fifty families,
moved north and settled on the land. However, we still retained
very close ties with the Wahhabi through marriage, reinforced at

festival and wedding and funeral times, and we used them as cameleers during the harvest and manure-gathering seasons.

My father, Ibrahim, was a great man who was feared and respected in the entire region. My father was not only the muktar, the head of the village, he was the agent of the landowners. Our family were sayyids, direct descendants of the Prophet Mohammed, and this gave us status above the others. In addition to Tabah, there were smaller villages of former Wahhabi Bedouin in the area and he controlled them as well. My father's power came from the fact that he ran the legal, clerical, and police apparatus and was endowed to verify the documents that spelled out the property and inheritances of the villagers. He was the only one in the area who had made the Haj, the pilgrimage to Mecca. A painting and the date over the front door of our house commemorated the glorious event.

At first he was known as Ibrahim al Soukori al Wahhabi, to denote his clan and tribe, but Arab names change with the birth of male children. Unfortunately, my parents' first two were girls and this was a small disaster. Everyone, particularly the women at the village well, whispered behind his back that he was Abu Banat, A Father of Daughters, a most terrible insult.

My father threatened to get rid of my mother, who had brought this humiliation to him. She begged for a final chance, and by Allah's will their third child was a son, my oldest brother, Kamal. After Kamal's birth my father could then assume the honorable title of Ibrahim Abu Kamal, which means "Abraham, father of Kamal."

Three more sons followed Kamal and my father basked in glory. But alas, there were three more daughters before my own birth. One of my brothers and two of my sisters died before I ever knew them. My brother died from cholera. One of my sisters died of the stomach and the other from a chest ailment. They all died before their first year. It was usual for a family of ten to lose three or more children, but my father felt particularly blessed to have four sons who survived.

My two oldest sisters were eventually contracted into marriage. They married in the Wahhabi tribe but to men from distant villages. As was the custom, they went off to live in the home of their husband's parents.

My father was only a young man, in his early twenties, when

he declared himself muktar, "the elected one." His father had been muktar and when he died there was to be a new election. The sheiks of the other four clans had agreed that the eldest among them would take over the position. However, my father disagreed and the story of his courage and greatness has been told many, many times.

Ibrahim had been born five years before the turn of the century. When he became muktar he had achieved the most exalted position in the village, for he no longer had to work. In a short time, he had three sons, one remaining daughter, and a wife, all of working age. He had the best and most of the land, collected the rents, and governed six villages. He did not even wear field shoes but shoes that others wore only on the Sabbath.

My Uncle Farouk was a slave to my father. He and my father owned the village café and store together. Uncle Farouk had been a sickly child and had been left in the kitchen to die, but as the fate of Allah would have it, he was discovered by some Christian missionaries who had a nearby settlement and they nursed him to health and also taught him to read and write. He was the only truly literate person in Tabah and my father was able to use Farouk's great powers to his personal advantage.

Ibrahim would make a perfunctory round of calls each day on his way from the house to the café, fingering his worry beads, reciting the Koran under his breath, and generally reinforcing his position. Most of the day he held court at the café, smoking his water pipe, greeting, and sincerely listening to complaints of the villagers. Mainly, he and the other men repeated stories from the past.

When my father came home each night, my mother and sister, Nada, washed his feet and he sat in an oversized chair. Just before the meal, my brothers came into the room, knelt, kissed his hand, and reported on their day's work. Uncle Farouk or some male cousins or friends were generally invited to the meal, which was eaten while sitting on the floor, and they ate with their fingers from a common plate. Later, my mother, Nada, and I ate in the kitchen from the leftovers.

My father owned the best horse in the village, a faint reminder of our Bedouin past. My next older brother, Jamil, was responsible for grooming him. Once during each phase of the moon my father rode off to settle matters in surrounding villages. He was an extraordinary sight to behold, galloping off with his special robes flowing out behind him.

Until the day I was abruptly weaned from my mother, my life had been pleasant enough. The only child left who was near my age was my sister Nada, who was two years older. I loved her very much. We were still allowed to play together because I was in the province of the women, but I knew that the day would soon come when I would be forbidden to have a friendship with a girl, even though she was my own sister.

Nada had great brown eyes and liked to tease and hug me. To this day I can feel her fingers rubbing through my hair. She took care of me, often. All the mothers worked in the fields and if there was no old grandmother to attend the children, they had to look out for themselves.

We had no toys except what we made of sticks and yarn, and until I saw the Jewish kibbutz I did not know that things like playgrounds or toy rooms or libraries even existed. Nada had made a doll of sticks and cloth that she named Ishmael, after me, and she would pretend to nurse it against her tiny nipples. I think she had her nursing fantasy because, as a girl, she had been weaned at an early age and I still had the privilege of my mother's breasts.

My mother continually tried to push me over the threshold into the room to join with the men, but I was in no hurry to leave the warmth and comfort of the women for a place I sensed was hostile.

Chapter Two

My father took as his second wife Ramiza, who was the youngest daughter of Sheik Walid Azziz, chief of the Palestinian Wahhabi Bedouin tribe. The great sheik was my father's uncle, so his new wife was also his first cousin. She was sixteen and my father almost fifty. After their wedding my mother was allowed to return to Tabah.

I never saw my mother smile again.

My father's bedroom had the only raised bedstead in the village. Everyone else slept on goatskin rugs or thin mats. The room that is usually built for a second wife had not been completed, so my father took Ramiza to his bed and ordered my mother to sleep in the adjoining room on the floor. There was an opening atop the door between the two rooms to allow the breezes to flow through the house, so everything that happened in the bedroom could clearly be heard in the next room.

I slept with my mother, folded up in her arms, my head between her breasts. When my father and Ramiza made love every night, my mother lay awake, only a few feet from them, forced to listen to them have sex, sometimes half the night long. When my father kissed Ramiza and groaned and spoke words of endearment to her, my mother's massive body convulsed with pain. I could feel her fingers claw at me unconsciously and hear her stifled sobs and sometimes I could feel her tears. And when I wept as well, she soothed me by stroking my genitals.

After many, many nights, when my father's initial passion for Ramiza had been spent, he invited my mother to return to his bed. But something had left my mother. She was cold to him and he could no longer arouse her. This infuriated him. In anger, he virtually cast her out of the house.

The Village of Tabah was a two-hour donkey ride to the town of Ramle and a three-hour ride to Lydda. Each town had two market days a week and the family owned a stall in the marketplace. Until my father took his new wife, my second brother, Omar, tended the stalls. Now Hagar, my mother, was ordered to

Ramle and Lydda four days a week to sell our surplus produce. She started out after the morning prayer at sunrise and returned very late in the evening after dark.

Hagar was one of the two best dayas, or midwives, in the village. She was greatly respected as a keeper of the formulas of herbs and medicines. These days when she went to the village water well or the communal ovens, there was snickering behind her back and cruel insults in passing.

As in any society where women are the chattel of men, they seek the path of revenge through their sons, and my mother selected me. Four days a week I rode on the donkey cart with her to Ramle and Lydda.

It was in the stall at the Lydda bazaar that I first saw someone use an abacus, a wooden frame holding sliding beads for adding and subtracting. The man was a leather merchant, a maker and mender of harnesses, and he allowed me to enter and play in his booth. We became friends and together we fashioned an abacus like his by using prayer beads. Before I was nine I could count to infinity and became faster than the merchant in addition and subtraction.

"Learn to count," my mother had been saying repeatedly.

At first I didn't realize what she meant, but she pressed me to learn to read and write as well. The leather merchant was semiliterate and helped me greatly, but soon I surpassed him again. After a time I could read all the labels on all the crates in the entire bazaar. Then I began to learn words in the newspapers we used for wrappers.

When I was free to play at home, Hagar ordered me to count all the houses in Tabah, all the orchards, and learn who farmed each field. After that she dropped me off in the outlying villages where my father collected rents and she told me to count their houses and fields as well. A family could own or sharecrop as many as ten or fifteen separate plots scattered from one end of the village's land to the other. With continued intermarriages, dowries of land to new brides, older people dying off, and dividing the land among many sons, it was extremely difficult to have an accurate record of who farmed what. Since most of the land was sharecropped, the farmers always tried to work an extra plot that was not accounted for or in other ways tried to cheat on their rent and taxes.

My father was barely literate himself and unable to contend with all the official documents, with their adornments of stamps and seals that spelled out boundaries, water rights, inheritances, and taxes. Uncle Farouk, who was partners with my father in the village store, the khan, and the coffeehouse, was far better able to cope with the mysteries of the documents. Farouk was also the village imam, the priest, and keeper of the official records for my father. My father didn't fully trust him and so he sent my oldest brother, Kamal, to school in Ramle as a precaution.

When my father collected the rents, he turned them over to the great landholder Fawzi Effendi Kabir, who lived in Damascus and who visited the Palestine district once a year to collect.

My mother had always suspected that Kamal and Uncle Farouk were working together to cheat my father, who got a percentage of the Effendi's rents as his agent.

When I had made my secret count of all the fields of the area, my mother pushed me out of the kitchen and told me to stick to my father like his shadow. At first I was fearful. Almost every time I slipped alongside him he would curse me off and other times he seized my arm and shook it or he would strike me. It was not that Ibrahim hated me or treated me any worse than he treated my brothers. Arab men can be very affectionate to their sons when they are little and dressed as girls and living with the women. But once they cross the threshold into the man's world they are generally ignored by their fathers. The relationship from then on is centered on obedience: complete, absolute, unquestioning obedience. It is the father's privilege. For this he allows his sons to work his fields for their living and when they take a bride, she comes into the father's house.

The father must be alert, too, that his sons are not cheating him, and so the tradition of paternal indifference is a way of life. In order to vent frustrations, male children have full leave to boss around all the females, even their own mothers, and they are allowed to slap around their younger brothers. By the time I was four I had already learned to order my grandmother around, and on occasion I would assert my male rights over Nada and even my mother.

The more my father ran me off, the more my mother pushed me back. I walked alongside my father so often that after a time he simply tired of my persistence and accepted my presence.

One day I summoned the courage to confront him. I told him that I had learned to count and read and write a little and that I wanted to go to school in Ramle. As the youngest son, I was due to become the goatherd in a few years and that was the lowest job in the family. He scoffed at the idea.

"Your brother Kamal knows how to read and write. Therefore it is not necessary for you. You will tend the goat flock by your next birthday and the rest of your life is already predestined. When you take a wife, someday, you will remain in my house with your own room."

This seemed final. I drew the deepest breath I had. "Father, I know something," I blurted out.

"What do you mean, you know something, Ishmael?"

"Something you should also know. A reason I should go to school in Ramle."

"Stop playing riddles with me!"

"There are nine hundred and sixty-two separate parcels of land in Tabah," I gasped out, nearly choking on my fear. "There are eight hundred and twenty parcels in the other five villages. These do not count the communal land that is farmed together."

Ibrahim's face grew somber, a hint that he was grasping my message. I controlled my trembling. . . . "In the account books that Kamal keeps, there are only nine hundred and ten listed for Tabah and eight hundred for the other villages."

I braced myself as I watched his face grow crimson. "You are certain of this, Ishmael."

"As Allah is my judge."

Ibrahim grunted and rocked back and forth in his large chair. He beckoned me to come close to him with a wiggle of his forefinger. I almost bit through my lip with fear. "What does it all add up to?" he asked.

"Kamal and Uncle Farouk are collecting rents for seventy-two parcels for themselves."

Ibrahim grunted again, reached out, and patted my head. I'll never forget it, for it was the first time he had done so since time began. He patted my face softly where he had slapped it so many times before.

"Will you let me go to school?"

"Yes, Ishmael. You go to school and learn. But you are never to

speak about this to another living soul or I'll cut your fingers off
and boil them. Do you understand?"

"Yes, Father."

It happened so fast I had no time to explain or even to flee.
Kamal, who was nineteen, seized me from behind in the barn and
flung me down, leaped on me and choked me and slammed my
head against the ground.

"You dog!" he screamed. "I'll kill you!" I kicked as hard as I
could, three times, four, five. He bellowed in pain, released me,
and doubled up on his knees. I scrambled to my feet and seized a
pitchfork. Kamal crawled to his feet, still doubled over, and
lunged at me. I jabbed out and hit him in the chest and he
screamed again, then staggered around the barn, careening off the
stalls. He found another pitchfork and menaced toward me deliberately.

"Dog!" he hissed.

"Kamal!"

He turned as our mother entered. "Do not touch Ishmael!"

"What do you know, crazy old woman! You sow! Ibrahim does
not even sleep with you!"

"He has called me to his bed tonight," she said calmly. "I will
have some interesting things to tell him."

Kamal had never been known as much of a fighter among those
of his own age and size. He had been able to defend himself only
because he was the muktar's son and could read and write. He
thought it over for only an instant, then dropped the pitchfork.

"You will never touch Ishmael again," my mother repeated.
She took the pitchfork from my hands, looked at us, one to the
other. "Never again," she repeated, then left.

"A day will come," Kamal said.

"We do not have to be enemies," I said. "There are still thirty
parcels I have not told Father about. If we go in on this together, I
will want half."

"It is very early for you to be playing such games, Ishmael," he
said.

"I want half. You will give my half to Mother."

"What about Uncle Farouk?"

"It must come from your half. Uncle Farouk had better be

careful because Father is ready to throw him out of the village.
Well, do you agree or not?"

Fuming, he shook his head in agreement and left.

When my mother and I slept together again in a few nights she
stroked my head and kissed my face a hundred times over and
cried of how proud she was of me.

So before I was nine I had learned the basic canon of Arab life.
It was me against my brother; me and my brother against our
father; my family against my cousins and the clan; the clan
against the tribe; and the tribe against the world. And all of us
against the infidel.

Chapter Three

"Sun, stand thou still at Gibeon; and thou, Moon, in the Valley of Ayalon." Thus, Joshua requested the light by which to smite his enemies.

The Village of Tabah occupies a small but strategic knoll in Ayalon, which has been described as both a valley and a plain. A German archaeological dig before the First World War determined that remnants of civilized man on this hillock dated back over four thousand years. If one were to come from the sea from Jaffa moving south and east toward Jerusalem, he would enter the plain through the twin guardian cities of Ramle and Lydda, where St. George the dragon slayer allegedly held court.

Ten miles into the plain one would come upon the knoll where the Village of Tabah stands sentinel as the gateway to Jerusalem. Beyond Tabah the road takes on a tortuous uphill route, snaking along the bed of a steep ravine known as the Bab el Wad. The Bab el Wad squirms a dozen miles to the outskirts of Jerusalem.

Before Joshua's battle, this was ancient Canaan, a land bridge between the powers of the Fertile Crescent Mesopotamia and Egypt. Then, as today, the land of Canaan lay like a morsel between the jaws of a crocodile, a passageway for invading armies. Waves of Semitic tribes drifted or swarmed into Canaan and settled to create a prebiblical civilization of city-states that were eventually conquered and absorbed by the nomadic Hebrew tribes.

After Joshua, the knoll of Tabah bore witness to the scourging armies of Assyria and Babylon, of Egypt and Persia, of Greece and Rome. It was the pale of the ill-fated Hebrew Tribe of Dan and the home of the errant Jewish judge, Samson. It knew the wheels of the Philistine chariot all too well.

It saw the great Jewish revolt against the Greeks, and here Judah, "the Hammerer," assembled his Maccabees for the assault to liberate Jerusalem.

It is said that Mohammed stopped at the knoll on his legendary overnight journey from Mecca to Jerusalem and back, riding his mythical horse, el-Buraq, which had the face of a woman, the tail of a peacock, and could gallop in a single stride as far as the eye could see. Mohammed, any villager will tell you, leaped from the knoll at Tabah and landed in Jerusalem.

Mohammed was followed to this place by the armies that swept out of the desert under the banner of Islam to evict the Christians from the Holy Land.

And Richard the Lion-Heart encamped here before his disastrous march to Jerusalem that ended his Crusade in a shambles.

The knoll of Tabah witnessed the British legions fighting their way to Jerusalem in the First World War.

Between those times, millions of pairs of feet of devout Jews, Christians, and Moslems passed here on their pilgrimage. Insofar as the pageant of history goes, the Village of Tabah rested on a hill that was.

The most recent of the captains of conquest were the Ottomans, who stormed out of Turkey to devour the Middle East in the sixteenth century and drew a curtain of darkness over the region for four hundred years.

Under the Ottomans, the Holy Land lay gasping, the rocks of her fields protruding like the baked bones of a monolithic mastodon, or from mucky, diseased swamp. As a minor backwater district of the Syrian province, Palestine had been devalued to bastardy and orphanhood. It had no status except dim echoes of its past. And Jerusalem, wrote the travelers of the day, was reduced to sackcloth and ashes.

Total cruelty, total corruption, and pernicious feudalism spelled out the infamous rule of the Turks. A few influential Palestinian Arab families did the dirty business for the Ottomans. One of these was the Kabir family, which was rewarded for its collaboration by large land grants in the Palestine district. One of its holdings covered a good part of the Valley of Ayalon.

In the eighteenth century the Kabirs took over several farming villages and peopled them with illiterate, impoverished, land-hungry Arab peasants, then proceeded to suck them dry. Tabah was the central village, with smaller ones scattered about the valley. The Kabirs had long abandoned permanent residence in the desolation of Palestine for Damascus, from which the Syrian province was governed. As landed gentry, they wintered in Spain and summered in London. They were known at the roulette tables of Europe and were frequent guests of the sultans of Istanbul.

Neither the Ottomans nor the Kabirs put anything into the land for centuries. Neither schools nor roads, neither hospitals nor new farming methods. Under the burden of a classic serf-landowner formulation, revenues began to dry up as villages collapsed in defeat. The stone-poor fellahin who worked the land were fleeced by day by the Turks, marauded by the Bedouin by night, and cheated by owners.

By 1800 the Kabir holdings in the Valley of Ayalon were severely in trouble. Villagers were constantly fleeing their own birth-to-death debts and the debts of their fathers. Drought, pestilence, and disease added to a misery that had brought the entire Holy Land to the brink of collapse.

Tabah had been a particular feasting ground for the Bedouin. The principal raiders were of the Wahhabis, who roamed away from their normal pasturages and fields around Gaza. They came in at the harvest time, looted the fields, prowled the snake road, the Bab el Wad, and robbed the pilgrims.

The Kabir family determined that the Soukori clan, of the Wahhabis, were the chief offenders. Around 1800 the head of the Kabir family sought out the sheik of the Soukori Bedouin and made him an offer that would change his stature from privation to position. If the Soukoris agreed to occupy Tabah, their sheik would become the land agent for all the Kabir properties in the valley. It was a none too subtle bribe that would supply the human fodder to work the land. A strong sheik could keep his people in place and assure the Kabirs their rents. Moreover, it would ensure that no further Bedouin raids would terrorize the valley.

The offer brought a major disruption to the Wahhabi tribe. For a clan of Bedouin to give up their nomadic ways was akin to giving up their freedom. The Bedouin had always considered himself the elite of the Arabs, the true Arab. The Bedouin had been the original driving force behind Islam, for it was their men who had filled the ranks of Mohammed's first armies and spearheaded the Moslem conquests.

The Bedouin owed no taxes, paid no landlord, recognized no borders. The Arabian Peninsula, from which he sprang, had remained remote and beyond the grasp of the early conquests of Egypt and Rome. In the punishing desert a cruel culture evolved that matched the brutal dictates of nature. While the world of progress passed him by, the Bedouin survived largely by plundering the vulnerable. Strong sheiks with no more compassion than the blistering sun showed little mercy to the weak. A system of absolute social order emerged, so that each man had a specific place in the tribe into which he was locked from birth to death. The only way to rise was to destroy the man above and dominate the men below. The demands of survival left no room for convocations of Bedouin to debate democratic principles, for the law of the desert was absolute.

The Bedouin was thief, assassin, and raider, and hard labor was immoral. Despite his raggedness and destitution, the Bedouin remained the Arab ideal, for he was the man with stars for a roof. The city Arab was considered of a lower order and the fellah who tilled the soil in the villages was the lowest of them all.

It was small wonder that when a strong sheik of the Soukori clan moved to the Village of Tabah, a fifty-year feud with the main Wahhabi tribe ensued. After five decades of intermittent bloodshed, the rift healed when other clans of the Wahhabi moved into Ayalon villages, opting for a less nomadic existence. If the scars of desert feuds never entirely heal, they were made more palatable by intertribal marriages and periodic reuniting to fight the threat of another tribe or the infidel.

The sheiks of the Soukori clan had succeeded one another as the muktars of Tabah for well over a hundred years.

1924

No sooner had Ibrahim ensconced himself at the café for the daily ritual of holding court, than his brother Farouk came in screaming.

"The Jews are coming!" he cried.

In a moment the village street was flooded with running, chattering people who all followed Ibrahim up to the high point of the knoll, from which they could look down the highway.

Ibrahim was handed a pair of field glasses belonging to one of the villagers who had fought in the Turkish Army. What he saw on the road was a line of huge flatbed trucks filled with materials such as barbed wire, shovels, fence posts, sacks of dried foods, and farming equipment. He had Farouk count them. There were twenty men and six women. The men were dressed in the blue of

Jewish collective farmers. The women's legs were naked to the thighs, a disgusting sight.

Another dozen men, whom Ibrahim had seen roaming through on occasion, were with them. These were on horseback and had rifles and crossed bandoliers of ammunition slung over their shoulders. They wore pale green uniforms, but several had Arab headdresses. Ibrahim knew them to be Shomer, the Jewish watchmen.

Then the convoy turned off the highway away from Tabah into an area that was swamp and marshland. One of the Jews had a megaphone and directed the others. In moments Jews with surveying instruments were staking out a square on some of the drier land. They were obviously in haste to lay out a defensive perimeter of barbed wire.

Ibrahim handed the field glasses to Farouk and walked away. "Have the elders come to the café," he said softly. In a matter of moments they had been gleaned from the fields and their places of rest.

"What do you think it means?"

"What do you see? That's what it means, you fool. The Jews are intending to build a settlement across the road."

"In the swamp?"

"But it is worthless land, Ibrahim."

"Do you think they have purchased the land?"

"Yes," Ibrahim answered, "they always do everything legally. But if we do not stop them here, there won't be an Arab village left in this valley. Effendi Kabir will sell them everything. We must give them a reception tonight."

There was unanimous agreement. A young boy pushed his way through the wall of gathered villagers and made his way excitedly to the muktar's table.

"A Jew is coming on a horse!" he cried.

Everyone looked to Ibrahim. He stood menacingly and the crowd parted before him. With a wave of the hand he commanded everyone to stand fast and made his way into the square alone.

In a moment a solitary rider on a magnificent, dappled Arabian mount trotted in. The man was of medium build, with a neat blond beard and blue eyes. He seemed rather old to be a Shomer; perhaps he had seen forty years. He bore no arms. Ibrahim understood immediately that the rider knew Arab custom, for once he had entered the village, the village was honor-bound to protect him, even if he was a Jew. He dismounted as smartly as he had handled his horse and tethered it near the well and walked toward Ibrahim with a hand extended.

Ibrahim held up his hand for the man to stop a distance away from him.

"I am Gideon Asch," the man said in perfect Arabic. "We have purchased several thousand dunams of land over the road from the Effendi Kabir. We hope to be able to make a farm out of it. I take it you are the muktar?"

"I am the muktar," Ibrahim said icily as everyone behind him inched in. Ibrahim was extremely quick in sizing up a man's courage. The Shomer had a reputation for bravery and this one obviously had his share. Ibrahim was now obliged to show his own courage and perform with the might of a fearless muktar.

"They are nice young people over there," the man called Gideon Asch continued, "and we hope that we all become good neighbors."

In the silence that followed, the men began to encircle the Jew, cutting him off from his horse and then, as if on a signal, everyone began shouting and shaking their fists at him at once. Ibrahim held up his hand again for silence.

"Our water truck was delayed," Gideon continued. "I was hoping we could draw some from your well."

"Not one drop," Ibrahim hissed.

This brought on a mixture of laughter and renewed shouting. The Jew walked toward Ibrahim and only stopped when he was so close their noses nearly touched.

"You will have to change your minds," Gideon said, "and the sooner you do, the better for all of us." Having struck everyone silent, he spun around and walked right at the men who enclosed him. They separated. He took his horse by the reins and led it to the well and allowed it to drink, then dunked his own face in it. Everyone looked to Ibrahim, confused, as the Jew mounted.

"You are not welcome," Ibrahim shouted, shaking a fist. "If you enter Tabah again, you will not have our sanctuary. In fact, I'll cut off your balls and stick them in your eyes."

Then the Jew did an astonishing thing. He laughed, saluted in a mock manner, and spurred off.

Ibrahim knew instantly that his people were in for serious trouble. The Gideon person was reckless, fearless. Ibrahim didn't like it. He had heard that the Shomer were as clever and brave as Bedouin. But Ibrahim was the Muktar of Tabah and he had absolutely no choice but to play out the game. If he didn't, they would replace him. Well, he would order an attack, and then let nature take its course.

Chapter Four

Gideon Asch had not ridden into Tabah simply out of nowhere. He, too, was a long-standing partner in the history of modern Palestine.

Some Jews had been able to find their first taste of true equality by immigration to America; however, most Jews in nineteenth-century Europe remained locked into a repetitious cycle of anguish. They looked, as they always had, to a return to Palestine. This longing had never left their daily prayer and was reemphasized in the yearly Yom Kippur greeting, "Next year in Jerusalem."

Into the weary land of Palestine there came a sudden stir. By hook, by crook, and by bribery, religious Jews were entering Palestine in great numbers. For the most part they were poverty-stricken Hassidim fleeing centuries of terror and persecution at the hands of the Russians and Poles. In the mid-1800s they turned Jerusalem into a Jewish majority, which it has remained ever since. They settled in the other holy cities of Hebron, Safed, and Tiberias to study, pray, and await the Messiah, and lived off Jewish world charity.

These numbers were followed by ordinary Jews of a pioneering nature also taking flight from the horrors of Christian Europe. With the help of wealthy philanthropists this second wave established a number of farming villages. Their success was minimal, for to Jews, unable to own land in most countries, farming was a strange and unknown occupation.

The Ottoman court in Constantinople, later Istanbul, looked upon this new Jewish settlement of the Palestine district with favor, for it meant an infusion of money: more taxes to collect, more bribes to elicit. But the Jews brought some things with them that had been sorely lacking: tenacity, vitality, and a love and longing for the Promised Land. They came to this backwater Palestine district, which was neither fish nor fowl, neither Syrian nor Ottoman, neither Arab nor Jewish, but a no-man's-land, hemorrhaging to death. The great return of the Jews represented a last thin thread of hope for them as well as for Palestine itself.

In the year 1882 Sarah and Samuel Asch emigrated from Romania with a group of other young people under the auspices of a foundation established by the Rothschild family. They went north into the Galilee and took over a settlement, Rosh Pinna, that had been abandoned by Hassidim who had been forced out by the Bedouin.

By using Arab guards and a great deal of Arab labor, Rosh Pinna held on but never fully prospered. The settlement teetered, hitting and missing with experimental crops, suffering from isolation and constant marauding. Baron Edmond de Rothschild sent experts from his French farms, but they failed because of an ill-conceived attempt to transplant a European type of peasantry.

In 1884 Sarah and Samuel had a son, one of the first Jewish children born in that part of the Galilee since ancient times. From the moment of his birth, Gideon Asch was to become the future.

After the turn of the century, on the heels of terrible and massive Russian and Polish pogroms, a new breed of Jews began finding their way to Palestine. They came out of the ghettos in organized groups, intensely bound to the ideal that only through personal sacrifice and Jewish labor could Palestine be redeemed.

Absentee Arab landowners were only too happy to dump useless acreage on them for outrageous prices. In the Valley of Jezreel, in the Galilee, on the Plains of Sharon, in the Valley of Ayalon, and on that ancient coastal route of the Via Maris dozens of collective Jewish settlements called kibbutzim took on the chore, and the sweet voice of springtime was once again heard in Palestine. The desolate, desperate land, whose fields had been raped, feudalized, and abandoned by Ottoman and Arab, were now being brought back to life. Festering malarial swamp, unmerciful rock, desert, and denuded earth gave way to carpets of green, and the energy of building was heard and millions of trees grew where none had grown for centuries. A blossoming of culture and progress erupted from Jerusalem. North of the ancient port of Jaffa a new Jewish city sprang out of the sand dunes: Tel Aviv, the Hill of Spring.

Their cleavage from the past brought on all kinds of changes for the Jews. An entire new social concept emerged from the kibbutz, where one came as close to complete communal living as could be humanly conceived. One of these changes was the concept that the Jews be able to defend themselves. In the beginning a small corps of Jewish horsemen roamed from settlement to settlement, putting down trouble. These were the watchmen, the Shomer. They took on the language, knew the habits, and often looked like Arabs themselves.

By 1900, when Gideon Asch was sixteen, he had become caught up in the new Jewish idealism and was among the Shomer protecting kibbutzim and other types of settlements in the Galilee.

Gideon first impressed the Bedouin by his ability as a horseman and enhanced his reputation by regularly beating the Bedouin champions in races and competitions.

He left the relative comforts of Rosh Pinna to live on the move. In the early years of the new century, Gideon commanded a roving unit of a dozen Shomer who went out with the pioneers as they established settlements, often in remote and isolated places and often in the midst of hostile Arab and Bedouin populations. The Shomer were there on that first crucial night to beat off the inevitable Arab attack and Gideon stayed on to establish defenses. He moved fearlessly among the Arabs in an attempt to befriend them. When one settlement was secure, he moved to the next.

Although he was in an adversary position, the respect grew between Gideon and the Arabs, particularly the Bedouin. He saw them as a continuation of the People of the Book. Often as he rode alone through the Galilee, it was three thousand years ago and he might have been one of Solomon's captains coming upon a Canaanite village. Sensing that he had no fear of them, many Arabs developed a strange loyalty toward him. Whether in a muktar's village home or in the tent of a sheik, the blue-eyed horseman was entirely at home.

Gideon knew many Arab women. Of course this was dangerous for him, but he was young and reckless and, above all, entirely discreet. While no Arab man ever knew or suspected, Gideon had a fairly large contingent of well-wishers among the women all over the Galilee.

How could such a thing happen? Well, it is a known truth that jails were built for men, and few Arab villages of any size did not have two or three of their members serving a sentence, generally for stealing, smuggling, or a knifing. As often as not, they left a wife a few months pregnant. There were others, widows and poor souls unable to bear children. These were safe.

Every village had a nearby cave or hiding place where Gideon would go out to rest and soon be "found," frequently a half a dozen times a day. He had the strength of youth. They were very natural with him and for the moment seemed released from the eternal shadow of shame. He seldom failed to ride off content and they seldom failed to giggle and to smile inwardly as they watched out of the corner of an eye as Gideon galloped away.

By the onset of the First World War, Britain and France were casting an envious eye on Turkish-held territories in the Middle East. The two emerging international imperial powers saw the region as a crossroads. Key to that power was the securing of the Suez Canal. British control stopped at Egypt and at the Canal itself. Turkish control began on the opposite bank in the Sinai and Palestine. That the Sinai was to become a battlefield was predestined.

In Turkish-held Palestine, Jewish aspirations for a national homeland had been growing rapidly and had gained the support of world Jewry and the attention of the world's capitals. Although it was perilous for the Jews of Palestine to stand against the Turks, they did so en masse, by enlisting in the British Army. In order to lock world Jewry into the Allied cause, the British foreign secretary issued the Balfour Declaration, favoring the establishment of the homeland in Palestine. The Balfour Declaration was later canonized into international law and recognized by the entire world, save the Arabs. By the eve of the First World War, the Arabs had formulated a nationalism of their own, to commence when the yoke of the Ottomans could be shaken.

British Intelligence agents slipped into Palestine to set up espionage networks in advance of their armies and to find men to engage in highly specialized work.

Gideon Asch was secretly commissioned as a lieutenant in the British Army; his mission was to go into the Negev and Sinai deserts to chart the wadis, the water holes, the sparse patches of shade, the sheer passes—all for the coming battle against the Turks. Asch was born a desert rat, able to disappear among the Bedouin and sink deeply into the vast brooding reaches of the

wildernesses of Zin and Paran, where Moses and the Hebrew
Tribes had wandered for forty biblical years. He followed those
routes of the Bible through the parched dry beds, piecing bits and
clues together of how one can survive and travel in such a landscape. His blue eyes would turn to slits under the blinding glare
and his fair skin would become sand-pocked and leathery.

He became a friend of the Wahhabi tribe and its sheik, Walid
Azziz, and he roamed for weeks with their legendary tracker,
Nabil.

One day, toward evening, Nabil and Gideon came upon a small
clump of scrub oak in an otherwise bleak desert terrain. A lone
Bedouin sat by the scrub, making a covering tent over his head
with his robes. Alongside the Bedouin was a clay pitcher of water
and some stale bread.

Nabil called to him, then approached the Bedouin, who was in
a semi-trance from the glaring heat. They spoke, and he returned
to Gideon.

"Who is he, Nabil?" Gideon asked.

"His name is Mustafa. He is of the Sulikan tribe."

"Why does he just sit there?"

"He says he is waiting for a friend. He said his friend told him
he would be coming through this way."

"How long has he been sitting?"

"Several times around the sun."

"Doesn't he know when his friend will come?"

"He said sooner or later."

"Do you mean he just sits, day after day, not knowing?"

"He knows his friend will come. When his friend comes is not
important. He has nothing else to do."

Just before eventide, Nabil sniffed out a camel caravan. He
rode his mount in circles with seeming aimlessness until he
picked up tracks. Nabil dismounted and placed his nose and his
lips on the ground in the tracks.

"They passed here not too long a time ago," Nabil said.

"How long?"

"Not long."

"A few hours?"

"Perhaps."

"Many hours?"

"Perhaps."

"Three, four, five hours?"

"Perhaps."

"Enough time for the sun to come up and down?"

"No, not that long a time."

"How many camels do you make out?"

"Several."

"Five?"

"Perhaps."

"Fifty?"

"Perhaps. The tracks are deep. They are heavily loaded."

"Where will they be going?"

Nabil squinted around the horizon. "There," he pointed. "A water hole belonging to the Sulikans. They must be Sulikans or allies of the Sulikans."

Gideon studied his map for a nearby water hole. It showed none.

"How far away is the water?"

"Not far."

"One day? Two days?"

"Perhaps."

"How many miles?"

"Miles? Oh, miles." Nabil tugged at his ear. "Four hundred miles."

"No, dammit. It can't be. How many times for the sun to come up and down before we reach it?"

"When the sun rises here until it crosses to there," Nabil said, sweeping his hand in a heavenward arc.

As the fire died, Nabil recited poetry while Gideon lay concentrating on the sky and the darting specks of comets. It was this kind of moment that made the desert real. Gideon was all of them from the beginning of time. He was Moses and Abraham looking up to the same sky, pondering man's earliest mysteries and begging for answers to the puzzlement of the universe.

> *"I was the jackal who could prey at the edge*
> *of the camp.*
> *I was a great horse who raced Mohammed's*
> *mighty mount.*

I was a camel, the first in a line of many.
I was all who looked at the stupid two-legged
beast called man and saw him as stupid.
I lived like a king in my own wild ways,
and they struggled."

Nabil stopped short and cocked his head. "Listen," he said. "I hear nothing."

It took several moments for the breeze to carry the sounds to him. "How far are they," Gideon asked, "and how many?"

"Why must you always ask things for which there are no answers, Gideon?"

"Well, suppose they were an enemy. If I knew how many of them there were and how far away they were, I would know how to get ready."

"What difference how far?" the Bedouin said. "In the desert you must always be ready and how many will be, will be. You can't change their numbers." He listened and reckoned there were many camels and that they had reached the water hole.

"When the sun comes up we will reach the water hole," Nabil said. "Do not go and drink from it. We move toward it slowly. Then we sit on the edge and hold the horses so they do not drink. They will be watching us from afar, and if we drink without permission they will shoot. After a time they will appear. They will tolerate me as a Wahhabi, but they will like you very much because of the strange color of your hair and eyes. Then, they will invite us to drink."

Three days later they retraced their tracks and the Bedouin named Mustafa was still sitting under the shade of his robe waiting for his friend.

After four hundred years of Ottoman misrule the feeling of the Arabs toward the Turks was one of oppressed to oppressor despite the fact that they were fellow Moslems. Clandestine Arab movements were afoot against the Turks as the war entered the region.

The key personality among Arab dissidents was Sharif Husain, head of the Hashemite clan from the Hejaz sector of the Arabian Peninsula. The Hejaz held a coastline of nearly a thousand miles

along the Red Sea that connected to the vital British lifeline of the
Suez Canal. The Hashemites, who were direct descendants of
Mohammed, had been accorded the honorary position of "keeper
of the holy places" of Medina and of Mecca, with Islam's most
sacred shrine, the Ka'aba.

The British game was to try to lure the Hashemites into a
rebellion against the Turks, and thus Arab nationalism was born.
Sharif Husain entered into a correspondence with the British
high commissioner in Egypt to determine the price for an Arab
rebellion.

The British led Sharif Husain to believe he would be made
king of a Greater Arab Nation in exchange for his co-operation.
The letters were a sham. The British and their French allies secretly had other ideas for the future of Arab lands.

On May 9, 1916, the British and French entered into a clandestine treaty on how they intended to carve up the region. The
treaty was the Sykes-Picot, named for the negotiators. Always
described as infamous, the treaty ignored both Jewish aspirations
and Sharif Husain's personal ambitions. And so Palestine became
the "twice promised land."

To pay the passage for their aspirations and the promise of the
Balfour Declaration, the Jews of Palestine supplied a Jewish Le-
gion to the British Army. One of these units, the Zion Mule
Corps, engaged in fierce combat at Gallipoli.

On the Arab side, Sharif Husain and his sons promoted some
effective guerrilla sabotage on the Trans-Jordan rail line, the Hejaz Railroad, a vital Turkish route. This Arab "revolt" of a few
thousand men was led and later glorified by the British officer
T. E. Lawrence.

Sharif Husain modestly declared himself King of the Arabs, a
title reduced by the British to King of the Hejaz. Later, Husain's
son Faisal entered Damascus and had himself proclaimed King of
Syria, a title that he believed would automatically include the
Palestine district.

By Christmas of 1917 British forces under General Allenby had
conquered Jerusalem, and both Arab and Jew went to the allies to
collect their IOUs.

Faisal wanted a large Jewish settlement in Palestine, so long as
he ruled it, just as the Turks had wanted it for the Jewish infusion

of money and progress. But the French grabbed off Syria and
booted Faisal out. No longer King of Syria, Faisal reversed himself and condemned the Jewish settlement of Palestine.

In the end, the British were to commit a series of perfidious
acts that not only denied Jewish and Arab claims but stole the
Palestine district away from their French allies.

The British arranged for themselves to rule Palestine through a
mandate of the League of Nations. After a series of international
conferences and treaties the British Mandate was bound by law to
honor the Balfour Declaration and a Jewish homeland. However,
the war was done and Palestine's location as a flank on the Suez
Canal was more important to them than honoring the promise to
the Jews. When in the early 1920s oil was discovered on the Persian Gulf and British interests increased, they drifted further
away from their commitment.

The eastern side of the Jordan River held a vast area of this
Palestine Mandate that was inhabited mostly by Bedouin. The
British, to protect their interests, created a puppet state called
Trans-Jordan. This area consisted of 75 percent of the land mass
of the Palestine Mandate. Before 1921 there was no such thing as
a Jordanian people or nation. They were all Palestinians. The
Jordanians were an invention of the British Colonial Office.

In order to temper the Arab thirst for nationalism, the British
threw them a couple of bones. Faisal, the deposed King of Syria,
was made a puppet King of Iraq, ruling under British direction.

As for their new colony of Trans-Jordan, the British reached
down into the Hejaz once again and plucked up Abdullah, another of the sharif's sons, and declared him Emir of Trans-Jordan.
As Hashemites from the Arabian Peninsula, both Abdullah and
Faisal were strangers in the lands they now ruled under British
direction.

As for the Sharif of Mecca, who had envisioned himself ruler of
a nation that stretched from the Red Sea to the Persian Gulf, and
included Iraq, Syria, Palestine, the Sinai, Lebanon, and the Arabian Peninsula . . . he ended up with nothing and fled into exile
when the conquering Saudi family ran him out of the Hejaz.

The British, who had lied to Arab, Jew, and their own French
allies and who had created a phony kingdom in Trans-Jordan,
now moved into the Palestine Mandate. Palestine had suffered
terribly during the First World War. Twenty thousand in Jerusa-

lem alone had died of hunger and disease. At first the freedom from Turkish corruption came like a breath of pure air under British administration. That was not to last.

The future of the mandate was spelled out early. A new force arose, the Heusseini clan, an old and powerful Palestine family. They were led by Haj Amin al Heusseini, a Moslem fanatic. Riots broke out in the early 1920s against further Jewish immigration. So vile was the bigotry behind the riots and so obvious was Haj Amin's attempt to take over Palestine that the British forced him to flee and sentenced him to fifteen years *in absentia*.

For Gideon Asch, a decorated British officer, a new era had come. The problems of protection had increased manyfold in the wake of the Arab riots. The Shomer were no longer of sufficient strength to control the situation. In Jerusalem a Jewish Agency governed its own population in Palestine and quietly went about the business of creating a defense force. Based on the principle that every settlement should be able to defend itself—the Haganah, a semi-legal, semi-underground army emerged in the early 1970s.

Gideon was called up to Jerusalem and asked to take over the building of the Haganah force in the Valley of Ayalon. For three decades he had been a wanderer on horseback. Now was the time to settle. He agreed to the assignment and chose to join a new kibbutz as a permanent member. The kibbutz was to be called Shemesh, which meant "sun," for this was the place where Joshua had beseeched the Lord to make the sun stand still. Shemesh also means "Samson," the name of the ancient Jewish judge. Shemesh was to be located ten miles up the road from Ramle opposite an Arab village named Tabah.

Gideon Asch returned from his visit to Tabah to the spot where his three dozen people rushed to lay down a square perimeter of barbed wire before nightfall. They questioned him excitedly about his visit to the Arab village. He related his stormy meeting with the muktar named Ibrahim.

"They'll attack tonight," he said. "We've not time to get reinforcements. Dig in with all you have."

Chapter Five

When Gideon Asch made his departure from Tabah, the village flamed to life with a sense of exhilaration. This was an unexpected great moment. It was the core of being for an Arab man to prove his courage. A gift from Allah! Rifles of a dozen vintages and models came from hiding places. There were Boer War rifles and Turkish and German rifles from the world war. There were British Enfields and American Springfields. There were bandoliers of ammunition hidden in crates deep in the fields and orchards. Daggers were pulled from the cottage walls and polished until they glinted.

Throughout the day men from the outlying villages drifted into Tabah and made for the café, where the young muktar, Ibrahim, embraced them. Each held up his weapon with a quivering fist, declared his loyalty, and assured the muktar of his pending valor.

"We shall shave the Jews with a hatchet."

"Their mothers' milk is camel's piss."

"No Jewish dunghills in this valley!"

"Death to the Jews!"

A cheer arose as Salim, the sheik of one of the smaller clans, made his way to the café. Salim had been in the Turkish Army during the Great War. The villages around the Ayalon Valley had been fueled with stories of his fighting prowess for six years. No accounts of his many battles were more graphic than that of a hand-to-hand fight during which he had hacked his way through a wall of British flesh to get to a machine gun nest and grenade it to oblivion. What was generally unknown was that Salim had never risen above the rank of corporal, had never been anything more than an orderly to a Turkish colonel, and had never gotten within fifty miles of a battlefront. A knife scar from a brawl over a belly dancer had been converted into a wound caused by a bullet that had grazed his flesh and was backed up by a medal for valor he had traded for at the Istanbul bazaar.

Everyone felt a sense of security as Salim was invited by

Ibrahim to join him at a council of war with the other muktars
and sheiks.

Outside the café at the water well children played "war" with
sticks as the gathering swelled and the frenzy grew. Bones would
be crushed this night. There would be a swamp filled with dead
Jews. The loot would be staggering. Save one of the Jewish
women for men's sport. It would be an eternity before another
Jew tried to build a settlement in this valley.

Inside the café everyone argued strategy at the same time.
Come from behind them through the swamp. No, the swamp was
too mucky. Surround them on three sides. No, we'll start shooting each other. Fists banged on tables and arguments flared and
sheiks reached for their knives.

All plans were given to Salim, who merely tried to look
thoughtful. At last Ibrahim heaved a deep sigh and explained a
simple strategy.

At dark, roadblocks would be set up to stop British reinforcements, which could not arrive until dawn. The roadblocks would
also cut off any Jewish retreat. Over a hundred men would attack
in a frontal assault in three waves. Ibrahim would lead the first
wave. Salim would lead the second. Fighting broke out as to who
would lead the third wave. Ibrahim selected a sheik by simply
pointing his forefinger.

When they reached the barbed wire, they would cross it by
throwing goatskins over it. The Jews would be quickly annihilated and the fighters would melt back to Tabah and hide their
weapons. Just before the light of dawn, the old men and the
women and children would come in, strip the bodies, and carry
off the Jews' weapons and their equipment. Ibrahim himself
would divide the spoils later.

It was declared a magnificent plan. Hands were clasped and the
war council went outside the café to organize their men. Farouk
called them all to the mosque and after prayer he declared it a
jihad, a holy war, to which the assemblage intoned in unison,
"Death to the Jews."

Victory was a certainty to everyone . . . except Ibrahim. The
dozen ex-Shomer, who were now called Haganah men, disturbed
him. In all the Arab attacks on all the Jewish settlements in the
Galilee, few had succeeded in driving them out. His men, although five times the number of the Jews, had never made a fron-

tal assault in their lives. Most of all he was wary of the Jews'
leader, the Gideon person. The man had defiantly drunk from the
village well before them all. He might know the soldiering business too well. The Shomer had a reputation as fighters and most
of them had served in the British Army in World War I. Yet a
muktar had to do what a muktar had to do.

At eventide, when the air became still and stuffy, Ibrahim and
his council went up to the knoll to see what might be seen. They
were able to observe a part of the barbed wire enclosure. The
Jews had lit smudge pots to drive off the mosquitoes and they
were so exhausted they fell asleep on their flatbed trucks. It was a
repugnant sight to watch the men and women unashamedly
sleeping next to each other.

As darkness crept up, the air on the knoll became scented with
hashish smoke from the village square below, and the fighters
became braver by the moment. When the daylight was gone, they
slipped out four or six at a time, the epitome of stealth.

Ibrahim took his position at the head of the first wave some
three or four hundred yards from the barbed wire. Dimly heard
shots from the highway signaled that the roadblocks were in
place. The second wave positioned itself behind boulders on high
ground to give covering fire, in case the Jews shot first.

Ibrahim slipped out in a low crouch, followed by his men.
Things started going wrong immediately. The scavenger group
in the rear was making too much noise. The older men were
relating their moments of fighting greatness; the women and children chattered loudly in anticipation of the loot. The second
wave, which was supposed to cover the advance of the first wave,
opened fire too soon, destroying the element of surprise. Moreover, they were firing short, right into the backs of Ibrahim and
his people. Farouk, who had declared a holy war only hours earlier and who was just behind his brother, threw his rifle down
and bolted, and three men followed him.

Then came an awesome and puzzling quiet.

"Do you suppose they are all killed?" someone whispered to
Ibrahim.

"Shut up, you son of a donkey!" Ibrahim snapped.

"Why don't they shoot?"

As another of his men began to crawl backward, Ibrahim stood up and raised his rifle. "Allah akbar!" he screamed over and over, "God is great!"

"Allah akbar!" resounded in the valley.

Everyone poured out behind Ibrahim, storming in confusion toward the barbed wire. They knelt, fired, and ran, knelt, fired, and ran. Their battle cry crescendoed.

Still no return fire from the Jews!

"To the wire!" Ibrahim screamed.

When they were within fifty feet, an awesome thing happened. The sound of deafening sirens erupted from the Jewish side, drowning out all other noise. Then the Jews filled the sky with flares, turning night into day, as the Lord had once made the sun stand still for Joshua. Caught in the sudden light and noise, the Arabs froze like deer hit by a spotlight.

Then the Jews poured out a disciplined volley and, although they fired it into the air, several of the villagers went down in fright. A second volley into the air found the second and third wave running into the first wave, which was in headlong retreat.

The battle was done.

The scavengers waiting on the fringe saw their sons, fathers, and husbands tripping, gagging, crawling, running over the highway back into Tabah.

"What happened?"

"They slipped in over three hundred Haganah men after dark!"

"We were hit with machine gun fire!"

"There were hundreds of British soldiers hiding among them!"

"They used poison gas!"

"We were badly outnumbered!"

Dawn found Ibrahim sitting alone on the top of the knoll, looking down on the Jewish camp. His humiliation had been absolute. At first those men who had fallen were assumed to have been wounded, but they had merely thrown their rifles away and fled. When at last he came down into the village, those who had not gone to their homes gathered at the café sheepishly. Strangely, as Ibrahim walked to his own home they broke into cheers.

"We gave them a lesson they'll never forget!"

"I killed at least three of them!"

"I cut a tongue out with this," another said, brandishing his dagger.

Ibrahim turned at his door. "You were very fierce, all of you," he said. "It was a complete victory, spoiled only by the fact that those Jewish cowards brought illegal British help . . . otherwise . . . well . . . don't ever forget the British did this." They cheered again and he went into the house and let the legend take its own course as he collapsed on a bed of weariness.

Chapter Six

Ibrahim went to the knoll atop the village day after day and brooded alone; it was a rather pleasant place to brood. Like most Arab villages, Tabah had a tomb where a saint or a prophet had allegedly preached, lived, or died. Tabah's tomb, a tiny white-washed, domed structure, sat at the highest point of the hill beneath the village's solitary tree, a withered oak. Legend had it that the saint, an obscure soldier who had fought the battle with Joshua, established the village afterward as a fortified position against the Philistines and later, as a guard post to Jerusalem. Mohammed had leaped to Jerusalem from there as well.

Ibrahim erected a small, one-pole Bedouin tent of strips of woven goat and sheep wool to protect him against the midday sun. He permitted only two persons to enter his solitude: Hagar, his wife, to bring him food and drink; and Farouk, to discuss village business.

He brooded about both of them. He had always detested Farouk for his weakness. Farouk was his older brother, and had he been a man of any courage he would have seized the position of muktar. Farouk's cowardice in the attack on Shemesh Kibbutz put a capstone on Ibrahim's loathing. He felt that Farouk had always taken advantage of his ability to read and write and he suspected his brother cheated him. He swore that when he had a son he would send him to school so Farouk would not have that mystical hold of literacy over him.

Ibrahim brooded about not having a son. Hagar had failed him with two daughters. She was with child again and the gossips seemed to be hoping to pin the ignoble title on him permanently. He had already told Hagar that if she did not give him a son he would call off their marriage.

Ibrahim brooded about the "victory" over the Jews, which, down at the café, grew more fanciful each day. His men had fought like females. He knew they would never be able to dislodge the Jews. Yet as the days passed, tales of courage in the attack on Shemesh became wilder. To prove their disdain for the lowly Jews, men would leave the café every day, climb to a high spot overlooking the Jewish fields, and fire off a few rounds from a safe distance of several hundred yards. Although they were out of range and never hit anything, it added fuel to the day's conversation.

Ibrahim brooded as the realization sunk in that the Jews were going to make a successful settlement of Shemesh. He watched them through the Turkish field glasses as they went about preparing the swamp. Within the week, stone walls had been erected as a new perimeter and these were anchored by high watchtowers. A generator not only lit floodlights to allow them to work through the night but made a future attack all but impossible.

The sound of their building never stopped. The original tent city gave way to communal buildings of stone. There was a hospital tent; he kept count of the Jews who were stricken with malaria. Sometimes half of them were down at the same time. It did not stop them. Parties of other Jews came several times a week to help with other aspects of the work.

The Jewish land was mainly a few thousand dunams of swamp and marshlands, a vicious place inhabited by snakes, mosquitoes, and other slimy creatures. Ibrahim wondered how anyone could make anything grow there. Much of their work was a mysterious digging of two large canals at points where the land tilted downward toward the coast. These canals were dug on either side of the swamp, then dammed up. There was a crisscross of smaller ditches that worked their way toward the larger canals.

The second section of the Jewish lands was a hill that ran right up against Tabah's olive orchards to a common boundary. It was filled with ancient derelict terracing of the kind that the Hebrews had constructed thousands of years before. This was like a miniature of the mammoth terraces in the Bab el Wad and those of biblical fame in Judaea.

Stones were a constant commodity in the fields. The Jews collected and carried them by oxcart to the base of the terrace. From there they were taken by hand, much like the Hebrew slaves had done in building the Egyptian pyramids. They were carried to places where time, flood, sun, earthquake, and natural erosion had broken down the terrace walls. The restoration took on the look of the steps of a giant staircase. Each step held back a small plot of earth large enough to plant orchards, vines, or even grain.

The new walls were intended to keep the topsoil from being washed away and utilize land that was otherwise useless. Tabah also had terracing, but a good part of it had been broken down for decades and had never really been restored.

The Jews brought in strange trees, and Ibrahim made Farouk come up and count them. Farouk said there were hundreds, then thousands, and his mind soared, so that he saw millions, perhaps even billions.

"What do they think they can do with those trees?" Ibrahim muttered. "Drink up the swamp?"

"That is what they are saying happened in the Valley of Jezreel," Farouk answered.

"They cannot change what Allah has willed. It can never work. They are idiots."

"I heard in the market at Ramle," Farouk said, "that the trees have come all the way from Australia and they are always thirsty."

"Australia? Don't they have savages in Australia?"

"I don't know."

"Where is it?"

"Someplace past India. As far east as the earth goes east before it turns into being west."

"I do not understand this," Ibrahim said. "Do they really believe those trees will grow here. Look around, Farouk, do you see any trees in this valley other than this poor oak who lives only for our patron saint?"

"No," Farouk agreed. But Farouk always agreed with his brother.

Six months after the Jews arrived an amazing event occurred. The Jews broke the earthen dams that separated the canals from the swamp. Ibrahim's eyes opened like saucers as the connecting ditches sent the putrid waters oozing into the canals. Soon the canals were bulging and running downhill and before his very eyes the level of swamp began to drop. Within days he could almost see the Australian trees grow fat with the fetid juices of the swamp. As the swamp dried under the hot valley sun, incredibly black, rich topsoil appeared. A great deal of it was carried up to the terracing while the rest was reditched and turned over to drain off every last vestige of the swamp.

The canals had emptied into a lower marshland. Ibrahim wondered why they did not let it run down to the sea and ordered Farouk to find out.

"It is some kind of sheer madness," Farouk said when he had learned the answer. "They are leaving it as a resting place for migrating birds."

It enraged Ibrahim that the Jews sang and danced every night. It enraged him that they were able to sing and dance after the energy they had put into their daily work. When he compared it with the slow way of life and lethargy of Tabah he realized that two strange worlds were heading into a conflict.

What the Jews had done had greatly discouraged the villagers.

"We will never get vengeance," Farouk whimpered one day.

"We shall get our vengeance," Ibrahim retorted angrily. "The Jews can perform all their little tricks. They have endless money, while we have none. They can hide by night in their stockade because they are cowards. But sooner or later they must come out of hiding and plant crops and the crops must be harvested. Then they shall learn the code of the Bedouin. Wait . . . patience moves mountains."

What Ibrahim brooded about most was the frightening pattern of land sales. At first swampland and eroded fields were being dumped on the Jews. That was all right in the beginning because he and every sheik, muktar, and fellah did not believe the Jews' soil was tillable. Sooner or later the Jews would give up and leave. It did not happen.

All over the region eviction notices were being given to entire Arab villages by the agents of absentee landowners. Some of the villages had been there for generations, even centuries. The peasants were given a few weeks to simply pack up and leave. Some went quietly, others forcibly. They went with no place to go and nothing to go to. Even the chance for marginal existence had been cut out from under them by their Arab brethren. In a matter of a few months after an area had been abandoned the land was invariably sold to the Jewish Land Fund at outrageous prices. A land boom was on because an unexpected vein of gold had been discovered by greedy men. It took no mental giant to figure out that a dunam of land sold to the Jews would bring more profit than if it were sharecropped for fifty years by the fellahin.

Ibrahim watched with mounting tension as his own landowner, Fawzi Kabir, sold off parcel after parcel in the Ayalon Valley until all that was left was Tabah and a few outlying villages.

Suddenly the land sales stopped. Tabah had been spared. Why, Ibrahim wondered? Tabah's fields were the richest in the valley and would certainly bring a king's ransom. Fawzi Kabir did not do it out of kindness.

Ibrahim brooded about this as he had never brooded in his life. Slowly it began to occur to him. Kabir was in constant strife with other great Palestinian families for financial and political control of the country. Tabah sat in a preeminent strategic position. Any takeover by one of the dominant Arab families would require a consolidation from Jerusalem to the key Arab towns of Ramle and Lydda. Tabah blocked that ambition. In order to control Palestine itself, someone would have to make a deal with Fawzi Kabir.

One day Farouk came up to the knoll to remind his brother that Fawzi Kabir would soon be making his annual trip to Jaffa to collect his rents. Farouk looked forward to the trip as the highlight of the year, for it meant a week in the fleshpots of Jaffa.

"Go to Jaffa," Ibrahim told his brother, "and see Kabir. Tell him that if he wants to collect his rents he is to come to Tabah for them."

"You are telling the mountain to come to Mohammed! He will sell everything out from under us, if he doesn't have us slaughtered first."

Ibrahim smiled sweetly. "He will come," he said.

Chapter Seven

Fawzi Kabir was an Ottoman remnant who still carried the old Turkish title of Effendi. For well over a century the Kabirs had been one of the most powerful families in the Palestine district. Their loyal service to the sultans in Istanbul had been generously rewarded. The Kabir clan had been granted, or otherwise acquired, over a million dunams of land in various parcels from Gaza in the south to the Bekaa Valley of Lebanon.

The Kabirs had made Damascus, administrative capital of the province, their home and headquarters since the beginning of the century. In Damascus there was always room for one more Kabir in a lucrative government post, and sons, cousins, and other relatives were deeply integrated into the Establishment. When the Turks were forced out of the region, the Kabir fortunes declined.

The French were now in Damascus and could be dealt with. They knew the oblique art of giving and getting favors and "how the world worked." While the Kabirs continued to fare well under French control in Syria and Lebanon, the Palestine district was another matter. British civil servants, for the most part, kept business aboveboard and free of bribery.

Since the British had taken control of the mandate, Fawzi Kabir had been receiving bills for taxes and petitions from his villagers for things like better roads, schools, and farming methods. A couple of Christian Arab villages asked for clinics and one had the temerity to inquire about electricity.

Fawzi Kabir had paid virtually no taxes under the Turks and, in turn, the Turks had given virtually no services to a peasantry that walked a tightrope over a chasm of destitution.

Kabir had political troubles in Palestine as well. His archrival for power, Haj Amin al Heusseini, who had fled to escape a fifteen-year prison sentence, returned. The British not only exonerated him, they appointed him the Mufti of Jerusalem, the highest Islamic post in the mandate.

Another political enemy popped up in the form of Abdullah, who had been brought from the Arabian Peninsula by the British and crowned emir of the newly formed state of Trans-Jordan. Abdullah harbored ambitions of annexing Palestine to his kingdom.

With his agricultural income shrinking, a British demand for taxes, demands of the villagers for schools and roads, and serious political enemies, Fawzi Kabir went into a reevaluation.

It was the Jews who salvaged his Palestine situation. After the world war, Jewish immigration increased dramatically and world Jewry was supporting the settlers with mammoth investments and donations.

Under the Turks tenant farming had been good business. Under the British it was fast reaching a point of diminishing returns. Fawzi Kabir sold off all his lands in Palestine save his orange groves in Jaffa and acreage in the Valley of Ayalon, which were of strategic value.

The Jews were developing the country at an astonishing rate and investment opportunities abounded. Tens of thousands of Arabs began to drift into Palestine from all around the Syrian province as work became available, and the centuries-old face of stagnation was lifted. The bulk of the Palestinian Arab population immigrated to the country on the heels of Jewish immigration.

Fawzi Kabir's investments changed from land to such enterprises as the new port development in Haifa, where there was talk of an oil pipeline terminal from Iraq, and a refinery. He invested with some Egyptians in a great new hotel to be built, the King David Hotel, where the wealthy and famous would be guests on their pilgrimages. In the all-Jewish city of Tel Aviv he was involved in a bank with a Hebrew name. As an Arab, his investments had to be kept secret from Arab and Jew alike.

Every year, when Fawzi Kabir set out by train from Damascus in a springtime trek to see his tenants and collect rents, three private cars were attached to the regular train. The first car held his immediate family, one or two of his wives and several of his favorite children. The other cars held staff, bodyguards, a few male and female mistresses. The route took him to the Bekaa Valley township of Zahle in the Lebanon, where the peasants of twenty-six villages paid their dues. The train proceeded to Beirut, which was quickly becoming a principal mercantile and banking center under the French and where he was involved in numerous new enterprises.

They continued to Haifa, with its large Arab population. The granary, port, oil terminal, and urban property were his interests. His lands in the Galilee paid their rents at Haifa.

The train followed the Mediterranean to Jaffa, where the Effendi collected from his Ayalon Valley villages, and then on to Gaza to the most profitable of all his agricultural ventures, twenty thousand dunams of orange groves.

The trek ended in Port Said and co-ordinated with the arrival of a passenger ship coming through the Suez Canal. From here the retinue continued by ship to a summer palace in Spain. So long as the land holdings had been the major income, the annual show of pomp and power was necessary. Peasants were allowed to make complaints by petitions, which were rarely acted on. Patronage was handed out with a token gesture, here and there, to reiterate the Effendi's "compassion."

Kabir was glad that his land holdings had shrunk in Palestine to the Ayalon Valley and Gaza. He was finding the journey wearisome. This year, 1924, would be his last such full-blown expedition.

When the Effendi's train pulled into Jaffa and the entourage transferred to a villa for a week's stay, Kabir learned from a terrified Farouk al Soukori that his brother Ibrahim was refusing to come down with the rents and that he was going to have to travel to Tabah to collect them. Under the Turks this would have spelled suicide, but in today's world, well, things were different.

A convoy of three Duesenbergs turned off the highway and banged its way up the potholed dirt road to the village square. For the occasion, Ibrahim had erected on the knoll the large four-poled Bedouin tent that was stored in the saint's tomb and was broken out only for a monumental occasion. A line of men all passed through with greetings and complaints before Ibrahim and the sheiks and muktars began a three-hour-long ritual feast. Ibrahim and Kabir showed nothing but warmth and brotherhood before the others. The Effendi realized that the young leader was enhancing himself in everyone's eyes.

At last they retired to Ibrahim's house alone. Ibrahim had purchased two overstuffed chairs for the occasion, and as they engaged in business Fawzi Kabir's pudgy fingers moved nonstop from the fruit bowl to his mouth. His devouring of grape and plum was interrupted only by conversation, a belch, and an occasional pause to lick his juicy fingers.

"All right, Ibrahim. I have come to Tabah. I have eaten in your tent. Now, let us put parables aside. What is the reason for this very dangerous summons?"

"My people are all very obviously frightened about the land sales. Your coming to our village was the only way to reassure them."

"To be honest, I was surprised when you were able to be elected as muktar," Kabir said. "For a moment I thought the Soukori hold had been broken. Had it been broken," he shrugged, "I would have had to deal with a half-dozen squabbling sheiks. Maybe I would have sold Tabah as well. The alliance between the Soukori clan and my family has been very successful."

"Never quite an alliance in the true sense," Ibrahim said, smiling.

"A favorable relationship then."

"I knew if you came to Tabah you would go to lengths to keep Tabah . . . as a hedge to protect your investments. If I am expected to hold this highway for you, then a real alliance must be made. We have a mutual enemy, the Mufti of Jerusalem. For years the Heusseinis have all but enslaved Wahhabis and committed all sorts of indignities upon us."

"You are a very clever young man, Ibrahim."

"As the Bedouin would say, the enemy of my enemy is my friend."

"I shall be blunt then," Kabir said. "Your attack on Shemesh Kibbutz was less than impressive. I am wondering how you will fare against the Mufti."

"My men are poor fellahin. They are not soldiers. However, it would not be out of the question for me to hire fifteen or twenty men who had been soldiers with the Turks or British. We have plenty of land for an encampment and I will assure their loyalty by putting Wahhabis in charge of them."

The Effendi stopped eating and wiped his hands clean with a handkerchief, then withdrew a pencil and pad of paper and calculated. "It makes no sense financially. Every lira I take out of Tabah will go for such a guard."

"Perhaps we can figure something out," Ibrahim said.

"I'm sure you have a plan."

"Let us say the eight hundred dunams I am now sharecropping from you are turned over to me."

"You are a bit of a thief, Ibrahim."

"And there are another five or six hundred dunams in swamp that are useless now. I want those too."

"You have been watching the Jews."

"I want nothing from the Jews except their Australian trees."

Kabir fought his way out of the deep chair. "It is too steep a price," he said.

"Think about it," Ibrahim said. "I will make no alliance with the Jews, but they, too, are the natural enemies of the Mufti. With them on one side of the highway and with Tabah on the other with an excellent guard . . . Think about it. . . . Just how important is it to you to keep the Mufti bottled up in Jerusalem and not let him get to Lydda and Ramle?"

Kabir bent over and fished the last few grapes out of the bowl. "Impossible," he said and walked to the door. He stopped and turned. Then he thought, If you want something from a dog, then start calling him master.

"Done!" Kabir said suddenly. "One condition. This guard you are going to form. Neither they nor your villagers are to make trouble with the Jews. The Jews may not be our allies, but they serve a mutual interest. Better the Jews than the Mufti."

"But I will not make friends with them," Ibrahim insisted.

"Who is a friend? Who is an enemy? Who is an ally?" Kabir shrugged. "It gets very complicated with us. But it is our nature. You and I understand each other, Ibrahim."

"It would be a good idea," Ibrahim said, "when we leave my house that we walk to the village square arm in arm, as brothers. It will make an impression."

Fawzi Kabir smiled. He had been fleeced by an illiterate with Bedouin as ancestors. Yet he would leave Tabah with a very strong alliance, a key piece of insurance for the several million pounds he had invested in Palestine. He opened the door, then pinched Ibrahim's cheek. "Just remember one thing. Don't ever summon me again."

Chapter Eight

The fortunes of Ibrahim changed drastically after the visit of the Effendi Kabir. The remaining fellahin of the Ayalon Valley knew that Ibrahim was their protector. He had made a powerful man travel to him, a courageous indignity to impose on such a figure. The word spread like the desert winds as to how Ibrahim had convinced the Effendi to retain Tabah.

This was a windfall to Ibrahim, who no longer had to pay rents but owned his land outright. Yes, Ibrahim had made things good for himself, but he deserved no less for what he had accomplished. As a crown to his run of good fortune, Hagar gave birth to a son, Kamal.

The most prestigious and highly visible symbol of power that an Arab man craved was his now, a personal bodyguard of a dozen vicious warriors. His sheiks and muktars were now far less inclined to squabble with him over minor matters. His domain was over two hundred families numbering fifteen hundred people. He was in unqualified control, a tribal chieftain in the fullest sense.

After the autumn harvest of 1925 Ibrahim announced that he was going to make the pilgrimage to Mecca and became the first peasant of the valley ever to do so. Upon his return he changed his name for a final time, taking the ultimate title, Haj, for he had been to Mecca.

All of this did not bring him complete happiness. He continued to spend long hours on the knoll and sulk about the Jews of Shemesh and the other Jewish settlements in the region. A chilly atmosphere between Tabah and Shemesh continued, with Farouk dealing with the necessary problems that arose between them. Within a few years the Jews brought in harvest after harvest and the swamp all but vanished.

Ibrahim had promised to hit the Jews when they had a crop to harvest, but he was not true to his word. It was not only the restraints that the Effendi Kabir had imposed, it was also the knowledge that even with his personal "militia," he had no chance of upending the Jews. Inside Shemesh and every other kibbutz in the Ayalon, the Haganah under Gideon Asch had created a force completely able to defend itself. It was even rumored that the Jews were manufacturing arms in clandestine factories in the kibbutzim. By spring of 1927 Shemesh began a large poultry house that was lit throughout the night to force egg production. Later in the year they enlarged their cattle and dairy operations to supply product as far away as Tel Aviv and Jerusalem.

Although Ibrahim had forbidden it, minimal contact between his fellahin and the Jewish farmers was maintained. This was particularly true of several hundred yards where their fields ran together. Although the Jews had erected fences of cactus, thorny jujube, and opuntia, they could be penetrated for the theft of a few chickens or fruits from the terraces.

On occasion the Jews and fellahin conversed and even traded. This tentative peace exploded in the late harvest of 1927.

A male Tabah villager named Hani had slipped into the Shemesh terraces at grape harvest time and waited until the last of the Jews returned to the kibbutz, then proceeded to do some harvesting of his own.

Hani was spotted by a woman of the kibbutz, but before she could summon help he seized her and flung her to the earth and in panic beat her badly about the head. Seeing her on the ground and hurt, with her legs open, Hani was overcome with lust. He tore her clothing off and attempted to rape her. She was able to beat him off by screaming and biting and kicking before she passed out, but she had been severely injured, with her nose broken and several teeth knocked out. To make the affair more enraging, it became known that she was pregnant at the time.

Within hours Hani had fled to the south and safe haven among his Bedouin cousins while the village girded for an expected reprisal attack. There was none, but the British police came. Although the villagers sealed their lips as one, Hani's name was already known by the police. The British left empty-handed, but throughout the day tension heightened as activity from the kibbutz came to a halt and the silence from over the highway became ominous.

The shocking thing for Ibrahim was the realization that someone in Tabah had informed on Hani to the Jews. Informers were a necessary way of life so that tribes and clans could watch one another, but until that moment Ibrahim had not realized the Jews could purchase his own people.

Ibrahim paced the knoll the entire night, with his personal army deployed. He was baffled. Hani was safe among the Wahhabi. The British would never find him. Was it not mandatory that the Jews seek vengeance? Why did they not attack? A few hours after sunup he had the answer. A stream of screaming villagers led by Farouk and Hagar reached him.

"The well is dry!"

Ibrahim's mouth also went dry.

"We have no water!"

"We shall die!"

"Save us, Haj Ibrahim!"

"Stop screaming like females and saddle my horse!" Ibrahim commanded, and shouted the names of two of his bodyguards to accompany him. Minutes later he stopped at the guard post of the main gate of the kibbutz. A single unarmed man emerged from the guardhouse.

"I demand to see your muktar!" Ibrahim shouted.

The guard called over a second man and they put their heads together. "We have no muktar," the second one said in halting Arabic. "Tether your horses and wait."

In a few moments he returned with a rather sturdy and buxom, but not totally unattractive, woman. Ibrahim and his guards looked at each other, puzzled.

"I am Ruth, the secretary of Shemesh," she said in atrocious Arabic. "What do you wish?"

"This is impossible! You are a woman! I cannot deal with a woman! I am Ibrahim, the Muktar of Tabah!"

"Perhaps you came to see the girl who was beaten up," Ruth said.

"I demand to speak with Gideon Asch!"

The three Jews conversed among themselves. "Gideon said you would probably be coming and asking for him. Leave your arms with Shlomo. You can have them back when you go," the woman said. Ibrahim grunted in frustration, handed his rifle to the guard, and ordered his men to do likewise.

"Shlomo," Ruth said firmly, "see if they are carrying knives or pistols."

Ibrahim continued snarling, then held his arms apart and allowed himself and his men to be searched.

"They are clean," Shlomo said.

The woman made an authoritative nod and Shlomo opened the gate. "You may enter with your horses," Ruth said. "Do you know where the brook drops to the small waterfall?"

"I know."

"Gideon is waiting there for you."

At a very pleasing place where the stream fell some ten feet into a small pool, then continued downstream, Gideon Asch stretched comfortably under the shade of a eucalyptus. He stood as the sound of hoofbeats reached him and saw the three riders storming toward him. Ibrahim leaped from his horse, breathing hard and shaking his fist at him. "I warn you! I have two thousand armed men in this valley and another ten thousand Wahhabi who will rush here to my side. If our well is not filled by the time the sun is high this valley will be soaking in Jewish blood!"

"Hello, Ibrahim," Gideon said. "It has been a year since you granted me the hospitality of your village. Well, it is an impressive army you have, but you don't get any water. It belongs to us."

"You are a Jew liar and I fart on your beard!"

"Your great benefactor, Fawzi Effendi Kabir, sold us the water rights to the Brook of Ayalon when he dumped this swampland on us. Tabah will always have sufficient water as long as you behave."

"Liar! You will die before anyone else does!"

"Get on your lovely horse and ride to Lydda, Haj Ibrahim. It is all registered at the land office."

Ibrahim was dumbstruck and severely shaken. Usually when he was upset he ranted and cursed to cover it up. He groped for some kind of words to hide his shock as his mind raced. He knew that if the Jews really did own the water rights he might have to give up Hani, the would-be rapist, in order to fill the village well!

Gideon suddenly issued a terse command for Ibrahim's guards to leave. They were startled into turning their horses around. "You go as well," Gideon said, "our meeting is done."

The Jew had him trapped. He had no choice. He gained control of his rage, for he knew the next moments could be crucial. He also knew Gideon was not of a stripe to be bullied and when one does not give way to intimidation another course must be followed. With a flick of the hand and a few words he ordered his men to leave.

"Please," Gideon said pointing to a pair of large flat rocks suitable for sitting. "I come here often, just as you go up to your knoll. We have a great deal to talk about. Do you indulge in a little wine?"

Ibrahim looked about as though he were being spied upon. As a Moslem, he was forbidden to drink. "First we talk," he said.

Gideon sat on one of the rocks. "He who is one day older than you is one day more clever. The Effendi Kabir dealt to you with a crooked hand," the Jew said.

Ibrahim stifled the urge to admonish Gideon, for one does not permit a Jew to speak ill of a brother Moslem. In his stomach he knew that Fawzi Kabir had betrayed him by selling the water rights to the Jews. He had done it to force Tabah to fight against the Mufti of Jerusalem. How to get around it? Would the Jews show mercy? Before I eat him for dinner, Ibrahim thought, he may eat me for lunch.

"I want Hani," Gideon said.

"He was in his own fields when he was attacked by a dozen of your men," Ibrahim spouted automatically.

Gideon shot back a disarming smile, the same smile of disdain he had shown three years earlier. "If that is the case, then let justice take its course. He will get a fair trial."

"No. The whole story is an invention for you to have an excuse to cut off our water."

"You have two choices," Gideon said, ignoring Ibrahim's litany. "I know that Hani is hiding among the Wahhabis. I have eyes and ears in your own village. I also have eyes and ears among the Wahhabis. I have eaten forty days and nights of meals in the tent of Sheik Azziz. We are brothers. Either Hani is returned and faces trial, or my friends among the Wahhabis will see to it he is fed to the desert."

Ibrahim was fast being maneuvered by the Jew into a position of weakness. He knew that Gideon knew he could never agree to return Hani to be put on trial. Ibrahim would lose face among his people. It would be far better to let Gideon's Bedouin friends take care of him. That would make him share a secret with Gideon. He would owe the Jew a favor. With the Jews owning his water he would be in double debt to them. You can pass in front of an enemy when you are hungry but not when you are naked. . . .

"Hani can go piss up a rope," Ibrahim said. "Let the vultures pick at his bones."

"The Wahhabis will get the message by tonight," Gideon said.

"No one must know," Ibrahim said.

"The desert hides everything," Gideon answered.

"You cannot take advantage of us because Kabir cheated us," Ibrahim pleaded. "We have been in Tabah over a thousand years." He exaggerated by several centuries.

"For your water you must pay a price," Gideon said firmly.

"But we are very, very poor."

"I understand you have become quite wealthy personally."

"I will not pay blackmail," Ibrahim said, with his valor slowly seeping out of his pores.

"Unless you have figured a way to strike water from the rocks, then start packing."

"What is your price?" Ibrahim whispered, with fear crawling all over him.

"Peace."

"Peace?"

"Peace."

"That is all?"

"That is all. The valve that sends water into Tabah shall remain open so long as you stay out of our fields, stop shooting at us, and never again lay a hand on any of my people."

Ibrahim quickly regained his valor. "What will you give me if I meet your demands?"

"Just water."

"I must have a paper to show everyone. Give me a paper and I will agree."

"We have already legalized your rights. They are on file at the land office. Your water depends on your keeping the agreement. Is there anything we don't understand?"

"I understand," Ibrahim capitulated. He was so relieved he shook Gideon's hands in a manner that consummates a bargain. "How do we know there will be enough water. The stream runs low in the hot months and we see you are building one of those gigantic water towers."

"We have been measuring the brook for two years. There is

enough for present needs. However, we are opening new acreage and plan to experiment with overhead sprinkling irrigation. Below the terracing we will be building a dam and reservoir. With the winter flash floods there will be enough water—for peaceful neighbors—for this century."

A dam! A reservoir! These were staggering things to contemplate. The Jews were ingenious!

"As long as you are here . . . Your shepherds have broken the fence on your south pasture where it meets our northern fields. Your goats are ruinous. They dig for water with their hooves and destroy the fragile vegetation."

Ibrahim was careful not to be offensive. . . . "But these goats have survived here for thousands of years."

"The goats have but the land hasn't," Gideon said. "I notice you have been drying up swamp and I understand it is your personal land. If you are looking for high profit I suggest you get rid of the goats entirely and try some of the cattle we have brought in."

Ibrahim came to his feet determinedly. "Understand this, Gideon Asch. I have made a bargain with you because I have no choice. We want nothing but our share of the water that was stolen from us. We do not want your cattle, your machinery, your medicine. You are deceiving yourself if you really think this is a land of milk and honey, just as the spies of Moses deceived him. Canaan has always been dust. The ancient Hebrews fled Canaan to Egypt because of drought."

"Perhaps we've learned something in the last three thousand years," Gideon said, "and perhaps it's time you started learning."

"And perhaps you will learn that what the Prophet has willed to dust, will be dust. Wait until there is no water for any of us. Wait till the earthquakes come. Wait till your medicine cannot cure the scourges. Wait till the sun breaks the rocks. They will break your spirit as well."

"Perhaps even Allah needs a little help," Gideon answered. "It is time you stopped picking at the bones of dead earth."

"You are a fool, Gideon Asch."

"We're going to be neighbors for a long time, Haj Ibrahim. I was hoping you wanted something better for your people."

"Not from you," Ibrahim answered, and mounted his horse.

"We must meet. We must agree to talk about things like fences and pestilence. Things that concern us both," Gideon said.

"How can I meet when you select a woman as your muktar?"

"We choose our leaders. Our leaders do not choose us," Gideon said.

"It is a very bad system. It will never work," Ibrahim said. "I will meet, but only with you and only at my knoll."

"Once at the knoll. Once here at the stream," Gideon answered.

As Ibrahim rode off he wondered why he was more angry with the Jew than he was at the Effendi Kabir. From Kabir this kind of trickery was expected and understood. But charity from the Jews? Never!

Ibrahim rode into a terrified assemblage at the café. He sat calmly at his table outside the door as Farouk groveled and put a finjan of coffee before him. He poured it deliciously slowly and sipped as he studied the fear-filled eyes before him. "The Effendi has sold our water to the Jews," he said. He held up his hand before mass hysteria could break out. "However, I told the Jew to have our well filled by the time the sun is high or fifty English warships won't save his ass."

"What happened!"

"The Jew got the message. I gave him a choice of having the hairs of his beard pulled out one at a time or by the handful."

"Is it war?"

"No. He pleaded for peace. I gave him mercy!"

"Haj Ibrahim!" someone called from the back of the crowd. "Water is filling up in the well!"

Cheers and whistles of joy and triumph ascended.

"Haj Ibrahim is great!"

The father of Hani pushed through to the table. "My son, Ibrahim. What of Hani?"

"Oh yes. I told him that a fine boy like Hani could not do such a thing. He is merely visiting relatives. The Jew agreed to remain quiet on the subject and after a time Hani can slip back into Tabah."

"May Allah bless your every breath and footstep, Haj Ibrahim."

Ibrahim went to the knoll after evening prayer. With all the trees he could no longer see into Shemesh Kibbutz. Damned, but he liked Gideon Asch! If only his son, Kamal, turned out like Gideon . . . why . . . why . . . the two of them could conquer all of Palestine.

Chapter Nine

Autumn 1929

Haj Amin al Heusseini, the Mufti of Jerusalem, assumed the pulpit. The mosque stood on a great plaza that had been the Temple Mount of Solomon and Herod. Since Islam it had been the site of Al Aksa Mosque and the Dome of the Rock, where Mohammed made his legendary ascension to heaven. Known now as the Haram esh Sharif, the Most Noble Sanctuary, it was considered the third most sacred site in all of Islam.

"The criminal Jews are going to take the Haram esh Sharif by a signal of a ram's horn blowing on Yom Kippur. They are going to destroy the Dome of the Rock and this mosque and rebuild their temple!" the Mufti shouted.

"Death to the Jews!" the congregation responded.

"Hatred of the Jews is sacred!" cried the Mufti.

"Death to the Jews!" they chanted.

Out they poured, brandishing knives, clubs, and hidden pistols from beneath their robes. Frothing, enraged by the sermon, the Arab mob fell upon the Jewish Quarter of Jerusalem's Old City nearby, a quarter inhabited by defenseless Hassidim. They tore into the little room-sized synagogues and burned Jewish holy books, smashed up shops, urinated and defecated on Torah scrolls, pulled beards, clubbed and garroted, and when it was done, thirty Jews had been murdered.

"The Jews have destroyed Al Aksa!"

The word roared over Palestine from mosque to mosque accompanied by crudely faked photographs.

"Death to the Jews!"

In the holy city of Safed in the Galilee, where the oriental Jewish scholars studied the mystical books of Cabala, eighteen were massacred.

"Death to the Jews!"

In Abraham's city of Hebron, where Jew and Moslem jointly worshiped at the tombs of the patriarchs, the burial place of Abraham and many biblical characters, the Arab mob murdered and dismembered sixty-seven unarmed and undefended men, women, and children.

Other attacks were co-ordinated as the Arabs spilled out of their mosques in Jaffa, Haifa, Beer Tuvia, and Hulda, spurred by the infamous lie that the Jews were taking over the Haram esh Sharif.

Using the pulpit and the power and position of his title as Mufti, Haj Amin al Heusseini moved through the decade of the 1920s and spread his tentacles into every corner of Palestine. He was a landowner of enormous properties, which were share-cropped in a feudal tradition. The Mufti's domain was a destitute, illiterate fiefdom of desperate serfs who were easily aroused and manipulated into religious frenzy inside the mosque.

While the Jewish Agency flourished, the Mufti blocked creation of an Arab Agency, which would have caused him to co-operate with rival clans and diminish his personal ambitions. This left the Arab community with an impoverished and ineffectual health and education system and no plans for future progress.

Instead, the Mufti maneuvered. Arab life was completely centered around the Moslem religion. A Supreme Moslem Council was the major body controlling religious funds, religious courts, the mosques, moneys for orphans and education. Haj Amin al Heusseini seized the presidency of the Council, which, in addition to his title as Mufti, gave him a hammerlock on the Arab community.

As president of the Supreme Moslem Council he had vast funds at his disposal without having to make a public accounting. He likewise controlled the appointment of preachers, mosque officials, teachers, and judges. So broad and dominating had the Mufti's powers become that he immodestly added the word "Grand" to his title and thus became the Grand Mufti of Jerusalem. The calm of the decade had been deliberately broken when he turned loose his ragged legions in a raw play for absolute power.

Although the carnage had been great in undefended Jewish holy cities, the Mufti's gains had been limited. He had struck at isolated pockets of pious scholars and rabbis and against rival Arab clans. The rioters, however, gave wide berth to the Jewish farming settlements, which were simply too tough to be attacked.

The Mufti tried and got nowhere in the Valley of Ayalon against the Jewish kibbutzim. Gideon Asch, the Haganah commander, had secretly armed and trained all males and females of fighting age. His area remained very quiet during the 1929 riots. A good part of the relative calm in Ayalon was due to the Muktar of Tabah, who ordered his people not to get involved in the Mufti's "holy war."

Although Shemesh and Tabah did not co-operate in or co-ordinate defensive matters, there was always ongoing business to discuss and most of the original coolness changed.

Haj Ibrahim personally did not set foot in the kibbutz proper. On those occasions when he visited Gideon he would enter the gate and ride through the fields to their rendezvous point by the stream. Likewise, Gideon visited him at the knoll but never at the muktar's home.

The two men seemed to find their times together a welcome respite from their burdens of office. Haj Ibrahim was constantly disarmed by the coolness of the Jew, who he felt was half Bedouin anyhow. He respected Gideon. He respected the way he handled a horse and spoke Arabic. He respected a fairness in Gideon that he was not able to practice himself. What he liked most about talking with Gideon was a new aspect of his life: an ability to speak to another person about his own hidden thoughts. Haj Ibrahim was an inner man of a people long conditioned never to speak inner feelings. His situation was even more lonely, for a muktar must never let anyone know his thoughts. A structure of silence was the rule of life. Public utterances, even to a friend or relative, were always based on what was expected to be said. No one spoke of personal longings, secret ambitions, fears.

With Gideon it was different. It was not so much like speaking to a Jew. It was more like speaking to a flowing stream or the leaves of a tree fluttering in the wind or to an animal in the fields, an abstract way of letting the tongue go a bit wild and not guarding every word. It was delightful. He and Gideon could argue loudly and insult one another and realize they didn't have to get angry with each other because of it. When Gideon was gone for long periods Ibrahim would send a messenger to Shemesh for an urgent meeting over an imagined complaint.

The afternoon drifted away at the stream. Haj Ibrahim took a swig of wine, placed the bottle back into the pool to cool, opened a tin, and unwrapped a small stick of hashish.

"Just a little for me," Gideon said. "I have to argue with bureaucrats later."

"Why don't the Jews enjoy hashish?"

"I don't know."

"We offer to sell . . . but . . . no one buys it. You enjoy it. Do they know you enjoy it?"

"Not really. At least they don't want to believe it. They accept the fact I'm a creature of the desert. They tolerate my Bedouin side," Gideon said.

Gideon took a long draw on the little pipe, emitted an "ahhh," and lay back on the ground. "We should be proud. The valley stayed peaceful during the riots."

"Who had a choice?" Ibrahim said. "Your hand controls the valve on our water."

"Suppose we didn't have the water arrangement. Would you have encouraged your people to riot?"

"During the summer heat my people become frazzled. They worry about the autumn harvest. They are drained. They are pent up. They must explode. Nothing directs their frustration like Islam. Hatred is holy in this part of the world. It is also eternal. If they become inflamed, I am but a muktar. I cannot stand against a tide. You see, Gideon, that is why you are fooling yourselves. You do not know how to deal with us. For years, decades, we may seem to be at peace with you, but always in the back of our minds we keep up the hope of vengeance. No dispute is ever really settled in our world. The Jews give us a special reason to continue warring."

"Do we deal with the Arabs by thinking like Arabs ourselves?" Gideon mused.

"That is the catch. You cannot think like an Arab. You, personally, maybe. But not your people. I give you an example. There is a clause in our water agreement we did not ask for. It says the agreement can be terminated only if it were proved that someone from Tabah committed a crime against you."

"But suppose the Mufti's men did it. Should that be a reason to cut your water off? We don't believe in punishing an entire village for something you did not do."

"Aha!" Ibrahim said. "That proves you are weak and that will be your downfall. You are crazy to extend us a mercy that you will never receive in return."

"The Jews have asked for mercy a million times in a hundred lands. How can we now deny mercy to others who ask it from us?"

"Because this is not a land of mercy. Magnanimity has no part in our world. Sooner or later you will have to play politics, make alliances, secret agreements, arm one tribe against another. You will start thinking more and more like us. Jewish ideals will not work here. You Jews have come in and destroyed a system of order we created out of the desert. Perhaps the bazaar looks disorganized to-you, but it works for us. Perhaps Islam looks fanatical to you, but it provides us with the means to survive the harshness of this life and prepare us for a better life hereafter."

"It need not be that life under Islam is meaningless on this earth and that you are only here for the purpose of waiting to die. Could it be, Haj Ibrahim, you use Islam as an excuse for your failures, an excuse to quietly accept tyranny, an excuse for not using sweat and ingenuity to make something out of this land."

"Come now, Gideon. What will happen when my poor people learn to read and write. They will begin to want things impossible for them to have. You get all the money you want from the world Jews. What will Fawzi Kabir give us without making a deal for himself? No, Gideon, no. The Jews are breaking down a way of life we are conditioned to. Don't you see . . . every time the outsider comes here he brings with him ways we cannot cope with."

"That's the point, Ibrahim. Islam cannot hide from the world any longer. With the Jews here, we can give you a window to a world you can't avoid."

Ibrahim shook his head. "It has always been trouble when outsiders come here and tell us how to live. First the Crusaders, then the Turks, then the British, then the French . . . everyone telling us our ways are no good and we must change."

"You're wrong about one thing. The Jews belong here. We come from the same father. We are both sons of Abraham. There must be a place in our father's house for us. One small room is all we ask."

"Look at the color of your eyes, Gideon. You are a stranger from a strange place."

"There have always been Jews and Arabs in Palestine and there always will be. We got our blue eyes wandering in a hostile world, and some of us need to come home."

"And we are being asked to pay for the crimes of the Christians against you," Ibrahim said.

"Pay? It's not your land, Ibrahim. You've given up on it long ago. You've neither fought for it, nor worked for it, nor ever called it a country of its own."

"You are trying to create a Palestine in your own image. You are pushing us into a world we do not know. We must have something we understand, something we can contend with. You are confusing us," Ibrahim said.

"Why don't you make a small start, like sending some of your children to our clinic? They don't have to die of the stomach or chest pains and they don't have to go through life blind from trichoma."

For the first time Ibrahim became annoyed and restless to end their meeting. "It is Allah's will that the weak among us be weeded out." He walked to where his horse grazed and took its reins. Gideon stood and sighed.

"We have a strong new generator in the kibbutz—"

"No," Ibrahim interrupted, "we do not want your electricity."

"What I had in mind was running a single wire over to your café. In that way, a radio can be installed."

"Oh, Gideon, you know how to tempt me. A radio . . . you know very well that it would make me only slightly less great than the Prophet in the eyes of the people."

A radio, Ibrahim pondered. Gideon was slowly but steadily building up an account of favors. Surely he would call in those favors. That is the way the world worked—but a radio!

"I accept," Ibrahim said.

"One more thing. I am taking a wife next week after the Sabbath. Will you come with your muktars and sheiks?" Gideon asked.

Ibrahim got on his horse. He shook his head. "No, it is not a good thing. My people will see men and women dancing together, eating together. It is not a good thing."

They galloped side by side to the kibbutz gate. The sentry spotted them and opened up. Ibrahim rode through, then turned. "I shall come myself," he called, "because you are my friend."

Chapter Ten

A classic commitment of aristocratic and wealthy German mercantile families had always been to send their third or fourth sons overseas. Large, wealthy, and influential German settlements were everywhere. The Germans had become particularly visible in Central and South America.

There had been an important German presence in the country beginning with the Teutonic Order, which had fought in the Crusades. In the mid-1800s the various factions in the crammed Old City of Jerusalem began to establish neighborhoods beyond the walls.

The first of these were the Jews, whose neighborhoods were built like stockades as a defense against Bedouin marauders. Connected apartments formed an outer wall with grilled windows. Entrance was gained through an iron gate, which was closed at sundown. A synagogue, school, clinic, and communal bakeries were built around a central courtyard.

The Germans moved beyond the Old City to construct an orphanage for Syrian children. This was followed by a lepers' hospital and a school for Arab girls.

In 1878, the German Templers, a vague sect, founded the German Colony southwest of the Old City. In contrast to the fortresslike Jewish neighborhoods, the German Colony had lovely individual houses on broad, tree-lined streets.

On a key ridge where the Mount of Olives joined Mount Scopus, the Germans built a landmark complex, the Augusta Victoria Hospital. In the Old City the German Lutheran Church of the Redeemer was constructed on ground they could acquire closest to the Holy Sepulcher, the site of Calvary and the tomb of Jesus. German presence in Jerusalem was magnified by a visit of Kaiser Wilhelm at the turn of the century amid dazzling pageantry. The Kaiser dedicated land purchased by German Catholics for a future Benedictine abbey on the traditional site of Mary's death on Mount Zion.

German importance peaked before and during the First World

War as allies of the Turks. The Augusta Victoria complex became their military headquarters and the city was flooded with German military men and engineers to build up Turkish defense capabilities.

For generations the ancestors of Count Ludwig von Bockmann had sent a younger son to Jerusalem to continue the traditional German presence. Young Gustav Bockmann had survived as a U-boat officer during the First World War and afterward took up the family responsibilities in Jerusalem. He resided in a gardened villa, one of the handsomest homes in the German Colony.

In the mid-1920s Bockmann was approached by German Intelligence to establish a small cover unit to spy on the British Mandate and co-ordinate with pro-German elements in surrounding Arab countries. Using a variety of import-export and trading companies and a German bank as cover, Gustav Bockmann proved adept at his assignment. On the surface, Bockmann was a respected businessman and pillar of the religious community through the Templers.

When Adolf Hitler seized power in the early 1930s, Bockmann made the transition to the Nazis with ease. Within a year of Hitler's ascent it was obvious that an all-out offensive against the Jews was under way in Germany. By 1934 and 1935 thousands of German Jews were fleeing the fatherland. Many of them found their way to Palestine.

This new wave of immigration set off a violent reaction by the Arabs, led once again by the Mufti of Jerusalem.

Haj Amin al Heusseini had gotten off free for perpetrating the riots and massacres of 1929 and entered the new decade as a rising star in the Islamic world. After organizing a showy Moslem conference in Jerusalem, he journeyed to India, Iran and Afghanistan, preaching a gospel of Jew hating.

Because the British had been timid with him, the Mufti now denounced them openly. Wherever anti-British sentiment was strong he picked up support. Throughout the entire Arab world, leaders were quick to join the swelling chorus of anti-Zionist, anti-British rabble-rousing. Inside Palestine nearly every pulpit in every mosque was turned into an anti-Jewish platform.

All of this was music to Gustav Bockmann's ears. Anything against the Jews was now part of the natural order of Nazi Germany. Anything that would cause problems for the British was also in keeping with Germany's ambitions. Bockmann carefully befriended and romanced the Mufti as a friend who was fighting mutual enemies.

A key source of the Mufti's moneys was his control of the Office of the Waqf, which administered religious funds. Although no new mosques bore the Mufti's name on their cornerstones, the Waqf treasury was kept anemic by illegal arms purchases and personal luxuries. A coalition of "moderate" Arab families surfaced against the Mufti and demanded an accounting of Waqf expenditures. It became apparent to Haj Amin al Heusseini that an outside bankroller, arms supplier, and political ally was needed. The German Colony of Jerusalem was bound to produce it.

Late in 1935 Gustav Bockmann was called to Berlin for a secret conference to help assess Germany's position in the Arab world and formulate long-range plans to undermine British- and French-controlled countries. Bockmann left Palestine, promoting the rising figure in the Moslem world, the Grand Mufti of Jerusalem, whose enemies were Germany's enemies. He returned from Germany jubilant.

The Mufti's villa stood on the northern road out of the city toward Ramallah. Bockmann was always rigidly German; a smile, so difficult to come by, was rare. Nevertheless, one was there as he was led to a splendid veranda overlooking the Mufti's orchards. The two men exchanged amenities, then settled down to the report.

"Your Eminence," Bockmann started, "the meeting was an outstanding success. Der Führer himself attended. I was given unlimited time with him."

Haj Amin nodded pleasantly.

"What we now realize," Bockmann continued, "is the extent of support Germany has throughout the Arab world. We have well-placed friends in Damascus and Baghdad and we have made great inroads into the Egyptian officer corps."

Sympathy for the Nazis was fine as far as it went, Haj Amin thought, but any other pro-German Arab could become a potential rival of his. He continued listening with little comment.

"Let me assure you that no Arab leader has caught the attention and imagination of Hitler as strongly as yourself. He is most impressed by your unceasing war on the Jews. He also clearly understands your unique value as a Moslem religious leader."

"Can you be more specific about what Germany intends to do regarding our particular situation?" the Mufti asked.

Bockmann cleared his throat for a long recitation. "The Nazis have only been in power for a few short years, but the results have been astonishing. There is a new spirit in the land, a feeling of national unity after the humiliation of the world war. Certainly in the next few years Hitler will unify the German minorities around Europe . . . in Austria . . . Poland . . . Czechoslovakia. All Germans will be under a single Nazi banner. The feeling is very strong that the French and the British are . . . how would you say . . . too demure, too decadent to stop a German advance on the European continent. Certainly within the decade there will be a German physical presence in the Middle East."

"By war?"

"I would think so. A short war. You are in the enviable position of getting in at the beginning to solidify your own claims."

"On the presumption that Germany dominates or is the influential power here," the Mufti said.

"Can it be otherwise?" Bockmann's voice had a touch of astonishment.

"How do you see things developing in Palestine?"

"Act one," Bockmann said. "The British Mandate is floundering. A carefully orchestrated Arab uprising, led by yourself, could collapse the mandate. Act two. With the British gone, the Jews are naked. With your proven ability you can unite the Moslem world against them and drive them out, eradicate them. Act three. A grateful Hitler would support your claims to leadership in the Arab world."

It was heady stuff. To do the German's bidding, would he be trading a British tyrant for a German tyrant? No, he had a special hold. No matter what Hitler ultimately did with organized religions, he would be extremely unwise to tamper with Islam. As Hitler's bridge to Islam, the Grand Mufti of Jerusalem would be in a position of immense power.

"By tradition," Haj Amin said, "Palestine also includes the eastern bank of the Jordan River, the so-called Emirate of Trans-

Jordan. One has to consider that we are also part and parcel of the Syrian province."

Bockmann snapped his head in a half bow. "Berlin looks favorably on your interpretation of the old Turkish boundaries."

"Dear Gustav," the Mufti said. "That is precisely what the British told Sharif Husain to get him involved against the Turks. Husain died in exile."

Bockmann stiffened. "You compare the word of Adolf Hitler to that of the British Colonial Office? We keep our promises to our friends." He cleared his throat, this time ceremoniously. "I am authorized to invite you to Berlin. Secretly, of course. A treaty supporting your claims will be drawn up."

Haj Amin arose and clasped his hands behind him and walked to the corner of the veranda, from where he could look beyond the Dead Sea depression to the hills of Trans-Jordan. "Abdullah," he said, "has an Arab Legion there that is British-trained, British-armed, and led by British officers. Are you sure the British will keep them still in the wake of another Arab uprising in Palestine?"

"We feel we can organize and help direct Arab opinion to bring unprecedented pressure on the British. In no way will Abdullah be permitted to cross the Jordan River."

"I'm not so certain. Abdullah is very ambitious."

"At worst, Your Eminence, it is a risk worth taking."

"Let me rewrite your acts," the Mufti said. "The British Mandate will not collapse all that quickly. They are weary but not dead. They will never give up the Sinai and the Suez Canal without a German invasion. If I call for an uprising and fail before Germany goes to war . . . Is that a risk worth taking? Before I even get involved in your act one, I have to eliminate this coalition of Arab families against me here in Palestine. Gustav, I do not have the resources."

Bockmann perched himself on the wide railing close to Haj Amin. He smiled once more. "I did not come from Berlin empty-handed."

The Mufti covered his delight and the conversation became head to head as though they were wary of eavesdroppers.

"I went into your problems at great length. I explained the high costs of running your continued opposition against the Jews and British."

That was what the Mufti wanted to hear!

"We are prepared to cover any . . . shall we say . . . indiscretions in Waqf funds." Haj Amin nodded and Bockmann went on quickly. "We studied the 1929 riots. This time you will have the funds and we will supply the dealers and routes to bring in several thousand rifles and millions of rounds of ammunition as well as explosives, grenades, automatic weapons, mortars."

A distinct look of approval emanated from Haj Amin. "Please go on," he said.

"Such key villages as Tabah and the road it guards will not stand this time," Bockmann said. "You will also have the means to make annihilation attacks directly against Jewish settlements."

A lone fly could be heard buzzing over the coffee cups.

"With all due respect, Your Eminence, you are a holy man. The situation calls for bringing in a first-rate military commander capable of recruiting a strong force of volunteers from various Arab lands."

"Kaukji," Haj Amin said instantly.

"Kaukji," Bockmann concurred.

The Mufti did not like it. Kaukji had been an officer in the Turkish Army during the war and had won an Iron Cross. Since the war he floated about as a mercenary. He had been involved in an abortive rebellion against the French in Syria and had fled. He turned up here, in Saudi Arabia, as an intelligence adviser, there, in Iraq in a military college. The German agents in Iraq were undoubtedly sold on Kaukji. He spoke fluent German, had a German wife and an Iron Cross. He had friends at court in Berlin. Haj Amin did not like the man personally; he was too ambitious. He fancied himself a German field marshal complete with a personalized uniform and a field marshal's baton.

But Kaukji was on the make and Haj Amin knew it. The so-called coalition of Palestinian Arab moderates had already contacted Kaukji. A secret meeting had taken place in Baghdad called by Fawzi Effendi Kabir, the Mufti's enemy. Kabir represented many businessmen and investors in Palestine whom Haj Amin wanted to eradicate. The Mufti also knew that Kabir had made secret investments in Jewish enterprises and wanted Palestine to retain much of its Jewish community. If he, Haj Amin, did not agree to take Kaukji, then certainly Kabir and his crowd would get him.

"If I agree to Kaukji," Haj Amin said.

"You must agree to Kaukji," Herr Bockmann answered.

"I see that all of this has been carefully thought out."

"It has."

"I will agree only to a meeting with Kaukji," the Mufti said. "He is to receive his orders from me. That must be clearly understood in advance."

"But of course, Your Eminence. There is another matter. We want you to start sending your boys to Germany for training. Not only is military and sabotage training vital, but your people must learn government operations to be able to move into key positions."

"You are saying we are incapable of governing ourselves?"

"We only wish to assist you in areas where we can be helpful."

It was utterly clear that the price for German help would be high, damnably high.

"We also feel," Bockmann finalized, "there is a great new value to the use of propaganda. It can be an extremely useful tool against the Jews and we are creating new techniques."

"Anything else?" Haj Amin asked.

Bockmann held his arms apart to indicate he had delivered all the messages. "It would not be terribly wise for us to continue meeting in the open." He turned at the door. "By the way. It is no trick smuggling arms into Jerusalem, but we are concerned with a place to hide them."

"The Crusaders used the Al Aksa Mosque as part of their headquarters," Haj Amin said. "There are large underground areas where they stabled their horses. These have been incorrectly described as Solomon's stables. The arms will be safe there."

"Ingenious, but the British could well become aware."

"My dear Gustav Bockmann, the British would never profane a Moslem holy place."

At last they managed a laugh together as the Mufti saw the German out.

Chapter Eleven

Between the ancient Arab port city and the new Jewish city of Tel Aviv stood a wasteland of hovels peopled by downtrodden oriental Jews, Arabs, and a purgatory of mixed marriages.

In the middle of evening prayers agents of the Mufti ran into the mosques of Jaffa, on signal, screaming that the Jews were slaughtering Arabs in Tel Aviv. The timing was exquisite, with every mosque in the city receiving the libel at the same time. The short fuse that every Arab carries in his guts had been ignited with consummate ease. Enraged mobs poured into the streets. The Mufti's operators were waiting to drum up a chant and lead them to the no-man's-land neighborhood between the cities. It was a maddened swarm that fell on the wretched quarters of oriental Jews and slaughtered nine, grievously wounding scores more. Within hours this always smoldering rabble had been ignited into a wildfire that swept over Palestine.

A day later, Haj Amin al Heusseini declared the formation of a new Arab Higher Committee with himself at its head to direct a general strike throughout the land.

The Higher Committee's first "communiqué" was an announcement appointing the brigand Kaukji supreme commander of the Palestine rebellion. He was immediately commissioned to recruit an army outside the country to take up the sacred cause.

With the Waqf funds depleted by the Mufti's excesses, Haj Amin looked now to the Germans for quick financial help. Herr Bockmann found his own budget overspent in the purchase of illegal arms. Money was needed at once for mercenaries to join Kaukji's Irregulars. Haj Amin responded by dispatching special collection squads to visit wealthy Arab families to extort "donations" for the "Strike Fund for Distressed Palestine." A prominent Haifa grain merchant was the first to refuse. He, his two sons, and his four guards were murdered during prayer in their family mosque.

In the countryside Mufti gangs pounced on the weaker and more isolated Arab villages. The Mufti's terrorists took for themselves the far-fetched title Mojahedeen, the Warriors of God. Everything was looted for "the cause," from livestock to personal belongings. The Mufti demanded men from the villages to be impressed into his forces. Many were simply taken from the fields and handed weapons. They went out and sniped at British traffic, cut power lines, set up ambushes, blew bridges. After a half dozen muktars were murdered for refusing to provide "volunteers," village after village succumbed to the terror.

Although the British had beefed up their forces to some twenty thousand troops, they were quickly manipulated into a defensive battle by a ghostlike enemy. The principal British deployment consisted of a network of large police barracks, named Tegart forts after the designer, which interlaced the land. It was the same strategy used by the Crusaders with mini-castles and the ancient Hebrews with fortified outposts on hills within sight of one another. During the day, the British were able to come out and patrol and launch raids, but by night they were forced to button up in the Tegarts and give the Mufti the freedom of the darkness.

As the rebellion increased in nocturnal savagery the British initiated massive but cumbersome assaults against lightly armed Arab gangs who would simply disappear into the scenery. The British assessed collective fines against known collaborators and even destroyed entire rebel villages, but they could not stem the Arab fury.

Within a few months Kaukji's Irregulars had infiltrated into Palestine, increasing the havoc. He had recruited a malicious corps from religious fanatics, criminals, a variety of adventurers, and prisoners who were granted early release to join the "holy war." With freedom of movement throughout the night, the rebels were able to select their time and place of attack, then vanish. Rebel bands grew bolder by the week. When a Tegart fort was finally overrun, the British realized they were in deep trouble.

In one of those queer paradoxes that made the mandate take on unreal aspects, the British turned to the Jewish Agency and petitioned the Haganah for help. The Haganah had stopped the Mufti from taking a single Jewish town or kibbutz. Unwritten but understood areas of co-operation between the Haganah and the British increased, changing the status of the Jewish army from semiillegal to semi-legal.

Even as the British and the Haganah assisted one another in fighting the Arabs, the two fought each other with equal bitterness on the matter of immigration. Desperation had increased among Europe's Jews. The Haganah went heavily into the business of smuggling them into Palestine, circumventing the British quotas that had been imposed as a result of Arab pressures. Hundreds of Jews entered as tourists and pilgrims and disappeared into the kibbutzim. Hundreds more came over with false documents for a sham marriage or to join nonexistent relatives. Still others beached themselves in small boats near Jewish seaside settlements. Others walked the tortuous routes from Arab lands and made illegal entry over the borders. Jew and Englishman shook hands with the right and hit each other with the left. Likewise, the Arabs had numerous sympathizers among the British officers and civil servants. It was a Middle East muddle of the first order.

As the rebels grew bolder a nervous eye was cast on the Valley of Ayalon and the road to Jerusalem. Haj Ibrahim had refused to contribute to the strike fund or to supply men. The expected happened.

Ghassan, the sheik of one of the smaller clans in Tabah, was kidnapped as he left the home of relatives in Ramle. Ghassan quickly broke under torture and agreed to co-operate to set up a trap for Haj Ibrahim's personal guard.

The bait was a Swedish blonde, the girlfriend of one of Kaukji's officers. She was of a breed of international fortune hunters who eventually lit on the gold coast around Beirut. Ghassan's story would be that he had discovered the girl and several of her girlfriends who had become stranded on the way to Cairo and were engaging in prostitution to work their passage.

Six men, half of Haj Ibrahim's guards, swallowed Ghassan's wild description of a night of splendor he had spent with them. At Ghassan's arrangement they deserted their posts in the middle of the night and slipped their way down to Ramle.

A buxom young blonde did indeed appear at the door of the designated house and bid them enter. They were discovered the next day in the Tabah village square with their throats slashed and their penises amputated and shoved into their mouths. The balance of Haj Ibrahim's militia deserted over the next few days, fleeing back to their own villages.

The next week the muktar of one of Tabah's neighboring villages was found decapitated in his fields. The defense of Tabah fell into the hands of a badly frightened and inept group of peasants. Although Ibrahim knew he was on the Mufti's death list, he refused to cross the highway to seek help from the Haganah in Shemesh Kibbutz or from his friend Gideon Asch. Only Haj Ibrahim's personal courage and all-night vigils kept the villagers from mass flight.

The next week was hellish for Tabah. Mufti raiders hid safely during the day deep in the caves of the Bab el Wad a half dozen miles up the highway. Under cover of night they came out and finessed their way around the Tegart fort at Latrun to the edges of Tabah's fields. The Mufti's Mojahedeen stalked their prey, picking off stray guards and howling terrifying obscenities. When villagers fled their posts they left their own fields and livestock naked for looting.

By the time a British patrol could be dispatched from Latrun, the raiders had slipped back into the wilds of the Judean hills. It was a land so fiercely rugged it had perplexed the legions of ancient Rome for years in trying to flush out Hebrew rebels. The deep ravines, impassable hills, and buried caves had given centuries of protection to hero warriors, smugglers, and thieves alike.

The British installed a token of permanent protection for Tabah, with roadblocks and frequent patrols, but they were thinly manned and could be easily bypassed. The British garrison had simply been stretched beyond effectiveness. The inevitable big raid to stampede Tabah could not be long in coming.

Gideon Asch had been assigned as the Haganah liaison with the British. His contact was Colonel Wilfred Foote, an old Middle East hand and close aide to the commanding general. Fink's, a zany little eight-table affair of a restaurant in downtown Jewish West Jerusalem, was the favorite place for British officers and a natural listening post for the Haganah. Fink's was one of those open secrets, a rendezvous and mart for exchanging information. David Rothschild, the proprietor, who often complained, tongue in cheek, that he was no relative of another family of the same name, nodded to Gideon Asch as he entered.

Gideon made his way up a squeaking stairs to a private room where Colonel Foote was waiting. Rothschild delivered a tray of schnitzels and beer and closed the door behind him as he left.

The main concern today was the critical situation in Tabah. Gideon had informers in the village whose main job now was to not let Haj Ibrahim out of their sight. If Ibrahim were assassinated, there would be little hope of keeping the peasants of six villages from taking wing.

At meal's end, Foote poured coffee, lit cigars, and changed the subject. "So far, no Jewish settlement has been in serious trouble," he said, "but those rascals are getting more brazen by the moment. If Kaukji were to knock over a single kibbutz, the recruiting lines in Baghdad would be a mile long the next day. I share the Jewish Agency's faith in the Haganah, but we are starting to run the risk of seeing the Mufti turn this thing around."

"If you stopped using the energy of the British Army in chasing down immigrants, you'd be much more effective against the real enemy," Gideon answered. It was the perennial Jewish complaint.

Foote blew a ring of smoke, perplexed. "So would twenty thousand more troops help," he said. "You know that General Clay-Hurst has his hands tied. He can neither get more forces, nor can he formulate political policy."

"What we want to know is," Gideon said, "if things get worse, will you keep the Arab Legion over there in Trans-Jordan?"

"If we allow Abdullah to cross the Jordan River, I daresay he'll never leave Palestine. It's also in Jewish interest to see that he stays put. As good as the Haganah is, it would eventually have to take on the Arab Legion. It's a damned good little army. Our situation is this. We can't do a hell of a lot more against the Mufti without having the entire Arab world cave in on us. We're giving serious consideration to some very bright ideas."

"Namely?"

"A young officer has recently joined the staff here. He's a bit of an off horse, one of those maverick types who pop up now and again. He's captivated the general with some quite original notions."

"What's his background?"

"Captain. Scottish ancestry. Deeply religious childhood, son of

missionaries. I say, he's rabidly in favor of Zionism and, inciden-
tally, he speaks Hebrew like a Jew."

"What does he know about the Arabs?"

"Long tour of duty in the Sudan. Bit of a desert rat. He's won
some measure of renown going on a one-man mission in search of
the lost Zarzura oasis in the Libyan Desert. And don't challenge
him on the Bible."

"What does he have in mind?" Gideon asked, smothering his
growing curiosity.

"A small elite force of Jewish night fighters given a free hand to
strike where and when necessary without written orders. No one
will ever be called to task over what they do. What do you think?"

"It's an interesting idea."

"Shall I ask him to join us?"

Gideon nodded. Colonel Foote pushed a buzzer, then lifted the
phone connected to the bar. "Mr. Rothschild, there's a chap at the
end of the bar . . . yes, a captain. Would you send him up? No,
no thank you, we have plenty of coffee."

A knock was followed by the entrance of a smallish but handsome dark-haired man in his early thirties. "You must be Gideon
Asch." He spoke in a most friendly manner. "I'm a longtime
admirer. I've traveled by your Sinai maps. Orde Wingate at your
service."

It was a lifelong friendship at first handshake.

"What are you up to, Captain Wingate?" Gideon asked.

The Scot smiled charmingly, but Gideon noticed that slight
hint of lovely madness in his eyes. "We have to take the night
away from the Mufti," he said. "You're half Bedouin yourself,
Mr. Asch. You know it can be done with a small, dedicated striking force. They must be good, very good, the best. They have
King David's tradition to uphold. I'll let them know that."

"How many boys do you have in mind?"

"Deborah and Barak routed a massive Canaanite army at the
foot of Mount Tabor with three hundred hand-picked men. He
was able to do it because he knew the Canaanites were illiterate
and superstitious and used the night and great noises as deadly
weapons."

"Captain Wingate. Suppose I'm able to sell this idea to the
Haganah and Ben-Gurion. We have an urgent situation in the
Valley of Ayalon. It will mean trailing fifty to a hundred of the

Mufti's men deep into the Bab el Wad. How soon can you address
yourself to it and how many men do you need?"

"Ten, twelve. They must speak Arabic fluently. I'll teach them
what the Bab el Wad means to Jewish fighters if you'll do the
tracking for us. Give me two weeks."

"I'll have an answer for you tonight," Gideon said.

"I jolly well told General Clay-Hurst you'd go for it," Foote
said jubilantly.

"Captain Wingate," Gideon said, "you didn't come upon this
by revelation in the middle of the night. What is your theory?"

"I am a dedicated Zionist. I believe this is Jewish land. I also
believe that the ways of using these valleys and hills and deserts
for defense have all been writ in the Bible. If there is ever to be a
Jewish nation in Palestine, I feel destined to be a part of making
it."

"What is the rest of your theory, Captain?"

"The Jews, we Zionists," he said, "will never be able to settle
more than a few million people here. That is reality. What is also
reality is the fact that such a state will always be surrounded by
tens of millions of hostile and unforgiving Arabs. You cannot
expect to hold them at bay forever. Sheer weight of numbers and
a Moslem society that perpetuates hatred makes that impossible.
If you are to survive, you must establish the principle of retaliation. For example, I am going to need several squads of these
night fighters to guard the Iraqi oil pipeline into Haifa. It covers
hundreds of miles and obviously a few dozen men can't protect it
from sabotage. What the Arab must understand before he cuts the
pipe is that he is going to face a reprisal . . . massive retaliation
—it is the key to controlling forces a hundred times the size of
your own."

"Captain Wingate," Gideon said, "what kept you so long?"

Chapter Twelve

Depending on whose grandmother was telling the tale, the olive press belonging to Ibn Yussuf of the Village of Fakim was anywhere from two hundred to two thousand years old. Four to five centuries was most likely. Ibn Yussuf's ancestors had made a meager but passable living from the press for generations.

The Village of Fakim was midway up the Bab el Wad, off the main highway, embedded in the plunging ravines and terraces of the Judean wilds. Despite its dire location, villagers came from miles around to avail themselves of Ibn Yussuf's press, which owned a magical reputation. Its product could not be matched. The more ancient the press, the more splendid the oil's fragrance, taste, and character.

Even the Jews, with all their modern skills, could not match Ibn Yussuf's oil press, and eventually representatives of kibbutz after kibbutz found their way into the hills for Ibn Yussuf to convert their crops. Ibn Yussuf scratched out a living, generally getting paid for his services in grain and other staples. One day the manager of the olive groves at Shemesh Kibbutz came to Ibn Yussuf with an idea that changed his fortunes considerably.

The idea was simple. Instead of accepting grain, Ibn Yussuf would charge a small percentage of the oil he produced. The kibbutz set up for him a one-building cottage industry to can the oil and they marketed it through their own co-operative. The size of the cans was either one or two liters and bore the words IBN YUSSUF'S OLIVE OIL in Arabic, Hebrew, and English. Beneath that was a sketch of the famed old press and the words FOUNDED IN 1502, FAKIM.

Ibn Yussuf and his wife were a childless couple, a considerable tragedy that bleached out their lives. Since he dealt with the Jews on a regular basis, he was convinced by them to allow himself and his wife to be examined at the Jewish hospital in Jerusalem. It was ascertained that a simple corrective operation performed on his wife could make her fertile. Afterward she bore him two healthy children, one of them the desired son.

The boy was nearly killed in a highway accident in infancy. Again it was the Jewish hospital that saved his life. Ibn Yussuf was a meek, humble little man, but his gratitude proved immense.

Gideon Asch found him in the normal course of events and over a period of years cultivated a special relationship. Since Ibn Yussuf was privy to the gossip from many Arab villages that used his olive press, he often knew in advance of any stir, any brewing against the Jews.

Fakim was also an excellent staging place for the raids of the Mufti's gangs and, more recently, of Kaukji's Irregulars. After an action the raiders would drift back to Fakim, ditch their loot and weapons in secret caches, and melt back into the Judean hills until the British pursuit gave up. The villagers were treated roughly by the rebels, ranging from common theft of crops to an occasional rape, but there was little they could do in the way of protest. On numerous occasions younger village men were impressed into service. Kaukji himself made several appearances as the village was turned into a semi-permanent base. Ibn Yussuf fared poorly. His one-room factory was the largest building in Fakim and had been all but confiscated for rebel meetings. Several hundred cans of olive oil were taken as "donations" to the "Strike Fund for Distressed Palestine." It was obvious that a buildup in and around Fakim was taking place, an indication that a major action was pending, and there was no doubt that Tabah was to be the target.

Meanwhile, twenty hand-picked young Haganah men, the cream of Palestine, had gathered at Shemesh Kibbutz to form the first Special Night Squad under Orde Wingate.

Wingate treated them to a preview of hell. He literally turned day into night by plunging them into soul-sucking all-night marches that included cliff and rock climbing in total darkness. Their bodies amassed lumps, cuts, bruises, and bloody feet from the brutal terrain and even more brutal hand-to-hand guerrilla training. He taught them stealth and cunning that could get them eye to eye with an unsuspecting fawn. Tracking, shooting, cliff scaling, knife fighting, strangling, crawling, underwater movement, fox and hound chases, judo, interrogation methods, patrol without compass or light: hit quick, deadly, no pity, no nonsense.

When they had succumbed to exhaustion, Wingate paraded before their prostrate bodies and preached Zionism in English and spoke long Bible passages in Hebrew from memory. He imposed upon them absolute knowledge of how to use each part of the land as it had been used by the ancient warriors of Judaea and Israel.

With Arabs, Jews, and British living in close proximity in a fairly heavily populated area, secrets were always on the open market. News of the strange English officer and his troops became part of the daily gossip. The squad was always under scrutiny as it left the kibbutz by truck. To keep their movements obscure, he taught the men to leap from the trucks at intervals while traveling at high speeds. They would hide in the roadside ditches, then go, one by one, to an assembly place unknown to the Arabs.

The twin hillocks at Latrun were the last sentinels before entering the Bab el Wad. On one side of the highway stood a British Tegart fort. On the other side there was a Trappist monastery that had won a measure of note for producing a cheap but excellent wine. The original site of the monastic settlement had been abandoned for a modern building. It was in the old abandoned monastery that Gideon and Ibn Yussuf were able to keep meeting away from prying eyes.

Gideon watched Ibn Yussuf coming through the fields toward the abandoned part of the monastery. Ibn Yussuf was a fragile man with tiny features encompassed by gray hair and a gray beard. He looked about to make certain he had not been followed, then entered the building. Gideon beckoned him from the doorway of a monk's cell. Out of sight but within earshot, Orde Wingate strained to listen.

Ibn Yussuf had pieced together the elaborate plan of Kaukji and his rebels to attack Tabah. Two diversions would co-ordinate with the main attack. In Lydda and Ramle the Mufti's preachers would incite riots to tie down the British garrisons there. A separate attack would be made on a remote Arab village with a handful of men to bring the British out of Latrun up a twisting dirt mountain road that could easily be blown up behind them and trap them for hours.

With the British tied down with riots and answering a false

alarm, the target area of Tabah would be clear. Gideon worked slowly with Ibn Yussuf to ascertain the number of troops, map co-ordinates, times, and places. Kaukji would be using up to three hundred men, an enormous operation. The importance of Tabah's demise was obviously the priority of the rebellion.

When Ibn Yussuf left, Wingate came out of the shadows and flopped on the hard wooden bedframe of a bygone monk. He stared long and blankly at the cobwebbed ceiling as Gideon looked through the slit of a window and watched Ibn Yussuf mount his donkey.

Whenever Wingate steeped himself in concentrated thought, he unconsciously withdrew a toothbrush from his trouser pocket and rubbed it softly over the hairs of his chest. He jerked himself to a sitting position suddenly. "How far do you trust that one?"

"I understand what you're trying to say, Wingate. They don't all lie and cheat."

"Oh sure, they'll do business with you for years, but when the crunch comes they'll sell you for tuppence."

"But they sell their own people for tuppence, as well," Gideon said. "If we expect to remain in Palestine, we're going to have to work out an accommodation."

"Ibn Yussuf and every last Arab is a total prisoner of his society. The Jews will eventually have to face up to what you're dealing with here. The Arabs will never love you for what good you've brought them. They don't know how to really love. But hate! Oh God, can they hate! And they have a deep, deep, deep resentment because you have jolted them from their delusions of grandeur and shown them for what they are—a decadent, savage people controlled by a religion that has stripped them of all human ambition . . . except for the few cruel enough and arrogant enough to command them as one commands a mob of sheep. You are dealing with a mad society and you'd better learn how to control it."

"It is so terribly against our nature," Gideon said sadly.

Wingate changed the subject abruptly. "The whole plan is too sophisticated for Kaukji," he said.

"I know that," Gideon agreed. "I am tempted to alert your command."

"Didn't you hear a damned word I said?" Wingate shouted.

"You're not giving a pep talk to one of the boys in the Special Night Squad."

"I'm telling you that since you Jews returned to Palestine you've never stopped hiding in your stockades. Now that we have the independence to act, you're becoming very tense. To hell with the British Army. Let them go chasing all over Judea. Good Lord, man, can't you smell the dirty hand of some British officer plotting this operation for Kaukji?" He sprang to his feet and paced, stopped before Gideon, and pointed his toothbrush under Gideon's nose. "Realize their thinking. Kaukji and this British officer . . . they're saying—are they not?—the Haganah won't budge out of Shemesh Kibbutz. The Jews think solely in defensive terms. Once the area is cleared of British troops, there is nothing to stop the attack on Tabah. The Haganah won't interfere. They're positive, utterly, utterly positive of it."

Gideon Asch was a man of fifty-three who still had the stamina to go tracking in the wilds with the youngest, hardest soldiers of the Jews. He had walked a lifetime through that labyrinth of the Arab mind, seeking accommodation, friendship, and peace. It had all eluded him. His first exhilaration with the Special Night Squads had been slowly overtaken by a sense of tragedy. The illusion of brotherhood with the Arabs was also overtaken by the reality that if the dream of Zion were to come to pass, the Jews must go on an offensive repugnant to their souls.

The cell became as quiet as though the bygone monk were meditating in it.

Gideon sighed ponderously. All right, they'd take the fight to the Arabs now because the Arabs would never stop persecuting them if they didn't. But how long, how terribly long would it go on? And during that time would the basic decency of the Jewish people be corrupted along the way? The road seemed incurably endless, but it was the price that the dream of Zion demanded.

"Well," Gideon said, "this is what we all came here for, isn't it?"

"Indeed, the moment of Zion is at hand."

"I'm not sure what plan that head of yours is concocting, Wingate, but Haj Ibrahim is a proud man. He would rather lose everything than accept our help."

"That, in one sentence, my friend, is the story of the Arab

nation," Wingate answered. "Well, I won't give Haj Ibrahim any options."

Wingate, garbed in the blue work clothing of a kibbutz member, climbed to the top of Tabah's knoll through the fields from the rear side to avoid the village proper.

"You there," he called to a daydreamer sitting near the prophet's tomb, "get yourself down to the village instantly and fetch Haj Ibrahim."

The peasant was startled to hear the sudden stream of perfect Arabic.

"Get along, do as I tell you," Wingate prodded authoritatively.

Fifteen minutes later Haj Ibrahim appeared and stopped behind the stranger who scanned the hills through binoculars. "Do you know who I am?" Wingate asked, neither turning nor lowering his field glasses.

"The crazy British officer."

"Precisely. But you'll note that I'm not in uniform. What I have to tell you is from one friend to another."

"Perhaps I allow a friendship longer to develop than you."

"No time for quaint sayings. You're going to get clobbered tonight and there won't be anyone home at Latrun to bail you out." Wingate lowered the glasses, turned, smiled, and walked past Ibrahim to another viewpoint. "By God, the chaps who put this village on this spot knew what they were doing. No real way to get close, except up this knoll from the rear. Even so, you can't defend it. Kaukji has too many men. They'll come on their bellies, using the tall grass as cover until they're fifty yards from where we stand. They'll start shouting obscenities and your men will be converted into quivering masses of immobile flesh."

"We will make an accounting."

"To Allah, perhaps. I suspect you're in the market for some good advice."

"If you mean asking the Jews to help, I won't have it."

"Wouldn't think of suggesting it, Haj Ibrahim." Wingate's deep brown eyes continued to be transfixed down the slope. "The wind will be coming from the sea," he said. "It will be blowing downhill. The grass is dry. It will ignite to appear like . . . like Joshua making the sun stand still. Things will get rather hot underfoot for Kaukji's men."

"Burn the fields?"

"Of course burn the fields, man; of course burn them."

"That is the most stupid tactic I've ever heard of," Haj Ibrahim said.

"Oh? I thought you'd rather fancy it."

"It's stupid."

"But Haj Ibrahim, that is what your great general, Saladin, did to the Crusaders at the Horns of Hittim. Maneuvered them against a bluff, caught them downwind in their armor, and burned the fields. Those who were not roasted alive or who choked to death tried to break out and get to the Sea of Galilee, for they were also parched, but Saladin stood between them and the sea." He turned away. "Of course, it takes imagination to be a Saladin." With that, Orde Wingate retraced his steps down the knoll and out of sight.

When darkness ended the fitful day, Kaukji's troops spilled out of Fakim and headed down the Bab el Wad on a trail that had once served as the Roman road to Jerusalem. Earlier in the day he had dispatched the diversionary unit to a small village deeper in the wilds, which would lure the British from Latrun. At the same moment in Ramle and Lydda the mobs in the mosques were being whipped up.

Orde Wingate moved his Special Night Squad out of Shemesh Kibbutz, sending them crisscrossing through fields and over hills in a crazy-quilt pattern. If they were detected, no one would be able to ascertain their direction. They assembled at the mouth of the Bab el Wad, found cover, and froze. In an hour the advance scout of the party reported back to Wingate that Kaukji's men were coming down toward them.

"Good, they are right on schedule," Wingate said. "Don't breathe, don't budge. Try to get a count of them."

The Jews were scattered on a steep little cliff directly above the old Roman road. They heard the tinkle of canteens and the clicking of dislodged rock, followed by the aroma of hashish. Then came voices, charging up their blood for the coming battle. Kaukji's rebels passed directly beneath the Special Night Squad and moved out of sight into the Valley of Ayalon.

Wingate waited a full hour after they had passed, then whistled

for his boys to assemble. They had counted somewhat over two
hundred and fifty of Kaukji's men who would take part in the
attack on Tabah.

Wingate spread a map. "We stay off the path. Keep in the hills.
Here at this point, two miles before we reach Fakim, we will set
up the ambush." The plan was to give a reception to Kaukji's
forces when they returned from the attack on Tabah. The men of
the Special Night Squad knew that in order to avoid detection,
the rest of the night would be one, long, murderous uphill climb.
Wingate glanced at Gideon, who nodded that he, despite his age,
would make it just fine.

At two in the morning, Kaukji's rebels fanned out at the base of
the knoll of Tabah and crawled upslope toward the village.

Haj Ibrahim had long second thoughts about his strange en-
counter with the British officer, then gathered his people and
ordered them to carry the village supply of kerosene up to the
prophet's tomb. Taking full credit for the plan, he had the perimeter soaked so the dry grass begged to be ignited.

At half past two, a rebel officer stood up near the top of the
knoll, held his rifle aloft, and screamed the ancient battle cry,
"Allah akbar!" A roar went up from the rest, followed by a volley
of fire and a charge.

Haj Ibrahim arced the first torch into the grass and fell to his
stomach. One after another his people ran to the perimeter, each
flinging a torch at the onrushers. Within seconds a grumble of
fire mixing with fuel belched into a roar and a titanic blaze leaped
heavenward. The wind swept over the knoll, pushing the fire
downhill toward the attackers almost instantly. Curses changed
to horrendous screams while one human torch after another ignited. Men leaped up and down as the ground turned into a
broiler. Some fell to the ground gagging from the rushing cloud
of angry black smoke, others tumbled downhill, frantically trying
to outrun the advancing wall of flame. They were cross-whipped
with hellfire and scattered in utter panic. Twenty-five men had
been burned or choked to death within two minutes of ignition.
Another hundred were badly charred.

The balance limped back into the sanctuary of the Bab el Wad
toward Fakim, dazed after an insane all-night retreat. By dawn

they began to enter a narrow defile a few miles from Fakim, overcome with exhaustion, barely able to hang on.

The Special Night Squad had arrived at the defile hours earlier
after the vicious forced march and were deployed in an executioner's ambush. The survivors of the charge on Tabah now faced
a pair of machine guns set up to mangle anything caught in their
crossfire. Those who survived the first burst flung down their
weapons and scattered through the hills, never to return to battle
again.

Chapter Thirteen

October 1937

The Office of the Waqf served as headquarters for the Grand Mufti of Jerusalem. It was located just outside the great plaza known as the Haram esh Sharif, the former Temple Mount of Solomon and Herod. The Haram esh Sharif held Islam's first major edifice, the Dome of the Rock, which dominated all else in Jerusalem. The mighty dome was thirteen centuries old. It was the site of Abraham's sacrifice, of the Holy of Holies of the Hebrew Temple, and the rock from which Mohammed made his legendary leap to heaven. Hovering in its shadows was a small replica of the Dome of the Rock known as the Mosque of the Chain, which had served as the model for the larger building. The Mufti claimed the Mosque of the Chain as his personal place of worship. Several times a day he crossed from the Office of the Waqf to attend to his spiritual needs.

He sat on his prayer rug in cross-legged meditation.

"Your Eminence!" a voice echoed behind him from the shadows.

The Mufti slowly opened his eyes and came out of his trance.

"Your Eminence!" the voice repeated, reverberating off the marble.

The Mufti turned to see Gustav Bockmann, dressed clumsily as an Arab. "Can't you see I'm at prayer!"

"You must go at once," Bockmann said. "The British are rounding up your council and all your commanders. There is a warrant for your arrest."

The Mufti grunted to his feet and looked about in confusion. "Quickly," Bockmann said, "you must hide."

The two ran out of the mosque over the Haram esh Sharif to its other great building, the Al Aksa Mosque, entered, and fast made their way down a narrow stone staircase into the hidden caverns beneath the building. The mustiness of the ages mingled with the scent of gunpowder that had been stored for the revolt.

"You must not move until I return," Bockmann instructed.

A day and a night passed until the German returned with several bundles beneath his arm. He brought food and drink, a shaving kit, and clothing.

"What is going on out there?"

Bockmann rattled off a long list of those in his council who had been hauled in. Some leaders had escaped, but a dragnet was over the entire country. The rumor had it that the British were going to ship the captives off to the Seychelles Islands, somewhere out in the Indian Ocean.

"Sons of dogs!" Haj Amin cried.

"We have a ship at anchor off Jaffa," Bockmann said. "You must remain here until the Arab Sabbath, when there will be thousands of worshipers in Al Aksa. It is our best chance to get you out of here."

"I don't like this dungeon."

"You can't move. Patrols are all over the Old City. All the gates are being closely watched."

Bockmann told the Mufti to shave off his beard and to wear the clothing he had brought, the white dress that Moslem women wore to prayer on Friday morning.

On the Sabbath the Haram esh Sharif was jammed with twenty thousand worshipers. Prayers broke up at midday and the human flood poured into the narrow lanes of the Old City, making detection extremely difficult. Haj Amin al Heusseini, buried in a mass of women pouring out of the Damascus Gate, easily escaped the scrutiny of the British.

He was then hidden in a crate among crates loaded with tomatoes destined for the Port of Jaffa; from there, onto a German tramp steamer and up the coast to Beirut, and then inland to Damascus. From Damascus, Haj Amin regrouped his leaders and continued to run the revolt in Palestine.

Orde Wingate's Special Night Squads firmly established a new era and a new principle. It could not be said that they alone defeated the Arab revolt, but they certainly took the starch out of rebel zeal. The time of the uncontested Arab night raid was over, forever. The Special Night Squads extended their operation, crossing the border into Lebanon, taking that sanctuary away from the rebels. Arab attacks began to dry up.

Kaukji's Irregulars had been woefully ineffective. Now faced with a stiff challenge, their stomach for action, gold, and glory

gave way to homesickness. They deserted in droves, fleeing Palestine for their own countries.

Unable to halt Jewish immigration or dislodge Jewish settlements, the Mufti turned his final energies to destroying his Arab
opposition. As the revolt ended its second year, Haj Amin's gangs
went on a murder binge and when it was done, eight thousand
Palestinian Arabs had killed one another.

With the Mufti gone and Kaukji's Warriors of God in full
flight, those anti-Mufti Arabs who had survived began to take
heart and spoke out against the revolt, and it started to fizzle.

In another year the Mufti's revolt began to collapse, but it had
succeeded in putting the mandate in disarray. From the very beginning the British had locked themselves into an impossible position. Palestine was the twice-promised land—once to the Jews
as a homeland through the Balfour Declaration and once to the
Arabs as part of the Greater Arab Nation.

Between the years of riots and revolts, British commissions of
inquiry investigated. Each would issue a White Paper, chipping
away at Jewish immigration and land purchases. Partition plans
surfaced. Under these plans the Jews were to get a small strip of
land from Tel Aviv to Haifa. A permanent mandate would be
given to Jerusalem as an international city. The Jews were inclined to agree to partition, but the Arabs flatly said no to everything. Most of those Arabs wishing to make an accommodation
with the Jews had been murdered by the Mufti's people.

At the zenith of the Arab revolt, a high British commission
concluded that Britain's ability to rule the mandate had been exhausted.

War was on the horizon in Europe and any British pretense of
remaining evenhanded in Palestine was exposed. In issuing the
commission's White Paper, the British completely renounced
their obligation to the Jewish Homeland. The British policy was
now to win favor in the Arab world at any cost in order to protect British interests in the region.

On the eve of the Second World War, millions of Jews were
desperately trapped in Europe. The White Paper cut off their
final avenues of escape by calling for a phasing out of all Jewish
immigration to Palestine and an end to all land sales. Although

the Mufti's revolt had been crushed, the British White Paper granted him a victory *in absentia*.

When war was declared against Germany, almost the entire Arab world spiritually allied with the Nazis. The betrayed Jews of Palestine declared, "We shall fight the war as if there were no White Paper and we shall fight the White Paper as if there were no war." Within days, a hundred and thirty thousand men and women of Jewish Palestine volunteered for military service with the British.

Haj Ibrahim was markedly glum. Gideon had left Shemesh Kibbutz on many occasions, to go to the desert or on training missions and surely to smuggle arms and illegal immigrants. Sometimes he would be gone for months. Each time Gideon left, Haj Ibrahim felt very uneasy. Of course, he never said so.

Tabah had been brutalized by the Arab revolt. Two dozen of his people had been killed or disappeared. Haj Ibrahim knew, within himself, that without the Haganah and the Special Night Squads the result for him might have been a disaster. He could never bring himself to think in terms of gratitude. On the contrary. Arab fighting Arab was an established way of life, hundreds and hundreds of years old. To be saved by the Jews and the British was a new humiliation.

"You are too old to go to war," Haj Ibrahim said to Gideon as he poured them coffee.

"Not this war," Gideon answered.

"If you have a hundred friends, throw out ninety-nine and be suspicious of the other," Ibrahim said. "Sometimes I know you are my only real friend. Relatives and members of the tribe are different. They cannot be real friends because they are rivals. Sons can often be your enemy. But the religion does not permit us to make friends with strangers. So, who is there? I am lonely. I cannot meet a man and have different thoughts without his being my enemy. At least we can . . . we can speak. . . ."

Gideon changed the subject, for Ibrahim was becoming maudlin. "Simcha is the new secretary of the kibbutz. You'll be dealing with him."

"He's all right. He's all right. We will get along. Surely the British are going to make a general out of you."

"No, nothing like that."

"A colonel?"

"Just an ordinary adviser on Arab affairs."

"You'll be very good at that," Ibrahim said. "I know why you must go and fight the Germans," he continued. "But to me, it doesn't matter who wins or who loses. I have no quarrel with the Germans. I am not angry with them. I don't know if I have ever really spoken to one, except perhaps a pilgrim." He sighed and grunted. "Now the Germans make us the same kind of promises the British made to win our support in the first war. I hear the shortwave broadcasts from Berlin. They say that the Nazis and Arabs are brothers. But everyone lies to us when a war comes. They will use our help, then leave us to rot, as the British did."

"If the Germans reach Palestine, at least you won't have to worry about the Jews anymore," Gideon said.

"I am not for the Germans just because of how they are treating the Jews," Haj Ibrahim said, "but I am not for the Jews. There are no Arab leaders left in Palestine and I don't trust the ones over the border."

"That covers just about everyone."

"Why is it that the only men we follow are the ones who hold a knife to our throats?" Ibrahim cried suddenly. "We learn we must submit. That is what the Koran tells us. Submit! Submit! But the men we submit to never carry out the Prophet's will, only their own. When you return, what of us, Gideon? We have not really had our war with each other yet. It must happen. You will keep bringing Jews into Palestine and we will protest."

"You are very upset!"

"These things are always in my head! I don't want the Syrians to come here! I don't want the Egyptians! I am now being left alone with these thoughts. The Jews are clever. You are sending thousands of your boys into the British Army to be trained as soldiers."

"I don't think they'll rush us into combat units unless they become desperate."

"But you will be prepared when the war comes between us. You have built a government within a government, and us? We will get the blessings of another Grand Mufti or another Kaukji or another king like that degenerate in Egypt. Why does Allah send us these men? I am sorry, Gideon. My thoughts go one way, then the other way. Whatever . . . whatever, I don't want anything to happen to you."

Gideon slapped the arms of the oversized chair, then pulled himself out. "Someone asked me once, do you have friends among the Arabs. I told them that I didn't really know. I believe I have a friend. It's a start, isn't it? You've trusted me, haven't you?"

"You are the only one I trust from either your people or mine."

"Perhaps if we Jews weren't overburdened all our lives with the fear of perishing . . . It dominates us! Always afraid of perishing. I'm fifty-three, Ibrahim. I've carried a gun since I was fourteen. Is it fair to know every minute of your life that forces out there want you dead and won't end it until you're dead . . . and no one hears your cry. . . . So I go to war because the Germans want us dead even more than you do."

"Come," Haj Ibrahim said. "We'll walk down to the highway."

Chapter Fourteen

1940

The focal point of village social life for the men was the radio in Tabah's café. With the world marching steadily and inevitably toward a second global conflagration, the radio took on an even greater imperative.

For Arabs these days it was pleasurable to enjoy a measure of vengeance. The governments of France and Britain, their arrogant overlords, had been struck politically timid and fearful. An emboldened Hitler seized Austria and then turned democratic Spain into a testing ground for his new arsenal of frightening weaponry while the democracies turned blind eyes and deaf ears.

In a conference at Munich the Arabs saw a pair of quivering and morally bankrupt democracies hand over the life of yet another free nation, Czechoslovakia. A few months after the sellout in Munich, Germany sealed her intentions by forming an alliance with Fascist Italy and together they poised to devour Western civilization. All of it brought joy after joy to Tabah.

"Have you heard, Haj Ibrahim! It is war!"

Haj Ibrahim could detect the first shifts of attitude among his people, who were awed as the German panzers mangled Poland in a matter of a few weeks.

It was Haj Ibrahim's position to give wise counsel and remain steady and not get caught up in the volatility of the villagers. He was the sure hand in a line of sure-handed men who had controlled the destinies of their village. Conquerors came and went and one got along with them. It was the endless struggle against nature that was more important, for that always remained.

Yet even Haj Ibrahim could not help but be sucked into the fever as Germany rolled up one incredible victory after another in the first half of 1940. A euphoria swept over Arab Palestine. Haj Ibrahim sent his brother, Farouk, all the way to Jerusalem to purchase maps of Europe and the Middle East and the café became a war room. Each new pin and line on the maps brought a repetition of discussion about German invincibility and the need for the Arab world to ally with them.

Gideon Asch went to war. The British traded on his unique
background with the Arabs and his knowledge of the Mufti and
put him on the mission of trailing Haj Amin al Heusseini. The
Mufti, having fled Damascus early in the war to the safer grounds
of Baghdad, was able to create new mischief as strong pro-German factions in the Iraqi military plotted to gain control of the
government, weakly run by a young regent.

Gideon Asch was white-haired and white-bearded and by dress
and mastery of the language was able to pass quite easily as an
Arab. Near the Mustansiriya College, perhaps the oldest university in the world, he established an excellent espionage ring using
Iraqi Jews as its heart. He purchased a number of Iraqis in key
government and military positions.

The moment that mainland France fell, the war was suddenly
and terrifyingly dumped on Palestine's doorstep. Most French
possessions were seized by the new Vichy government, which
collaborated with the Nazis. In an instant Syria and Lebanon
were in pro-German hands and the issue in Iraq hung in the
balance.

In North Africa, a second menace loomed against Palestine.
The great Western Desert straddled the borders of Egypt and
Libya, where the Italians had amassed a vast army—over three
hundred thousand men—with the ultimate mission of crossing
the desert and conquering Egypt, the Suez Canal, and Palestine.

Although the British were outnumbered by ten to one, they
audaciously went into an offensive that chewed up the Italians
and bagged tens of thousands of prisoners and took them deep
into Libya.

Once again Hitler had to rush to his partner's rescue. Early in
1941 a young German general named Erwin Rommel landed in
Tripoli, Libya, and with a highly mechanized force known as the
Afrika Corps won back the territory the Italians had lost. Rommel stopped at the Egyptian border to regroup because of an
overextended supply line.

But Palestine was in a nutcracker from the east and west.

Although the British had been badly bashed about, they
reached deep and scraped together a force of Australian, Indian,
and Free French brigades and launched an invasion of Syria and

Lebanon from Palestine. This was led by units of Jewish scouts, most of whom had served in Orde Wingate's Special Night Squads and all of whom had been under Gideon Asch's command at one time or another. This expedition flowed on a stream of intelligence supplied by Gideon Asch's unit in Baghdad and other Jewish espionage units that had been planted earlier.

At the same moment in Iraq, a pro-German faction seized control of the government. A hastily assembled British force stormed ashore at Iraq's only seaport, Basra, on the Persian Gulf—the port of Sinbad, his seven voyages, and *A Thousand and One Nights*. Basra was several hundred miles from Baghdad, so a second force from Palestine rushed overland, again guided by Gideon Asch's intelligence.

As the British reached sight of Baghdad the pro-Nazi Iraqis turned maniacal and at the last moment tore into the Jewish ghetto of the city. Four hundred Jewish men, women, and children were slaughtered. Gideon Asch was betrayed by a turncoat saving his own neck and was dragged off to be tortured. When the British broke into the city a frenzied Iraqi colonel chopped off Gideon's left hand. His war was done.

Haj Amin al Heusseini fled Baghdad, this time to neighboring Iran, a country floundering politically under the twenty-two-year old Shah. The British quickly marched into the country to secure it. As they did, the Japanese granted the Mufti asylum in their embassy in Teheran and later slipped him out of the country. Haj Amin al Heusseini surfaced again in Berlin. He spent the balance of the war broadcasting to the Arab world on behalf of the Nazis. He was also instrumental in helping to form a division of Yugoslavian Moslems who fought alongside the Germans.

With the successful occupation of Iraq, Syria, Lebanon, and Iran, the Allies had secured their eastern flank in the Middle East. On the Western Desert a ferocious battle of attrition raged back and forth between the British and Rommel's Afrika Corps. Enormous hordes of tanks used as chessmen ravaged one another.

Time and time again Cairo was bedecked in Nazi swastikas to greet the "liberators." It was not until October of 1942 when the British General Montgomery and the German Rommel faced off for the second time at an oasis called El Alamein a short distance from Alexandria.

The Afrika Corps was being beaten despite inflicting massive losses on the British. Rommel called for an orderly retreat to a position where he would be able to make a firm defense. Hitler, seeing his dream of the Suez Canal slipping, ordered his general to stand at El Alamein. By the time Rommel was able to withdraw, it had turned into a rout.

Chapter Fifteen

1944

The virility of Sheik Walid Azziz, chief of the Wahhabi tribe, was legend. No one knew his age for certain, but it was said that he was born during the great American Civil War. He had been a widower many times and each time replaced the deceased with a younger woman of child-bearing age. The last wife he took was under twenty as he passed seventy, and in the following ten years she bore him a brood of eight. He still had two living wives and an unknown number of concubines. Many of the tribe's widows looked to him as a surrogate husband and gladly came under his tent. Walid Azziz's total production was supposed to have been twenty-five sons and an equal number of daughters. His children formed the cement of many alliances through intermarriage. His sons and daughters also stocked the clans of the Wahhabis and assured his continued leadership.

For Walid Azziz the selling of daughters was a lucrative source of income. If a man had enough money he could buy the daughter of a sultan. He knew the exact value of all his women. He also knew how to keep a white coin for a black day by holding back those daughters who would bring the greatest price.

Ramiza was sixteen, the perfect age for marriage, and would unquestionably bring top lira. The son of a prominent clan chief had been a prime prospect. Unfortunately, after checking with the old midwives, it was ascertained that Ramiza had shared the same wet nurse as the boy when they were infants and marriage was therefore out of the question. Blood was one thing, for a great part of the Arab race is cousin marrying cousin. Milk was something else.

Haj Ibrahim had everything to make a man comfortable in life: sons, a large house, an obedient wife and a fast horse. Yet he was not fully content. Hagar had acquitted herself well, but Ibrahim seemed to grow more lusty as his wife grew more weary. After Ishmael it was certain she would bear no more children. He had four sons but was not pleased with three of them and Ishmael was too young to make a judgment on.

In the closeness of the village it was more difficult to keep concubines than in the freedom of the Bedouin camp or the maze of
the city. On occasion he visited Lydda to cavort with prostitutes,
but this was never fully satisfying.

Ibrahim had gone to the tribal country for the funeral of an
uncle, the sheik's brother. While there, he saw Ramiza. Walid
Azziz did not insist that the women be veiled, except in the presence of strangers. Besides, the sheik was in the daughter-selling
business and was not above having prospective suitors get a
glimpse of the faces of his most beautiful daughters.

Haj Ibrahim sent his brother, Farouk, as his representative to
negotiate for the girl. With a warning that "Walid Azziz has not
ruled our tribe for all these years because he cannot recognize a
mule from a horse," Farouk, who was always anxious to serve his
brother, promised to fleece the sheik in the bargaining.

The sheik suspected the purpose of Farouk's visit but was not
certain which daughter was wanted. He had set a price for each
one of them in his own mind. Before Farouk arrived he and the
elders determined that Haj Ibrahim had been born before the
new century. It would make him a man of some fifty years. Thus,
Walid Azziz felt that Haj Ibrahim would settle for one of his older
daughters, still fertile but less saleable.

Farouk was welcomed into the sheik's small, private, two-poled
tent, used to get away from the hubbub of his family in the great
tents. Farouk and the sheik exchanged remembrances of the recent fight against the Mufti and of their battles won: the salt of
men's conversation. As the moment of private consultation arrived, Azziz dismissed his pair of black slaves. After long jousting
Ramiza's name was delicately dropped. The old man was caught
off guard for a moment and went into a profound performance,
extolling the virtues of his other daughters.

"It is no use, Uncle," Farouk said, "Ibrahim is smitten. He saw
that her eyes were emissaries of greater beauties."

Azziz mulled mightily. He would have to make a decision on
this based on many factors. The tribe had had a run of very bad
fortune. Many of his best warriors had been killed during the
Mufti's uprising. An alliance with Haj Ibrahim would be of no
harm. Other needs were also pressing. Money for planting seed
was needed. Several of his camels had suddenly turned old, frazzled, and lame. With British military personnel running all over

the Negev and Sinai deserts, it was difficult to engage in the smuggler's art. Several of his best contraband runners had been caught and jailed. Because the war pay was high, many had deserted the tribe to work for the British Army. Most sent their wages back to the family, but several had run off to the cities. His own son had fled and had become a homosexual prostitute in Jaffa.

Could he find a better offer than what Haj Ibrahim was prepared to pay?

"Ramiza is an unblemished jewel," he said, grasping his heart.

With that gesture Farouk knew that negotiations were under way.

The sheik slapped his head and waved his arms wildly. "Allah himself has rarely feasted his eyes on such purity. I must be completely honest with you, my nephew. There has been inquiry after inquiry for Ramiza. One poor beggar after another has insulted me with his offer. She is a gift, a treasure. She can bear many children. She is also a weaver of baskets . . ."

Ramiza's assets were passionately drawn for nearly an hour.

The first part of the bargaining was to obtain for the prospective bride a personal fortune and trousseau. Although the moneys went directly to her, they would serve as an indication of what the sheik could expect for himself in damages for his "great loss." Ramiza was entitled to a specific set of gifts and benefits. She must have a room equal in size and furnishings to that of the first wife as well as a room for her children. She must be given the deed to a piece of land of her own in the event of her husband's death.

Haj Ibrahim had been wise enough not to send Farouk down to Gaza to barter for a sow. The bride's trousseau he offered was many times greater than was required. Seeing such initial generosity, the sheik felt his appetite suddenly sharpen. Ramiza would be given fifty dunams of land, more than Hagar had by double. It would make her a wealthy widow and assure her of a good second marriage.

With Ramiza's needs attended to, the time had come to compensate the father for his great loss. The bargaining raged for six hours amid breast beatings, cries of poverty, extolling of the bride's virtues, hinting at thievery, and a creeping of insults. One by one the sheik got the range of Ibrahim's limitations on gold and silver coins, crops, seed, numbers of animals. Farouk had managed to stay slightly below the limits his brother had placed. The scent of a deal began to permeate the tent. Farouk then played the clinching card.

With the war on and so many soldiers and military convoys passing through Tabah, the village had naturally gone into illicit arms dealing. Haj Ibrahim's final offering was two dozen immensely precious rifles of the newest models and five thousand rounds of ammunition. Farouk watched his uncle go dull-eyed, an indication the man was struck and was trying to hide it.

"We are very close," Azziz emoted. "Instead of six camels, I think in terms of eight."

"That is beyond all question," Farouk answered.

"But we are very close, Nephew, very close. I think in terms of keeping the seventh camel, but I shall sell the eighth . . . and the money from that will find its way back to you."

"I cannot hear of such a thing," Farouk opined sincerely.

"And instead of twenty-four rifles, let us say, thirty-five rifles and the proceeds of the sale of five of them will be yours."

Farouk closed his eyes and shook his head "no . . . a thousand times no," but Walid Azziz continued down the list, so that when he was done Farouk had obtained a small fortune for himself.

Farouk returned to Tabah elated and recounted how he had bilked the old sheik out of his favorite daughter at an immensely reasonable price.

A month later Hagar was unceremoniously told to visit her relatives in Khan Yunis on the Gaza Strip and not to return until she was sent for.

After she left, Haj Ibrahim organized all the village's women to start preparing a feast of glorious proportions. Several days later a majestic line of camels floated over the horizon toward Tabah. Haj Ibrahim, dressed in new robes, galloped out to greet them and led them into the village.

Tabah had a khan near the village center containing two large rooms: one for the women and one for the men. In the old days the village was a day's camel ride to Jerusalem and the khan had served as a hostel for Moslem pilgrims. These days cameleers came to Tabah several times a year to haul crops, and the khan was availed to them. On other occasions, such as a wedding or other large occasion, the big room was used as a gathering and banquet hall, instead of the tent.

The entire male population of Tabah had gathered in the square. Haj Ibrahim entered first, followed by the great Walid Azziz astride a horse and flanked by his two slaves on donkeys. The camels were tethered in the court of the khan and the two lines of men came together, firing rifles into the air, whooping it up, hugging, kissing, invoking parables and Allah's name. Gifts of the principals were exchanged. The sheik gave Ibrahim a silver dagger of pre-Ottoman vintage and Ibrahim presented the sheik with a handsome camel saddle.

During the men's greetings the bride had been whisked, unseen, up to the knoll by the prophet's tomb, where two large Bedouin tents were pitched, one for either sex.

When the men had rested from the journey and completed their encampment, they repaired down to the khan for the feast. Counting the men in the Wahhabi party and Ibrahim's clan sheiks, muktars, clansmen, and close friends, some eighty men reclined on the carpeted floor on an array of pillows and camel saddles, to be served by over a hundred women.

Neither the sheik nor Haj Ibrahim allowed religion to interfere with a little imbibing on such an occasion. Mouths were seared and stomachs turned into infernos with portions of arrack that brought tears to all but the most hardened.

It is said there were four ways of eating. With one finger to indicate disgust; with two fingers as a show of pride; with three fingers as an indication of normalcy; and with four fingers to show voraciousness. This was strictly a four-finger affair.

Haj Ibrahim had often lectured his villagers, admonishing them for giving parties beyond their means. It was an Arab downfall, a false means of proving one's self-image. Haj Ibrahim was not, of course, a man to be bound by advice he gave others. The Muktar of Tabah displayed his generosity and power and voracity by the enormity of his parties. Farouk often complained that his brother's banquets were taking them to the brink of ruin, but to little avail.

After the ritual handwashing, food came in battalions, regiments, and legions. A parade of the mezes led off the feast, with three dozen varieties of salads.

Stacks of pita bread, flat and round, were torn asunder to be swished around in the pasty salads while the rest was taken by finger. There was hummus and tahini of cold mashed chick peas, sesame seeds, olive oil, and garlic. There were steamed grape leaves filled with pine nuts and currants. There were falafel, deep-fried balls of crushed wheat and chick peas. There were plates of pickles, olives, cold and hot cabbage salads, lamb livers, cucumber salads, peppers, a squadron of eggplant dishes, yogurts, tomatoes, onions, a half-dozen varieties of cheese, lamb pastes, pomegranate seeds with almonds. There were small crusty pies of lamb and fowl and fish balls on skewers, and squash dishes and okra and leeks and a half-dozen different plates of mashed and mixed and whole beans.

Then came the main course.

Heaping platters, so heavy that the women could scarcely carry them, held spit-roasted chicken buried in couscous and other platters held rice filled with lamb's eyes and testicles surrounded by small spring lamb chops. They smelled of saffron and dill and sour cherries and lemon and herbs and cinnamon and garlic and tasted of crunchy nuts.

Then came melons, peaches, grapes, plums, bananas, and baklavas, the layered pastries of honey and nuts, and other thin, sweet, sticky cakes.

After a half-dozen servings of double-boiled, thick sweet Arab coffee laced with cardamom, fingers were licked clean to the accompaniment of an artillery barrage of belching as women cleared the tables.

Narghiles, the water pipes, were passed from smoker to smoker. Then came a contented retelling of great battles and events of the past.

During the latter part of the meal, Haj Ibrahim became visibly uncomfortable. At last his face broke into a broad smile as Gideon Asch entered. As Gideon embraced Sheik Walid Azziz a great howl of approval arose from the Wahhabis, for Gideon had eaten and slept in their tents for the proverbial forty days and was almost one of them.

Walid Azziz, who had not seen Gideon since the war, started suddenly when he saw that he had lost his left hand. And the ancient sheik did something few men had ever witnessed. He wept.

Chapter Sixteen

It did not take long for the party to disintegrate. Shortly after Gideon arrived and after the long journey and orgy of food, the old sheik suddenly looked as if he had been struck comatose. The villagers drifted off while many of the Bedouin toppled over where they had been sitting and broke into a chorus of snores.

Although many of the Bedouin were clansmen, uncles and cousins of the villagers, the villagers locked their doors tightly, hid their valuables, and counted their daughters.

Haj Ibrahim walked Gideon to a place out of the village proper near the highway where they could be alone. The muktar seemed terribly anxious.

"I was afraid you weren't coming back in time for my marriage," Ibrahim said.

"You know I wouldn't miss it."

"Tomorrow we complete the arrangement," Ibrahim continued. "She is an exquisite, magnificent flower, a fawn. I am very fortunate. What do you think about all of it, Gideon? Perhaps taking a second wife is something the Jews ought to think about. That way you can have many more children."

"It only means you'll have that many more plotting against you."

"Hah! No matter. My brother Farouk has been cheating me for years. I am certain that my oldest son, Kamal, is also cheating me. But I am a compassionate man. If a brother and a son spend their lives working for you and you are wealthy and they are poor, then they cheat you. Don't make your dog starve, I say, for someone else will give him a piece of bread and take him away. Believe me, I have gained enough wisdom to control a second family."

Haj Ibrahim cleared his throat a number of times, a clear indication to Gideon that he was wiggling up to a tender subject. "I have to bring up a very delicate matter. You are the only friend I can trust with such a confidence." Ibrahim became grim. "This is the most confidential revelation of my entire life," he said. "I am putting my greatest earthly secret in your hands."

"Are you sure you ought to?"

"I trust you, at least I think I trust you."

"Very well. What is it?"

Haj Ibrahim repeated his throat-clearing performance, then leaned very close to Gideon and lowered his voice, although no one was within earshot.

"The girl, Ramiza, is very young and I have been through many harvests." He emitted a deep, deep, deep sigh and did it over again. "It is vital that I make a great impression because this marriage is one of the most important to take place inside the Wahhabi tribe for many years. Gideon, my friend, in recent times I have had some failures."

"What kind of failures?"

The muktar waved his hands about and grumbled. "Failures of the most humiliating kind. It is certainly not my fault. I simply cannot find Hagar that attractive anymore. I know there has been women's gossip around the water well. Hagar has intimated that there is no longer satisfaction between us. I must make an important impression on my new wife or I will be ruined."

"You're speaking about your role as a man, a lover in bed, are you not?"

Ibrahim groaned long and shook his head. "I cannot understand it. It has only begun to happen since the last harvest and only once in a while."

Gideon nodded that he understood and felt for Haj Ibrahim's embarrassment. The centerpiece of an Arab man's existence was his masculinity. Known impotence was the most horrendous disgrace that could befall a man.

"What am I supposed to do?" Gideon asked.

"I know that your people at Shemesh have certain medicines that can correct the situation."

"Really, Ibrahim. Men have been searching for that magic elixir since time began. You have your own aphrodisiacs."

"I've tried them all. I even sent to Cairo from a magazine. They don't work. I am all right except when I get nervous and think too much about it."

Gideon shrugged.

"The stuff you give to your bulls and horses. The stuff that comes from Spain."

"Spanish fly!"

"Yes, yes, that's it. Spanish fly."

"But that's for animals. It would be dangerous for a man. No, no, Haj Ibrahim, nothing doing."

"If I get nervous and fail with this young girl, I leave Tabah, I leave Palestine. I go to China."

The consequences of failure loomed so large that Haj Ibrahim had been driven to expose his weakness to another man, the most intimate secret an Arab could have.

"I'll speak with the veterinarian," Gideon said.

"My good dear blessed friend! But you must swear by Allah," he said, putting his finger to his lips.

Two hours later Gideon returned to Tabah to find Haj Ibrahim alone in the square, pacing fiendishly.

Gideon took a packet from his pocket. "I had to argue like hell and lie a lot to get this."

Haj Ibrahim seized Gideon's hand and kissed it. Gideon opened the packet, revealing a gram of brownish powdery stuff.

"How does it work?"

"It's made from ground-up beetles and it irritates the skin. Use only a tiny pinch. Rub it around on the head of your prick." Gideon pressed his fingers together to indicate an infinitesimal amount. "Too much could be very dangerous. What is here is enough to last you for ten days. After that, you're on your own."

Haj Ibrahim rubbed his hands together gleefully. "I'll get her with child right away. Then everyone will know exactly how great I am."

After morning prayer, Farouk and the clan chiefs and elders assembled at Haj Ibrahim's house. They then paraded solemnly to the knoll and to the tent of Walid Azziz. Several of the more important members of the Wahhabis sat on either side of the old sheik. Camel saddles surrounded by dozens of embroidered pillows were on the floor in a semi-circle.

Farouk had brought a small chest of silver and gold pieces and a number of official documents. He cracked the lid, withdrew the first of the papers, and read it. It detailed the bride's fortune to be paid by the husband, the bride's price paid to the father, and terms for her return in the event she was not a virgin or did not bear him a son within three pregnancies or if she proved barren.

Farouk then turned over a deed giving Ramiza fifty dunams of land.

The chest of gold and silver pieces was placed before the sheik. This would be the next to final payment. A small percentage was held back in case she had to be returned. Farouk read another document spelling out the crops and animals that were to be turned over to the sheik.

There were nods from all the Wahhabi men to concur that the contract had been fulfilled and that Haj Ibrahim had shown outstanding generosity. The sheik stood, as did the bridegroom, and they clasped hands. Farouk, acting in his role of village priest, read the acceptance. It was repeated by Ibrahim and Walid Azziz three times. Farouk then read from the opening verses of the Koran and the marriage was done.

When the men had finished their business, a sea of village maidens converged on the women's tent, dancing, singing, and undulating. Undulation was taught to a girl early, for it developed the muscles that would later be used in childbearing.

Ramiza's bridal gown and headdress, trousseau and treasures were laid out for the women to inspect. Her own trove was a chest of Bedouin jewelry, simple silver round coins, and crude gemstones. The wedding gown was ornately embroidered with silver threads down the arms and sides. A square over the breast held intricate stitching of a pattern to identify her as a new member of Tabah. The frontal embroidery work was called "nun's stitches" because the nuns in Bethlehem taught young girls how to do it and Ramiza's costume closely resembled the Bethlehem pattern.

Haj Ibrahim, as promised, had not stinted on the trousseau. Ramiza's headdress held a small fortune of Ottoman coins stitched into it. Ibrahim had commissioned six gowns for her instead of the required three. Her belt had a large silver buckle and her mirror, a silver frame. The umbrella was imported from England and her coffer was of beaten copper made by a Jewish artisan in the Old City of Jerusalem.

It was a lavish dowry. Haj Ibrahim greatly increased his stature in the eyes of all the women. Within the hour every woman in the village had come to Ramiza's tent; they were properly impressed as a rain dance of undulating bodies, singing, and clapping resounded from the top of the knoll.

Only the single women were allowed inside the tent as the bride was dressed. One of Ramiza's sisters dressed her by ritual while another carefully folded her trousseau and replaced it in the chest. The girls applauded in unison as each new piece of clothing was put on the bride. The cosmetic bag was opened and her brows and eyelashes were darkened to a piercing, glistening, sensual coal color. Blue powder was traced on her face above and below her eyes so they had a cat's shine. Through it Ramiza remained as immobile and passionless as a painted doll. Her sister finished by splashing perfume over her and sprinkling all the girls in close proximity.

Ramiza's mother was called in to inspect her daughter. She entered singing and undulating as the girl's sisters veiled her and put on her cloak, then the headdress with its display of coins. Ramiza was led outside to where the married women had gathered.

She was placed atop a camel. For the first and last instant of her life, Ramiza was a princess. A sound of whooping was heard by women clucking their tongues quickly in a denotation of joy, and this changed to wailing and weeping.

Ramiza remained motionless, gliding slightly with the sway of the camel, and was engulfed by screaming children and crying women.

As she was assisted from the animal she got her first look at her husband, resplendent in his new robes. He nodded stiffly, fingering the magic powder in his pocket. Ibrahim walked in front of her as she followed him into the house, trailed by the sheik. Haj Ibrahim and the sheik took the two soft chairs, with Ramiza taking a stiff one alongside her husband. Ibrahim's sons, Kamal, Omar, Jamil, and Ishmael, and the daughter, Nada, were told to enter. They bowed to their father and kissed his hand, then kissed the hand of the sheik. They were introduced stiffly to Ramiza, who remained expressionless.

"You are welcome," each said in turn.

A parade of villagers followed, repeating that "our village is your village." By evenfall the tambours, reed horns, and dhamboura had heated up on the threshing floor. The men danced and feasted while the women served. They danced the dabkah. A line of eight or ten men moved together with arms on the next man's shoulders. Their bodies were rigid and they danced like wild dervishes, with swords flashing and war cries cracking the air.

Ibrahim had gotten rid of the children for the occasion. He took Ramiza into the bedroom, which was inundated with incense and shimmering light. She had never seen a bedstead before, nor a room like this.

Ramiza turned her head and giggled as she swayed between nervousness and curiosity. She dared a peek out of the side of her eye as Ibrahim lifted his robe and flung it aside. This was the moment that every woman waited for. From the time she was a little girl, talk of the moment of her husband revealing himself dominated all other conversation among the women. She peeked again and her eyes widened and her lips parted as she gaped at the thing between his legs. All her life it had been pounded into her that she was to fear his instrument. Would that thing hurt her? He was holding it in one hand and it was swollen. He rubbed something on it with his fingers and moved toward her.

"I want to see you!" he rasped.

His hands were on her, clumsily pawing at her headpiece as he half ripped her bridal costume off. The top of her was magnificent, with skin as smooth as precious oils and ripe breasts bearing large brown nipples. She took off her long pantaloons and stood rigidly as he continued to stare up and down.

His member began to itch fiercely, causing him to pant like a dog. He seized her, wrapped his arms around her, and clutched at her as control fled. Ibrahim pushed her onto the bed and jumped on top of her, becoming wild, thrusting crazily, cursing for joy, grunting, gone. Ramiza could not see, but could only feel, this large creature cover her and crush her. She felt the thing tearing at her hard, poking . . . through . . . between her legs. She let out a cry of excruciating pain.

Outside they danced and ate at the threshing ground. Haj Ibrahim could not help but keep on using Gideon's magic powder. It was sublime! It kept him up and going, over and over, sublime, sublime! He used the powder all night long until it was gone.

For Ramiza it was a long and hideous nightmare, just as her mother and sisters had told her it would be. Men were no good on the penetration night. Let time pass, her mother had told her, and you might catch a moment of pleasure for yourself now and then.

By daybreak Ibrahim was scarcely able to lift himself from the bed. For him it was a night never to be forgotten. The secret of the brown powder must have come from Allah himself. Ramiza's bridal nightgown, crimson with bloodstains, was proudly hung where the mirror reflected its image into the living room. All the visitors could now see the manliness of Ibrahim. This night was the moment of truth to all the Arab families, for if the bride had cheated sexually it would have become necessary to have her killed by her brothers, for their honor and the honor of the father depended on her virginity.

There had been occasions in Tabah when a girl was not a virgin and her husband collaborated with her by cutting himself and allowing the blood to drip on the bedsheet.

Girls who had lost their hymens either by masturbation as youths or by some rough game or accident as children had to travel to Lydda to obtain a physician's document of virginity.

There were those who were not virgins, and they had to dupe their new husbands. For a goodly price they could get one of the old widows practicing witchcraft to sew up chicken blood in a breakable skin and insert it into the vagina so that it would burst on penetration by the husband's finger or sexual organ. However, if the husband suspected, the blood could be examined by a midwife who was an expert on these tricks.

There was a percentage of girls whose hymens were elastic and did not break easily, and if such were the case the old daya, or midwife, was commissioned to break the hymen with her fingernail and then certify virginity.

The new husband, who had held nothing more delicate than a shovel or plough handle, could be rough and often leave infection. Or the daya, with her sharp, dirty fingernail, sometimes cut into the vaginal wall and caused hemorrhaging.

But this was not the fortune of Haj Ibrahim. In the morning he presented the bloody sheet to Sheik Walid Azziz, who held it up on the tip of his sword and galloped around their tents, waving it to the cheers of his people.

Haj Ibrahim accompanied Sheik Azziz and his bodyguards and slaves as they rode out ahead of the caravan as it left Tabah. The entourage stopped at a half day's travel mark and waited for the main body to catch up. The two men found shade on the fringes of the Negev Desert, one of those incomprehensibly cruel parches of earth where only a handful of people of a distinctive breed could endure. The belt of Islam held some of the planet's worst land, which ran from North Africa into the dismal places of the Pacific Ocean. It was that crushing part of the world where men could not beat the earth. Numbly they embraced Islam and its fatalistic outlook. Islam gave them something to grasp hold of in order to continue the struggle through life. This land bullied everyone who attempted to exist on it. So harsh, so brutalizing were the forces of nature that those people imprisoned upon it were convoluted into forming a society where cruelty was commonplace.

Brown spots and rising veins declared the age of Walid Azziz, an old desert chieftain whose hand had twisted more daggers into more bellies of enemies than the biblical Joab. Ibrahim and Azziz were men who had declared themselves leaders and proceeded to carve out mini-kingdoms. The tribe and its strongmen had always been the bulwark of Arab political structure.

Ibrahim needed information, perhaps guidance, but men even so close by blood relationship and position seldom spoke straight with one another.

"It seems the war will soon be over," Ibrahim said.

Walid Azziz, who had seen it all come and go for almost ninety years, merely shrugged. They all came, they all went. Only the Bedouin was eternal.

"Perhaps I am relieved. I'm not certain," Ibrahim continued. "I never did trust the Germans."

Walid Azziz said nothing. Early in the war the Germans had slipped one of their agents into the Wahhabi tribe and made the Bedouin all kinds of promises if they would stage a rebellion to co-ordinate with the Afrika Corps when it advanced on the Canal. Walid Azziz made vague and noncommittal promises, just as he had made vague and noncommittal promises to the Turks and the Egyptians and the British, all of whom had claimed sovereignty over the brooding spaces roamed by the Bedouin.

"I have been approached to help form a new All Palestinian Party," Ibrahim said, "and I have been asked if the Wahhabis will come in."

"You live like the center of a target. Villages are no good. I go to the desert. It makes no difference to me who tries to rule Palestine."

"But, Uncle, when the big war stops, a new one will begin here. The British will leave sooner or later. They have failed and they are very weary. We must be prepared to move in and take over Palestine."

For a long time Walid Azziz was desert silent. "Donkey piss," he finally said. "You rule your village. I rule the Wahhabis. The rest is donkey piss. No two Arabs can agree on the distance from here to that tree over there. We have been on this land since the sun has been in the sky and no Arabs have ever ruled Palestine. Be careful about political alliances now."

"When the British leave, surely the Jews will not be able to take on the entire Arab world."

"Perhaps not. Of all the infidels who have come here, none is more loathsome to us than the Jew. This mission against the Jew is like the milk of life for us. And now, for the first time in hundreds of years, there may at last be someone we can beat in a war. But what then? Will the Arab nations hand over Palestine to your wonderful new political organization? Or will Syria grab the Galilee and Egypt the Negev? Will the Arab Legion go back across the Jordan River or stay on the West Bank? And what of Kaukji and the Mufti? And how will our Palestinian nationalism end? It will end as it always ends, with the personal desire of one man to gain power. Be careful of alliances," he repeated, "and be careful of conferences; they always end up in screaming matches and threats."

The old sheik slumped back into silence. The caravan could be seen inching against the skyline at a distance of a few miles. Horizons, it seemed, were made to showcase camels' humps.

"Uncle," Ibrahim prodded. "It must come down to a war between us and the Jews. It is inevitable."

"Yes, we must fight them," Azziz agreed, "because they are infidels and we are Moslems. No infidel can be allowed to rule one inch of land where Islam exists. However, fight the Jews very carefully."

"What do you mean, Uncle?"

"All the rest of the foreigners have come to Palestine to exploit us. The Jews have come to stay. They have done well by the land.

They can be trusted more than anyone else, including ourselves. In the end we will get a better deal from a Gideon Asch than from the Syrians, the Jordanians, the British, anyone. Of course, out in public, you must scream and rage about Jewish presence. However, when you pick up a gun against them, make sure your aim is bad and make sure they know you never meant to hit anything. Allah forbid I have to go back under Egyptian rule."

The line of camels swayed toward them. The old man creaked to his feet, embraced his nephew, and mounted his horse. "We cannot function as nations. We never have been able to govern ourselves. Our way has always been men like you and me taking charge. Play with the Jews quietly. It is our best chance."

He turned his mount and spurred off to join the caravan.

Chapter Seventeen

My father emerged from the war as an imposing figure. Not only had he survived the Mufti's rebellion, he had administered an ignoble defeat to Kaukji's Irregulars. His burning of Tabah's fields, catching the enemy downwind, became a legendary battle that thousands, even millions of poems have been written about.

After my father's initial onslaughts of lust for Ramiza had been blunted, he wanted to return to the familiar comforts that my mother's large feminine body could offer and he summoned her back to bed.

Hagar did as she was bid, for she had no choice, but she made it clear, without using words, that Haj Ibrahim would never know her again with the same passion or share pleasures they had once known.

This enraged my father. His first threats were to divorce her and cast her out permanently. For a Moslem husband to rid himself of an unwanted wife was a very simple matter. However, Haj Ibrahim was pragmatic. Although Ramiza was beautiful, she was a Bedouin girl and much cruder than village women. She was inept and clumsy in running the kitchen and performing her duties. Haj Ibrahim said that one does not throw out the old cow until the new one starts producing milk. He wanted his comforts and meals properly administered. Therefore, my mother was allowed to remain.

At the end of the war I was nine years old. With my mother's prodding, I had approached Haj Ibrahim and convinced him to let me go to school. By learning to read and write, I could become familiar with the village records and documents and make certain Kamal and Uncle Farouk were not still cheating Father.

The school in Ramle was basic and primitive. Yet I was very proud. I was the first child from Tabah since Kamal to go to an Arab school. Uncle Farouk had been taught to read and write by Christian missionaries.

The school consisted of a single, dark bare room, peeling and chipped, with smells from the outside toilet often settling in on the hot windless days. The school yard was not much bigger than the classroom and was of hard-packed dirt. It could not be called a playground because there were no swings or slides or any sporting equipment. I did not know that these even existed until much later. Most of the time recess in the yard was spent eating our lunches, sitting huddled with our backs pressed against the wall to catch the shade. Once in a while some boys kicked a ball or played tag, but mostly we just sat in the shade of the wall or threw stones over it if we could find an old Jew passing by.

There were sixteen boys and no girls in the school, from age eight to twelve. I was the youngest but determined to be a great scholar because my alternative was the lowest job in the family, that of the goatherd. No one else wanted to learn as badly as I did, and often the other boys would fling me to the ground and beat me to try to make me stop studying so hard.

The teacher was Mr. Salmi, a skinny, nervous man with a shiny bald head and a thread of a moustache. He seemed to get more pleasure in using the blackboard pointer for beating us than he did in pointing out problems. Being the son of Haj Ibrahim, I did not get nearly the number of backside strokings as the other boys, but that only made them take out more vengeance on me in the yard. Within a few months I realized I had to be able to hold my own or be beaten out of the school.

I was never without a pocketful of stones and I could throw them as straight and as hard as the meanest Shi'ite Moslem rioting in the streets. I was very good. One day, when things had gotten particularly nasty for me, I filched one of my father's fine daggers from his armoire and hid it under my dress. That day when I was cornered in the yard, I flashed the dagger in desperation and swung it and barely scratched the face of the leader. They didn't bother me much after that.

We had only a few textbooks. Sometimes four of us had to use one book at the same time. Our courses were limited. Mr. Salmi was amazed at how quickly I learned. Often, when Hagar came to fetch me, Mr. Salmi would pat my head and tell her I was gifted by Allah. Mr. Salmi was the second adult man to ever pat my head, because we were mostly ignored by adults. Once my father did pat my head when I proved he was being cheated by Kamal and Uncle Farouk. I can never forget the touch of Mr. Salmi's hand. It felt very good. However, when we were alone and he patted my head, it made me very nervous because Mr. Salmi always gave me a strange look at the same time.

By the time I was nine I had memorized many surahs, or chapters, of the Koran. I practiced in all my free moments, so I could multiply and even do long division in my head without use of a pen and paper.

Aside from the Koran, there seemed to be two main topics of discussion. Out in the yard all the boys spoke about was fucking. The older boys bragged endlessly about their escapades while the younger boys listened to them in awe. I saw through them. They were making it all up. Even though I knew they were lying, I realized that it was important for them to make a manly impression. In fact, making a manly impression seemed to be the most important part of adult men as well. In Tabah, whenever I came into a group of older boys and unmarried men, all they talked about was fucking. Until I went to school all I ever heard about it was that it was dirty, dangerous, and against Allah's will. I knew there had been feuds between our own clans for years over boys and girls who merely looked at each other with passion. Touching a girl could be the cause of a fist fight or even a murder. In the yard one day one of the boys told us how his brothers had murdered their sister because the family had suspected her of fornicating without being married and she had dishonored them. I heard that it had happened in Tabah also, before I was born.

While the glories of sex were extolled all the time in the school yard, just the opposite was told in Tabah. "Stay away from the girls; don't touch a girl, don't smile at a girl, don't play with a girl, don't speak to a girl except on actual village matters. The honor of the family depends on keeping your sister a virgin. The honor of your own manhood depends entirely on your wife having her virginity on the wedding night."

It was so powerfully ingrained in us that boys and girls were absolutely frightened of one another. Yet it seemed that little else mattered to men except how many women they had slept with.

The other major topic in school was the Jews and what was called Zionism. In Tabah my Uncle Farouk was the village priest, or imam. He preached what my father told him to preach. No Sabbath sermon could ever be complete without words condemning the Jews for returning to Palestine. I did know that the Jews had murdered all the prophets and had lied about Abraham and had falsified the Bible. All of us kids knew that. Even though my father wanted nothing from the Jews, we were forced to live next to them, but we never had trouble. Hatred of Jews was not that strong in Tabah. I found out how really evil they were only after I began school.

When the Jews at Shemesh Kibbutz began to dig up antiquities in their fields, they built a museum to display them. Until then, when we found ancient potsherds, flints, and arrowheads in our own fields, we would go down to the highway and try to sell them to pilgrims and travelers on the way to Jerusalem. Once the Jews opened their museum we could sell them lots of what we found. If we found an entire broken pot, we would sell it one piece at a time, getting more and more for each new piece. The Jews spent hours putting the pot back into its original form.

Haj Ibrahim forbade any of the Tabah children from entering Shemesh Kibbutz. We were told that they sacrificed human babies and would more than likely slaughter and sacrifice us if we were caught inside their grounds. In addition to human sacrifices, the Jewish women ran around with their legs naked clear up to their sacred places and there were orgies going on all the time among people who were not even married. Every time we went to the kibbutz gate and asked for the man who ran the museum, our suppressed curiosity only made the tales of Jewish debauchery wilder.

Even so, no one of us kids was really afraid of the Jews. When we did pass or speak, they were always friendly enough. What puzzled me personally was the fact that my father would mount el-Buraq and go off riding with Mr. Gideon Asch for hours. I think a lot of the attitude of letting each other alone stemmed from their friendship. When my father held court at the café I would often hear him say, "we will work the problem out with my good friend Gideon."

If Tabah had a placid and resigned attitude about the Jews, Mr. Salmi didn't. Since most of our time in school was spent learning the Koran, Mr. Salmi usually ended up with a tirade about what the Zionists had done to destroy Palestine and why we must hate them. When Mr. Salmi got going on the Jews, his large Adam's apple bobbed up and down his skinny neck and his face often turned purple and the veins stuck out on his bald head and his voice rose to a shrill shriek.

"Mohammed is the final and ultimate prophet. He alone is the Messenger of Allah. All other religions are therefore null and void. The nonbelievers are infidels, always to be suspected and eventually to be destroyed. The Jews in particular are in a never-ending plot to destroy Islam through heresy, subversion, and cunning ill will. The Koran tells us that. Jesus was a Moslem and Allah saved him from the Jews. It is in the Koran. One day, when Judaism and Christianity and all the other religions of nonbelievers have been destroyed and all their followers have been burned on the Day of the Fire, then Islam will rule the world. Mohammed makes that very clear. Mohammed also commands every Moslem to the sacred duty of devoting his life to these beliefs."

We came to learn that Mr. Salmi was a secret member of the Moslem Brotherhood, which had been formed in Egypt and which killed anyone who opposed them. They were everyone's enemy, even Moslems'.

Mr. Salmi was the first to infuse into me the impurity of all religions except Islam. When Mohammed began preaching in Mecca in the seventh century, wealthy Jews inhabited the peninsula. Surely, Mohammed thought, the Jews, particularly those in Medina, would flock to him and recognize his claim as the final and ultimate prophet and would accept Islam as their new faith. They didn't accept Mohammed, just as they hadn't accepted Jesus, but kept right on practicing their heathen faith.

This outraged Mohammed, who put a curse on them forever. The Koran is filled with dozens of Mohammed's sermons about Jewish treachery. Mr. Salmi always ended the school day with a reading from part of a particular surah from the Koran berating the Jews. His bony fingers quickly licked the pages until he came to a marked place and his eyes lit up as he read with rancor.

It didn't take us long to get the idea from Mr. Salmi what the Jews were up to and why Mohammed detested them.

Surah 2, the second chapter, explains how it was really the Moslems who delivered the Jews from Pharaoh and how the Moslems divided the sea for the Jews to escape to Egypt and how the Moslems made the appointment for Moses to go up into the mountain for forty days and how the Moslems gave the Law to the Jews on Sinai and allowed them to become the People of the Book.

"From the very beginning," Mr. Salmi said, "the Jews lied when they said they discovered the Law and wrote the Bible. They lied when they said Abraham was a Jew. He was a Moslem."

The Christians were also nonbelievers, but we didn't have to hate them as much as the Jews. Jesus had been sent to earth by the Moslems and had been saved by Allah. Jesus became a prophet of Islam. We do not believe that Allah has any children with a human likeness and Jesus was not the Son of God, as the Christians claim. Therefore, the Christians also lied about Jesus and were also in for terrible punishments, for they, too, failed to recognize Mohammed as the final Messenger of Allah.

Early in the year, when Surah 3 was read, many of us were curious. One boy asked Mr. Salmi how Abraham could be a Moslem more than two thousand years before Mohammed founded the religion. The beads of perspiration leaped through Mr. Salmi's skin, wetting his entire head. Mr. Salmi's answer to that question was ten strokes with the blackboard pointer across the boy's ass.

Sometimes, when we sat in the yard, we tried to figure out Mohammed's message. We became confused over dates and names and many things did not match up. The Koran seemed very mixed up about the Virgin Mary, having her born several hundred years before Jesus, but I wasn't about to risk Mr. Salmi's pointer to ask.

Besides, it was useless to ask. Unless a man were a holy man or a great scholar, the Koran was impossible to follow.

Surah 3, verses 114 to 116, warns the true believers, that is, us Moslems, against befriending Jews because they are disloyal and how Jews are happy when evil befalls the true believer.

Surah 7 warns that Jews cannot sleep at night because of the vengeance that the Moslems will take out on them because of their plot against Allah.

Surah 16 shows that the Jews are corrupt because they have turned from Islam and therefore the Moslems correctly invoked punishment upon punishment on them.

From Surah 2 to the end of the Koran in Surah 114, Mohammed establishes all the rules for the believers to live by so they may join him in paradise. We all liked the way Islam declared eternal war on the nonbelievers and we all hoped to be alive when we won the war over them.

Mr. Salmi would often screech out, when his head was really dripping, that "in Arab lands we know how to deal with Jews and infidels. Surah 22 tells it better than anything else. Mohammed had been rebuked by the Jews of Medina and preached that 'turning the cold shoulder, they, the Jews, were led astray from the way of Allah; for them is humiliation in this world and on the day of resurrection the Moslems shall cause them to taste the punishment of the burning.' "

Once or twice before going to school I tried to ask questions about the Koran of my Uncle Farouk but was answered with a slap or, if I stayed outside of slapping range, a threat.

The only surah that most Moslems knew and understood was Surah 1, a simple prayer of seven lines. Like all the surahs, it begins with "In the name of Allah, the Merciful, the Compassionate." It is a prayer to Allah acknowledging him as the one having power of the Day of Judgment and beseeching the worshiper to stay on a righteous path. The rest of Islam and the Koran was left up to holy men to explain, for we had no formal priesthood.

Each day as my mother and I passed by Shemesh Kibbutz I became more and more curious. When my mother was allowed to stay at home again, my brother Omar took over the stalls at the bazaar. Omar was lazy and it was hard for me to depend on him to get me to school on time.

I was reading and writing so well that my father was beginning to see my great future value for him. I tried to inch up close to him every time I could, but Kamal was always at his side, blocking my path. But I was brave because I was becoming learned and I looked Father straight in the eye one night and asked him to be allowed to take the bus back and forth to Ramle. There was an Arab bus line, and after warning me never to ride the Jewish bus, my father agreed.

My curiosity about Shemesh Kibbutz intensified as Mr. Salmi taught us more and more about their heathenism. I could envision the terrible things going on there and often spoke to the other boys in the village about them. Although none of them had actually been inside the kibbutz, they all seemed to know everything about it.

My best friend was Izzat. He was my age, but there was a serious problem. His entire family had been ostracized by the villagers as punishment for his father's working in a Jewish field. None of us were supposed to talk to anyone in Izzat's family. Because we were best friends, I dared break the rule. Izzat always waited for me at the bus stop and we could take a long route back to the village so we would not be seen by the others. One day Izzat awaited my bus breathlessly and told me that he knew positively what was a true story. A married Jewish woman made love with another man. The husband found out, chopped off the lover's head, cut open his wife's belly, put the lover's head inside it, and sewed it back up.

This only made me more curious. I must admit I was most curious about the women who wore short pants that showed their legs. I had never seen a woman's legs except my mother's. I had never seen Nada's legs, for she wore long pantaloons down to her ankles and was as modest as the Koran admonished her to be. A dozen times a day my mother would warn Nada to keep her legs closed and tell her, "Shame." Until I was old enough to understand, I thought the word "shame" was part of Nada's name.

I found out by accident that Mr. Salmi actually went inside Shemesh Kibbutz one day every week to teach classes in Arabic to the Jews. I thought this was very strange.

For several weeks I slowly tried to convince Mr. Salmi that I could help him by teaching the younger kibbutz children simple things, like the names of trees and animals and plants in Arabic. He was teaching two classes, one to children and one to adults, and began to see the value of having me teach the children. He would have less work to do. Of course, I didn't tell him I was forbidden to enter the kibbutz. He finally agreed to let me go with him and assist him. It meant I would have to come home after dark, but my father rarely knew where I was and I was willing to take the risk that he would never find out.

I don't know what I expected, but I was awash with fear as we were passed through the kibbutz guard post. What I saw bewildered me. I saw for the first time so many things I had never seen before even though Tabah and Shemesh lived side by side.

I had never seen a green lawn.

I had never seen flowers that did not grow wild.

I had never seen streets without donkey or goat shit on them, even in Ramle.

I had never seen a real playground with all kinds of balls for the children and all kinds of things like swings and sliding boards and sandboxes.

I had never seen a swimming pool.

I had never seen a library with hundreds of books just for children.

I had never seen toys.

I had never seen a museum or a science room in a school with microscopes and magnets and burners and bottles of chemicals.

I had never seen a toilet.

I had never seen a medical clinic.

I had never seen a machine shop.

I had never seen anything like the big barn filled with tractors and tools and automatic machines that milked the cows.

I had never seen electric lights, except in the distance, out on the highway or lights from the kibbutz. I often wondered how they worked. There was a light bulb in our classroom in Ramle, but it didn't work.

I had never seen a painting made by a human hand.

I had never been in a room in the wintertime that was really warm.

I had never seen a pond where they actually grew fish to harvest.

I saw a great chicken house that was lit up all night to confuse the chickens so they wouldn't know day from night.

As you can well imagine, dear reader, I made myself invaluable to Mr. Salmi and by the end of the fourth visit I was teaching some of the smaller children all by myself because I wanted to keep coming back.

The Jews were very friendly. At first this made me suspicious that they were trying to lure me into a trap, but as time passed I began to trust them a little. I did keep out a sharp eye so I wouldn't suddenly be seized by them, and I always remained within shouting distance of Mr. Salmi.

There was a Jewish girl named Hannah who had come from Syria and spoke a little Arabic she remembered from her earlier years. She became my helper in the classroom. Like Nada, Hannah was a few years older than me. The first time she took me by the hand, I pulled it back instantly and my mouth went dry. Surely someone would see her touch me and I would be killed.

Then I saw the strangest thing of all. Boys and girls, older and younger than me, held hands and played. They formed circles and danced and sang together. Often they kissed and hugged. Perhaps this was the beginning of a secret orgy? I was so astonished about all the things I saw I even forgot about the naked legs of the girls. Hannah did not seem ashamed about hers.

What was most difficult to comprehend was the way Mr. Salmi acted when he was with the Jews. He laughed and joked while he taught them. He never did that with us in Ramle.

Mr. Salmi seemed to be good friends with many of the Jews. He often patted the children on the head when they gave correct answers. I saw him embrace some Jews the same way Arab men greet each other. I even saw a Jewish woman put her arms around him once and laugh, and her husband was standing right next to them! The Jews always sent him to catch his bus with a market basket filled with vegetables, fruits, eggs, and an occasional chicken. The very next day in Ramle he would go into a rage about his hatred of the Jews.

I think my mind started going crazy with confusion. Was Shemesh Kibbutz all a trick of Satan to lure us Moslems away from being true believers? After all, our mission was to convert them or kill them. That was what the Koran said. Oh God, I wanted to ask someone. One day I caught a glimpse of Mr. Gideon Asch and longed to speak to him. I dared not, for he might tell Haj Ibrahim I was there. He was friends with my father and therefore I could not trust him. All I knew was that someone hadn't been telling me the truth and that it was dangerous for me to learn the truth.

I became so obsessed with going to Shemesh I often dreamed about it. If the Jews did practice human sacrifices and held orgies, they did it so no one could see, and by the end of my fifth trip I began to doubt that they even did those things.

Despite the dangers, I determined to find out the truth, and that is when disaster fell. On that awful night I tried to slip through our yard into the kitchen, as I always did when I had been to the kibbutz. This night my father filled the doorway. I ducked under the first swing of his walking stick, but he caught

me with the backlash in my ribs and sent me sprawling and
screaming over the yard. He was atop me, immense as a giant, his
feet kicking into my body, his face contorted with rage, and
curses ringing off his lips.

"I will kill you if you ever go near the Jews again! May a thousand ants infest your armpits!"

He only stopped when Hagar ran out and threw herself over
me and begged for mercy. For several days I could barely move. I
crawled into the kitchen near the stove and cried all day. The sky
had come down on me. My father had taken me out of school.

This went on for a fortnight. Although the color of my bruises
began to fade, the pain in my heart would not. I finally heard my
mother confide to one of her cousins that she would have to put a
stop to it or I might starve myself to death.

For the first time since Ibrahim married Ramiza, my mother
was very nice to him. She brushed against him, undulating
slightly, touched his shoulder, and did the rest with her eyes. She
made suggestive remarks like she used to before Ramiza came.
She seduced my father with all the sensuality she could muster
and he invited her to bed that night. The next morning Haj
Ibrahim seemed a changed man. The anger against me was suddenly gone. My mother went to bed with him again that night.
The next morning my father, with a magnanimous flick of the
wrist, told me I could return to school.

Eventually I found out who had told my father about my going
to Shemesh. It was my best friend, Izzat. He had always waited
for me by the bus stop and became suspicious of the one day a
week I told him not to come. Izzat saw me leaving the kibbutz.
His family was like the village leper. No one had spoken to them
for years. Izzat thought that he could win a reprieve for them and
gain favor with my father.

It taught me a lesson: Never trust anyone, especially your best
friend. I didn't trust my brothers, particularly Kamal, who was
my greatest rival. I didn't even trust my mother even though I
loved her very much. She was always scheming and using me
against my father. I suppose I did trust Nada.

I only went back to Shemesh Kibbutz one more time . . . but
that is another story.

Chapter Eighteen

I did not want to be a goatherd, although there were some goats I liked. I was good friends with our yard goat, and when Ibrahim told me to help my brother Jamil slaughter her, I could not. Not only was being a goatherd the lowliest of all jobs, but I simply did not like to kill animals. Haj Ibrahim told me I must learn how to kill and he forced me on three occasions to slaughter goats. I did it because he was watching, but I ran off and vomited afterward and cried all night.

When I returned to school I was more determined than ever to become a great scholar. It was apparent that Mr. Salmi could not teach me much more. He was a poor man and had only a few books in his personal library. I devoured them quickly. I talked him into saving his newspaper for me to read after he had finished with it.

The Jews spoke their own language, called Hebrew. We spoke Arabic, of course, so when we had to deal with Jews we almost always did it in English. Neither we nor the Jews liked speaking English because the British ruled the country. However, so many signs and so much business was done in English that all of us knew a little of it.

Mr. Salmi could read and write in English, but he had no books. There were a few Jews in Ramle who had businesses around the bazaar. One, Mr. Yehuda, owned a junkyard and collected and sold old newspapers and magazines. He was a friendly old man and quite unlike the Jews in the kibbutz. Mr. Yehuda spent most of the day sitting in his tiny office and reading prayer books. He would let me scour his newspapers for the Palestine *Post*, the English-language paper. I worked it out so I could spend a half hour after school reading in the junkyard before taking the bus back to Tabah. It was a wonderment, and my learning English eventually saved the life of my family. Reading the Palestine *Post* had to be kept secret from my father because it was published by the Jews.

By the third year in school I began to write quite well. Mr.

Salmi encouraged me to write about my village and other things I
knew of. Almost every night I wrote another new story. Some of
them were in the form of poetry, like the Koran. We Arabs use
poetry a great deal to express ourselves. My writings became like
a diary of the daily life of Tabah and our religion and customs
and sorrows. Many of the stories and thoughts I kept to myself
because I could have gotten into trouble for thinking what I
thought of certain people and happenings. Many of the things I
write here now I learned many years later. It is very mixed up,
like the Koran itself, but I would like to tell you about us. You are
most welcome.

My Village of Tabah, like most Arab villages, was built on the
highest ground for defensive purposes from Bedouin raids or attacks from enemy tribes.

My earliest memories of Tabah were its smells. As I walked
barefoot in the dirt street, there was an ever-shifting current of
aromas, of the sharp food spices, of cardamom in the coffee from
the café, of incense at night.

Mostly I remembered the smells of dung. Any child of three
can tell the difference between the dung of donkeys, horses, cows,
goats, sheep, and dogs, all of which littered the streets, paths, and
fields and only disappeared during the winter rains. Then the
streets were always muddy.

Dung was very important for us. We not only used it to fertilize
our fields, but Hagar and the village women made large brown
flat cakes of it and dried it on our roofs. It was the principal
source of heat for cooking and warming our houses. Wood was
scarce and gathering it was a long and tedious chore, left mainly
for older women who had no families to take care of.

Every year in the springtime after the houses had dried out
from the winter rains, a new layer of mud and whitewash was
applied to the cottages to replace wear and mend cracks. The
mud was mixed with dung to give it firmness. Extra dung was
traded to the Bedouin, who did not have wood or enough of their
own dung for their needs. My father and a few others in the
village were wealthy enough to burn kerosene, but this was a
very luxurious item.

Every house in Tabah was built along the same lines: square
with flat roofs for collecting water in the rainy season and for

drying out crops in the warm weather. Mr. Salmi told me it was the same look that the villages had thousands of years ago. The houses of the poor, which was most of the village, were made of mud brick, and after the annual whitewash a light blue color was used to outline windows and doors. This was to ward off the evil spirits.

The houses were very close together, for defensive purposes. There were five clans from the Wahhabi tribe in Tabah and each clan had its own section of the village and each also had a separate part of the graveyard where the men were buried. Women were buried separately.

My father and Uncle Farouk had stone houses, as did the clan heads and certain other prominent villagers like the carpenter, the potter, the sandal maker, the basket weaver, and the cloth weaver.

There was one other stone house in Tabah, which was most unusual because it was built and owned by a widow. Her name was Rahaab and she was the village seamstress. In all Arab villages everyone is expected to marry and have children. Childless couples were looked upon as tragedies. Widows were taken care of by the sons, usually the oldest, who inherited their father's land leases and debts. Every village had some kind of widow like Rahaab who had no one to look after her, and there were always a few unmarriageables—cripples, idiots, and blind ones—and if they had no family the clan was responsible for them.

Rahaab was old and fat and toothless, but she owned a hand-powered sewing machine that had come all the way from England with the name "Frister & Rossmann" on it. The village women were jealous and afraid of Rahaab. It was not only that she made a good living, for her machine was going all the time, but it was rumored that she fornicated a lot. The Koran is very strict about the punishments for fornication, and those who do it are apt to go to the fire on the Day of Resurrection. My father turned a blind eye to Rahaab's fornication because she only did it with widowers and unmarriageables.

As ugly as Rahaab was, there were always a lot of males hanging around her stone house, mostly little boys like myself. She kept a big pocket filled with sweets and we would take turns at turning the handle on the big wheel of the sewing machine. Rahaab had a certain way of tilting on her bench so that she rubbed her tits against the little boys who were spinning her wheel and it would make our pricks hard. I remember the smell of oil that came from her machine and the fact she always sang when she sewed. She was the only woman I ever heard singing except at a festive occasion. I think Rahaab was the happiest woman in Tabah. She was the only woman who was allowed to travel to Ramle by herself, without a male escort. The women gossiped, and I think with some envy, that Rahaab paid younger men in the city to sleep with her.

The stone houses were the only ones with their own outdoor toilets. Each clan had a pair of abandoned houses that were used for toilets and to throw away garbage. One house was for the men and one for the women. I was glad my house had its own toilet.

Communal life centered around the village square, with its picturesque water well and a small overflow stream. The women washed the family clothing in the stream. Next to the well was the communal bakery, partly below ground because of the ovens. The water well, stream, and ovens were the main meeting places of the women for gossip.

By the opposite side of the square was our mosque, with its own small minaret. Uncle Farouk was the priest, or imam. He was also the village barber. One of the old clan chiefs acted as muezzin and climbed to the top of the minaret each day to call us to prayer.

On the third side of the square was the café, store, and khan, all owned jointly by my father and Uncle Farouk. The khan, a two-room hostel, had one room for men and one room for women and a place to hitch camels.

The khan was always ready to receive any members of the Wahhabi tribe. All Arabs are extremely hospitable and even the poorest home had a stack of mats to put down on the floor for visiting relatives. Moreover, the khan was used during those times of the year—harvests, festivals, for the dung trade—when the cameleers came.

I think Haj Ibrahim kept the khan for his own vanity too. It gave him a large gathering place for clan chiefs of other villages to come to Tabah to discuss communal matters or as a room where my father could throw his fabled parties.

If the water well and ovens belonged to the women, the café belonged to the men. The radio wailed from sunup to sundown with oriental music, sermons, and news from Jerusalem and Damascus. At nighttime we could hear from as far away as Baghdad and Cairo.

On one side of the café was the village store. Women were allowed on the store side to make purchases. Before the Jews came to Palestine everything in the store was foreign: tobacco from Syria, sardines from Portugal, matches, razor blades, and sewing needles from Sweden, tinware from England. There were a few medicines such as aspirin and baking soda but, as Moslems, we did not believe too much in them. Illness was caused by evil spirits and the healing herbs and special brews were made and kept by older village women. The most important item in the store was kerosene, but few families could afford it. At Shemesh Kibbutz the Jews had a cannery and canned many of their fruits and vegetables. My father did not allow them in the store. There was a story around that they would probably sell us poisoned cans so we would all die and they would get our land.

Everyone in the village owed money or some crop to the store. My father was very liberal at letting the villagers run up a debt on the theory that "a man in your debt cannot call you a dog, for he is the dog and must obey." More than once my father used a villager's debt to convince him to think accordingly on various questions.

The final part of the village square was a communal threshing floor. It was a favorite gathering place of younger people because it was one of the few places where boys and girls could come into proximity with one another without fear. At the threshing floor, with sheaves being unloaded and the two sexes working side by side to grind the grain, they were often almost forced to touch one another, however quickly and however slightly. It became a place of flirtations. Everything at the threshing floor had a double meaning: the casual touch, eye contact, and conversation. Because girls were not permitted to show anything of themselves except their hands and part of their face, they made their eyes do the work for them. No women in the world can say more with their eyes than Arab women.

Tabah was large enough to have its own market day every fortnight. Peddlers descended on the square by donkey cart, carrying their wares in great clay pots.

The jars and pots were works of art. Many had shapes resembling women, full-breasted or pregnant or straight and skinny.

There were mirrors, combs, and amulets to ward off jinn, the evil spirits. There were medicines and potions guaranteed to cure all ills and to make men virile. There were stacks of secondhand clothing, used shoes and harnesses, and tempting bolts of cloth.

Other peddlers repaired pots and ground knives and scissors and field tools. There were gunsmiths to repair our cache of arms. Every village had secret arms that they kept in the mosque or their "prophet's tomb." We knew that no Arab would steal from these holy places and we knew the British would not go into a holy place to search for them.

Once a year the Armenians came with their picture machines. Each home, no matter how poor, had a few photographs. It was usually a picture of the head of the house taken in full, flowing regalia, perhaps on his wedding day. No photographs of women were allowed. One of my father's greatest prides was his collection of many pictures that showed him in fighting or riding attire or shaking hands with some important official. There was one photograph with all of his sons.

There was another peddler who came only once a year. He had stacks of used magazines from many foreign countries. Most of them had pictures of naked women in them. My father kept his hidden in the big wardrobe closet in his bedroom, but all of us boys risked a look.

One path from the square led down to the highway and bus stop. Uncle Farouk kept a stand there that one of his sons ran. He paid the bus drivers to always stop at Tabah so he could sell the travelers a soft drink or fruits and vegetables. The children sold pieces of potsherds that the Shemesh museum didn't buy and they sold prayer or worry beads to the Moslems and crucifixes to the Christians. They told the travelers that the arrowheads were from the battle during which Joshua asked for the sun to stand still.

Other children, who had nothing to sell or nothing better to do, ran down to the bus stop to beg. They surrounded the travelers and pulled on their clothing for attention until the people had to beat them off like flies. We had the usual number of blind, deformed, and mutilated villagers who used their horrible appearance to extort money. Haj Ibrahim did not allow any of his sons or daughters to beg, but it was impossible to stop the others.

Inside the homes of most of the villagers the combined living and dining room had goatskin rugs on the floor and a long bench of mud brick to seat the family and visitors.

The kitchen held an open hearth for cooking. In the more affluent homes one could find a Primus kerosene stove, which the Jews manufactured in Palestine. A stone mortar and pestle was the main utensil. The rest of the kitchenware consisted of a few platters and tin tools and pots. The one fine thing everyone owned was the coffee finjan and cups.

Clay jars holding salt, coffee, beans, and other staples lined the wall. Other large jars or empty kerosene tins sat near the door and were used to carry water from the well. Attached to the kitchen were clay bins to hold grains, nuts, dried fruits, and other food that would not spoil.

Because of our wealth, our kitchen also had a caldron for preparing grape syrup and rendering the sheep fat that was used in most of the cooking.

The balance of the rooms were bedrooms. These were nothing more than large square cells with thin rush mats and goatskins for sleeping.

As more children came into the world and older sons brought new brides home, new sleeping cells were added. This way everyone was garrisoned in together in his own clan's sector of the village. One of our villagers, who had nine married sons, had fifty-two people in his extended-family house.

My father's house had many things the others did not have. In his living room were wooden, instead of mud-brick, benches filled with pillows covered with elaborate stitching that was embroidered in Bethlehem. We also had two very fine Western-type overstuffed chairs, one for Ibrahim and one for the honored guest. We were not allowed to sit on them.

We had glass over our windows, while the other houses had wooden shutters. My father had the only raised bedstead, and when he married Ramiza he had the only two bedsteads.

Beyond the cluster of houses and the village square came a confusion of small farming plots that had been divided and redivided many times through inheritance. The season of the year dictated the kind of crop. Winter crops of wheat, barley, horse beans, and lentils were mainly for our own subsistence. Fenugreek, or Greek hay, was grown for forage. Summer crops were for selling in the souk. We grew magnificent hand-watered melons, chick peas, sesame, and a large variety of vegetables.

Many of our fields and orchards were communal. Tabah had exceptionally rich land for Palestine. Our pride was our fruit trees and our almond and walnut trees and, mostly, our ancient olive grove. The year's final crop was the grape and this was also communal, as were the grazing grounds for the goat and sheep herds.

Until the time of the trucks the cameleers came up from the Wahhabi tribe several times a year to haul crops and bring in lime for replastering houses. The cameleers mainly traded for our surplus dung. Since the Bedouin were the greatest smugglers in all the world, our dung was usually paid for with hashish.

Every field, every prominent tree or rock or patch crossing had separate names such as "the place the old woman died," "the place of the spoiled figs," "the frog stone," "the widower's tree," "the prophet's tomb," "the place of the burning battle," "Joshua's mound," "the place of stitching," which was Rahaab's stone house.

My father had the only clock in the village, although he could scarcely read time and did not adhere to it. Each day at sunset he would set the clock at twelve, which made no sense. Time was kept by the location of the sun.

My father also had the only calendar, which he did not use either. Time of year was told in the ancient way by phases of the moon or the season.

My father was wealthy enough to burn kerosene for light. His lamp was much brighter than those that burned a wick of sheep's wool dipped in a bowl of olive oil. He did keep a small oil fire burning in his bedrooms to ward off the evil spirits.

Attached to each house was a barnyard containing the household donkey, cow, a milking goat, and perhaps a brace of oxen. Many of the oxen were jointly owned with other families of the same clan and a great number of family feuds erupted over their use. The farmers considered the household animals some kind of relatives. Often they would walk to the fields while holding conversations with them. Most of the barns opened into the house because the animals gave off heat from their bodies, which was essential in helping to keep the house warm. Beyond the barn was a small plot of vegetables and perhaps a few fruit trees and chickens. Chickens and eggs were the wife's domain. By tradition they were allowed to sell the surplus eggs and keep the egg money for themselves. All the little individual yards were walled off by cactus fences.

In Tabah everyone thinks of everyone else as a tribal brother or sister and the elders as aunts and uncles. Although everyone is supposed to be responsible for everyone else, for the Koran commands love among the believers, fighting within the family, the clan, and the tribe is the bane of Arab life. No clan or tribe is without many enemies.

I knew it was dangerous and difficult for me to go to school and aspire to things like writing poetry and stories and learning foreign languages, for it made my brothers very jealous. I was the only child in Tabah who aspired. Because we had no organized schooling or recreation, the children hung around the adults, each child tagging along with the man or woman whose position they would eventually replace.

Kamal stayed fiercely at my father's side because he wanted to become the muktar and head of the home and clan when Ibrahim died. Omar, who ran the stalls in the bazaar, would eventually become the store and café keeper and he could usually be found around my Uncle Farouk waiting on tables and selling behind the counter. Jamil, who would be the principal farmer, stayed with a cousin who was foreman of our fields. As I slowly gained my father's confidence, the danger from my brothers grew.

For the peasants of Tabah, the land, the village, the family, and the religion were one and the same. The village awakened to morning prayer, which was called for from the minaret by the muezzin. We had breakfast of pita bread, goat's cheese, olives, figs, thyme, and coffee and everyone went to work, except my father.

Because we lived so close to each other it was inevitable that fights broke out all the time. Each of the five clans had its own sheik who was also a village elder. Fighting inside a family or clan could usually be contained by the sheik. It was when two clans disputed that a blood feud could form that could last for generations.

Haj Ibrahim was a powerful muktar. His dispensation of justice was swift and final. The best way to keep a man in his place was to have communal humiliation imposed upon him and his family. To an Arab, humiliation is the ultimate punishment.

The humiliation of Izzat's family had been particularly harsh. His father, Tareq, was a member of our own Soukori clan. Between harvests most of the men had to find outside work. Many went to Gaza when the orange crop was being picked and they could stay in nearby Wahhabi tents. Others, with relatives in Jaffa, worked the docks during shipping seasons. Since the Jews now had many settlements, it was easy to find extra work in their fields during the harvests and still be close to home. However, Haj Ibrahim had forbidden anyone in Tabah to work for the Jews. When Tareq broke the ban my father forbade him to enter the café, cut off his credit, forbade him to enter the mosque, to join festivals, or to share equally in communal income. His poor wife was so berated by the women at the water well and the ovens that she would only go there when the others had left. The village boys were forbidden to play with Tareq's three sons, although I did keep on being friends with Izzat.

After nearly three years of it, Tareq went berserk and ran off to Trans-Jordan, abandoning his family. Such a separation from kin in the Arab world is living death.

Men and women were locked into lifelong roles from which there was no chance of change or escape. My father explained that only through blind acceptance could one expect to get through this life without going mad. Many people went mad anyhow.

One only had to enter a house in Tabah or the café or the ovens to realize that no one got pleasure from their toil. Work was considered to be the worst curse in the world. My father did not have to work and had reached the highest station in Arab life. Work was a reason to survive, but there was no reason to improve one's house or land, for few owned them; most were simply bound to them.

Although the women had a secret subculture, they were destined to go from birth to death with no permission to have pleasure. They were always separated from the men on social occasions. They could not sing or dance at weddings, except off by themselves. They could not travel without a male member of the family accompanying them to oversee the family honor. Some male villagers went to a cinema in Lydda once or twice a year, but this was forbidden to the women.

The men were able to gather at the café or at a celebration of a saint's birthday or a wedding or a funeral. A lot of frustration was vented on these occasions. The only time women could gather was at their daily work. Almost every day there was a fight among the women at the well or the ovens. Their language often became more vicious than the males'.

Our seasons were very specific: wet or dry. By March the rains had stopped, and this was the time to prepare the soil, set out new vines, and plant new trees. Getting rid of the winter's dampness was a huge chore. None of our homes, even the stone ones, were warm enough or dry enough. Many children died of the cough when they were infants. After the rains all the household goods, sleeping mats, clothing, goatskin rugs, and quilts were moldy. These were set on the rooftops to dry while the houses were repaired.

Garden plots were planted and the sheep sheared. Many of the older women still spun wool with hand spindles. The damp wool was discarded from our sleeping quilts and new wool stuffed into them.

By midsummer we were harvesting. When the grain crop came in, a sense of urgency swept over Tabah. Everyone turned a hand to work, except my father and some of the village elders, for we were in a race against rain and the dread of rotting grain. We feverishly sorted the grains, dried them on the roofs, and took them to the threshing floor, working day and night.

Our winter needs in grains, lentils, and beans were sorted on goatskins and stored in the large clay bins attached to the house. Rents were paid with half the crop, and what was left over after personal needs was sold in the souks.

Spoilable crops such as eggplants, tomatoes, and figs were dried in the sun so they could be stored for the winter.

By September we made the final harvest, a communal gathering of grapes. Many were sold to the Trappist monastery at Latrun, a few miles up the road. The monks were crazy, but they made a famous wine. None of them was allowed to speak except the superior.

The village men trampled the balance of the grapes. It was considered to be work too immodest for women, who would have to show bare legs above their knees. The grape juice was boiled in open hearths. At the same time the sheep, which had been carefully fattened on mulberry leaves, were slaughtered and their meat was boiled down to extract the fat. The Valley of Ayalon was permeated with the smells of the fires: The grapes and the sheep fat, and the smoke from them hung low on windless autumn days.

The poorest of our lot moved the goat herds up into the Bab el Wad for the winter. Often wives and children traveled with the men and lived in caves. They paid cave rent and pasturage fees by collecting and sacking goat dung.

When we were all tucked in and awaiting the rains, the women used the time for mending, sewing, and embroidering their fancy dresses. The women of Tabah had a unique geometric pattern of embroidery down the front of their black gowns. Men would repair tools and harnesses, but mostly they would sit around the café, listening to the radio and repeating stories of great courage in battle or greater prowess in bed. Repetition in tales and poetry, repetition in the shapes of our houses, repetition in the music over the radio, repetition in everything was our life.

In the relaxed atmosphere of the wet season many babies were made, new marriage contracts completed, and the subsequent weddings helped alleviate the boredom. That was the time of the year my father took his second wife.

I remember it because the beginning of the wet season was the time the Armenians came to take pictures and the circumciser came and cut off the foreskins of all the boys who had been born that year. They all lined up in one of the rooms in the khans, held in their mothers' arms. Soon every one was shrieking and bleeding from the pain. Fathers congratulated one another while the mothers soothed the pain with sheep fat and fondling.

I cannot leave the story of my memories of Tabah without writing something about Islam, the Koran, the Sunna, and jinn.

Islam means "the submission to God's will."

A Moslem is "one who submits."

Mohammed was an impoverished and illiterate camel driver from Mecca who married a rich widow. This allowed him to

pursue his calling. He received his mission by going up to Mount
Arafat for forty days and receiving instructions from Allah Himself.

The Koran, a collection of Mohammed's sermons, was not
written until many years after his death, by people who had listened to him and were divinely inspired to remember everything
he said. Since he was the final prophet, all other religions were
therefore obsolete.

Mohammed was awakened one night by the angel Gabriel in
Mecca and was told he was to take a night journey to paradise. To
prepare for the journey, the angel slit Mohammed's body open,
removed his heart, and washed it; when it was replaced it was
filled with faith and wisdom. Mohammed then mounted a sort of
horse, a mare named el-Buraq. I say a sort of horse because the
mare had a woman's face, a mule's body, and a peacock's tail. This
amazing animal could travel as far as the eye could see in a single
stride.

The Koran has a passage that mentions "the fartherest place."
Jerusalem is never mentioned by name, but the early wise men
figured "the fartherest place" was Jerusalem.

Reaching Jerusalem, Mohammed tethered el-Buraq to the Western Wall of the Temple of Herod and ascended to the Temple
Mount. Here he discovered the great rock of Abraham's sacrifice,
which had also been the altar of the Hebrew Temple. Mohammed
then leaped from the rock onto a ladder of light that led to paradise. The rock started to follow Mohammed, but Gabriel, who
had flown to Jerusalem ahead of Mohammed, ordered the rock to
stay put and the rock obeyed. Later, a great shrine was built over
it, called the Dome of the Rock. Nearby, the Al Aksa Mosque was
erected. Al Aksa means "the fartherest place."

El-Buraq was waiting for Mohammed when he got to heaven.
Once again aboard the mount, Mohammed rode through the
seven paradises of heaven. He met the patriarchs and the
prophets of the Book and saw all the angels at prayer. He said
that Moses was a fairly reddish-faced man and that Jesus was of
average height and had a lot of freckles, as did Solomon.

Quickly gaining all the knowledge and wisdom of the saints,
angels, and prophets, he was allowed a private audience with Allah and was the only man to ever see Allah unmasked. Mohammed and Allah spoke at length to define the various aspects of

Islam. Allah wanted the people to pray to Him thirty-five times a day, but Mohammed argued Him into letting them pray a more practical five times daily. After his visit Mohammed returned to Mecca the same night.

The Koran has many other things besides punishments and rewards. It gives us instructions about fornication, adultery, disobedient peoples, alms, murder, corruption, insults, debtors, the pit, divorce, blame casting, dowries, persecution, fasting, the Day of the Burning, fighting, backsliding, backbiting, covetousness, gambling, infanticide, burying infants, heathenism, inheritance laws, how to sleep, menstruation, parental duties, wet-nursing, marital intercourse, oaths, dissension, orphans, eating in other's houses, prayer times and requirements, the evil eye, ownership of horses, suckling, the scene of the judgment, prohibition of wine and alcohol, renegades, retaliations, satans, repentance, slanderers, treatment of slaves, widows' wills, thievery, suspicion, usury, cunning, transgression, omens, diets and food laws, prayers of the evil, sexual abstinence, unscrupulous business practices, vanity, raising the dead, sexual dishonor, eunuchs, motherhood, regulations for keeping concubines, bloodclots, enemies, evil spirits, why Mohammed must be believed, vanquishing the Greeks, veiling the woman's face, cattle, fraud, niggardliness, idolatry, Allah's powers of imposing death, hypocrites, breaking bonds with kin, temptation, avarice, ritual washing, head shaving and other rules for pilgrims, fate of sinners, those who disbelieve, conspiracy, treatment of enemies and women refugees, lewdness, pregnant camels, slinkers, rain, perversity, plots and counterplots, world unity, and mercy.

Of course this only touches the vast number of other subjects the Koran instructs us on. Every house owned a Koran, but almost no one knew how to read it. Most people knew the required daily prayers and bits and pieces of the Book. The rest of it had to be taught by people like my Uncle Farouk because we have no formal clergy. Uncle Farouk didn't seem to be too clear, but his sermons were accepted.

There are Five Pillars of Islam. The first pillar is the Moslem's total submission to Allah. He must say, in all sincerity and belief that "There is no God but Allah and Mohammed is His Prophet."

He must pray five times a day after ritual ablution and do the prescribed genuflections, kneeling, and bowing to Mecca and prostrating himself. Many times during prayer the words "Allah akbar," "God is great," are recited.

The Moslem must pay a purification tax for almsgiving.

The Moslem must fast during Ramadan, the ninth month of the Islamic calendar and our holiest time, for that was when the Koran was sent down to direct our lives. During Ramadan the gates of heaven open and the angel Gabriel asks grace for everyone. Old people in particular pray very, very hard for forgiveness of their sins, since they will be the ones trying to get into paradise the soonest. Although it is never seen by human eyes, everyone knows that even the trees kneel toward Mecca during Ramadan.

We must fast during the daylight hours for the entire month. We tell day from night by a thread. If you can see a white thread, then it is night. If you can see a black thread, then it is daytime.

Ramadan is when new clothing is purchased and everyone gets a haircut from Uncle Farouk and everyone takes a bath. Most of the daylight fasting hours are spent in the mosque, praying. In Tabah we allow women into the mosque, but only on one side, in the rear, and out of sight of the men. During these hours there is complete abstinence from food, drink, smoking, and, worst of all, from sex. Pregnant women, wet nurses, the very aged and ill, travelers, and small children are exempt from fasting by Allah's grace.

Late in the daylight hours people can start going crazy. Majnun, the spirit that makes you crazy, is in its full glory during Ramadan. Men, weak from hunger, thirst, and the sun, flare into fighting at the slightest pretext. My father is very busy keeping order during Ramadan. It is forbidden to cheat by eating. If anyone is caught he and his family are ostracized until the next Ramadan.

The night meal can go on for hours. They gorge themselves until they become bloated and start vomiting. Just before the sun comes up a second meal is eaten, but people are so stuffed from the night meal the morning meal becomes an ordeal. Everyone is glad when Ramadan is over.

Most important to Moslems is the Sunna. Although the Sunna is not formally written down, it cannot be divorced from the Koran. It is an interpretation of the values of the Koran by experience and tradition. Those who believe in the Sunna are called Sunni Moslems. Everyone in Tabah was a Sunni. The Sunnis make up most of the Islamic world.

The main Moslem group other than Sunnis are called Shi'ites. Shortly after Islam rose in the seventh century, the center of its power shifted from the Arabian desert to the cities. First Damascus became the center of Islam, then Baghdad, then Cairo, and much later, Istanbul. The caliphs, or leaders of the Islamic world, were no longer from Mecca or Medina but from the most powerful Islamic country at the moment.

The Shi'ites believed that the caliph, the leader of Islam, should always be a descendant of Mohammed and Caliph Ali. They beat themselves with whips to prove their devotion and looked for martyrdom and did other crazy things. The Shi'ites often hated the Sunnis more than they hated the infidels. They always started riots. Palestine didn't have many Shi'ites, praise Allah, but there were plenty of them in Iran and they were hated, distrusted, and feared by us.

Once I got the courage to ask Mr. Salmi if the Shi'ites, Alawites, Druzes, and Kurds were really Moslems and he managed to mumble, "Well, just barely."

The fifth and final pillar of Islam says that every Moslem must make the pilgrimage, or Haj, to Mecca once in his life. In Mecca there is a Black Stone in a shrine called the Ka'aba. This is the most sacred place in the world. It is said that our father, Abraham, whom we all know was a Moslem and not a Jew, gave the mission to his son, Ishmael, to found the Arab race. I am named after Ishmael, just as my father, Haj Ibrahim, is named after Abraham.

The Ka'aba had once been a pagan shrine but Mohammed changed all that after he got his message from Allah and when he got mad at the Jews. In the beginning all Moslems faced Jerusalem when they prayed. When Mohammed made the Ka'aba the center of Islam he ordered everyone to pray facing Mecca instead because the Jews had not accepted him.

The final thing I will say about Islam concerns jinn, which are very important to us. They are evil spirits capable of looking like an animal or a person and have supernatural influence. The Koran says that "We have created man from potter's clay, of mud ground down; the jinn we created previously of fire of burning heat." The Sunna has taught us to fear jinn because once one of these spirits gets inside a person it can cause all the illnesses in man. Once a person is afflicted, nothing but the will of Allah can make that person well again.

All Moslems realize they have no control over their own lives and destinies. Illness, death, drought, pestilence, earthquakes, any disasters must be fatalistically accepted as the will of Allah. Only by being a believer, accepting Mohammed's word, accepting Allah's will, can we get into paradise. So life on this earth is really not to be enjoyed, but it merely makes us prove ourselves worthy of joining Mohammed forever in heaven.

I am a devout Moslem, but sometimes some things are hard to understand. If Allah is merciful and compassionate why is He so consumed with horrible punishments and why must Moslems be committed to a holy war to destroy other people who are nonbelievers? Why can't Islam share the world with other people?

Chapter Nineteen

Hagar often complained that she dreaded the day her sons would marry and bring wives into our house because she didn't want to share the kitchen with anyone. Haj Ibrahim changed all that when he took Ramiza as a second wife.

In the beginning we were very cold to Ramiza, particularly after my father banished my mother to the marketplace stalls. The only person in our house who seemed truly happy was Haj Ibrahim, but he was oblivious to our feelings. My mother's humiliation had devastated her and made us very wary of our father.

Change toward Ramiza came slowly. She was so beautiful alongside my mother it made it even easier to hate her. At first we thought she was arrogant because she was so quiet. Little by little we realized that she was very shy and not terribly smart. Haj Ibrahim wondered aloud, from time to time, if the old Sheik Walid Azziz had duped him in selling him Ramiza. The chances were that Ramiza had never sat down with her father and had a conversation with him. The old sheik had no way of knowing if Ramiza was clever or stupid. He had so many daughters he scarcely knew all their names and the only criteria by which they were judged were their appearance, obedience, the preservation of their virginity, and the bride price they would bring.

Ramiza had lived as a nomad all her life. With so many women about to do the sheik's bidding, a lazy girl could slip out of many duties. It became clear that Ramiza had not been sufficiently trained. She had a miserable time trying to fill in for my mother in the kitchen. We had many more kinds of foods and spices than the Bedouin and she botched most of the meals she prepared. Nada was the first to take pity on her. Although Nada was only ten, my mother had trained her well and she saved Ramiza from many a tongue-lashing from Haj Ibrahim.

After a few months Ramiza became pregnant and the first burst of my father's ardor diminished rapidly. He yelled at her frequently and at times punctuated his displeasure by slapping her. Nada and I would often find her weeping softly in a corner of the kitchen and muttering her puzzlement.

When Ramiza's room had been completed in the spring and a second bedstead installed, only then did he allow my mother to get off the floor and return to her bedroom.

Neither Ramiza nor my mother was giving him much sexual satisfaction and it angered him. However, he did return Omar to tend the stalls so he could get Hagar back into the kitchen; he gave her specific orders to teach Ramiza how to cook and take care of her duties properly.

When Hagar returned to her kitchen she scarcely spoke to Ramiza but admonished her constantly as "that dirty little Bedouin wart." Ramiza began to show her pregnancy and became sick in the mornings and whimpered constantly. Hagar slowly began to be humane to her. I think that their friendship truly started when both of them realized it was no great pleasure or honor to sleep with Haj Ibrahim and derogatory little remarks crept into their conversation about the crudeness of his lovemaking. Then the two women began sharing secrets as a mother to a daughter. I believe Ramiza liked Hagar better than she liked Haj Ibrahim. She clung to my mother's skirts to keep from making mistakes and every now and then Hagar took the blame for something Ramiza had done wrong.

One day Hagar was midwifing. I was home from school with a fever and had tucked myself away in my favorite spot in the kitchen where I was out of everyone's sight but still had enough light to read by. Ramiza was about seven months pregnant and huffing and puffing about. She finally grunted to a seat on the milking stool and listlessly pumped the churn, making cheese of goat's milk.

Nada scratched herself unconsciously between her legs, a kind of scratch that would have brought a sharp slap and rebuke had Hagar been present.

"Do you feel anything there?" Ramiza asked.

"Where?"

"In your sacred place where you just scratched yourself."

Nada quickly dropped her hands and her cheeks turned crimson.

"Don't worry," Ramiza said, "I won't tell on you."

Nada smiled gratefully.

"Well, does it feel good?" Ramiza asked again.

"I don't know. I think it feels good. Yes, I guess it does. I know it is forbidden. I must be more careful."

"You might as well go on feeling yourself as long as you like it," Ramiza said. "I suppose you must still have one."

"Still have what?" Nada's eyes widened with fear. "If you mean the membrane of honor, of course I still have it!"

"No," Ramiza said. "The little button hidden beneath the membrane of honor. Do you still have it?"

"Yes, I still have it," Nada said haltingly. "I have felt the button."

"Then you must enjoy it as long as they let you keep it."

"What do you mean? Won't I always have it?"

"Oh, I'm sorry," Ramiza said. "I shouldn't have told you."

"Please, you must tell me . . . please . . . please . . ."

Ramiza stopped churning and bit her lip, but after looking at Nada's pleading eyes, she knew she had to tell. "It must be a secret. If your parents knew I told you I would get a severe beating."

"I promise. May the Prophet burn me on the Day of the Fire."

"It is the pleasure button," Ramiza said. "Girls are not supposed to keep it."

"But why?"

"Because, as long as you have the pleasure button, it makes you look at boys. One day you might even let a boy touch it and if you enjoy it you may not be able to control yourself. You could even let him break your membrane of honor."

"Oh no! I would never do that!"

"The button is evil," Ramiza said. "It makes girls do things against their will."

"Oh . . ." Nada whispered. "But don't you have your button?"

"No, it was taken from me. I did nothing wrong, but it was removed to take away temptation. They will take yours too. Once it is gone you will not care about boys and you will be a virgin for sure when you marry and can never dishonor your family."

Nada's blazing curiosity faded to a rising of fear. She had always liked it when she rubbed against a boy. She liked it when she knew she would be working at the threshing floor or when she carried water to the fields for the men. Hagar had warned her a dozen times a day during the threshing season about touching boys. She did not realize it had anything to do with the pleasure button. "What happened to you?" Nada finally brought herself to ask.

Ramiza patted her large belly and told the baby to be still. She was quite uncomfortable and it was difficult for her to work, but she did not want Haj Ibrahim yelling at her. "They come at night," Ramiza said. "You never know when they will come. The daya, the midwife of the clan. She is the one who takes the button."

"But my own mother is a daya," Nada said.

Ramiza grunted an ironic little laugh. "Then they will use another daya. She will come with your aunts. They always come for it when you are asleep. They put something in your food to make you sleep so you won't be alert. There will be six or eight of them. They will grab you by the arms and legs so you can't move. One of them will cover your eyes with a black cloth and another will stuff something in your mouth so you can't scream. They will carry you to a secret tent they have prepared. Your aunts will hold you fast on the ground so you can't move and then they will spread your legs apart as wide as they can. At the last moment I managed to fight my hands free and screamed for my mother and pulled off my blindfold. When I looked up, I realized that it was my mother who was holding my head down. The daya has a very sharp knife and while they hold your legs apart she hunts for the button with her fingers until it pops up, then she cuts it off!"

Nada screamed. I wanted to run to her but knew that would only cause trouble, so I scrinched up into a ball so I wouldn't be discovered.

"I've made you very upset. I didn't mean to do that. They made me swear I would not tell any of the other girls or they would cut my tongue out . . . only, that was when I was living in the desert. I thought it would be all right to tell you."

Ramiza grunted up off the stool and waddled to Nada and patted her head. "Poor Nada," she said.

Nada's great brown eyes looked up to Ramiza hauntingly. "Does it hurt much?"

Ramiza shook her head and sighed. "I bled much worse than the worst menstruation. For several seasons I was in pain every time I tried to pass my urine. I was very sick from it. Finally I

was allowed to see a British doctor in Beersheba. My father
wanted to keep me alive so he wouldn't lose my dowry."

"Did . . . did it make you stop thinking about boys?"

"Yes, and I obeyed from then on, whatever they told me."

"Do you have any fun with my father?"

Ramiza went back to the stool and churned. "At first it was fun
just to see what the mystery was all about, but you are not supposed to have fun. You can pretend to have fun because that
makes the man feel very important. After a few times, there is no
fun. It really doesn't matter whether Hagar sleeps with Haj
Ibrahim or I do. I wish she would sleep with him more."

Nada and I were the youngest and I was still allowed to sleep
in the same little cell with her because my three brothers were
already too crowded. I didn't know how much she slept anymore.
Any tiny little noise would bring her up trembling in the night.
By day she would doze off during her chores and large circles of
weariness formed beneath her eyes. When she did sleep at night
she twitched all the time and often she cried out.

She would not eat except out of the common plate and not until
Hagar or Ramiza ate first. She became weak and frightened to
such an extent that I finally told her I had heard the conversation.
I begged her to speak to Hagar about it. It came down to a question of Nada falling seriously ill from exhaustion and fear. One
day I threatened to tell Hagar myself. In order to spare me a
beating she finally went to Hagar. I waited in the barn.

She came out to me after a time, her face wet with tears and
sweat and still trembling.

"What did mother say?" I asked anxiously.

"I don't have to have mine cut off," she sobbed. "They only do
it here to girls who have dishonored the family. I promised I
would do nothing to shame us. I promised I would never look at a
boy or let a boy touch me until my wedding night."

I guess I started crying too. We held each other and sobbed
until she realized we were holding each other, then she pushed
me away and a look of terror came to her. "It is all right, Nada," I
cried. "I am your brother. I will not harm you."

Chapter Twenty

If it took Ramiza time to gain acceptance within the family, it took longer to win the approval of the village women. Until her period of trial was over she was accused of carrying the jinn. Any misfortune in the village was blamed on her, for bringing the evil spirits to Tabah. She had a lot to overcome. Since Ramiza was the only second wife, the village women generally sympathized with Hagar. Ramiza had the unfortunate fate of being very young and exquisitely beautiful as well.

At the communal ovens family intimacies were exchanged by weary, bored, and frustrated wives. Women fled to the ovens for shelter from fights with their husbands. While there was some release in this place of female social privacy, the endless cycles of monotony and labor often exploded into violent quarrels, with obscenities filling the air and spitting and slapping and kicking commonplace.

Ramiza was a ready-made target for slurs. Their jealousy of her could be added to her suffering. As Ramiza's time to give birth drew near, acceptance of her was grudgingly given. Childbirth was one of the rare occasions when women were allowed to congregate and celebrate without serving the men. When Ramiza's time came due, my mother once again left Tabah for an extended visit with her family.

The word spread quickly that Ramiza was feeling her first pains and our house became the center of an occasion. All of the village women gathered, except those who were menstruating, for their blood was unclean and they were not permitted over the threshold. During the time of a woman's period she was also forbidden from entering the mosque, visiting the graveyard, or fasting during Ramadan.

Ramiza was taken into the living room for the delivery. She appeared to be little more than a child herself. The daya sat her on the floor on a goatskin rug. One of her aunts, who lived in Tabah, sat on a stool behind her, holding her head and bracing her between her legs. On either side she was attended by cousins.

The room was in general chaos, with women and little children running in and out at random. I was still young enough to watch it all from a careful distance at the kitchen door.

The lower half of Ramiza's body was covered with a quilt, although she still wore ankle-length bloomers. The daya made several inspections under the blanket, feeling about after greasing her hand with sheep's fat.

With each new sharp pain the women would shout in unison for her to "heave" and "bear down." After a pain diminished they would chatter about the problems they had had when they had given birth. As the pains grew sharper and came more often, Ramiza began to scream for her mother. I could not understand why she wanted her mother after her mother had helped take away her button of pleasure. It was Nada who took a place alongside Ramiza, held her hand, and washed her perspiring face.

After several hours and many inspections the daya drew back the quilt and removed Ramiza's bloomers. A quiet swept the room as the tension mounted. In a burst, a blur, and a scream, it was there! I had a half brother! The daya wiped off all the blood and mess and cut the cord. While the baby was still naked and screaming, it was passed around from woman to woman for everyone to gush over.

I ran to the café to tell my father. He basked in his new glory. Ramiza's baby came just before the circumciser made his annual visit, so the baby's foreskin and first soiled diaper were placed in the transom over the front door, just as my foreskin and diaper and those of my brothers had been placed and still remained.

Ramiza's stomach was tightly bound and she was given the traditional forty days to abstain from sex. Hagar was ordered back immediately to comfort my father and cook for him and Ramiza was left in her room with her son.

It was not as though she had given birth to a baby, but more like she had acquired a playtoy, something of her own. She had never really had anything of her own before. Hagar became impatient, for it was soon apparent that Ramiza was not too capable of caring for an infant. However, my mother was not allowed to interfere.

When Ramiza was able to get up and about, things went sour, quickly. Her milk did not satisfy the baby, so a wet nurse had to be brought in. The baby screamed constantly and Ramiza's confusion turned to panic, then constant weeping. Hagar was still not permitted to get things under control.

When the forty days of sexual abstinence passed the situation worsened. My father was once again passionate to have Ramiza, but she was still in pain and unable to have sex. One night my father forced himself into her, but she bled profusely afterward. Ramiza and the baby were usually left alone and they stayed in their room all day. Nada brought her meals, but my father was so angered he insisted no one pay attention to her.

He uttered aloud now that he wished he had never married her. We all knew the only reason he didn't terminate the marriage was out of fear of insulting Sheik Azziz.

The baby was three months old when the rainy season came in full blast. It poured outside and it was the third night running that the house was to get no sleep from the infant's screaming. Haj Ibrahim was spending more and more nights away from Tabah. The gossip at the ovens had it that he was visiting prostitutes in Ramle.

This night he was home and in a fury. He yelled to Hagar to go to Ramiza's bedroom and restore order. Neither Nada nor I had been able to sleep and followed Hagar into Ramiza's room.

The scene was appalling. Ramiza was propped up against the headboard, her hair askew, her eyes like those of a mad woman, and she bit at her fingers and grunted like a wounded animal. The baby shrieked, coughed, and gagged. Hagar rushed to the crib and threw back the quilt. It was a filthy mess. The baby had not been cleaned, perhaps for days. There was a hole in the bottom of the crib where excrement was dropped into a pot, then later dumped outside. It had not been used. The baby was covered with his own shit and had eaten some of it. Hagar feverishly cleaned everything up and tried to make the baby vomit. Although she was a keeper of herbs and potions of the clan, she knew she had nothing to alleviate the situation. Then she, too, became hysterical after she reported to Haj Ibrahim that the child was very ill, running a high fever, and obviously having terrible stomach pains.

Haj Ibrahim cursed Ramiza abusively for allowing jinn to enter the house through her. Nada joined the hysteria as my brothers cowed out of the house. The elder daya was called in to see if she could exorcise the jinn, but she was equally helpless.

With Hagar and the daya both screaming at my father, he relented and ordered me to take the donkey and go to the British
police fort at Latrun. From there I was to get one of the soldiers
to telephone Ramle for an Arab doctor.

I begged my father to be allowed to use his horse, as it would be
much faster, but he angrily cursed me for even suggesting that I
take his horse out in such a downpour. I remember the donkey
ride to Latrun only in blurs, kicking the animal and begging it to
move faster.

I covered my face as a spotlight blinded me.

"Halt! Who's out there!"

"I am Ishmael, the son of the Muktar of Tabah," I cried.

"Corporal, get the duty officer. There's a little Arab kid at the
gate and he's soaking wet!"

I remember being led by the hand to a large frightening room
where an officer of obvious power sat behind a desk. Other
soldiers took off my wet clothing and wrapped a blanket around
me and brought me a bowl of hot soup as I tried to get out my
story in my poor English. Then there were telephone calls.

"The doctor at Ramle is out at a distant village and they don't
know when he'll return."

There were more phone calls.

"One of our doctors will come down from Jerusalem. It may
take a while in this rain."

"No!" I cried, "It must be an Arab doctor."

"But Ishmael—"

"No! My father will not have it!"

"Try Lydda, Sergeant. Radio our police station there and see
what they can do."

The report from Lydda was no better. The doctor was not to
be found and the small hospital only had a night orderly. The
nearest Arab doctor was in Jaffa and in such a storm it would be
early morning before he could reach the village. The soldiers offered to hold the donkey and to drive me back to Tabah in a
truck, but I was now frenzied. My clothes had been drying over a
stove. I dressed and ran out of the office and the building and
pounded on the gate.

"Come back here, boy!"

"Let him through. He's frightened of his father."

It was utter blackness outside. Water from the rains gushed down from the Bab el Wad, covering many parts of the road. It was very difficult to see where I was going. Although I tried to stay on the side of the road, several times I was almost hit by passing cars that sprayed me like buckets of water flung into my face. The only time I could really see anything was from the headlights of the cars, and I would quickly move to the ditch of the road for safety and try to get a glimpse down the road. It seemed like the whole month of Ramadan had come and gone before I was able to make out the first white houses on the hill of Tabah.

At that instant the headlight of a car fell on the sign that read SHEMESH KIBBUTZ. I was drawn toward it, mesmerized. I knew I was forbidden to enter, but if I begged the Jews not to tell my father, perhaps they could find an Arab doctor for me. Then spotlights blazed through the rain from the guard post of the kibbutz, once again blinding me. I was suddenly surrounded by a number of Jews holding rifles on me. They took me inside the gates.

"What is he saying, Avi?"

"Something about a sick baby."

"Does anyone know him?"

"Isn't he one of the muktar's children from Tabah?"

"Someone get Gideon."

"What's going on over there!"

"It's a child from Tabah. He keeps repeating that a baby is very sick."

I must have fainted. The next I remember was being in the seat of a truck with Mr. Gideon Asch holding his arm around me and another man driving, trying to get up the muddy street to the center of the village. The truck spun and slid all over the place.

"They live up there!"

"The road is impassable. We'll have to walk."

I fell down into the mud and was unable to get up. Mr. Gideon Asch swept me up in his good arm and the three of us, running, slipping, and falling, made our way up the path to my father's house. The two Jews pushed through a number of people who had gathered outside in the rain.

Mr. Gideon Asch and the other man were standing inside the living room. I was set down and I swooned into Nada's arms but

managed to remain conscious. Mr. Gideon Asch explained that
the man with him was a physician.

Haj Ibrahim stood across the room, blocking the doorway to
Ramiza's room. After a strange silence Hagar and Nada and my
father and the daya all started yelling at once.

"Calm down everyone!" Mr. Gideon Asch bellowed over ev-
erybody's voice.

"Where is the baby?" the doctor asked.

Haj Ibrahim took a couple of menacing steps toward me and
raised his fist. "I told you! I told you to go to Latrun!"

"Father! We could not get a doctor from Ramle or Lydda!" I
cried in defense. "I did not know what to do."

"Please let me see the baby," the doctor pleaded.

"No!" my father roared. "No! No! No!" He pointed menacingly at me. "You bring them here to show them how inferior we
are!"

"Ibrahim," Mr. Gideon Asch pleaded, "I beg you to calm
down. Stop talking like a fool. There is a child's life at stake."

The women began wailing convulsively.

"No pity from the Jews! No pity! No mercy! I will not have
you coming into my home to prove your superiority!"

Mr. Gideon Asch made a move toward the bedroom, but my
father blocked the way. "Don't do this, Ibrahim! I implore you!
Ibrahim!" My father did not budge. "You are committing a grave
sin."

"Hah! The sin is to receive mercy from a Jew! That is the sin!"

Mr. Gideon Asch threw up his arms in defeat and shook his
head at the doctor. My father and the women howled louder, he
to make them go and they to keep the doctor there.

An unreal silence suddenly descended. Ramiza, chalky-faced,
ghostlike, mouth gaping in a trance, walked in with the baby in
her arms. The doctor pushed my father aside and took the baby as
Ramiza crumpled to the floor and the women fell around her.
The doctor held his head against the baby's chest, slapped it, then
breathed into its mouth, opened his medical bag, and listened
again.

"The child is dead," the doctor whispered.

"This place is filled with evil spirits," my father said. "It is
Allah's will that the baby die."

"Allah's will my ass!" Gideon Asch gnarled. "That child died of filth and neglect! Come on Shimon, let's get out of here."

They plunged from the house into the awful downpour, with Haj Ibrahim roaring after them and shaking his fist. I did not hear any of the rest of it, but others did.

The two Jews slid and struggled for balance down the path of rocks, glazed by the rain, with the muktar behind them. "How we live is how we live! We have survived here for thousands of years without you! Our existence is as fragile as the mountain tundra! Why is it that you must always come in from the outside and tell us how to live! We don't want you! We don't need you! Jew!"

Gideon slammed the door on the driver's side and groped for the ignition. The doctor jumped into the opposite seat as Haj Ibrahim pounded on the door and continued to shout.

Gideon closed his eyes, fought back tears, and for an instant dropped his head against the steering wheel. "Jesus Christ," he muttered. "I left my artificial hand at home. I can't drive this damned thing."

Before the doctor could get to the wheel, Gideon had flung the door open and walked down toward the highway.

"Go fuck a dead camel!" Haj Ibrahim screamed, "fuck a dead camel!"

END OF PART ONE

Part Two

The Scattering

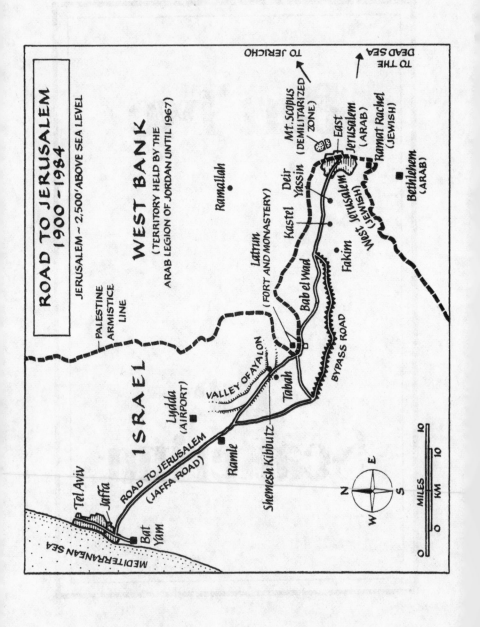

ROAD TO JERUSALEM
1900 - 1984

JERUSALEM ~ 2,500' ABOVE SEA LEVEL

- - - PALESTINE ARMISTICE LINE

WEST BANK
(TERRITORY HELD BY THE
ARAB LEGION OF JORDAN UNTIL 1967)

ISRAEL

MEDITERRANEAN SEA

Tel Aviv
Jaffa
Bat Yam

ROAD TO JERUSALEM
(JAFFA ROAD)

Lydda
(AIRPORT)

Ramle

Shemesh Kibbutz

VALLEY OF AYALON

Tabah

Latrun
(FORT AND MONASTERY)

Bab el Wad

BYPASS ROAD

Ramallah

Kustel

Deir
Yassin

Fakim

West Jerusalem
(JEWISH)

Mt. Scopus
(DEMILITARIZED
ZONE)

East
Jerusalem
(ARAB)

Ramat Rachel
(JEWISH)

Bethlehem
(ARAB)

TO JERICHO

TO THE
DEAD SEA

N
E
W
S

MILES

0   10

0   10   KM

Chapter One

1946

It was a day of great sadness for me when I left school, but the decision was mine. I had turned ten years of age and knew more than anyone in the classroom, including Mr. Salmi. At first Mr. Salmi used me to read surahs from the Koran while he sat in the back of the class and napped. Then he put more and more responsibility on me to teach. I wanted to learn. I had taught the Jewish children in Shemesh Kibbutz, but I learned more from them than I taught.

The real reason I chose to leave school was because I was creating a place for myself at my father's side. This gave me the courage to finally cross out of the world of women and the safety of the kitchen into the fearsome world of men. My mother's plotting was behind the move.

From the moment the great Second World War ended, things went very badly in Palestine. As the respected Muktar of Tabah, my father had to ponder all the time. The news over the radio and in the Arab newspapers became violently anti-Jewish. My father said many times to me that our people were more easily moved by words than by ideas and more moved by ideas than by logic. He had depended upon Mr. Gideon Asch to explain the Jewish side of things. Since the night Ramiza's baby died Mr. Gideon Asch never returned to Tabah, so my father was left with one point of view.

Each night there was a ritual in our house. Kamal read the Arab newspapers to my father. Haj Ibrahim would sit in his personal great chair while Kamal sat on the long bench, which was for the rest of the family and unimportant guests. Kamal was a poor reader and when my father got impatient it made matters worse. Kamal would stutter when he didn't know a certain word.

"You're so dumb you couldn't find your ass with both hands at high noon," my father often roared.

But Kamal would rather eat a mile of donkey turds than ask me about pronouncing a word. Hagar observed all this.

"You will read for your father very soon," she promised. She went into a seduction of Haj Ibrahim and sure enough, after a few nights, he asked me to replace Kamal in reading to him. It was the most important day of my life up until then.

It was not difficult for Hagar to get my father into her bedroom and away from Ramiza. Ramiza was frightened all the time. She bit her lips and fingernails and slinked about like a cowering dog when my father was near. She listened keenly in case he issued an order, when she would jump to bring him his pipe or whatever he asked for and grin like an idiot when she handed it to him, hoping to get a nod of approval. She worked furiously at her chores, to avoid being yelled at, and virtually clung to my mother and Nada. At the slightest sign of friction she'd run off and weep. Ramiza became too timid to go to the village well or mingle with the women by herself.

We kept her as one keeps a feeble-minded sister. Hagar ceased being jealous and at times showed her kindness. My father did keep going to Ramiza's bedroom, but there was gossip that he only wanted to look at her naked and make her dance for him. Once I overheard Hagar tell her to pretend to enjoy sex; she instructed her on certain kinds of movements to make with her body and on how to groan as if she were in ecstasy.

Kamal was absolutely furious at me for taking his place as the reader. His method of getting revenge was to marry in the hope of having a son so he could establish himself with a line of heirs. He married a Tabah girl, the daughter of a clan sheik. Her name was Fatima and she was homely. However, she had a pleasant way about her and she was plump, which many Arab men like very much. Haj Ibrahim was able to get her at a good price. The wedding was nowhere as grandiose as my father's marriage to Ramiza had been, but Kamal was no treasure either, so they suited each other. Fatima became pregnant immediately, but fortunately for me and my mother's ambitions, the baby was a girl.

Fatima was one of those bossy women one rarely sees. When Kamal ordered her around she obeyed, but she always got even with him. It appeared that Kamal was actually afraid of her. This was a joke because it only made Kamal look weaker in my father's eyes.

Now that I was out of school I could spend my time studying the village books and records. This put Kamal at my mercy. I kept pretending to find new parcels of land on which no rents were paid. I say I pretended to find them because I had known about them all along. I had a secret pact with Kamal to share the rents on these parcels. Kamal remained too frightened to reveal our agreement to Haj Ibrahim. This left the way clear for me to "stumble" on a new parcel when Hagar or I wanted something from him. Maybe Haj Ibrahim knew all along that I was cheating him because he certainly made enough remarks about Farouk and Kamal playing loose with the books. In all sincerity I did not feel too badly about it because I gave the money to my mother.

One night, just after the war ended, Radio Damascus broadcast news that death camps had been discovered in Germany and Poland. Many millions of Jews had been gassed to death by Adolf Hitler and the Nazis. In the following days all the newspapers were filled with the revelation and every night on the radio it seemed another new death camp was discovered. Radio Cairo said that Churchill, Roosevelt, and the holy Pope in Rome had already known about the death camps during the war but kept quiet about it and let the Nazis kill the Jews without protest.

It was strange and shocking news for us. We had been living side by side with Shemesh Kibbutz for over two decades with no serious trouble and only ordinary hatred of the Jews. The death camp news brought an odd reaction from the villagers. It was as though their true emotions about Jews had been locked deep inside a cave with the entrance blocked. The rock had been blasted away and thousands of bloodthirsty bats poured out. I did not even know my people from the joyful way they were reacting.

I was still going to school at the time and in Ramle there were street celebrations over the death camps led by members of the Moslem Brotherhood. Mr. Salmi read surah after surah from the Koran to prove to us that the death camps were the fulfillment of Mohammed's prophecy of the Day of the Burning for the Jews. It was all in the Koran, Mr. Salmi reasoned, so Mohammed obviously had a magical vision from Allah, and it proved the major point of Islam: what would happen to nonbelievers.

Uncle Farouk usually preached very dull sermons on the Sabbath, sermons about the great benefits that would come to the believers in death, or about giving money to the poor, or instructions on daily life. After the death camp news he began preaching

from some of the most frightening surahs and verses: those dealing with the destruction of the Jews. My father, who always approved my uncle's sermons in advance, sensed the new attitudes
of the villagers, for he allowed the sermons to continue, Sabbath
after Sabbath. The easygoing relationship with Shemesh was suddenly filled with suspicion and a tension I had never felt before.

Although the Arab press had jubilantly reported the genocide,
they now did a complete turnaround. For months the newspapers
had printed photographs of the gas chambers and ovens on the
front pages. Overnight they said that the genocide never really
took place, that it was all a trick of the Zionists to win the sympathy of the victorious Allies. Now the Allies would let all the Jews
in Europe come to Palestine.

This was my first experience of seeing my people believe one
thing one day and believe exactly the opposite the next. As
quickly as the people in Tabah had accepted and had been elated
over the burning of the Jews, they accepted that it had been a
Zionist plot all along.

Haj Ibrahim was not certain. He did not get caught up in the
instant emotionalism as the others did, but wanted to think it out.
It was difficult for him, for he did not have Mr. Gideon Asch to
speak with. Whatever did take place in Europe must have been
very bad, for there was a rage brewing all over Palestine, a rage
more fierce than during the Mufti's revolt.

Jews began forcing their way into Palestine from Europe because they claimed they had no other place to go. If there had
been a genocide, these people would have to have been the survivors. If the genocide was a Zionist lie, then these Jews were deliberately being sent into Palestine to displace us.

Haj Ibrahim had many failings, but he did not bite at words.
He was the only man I knew in Tabah to question the radio or
the newspaper or even the clergy, and try to find logic and truth.
So my father mumbled aloud and posed questions to himself
while I read to him.

He was suspicious of how the Arab press had changed the entire story of the genocide overnight. He was suspicious because
the British were doing everything in their power to stop the Jews
from entering Palestine. Thousands upon thousands of British
combat troops were arriving in the country. It made no sense to
my father. He knew that many thousands of Jews had fought for

the British in the war. If these had been Arab troops, he reasoned, the Arabs would expect the reward of ruling Palestine. The British had won and the Jews had helped immensely. Why then were the British keeping them out? He had studied maps all during the war and he had incredible native instincts. Haj Ibrahim reasoned and concluded that the British had too much invested in the region, in the Canal, in creating Trans-Jordan, and mainly in the oil fields of the Arabian Peninsula. Because these were in Arab lands, the British had to yield to Arab pressure, and their investment, particularly in the oil, was more important to them than any Jews.

At last my father called me to the prophet's tomb early one day in 1946. He made me swear I would keep a secret. Omar, who tended the stalls in the souks, was to purchase a Palestine *Post* every day and I was to read it to Haj Ibrahim. It was the newspaper of the Jews and it gave a completely different story from that which was in the Arab press or on the radio. It was the first time we even heard of the war crimes trials at Nuremberg.

When he had pondered the question fully, my father reached a decision. He told me one night that the genocide had really taken place. "Now we Moslems will have to pay for the sins of the Christians. The Christians are very guilty about their behavior, even the Allies, who kept the secret. They want to wash their hands of their sins and they will do so by dumping the survivors in an Arab land. It is a black day for us, Ishmael."

I didn't think it was a black day because I didn't quite understand him. I had planned the day very carefully. I "discovered" two new parcels of land not paying rents and I had read very well in both English and Arabic. Despite his bad mood, I decided to confront him.

"Father," I said, "my backside grows very sore on the bench while I am reading to you. I would like to sit in the other big chair."

Well, he knew what was up. None of my brothers and certainly no women were allowed the privilege of that second chair, which had been reserved for honored guests. What I had asked of him had far-reaching implications. He thought about it for what seemed like an hour.

"Very well, Ishmael," he said at last, "you may sit next to me, but only when you read."

Chapter Two

Gideon Asch's war ended abruptly with the British conquest of Iraq. He had lost his left hand in an Iraqi prison after trying to defend the Baghdad ghetto. He was bitter because British troops had reached the scene of the Arab massacre and did nothing to stop it, nor anything to investigate it afterward.

Gideon scarcely had time to recover from one war before he was plunged into another: a dark war of illegal immigrant runners, underground fighting, political struggle, arms smuggling. A war of polished conference tables and clandestine meetings in dark seamy harbor-side hotels.

Gideon was made an aide without portfolio to David Ben-Gurion, who headed the Jewish Agency of Palestine, their quasi-government. He was to be involved in many kinds of operations in many places at many times.

Gideon's first task was to attempt to capitalize on the contribution Palestine's Jews had made during the war. Upward of thirty-five thousand men and women had worn the British uniform and by the war's end had carried their own banner into battle in Italy.

He quickly tried to point out that the overwhelming majority of the Arab nations had not lifted a finger in behalf of the Allied victory and had no right to scream for the political spoils. It was the Jews who had fought the Nazis without reservation.

Gideon was a native Palestinian who was more at home in a Bedouin tent than in a Left Bank café. Christian Europe was sometimes a distant notion. He greeted the news of the Holocaust with disbelief at first, then sank into a terrible depression.

The stench of the human slaughterhouses permeated Europe as the lid was lifted on the cesspools of Auschwitz and Buchenwald and Dachau and Bergen-Belsen and Majdanek and Treblinka and dozens of other death camps.

Europeans were civilized, Gideon had always been taught. Christians were certainly nowhere as cruel as Arabs and Moslems. For Gideon and the rest of the Jews, the illusion had been shattered. What an advanced, civilized Western culture had done to an innocent, defenseless people was without precedent in human annals.

A pitiful handful of survivors, a few hundred thousand out of over six million, climbed out of man's foulest pit. Even as the victorious Allied captains and kings and their armies departed the fields of battle, the gates of mercy were slammed in the faces of the living-dead remnants of European Jewry. In their ranks had been thousands of great and near great and noble names who had made an incredible contribution to the world; a race of people that had done as much for the betterment of the human race as any people of their size.

There was little time to mourn. Gideon and the Yishuv plunged into salvaging what could be salvaged, building for the inevitable war with the Arabs. He was first assigned to help beef up the Palmach, a striking force of young, handpicked Haganah Jews. Many of them had been members of Orde Wingate's Special Night Squads.

When Winston Churchill was voted from office, the new British Labour Government chose as its foreign secretary a rather heartless bullyboy and Jew-baiter named Ernest Bevin. Crudely he told the survivors of Hitler that he would not allow the Jews to push to the head of the queue and ordered the Royal Navy to blockade Palestine against refugee ships.

Desperate to flee the graveyard that was Europe, the survivors were to find no place in the world that would offer them refuge, except for the Yishuv in Palestine. Those who had survived Hitler were to board unseaworthy boats and be further victims of the outrage of British warships ramming them on the high seas and boarding and bludgeoning them into submission. They arrived in Palestine under British bayonets and were locked in new concentration camps.

The Haganah plunged into the battle of Aliyah Bet, the "illegal" immigration. Gideon Asch was commissioned to establish an underground operations unit to purchase refugee boats, find Jewish naval veterans from around the world to form crews, and seek out sympathetic ports in southern France and Italy to begin their blockade runs.

In Palestine itself the Jewish Agency restrained the Haganah in order to be able to keep a political dialogue going with the British. At the same time they covertly trained the Palmach under the cover of the kibbutzim. Although the Haganah kept its powder dry, the Yishuv had two smaller armed bands operating outside of Jewish Agency jurisdiction and these were furious and volatile.

There was the Irgun, led by a Holocaust survivor named Menachem Begin, and a smaller group known as the Stern Group. Gideon Asch was trusted by both organizations and was assigned as a liaison to them. For a time Gideon was able to keep a semblance of co-operation between the Irgun and the Haganah. But that time passed, as the new British policy became apparent.

No amount of argument Gideon tried to put forth could keep the Irgun and Stern Group from unilaterally going to war against the British, and they stung them with bomb and ambush. As the Royal Navy prowled the Mediterranean for refugee runners, more thousands of British combat troops poured into fortress Palestine to stem what was expanding into a Jewish revolt.

The treatment of the survivors became so inhumane that the Jewish Agency could no longer remain silent and keep its credibility. Gideon, who had tried to restrain the Irgun, now led a group of hard-line Haganah commanders to pressure Ben-Gurion into action and the Haganah was finally unleashed!

In their initial operation the Haganah attacked a British concentration camp set near the ruins of a Crusader fort at Athlit, on the Mediterranean. Executing a textbook strike, they liberated over two hundred illegals and dispersed them in the kibbutzim. This was followed by attack after attack on British installations: police forts, radar emplacements, munitions dumps, naval bases, communications centers. The British answered with more fresh troops until their garrison contained upward of a hundred thousand men.

By 1946 Palestine was in chaos.

In May of that year Foreign Secretary Bevin made a series of treacherous declarations. After initially agreeing to accept an immediate hundred thousand refugees into Palestine, he reneged, reversed his position, and declared an end to all Jewish immigration! He further declared an end to all land sales to the Yishuv and rejected all Jewish political claims in Palestine. Henceforth, Bevin stated, any refugee boat caught on the open seas would be escorted by force to the Island of Cyprus, the victims to be interned in new concentration camps established there.

A month later His Majesty's forces made a gigantic sweep of Jewish Palestine, arresting a thousand of the Yishuv's leaders, the heads of the Jewish Agency, and Haganah commanders, with Gideon Asch among them. The young Palmach commanders were thrown into a camp at Rafah, while members of the Irgun were interned in the Acre Prison. It had once been the Ottoman fortress that had turned back Napoleon and was now one of the toughest penal institutions in the Empire. It bulged with prisoners from the Haganah, Palmach, Irgun, and Stern Group.

British units pounced on and scoured kibbutz and village for arms caches. Tel Aviv was cut off by two divisions of troops that dragged the city for guns, illegals, and Jewish fighters.

The Irgun, now operating independently, replied by blowing up British headquarters in Jerusalem's King David Hotel.

With the disappearance of all semblance of order, the British feverishly backed down and called for a truce with the Jewish Agency. The Agency was reinstated and its leaders were released from prison. In turn, the Agency halted Haganah operations and called for negotiations. Despite the Haganah's efforts to unify the dissident forces, the Irgun and Stern Group announced from their covert headquarters that they would not be bound by the truce.

1947

His Majesty's government was faced with two alternatives. They could throw more might into Palestine and stop the Jewish revolt by raw power and suppression. In the end the British had no stomach to commit the atrocities required to remain in power and fell back to their second alternative, a position of negotiation.

The year was ushered in by a British partition plan that called for Arab, Jewish, and British cantons under supreme British rule. They had drawn ridiculous borders. Both the Jewish Agency and the Arab leaders rejected the plan out of hand.

It was apparent that Britain's ability to rule had been exhausted. A month later the British lion was brought to its knees with the announcement that it was turning the entire Palestine problem over to the United Nations. Nonetheless, the blockade of the Palestinian coast continued as desperate, half-maddened survivors filled up the concentration camps on Cyprus after being turned back within sight of the shores of the Holy Land.

In the most audacious of all raids, the Irgun broke into the Acre prison and liberated their comrades. During this period the British hanged several Irgun fighters and the Irgun retaliated by kidnapping and hanging two British sergeants.

In July of 1947 the British played their ugliest card in the mandate by returning a refugee boat with nearly five thousand aboard to Germany, the graveyard of the Jewish people.

November 29, 1947

The United Nations General Assembly convened at Lake Success, New York, to vote on their own partition plan to divide Palestine into separate Arab and Jewish states. The Arabs, who had refused to come to the table to negotiate throughout the tortured history of the mandate, remained consistent. They rejected the plan before it came to a vote.

The Jewish Agency, realizing it could gain no more, agreed to accept the plan.

With Britain having wiped her hands of Palestine, the United States of America was suddenly and vividly in the picture.

As the Arabs rushed to their new friends, the Russians, they did so confident that the partition plan would be defeated. In an ideological reversal of three decades since the Russian Revolution a young Russian delegate named Andrei Gromyko announced to a startled world that the Soviet Union was going to support the Americans in the partition.

Even so, the United Nations was made up largely of small states, a third of them in Latin America and all of them susceptible to oil blackmail.

It all came down to a moment of truth in the postwar world. One could smell the tension in Tabah as the village men gathered in the café in the middle of the night to listen to the broadcast on the partition vote. Even the women dared to inch around the outside of the café.

With their usual prebattle bravado the villagers had lulled and convinced themselves the partition had to fail. Only Haj Ibrahim faced reality.

"We are about to witness a guilty world being manipulated by the Zionists," he admonished.

The fellahin of Tabah did not agree.

They are forever postponing reality and decision, their muktar thought. Despite the favorable signs of enormous pressure by the Arab states, Haj Ibrahim knew quietly that the combination of America and Russia was probably too great to overcome.

Then the votes came in. As nation after nation cast its ballot, the villagers began to feel the despair creep over them. Haj Ibrahim did not even wait for the final tally. He arose morosely, said, "It is the will of Allah," and left.

At Lake Success, a devastated British Government, which had abstained, watched red-faced as their wartime allies turned on them. The final count was thirty-three to thirteen, with ten abstentions, in favor of partition. His Majesty's delegate arose and announced that Britain would not co-operate in implementing the partition and would withdraw her forces from Palestine by May 14, 1948. Thus ended the shameful episode of the mandate.

Within moments of the vote the fellahin of Tabah had unearthed their cache of arms and fired angrily into the air, swearing revenge. All over Arab Palestine this was echoed with an eruption of country-wide riots and a general strike. But alas, the night no longer belonged to them.

Tabah's new and powerful radio receiver was able to get broadcasts from every part of the world. They heard the Arab and Moslem prime ministers, presidents, kings, the Moslem Brotherhood, the Moslem Youth, and the Moslem clergy all spew forth public venom. With each declaration of support the fellahin of Tabah became heartened and shouts of agreement followed every new blood-curdling announcement.

Cairo: "The Zionist invasion is like that of the Tartars. If the Jews dare to declare their independence on May 14, they shall be so ravaged that it will make Genghis Khan seem like a man of peace. There will be new pyramids of skulls . . . Jewish skulls!"

Damascus: "Arab weapons will make this so-called partition plan just so much worthless ink on paper."

Baghdad: "Revenge and hatred of the Jews is just and legitimate. We shall proudly uproot this Zionist cancer from sacred Arab soil."

Kuwait: "O Arab brothers in Palestine, take heart. We shall cause history to repeat itself. We have rejoiced over the devastation of the Jews, whose filthy economic cunning led to their massacre in Europe. We shall finish Hitler's work."

Saudi Arabia: "May the greatest of Islamic dogmas light our way into the battle of the extermination of the Jews."

Trans-Jordan: "The Jews are wild beasts, bloodsuckers, traitors, enemies of mankind. The world has scorned, rejected, and expelled them. If they try to establish a Zionist state, it shall be eradicated by blood and victims."

Libya: "We shall drench Palestine with rivers of Jewish blood. We shall crush Jewish bones and use them for fertilizer."

Yemen: "We live and die with Arab Palestine. We shall strew Jewish entrails over the land."

Tunis: "May the Prophet strike us blind, nay dead, if we permit a Jewish state in the midst of sacred Islamic soil."

Lebanon: "Victory is ours! We shall throw every Jew and every Jewish baby into the sea with its mother."

Haj Ibrahim alone understood the difference between rhetoric and action. The Arab language was now its saltiest and filled with an overkill of wild phrases. To a listening stranger it could be the most fearful use of language they would ever hear. To the Arab masses it was a siren song from a distant mirage. Words painted elaborate pictures, but like a mirage, the words were illusions. Haj Ibrahim had long ago realized that fantasy and reality were one and the same thing among his people. The fantasy had to be kept alive at all costs.

He also knew that he alone would have to make a decision for all of them, for none would undertake responsibility.

Each night a fever arose from the café of Tabah. "Jihad! Jihad! Jihad! Holy War! Holy War! Holy War!"

Riots and massacres ripped through the Arab world, turning their fury on small and defenseless Jewish populations. Synagogues from Aleppo to Aden buckled under the torch. In those Arab lands yet under British rule nothing was done to stop the massacres.

As the Arab rage crescendoed, the United Nations, having given the Jews their "pound of flesh," threw up their hands en masse and cried, "Neutral!"

The world's military experts unanimously concluded that the Jews would be overrun. In the end they would probably be squeezed into an enclave around Tel Aviv. At such time, when the remaining Jews had their backs to the sea and annihilation before them, perhaps the United Nations could step in with some kind of humane gesture to evacuate what was left of the Jews.

It was the day of Christian Christmas. You must know the commotion caused when Mr. Dandash's black Mercedes fought through the potholes to the village square. The village boys engulfed the car as his chauffeur shooed them back. They all gave a respectful salute as Mr. Dandash emerged.

I recognized him instantly as one of the Effendi Kabir's aides. I stepped forward and announced to him that I was the son of the muktar because I knew he would want to see my father. I led him to the prophet's tomb, where my father was contemplating away another day.

Haj Ibrahim looked up. His eyes wore dark circles, large circles telling of nights with little sleep. He arose and embraced Dandash in the familiar Arab manner. They did not like each other; their embrace was too sincere.

"I have come from Damascus with a message from the Effendi," Dandash said.

"Yes?"

"The Effendi requests your urgent presence in Damascus. He has sent a car for you."

My father gave Dandash a fishy-eyed look, clearly one of suspicion. I could almost feel my father thinking . . . *I will not go to Damascus to be assassinated.*

"I have no papers to cross the border," he said.

"It has all been arranged," Dandash answered. "And be assured that the Effendi guarantees your safety under the tradition of protection to a guest."

"The Effendi also guaranteed us our water, which he sold to the Jews."

"I suggest that you had better be reasonable."

My father did not know the details, but it was rumored that Kabir had liquidated most of his holdings in Palestine and had transferred millions to Switzerland for safekeeping. It would be no trick for him to sell off the land of Tabah and the other villages nearby. He had no choice but to answer the summons. "I am honored," he said. "When shall we leave?"

Chapter Three

Haj Ibrahim had never seen an automobile as imposing and luxurious. When the driver cleaned it off from the trip it shined so that one could see one's face as if in a mirror. The inside smelled of fine leather and it drove with enormous power. Nonetheless, Haj Ibrahim was quite uncomfortable. The Effendi had never done anything so grand as to send an automobile all the way down from Damascus. What was he up to?

Obviously it had something to do with the partition plan. Political and military alliances were being made between old enemies, and Kabir was a cat who always landed on his feet. Even though Kabir had transferred much of his wealth out of Palestine, he would certainly keep a foot in the door.

Haj Ibrahim would find out soon enough. For the moment he was made more uncomfortable by the driver as the car pushed its way up the winding, crooked Bab el Wad, throwing them rudely from side to side on the turns that came up every few seconds. Truck traffic spewed smoke and coughed along at a snail's pace. The Mercedes would roar up behind a truck and the driver would tattoo his horn impatiently, then make a hair-raising pass into the lane of oncoming traffic. Dandash seemed relaxed, even bored, as he fiddled with the radio, which alternated between hotly delivered news and high-pitched oriental music.

Haj Ibrahim did not go to Jerusalem often. He studied the high banks on either side of the road filled with likely places for snipers and ambush. It had been thus for three thousand years of wars. The road would be more important than ever in anyone's military plans.

Where the Bab el Wad flattened out briefly at its summit, the British had set up a roadblock. Fifty cars were held up in two lines, one of Jews and one of Arabs. Mr. Dandash ordered the driver to go around the line directly to the checkpoint. Because of the obvious importance of the Mercedes, no one waiting in the Arab line voiced objections. Dandash stuck his head out the window and spoke a few terse, well-chosen words to the officer in charge and the barrier was opened immediately for him to pass through. Haj Ibrahim marveled at such power.

The highway took a downward plunge into a deep valley before starting the last climb to Jerusalem. On either side there was a smattering of Arab villages. To the left, in the distance, a tall hill arose that held the traditional Arab tomb of the prophet Samuel. It was from that particular hill that Richard the Lion-Heart was compelled to end and dismantle his Crusade. From there the British king had stared into a Jerusalem he would never enter.

As they took the final long hill up, homes made of the subtle pink Jerusalem stone revealed themselves glaringly under a midday sun. They broke into the suburbs, with an Arab district on the left of the highway and Jewish West Jerusalem before them. Moving down Jaffa Road to the central business district of the Jews, they snarled along behind a regiment of slow-moving traffic. Undisciplined Hassidim crossed the street in front of them at random with their side curls flopping up and down beneath broad-rimmed black beaver hats. Arab donkey carts, buses belching smoke, and a Mardi Gras mixture of unlikely peoples thickened near the Old City Wall.

A jungle of barbed wire and British presence blocked the way where Jaffa Road met the Jaffa Gate of the Old City. Dandash personally had to leave the car to find an officer to get them through.

They skirted the Old City, then turned abruptly onto Jericho Road and the welcome sight of all-Arab suburb. Once they cleared the outlying villages, the car took its downward trek into the bleak landscape of the Judean wilderness: the wilderness where David hid from Saul, the wilderness of the Essenes, of John the Baptist, and the wilderness of Christ. Ever downward they drove toward the lowest point on earth. A British convoy tore uphill, passing them in a race for Jerusalem, as military convoys will, with a sense of the utmost urgency.

With the traffic thinned, the chauffeur floored the pedal, slowing only to slam on the brakes and swerve past a suddenly appearing old truck or cart. A blinding afternoon heat blazed off the desert floor, sending up little waves rippling off the rocks. Haj Ibrahim was astonished that the inside of the automobile had remained cooled by some kind of miraculous device.

Through a Jericho lolling in stagnation, they skirted the northern tip of the Dead Sea and zipped along an empty straight road at breakneck speed. They were in a deep depression of the earth known as the Great Rift Valley. In the background on both sides of the river rose a backbone of sentinel mountains, one in Palestine and one in Trans-Jordan.

Across the river, Moses had died after seeing the Promised Land and Joshua had staged the Hebrew Tribes for their invasion. This had once been the ancient King's Highway, a vital caravan route from Damascus to its terminal at the Gulf of Aqaba, from whence Solomon's ships departed for Africa and the Orient.

On May 14 of the coming year of 1948, the British would withdraw from Trans-Jordan as well, leaving only an officer corps for the Arab Legion. The Emir Abdullah, who had already crowned himself king, now ruled a territory known as the Kingdom of Jordan. It would be a bogus kingdom, one of the weakest and poorest in the Arab world.

Everyone knew that Abdullah talked with the Jews and was only mildly interested in getting mixed up in a war with them. Despite his moderate hatred of the Jews, he did covet Jerusalem and longed for it to be annexed into his kingdom. He felt there was an excellent chance of obtaining both East Jerusalem and some lands on the West Bank by negotiation with the Jews. Unfortunately, he was an Arab monarch and under fierce pressure from the larger Arab states to join the conflict.

Although Abdullah was small and would be prone to yield, he had perhaps the best single army in the Arab world. Egypt, Syria, and the Saudis wanted to use Abdullah's Arab Legion, even if they were also wary of Abdullah's ambitions.

The British-armed, British-trained, and British-led Legion was likewise commanded by a British general. Its potential in the future war struck fear into the Jews. Abdullah was dancing on the head of a pin.

Evening found them travel-weary as they entered Tiberias. This town on the Sea of Galilee was of great historic importance to both Jew and Arab. At the nearby Horns of Hittim, Saladin the Kurd had all but destroyed the first Crusader kingdom in an epic battle.

The Galilee remained relatively quiet during the Roman period while the rest of the nation waged rebellion. Jews who had been driven out of Jerusalem fled to Tiberias as a refuge. Here great rabbis and scholars worked and studied down through the ages and made Tiberias one of their holy cities. The tombs of many of the rabbis who had kept Judaism alive embraced the lake and were scenes of great religious gatherings.

A hundred years earlier, during Ottoman times, the city was ravaged by an earthquake and was largely rebuilt by the Jews. They used the unique native black basalt rock as the main building material, which gave the town a look as uncommon as Jerusalem's pink stone.

As was the case with all towns and settlements in the region, the sun took a vicious toll on human energy. The Jews had the better of the energy and used it to establish a string of green kibbutzim and villages. Their strong presence in the region enabled the Jews to maintain relative peace and a balance of order.

Haj Ibrahim was surprised when Mr. Dandash ordered the driver to continue on past the Arab old town on the sea to an isolated Jewish hotel farther down the road. It was called the Gallei Kinneret and was owned and operated by a German refugee lady. They pulled into the driveway and halted. The driver emptied the trunk and was ordered to find himself a room at an Arab hotel and report in the morning.

"I do not wish to insult your hospitality," Haj Ibrahim said, "but I would feel more comfortable going with the driver to one of our own."

"But I have specific instructions from the Effendi," Dandash said sourly.

"It is also a matter of principle with me," Ibrahim added.

"As you wish," Dandash said, annoyed, "I will see you in the morning."

Haj Ibrahim had only been to Tiberias once before in his life and that was many years ago as a boy. The lake was heady stuff. He and the driver took their meal at a seafront café and watched the moon rise enchantingly above the hills on the opposite side. These were the Golan Heights of Syria, a high plateau hovering directly above the lake's eastern shoreline.

In Tiberias, as in all of Palestine, the conversation centered about the coming war with the Jews. The driver soon let it be known to everyone that Haj Ibrahim, the famous Muktar of Tabah, was with him. They all knew of the man who had used Saladin's tactic of burning the fields to defeat Kaukji's Irregulars.

They gathered about his table to exchange gossip and views. It was perfectly clear that the Syrians would come down from the Golan Heights and seize the lake, then drive across the Galilee and capture Haifa, with its large mixed population, helping pin down the Jews in advance of their army. From here it was so easy to envision.

Another sleepless night plagued Ibrahim. From a small stone balcony of his hotel room he stared at the lake as the moon danced its way to oblivion and the hills of Syria disappeared from sight.

Gideon Asch had come from a town near the northern end of the lake. It was on Ibrahim's mind. They would be passing close to it tomorrow. Oh how he missed Gideon. Gideon always knew what was taking place behind the scenes. He wanted to see Rosh Pinna and he wanted to see the house in which Gideon had been born and raised. What would Gideon tell him now about Arab maneuvering?

Certain things were becoming quite clear. A week earlier he had visited the Wahhabi tribe for a wedding. The Wahhabis roamed the northern Sinai and little escaped their eyes and ears. His uncle, the great Sheik Walid Azziz, had told him that Egypt was starting a military buildup in the Sinai. It was scarcely a secret that Egypt would attack Palestine from the south.

Because he knew the Arab mentality, Ibrahim was distressed. No Arab nation would go to war for fellow Arabs without a reward.

Syria, over the lake, had always kept up a vague claim to all of Palestine on the grounds that Damascus had been the political and administrative center for both countries and for Lebanon as well. Syria would certainly grab the Galilee and Haifa for itself. In that manner it would have Lebanon surrounded on three sides, with the Mediterranean on the fourth.

Egypt? It would claim the Negev Desert, the Gaza Strip, and Beersheba at the head of the desert as well as Tel Aviv and Jaffa.

Abdullah would not be able to resist the temptation of ruling over Jerusalem and the west bank of the river.

Palestine would be cut up among them. And what of Iraq and the Saudis and those states that did not border Palestine? They would be in it to restore Arab manhood and for the looting and destruction of the Jews.

Would these nations, each with their own interests in a piece of Palestine, allow the Palestinian people to form a nation? There would be little left for the Palestinians when it was done, and whatever autonomy Haj Ibrahim's people got depended upon whom they co-operated with. The warlords of Cairo, Damascus, and Amman were not even considering the Palestinian Arabs.

Was his mind wavering? Revelations came easily on the Sea of Galilee. It seemed so utterly plain to him. It was what Gideon would have told him. He would have argued with Gideon. It was difficult to talk himself out of what he had discovered.

How then did the Effendi Kabir plan to play it? What did he have in mind?

Chapter Four

Morning found them speeding north along a shoreline of immense historical and religious dimensions. Beyond the place where Jesus walked on the water, a long sloping hill drifted back from the lake. Beatitudes! The Sermon on the Mount. The meek shall inherit the earth. Past the ruins of the ancient synagogue at Capernaum where Jesus preached as a rabbi, the Sea of Galilee abruptly ended.

"I should like to see Rosh Pinna," Ibrahim said.

Dandash looked at his watch, shrugged, and instructed the chauffeur to take the short detour. The village of Gideon Asch's birthplace on the lower slopes of Mount Canaan had not changed much since it had been founded. It was sleepy but tidy. The people here farmed their own land and homes, in contrast to the communal aspects of the kibbutz.

These continuous thoughts of his former friend puzzled him. Why do I think so much of Gideon these days? Because I need him, I suppose. Haj Ibrahim could visualize Gideon as a lad lazing in the shade of the giant tree with a book in his lap . . . or mounting his stallion in defiance and reaching out beyond this lovely place to join the surging new order of things.

"Can I help you?" a Jewish farmer asked.

Ibrahim was about to ask to see the home of Gideon. "No," he said, "it is just so very pleasant here."

On social occasions Jews and Arabs were extremely hospitable to one another hereabouts. "You will stay for lunch?"

"It is not possible," Dandash interrupted, "we must be in Damascus today."

They entered the car and closed the doors. "Shalom," the farmer said.

"Shalom," Haj Ibrahim answered.

Again on the main highway, they turned east and climbed toward the Syrian border. From the bottom of the earth they ascended some three thousand feet onto the plateau of the Golan Heights. At the British side of the border they left the car for a

stretch and a meal from the picnic basket that had been prepared
at Dandash's hotel.

Haj Ibrahim stared down at the lake, which appeared to be
little more than a large pond from this height. He could see halfway across the entire Galilee to the hills of Nazareth and south
for many miles down the Great Rift Valley where the river fell
from the Sea of Galilee to the Dead Sea. The strings of Jewish
settlements along the lake appeared so tiny and helpless from
here. Syrian artillery could sit on this mountain and simply rain
down their fire. The Jews had no guns that could reach this far.
Certainly the Jews would never be able to scale the clifflike sheer-
ness and capture the place. Even his fellahin in Tabah could hold
such high ground against a brigade of the elite Palmach. It took
no Saladin to figure out that the Jews would be driven underground by the barrage, after which Syrian tanks and infantry
would merely have to sweep down and eradicate them. Of all the
military positions in Palestine, Haj Ibrahim could not envision
one that gave the Arabs a greater advantage.

The Syrian officer at the border town of Quinetra groveled
before the imposing automobile and, after a brief word with
Dandash, snapped off a smart salute, shouted a command to open
the gate, and watched the car as it bolted into the town.

Quinetra had been built up as a military staging town because
of its impeccable strategic credentials and because it straddled an
oil pipeline that originated in the Persian Gulf almost a thousand
miles away. The flurry of military vehicles, a field of neatly
parked tanks and mobile artillery pieces, and hundreds of Syrian
soldiers on the street all bespoke coming war.

Once through the town they skirted the bottom of a snow-
capped Mount Hermon, a great lonely peak whose broad base
touched down into Palestine, Syria, and Lebanon. The mountain's lower slopes held a collection of villages of the mystical
quasi-Islamic Druze sect, impoverished Shi'ite Moslems, and a
smattering of Christian Arabs.

Now out on a flat ugly gray volcanic desert plain of the Golan,
they linked up to the Amman highway, and before Haj Ibrahim
could prepare for it, there suddenly rose before him the spires of
the glorious Umayyad Mosque of Damascus, next in sacred rank
to the Dome of the Rock. Damascus, the city of Abel and Cain
and the Apostle Paul and the birth of Christianity, was claimed as

the oldest on earth. It rose from the surrounding desolation as a gigantic oasis. Damascus, which had once ruled an empire larger than Rome's, continued to live on glory a thousand years departed.

Haj Ibrahim's calm fled him; his prayer beads were fingered at a feverish pace as they reached the outskirts of the city. Next to his arrival in Mecca, he had never experienced anything like this. His awe was counterpointed by Dandash's sullenness and the chauffeur's bullying his way by horn. An Arabic hodgepodge of minarets and domes, of the old walled town with its crumbling casbah packed with humanity, was breached by modern glass skyscrapers and wide boulevards telling of recent French influence. Everything was hazed by an eternal pall of ash and sand that constantly blew in from the desert.

Damascus was made possible by the River Barada, which gushed down from the mountains of Lebanon, then broke into hundreds of streamlets that had been converted into a patchwork of canals. The waters had enriched a greenbelt called El Ghouta. This district had been likened in Arabian fantasy to the Garden of Eden. El Ghouta held an unlikely mixture of gardens and grand villas, of casinos and farms and orchards that fed the city, of parks and recreation areas.

It was in El Ghouta that the Effendi Kabir dwelled in a square villa of demicastle proportions. A quarter of a mile down the gated and guarded entrance they drove through a small blizzard of fruit orchards and into a garden of thousands of Damascus rose bushes, then burst on the villa with its facade of orange-peach colored Algerian marble framed in Persian tiles.

Haj Ibrahim's head became light and fuzzy as Fawzi Kabir greeted him with no less exuberance than if he had been welcoming a Saudi prince. The enormity of the welcome snapped Ibrahim into alertness and made him doubly suspicious. He knew full well that he had been summoned for something of great importance.

His awe of every new aspect of this fairyland was now tempered by continuous voices of caution. It was dream stuff, his preview of paradise, but he realized Kabir's hospitality would have a steep price.

Dinner found them in a room straight out of *Arabian Nights*, designed for partying. Large embroidered cloths formed a tent on the walls and ceiling, interspersed with mirrors. The floor was covered, not with thin oriental rugs, but deep plush Western carpeting. Pillows and low tables added a sense of Roman debauchery. The two men ate alone, save a quartet of handsomely muscled young servants and a pair of guards uniformed like old Turkish Janissaries with bloomered pantaloons to the ankles, wide red sashes about the waist, and fez head coverings. At the meal's end two servants carried in a six-foot silver platter of fruits, nuts, cheeses, and European chocolates, pastries, and candies that seemed half as high as Mount Arafat. Kabir clapped his hands, delivered an order, then dug into the great mound of afterdinner delights.

Lo and behold, a quintet of musicians appeared, and as they whined out a repetitious melody a belly dancer slithered in from nowhere and began to gyrate before them.

In Allah's name! What does this man want of me! I must be alert beyond alert! This could all be a softening-up process to lull me off my guard and then assassinate me. Why does he want to kill me? Oh yes, I made him travel to Tabah once. Although that was a quarter of a century ago a man like Kabir would never forget such an insult! Nonsense! He is only trying to be a good host . . . on the other hand . . .

The Muktar of Tabah gaped as the woman wiggled her torso toward them, then danced directly above where he was reclining. She was not an Arab, for her skin was a Western white and her hair was gold and her eyes, blue. Kabir leaned over, propped on an elbow, and put his lips close to Ibrahim's ear.

"Her name is Ursula. She is German and extremely clever, very talented. She is one of my favorites. Can you believe she learned to dance like that in less than a year? She will visit your room tonight. Keep her as long as you wish." Kabir paused slightly to crack a walnut and his eyes roved to the male servants standing at attention. He nodded toward a young man of startling, sensual feline beauty. "Or take them both."

Ursula pumped a beautifully curved, firm, delicious hip an inch from Ibrahim's nose and met the warm, uneven breath huffing out of him. She turned ever so slowly so that her sacred part was all but in his face.

"Why was I brought here?" erupted from Ibrahim.

"Time enough for business tomorrow," Kabir answered. "It has been a long day for you. I hope the night is equally long."

The music abruptly halted, as oriental music often does.

This cannot be true, Ibrahim thought as he lay back on a satined bed in a room fit for Mohammed himself. It was dimly lit and floating little lines of incense twirled to the ceiling.

I know! She is the one assigned to kill me. I must be extremely careful.

His heart thumped audibly and tried to leap through his throat as he sensed movement behind a latticework that divided the room. He could barely see through it but could make out the girl on the other side. She feather-stepped her way into the room, gowned in filmy transparent chiffon, and came to a halt at the foot of the bed and unabashedly revealed herself, stitch by stitch, with agonizing deliberateness.

When her gown dropped to her feet, she came over the bed toward him on all fours. Haj Ibrahim seized her, threw her on her back, and his thrusts were rapid, powerful, and inflamed. In a moment he dropped back, gasping and perspiring. He had never touched flesh like hers. It was madness.

Ursula survived his first assault graciously. The next time he took longer and was not as rough. He collapsed for a second time, finished for the night. The girl lay tightly beside him and her fingers wove elfin circles about his skin.

"You are so gentle," he said at last. "You hate me. I made love all wrong." He was surprised by his compulsive burst of guilt.

"You must learn to allow yourself to be touched," she said.

"I did it wrong."

"Stop that. Learn to be touched. Learn to enjoy your own stillness."

Haj Ibrahim gasped several times. Everything was running together: the long drive from Tabah, the spell-binding arrival in Damascus, this night of paradise, Gideon's home, the moon rising over the Golan Heights, tanks, cannons, Tabah . . . Tabah . . . Tabah . . . the road to Jerusalem.

"I must confess that for the first time in my entire life, I am somewhat tired," he said.

"Not to be so certain," she answered.

Ursula sat up, opened a bedside table drawer and withdrew a

little jeweled box, opened it and took out a stick of hashish and crumpled some in a pipe.

Aha! Now that I am weak she will give me hashish dipped in poison.

Before anxiety overtook him he saw her light the pipe and draw a deep, hungry puff, then offer it to him. He smiled, almost aloud, at his own foolishness. As he relit the pipe for a second draw, her hand brought his down.

"It is very strong," she warned.

"Yes," he said in delight, "yes." The room swirled and the aroma of frankincense glazed his mind. Everything about him was satin. Ursula's touch had now become incredible. He never realized such finesse existed. She licked him entirely, endlessly. What he thought was dead between his legs began to come alive again.

"Don't move, don't grab me," she instructed. "Accept."

"I will try, but you are driving me out of my mind."

"Try. You are a good man."

"I'll try," he repeated.

She bathed herself in scented oils before him under a dim light, then bathed him. As she slithered atop him she admonished him again softly to remain still. He allowed himself to be taken over. Ursula was in control and loved him and loved him and loved him until he was holding a volcano at bay inside himself. This time she joined in the delight, forcing him to submit to her in tiny stages until the volcano could no longer contain eruption and the most blissful of all weariness overcame him.

"Ursula," he whispered later.

"Yes?"

"Why did he bring me here?"

"I should not tell."

"Please."

"Tomorrow you will meet with Kaukji and Abdul Kadar Heusseini."

Ibrahim sat up, his fogginess dispelled instantly. "But they are my blood enemies. They are Kabir's blood enemies!"

"It seems that all Arabs are to become brothers, now."

Haj Ibrahim grunted in dismay. Ursula put the pipe in his mouth again and lit it. He took a very deep draw and fell back on the pillow and she was beside him.

"I will begin to worry tomorrow," he said.

Chapter Five

The voice of the muezzin, wailing out to call the devout to prayer, pierced the air as night turned to day. Haj Ibrahim awakened to it automatically, as he had done every day of his life. He blinked his eyes open slowly. He was very groggy. Damascus! The Effendi Kabir! He bolted upright and his head pounded from the night of hashish, wine, and lovemaking.

He looked quickly to his side. She was gone, but he could still smell her fragrance and the pillow was indented where she had slept. He moaned an enormous sigh of remembrance and smiled, groaning equally at his hangover, smiled again, and threw the sheet back. It probably never even happened, he thought. Even if it had been a dream, it had been worth it.

Haj Ibrahim unrolled his prayer rug, laid it down facing Mecca, and bowed.

> "In the name of Allah, the merciful, the compassionate.
> Praise belongs to Allah, the Lord of the worlds,
> The merciful, the compassionate.
> Wielder of the Day of Judgment.
> Thus do we serve, and on Thee do we call for help;
> Guide us the straight path,
> The path of those upon whom Thou has bestowed
>   good,
> Not that of those upon whom anger falls, or
>   those who go astray."

When the prayer was done he arose gingerly, for he ached in many places. "I have prepared a bath," a woman's voice said behind him. He turned to see Ursula by the door and his heart raced. "I've ordered breakfast on the veranda. Your meeting is not until later."

She helped him down three steps into a great marble caldron of a tub. They sat with hot foam up to their necks. She sponged him off pamperingly.

"You naughty old man," she said, "five times. The last ones were so very good. You are a marvelous student."

Their conversation on the veranda was in snatches . . . she told of Berlin and air raids . . . the terrible artillery bombardment . . . the terror of the Russians entering the city . . . a young girl hiding in the rubble . . . rape . . . starvation and destitution . . . escape . . . Beirut . . . blondes, they like blondes . . .

"War," he rasped, "I don't want this war. There must be another way."

"You are in trouble here, aren't you?" she said.

"Yes, I believe so. Fawzi Kabir did not send for me to reward me for being a good Moslem."

"I don't know if I'll be able to come back tonight," she said, "but I can remain with you until your meeting."

"It is not necessary," Haj Ibrahim replied, "I must meditate. Besides, I've had my preview of paradise, thanks to you. I would be the worst kind of fool to think I could find it again on earth. I want always to be able to think back to the one moment of perfection. I don't want to take a chance that something could go wrong tonight and change that memory. Do you understand that?"

"You are a good man, Ibrahim. And wise, as well. After all, I am really only a prostitute."

"Allah has given me many things in many different kinds of ways. I accept that He sent you as some great reward. Do not berate yourself. Any woman who can give a man a look into paradise is a good woman."

"I don't think I have blushed since I was a little girl," Ursula said.

"I don't want you to go quite yet," he said. "I have learned something of importance. It is very difficult to teach me anything. No one among my people could even presume they could teach me. It is I, Ibrahim, who must make the decisions for everyone else and I alone out of a hundred men who will take any responsibility. I have a son, Ishmael. He is my single hope, but he is very young. He is brave and he is cunning, so he may become a leader. He is also clever. He already knows how to manipulate me. Ishmael reads to me so I can be informed. But in the end, I must make all decisions according to Sunna, according to tradition. To live by tradition, one cannot gain too much knowledge for himself. Knowledge clashes with tradition. I have followed the Koran by surah and verse. To do that you must shut out much inquiry. Forgive me, Ursula, I am rambling."

"Please go on."

"It is to say I have learned something last night. A friend has been trying to tell me for years to open my mind, my soul. The Koran tells me not to do that, but only to accept everything in life as fate and Allah's will. I reached out last night. You gave me my first true look into this frightening world the Jews have brought to Palestine. I accepted mercy and compassion from a woman. I now know my first woman and acknowledge that she . . . you . . . knows more than I do about many things. Do you understand what it means for Haj Ibrahim, the Muktar of Tabah, to accept that from a woman?"

"I know of Arab men," Ursula said with a tinge of tiredness creeping into her voice.

"Do you know what it means?" he repeated. "To suddenly open a door to a forbidden room? I have battled with a man who is probably my best and maybe my only friend. Oh, I have friends, many friends. But a man I trust . . . I do not even trust my son, Ishmael." His voice became pained. "The man is a Jew. See, I am now even speaking to a woman about my private thoughts."

"What is it, Haj Ibrahim?"

"What is it? We should sit down and talk to the Jews. The Grand Mufti of Jerusalem established the pattern of hatred. Maybe it was established before him. Maybe it has always been part of us. I learned last night from a woman, you see, and I have shut out the truth and the truth is that we can learn from the Jews . . . and we can live beside them. If there was a single voice in our world inclined to moderation, it would be stilled by assassination. That is our nature. This war will be very hard for my people and I am the only one who will make the decisions."

He reached out and patted her hand and smiled, sadly. Haj Ibrahim had responded to the summons from Kabir by bringing along his finest robes and by wearing his finest jewelry. It was not the jewelry of a rich man, but the pieces were antique Bedouin, primitive, but powerfully lovely. He took a ring from his small finger, opened her palm, placed it within, and closed her hand.

"Please," he said.

"Thank you, I'll treasure it," she whispered.

"Now, if you please, I must meditate."

"Haj Ibrahim."

"Yes?"

"Please be careful of Kabir. He is treacherous."

A brackish streamlet of the Barada River slugged its way past the veranda. The fragrance of the Damascus roses hung on silenced air. Haj Ibrahim sat and contemplated. Since Ishmael had been reading to him, he had learned many new things and reasoned out others.

Haj Amin al Heusseini, the Grand Mufti of Jerusalem, was his blood enemy. Now the Mufti was wanted by the Allies as a war criminal. He jumped a "gentleman's" detention by the French and escaped into the Arab world, which showed no embarrassment at sheltering him. Indeed, he and his philosophies were revered. Unable to return to Palestine, the Mufti directed his continuing vendetta against the Jews from various Arab capitals.

The instant the United Nations voted for the partition of Palestine, the Mufti appointed a nephew, Abdul Kadar Heusseini, to enlist and command a force of volunteers in his behalf. The Heusseini tribe and clans were mainly in the Jerusalem area. The volunteers were to be known as the Army of the Jihad.

Abdul Kadar knew almost nothing about military matters, but he was popular from Hebron to Ramallah along the West Bank. He had become the surrogate of his uncle and titular leader of the Arabs in Jerusalem, Judea, and Samaria. Ibrahim knew that the militia he was recruiting consisted of a potpourri of unemployed workers, youth clubs, fanatics from the Moslem Brotherhood, farmers, and tradesmen. They knew even less about military matters.

A few thousand Palestinian Arabs had received British training in the war and another few thousand were members of the police and border guards. This Army of the Jihad would consist of five or six thousand men with small arms and without real organization or leadership.

During the Mufti's revolt a similar militia calling themselves Mojahedeen, the Warriors of God, had very limited success against the Jews, mainly on the vulnerable Jerusalem road. Their greatest victories were over fellow Arabs and came by assassinating and massacring the Mufti's political opposition. Certainly this new Army of the Jihad would have minimal effect. In Haj Ibrahim's mind it could be all but written off.

His thoughts turned to another old worm who had come out of the woodwork. Kaukji, who was either Lebanese, Syrian, or Iraqi, had spent the war in Nazi Germany. His Irregulars had had a miserable record during the Mufti's revolt. They were a ragtag band of brigands who evaporated every time a battle heated up.

Haj Ibrahim was more concerned about the defeat he had administered to Kaukji. He knew he was a candidate for Kaukji's revenge, for one does not forget in this world.

Haj Ibrahim also knew that in the fanciful Arab mind the terrible record of Kaukji could convolute defeat into victory. Somehow Kaukji still remained a respected military figure in the Arab world. Always on the prowl for spoils, Kaukji announced formation of an Arab Army of Liberation to be recruited from Morocco to Oman, an army of many thousands of volunteers. They would be supported by a variety of Arab treasuries.

Tens of thousands of Arabs answered his call on the night of the partition vote, swearing to volunteer. Their anger was quickly spent. In the end, a few hundred idealists found their way to the Army of Liberation's recruiting offices.

With his ranks empty, Kaukji set out to purchase an army. He found the best mercenaries available among the Arabs. Bonus money always brought a response, but this time the response was poor. He found former Nazis hiding among the Arabs, British deserters, Italian deserters, and he bought officers from standing Arab armies. He then appealed beyond the Arab world to Islamic nations and this brought another few thousand from Yugoslavia, the Moslem parts of India, Africa, and the Far East. He obtained early releases of criminals from prisons in Baghdad, Damascus, Beirut, and from Saudi Arabia. He signed on several companies of the Moslem Brotherhood, who were men of intense hatred but totally undisciplined. Kaukji hoped for ten thousand men. He was over two thousand short. His self-ordained sacred mission was to enter Palestine and grab off whatever he could. He had four and a half months to operate before the regular Arab armies invaded.

It was obvious that both commanders were in Damascus scouring for arms and money. What then? Haj Ibrahim pondered. Ab-

dul Kadar and Kaukji loathed one another. It was beyond com-
prehension that they could operate with a unified command. It
was beyond doubt that each of them had made side deals with
Abdullah, the Egyptians, and the Syrians. Who was in bed with
whom? Where did the Effendi Kabir fit in?

Did the Arabs have a policy or just a series of secret deals? Did
they really know what they were after with any clarity? Were
they in agreement on any single question except the abstract
mania of destroying Jews? With so many Arab armies and militias
in Palestine, was it not logical that if the Jews were defeated it
would only lead to an even bloodier mess of Arab fighting Arab?
Haj Ibrahim had followed Arab conference after Arab conference
and knew the only thing that ever came out of them was time-
tested anarchy.

And what of the soldiers of the Army of the Jihad and the
Army of Liberation? They were men like his own villagers in
Tabah, coffeehouse fighters, impoverished men of little self-esteem with no real training and less stomach for the bitterness of
bayonet combat.

Ibrahim did not know the entire strength of the Jews, but he
had long respected their tremendous organizational capacities,
their commanders, and their unity of purpose. Against the British the Haganah had had startling success. Against the Arabs they
were undefeated. Tens of thousands of new Jewish veterans of the
war filled their ranks. The stationary defense of the kibbutzim
would be able to turn back anything Abdul Kadar or Kaukji
could throw at them.

The Jews also had several battalions of young, hard Palmach
men.

The Jews also had reality in their planning instead of fantasy
and the support of the Yishuv in place of intertribal disarray.

In the end it would not be Kabir, Kaukji, or Abdul Kadar who
paid the price but the fellahin of Tabah and the struggling peasants and townsfolk of Palestine.

"Haj Ibrahim."

He turned and looked into the ever-mournful face of Dandash.
"The Effendi is ready for the meeting."

Chapter Six

"Brother."

"Brother."

"Brother."

"Brother."

The office of Fawzi Kabir held a conference table around the likes of which kings and foreign ministers would debate. Haj Ibrahim was determined that the setting would not intimidate him as he was placed opposite Abdul Kadar Heusseini and Generalissimo Kaukji, resplendent in a new field marshal's uniform.

"Before we begin," Kaukji said, "I want Haj Ibrahim to know that I never have nor ever will hold thoughts of personal vengeance against him or the people of Tabah for the time he outfoxed me. We are now all brothers facing a common enemy."

The common enemy is ourselves. Ibrahim nodded and smiled to Kaukji.

"What the generalissimo said goes for the Heusseinis as well," Abdul Kadar added. "My uncle, the Grand Mufti, bears no grudges. There can no longer be the luxury of petty feuds among us. The greater cause is too urgent."

Again Ibrahim nodded.

Fawzi Kabir cleared his throat, balanced his fat little body on the edge of his high-backed leather chair, pursed his lips, and pushed his fingertips together. "Times have changed drastically since the Mufti's revolt. Then, even I had a different viewpoint. When these two brothers came to me I was only too happy to join the new order of things. Today, there is but one issue and one enemy. Unity in the Arab world is paramount."

"When have we ever had unity?" Ibrahim asked.

The three stared at him, annoyed. Kabir felt he would be difficult from the outset. "We found unity the day, the minute the partition plan was voted. The world shall see how the Arab brothers can stand shoulder to shoulder."

"When have we had Arab soil desecrated by the threat of a Zionist state?" Abdul Kadar added.

"I myself have had many differences with the Mufti," Kaukji continued the litany of brotherhood, "but 1939 was 1939, and 1947 is 1947."

But it is the same old cast of players. The leopard does not change his spots or the camel discard his hump at the water hole. What has changed? All three men are seething with ambition. Do they really believe they are now allies?

"The strategic aim of our two, shall we say, liberation armies," Kaukji said, assuming the air of a man who believed himself to be an outstanding military mind, "is obvious. Abdul Kadar and I shall seize as much of Palestine as is possible before the formal invasion by the regular Arab armies of Egypt, Syria, Jordan, and Lebanon."

"Excuse me," Haj Ibrahim said, "I am but a simple and humble fellah, not versed in military matters. But your volunteers, pardon me, your armies, are of the same general composition as they were ten years ago. Today the Jews are better trained, better armed, better organized, and better commanded than they were ten years ago. Ten years ago you were unable to dislodge a single Jewish settlement. What makes you believe, united though we may be, that it will be any different this time?"

He is being troublesome, Kabir thought, very troublesome.

"We did not succeed the last time," Abdul Kadar said, "because we spent our strength fighting each other. That condition no longer exists."

By Allah's beard, I really believe he has talked himself into believing the camel will leave his hump at the hole. He believes we have changed our nature, overnight. Dear brother, Abdul Kadar, you don't know donkey shit from mother's milk.

"There are many other differences," Kaukji said, jumping in quickly. He laid his riding crop on the table and stared at the ceiling and gestured with his hand as though lecturing abstractly to cadets. "Namely, one. This time the Jews will not have the British to save them. We have been assured by the highest levels of the British command that they will not interfere with the operations of the two volunteer armies, even though the British are still in the country. We have been further assured that, as they withdraw, they will turn over all major strategic positions to us. By May fifteen next year when the British are out, there will not be enough Jews left for them to declare independence, or even a quorum to give prayers for their dead."

Kabir and Abdul Kadar allowed themselves a laugh.

Kaukji nodded and went on. "Point two. This time we are bringing in tanks, artillery, heavy weapons of all types that we did not have previously. We will hit the Jew with a firepower he has never tasted before. Once I have captured a half dozen of their settlements, and no question of that, I envision a panic sweeping over them. We shall give them the sea to flee into."

Kaukji quickly held up his hand to silence Ibrahim. "Three," he said, "this time we have the armies of the entire Arab world to back us up. Even now we have officers from the regular armies and we can slip in units of regular armies and integrate them into the forces of Abdul Kadar and myself."

"The British have a hundred thousand troops in Palestine. Yet the Jews have forced them to give up the mandate," Haj Ibrahim retorted.

"But," Kaukji answered, "the British played games with the Jews. We will not show them the same mercy. A hundred thousand Arab troops in Palestine and a hundred thousand British troops in Palestine are not the same."

"I'm sure you are prepared to take heavy losses," Haj Ibrahim pressed. "The Jews will not go down easily."

"We may lose thousands, tens of thousands, hundreds of thousands, but we will gain victory if it takes the last drop of Arab blood," Abdul Kadar intoned.

Aha! The last drop of blood. When have I heard that one before. Like the hundreds of thousands of men who said they would enlist in the Army of Liberation and ran out of stomach before they got to the recruiting office? The three of them have drunk too much of the wine of words. They are intoxicated by their own rhetoric. Perhaps not Kabir. He alone is working out a reality for himself. But Abdul Kadar and the generalissimo? They do not know where one command begins and the other ends. They will be fighting with the same old unskilled gangs. The Jews will be brave because bravery often comes from the lack of choice. But who among these three knows which one has made secret alliances with which Arab leaders?

"I would be the last man in Islam to question the field marshal's wisdom, but, in the event your armies do not meet with the initial success hoped for and the regular Arab armies are called upon, what will be their price? I ask you, Abdul Kadar, what will

Abdullah want in return for bringing the Arab Legion over? Jerusalem? Or do you expect him to hand it back to you on a platter? Will they all pack up and leave and say to us, 'Here, brothers, we give you Palestine'? Or perhaps they might want a few, you know, border changes for their participation."

There was a shrieking silence. Faces reddened.

Kabir stepped in quickly. "It is a simple matter. After the Jews have been destroyed, by whatever means and by whichever armies, we shall call a conference and work out an agreement. There will be enough spoils for everyone."

When has Abdullah ever agreed with Egypt on anything? When has Syria agreed with Lebanon? When has Iraq agreed with anyone? How long will the conference last? A thousand years?

"The main point you are missing, Haj Ibrahim," Abdul Kadar said, "is that we are unified and that we will win. What is the final difference so long as we are ruled by Arabs and not Jews?"

"Pardon my ignorance, my brothers, but I was under the impression that Palestine was going to be liberated for the Palestinians," Haj Ibrahim retorted. "I think the time to hold the conference is now, before anybody starts shooting, and make certain we all have a clear picture of who is in it for what."

"So let me summarize," Kabir said, evading Ibrahim's charges and questions. "The Jews, one way or another, have no possibility of surviving." Abdul Kadar and Kaukji nodded in agreement.

"So now that we have crushed the Jews, at least in this discussion, why was I summoned here?" Haj Ibrahim said acidly.

The other three exchanged glances.

Kabir did a throat-clearing, finger-tapping, moustache-twisting routine. "All our military minds agree, and I concur, that the key to ultimate victory will be to cut off Jewish Jerusalem," he said, and deferred to Kaukji.

"This round," Kaukji said, "my army and Abdul Kadar's Army of the Jihad will be in perfect co-ordination and we will throw everything into blockading them. You know the Bab el Wad. Not a single Jewish truck will get through."

"The Army of the Jihad," Abdul Kadar said with rising emotion, his finger pointing and shaking at the air, "will have many thousands of men in Jerusalem and along the highway. But I will also have over a thousand men in Lydda and Ramle to seize the airport!"

"We shall set up very sophisticated communications," Kaukji cut in, "and every time a Jewish car, truck, bus, or convoy leaves Tel Aviv, we will know the instant they reach Lydda and we will alert thousands of men already in position to stop them. How? Every Arab village from Ramle to Jerusalem must be opened to our observers and our troops."

"I see three problems," Haj Ibrahim said in a subtle mockery of Kaukji's earlier dissertation. "One. Tabah commands a key position on the road. So does Shemesh Kibbutz. Two. Shemesh Kibbutz controls our water. Three. Shemesh Kibbutz knows everything that is going on in Tabah. I regret they have excellent information supplied by spies of my own clan and tribe. If the Jews know we are co-operating openly with your . . . er . . . armies, they will attack us."

"This brings us to the point of the meeting," Kabir said. "It is a difficult point, a very difficult point. Generalissimo Kaukji has conferred with the chiefs of staff of all the Arab states. We consider that it would be better to remove our people from a number of sensitive strategic locations."

"You must evacuate Tabah," Kaukji said, "in order to give our forces a free run of things."

So that was it! Oh, Allah, how could you let this befall me! It is madness! It cannot be true! No! No! Evacuate Tabah! In behalf of these fools!

"You must evacuate," Abdul Kadar repeated.

"But where shall we go?" Haj Ibrahim mumbled as if in a stupor.

"You have a great tribe in the desert. They are your cousins."

"But the Wahhabis live in privation. They cannot take in and feed two hundred more families."

"Let me tell you very confidentially," Kabir said. "I am negotiating with both the Syrians and Abdullah. They have expressed a definite willingness to take under consideration having you as guests until our armies have completed the job. We are suggesting that a number of other villages, even cities, evacuate. Obviously, we will make suitable arrangements for everyone."

"But you said they are only considering taking us. No one has said they will take us. I must hear it from Abdullah himself. Why doesn't he have someone here? I cannot simply pick up a thousand people and go nowhere."

"Haj Ibrahim, this is war, holy war. You have no choice. Now listen, my brother. It will be a short war, a few weeks, a few months at most," Kabir oozed. "I say, sitting before you in the presence of Generalissimo Kaukji and Abdul Kadar Heusseini of Palestine's most noble family . . . and I swear to you on Allah's name that when you return, one third of the land of Shemesh Kibbutz will be yours."

Haj Ibrahim was numbed and enraged but also wise enough to realize when a decision beyond his control was being imposed. He had neither room to maneuver nor bargaining points.

"My army will be crossing the border in a few weeks, after the new year," Kaukji said. "After I have captured a number of settlements and stampeded the Jews, Abdul Kadar's Army of the Jihad will unite with me and squeeze off Jerusalem. There is no way the Jews can defend all the roads . . . unless some of our brothers choose not to co-operate."

"We will advise you," Kabir said, "exactly when to evacuate. You will take your people directly to Jaffa."

"Jaffa? Why Jaffa?"

"To put them first in a safe place. In the event you are unable to get to Gaza by road, you will have an alternative, to leave by sea. Either you go to Gaza or when my negotiations with the Syrians are concluded, you can be shipped up to Syria. I have funds for a boat and instructions for you in Jaffa."

"But resettlement will cost a fortune." Ibrahim protested.

"I pay, I pay," Kabir said.

"In return for what? Your charity is not exactly legend," Ibrahim retorted.

"I pay for an Arab victory!"

"Very well, but before I leave for Jaffa, I must have the funds in my hands," Ibrahim said.

"Of course, of course. One thousand British pounds."

"To evacuate and resettle over two hundred families? I cannot go with less than five thousand."

"We will work out these minor details," Kabir said, switching subjects. "You will all be back in Tabah in time for fall planting. And most importantly, you can live forever without fear of a Zionist state."

Here are my leaders. The vanguard of more leaders reeking of personal ambition and greed, maniacal for power. They have their cause now, their noble cause. I am as much to blame, for I have never really thought in terms of peace with the Jews. None of us is capable of even thinking in such terms. But there is no real plan, no organization, no stated set of goals; only to recruit an armed mob and dupe themselves into believing it will overrun the Jews. What donkeys! What fantasy-chasing idiots! They are leading my people into an eternity of suffering.

Haj Ibrahim declined the Effendi's further hospitality and asked to be returned to Tabah.

When he was gone the other three reduced their agreement to a written contract overseen by Dandash. Kabir would give the two armies letters of credit to purchase arms. He would use his personal contacts in the Arab governments and Arab financial institutions to raise money to continue recruiting volunteers by offering large bonuses. Further moneys would continue to come to pay for the troops' salaries and for operations.

As payment for this, Kabir was to be assured of the return of all his lands in the Valley of Ayalon. Most importantly, he was to receive title to Shemesh Kibbutz and fifteen other Jewish settlements. The Jewish lands were a gold mine. The strategic location of his fiefdom would put him into a position of a major political power in any future division of Palestine.

Dandash was sent off to put it to formal documents.

"What of Haj Ibrahim," Abdul Kadar said. "Will he evacuate? There has always been the rumor that he co-operated with the Jews during my uncle's rebellion."

"Haj Ibrahim is a pragmatic man. He will take his people to Jaffa when we tell him to do so."

"That fart eater will pay for what he did to my men," Kaukji said. "I have waited ten years for my vengeance."

"I am directing him to Jaffa for you, am I not?" Kabir said. "Once he is in Jaffa, he will be in your hands. I see nothing. I hear nothing. I speak nothing."

"Now then," Abdul Kadar said, "the first moneys due us."

"It has been held up by some minor bureaucrats. Do not give it a second thought. I will take care of everything."

Chapter Seven

"There will be no negotiations, no settlement, no recognition, no peace with the Jews. All solutions that do not give us Palestine in its entirety are rejected. Our policy issues will be settled at the point of a gun." Thus spoke the entire Arab world, which generally ended each new statement with a battle cry of the ancient Romans: *"Perish Judea!"*

Arab Palestine mobbed and struck. In cities with mixed populations, accordions of barbed wire set up demarcations of communities. The British, neutral in theory but pointedly pro-Arab in reality and action, continued to blockade the Palestine coast. The country's only large airport at Lydda was due to go into the Jewish state, but the British permitted a large buildup of Arab irregulars to control it, within range of their guns.

As in the past, it was the hit-and-run raid and ambush on the highways where the Arabs would have their best results. It began with the ambush of a Jewish bus near Lydda and the massacre of the passengers.

A sudden chilling, rapid, and unforeseen panic swept the Arab community. As they observed the Heusseinis and Kaukji preparing for war, a flash flood of fear raced through them. The wealthy and influential Arab families, the leaders of the community, recalled the days of the Mufti's revolt. The militias had been the same two forces who had all but destroyed their brother Arabs a decade earlier. The Palestinian Arabs knew they were in for blackmail, extortion, and murder from Abdul Kadar and Kaukji.

By the dozens, hundreds, and thousands, the crème de la crème of Arab Palestine liquidated their holdings, withdrew their savings, and fled the country. The Arab community was suddenly stripped of its doctors, lawyers, landowners, social leaders, politicians, professors, principal merchants, bankers, manufacturers, intellectuals, and writers. Within weeks of the partition plan, some thirty thousand families, representing over a hundred thousand people, simply quit Palestine, opting to sit out the coming war in the more comfortable surroundings of Beirut, Cairo, or the European continent.

No warnings had been issued and no shots had been fired at them by the Jews, but they showed neither the desire nor the courage to enter the struggle to liberate Arab Palestine. They had no feeling whatsoever for a Palestinian nation, for there had never been one. They knew that an Arab victory would mean a state of chaos in which they would be victims rather than victors. This Palestinian Arab leadership simply abandoned its country in a self-serving manner, uncaring for the balance of the population.

Commerce, education, social and medical services, agricultural marketing, banking and communications halted, building stopped and factories suddenly closed, and ideology within the Arab community collapsed. This self-imposed exile of the rich and the important stripped those who remained of any kind of responsible leadership. Small wonder that the ordinary fellah and the little merchant were utterly devastated by their departure. Witnessing the desertion of almost every prominent and respected person in the community, other families began to simply drift out of the country. This was the opening chapter of a ripple effect that exploded into universal flight, a flight that resulted in a refugee problem that was to consume the Palestinian Arab.

A British patrol entered Tabah on a routine search. The lieutenant in command went into the café and ordered Farouk outside, beyond earshot of the others.

"Fawzi Kabir is in Jaffa in his villa," the officer said. "He wants to see you as quickly as possible. When shall I say you will be there?"

"I can come the day after the Sabbath."

"No one is to know, particularly your brother," the lieutenant said.

"Yes, of course."

"Will there be any suspicion?"

"No no. I will simply tell Ibrahim that with the shortages building up I want to get to Jaffa for supplies."

"No one—repeat, no one—is to know who sent for you."

"I understand. But what does the Effendi want of me?"

The officer shrugged. "I only carry the message," he said.

Kabir's people had been on the lookout for Farouk and spotted him the instant he debarked from a bus at the Clock Tower in the center of Jaffa. He was whisked off in a car with its curtains drawn.

Kabir's villa was across from the Scotch House Hotel above the port. Farouk had been there on many occasions to pay the annual rents of Tabah, but never surreptitiously. Every time he was to see the Effendi, his nerves betrayed him. This secret summons had him in a hand-sweating, stomach-growling tizzy.

Farouk was welcomed with uncustomary warmth. This increased his suspicions.

"How does it go in Tabah, brother?" Kabir asked.

"It is very tense."

"What is the general attitude of the men?"

"We are coming under a great deal of pressure from Abdul Kadar to join his militia."

"Have any joined?"

"Some have secretly pledged. They must wait until Haj Ibrahim gives them the blessing."

"And your brother. What does he have to say about this?"

"Since he has returned from Damascus, he says very little. Of course he is enraged about all the wealthy families who have abandoned us."

"Yes, their flight has raised havoc with commerce. I will have a terrible problem getting my orange crop shipped out this year. We shall not forget the cowardly behavior of those who fled. When the war is over, there will be many new leaders in Palestine."

Farouk bowed his head twice in agreement.

"I understand there has been talk of evacuation among all the Arab villages of Ayalon," Kabir said.

"Oh no, Effendi! We are prepared to fight to the last drop of blood."

"Tabah?"

"Tabah will lead the fight."

"Suppose there are circumstances beyond your control that may force you to leave Tabah for a short time. Has Haj Ibrahim mentioned anything about that?"

"No. As I said, he speaks very little but he ponders."

"What of the others in Tabah? The sheiks?"

"We will fight to the end."

Fawzi Effendi Kabir reached out and took Farouk's hands in his and looked him directly in the eyes. Farouk was terribly uncomfortable, fearful.

"As brave as your people are, I want you to tell me the real talk among them. Let me assure you that the truth is extremely important. It could mean a great deal to you." Farouk whined out a nervous sigh. The Effendi continued to grasp his hands. "The truth," Kabir repeated. "Try."

"Most of the talk is of evacuation. Everyone is frightened. The truth is that we are only waiting for word from Haj Ibrahim."

"Un-huh. So what I tell you must be strictly between you and me. It is very secret information. Do you understand me, Farouk?"

"Yes. Yes, indeed," he answered.

Kabir lowered his voice to his most confidential tone, a shade above a whisper. "Kaukji will cross the border soon with twenty to thirty thousand men. They will be led by regular officers of the Syrian and Egyptian armies. He will have airplanes."

"Airplanes? But who will fly them?"

"Moslem pilots from India. He will have tanks, artillery, heavy machine guns, flamethrowers. The Arab Army of Liberation is loaded to here," he said, withdrawing his hands and pointing to his teeth. "Kaukji wants Tabah badly. You know why."

"But . . . but . . . but I had nothing to do with the burning of the fields. I am only the poor brother."

"For certain you are innocent and Field Marshal Kaukji owes me many favors. He will go as hard or as softly as I tell him."

"I was against the burning of the fields. It was a tactic of horror —brutal, inhumane. But you must remember, I only keep the village store."

"The generalissimo is aware of that. I have told him so."

"Thank you, Effendi. Thank you. May Allah insure your every step. May you live a thousand lifetimes in paradise."

"Farouk, my brother. I must tell you something else of a very confidential nature. I asked your brother to come to Damascus to co-ordinate a plan of action with Abdul Kadar and General Kaukji. Haj Ibrahim told us that there was no way Tabah could defend itself. He demanded the right to evacuate Tabah and all the other villages around."

"You are destroying me with pain," Farouk moaned.

"No no, my brother. Listen. I do not wish to see Tabah fall, Allah forbid, to the Jews. As I said, Kaukji will do my bidding. I have a plan in mind."

"Yes?"

"I have told you I have spoken to Kaukji about you. He assures me that you will be spared. You will be given advance warning if he is to attack."

"But if Tabah is evacuated?"

"That is the point I am coming to. You will remain in Tabah when the others evacuate."

"Me? Remain? But how can I do that? Haj Ibrahim will be very suspicious."

"You will convince your brother that someone must remain in Tabah in order to establish future claims to the land. When he leaves, you and ten or twenty families must stay behind."

"But Haj Ibrahim is the muktar. He is the leader. If anyone is to remain in Tabah, he will be the one to take that responsibility."

"No. He must lead the flock. You know that he will not entrust anyone else to take the people to Gaza or Syria or wherever they will go. You will volunteer to remain."

"All right," Farouk said, "I would be safe from Kaukji, but what, Allah help us, if the Jews capture Tabah?"

"So the Jews enter Tabah. Put up white flags and do not fight. If someone remains in the village, the Jews will not force you out. That is their weakness. Even if the Jews, Allah forbid, do capture Tabah, they will respect your presence. But let us look beyond. The Jews have taken Tabah. Not a great tragedy because in May of next year the regular Arab armies will liberate it. And when they do. . . ." Kabir handed a bank deposit book to Farouk. "Barclay's Bank. Barclay's will be in Palestine, no matter who is in Tabah. I have deposited four hundred pounds in your name."

"Four hundred pounds! But when the Arab armies liberate Tabah, Haj Ibrahim will return."

"I think not," Kabir said ominously.

Farouk paled. The passbook shook in his hand.

"You have barked on all fours as your brother's dog for long enough. You are the older, the wiser, the one who reads and writes, the one who keeps the village records, the one who is the spiritual leader. Ibrahim robbed you of your rightful place as muktar and he has lived like a prince from lands that should have been yours. This is the moment you no longer have to lick his feet and call him master. All you have to do is convince your brother you should stay behind with a few families."

Kabir then applied the clincher. "After the war, I am laying claim to all the lands the Jews stole from me. That includes Shemesh Kibbutz. One third of their land will be turned over to you personally."

"One third of Shemesh Kibbutz!"

"One third."

"If Haj Ibrahim ever learns about this, he will kill me."

"Those who flee will have no chance of returning. We want men of character to lead the new Palestine."

"Effendi, I do not wish to seem ungrateful, but what if the Arab regular armies are defeated?"

"All the Arab armies defeated! It is not possible."

"I realize it is not possible, but suppose, by some very strange quirk, they . . . lose?"

"You are right, Farouk. One cannot be too careful. We must think of all possibilities. I have spoken to Ben-Gurion personally."

"Ben-Gurion!"

"Ben-Gurion. He tells me that the Jews will do nothing to those Arab families who remain. If the terrible catastrophe of a Jewish victory happens, then you will still have Tabah. In such an unlikely event of a Jewish victory, you and I will split all the lands of Tabah fifty-fifty."

Farouk thought about it. Fawzi Effendi Kabir had figured things out so that he was going to end up with something no matter who won or who lost. An Arab victory meant that he, Farouk, would end up as a great landholder and the muktar. Arab defeat meant that he, Farouk, would still end up as the muktar with half of Tabah's profitable fields. All it hinged on was his telling his brother a small untruth. Either way, Haj Ibrahim would not be able to come back to Tabah. He broke out in perspiration. He could justify everything, for if he did not do what Kabir wanted, he would also be finished.

Farouk suddenly grabbed Kabir's hands and kissed them and pocketed the bankbook. "I must leave and find supplies or otherwise there will be some suspicion."

"Just give me a list of the things you need," Kabir said. "I will have your supplies gathered by morning. Tonight I wish you to be my guest. I have planned some interesting entertainment for my new friend and ally."

Chapter Eight

Late in the autumn of 1947, Gideon Asch was assigned by Ben-Gurion to head a committee of Haganah commanders and Jewish Agency executives to formulate a number of alternate plans in the event of war. As each area commander reported in on his capabilities, a grim set of prospects piled up on his desk.

His daily time with Ben-Gurion usually came after normal working hours, often in the living room of the Old Man's flat in Tel Aviv.

The central question was how much of Jewish Palestine could be defended. What would be acceptable losses? Jerusalem was terribly vulnerable. What would the Arab villages along the Bab el Wad and near Latrun do? How to defend isolated settlements, such as those in the Negev Desert who would be facing the regular Egyptian army?

Should the Yishuv plan to shrink back into their highly populated regions and fight from a more defensible line? Gideon leaned in that direction and had the Old Man's ear. The Young Turks were brazen enough to believe that every Jewish settlement should fight to the end . . . concede nothing . . . evacuate no one.

As the various plans were refined, a moment of decision came to hand.

Even now the road to and from Jerusalem was becoming difficult to travel safely. It increased the problems of running the Jewish Agency tenfold. At last Ben-Gurion agreed to move many of the Agency's offices to the greater safety of the all-Jewish city of Tel Aviv, which was on the coast and adjoined Arab Jaffa. A small turn-of-the-century house in a former German colony in Tel Aviv had become headquarters for Ben-Gurion and the military.

On the night of decision, Gideon arrived early to review the options once again. The pages of Plan D seemed to glare from the conference table as though a light from an unseen force were shining on it. Without words, Gideon knew that Ben-Gurion had

dug in; when that happened he could be immovable. Plan D audaciously called for the defense of every Jewish settlement, no matter how vulnerable or isolated.

"At worst, it is suicidal," Gideon said at last. "At best, it is a
dangerous gamble."

"I know what you think, Gideon," B.G. retorted tersely.

They began to arrive from the Galilee, from the Negev, from
the mixed cities, from the settlements. When the backslaps were
done and the tea finished, Gideon went into a long review of the
situation.

Aside from the larger cities with mixed Arab and Jewish populations, there were some three hundred exclusively Jewish settlements in Palestine. Each had a Haganah unit, consisting mainly
of citizen-soldiers. The bulk of the Jewish population lived in a
belt from Haifa to Tel Aviv. This would be the principal defense
line.

However, some fifty settlements were either in densely populated Arab areas or in remote locations, such as the Negev Desert
and the Dead Sea. To defend these meant stretching supply lines
beyond their means. The Arabs would have their best success
slicing up the roads. In order to carry on normal transportation,
the Jews had been forced to armor plate their vehicles and move
them in large convoys. It would add to an already overtaxed supply line. Militarily it made little sense and many of the Haganah
commanders were dead set against it. They argued hotly for the
evacuation of these more isolated settlements. This would enable
the Yishuv to consolidate, shrink their communications and supply lines, and set up a defense in a tighter area.

Ben-Gurion doggedly shook off the advice. "We will not give
up a single settlement without a fight!"

"But, B.G., we are overextended."

"The first settlement we cede without a battle will only encourage the Arabs and demoralize every Jew in Palestine," the
Old Man answered.

"But the first time we lose a settlement in battle will demoralize us even more!" Gideon Asch shouted from the end of the long
table.

"If we cannot win this battle for the roads," B.G. retorted,
"then we cannot have a state." He arbitrarily halted further de-

bate for the moment and asked the various section chiefs to give their assessments.

The head of manpower gave a shaky picture. The Haganah had nine thousand battle-ready men in the eighteen- to twenty-five-year-old age group. These troops would largely carry out a defensive mission. Their units would be called upon to hold the settlements and towns against the initial Arab assaults.

The Haganah's striking force, the Palmach, was pumping its numbers up to a final capacity of three to four brigades with a total strength of several thousand men.

This was the core of their fighting capacity. In an all-out war against five regular Arab armies, the Yishuv could count on raising perhaps another twenty thousand men.

The Irgun and the Stern Group had a few thousand men, mostly urban guerrillas, but they operated independently and would only co-operate with the Haganah on a case-by-case basis.

The grim fact was that they would be outnumbered by the Arabs by a ratio of at least five to one. If the Arabs were determined, they could draw from a vast population pool and throw endless reinforcements at the Yishuv.

The ordnance chief followed with an even more sobering report. The Haganah arms inventory consisted of ten thousand rifles and a few thousand submachine guns, light machine guns, and mortars. To complicate matters, the rifles required a number of different calibers of ammunition. The Yishuv had nine single-engine aircraft of the Piper Cub variety and forty pilots. They had no fighter planes, no bombers, no tanks, no artillery, and no vessels. They would be outmatched in firepower by the Arabs by a ratio of a hundred to one.

Ben-Gurion next turned to the underground arms procurement head. Agents had been combing the world but were having little success. One hopeful sign was an initial discussion with the Czechs, but what might come out of it appeared to be too little and too late.

Finances? They were flat broke. Golda Myerson had been dispatched to America in a desperate mission to raise funds, a small ray of hope as the Jewish community of that country raised several million dollars.

"What Golda has done has been a miracle," the financial director said, "but when it comes right down to it, it amounts to a few days' oil revenues for the Saudis. The Arabs can outspend us by as much as they choose: a thousand to one, ten thousand to one, a million to one."

"Now, Gideon," Ben-Gurion said, "maybe you have a little good news."

Gideon shuffled his papers but scarcely needed to refer to them as he reported on the strength of the Arab Irregulars and their probable strategy.

"I count less than three thousand full-time men in Abdul Kadar's Jihad Militia," Gideon said. "However, half of them are deployed in the Ramle-Lydda area. This means they will make an all-out fight for the airport. In our early strategy we must be prepared to commit the Palmach. If we don't capture the airport, it would spell a catastrophe."

The chief of operations, a young Jerusalem archaeologist of thirty years, agreed that Ramle-Lydda and the airport was second only to West Jerusalem.

Gideon continued. "The balance of the Jihad force is around Jerusalem. But we must remember Abdul Kadar can drum up as many as ten thousand coffeehouse fighters for any given action. All of them have arms of some type. If he smells a soft spot in our defense, he might overrun it by his sheer numbers. He can hurt us in three ways. First, the roads. He can line up a thousand men along the Bab el Wad against any given convoy."

"For us to clear the Bab el Wad and the Judean hills," Yigael Yadin, the chief of operations, said, "we would have to use an entire Palmach brigade."

"We might have to," Gideon replied. "Abdul Kadar's obvious strategy is a blockade of West Jerusalem and the starvation of our people."

"It would be the mortal blow to the Yishuv," Ben-Gurion said.

Yadin, who was a Jerusalemite, whose family lived in the city, and whose father had discovered the Dead Sea Scrolls, was adamant. "I would love dearly to be able to commit a Palmach brigade from Latrun to Jerusalem, but it is not possible. We may have to think in terms of a Jewish state without Jerusalem."

There was a silence of someone sprinkling ashes.

"It cannot happen," the Old Man said.

"I hope not," Yadin agreed.

Ben-Gurion nodded for Gideon to continue. "The four most

vulnerable settlements in Palestine are the Etzion Bloc," he said, in reference to four kibbutzim of ultra-Orthodox Jews located in all-Arab territory fifteen miles south of Jerusalem. "Abdul Kadar can butcher us there. The Etzion Bloc is my major objection to Plan D. I think we have to evacuate it."

Several commanders jumped up in disagreement. The debate heightened.

"Quiet, quiet. Let Gideon finish."

"West Jerusalem is already our greatest problem," Gideon insisted. "How the hell can it supply the Etzion Bloc?"

"I disagree! Abdul Kadar cannot take the Bloc."

"Then I suggest that you personally lead the first convoy that tries to break through to them," Gideon retorted. "Suppose the Etzion Bloc holds against the Irregulars. Suppose some of the isolated settlements in the Negev and Galilee hold during the first phase. What then? What happens in phase two when the Arab Legion crosses the Jordan River and the Egyptians invade from the south?"

"Forget Plan D for the moment. I want your assessment of Kaukji."

The Old Man was being stubborn beyond stubborn. Gideon sighed a deep sigh and shrugged his shoulders. "Kaukji has put together a force of eight thousand men: a thousand Syrians, five hundred Lebanese, two thousand Iraqis, five hundred Jordanians, two thousand Saudis, and two thousand Egyptians. They are laced with a number of regular officers from the standing armies of these countries. In addition, we may be looking at a few thousand Moslem Brotherhood and several hundred highly trained troops in the form of British deserters, ex-Nazis, and European mercenaries. Kaukji will have some armor and a half-dozen artillery batteries."

"How good are they?"

"They are more than adequate for their particular mission. Their strategy is no secret. Kaukji will cross and try to pick off some of the most isolated settlements in the Galilee. None of these settlements can depend on reinforcements from us. If Kaukji captures a village or kibbutz, there will be a massacre. I am sure that Kaukji deeply believes he can create a panic and flight of the Jews in Galilee through such a massacre."

The intelligence chief nodded in agreement.

"During phase one, which we are now entering," Gideon continued, "the British are going to adopt a benign attitude. They will allow Kaukji's Arab Army of Liberation to cross into Palestine unchallenged and permit them to establish a headquarters in a heavily populated Arab area, probably around Nazareth."

"Are you saying that the British will stand by idly if Kaukji engages in a massacre?"

"Well, we come down to personal evaluations," Gideon answered. "My own opinion is that they will not lift a finger. Kaukji is going to be permitted to operate openly. The British might do this and that to play out their game of being even-handed, but there's no truth to it. Even if Kaukji is unsuccessful in taking a settlement, he is going to do tremendous damage to us on the roads."

Once again the fallibility of Plan D came under attack. Why give Kaukji such tempting targets as small isolated kibbutzim? It was high-risk business.

"Declaration of the state is high-risk business," Ben-Gurion retorted. "War is high-risk business. Only by making the Arabs pay for every inch can we blunt their ardor."

It was obvious that the Old Man was not going to back down. A final assessment was made by the chief of intelligence. Supplies for the Arabs was a simple matter, for they had the entire Arab world as a hinterland and could simply move arms over the border. If the Saudis opened their purse strings, the parade of Arab arms would be endless. On the other hand, the Yishuv had to bring in every bullet from over the sea. This, along with Arab population advantages, painted a bleak picture for the Jews. It all depended on just how much stamina the Arab armies had.

For the most part, they were far from being modern armies, but they did have tanks, long-range guns, motorized units, combat aircraft, and, in fact, everything the Jews did not have.

The force the Haganah feared most was Abdullah's Arab Legion of ten thousand trained professionals including the Trans-Jordan Frontier Force, with modern weaponry under the command of a skilled cadre of British officers.

Plan D was argued far into the night. Ben-Gurion prevailed. His only concession was that in such places as the Etzion Bloc, the women and children would be removed. It was past two in the morning when the plan was adopted. This left one major question to be discussed. What of the Arab civilian population? What of their continued flight out of the country?

On this issue everyone deferred to the Old Man. He was the spiritual father of this unborn nation. His philosophy would set its tone and its standards.

"The Arabs have begged for this war," Ben-Gurion said. "But we have too many other priorities to engage in endless quarrels with them. We must win the war and come out of it with a viable state. There are so many things a Jewish state must accomplish, for we and our moral standards must be the light of mankind.

"Yet we are the worst kind of fools if we think we can carry out our schemes of grandeur in the midst of hostile neighbors. We must have peace and we must live with the Arabs if our state is to flourish as something more than a fortress.

"Never," he said, smashing the table with his fist, "will we adopt any policy to drive the Arabs from Palestine. In those places that spell strategic life and death for us, such as Ramle-Lydda, as Latrun, as West Jerusalem, we will fight them with everything we have. If the Arabs choose to run, I will not beg them to stay. If they leave Palestine, I will not beg them to return. But under no circumstances will we force out a single Arab who wants to remain. Defeat will go down hard for the Arabs. I pray they will consider their own brothers and sisters who fled from Palestine in the same manner that we care for our brothers and sisters. I pray the Arabs will give them a chance at a decent life. But when a man leaves his home during a war which he started, he cannot expect us to be responsible for his future.

"It is late and we are tired, comrades. One final policy. We must always keep the door open to negotiation and peace. Someday an Arab leader will walk through it and sit down and talk with us. Gideon, I note that you doubt me . . . but we shall see."

Chapter Nine

January 10, 1948

The River Banias flowed down from Mount Hermon over the Syrian border to help form the headwaters of the Jordan. Nearby stood the kibbutz of Kfar Szold, six years old, named for Henrietta Szold, the American woman who had founded the Hadassah.

Generalissimo Kaukji selected this as his initial target. He crossed with three battalions, including the First and Second Yarmuk, named for an ancient battle in which the Arabs had defeated the Byzantine Empire.

Eager to report a first quick victory, little was made in the way of plans and the kibbutz proved more than capable to the task. Kaukji retired quickly to the Syrian side.

COMMUNIQUÉ #1, ARAB ARMY OF LIBERATION
Praise Allah, the compassionate, the merciful. At 0700 of January 10, small elements of the Yarmuk and Hittim battalions engaged in a training exercise against Kfar Szold. As the exercise progressed, it was apparent that the settlement was unable to hold. I ordered an all-out attack, but this was interrupted by British forces in the area, compelling us to retire. Victory is plainly in sight.

F. Kaukji, Field Marshal,
Arab Army of Liberation

Stung by the defeat and aware of the necessity of a fast win, Kaukji and his officers opted for what they felt to be the softest target in the Galilee. He moved up into the Golan Heights under the cover of Syria, then came down where the Yarmuk River connected to the Jordan below the Sea of Galilee. Fifty miles south of his initial target, they reached the outer fields of Tirat Tsvi, the "Castle of the Rabbi Tsvi." The kibbutz was totally isolated on a dead-end road. Its members were Orthodox Jews who numbered but a hundred and sixty men and women of fighting capability. Aside from their rifles, the kibbutz had a single two-inch mortar. Reinforcements were not likely and the kibbutz could be easily ambushed.

Kaukji pitched his command tent on a hillside above the kibbutz and, as he examined it through field glasses, he bemoaned the fact that he had not picked it as his first target. It was a delicious pomegranate, ready for the plucking.

Once again eagerness overcame the Arab Irregulars. Under pressure to avenge his first embarrassment, Kaukji massed his thousand troops to come at the kibbutz in a frontal assault of three waves.

The defense of all the kibbutzim was on a general plan. The settlements were circular in shape, with the children's nursery and school in the middle, along with the shelters. Beyond the outer buildings ran a line of trenches and barbed wire. This was much like the covered wagons of the American prairies which closed in a circle against Indian attack. The fields of Tirat Tsvi and most of the other kibbutzim were ceded to the enemy because there weren't enough people to defend these outer perimeters.

A couple of prudent officers argued with Kaukji that they should send out patrols to probe and to generally soften up the kibbutz with mortars and artillery, then advance beneath a covering curtain of machine gun fire. If they were pinned down, reinforcements could then go into flanking movements. It sounded too complex and slow. The generalissimo was frothing for a victory.

At dawn his Irregulars were summoned to charge with bugle calls and bloodcurdling battle cries. They stormed over open, newly plowed fields. Within moments, any semblance of an organized attack disappeared. Officers, trying to control the movement of their men, ranted at them to no avail. Then the sky opened up, sending down a torrent. The field turned into a quagmire.

The Orthodox Jews of Tirat Tsvi remained extraordinarily disciplined and held their fire. What managed to reach their perimeter was a rain-soaked, muddy mob. The Arabs were cut down coldly as they hit the barbed wire. The second wave was dispirited and the third wave quit before it was halfway across the battleground.

From his hillside command post, Kaukji looked on in horror.

He and his officers tried to rally their forces for a new assault but it was puny. The men had had enough.

Kaukji moved his troops into Palestine to the all-Arab city of Nablus, which had been the site of ancient Shechem of biblical distinction. The British in the area closed their eyes to the presence of the Irregulars.

COMMUNIQUÉ #14, ARAB ARMY OF LIBERATION, JANUARY 25, 1948

Praise Allah, the compassionate, the merciful. As its final training exercise under combat conditions, small units practiced in the area of Tirat Tsvi Kibbutz. It was necessary to engage in these war games to familiarize our troops with their weapons and our tactics. The exercise was an unparalleled success. We toyed around with the kibbutz for several hours, probing and using various maneuvers which we will employ in future combat. I declare the Arab Army of Liberation now ready to crush many Jewish settlements. Victory over the Zionist dogs is at hand.

F. Kaukji, Field Marshal,
Arab Army of Liberation

Just about the same time, Abdul Kadar Heusseini's Army of the Jihad went into its initial action. The target was a surprise to no one. The Etzion Bloc lay in all-Arab territory in the jagged hills and valleys of Judea, halfway between Bethlehem and Hebron.

Abdul Kadar did not attack but held back and pumped fire into the settlements. His aim was siege: to starve them and force them out of ammunition. This could be accomplished because of a British promise of nonintervention and because the mountain road to the Bloc was easily ambushed.

The Palmach, already stretched to breaking, managed to spare three dozen men, who worked their way into the Bloc under cover of darkness. With their arrival, Jewish resistance stiffened. As the siege continued, supplies ran perilously low. It became incumbent upon the command in Jerusalem to either give up the Bloc or try to get a convoy of supplies through to them.

The convoy was formed. As soon as it left Jerusalem, it was in "Apache" territory, with every house in every village a potential gun post and every turn in the tortuous mountain terrain a potential ambush point. The convoy reached the Bloc, but was trapped on its return trip. All forty men and their armor-plated trucks were destroyed.

Abdul Kadar then probed the perimeters of the Bloc and came to the realization that any final attack would have to end in a bayonet-tipped, hand-to-hand fight. With his own men growing bored and wary, he withdrew.

Both Abdul Kadar and Kaukji had failed in their initial thrusts. But the Jews were taking casualties, losses they could not sustain with their meager reserves. In Jerusalem it had become the day of the bomber. British soldier-deserters, thinly disguised as Arabs, assisted in a number of terrible bombings. One car bomb destroyed the Jewish Agency Headquarters, while another bomb got the Palestine *Post*. A third bomb was planted in the heart of the Jewish business district and went off without warning in a crowded midday explosion, taking an awful toll of civilians.

Retaliations by the Irgun and the Haganah destroyed Arab headquarters in both Jaffa and Jerusalem.

It was a time of the boom, the bouncing earth, shattering glass and flying debris, of screams and blood and sirens. Of people being dismembered and packed into bags.

When the British withdrew from their Tegart fort in the Arab city of Nazareth, Kaukji moved in and claimed it as his headquarters. The town was largely populated by Christian Arabs who had decided not to get involved in the fighting on either side. Unable to recruit or get co-operation, he turned his men loose on a spree of looting and intimidation. Many of Nazareth's churches were broken into and sacred relics were carted off. The Christian Arabs taunted him to return to battle and get out of their city.

Across the border, Kaukji had serious problems as well. His original backers, consisting of financiers, Arab organizations, and governments, were losing their enthusiasm.

As he became frantic for a victory, he knew it would have to be a major one. This time he selected an objective of vital strategic value to silence his critics. Kibbutz Mishmar haEmek, "Guard Post of the Valley," dominated the Haifa-Jerusalem highway. Its capture could effectively cut the Yishuv in half.

The kibbutz was manned by a small Haganah unit and, in addition to its rifles, owned a single light machine gun and a single mortar.

Kaukji moved cautiously onto the high ground around Mishmar haEmek with two battalions of troops numbering around twelve hundred men. This time he introduced a new dimension, a dozen field guns. They pounded away and, although their gunners were not accurate, the kibbutz was taking heavy damage and the shell fire was demoralizing. He sent out infantry probes in cautious, disciplined squads. The kibbutz pushed each patrol back. Kaukji then ringed the place and threw hundreds of rounds of artillery into it throughout the night.

By the following morning, the British were compelled to act. They arrived at the kibbutz under a flag of truce and offered to evacuate the wounded, women, and children and negotiate a surrender. The children were taken out, but all the adults remained.

During a second night of barrage, a battalion of the Haganah which had been training in the area, slipped into the kibbutz. This was followed by the First Palmach Battalion, which had force-marched all night and arrived just before daybreak.

The artillery became quiet with daylight, but the Arabs moved in stealthily from several directions. As they reached the perimeters and regrouped for an assault, they themselves were assaulted.

For the first time, Jews in battalion strength were loaded and ready. They poured out of the kibbutz and stormed at an enemy who was taken by complete surprise. The Arab Army of Liberation plunged into headlong retreat with the Haganah and the Palmach on their heels, not permitting them to break off the action. Kaukji desperately attempted a truce, but there was none to be had. The Irregulars were in full flight. The Jews did not stop chasing them until they reached Megiddo, five miles away. There the Haganah and the Palmach regrouped quickly at the archaeological tel that was the mythical site of the New Testament Armageddon. Beyond Megiddo was a defile called the Wadi Ara, a passageway for invading armies from time immemorial. As the Jews pressed the attack again, Kaukji's Battalions of the Yarmuk vanished.

COMMUNIQUÉ #56, ARAB ARMY OF LIBERATION, APRIL 14, 1948
Praise Allah, the compassionate, the merciful. This is a day of infamy. Our forces had reduced Mishmar haEmek to rub-

ble. As we made our final assault, we were to learn of an
utmost treachery. During the night, British units in regimen-
tal strength slipped into the kibbutz disguised as the
Haganah. As we reached their outer defenses, artillery fire
from over a hundred cannons hurled thousands of shells into
our ranks. Eighty hidden tanks, with their British markings
painted over, advanced on us. Our courageous warriors
stopped the infidels in their tracks, only to be further assaulted by British fighter aircraft and bombers. Outnumbered and outgunned by vast margins, we had no choice but
to make an orderly retreat. It was learned by my intelligence
that the Zionists had paid a hundred thousand pounds to the
British for their participation. Fear not, my brothers, we
shall never forget and we shall have our vengeance. One cannot speak too highly of the bravery and dedication of the
soldiers of the Arab Army of Liberation who now rest in
safety. We shall return in greater numbers and victory will
not be far behind.

> F. Kaukji, Field Marshal,
> Arab Army of Liberation

From this point on, Kaukji sent back bitter communiqués to
the Arab capitals, complaining of the lack of support, complaining of massive desertions as his militia dwindled, complaining about the lack of finances to meet his payroll. He limped
into the Bab el Wad, where his remnants hooked up with Abdul
Kadar's Jihad Militia. Here, at last, he hoped to be able to find
some success against Jewish convoys to Jerusalem.

As the British withdrew from location after location, one side
or the other gobbled up their police forts. The Yishuv received
their first load of arms from Czechoslovakia at a secret airstrip in
the Negev Desert. The coastal blockade loosened and a Polish
ship got through to the Jewish port of Tel Aviv with heavier
weapons. These were quickly distributed to reserve units, which
had been training with sticks for rifles and rocks substituting for
grenades.

With the new weapons, the Haganah was able to move deci-
sively in the cities with mixed populations, witnessing a strange

collapse of Arab resolve and a panic devouring the Arab populations.

Haifa: The major port city of Palestine, Haifa rose from the Mediterranean up Mount Carmel, offering a San Francisco-like vista from the high hills. The Arab town was clustered around the port, with the Jewish town on the upper slopes of Carmel.

Because it was the country's major supply depot, fighting and road sniping had been going on incessantly among all three sides. The Arabs were well organized and armed. The Jews had a unit of Haganah under the command of Moshe Carmel that came to be known as the Carmeli Brigade.

An Irgun bomb exploded in the Arab Quarter of the city, which led to an Arab riot at the nearby oil refinery in which forty Jews were massacred. The battle lines were drawn as outrage and counter-outrage ensued until any hope for a peaceful solution vanished.

The Arabs packed their section of the city with Irregulars and mercenaries, as well as units of their home militia, giving them a decided numerical superiority.

But the Carmeli Brigade was on the high ground. As the British began their withdrawal, the Haganah struck in Operation Siccors. After an all-night attack on the Arab quarter, the Arabs were split into four parts and the fight was out of them. The British stepped in and arranged a truce.

Carmel met with the Arab mayor and set out his demands. He required the Arabs to lay down their arms and turn over all non-Palestinians and foreign mercenaries. No demand was made for the Arabs to evacuate their civilian population.

Asking for time to consider the terms, the mayor rushed to confer with Kaukji's top officer in Haifa. That officer assured the mayor that Kaukji was about to open an offensive from Nablus to Haifa. He urged the mayor and other Arab civic officials to take the Arab population out of the city so they would not be caught in the middle of a major confrontation. As soon as the Jews were driven out, the Arabs could return and take over the Jewish part of Haifa as well.

For the most part, the Arabs and Jews of Haifa had gotten along well. There was a great deal of commerce between them and a smattering of neighborly relationships. A delegation of

Haifa's Jewish leaders met with the Arab leadership and tried to persuade them to remain, citing Ben-Gurion's policy.

The Arabs chose to evacuate. The British continued the truce and in the next five days nearly a hundred thousand Arabs took to the roads and headed for Acre. A few thousand chose to remain and they were left unharmed.

The Arab population of Haifa ran without cause. Fears of annihilation were merely echoes and reflections of their own designs. They and their leaders had promised death to the Jews. The Arabs were consumed with fear that the Jews would do to them what they planned to do to the Jews. Their terror was played upon by their own leaders, who urged them to flee in order to clear the way for their armies. The Haifa exodus was repeated in Safed and Tiberias, where Arab populations bolted after short battles.

The Arabs had already witnessed a mass flight from Palestine of the leaders of their community after the partition vote. An unstoppable movement was forming. By the thousands, they took to the roads without a threat having been made and without so much as a shot being fired at them. The scattered movement exploded into a stampede.

Arab Palestine had all but lost the first round. In order to salvage their situation, the new strategy was to put every resource into the road battle to shut off Jerusalem from the rest of the Yishuv and starve out the Jewish population. If they could accomplish victory in Jerusalem, all of the early Arab failures would be nullified. Jerusalem was the heart of the Yishuv and to the Arabs it symbolized the head of the snake.

As this most vital battle shaped up, the Yishuv was shaken to its boots when the Arab Legion broke its promise and crossed the Jordan River. The beleaguered Etzion Bloc fell to the Legion after a murderous fight. Most of the survivors were massacred; a few were taken prisoner.

Arabs stormed out of Jerusalem and Hebron and Bethlehem to loot and level the Etzion Bloc, destroying its orchards and fields and desecrating its synagogues. On the eve of the Jewish declaration of independence, the Yishuv went into agonized soul-searching to find the courage to declare their freedom after this taste of things to come from the Legion.

Chapter Ten

The noose tightened around West Jerusalem. A hundred thousand Jews came under a virtual blockade. A thin, wheezing lifeline through the Bab el Wad was choked off, forced open, choked off.

Inside the Old City wall, two thousand ultra-Orthodox Jews refused to quit, although surrounded by fifty thousand Arabs and separated from their own population.

Supplies had to come from the coast through a thicket of Arab strongholds, then into the vulnerable Bab el Wad. The British made little pretense of patrolling the road.

In preparation for the siege, the Jews had made a survey of all cisterns in their part of the city. Because of periodic drought and perennial water shortages, rainwater had long been trapped on the flat rooftops of the houses and channeled into underground concrete holding tanks. Many houses had them, but they had long been out of use since a modern water system had been installed with pumping stations near the coast.

Chemicals had been put into the cisterns to preserve the water and they were capped with cement covers. It was determined that the cisterns held some three months' supply of water if rationed at the rate of ten gallons per family per day.

The plan came none too soon, for the Arabs blew up water pipes all along the line into West Jerusalem and the British declined to get involved in rebuilding or guarding them.

Each day water trucks opened a given number of cisterns and distributed what became liquid gold. Each housewife set aside one gallon for essential drinking and cooking. The balance went through a series of declining usages so it could be recycled several times for personal washing or cleaning the most necessary cooking utensils. A tad was allowed for brushing teeth, laundry came last, and the final daily use was the toilet's single flushing. There was no water for showers, gardens, or effective sanitation. In the ensuing months, Jerusalem's streets became filmed with desert dust. As the Jews slowly dehydrated, their city took on a death-like browned-out look.

There was no fuel, except for hospitals, the military, and bakeries. Candles replaced electric lights. The Jerusalem housewife did her cooking on a communal bonfire. Because there never had been much timber in the region, people dismantled wooden railings and window sashes and chopped up furniture.

The only edible greens were dandelions. The ration fell to a borderline starvation level of six hundred calories a day. A makeshift airstrip that could only accommodate a small single-engine plane was where the Yishuv's "air force" made daily runs of baby formula, emergency medicines, small arms, and the Yishuv's leaders.

Strategically the Jews were in impossible shape. The region was ponderously Arab. The Haganah had its troops spread so thin in trying to protect a bulky urban area that its lines sprung leaks all over. The arsenal consisted of five hundred rifles and some odds and ends, including the Little David mortars which had been used so effectively in Safed. These "Davidkas" were moved from location to location to make the Arabs think the Jews had many more of them.

It became incumbent upon the Jews to consolidate their area. The Haganah managed to capture an Arab suburb of Katamon, which eliminated an enemy enclave in their midst and straightened out their lines. Other Haganah attempts failed. The attack on the high ground at the Prophet Samuel's Tomb, which could have protected incoming convoys, was beaten back.

Another attack was made on the Victoria-Augusta complex to have a direct connection to Jewish establishments isolated on Mount Scopus. When this attack failed, Hebrew University, the National Library, and the Hadassah Hospital were cut off from West Jerusalem. To reach these institutions, convoys had to travel through a series of hostile Arab neighborhoods. To keep the institutions functioning and to save the buildings from being looted, the Yishuv reluctantly agreed to accept a demilitarized status for them.

In its first operation to break the blockade, Haganah units from Tel Aviv moved on Abdul Kadar's hornet's nest of Irregulars in the Lydda-Ramle area, blew up their headquarters, and cleared the road of sniper locations. But there was still a long, bloody way to go to get to Jerusalem.

Of late, Colonel Frederick Brompton had been meeting with Gideon Asch several times weekly at the Latrun Fort. Each acted in a liaison capacity to convey urgent business to the other's command. Brompton had been selected for the job because he was a bureaucratic neutral, the epitome of British evenhandedness.

"Very nasty business, this bomb you set off in Lydda," he said. "We have it that you are very quietly moving a Palmach force out of Shemesh Kibbutz and deploying it along the Bab el Wad. If I were a military man, I'd say you are going to take a crack at forcing the road open."

Gideon threw open his arms in innocence.

"It's going to be damned costly, damned costly," Brompton said.

"Perhaps if you made more than a token effort to patrol the highway . . ." Gideon said.

Brompton returned a gesture similar to the one Gideon had made.

"All right, Colonel. Let's get down to business. We have two priority questions. First, we continue to protest the Arabs arming the Temple Mount. We now count twenty machine guns and mortar emplacements and an observation post on the top of the Dome of the Rock. And if anyone lit a cigarette in the cellar of the Al Aksa Mosque, it would blow up the entire city."

"You know how it is, Gideon, old man. The Arabs have never had respect for anyone's holy places, including their own."

"Like hell, Brompton. God forbid if the Jews were to put one well-placed shell into the Dome of Al Aksa. They'd have the world at our throats in a religious fever."

Brompton gave the tiniest of laughs.

"I was about to mention arms stashes in every hospital and school in East Jerusalem," Gideon continued.

"You're not going to teach the Arabs fair play or democracy at this date, Gideon. There are some things we would not do in order to keep the Mandate. God only knows, we may lose the Empire because even in war there are some boundaries to humanity. It's a game with them, a dirty advantage. They'll take it. You'll just have to smile."

Brompton suddenly showed nervousness, quite unlike himself. Gideon reckoned that there was some weighty business on the man's mind he had not yet come to. "What else is on your agenda?" Brompton asked.

"The water line. We cannot rebuild or guard it without your help."

Brompton was visibly irritated.

Gideon came to his feet. "Shit!"

"Sit down, Gideon. Sit down, please," Brompton said, applying an oversized dollop of English calm. "I told you at the time of the partition vote that our position has changed from one of governing to one of neutrality. On the one hand, you believe we are decidedly pro-Arab. It may come as a surprise, but the entire Arab world accuses us of being blatantly pro-Zionist. In truth, the chaps in our command are divided down the middle."

"I didn't ask you for a dissertation on British fairness. I asked you about water for a hundred thousand people."

"We cannot be involved in rebuilding the pipeline. We are withdrawing our forces at a very rapid rate. We have neither the manpower nor the desire to do so. It is clearly no longer our mission to keep either side from building up their forces or fighting one another. We are leaving and there is going to be an all-out war after we pull out. We have continued, on a case-by-case basis, to step in and try to spare the civilian populations. We have escorted Arab populations out of Haifa and Tiberias and elsewhere. You have refused similar offers to evacuate. But let me emphasize that we are not out to stop Kaukji and we are not out to stop the Palmach. Forgetting all the nasty business we've done to one another in the past, all we want now is to get out."

"Without muddy hands," Gideon said.

"Without muddy hands," Brompton agreed.

"You're a bad card player, Colonel," Gideon said. "What's really on your mind?"

Brompton cleared his throat defensively. "I'm about to tell you something you already know. Your situation in Jerusalem is impossible. The Etzion Bloc is finished. The Jews in the Old City are doomed. Perhaps the Jewish Agency says these are acceptable losses, then what? If you manage to hang on until May 15, when we get out, you're looking at the Arab Legion within one day's march of Jerusalem. With the Egyptians coming in from the south and the Syrians and Iraqis from the north, they plan a very tumultuous convergence on Jerusalem. Gideon, Plan D is dangerous . . . nay, suicidal."

Gideon did not speak of his own vigorous opposition to Plan D. Undoubtedly the British command was of the same opinion and was wary of the consequences of the Yishuv's stubbornness.

"I am authorized to speak for the British Government from the prime minister on down and to personally implore you to take your population out of Jerusalem."

"Why this sudden pang of conscience?"

"Straight on, Gideon?"

"Straight on."

"Once an Arab has an upper hand in battle, he has only one driving force—total annihilation. We are obliged to go on record as having warned you to evacuate West Jerusalem because we will not take the responsibility for the massacre of twenty, thirty, forty, eighty thousand civilians."

"Do you fear for us as human beings or do you really fear being held up to the world with blood on your hands?"

"As I said earlier, we are split down the middle. But in any event, we do not store arms in cathedrals and we are not Nazis."

"Yes, I understand you," Gideon said.

"Then surely you know there is an eighty percent chance of the greatest single massacre in two thousand years."

"We are so aware."

"For God's sake, Gideon, you must impress this on Ben-Gurion. How can he live as a man after he has permitted such a thing to happen? How can any of your dreams of nationhood survive such a catastrophe?"

"I'll certainly give the Old Man your message. There's a problem, you see. The same problem we had in Europe. We have no place to evacuate *to*. Or am I to assume that your warning comes along with a magnanimous gesture by His Majesty's Government to open your arms and take in a hundred thousand Jews or a half-million Jews in the event of an all-out Arab victory? We don't have to emigrate to England. What about sending us to Uganda or India or the West Indies? Perhaps you can convince the Americans or Canadians to give us refuge. Or how about all the rest of the sanctimonious Christian democracies. Ah, Colonel, you are a

naïve man. We Jews know that not a single tear will be shed over
our demise."

Gideon arose and made for the door.

"Gideon."

"Yes, Brompton."

"I am personally very sorry about this."

"Never mind. Being a Jew has always meant that we are a
people who dwell alone."

The Yishuv's answer came instantly. Ben-Gurion ordered the
Bab el Wad opened. Heretofore the Palmach had operated only in
small units, squads, and platoons. The Jewish command set into
motion Operation Nachshon, named for the first man with Moses
who leaped into the Red Sea to test the waters. The Har El (God's
Hill) Brigade of the Palmach was given the gut-wrenching mission of opening the Bab el Wad long enough to get some supply
convoys through to Jerusalem. At the same time, the Yishuv
started building secret roads to bypass Latrun and run around the
back of the Bab el Wad.

The most strategic position at the Jerusalem end of the highway was an Arab village built on the ruins of Roman and Crusaders' forts, the Kastel. Its high ground completely dominated the
road and had been the major staging area for raids on Jewish
convoys.

Using years of intelligence gathered by Gideon Asch, units of
the Har El Brigade splintered, traversed the treacherous landscape by night, and seized many of the key points along the road,
ejecting the Arab Irregulars.

At the same time, a company of eighty Har El men inched its
way up the long, steep hill to the Kastel undetected. They were
able to effect total surprise. The battle was over in minutes and
the villagers took flight.

With the Kastel momentarily in Jewish hands, a frenzied,
around-the-clock operation ensued. Supplies were loaded aboard
trucks all over Jewish Palestine. By April 30, three large convoys
had slugged their way into Jerusalem.

Word of the capture of the Kastel flashed from Arab villages to
Jerusalem with disbelief. A fever instantly swept over the Arab
community all the way down to Tabah. Although Haj Ibrahim

gave no blessings and declined to join, dozens of his fellahin
rushed to answer the call to retake the Kastel.

When enough men had gathered at the base of the hill, they
charged up haphazardly, only to be hurled back. Without a determined and knowledgeable leader to rally them, the Arabs became
unable to organize or sustain a drive and, after some further long-
range potshots, they drifted off back to their homes.

Abdul Kadar Heusseini came under immediate pressure to retake the Kastel, which had been turned over to a unit of ninety
older Haganah reservists from Jerusalem. Within a few days after
losing the Kastel, Abdul Kadar assembled a force of Jihad men,
deployed them intelligently, and moved up the hill cautiously and
under covering fire. He established positions in secure places and
pinned down the outnumbered Jewish defenders.

A desperate call went out that their ammunition was perilously
low. They could not hold off an Arab attack. At that time, a
tramp steamer had gotten through the British blockade. Its cargo
of arms was quickly unloaded and a truck made it as far up the
Bab el Wad as possible. When it was stopped by an Arab ambush,
a dozen Palmach removed fifty thousand rounds and took a circu-
itous route into the hills. They slipped through Abdul Kadar's
lines when the defenders were virtually down to their last bullet.

Abdul Kadar ordered an attack, with himself at the head of his
troops. They were hit with a sudden barrage and the field was
strewn with their dead. The Irregulars withdrew and the
Haganah sent out a patrol to examine the field. Among the Arab
dead, they discovered the body of Abdul Kadar Heusseini.

Every Arab village from Hebron to Nablus rushed men to the
Kastel by taxi, bus, car, and truck. Half the fellahin of Tabah—
save Haj Ibrahim—were in the mass that surged up the hill in a
human tidal wave.

The Jewish commander kicked his weary men awake, threw
boxes of ammunition to them, fired his gun, cursed them, shouted
orders. They simply could not shoot fast enough to stop the Arab
surge and they retreated.

The emotion that had triggered the Arab rampage now erupted
into pure grief upon locating the body of their fallen leader. Firing into the air, weeping madly, and shouting oaths, they carried
the martyr down and took him to Jerusalem. In one of the most
bizarre incidents of the war, the Arabs left only a handful of men

to defend the Kastel, for they had really come for the purpose of finding Abdul Kadar. The Haganah quickly returned and this time they stayed.

The funeral of Abdul Kadar, whose open pine coffin was passed over the heads of tens of thousands of hysterical Arabs, was an ultimate display of Moslem rage and grief. They swarmed through the Damascus Gate into the Old City, jamming every inch of the thin alleyways, and accorded him the ultimate honor of burying him on the Haram esh Sharif near the Dome of the Rock.

When their burst of anguish and anger had simmered, the villagers of Tabah became shatteringly sobered. They had swept themselves into battle and waived their longstanding peaceful existence. Their sudden impulse to battle was now smothered by a dark fear.

The Kastel was firmly in Jewish hands and Tabah, once neutral, was now an enemy village. They were no longer immune. What was taking place all over Palestine was now happening to them. They dreaded the thought of the moment when the British would withdraw from Latrun. They would be naked, with a powerful Jewish settlement a stone's throw away. Every day the talk was of Arab villages, towns, even cities being abandoned. The families of Tabah began to break and run.

Haj Ibrahim could no longer merely ponder. People were leaving; he was under pressure from the Irregulars to establish observation and sniping posts. No money had arrived from Fawzi Kabir. The moment when he would receive orders to abandon Tabah was close at hand. The weight of it crushed him. Was there a chance—any chance—that they could ride it out without being destroyed by one side or the other?

He donned his finery, walked down the hill, crossed the highway, and stood before the guard post of Shemesh Kibbutz and asked to see Gideon Asch.

Chapter Eleven

One could tell Gideon Asch's cottage apart from the others. As one of the few remaining founders of the kibbutz, he was accorded the distinction of having his own hot water storage tank on the roof. The cottage was a Spartan two-room affair—a small bedroom and a larger multipurpose living, dining, and office room. His hours away from the kibbutz did not allow him to eat often at the communal dining room, so the members had voted him a small kitchen. A final note of his importance was a pair of private telephones on his desk.

Gideon responded to a knock on the door by lifting his eyes from the eternal stack of papers.

"Come in."

A guard held the door open as Haj Ibrahim entered. He asked Ibrahim to hold his arms apart and started to frisk him.

"That won't be necessary," Gideon said.

The two men had not seen each other for almost three years and an awkwardness prevailed. Gideon arose and extended his hand. As Ibrahim took it, they went into a bear hug and slapped one another on the shoulder. Gideon waved him to a seat opposite his own at the desk.

"Your sons are faring well?"

Ibrahim nodded. They became quiet. Aside from the austerity of the place, Ibrahim was taken by the fact that every available space held books, hundreds of them, crammed into every corner.

"I have often wondered how you lived," Ibrahim said. "There are many books here. I even see books in Arabic. How many languages do you read?"

Gideon shrugged. "Five . . . six . . . seven."

"That is very impressive. Ishmael reads to me from the Palestine *Post.*"

Gideon smelled the tension but remained patient as the Arab tried to pick up the elusive threads. He opened the bottom drawer of his desk and took out a bottle of Scotch whiskey and shoved a glass over the desk.

"Compliments of our British protectors."

Ibrahim held up his hand in protest. "You know that stuff will destroy me."

"Some wine?"

The muktar declined. Gideon opened another drawer, poked around and found a stick of hashish, and tossed it toward Ibrahim. "You smoke. I'll drink," Gideon said.

"The guards?"

"They don't know hashish from horseshit."

Two belts and two puffs later, the tension had melted. Ibrahim groaned and dropped his head into his hands. "This whole thing is like trying to pave the sea."

"What can I say? We don't want this war, Ibrahim."

"I wish I were a Bedouin. They know every trick of survival." His mind floated after another draw on the pipe. "I saw Rosh Pinna. I was passing through."

"On your way to Damascus, where you met with Fawzi Kabir, Kaukji, and Abdul Kadar, who is, for better or worse, no longer with us. I assume they didn't summon you to wish you well with your olive crop."

"It is so humiliating seeing my people run like this. Perhaps humiliation is not so important to the Jews. After all, you have been humiliated in many places in many times. To us this humiliation is crushing."

"What is it, Ibrahim?"

"I am under terrible pressure to evacuate Tabah."

"I know."

"If I take my people out, even for a short time, will I be able to bring them back?"

"If we abandoned Shemesh Kibbutz, would the Arabs allow us to return?" Gideon countered.

"No, of course not. Gideon, what can you tell me?"

"We have no policy to run the Arabs out of Palestine. No responsible man among us has any illusion that we can create a state without peace with our neighbors. God knows, we do not want to condemn ourselves and our children to generations of bloodshed. We have tried to reach every Arab leader. They are all committed to war."

"Can you tell me . . . have you made deals with any Arab villages? Will any of them stay?"

"We have made deals. Even with villages in the Jerusalem corridor."

"What kind of deal?"

"Don't go to war against us and we won't go to war against you. Simple enough. One of these days, you'll learn that the Jews of Palestine have a better future planned for you than your blessed Arab brothers over the border."

"Suppose I ask for the same deal for Tabah?"

Gideon arose and grunted. "You've become an enemy village. Some three dozen of your people are in the Jihad Militia. More than fifty were in the attack on the Kastel. Irregulars come to and go from Tabah at will. In other words, you are an active participant in the attempt to starve out a hundred thousand people in Jerusalem. Ibrahim, I don't want to recommend an attack on Tabah, but once a war starts, forces beyond anyone's control take over."

"I am crushed," Ibrahim said. "It is the Arabs who are forcing me out."

"I know."

"The village is on the brink of panic. If one loud shot is fired into the air, everyone else will take flight."

Gideon studied the distraught man, now being helplessly swept up in that sea's tidal wave of events. Hatred of the Jews had been building in Tabah since the world war. Many would be opposed to neutrality, others too frightened to implement it. But God help them all if they ran.

Ibrahim moved his hands pathetically and reeled to his feet. Gideon scribbled some numbers on a piece of paper and handed it to Ibrahim. "These phone numbers will reach me. If you get into personal trouble, I will try to help."

"If only you and I could sit down and talk this out," Ibrahim said in a faraway monotone. "We could work things out between us. We could make peace."

"We'll always be ready when you are."

One of the phones rang. Gideon listened to an emotional voice babbling in Hebrew. He said he would come right away and set the receiver down. He gave Ibrahim a terrible look.

"The Irgun hit an Arab village near Jerusalem. Deir Yassin."

"What happened?"

"There was a massacre."

Gideon Asch arrived at Deir Yassin within the hour. He was under instructions to make an immediate assessment of the situation. The village had been cordoned off and Colonel Brompton was on hand. He trusted the Englishman's briefing, for it matched what he already knew, and he dispatched an aide, a young Palmach officer, back to Jerusalem with an initial report.

Gideon then went through the grisly business of a personal inspection of bodies, speaking with the wounded, and reconstructing the events of the nightmare.

The smell of burning flesh and putrid smoke of battle was overpowering, as was the soft steady drone of numbed weeping, punctuated by outbursts of rage and hysteria. He made a feeble offer for use of Jewish medical facilities, but the wounded were too terrified. The shrill of sirens racing back and forth overcame him. It was all he could do to keep from breaking down.

It seemed that something of this sort was bound to happen. After the Haganah opened the road long enough for three convoys to get through, the Arabs closed it again. Among the string of Arab villages used as staging points against Jewish traffic, the village of Deir Yassin, on the edge of West Jerusalem, had been one of the most hostile. Looking for a victory of their own to match Haganah successes, the Irgun had assembled a hundred men and targeted the village for capture.

But the Irgun's intelligence had been faulty. They felt they could stampede the population out, as had been the case at the Kastel. They did not know that a large contingent of Jihad Militia was in Deir Yassin at the time. When they attacked, resistance was fierce. The soft target became hard as fighting intensified. The Irgun was at that time an urban guerrilla force neither trained for nor skilled in field combat. Their advance was slow and each captured house was blown up.

As the Arab militia fell back, they became entangled with the ordinary villagers. Panic broke out as the villagers tried to separate themselves and flee, but the militia used them as cover. Civilians were caught in a vicious cross fire and broke in all directions in the mayhem. At this point, the Irgun's discipline collapsed in confusion, then decayed into frenzy. The Irgun pressed in, shooting at anything and everything that moved.

Gideon finished his survey, then fled into an empty house and retched. Colonel Brompton came into the room and closed the door behind him as Gideon pulled himself together.

"The final count seems to be in excess of two hundred and fifty killed," Brompton said. "Half of them are women and children."

Gideon's face was wet with sweat. He jerked out his shirttail and wiped it, then dropped his face into his hands. "We are denouncing this affair," he said. "The Haganah had nothing to do with it."

"Ah yes, but you are still responsible, are you not?"

Gideon clenched his jaw and nodded. He knew the Jews were responsible. He held up his handless arm. "The Baghdad ghetto. Ever hear of it? All my life I have lived with massacres. Only this one is different. The Jews committed it. Does that clean the slate of a hundred Arab massacres?"

"Is that all you're worried about—keeping score?"

"Of course not. A defensive reflex. I've lived among the Arabs. I've loved them. Even though I've lost most of that love, I've continued to believe we could create something side by side . . . progress . . . an irresistible quality of life . . . decency . . . respect for one another. We would set an example and when the others saw it . . . they would come and speak peace to us. I am a Jew, Colonel, and I am tormented that we have been driven to do such things to survive. I can forgive the Arabs for murdering our children. I cannot forgive them for forcing us to murder theirs."

"So the purity of the Zionist dream becomes tainted with the ugliness of reality," Brompton said. "Digging ditches, rolling back swamps, and singing around the campfire isn't quite the same as declaring one's independence. As long as you stayed in your synagogues and prayed and took your persecutions in silence, you could demand of yourselves an ethereal set of standards. You demand your own destiny, for better or worse, and that requires getting messy hands."

"All right, we've done a ghastly deed. But the Arabs will blow this thing all out of proportion."

"And they will continue to do so for a hundred years," Brompton said. "The first Jewish massacre of Moslems. You've presented them with a splendid rallying point and an eternal footnote in history."

"God knows, we did not want anything like this to happen."

"Fair fight and all that? If I'm not mistaken, you preached the gospel that once battle starts events overcome one. You could have prevented this, Asch."

"How!"

"By controlling the Irgun. They're your people. They're your responsibility."

Gideon leaned against a window and looked outside to the rows of corpses on litters being removed by soldiers wearing gas masks. Gideon clenched his jaw against the shock of physical pain.

"So all your years of impassioned idealism and righteous dreams will be severely tested. You've given us a lot of sanctimonious advice. I'm going to give you some," the Englishman said.

Gideon turned and looked at him squarely.

"When you see Ben-Gurion, you'd better impress upon him that he has to dissolve and absorb the Irgun. If you continue to allow a private little army in your midst, you'll end up with the same anarchy that pervades the Arab world. Allow it to continue, as the Irish have with the IRA, and you'll condemn yourself to everlasting chaos."

"We are aware. It is but one of many problems."

"But none is more important," Brompton answered. "There can only be one central authority."

Later in the day, Gideon's aide returned from Jerusalem and he found Colonel Brompton once more.

"A press conference is being called in Tel Aviv now," Gideon said. "The raid on Deir Yassin is being denounced. We have also contacted the Irgun. They repeated their accusation that the village has been the principal base of operations against Jewish traffic. They also claim they had warned the muktar and the village elders on six separate occasions to stop it. They warn further that if the Arabs use villages as military bases in the future, they had better remove their civilian populations from them first."

"Well, that's drawing the old battle line, isn't it?"

"Strange, isn't it, that we Jews are once again stuck with a dirty job no one else wants? You and all your snide friends in all the foreign offices know in your hearts the cruelty, the evil that emanates from the Moslem world. But you are afraid to hold Islam up to the light and tell your people, 'Look, this is what we have to live with.' No, let the Jews do it. We once again man the barricades alone, berated by our smug, so-called allies of the Western democracies. Islam is going to turn this world upside down before this century is out and you'd better have enough guts to deal with it. It's lonely here, Brompton. It's lonely."

Frederick Brompton avoided the angry glare of Gideon Asch. "Shall I escort you back to Jerusalem?"

"Please."

"Well, Asch, the first massacre is always the worst."

"If you are saying that this thing will ever become acceptable for the Jewish people, you are wrong. We're not afraid to examine ourselves. We won't hide our dirt."

"So be it, but I am afraid the Arabs have mortgaged their future generation for revenge."

By the time Haj Ibrahim had returned from Shemesh Kibbutz, the entire village population had gathered in the square and others were pouring in from the outlying villages. A roar of relief went up upon seeing their muktar.

"Haj Ibrahim! There has been a terrible massacre!"

"The Jews murdered everyone in Deir Yassin!"

"Thousands slaughtered!"

"They cut off the limbs of babies!"

"Old people were thrown down the wells to drown!"

"They cut open pregnant women and used the fetuses for target practice!"

"The Jews are attacking Tabah next!"

Ibrahim called a meeting in the khan of the sheiks and elders. It was chaotic. Everyone complained, but no one put forth an idea. Fear could be seen and smelled as well as heard. Ibrahim had come to a lonely conclusion. He decided to make a last-ditch stand to hold the village. It meant defying Fawzi Kabir, ridding Tabah of the Jihad Militia, and extracting a promise from Gideon not to attack. He ordered everyone to return to their homes and fields. They reluctantly obeyed.

As Haj Ibrahim set about desperately to get things turned around, the Arabs got their revenge for Deir Yassin. A convoy of medical personnel left West Jerusalem to relieve the staff at the Hadassah Hospital on Mount Scopus. It had to pass through Arab East Jerusalem on a road under British control. Within a hundred yards of a British encampment, the Arabs ambushed the unarmed

Red Cross convoy in broad daylight and murdered seventy-seven
doctors and nurses. The British made no response to the attack.

But the Jews did not flee Jerusalem or elsewhere.

The Hadassah convoy massacre seemed to have a boomerang
effect on the already frantic Arab population. Having wrought
vengeance, they now feared the Jews would retaliate in kind and
their fright began to rise to epidemic proportions.

Although Haj Ibrahim had ordered his people to stand pat,
they started to slip away and run. A dozen families one night,
another dozen a second night. He had lost control of the situation.

On the third morning at the mosque, he studied the remaining
families face by face and he knew he could no longer hold them
together. At the end of the prayer, he ascended the pulpit and
ordered everyone to gather in the square with their belongings
and prepare to evacuate Tabah and the Valley of Ayalon.

Chapter Twelve

Can there be a scar deeper in the life of a twelve-year-old boy than the memory of the fellahin of his village laying down their tools by the prophet's tomb? They left them there because the tomb was on sacred ground and only the most vile of villains would steal from such a place.

"We will be back in time for the harvest. Cairo assures us of that."

"Yes, perhaps within a week."

What to save? What to leave? What difference did it make when one abandons one's fields and one's cottage?

My father sat at his table in front of the café, calmly answering questions, giving orders, and trying to make a plan.

He reckoned that our movement would be very slow and counted on three days to reach Jaffa. He dispatched several men from our clan to find a suitable field or grove for us to camp in the first night near Ramle. I sat beside my father with some of the village records, trying to make a count of the number of people involved. It came to somewhat over six hundred who had not already left.

He ordered all donkey and ox carts to be assembled in the village square, loaded with enough food for four days. Everything of value should be taken, for it would have to be sold when we reached Jaffa. Each family was allowed one or two goats or sheep to either be slaughtered for food or sold at the Jaffa market. Otherwise, only bare necessities would be allowed.

The Effendi Kabir still had not sent the funds he had promised, so each villager would have to sell everything down to the shirt on his back in order to charter a ship to take us to Gaza.

The women ran back and forth from their homes to the carts, loading them and weeping hysterically as they did. When the carts were full, the women filled sheets and blankets, knotting the ends together so they could balance them on their heads.

"Yes," my father said, "all guns and ammunition must be taken."

"How much water, Haj Ibrahim?"

"Two jugs for each family and enough to water two animals."

"Will the Jews seize the village? Will they blow up the houses after they have looted everything?"

"We won't know until we return," Ibrahim answered.

"Will they open the graveyard?"

"I don't think so."

"What about this jewelry?"

"Take it if it can be sold."

"Chickens? Dowry trunks? Photographs? Seeds?"

"Blankets . . . take plenty of blankets. It will be cold at night."

"Koran?"

"One for each family."

"Surely the Jews will steal everything growing in our fields."

"If the Jihad Militia doesn't get to them first."

"I have six daughters. Who will protect them?"

"Each clan will set up its own guard."

As the square bulged and panic and frustration heightened, men began cursing and fighting one another while the women did the work. Wild stories of the Deir Yassin massacre poured in. They said all the old men had been decapitated, all the young men had been castrated, all the women had been raped. The Irgun was coming.

Some had relatives in Jaffa, but most would need shelter. My father had a close cousin there who was a successful merchant and we were depending on him heavily. Ibrahim wanted to go on ahead to find housing and to charter a boat, but he feared leaving us alone.

British jeeps dashed back and forth from the Latrun Fort offering help, offering no help. They would clear the road as far as Ramle but would escort us no further. We were apprehensive at the thought of a thousand Jihad Militia in the vicinity.

"Do not fear. Do not fear. We will keep together," my father said.

I walked with my mother through our house what seemed like a hundred times, partly to look at it and weep and partly to see if there was one more thing she could load on our carts. I had made it my sacred duty to watch after Nada. We had not been allowed to play with each other or touch for a long time, but I still loved her and she loved me. I would defend her against everything with my dagger.

I saw my father go into the store with Uncle Farouk, closing the door behind them and discussing something heatedly. I slipped in through the back and listened.

"We will have two or three empty carts left," Ibrahim said. "Take from the shelves the most vital necessities. Give anything else away to anyone who has room."

"But you are crazy, Ibrahim," Farouk argued. "We could fill up fifteen or twenty carts if we had them. What you are telling me is to leave almost everything here to the Jews. If we could empty all the shelves and take the goods to Jaffa, along with forty or fifty head of sheep, it will bring us money that we very desperately need."

"Perhaps Mohammed is going to send an angel down to fly it all to Jaffa?"

"Have I not been in charge of arranging transport for our crops for twenty years?" Farouk argued. "I know where there are trucks. I know where there are buses. There is a bus at Beit Jarash. I can pluck it like so. Give me fifteen men. I raid Beit Jarash tonight. We rip out the seats, load up the entire store, and take out livestock in whatever room is left. We will meet you on the road by midday tomorrow."

"The Jihad will take the bus in five minutes."

"Not with fifteen armed men on the roof."

The plan seemed to make perfect sense, but my father was leery of my uncle. Ibrahim had almost a thousand pounds in the bank in Jaffa. Some of it was his money and some of it had been deposited in behalf of the villagers. The account had been entrusted to Farouk.

"Give me the bankbook," Ibrahim said.

"Of course," my uncle answered, somewhat miffed. He unlocked the cash drawer, fished about, then handed my father a savings account passbook from Barclay's Bank. My father thumbed through it to the last page, squinted and seemed satisfied that the correct amount was on deposit.

"I would like to personally lead the raid," my father said. "But if we do not leave here by midday, I'm afraid there will be total panic. They won't get much farther than the main road without me. Take four men from each clan, young men without family ties. I want Amjab from our clan to plan and lead the raid. It cannot be messed up."

"You are wise, Ibrahim. There are bound to be shortages in Jaffa. We can sell everything off for a fortune." He left to gather his raiding party. My father suddenly seemed about to collapse. He leaned against the wall, moaned and began to weep very softly, then he saw me and quit.

"It is madness," he whispered. "We do not have to leave Tabah, Ishmael."

"Then why, Father?"

"You cannot stop a frightened dog from running, even from his master's voice. They are my children out there. They are innocent. They will be cheated. They will not be able to make decisions. They will die of hunger and thirst. They will be robbed. The women will be raped. I am all that's left. I must protect them."

"The Jews must be savages," I said.

"It is not the Jews I am afraid of," he answered strangely.

"Even after Deir Yassin?"

"Even after Deir Yassin. Men of self-esteem do not abandon their homes and fields without a fight. Allah sent me to take care of them."

"Do you trust Uncle Farouk?"

"As long as I have the bankbook." As suddenly as my father had faltered, he stood erect and puffed out his chest. "Saddle el-Buraq," he ordered of me, "and bring him to the square."

The activity had drummed up a cloud of dust that mixed with the confusion and constant wailing and cursing. One of the sheiks stood on a low stone wall near the well and screamed, "Is there no one who will stay and fight!"

"We cannot stay," someone cried. "If we remain, we will be hanged by the Arab armies as collaborators."

I will never forget my father walking among them like a saint, calmly checking everyone's cart, and answering questions. He instructed the men to drive the carts and the younger children to pile on top of the belongings. The women would follow on foot, carrying belongings on their heads and infants in shawls on their hips. My father set a picket of guards as I brought him his horse. He mounted.

"Do not look back," he said and set everyone into motion. On

the highway, several jeeps filled with British soldiers stopped
traffic as their sirens wailed. There was no movement nor anyone
to be seen as we passed Shemesh Kibbutz.

Within moments, carts began to break down, causing us to
stop. Those that couldn't be repaired immediately were ditched
and their contents spread among other carts that could scarcely
hold them. Time and again we moved to the ditches as bus and
truck traffic drove us off the highway. Off in the distant hills we
could hear gunfire and then a windstorm consumed us.

When the villagers were out of sight, Farouk came down from
Tabah, crossed the highway and went to the kibbutz gate, and
asked to see Gideon Asch.

"Everyone has left except for myself, fourteen men who have
agreed to remain, and a half-dozen trusted families who have
stayed hidden. We claim Tabah as our land. I do not have the
forces to stop either you or the Jihad from taking the village. I am
at your mercy."

Gideon saw through Farouk's scheme immediately. The
Haganah would use the village's height for an observation post
and would defend the position. With villagers remaining, the
Jews would probably leave most of the place intact. If the Jews
won, Farouk could claim all of Tabah.

If the regular Arab armies conquered the Valley of Ayalon,
Farouk would be there, not only to greet them but probably to
claim Shemesh Kibbutz as well. Such was the way of Arab brotherhood, Gideon thought.

"I am moving a platoon of the Palmach into Tabah," Gideon
said. "Tell your people they will not be bothered. Report any
movement of the Jihad to me immediately."

Farouk bowed many times solicitously and assured Gideon of
his loyalty.

"Does your brother have any idea how beautifully you have
fucked him over?" Gideon said.

"How can you say such a thing when I, alone, had the courage
to remain?"

"Yeah . . . sure. . . . You can go to the mosque now and pray
for the side that brings you the most."

"For the time being," Farouk answered, "I will act as muktar
and handle all village affairs."

Chapter Thirteen

The unraveled line of broken and rattling carts, braying asses and oxen, women afoot bearing immense bundles on their heads and infants in shawl slings, and weeping stragglers inched toward Ramle. It was more of a sprawl, a sullen mass, a broken array incongruously led by a man, my father, resplendent in his finest robes astride a stallion of magnificent dimensions.

We reached the edge of town just before dark and were rudely shunted to a large field with a cactus fence about it and guarded by the nasty-tempered Jihad Militia. These were our own men, ordinary villagers and townspeople, who in regular life were gentle and warm. But in an armed band with a self-proclaimed authority, they had turned into something ugly.

My father's horse was eyed enviously and I could see my father sizing up the guards immediately. People from other villages— thousands of them—were already in the field. It was a sea of human misery. There was no water or sanitation.

Haj Ibrahim staked out an area and set a guard, then called the sheiks together.

"Pass the word," he ordered. "Do not eat but a few bites. If the others here find out we are carrying a quantity of food, we will be raided."

My father was well known in Ramle. Many merchants owed him favors and there would never be a better time to call them in. He put Omar in personal charge of his horse and took me, Jamil, and Kamal into the town to try to collect.

The shops were shut tight, with their iron grills rolled down and padlocked. Many bore signs reading: ENGLISH POUNDS ONLY. The souk, where the family had held a stall for decades, was reduced to selling little more than garbage. Anyone with anything was obviously hoarding it. Ibrahim reconnoitered the back alleys, where trading was done in whispers and prices were outrageous. He tried homes. Everyone who had done business with Tabah must have heard of our evacuation and had deliberately made themselves scarce. Suddenly my father had no friends left in Ramle.

We returned to the field empty-handed while a numbness overcame me. The children cried with hunger, but the word was out not to show that we carried a large amount of staples. Everywhere eyes were probing.

We huddled around a grubby little fire near the highway. Jihad vehicles raced back and forth. Many of the soldiers fired into the air. My father commented that they were doing it because the sound of their own guns made them believe they were brave. The great airport of Palestine was nearby and there would soon be a fierce battle for it, so the Jihad was pumping up its courage.

The fire glowed down to ashes. An eerie silence encompassed the field. Haj Ibrahim sat stone-faced, trying to comprehend what had befallen him. As always, I sat as close to him as I could manage. Our family was huddled together on the ground, sleeping fitfully. My father began to wonder aloud.

"I should have listened to Sheik Azziz," he mumbled. "He is keeping the Bedouin clear of everyone's armies, Jew and Arab alike. He will survive. What will happen when he finds six hundred of us dumped on the Wahhabi doorstep? How can the desert provide? Look what we have been brought to, Ishmael."

"We can still go back," I said.

"You cannot make a waterfall flow uphill, my son," he said. "As Arabs, we must pay the price for foolish pride. It would have been simple to allow a few Haganah into Tabah with my blessing. I think Gideon did not lie when he said the Jews were more like brothers to us . . . than that Jihad Militia. Still, we must pray that the Arab armies crush the Jews."

He nodded, dozed, awoke, and mumbled again.

"A good thing Farouk is coming with livestock and stores. We will need every lira we can get our hands on . . . we must find new land right away . . . perhaps I will stay in Jaffa and open a store . . . I am tired of leading people . . . at least we know the Jews can never take Jaffa."

"Father, you are very tired. Sleep. I will guard the family."

"Yes, Ishmael . . . I will sleep now . . . I will sleep."

The confusion of the first day was embittered by a frosty morning. There was hunger throughout the field and my father's first command was not to eat. Despite our guards, many families reported their carts had been looted.

Haj Ibrahim found a meeting of muktars from a half-dozen villages trying to make sense out of the morning rumors. Each village seemed to be heading in a different direction to get to their closest tribal unit in Arab territory. No one knew which route was safe, which was closed by fighting. We had only one choice— Jaffa. That was where our money was banked and where Uncle Farouk would be coming with the busload of supplies and livestock.

One by one the field emptied of its clans, all seeming to strike out on a different route in an atmosphere of universal uncertainty. There was no Arab authority of any kind to give advice on the roads or dispense food rations. The British were nowhere to be found.

"We must push hard, very hard today. We must reach Jaffa."

Out on the road again, we became part of a horde spilling toward the illusion of safety. By the end of the second night, we reached the edge of the city and, although we were beyond weariness, the sight of the lighthouse and minarets buoyed our spirits. There were British about and we were herded into a large park near the Russian church on the outer edge of the city. As my father set up a perimeter around our people, he reckoned that some of the livestock could be slaughtered for a meal. I could see, though, that he was desperately concerned that Uncle Farouk had not linked up with us. When questioned, he waved it off.

"You saw the roads and the confusion. Perhaps it will take him a bit longer than we planned. Certainly he will be in Jaffa by morning."

With that Ibrahim set out, with me tagging along, into central Jaffa to the home and business of our cousin, Mr. Bassam el Bassam, who owned a trading company. Farouk had purchased village supplies from him for over twenty years. My father had lent him money several times during lean years and other times he had given crops on credit for Mr. Bassam to export. In our world, which operates on the building up and paying off of favors, Bassam el Bassam was overdue and he knew it.

Although he greeted my father with traditional warmth, one could tell he was not very happy with the situation. Behind his small storefront was an office and warehouse permeated with the

smells of hundreds of flavors of spices and coffee and guarded by
Bassam el Bassam's personal cadre of six men.

When the coffee was brewed, the two tried to sift through the
rumors and make sense out of the sudden mass flight of the Arab
population.

"I don't know where it started or how it started," Mr. Bassam
said. "The mayor of Haifa was the worst fool. He was ill-advised
to take a hundred thousand of our people out of the city."

"But his alternative was to submit to a Jewish victory," my
father said.

Mr. Bassam threw up his hands. "I have cousins who remained.
They are a hell of a lot better off than you are at this moment. I'll
tell you when it really started, Haj Ibrahim. It started two minutes after the partition vote, when our rich citizens bolted from
Palestine to protect their comforts."

"What is the situation here?"

"There are seventy thousand or more Arabs in Jaffa. We are
well armed. However, Jaffa is like a piece of meat wrapped inside
a piece of pita bread. Tel Aviv is to the north and below us is the
Jewish city of Bat Yam." He leaned close to my father to give a
confidence. "I have spoken to one of the Haganah commanders
who has been a good friend. The Jews say they have no plans to
attack Jaffa. This has also been confirmed by my very good British friend, Colonel Winthrop. Jaffa is outside the partition boundaries of the Jewish state and the British are determined, as their
last act, to see that it remains in Arab hands."

"Tomorrow, first thing, I must go to Barclay's Bank," my father said. "You will come with me?"

"Of course."

"And tomorrow, when Farouk arrives, we will have a great
number of stores to sell, as well as livestock. There are also family
valuables. We want to convert everything into cash and charter a
boat for Gaza as quickly as possible."

"Leave everything to me and be assured, my brother, that I do
not take one lira in commissions. I will buy back your stores at a
fair price and I will find you an honest trader for the livestock.
The personal items would be better disposed of on the open market."

"I hope our stay in Jaffa will not be an extended one," my

father said. "What are the possibilities of obtaining a boat to Gaza for a humane price?"

Mr. Bassam meditated aloud as he ran through the possibilities in his mind. "A number of small Greek ships are working the coast. Many of them from Cyprus I know personally. But one cannot be too careful. You know how the Greeks are. They are taking deposits and never showing up. Other boat owners are letting passengers starve. You let me do your bidding, Haj Ibrahim."

Letting Bassam el Bassam do our bidding was not what my father had in mind, but the transaction would be impossible without him. "How much will it take?"

Mr. Bassam perspired over that one, talking to himself, arguing with the right hand against the left hand. "Well over three hundred and fifty pounds with that crowd you have."

"But that is thievery. Gaza cannot be more than a day's sail."

"It is not the length of the journey but the dangers. The boat owners are running the game. It would be better to pay a bit more and have a reliable charter. I have been on this waterfront all my life. I will find a safe boat. Unfortunately, I might have to put up a deposit."

"We shall sort that matter out after Farouk arrives and when I have been to the bank. A final question. Is there any possibility of shelter?"

"It is not out of the question. The neighborhood that is closest to Tel Aviv has been virtually abandoned. There is quite a bit of sniping going on, but the area is generally safe. I have scouted out two or three streets close together that are all but empty. I advise you to sell everything for cash as quickly as possible. Look at my warehouse. It has been almost stripped. There are four or five separate militias running around taking what they wish at gunpoint. There is no order. Our own police are either helpless or are taking baksheesh," he said rubbing his fingers together to indicate the bribe.

"But a good part of our resources are in food," Ibrahim said.

"Sell it. The Christian churches have gotten together and established a relief kitchen at St. Anthony's Church. You can be assured of one meal a day for your people. As for yourself, you will be my honored guest."

Haj Ibrahim thanked Bassam el Bassam and allowed that he

would partake of a meal with him now and then, but he wished to stay close to the villagers. He would, however, be grateful if Bassam stabled his horse.

"El-Buraq goes with me to Gaza," he said.

My father and Mr. Bassam were able to locate an entire square block of empty houses on the northernmost fringe of the city in a district called Manshiya. It was an extremely poor neighborhood of tiny dilapidated houses crushed against one another on filthy, unpaved streets. It had been the worst of dens, a former place of cheap prostitutes, smugglers, thieves, and beggars. Most of the houses smelled of urine and defecation and were broken beyond repair. It wasn't much, but it was better than camping in the open, with envious eyes staring at us all the time. It seemed that my father alone, among all the muktars now in Jaffa, had made adequate preparations for his people. Most had left everything behind and fled. Thousands around us had absolutely nothing, were desperate and became more dangerous by the hour.

"Two streets away," Mr. Bassam said, "is an open market. The Jews still cross over from Tel Aviv to trade. Business is flourishing. You will get your best price for jewelry and personal items."

It was very late when we returned to our encampment in the park. My father ordered everyone to be ready to move at daybreak. He inquired about Farouk, but was told that heavy fighting had broken out on the highway and he was most likely held up.

By dawn we moved to the Manshiya quarters. We staked out a compound, so we would be huddled together. A few blocks to the north, the Jewish city of Tel Aviv began, with a quarters inhabited mostly by oriental Jews from Yemen. The streets between the two cities once held a mixed neighborhood where some Jews and Arabs had intermarried and lived in squalor. It had become an abandoned no-man's-land.

We had no idea how long we would be in Jaffa. We could no longer feed our livestock, so my father ordered it all rounded up, selected two of the village's sharpest traders, and sent them off to sell it. The women were told to take personal belongings to the market and sell them as well. All the women had collections of heirlooms and dowry jewelry, but it was inexpensive and of low value. The money was to be brought back to Father. By nine o'clock everyone had returned from their selling forays and had dropped the cash in a blanket before Ibrahim. I counted it. The final amount came to a disappointing sum of just under two hundred pounds. It was not nearly enough to charter a boat, much less have anything left to feed us in Gaza or purchase land for temporary resettlement.

"At least we have this," my father said, patting the bank passbook under his robes. "It is very important now that Farouk gets here soon. The village stores and the herd will give us a margin of safety."

We received the news that the fighting on the highway had stopped and normal traffic in and out of Jaffa had resumed. My father was most eager to return to Bassam el Bassam, for surely Uncle Farouk had gotten through and had contacted him by now. We arrived at the trading company just before ten o'clock when the bank would be opened. No news of Farouk.

"It is mayhem. It is mayhem," Mr. Bassam said. "Farouk is clever. He will get through."

"There is no village without a dunghill; I am smelling ours now," my father said. "I do not like it."

"Come, we go to the bank. We worry about Farouk later."

It was fortunate that Mr. Bassam was with us, for everything in the bank was crazy. It seemed like ten thousand people were trying to get their money out at once. Mr. Bassam knew the manager, an Englishman named Mr. Howard, and we were whisked through the mob into his private office.

Mr. Howard was dressed in a fine Western suit and seemed obliviously calm, removed from the chaos.

"You know Haj Ibrahim's brother, Farouk al Soukori of Tabah," Mr. Bassam said.

"Yes, of course. I've had the pleasure," the banker said.

"We wish to withdraw our money," Haj Ibrahim said. "Seven hundred and fifteen pounds. Some of it is mine, some of it belongs to the villagers."

"You do realize there are branches of Barclay's everywhere and it would be prudent not to put all your eggs in one basket, so to speak. Do you know your destination?"

"Gaza."

"If you withdraw only part of your funds, enough to safely get you down south, I could give you a letter of credit that would be honored in Gaza."

"I do not understand such things, Mr. Howard."

"Mr. Howard is only looking after the safety of your money," Mr. Bassam said. "I assure you that it is a proper transaction."

"I appreciate your interest. However, I will feel much better if I can touch a lump in my pocket."

"As you wish. Do you have your passbook, Haj Ibrahim?"

My father reached inside his robes, withdrew it as though it were the magic key to life, and handed it over the desk. Mr. Howard's face went into an immediate frown as he accepted the book and thumbed through it. My father and I knew instantly that the banker was grossly uncomfortable.

"Is anything wrong?" Ibrahim asked.

"The account has been closed."

"But that is not possible. The sum on the last page says we have over seven hundred pounds in your bank."

Mr. Howard cleared his throat and looked at my father with great pity. As Ibrahim paled, he realized calamity had befallen him.

"The final withdrawal has been very cleverly erased. But you see the stamp here on the first page as well as below the last deposit and you'll notice the corner of the book has been clipped off."

"I cannot read what the stamps say. They are obviously in English."

Mr. Howard handed the passbook to Mr. Bassam. "It says the account is canceled, Haj Ibrahim." My father snatched the book and handed it to me. I could not look him in the eyes to confirm it.

"I'm terribly sorry," the banker said. "Terribly sorry, indeed."

My father seethed all the way back to the trading company, then exploded in Mr. Bassam's office.

"I am returning to Tabah tonight! There will be a big funeral for a mouse!"

"I know it comes as a terrible shock, but there has been fierce fighting all over the area."

"Don't worry. I can get through anything. I will not rest until I have my hands closing around his throat! I will rip out his Adam's apple!"

"What if something happens to you, Father?" I cried. "If you are gone, we will be abandoned!"

"I must kill him!"

"There will be all the rest of your life to plan that properly,"
Mr. Bassam said.

"I can never know a night's sleep until this is avenged!"

"Father. Does it not make sense that Uncle Farouk knows and
fears you will return? Does it not follow that he is going to spend
the next days in hiding?"

"Your son makes perfect sense."

My father had been the one man in Tabah who sometimes
responded to logic. Our only hope was that he would respond to
it now. I knew that once he left, Mr. Bassam's co-operation would
be gone. We could not do without him. It took an hour for the
heat of his boiling blood to lower to a simmer.

"What can I tell our people?" he moaned. "What is there left to
say?"

Chapter Fourteen

It was openly announced by the Haganah that Jaffa would not be attacked if the Arabs stopped sniping at Tel Aviv from their tall buildings and if they stopped ambushing the roads in and out of the city. A tentative truce prevailed, but Jaffa remained a bone in the Jews' throat, an all-Arab enclave in the most heavily populated Jewish region.

Mr. Bassam el Bassam confided to my father that he hoped the Arabs of Jaffa would accept the partition, avoid battle and the fate of their brothers in Haifa. He counted heavily on the fact that a great deal of British prestige was at stake in keeping Jaffa an Arab city.

Several days after our arrival, we had mixed emotions as units of both the Jihad and Kaukji's Irregulars entered the city and deployed mainly in the Manshiya, where we were, the closest district to Tel Aviv.

The militias wore out their welcome immediately. They confiscated whatever they wished. Shops were broken into and looted, men were beaten trying to protect their property, cats and dogs were shot for target practice, warehouses on the docks were raided, and any places selling or serving food were forced to close. Worst of all, they shattered the truce with the Jews by shooting at Tel Aviv around the clock.

One night followed the other and found us cringing and clawing at the floors of our hovels as bullets smashed through the meager protection of crumbling plaster. During the hours of darkness, my father tried to answer hysterical calls.

The Haganah responded with an operation that cleared the environs of Jaffa of Arab villages and sealed the city in. Tel Aviv was to the north, Bat Yam to the south, and a brigade of Haganah now controlled the east-west highway. They upped their firepower into us from Tel Aviv and the villagers of Tabah took their first casualties. An older woman and a child were hit by gunfire and badly wounded. Then we got the chilling word: a unit of six hundred Jewish Irgun troops were positioned opposite us.

My father ordered our men to immediately search for safer shelter deeper in the city, even if it meant we could not all stay together. Every man would be responsible for his own family. Unaccustomed to taking such personal responsibility, our men were plainly frightened. As long as we clung together, we had a sense of security. Splitting up the village meant the loss of tribal warmth. One could not remember when Haj Ibrahim did not make all the decisions. Yet they had to obey because the shooting throughout the night had become unbearable. No one slept. Women wailed and babies screamed, shattering our nerves. The fighting was escalating every day.

Our men departed with a final instruction to move their families immediately and that night they were to meet with Haj Ibrahim at the central Clock Tower and give us their new locations. A few guards were left to protect the women while the others scattered. In our family, Jamil and Omar were commissioned to search for shelter, Kamal to stay and guard.

Mr. Bassam arrived shortly afterward with a glimmer of welcome news. So many people had already fled Jaffa, a small surplus of escape boats had developed and captains were hanging around the port and the Clock Tower bargaining for passengers. Mr. Bassam believed he had a suitable boat for us.

Nada and I were told to find containers and wait until the fire hydrant was opened a few blocks away and to collect water for the family. My father then left with Mr. Bassam to meet the boat's captain.

Nada and I found some empty gallon-sized olive oil cans near the flea market. She could balance hers on her head so beautifully. I made a yoke with a long pole, so I could carry two on my shoulders. By the time we got to the fire hydrant, the line was very long. From where we waited, we could look back to our hovel through open spaces created when homes had been leveled.

Suddenly two trucks filled with Kaukji's soldiers roared past our hydrant—almost hitting us—and screeched to a stop on our street. The militia jumped from the trucks and spread out, shouting orders I could not understand from this distance. There was a burst of firing and women screaming.

In a moment, the men who had been left to guard the women were running away toward us. I spotted Kamal without his rifle and chased after him, finally throwing myself on him and bringing him to the ground. He was awash with terror.

"They have sealed off our street! They are looking for Father!"

I realized instantly that it was Kaukji, seeking revenge for the burning of the fields a decade earlier, for I had grown up hearing the story of the battle every night of my life at the café. For the moment, Father was safely with Mr. Bassam. Kamal was frightened to the point of being deranged. I could not trust him with the task of reaching Father. First, I feared for my mother, Ramiza, Fatima, and her baby.

I ordered Nada to take cover in a nearby shelter. She clung to me and begged me not to return to the house. I was forced to beat her off me. It was the first time I had ever struck her, but the situation required me to act quickly.

I was small and I was fast and I slithered my way back, darting from cover to cover. I got as far as the adjoining street and stopped to study the situation. If I could only cross the street and get up on a rooftop, I could see what was taking place on our block and also work my way back to our hovel.

I sprinted over the street and for an instant I was frozen by the sight of bullets kicking up around my feet. I plunged into a house through its paneless window and scampered up to the roof before anyone was able to follow, then crawled on my belly down four houses and dared a look into our street.

The women had been rounded up with the children and were surrounded by a dozen soldiers who were herding them at bayonet point. I could tell by their uniforms and accents that they were Iraqis from Kaukji's irregulars. Other soldiers had shut off the ends of the street and others were going from house to house, kicking in doors. I looked desperately into the pack of women and children. Hagar, Ramiza, and Fatima were not there!

I worked my way down the rooftops very cautiously until I could get a look at our place. It was blocked off by soldiers. There was a small crawl space between our house and the adjacent one. I dropped down from the roof and froze on the ground until I was certain I had not been seen, then I slithered up to the window.

The sight inside was utter horror! There were eight or ten soldiers or more and an officer with a pistol. Hagar held her arms about Ramiza and Fatima, who cringed against her. The officer pointed to a ghastly burn scar on his face. "A present from Haj Ibrahim. I have waited for ten years! Where is he?"

"I don't know," my mother answered softly.

The officer fired the pistol at their feet. Hagar stood fast while the other two whimpered and clung more tightly to her. He fired again and again and taunted her by putting the pistol against her head. Fatima's baby shrieked!

"I don't know . . . I don't know," my mother answered again and again.

"On your knees, you old whore!"

The officer threw up his hand in disgust and his soldiers fired a dozen shots around them. The officer's face became wet with perspiration and he began to pant and snarl, then opened the front of his trousers and took his prick out.

"Take off your clothing, all of you!"

"Do what he says," Hagar said to the other two. "Do not fight them."

"I am menstruating," Fatima whispered.

"Never mind. Submit to them. If we are found bruised, it will be worse for us later."

I slammed my eyes shut as my mother lifted her dress and I could hear the soldiers howl with delight. The women were being thrown to the floor. The soldiers were laughing and shooting, but no sounds came from the women. I felt myself the most terrible coward who ever lived, for I shook with fear. What could I do? Allah must understand! There was nothing I could do! Nothing! Nothing! Nothing!

I should not have looked again, but I could not help it. The three were spread out and naked. The soldiers did not even bother to take their pants off, but lowered them and plunged atop the women, grunting like animals, slapping flesh, slobbering kisses, pounding, dripping, staggering off as the others stood around with their pricks in their hands. Fatima was passing blood from her legs.

I doubled over and shut my eyes and clamped my hands over my ears. Coward! Coward! Coward! Allah! What can I do? Think, Ishmael, think! If Father returned, they would kill him after forcing him to look at the terrible sight! I had to get to him and warn him! No! I must not leave my mother! Go! Stay!

Would they never stop? Ibrahim, do not come back! Please do

not come back! How long will it go on? How long? Then they staggered from the house. I took my hands from my ears and heard the officer command his men to watch the place from hiding and keep the women as bait.

I knew I was scarred forever from the sight and the dishonor. Yet somehow I had to put aside my own terrible vision to save our lives. I forced myself to forget for the moment what I had witnessed and I crawled up to the window. Ramiza and Fatima were crumpled on the floor. My mother was in a daze, but still she comforted them. She wiped the blood from Fatima, then held them in her arms and rocked them back and forth.

"Mother!" I whispered.

Her eyes widened in terror upon seeing me.

"Do not fear. I will never tell Father. No one will know."

"Oh, Ishmael!" she cried. "To see your mother in such shame! Get me a knife! I must kill myself!"

"Mother, no!"

"Ishmael, run! Run! Forget what you have seen. Run!"

"Mother, don't weep. It is over. Mother, please. We will live!"

"I don't want to live!"

It was no use. I did not care any longer. I jumped into the room and slapped her in the face. She stopped her weeping and gaped at me.

"Will you listen now?"

She did not answer and I slapped her again. Slowly she shook her head that she heard me.

"Do not move until darkness. Clean yourselves up. The shooting from Tel Aviv will start again after dark. The guards are smoking hashish. They will not be alert. When the firing starts, slip out one at a time and run for the market. After you gather, then go to the Clock Tower in the center of town."

She clutched at me and looked up. Her eyes were red and her face was streaked with tears. "Oh, Ishmael!"

"Did you understand me, Mother?"

"Yes, but Ibrahim . . ."

"He will never know. Never. No one will ever know."

She touched my face, her hands shaking. I gripped them and held them steady and begged her with my eyes to obey me. At last she said she would. I kissed her and wiped her cheeks. "Make yourself look nice now. I go to warn Father not to come back. All he will ever know is that the soldiers questioned you—nothing more."

I ran. I heard firing behind me, but I didn't know if they were shooting at me or not.

I found Nada and Kamal and told them only that the soldiers were holding the women hostage to set a trap for Father. I ordered them to stay and watch for Jamil and Omar in case they returned. We would all meet later by the Clock Tower. I made haste to save my father.

Chapter Fifteen

Bassam el Bassam assured Haj Ibrahim he had traded fairly with the Greek Cypriot, Harissiadis, for almost twenty years. His price for a charter to Beirut of four hundred pounds was eminently fair. Haj Ibrahim objected to the destination.

"I have just come back from a run to Gaza," the Greek said. "I will not go back there for five thousand. The Egyptian Navy is in the waters. They shoot at anything. They all but sank a refugee boat three days ago. I have made five round trips to Gaza and enough is enough. It is too dangerous. I would not even consider taking you up to Beirut, but it happens to be on my way home to Cyprus."

"But we have no relatives in Beirut," Ibrahim said.

"You have a safer coast and I am giving you a fair price for six hundred people. Yes or no?"

"Harissiadis is giving you a break," Bassam reassured.

The bulge in his pocket was not what he had hoped. He had only one hundred and eighty pounds. Seven hundred had flown out the window with the visit to Barclay's Bank and an equal amount had been lost when Farouk failed to show up. Ibrahim threw up his hands. "It's madness. I don't know why I left Tabah. Beirut. What is Beirut? How much time do I have to raise the money?"

One could see that the Greek was disappointed. He had been led to believe that Haj Ibrahim already had sufficient funds. "The truce here has been broken. The fighting increases. Who knows if there will be an assault on Jaffa? Do you know? Does Bassam know? No one knows. I will take a chance. Twenty-four hours."

"Tomorrow," Haj Ibrahim said. "I will pay half when my people board and half when they arrive in Beirut."

The Greek shook his head no.

Ibrahim took the bankroll from his pocket and laid it on the table. "That is every lira we have," he said.

"How much is there?"

"Just under two hundred."

Harissiadis shrugged in sympathy. "Can I tell you the truth? It will cost me almost three hundred and fifty. To get a crew for such business, I've had to pay double and triple bonuses." He whipped out a pencil and scribbled furiously, bit his lip, and sighed. "Three hundred and twenty-five and, believe me, I lose on the deal."

Haj Ibrahim reached under his robes and took out two wrapped packages and laid them on the table, then unwrapped one, a five-kilo slab of hashish. Harissiadis crumpled a corner in his fingers, sniffed it, and put it to his lips. "Twenty," he said.

"You are stealing," Mr. Bassam said.

"They give this stuff away in Lebanon. I sell it on the dock in Athens for maybe thirty."

"Twenty," Ibrahim agreed.

"What else do you have?" the Greek said. Ibrahim pointed to the second package. It was unwrapped and contained Ibrahim's most magnificent possession, a bejeweled dagger some three centuries old.

"I do not know if such a thing is junk or real."

"It is a treasure," Bassam said. "It is worth one or two hundred."

Harissiadis looked the dagger over. "Twenty and I take a risk."

"I cannot let it go for that," Haj Ibrahim said. "Perhaps I keep it. I have a special use in mind for it."

"We are still over one hundred pounds short," the Greek said.

Ibrahim arose, opened the door to the warehouse, and nodded in the direction of his stallion. The Greek's eyes widened at the sight of the animal.

"I will buy the animal," Mr. Bassam said quickly. "I will give you one hundred fifty."

"One hundred fifty for el-Buraq?" Ibrahim said in disbelief.

"Another twenty-five. Times are terrible. Things are very bad," Bassam moaned.

"Pay him," Haj Ibrahim said. Mr. Bassam el Bassam peeled the bills from a grapefruit-sized roll and gave Ibrahim the balance.

They shook hands on the deal and set a time.

"One more thing," Harissiadis said. "No rifles, no handguns, no knives. My crew is honest. I am an honest man. And don't hide weapons beneath your women's skirts. Everyone will be strip-searched when we reach Beirut. The authorities there are taking anything and everything of value from the refugees. I can tell you for a fact that the Egyptians cleaned out everyone in Gaza."

"We are naked without our weapons," Ibrahim said.

"If you take weapons and they are found—and they will be found—I will no longer be able to have Beirut as a port of call. I cannot live without Beirut," the Greek said. "One final thing. I can supply water, but you must bring your own food."

"We sold everything," Ibrahim said. "We have been eating from the Christian church." He turned to Bassam el Bassam. "I think that for the price you took my horse, as cousins, you can contribute a few hundred kilos of grain and fruit and milk for the babies."

Haj Ibrahim's eyes conveyed a message to Bassam that he might be the first to taste the jeweled dagger. "But of course," Bassam said. "I shall supply the food with pleasure."

I arrived at the trading company a few minutes after the deal had been closed and gasped out that Kaukji's soldiers had been looking for him, but said nothing of the rape I had witnessed. With good fortune, the family would all assemble at the Clock Tower later.

Bassam slapped his forehead and cursed. "It will not be possible for you to get on that boat."

"But . . ."

"The port will be watched. They'll find you."

"Then we go by foot."

"All roads are closed, Ibrahim."

"We're trapped," my father whispered.

"Let the villagers keep the charter. The Iraqis will search them for hours before letting them board. That will keep them busy. You must go into hiding."

"I cannot be separated from my people!"

"Can you tell me another choice?"

"Father," I said. "We must do as Mr. Bassam says."

Ibrahim was beaten and he knew it. He did not even have time for the luxury of bewailing his fate. Bassam took him to the basement of a fish market near the docks, where he would be safe for a few hours, then set out to find a permanent refuge. I would meet him later with instructions.

By Allah's grace, the entire family made it to the Clock Tower. Many of the villagers were already milling about in the crowd. I gave them instructions about the time, place, and name of the boat and this was whispered from ear to ear. They then moved out, deftly avoiding the searching eyes of Kaukji's soldiers.

I had checked out the Great Mosque across the street earlier. Many people from many villages had crushed into it, seeking refuge. As our villagers began to drift off, I ordered my family to go into the mosque, lose themselves in the crowd, and wait for me. The square was still crowded, but as it turned dark many of the soldiers drifted toward the Manshiya district and gunfire between the two cities started up.

It turned late. I was stricken with fear. Just as I was on the verge of quitting my post, I spotted Mr. Bassam. He walked past me and, after waiting for a moment, I followed. He ducked into a narrow alleyway and I went after him. He was in shadows. I could not see him.

"Ishmael."

"Yes."

"Is your family safe?"

"Yes, they are hiding in the mosque."

"Good. I have taken your father to St. Peter's Church, past the lighthouse. Do you know where it is?"

"I am sure."

"Find your family. Go to the back entrance. Brother Henri is a Christian Arab and a good friend. They have agreed to give you sanctuary."

"Are you all right?" I asked.

"I am not sure. I believe my home and store are being watched. I may try to slip on the boat. I am not sure."

With that he was gone.

Our entire family had two tiny monk's cells, but from the windows we could see the port and the sea and up the coast to Tel Aviv. Late in the afternoon, we saw Mr. Harissiadis's boat, the *Kleopatra*, chug into the harbor.

I slipped out of the church and worked my way down the hill to the lighthouse near where it was docked. Everyone from Tabah sat about, jammed close to the dock. There must have been a hundred of Kaukji's men moving through them, shaking them down, roughing people up, searching for Haj Ibrahim. There were deliberate delays by port "authorities" when they could not find my father. Mr. Harissiadis ranted that he must get under way.

Then the word came that all hell had broken out on the front between Tel Aviv and Jaffa. The Iraqis were called away and the villagers flooded aboard the ship, cramming every inch of deck space. There was no way I could risk having the family make a last-minute try to board, so we were stranded in Jaffa. At last the *Kleopatra* pulled away from dockside. I ran up the hill toward the church as the ship moved below me. It reached the end of the quay and headed into open sea.

I went back to St. Peter's. From our window, the family could see tracer bullets streaking back and forth between the two lines. The fury of the fighting told us that this was not another night of sniper fire. A full-scale battle was under way.

We were able to make out the *Kleopatra* until it fell below the horizon with the sun. And then . . . they were gone.

Chapter Sixteen

The Irgun, acting solely on its own, had launched an all-out attack on the Manshiya district of Jaffa. They had neither permission, co-operation, nor co-ordination from the Haganah, but sought a spectacular victory to gain equity. A conglomerate of Arab militias were well entrenched and beat back attack after attack. The Irgun fought hard, capturing some houses on the outskirts of the district, but again their lack of formal military training and leadership hindered them. They had neither the plan of execution nor the wherewithal to consolidate their gains and by dawn they had been driven back to Tel Aviv.

In order to stave off an ignoble defeat, the Irgun appealed to the Haganah for help. As battles heightened all over Palestine, the two Jewish forces engaged in more and more irritating little conflicts. A grand showdown about who had the authority in the Yishuv would not be long in coming.

After a quick meeting, the Haganah agreed to bail the Irgun out, provided the Irgun accepted the Haganah's command of the Jaffa front. The Irgun agreed and attacked the Manshiya again with Haganah support, cutting it in half.

At the same time, the Haganah tightened the lines around Jaffa. Their objective was to remove all Arab resistance between Jaffa and Lydda, so they could have a clear shot at the airport without fear of Arab reinforcements.

Jewish plans to capture Jaffa sat like acid in the British stomach. Saving the Arab city had become something of an obsession with them. Although they had been pulling out of Palestine in droves, they sent out an emergency order to immediately return some units from Egypt and Cyprus.

After an appraisal of the situation, the British command reckoned that the Jews had Jaffa bagged and there was nothing, really, that they could do about it. Their mission then became to force an exit open to allow the Arabs to escape, if they wished. There was but one avenue left down the southern highway to safe Arab

country around Gaza. The Jewish city of Bat Yam blocked the
way.

The British struck Bat Yam with an authoritative artillery barrage and strafing from the air, then pushed in tank patrols to clear
the road. It was like uncorking a highly charged bottle of fizz
water. The Arabs gushed from Jaffa, plunging south in a tumultuous exodus. The Haganah allowed the Arabs free passage to the
south, deftly avoided battle with the British, and continued reinforcing their encirclement of Jaffa on the other fronts.

From our monk's cells at St. Peter's Church, we were on high
ground and could witness the gunfire and shell bursts throughout
the nights. On the third day of battle, Brother Henri brought us
the devastating news that Bassam el Bassam was gone. He did not
know if Bassam had fled or had been murdered by the Irregulars
for helping us.

Brother Henri told us the British were still holding the road
open through Bat Yam and suggested we try to lose ourselves in
the flood of refugees. My father rejected the offer, telling Brother
Henri a small untruth. There were only two ways out of Jaffa—
the single road to the south and by the port. My father pointed
out that Kaukji had men posted in both places searching for him
and were checking everyone with great scrutiny.

Secretly my father favored staying put in St. Peter's. He had
confided in me that when the British finally withdrew, the Jews
would capture the city. While he was afraid of Kaukji's revenge,
he had no fear whatsoever of a Jewish massacre.

What was really in the back of my father's mind was the hope
that the Jews would take Jaffa, which would allow him to return
to Tabah and pay a visit to Uncle Farouk. It was what he lived
for. If the regular Arab armies defeated the Jews later, what of it?
He would have settled his score with Farouk.

Two days later, Brother Henri came to us in a state. Kaukji's
men had been snooping around the church, asking questions
about us. The monk quivered and said that the church could no
longer grant us sanctuary. We had to move.

Haj Ibrahim reckoned that our last hope was Gideon Asch. He
had saved the phone numbers Gideon had given him, but Brother
Henri said that all telephone lines from Jaffa had been cut. My
father and I concocted a desperate plan.

Late in the afternoon, I slipped out of St. Peter's and made for the Manshiya, edging through the narrow streets toward the front lines. I felt safe, in that one more little kid running around wouldn't get much notice. Moreover, there were boys in a youth militia, my age or only a few years older, who were in the fighting.

I had become an urban rat. It was no trick for me to work my way to find the best possible observation point. I had an instinct. Something in my gut told me that the flea market between the two cities might still be operating, despite the heavy gunfire from both sides. I was right.

From my rooftop, I could clearly see that the market was crowded and there were no soldiers in it. Everyone who was leaving was selling off anything they couldn't carry. As though by magic, I was wandering around in a free-trade zone. I had a last piece of Ramiza's jewelry as a bargaining piece and a note I had written in English.

I moved along the stalls, listening carefully and sizing up the merchants to see if there was anyone I felt like trusting to deliver my note. There wasn't. Everyone would try to take advantage of me because I was so young. They would steal Ramiza's bracelet and leave me cheated.

I inched around some of the Jewish merchants, but my Hebrew was faulty and most of them didn't speak English. Those who did I didn't trust. It would have been madness to approach an ordinary Jewish shopper. What to do?

At the far end of the market, there was a fence and an opening where people went back and forth. Jewish soldiers were on the far side of it, checking everyone's papers as they left the market. That was it. My only chance.

It took me an awful long time to screw up my courage. Come on, Ishmael, I said to myself over and over, go through the fence. I edged up to it, commanding myself not to be frightened. Do *not* run for it, I said. I will be shot if I run. Find a big person crossing to the Jewish side or two or three of them and slip in behind.

There it is! My chance! Now! *Go.* I hopped onto the tailgate of a peddler's donkey cart as though I belonged and I was on the Jewish side! The peddler did not notice. Inch by inch and foot by foot, we penetrated the other side and came up on their guard station.

Then a hand grabbed my arm and jerked me off the cart. A Jewish soldier looked down at me angrily. I thought my time to die had come.

"You can't come over here!" he said to me in Hebrew.

"Do you speak English?" I asked.

He pushed me aside and waved for me to go back to the other side. I went right back up to him. "English!" I cried. "English! English! English!"

By Allah's grace, I had caught the attention of another soldier. "What do you want, boy?" he said in English. I drew a breath, closed my eyes, thrust my hand in my pocket, and took out the note and handed it to him. He unfolded it curiously, read it haltingly, and scratched his head.

I am Ishmael. My father is Haj Ibrahim al Soukori al Wahhabi. He is the Muktar of Tabah. He is very good friends with your great commander, Mr. Gideon Asch. We were told to call him at these phone numbers if we got into serious trouble. We are trapped. Will you telephone Mr. Gideon Asch for us? Thank you.

By now an officer had drifted over curiously. He read the note and all three of them studied me.

"It could be a trick," one said.

"What kind of trick? If Asch doesn't know who these people are, he won't come."

"Please!" I cried. "Please! It is no trick! Kaukji is trying to kill my father."

"Wait here, boy," the officer said. He went into a small house that was being used as a command post. In a moment another officer came back with him. He seemed to be in charge. He read the note and scrutinized me, puzzled.

"We were neighbors," I said. "Kibbutz Shemesh and Tabah. Neighbors."

"All right," the officer in charge said. "I will phone him tonight. You come back tomorrow."

"No," I said. "I cannot leave without seeing Mr. Gideon Asch."

"Well, you can't stay here. The market will close in an hour and there'll be shooting around here."

"Please!" I cried. I took the bracelet and offered it to him. The officer looked it over and handed it back to me.

"Put that back in your pocket," he said. "Come with me."

The rest of it seemed to be a blur. We passed through the roadblock at the guard post with the officer holding my hand. In a moment we were driving in a battered car toward Tel Aviv. "I am from the Irgun," the officer said.

Now I am dead for sure.

"I will take you to the nearest Haganah command post."

In a moment we had crossed into another poor neighborhood and stopped before a row of houses bustling with soldiers. I had felt naked and terrified, but somehow the fear began to vanish. No one threatened me, questioned me, or touched me. I was looked upon with a glance of passing curiosity. The Irgun officer, in particular, seemed very sympathetic.

Inside one of the larger houses, I was taken to the door of a room guarded by a soldier. The Irgun officer spoke to the guard and he let us into the room. A Haganah officer behind a table seemed more important than anyone. He spoke to me in Arabic and, after I told him the story, he took me down the hall. I was let into a room that was empty except for a couple of chairs and was ordered to sit down.

For a long time, the Haganah officer asked me many questions about the names of my family and questions about Tabah and Shemesh Kibbutz. He asked me over and over why my family had not fled through Bat Yam. He was very suspicious and I realized this was because I was so little and was an Arab peasant and could speak three languages. Finally he asked me if I could give a secret message that only Gideon Asch would know. I thought about it a long time, for this was the final key to our survival.

"Tell Mr. Gideon Asch that I went to fetch him the night Ramiza's baby died."

"I don't know how long this will take," the Haganah officer said. "You stay put. Don't try to leave."

In a few moments a soldier came with a bedroll and some food. I did not realize it, but I had not eaten much since we had left Tabah and I ate so fast I became sick. Many times soldiers came into the room and looked at me. They were all very kind and soon I was not as suspicious as I had been. Even though heavy shooting started up, I was very tired. I did not want to sleep or lower my guard, but it was difficult to keep my eyes open.

"Ishmael."

I opened my eyes. Mr. Gideon Asch knelt beside me. I had never done such a thing before in my life, but I threw my arms about him and wept. I tried to speak in all three languages at one time between my weeping and choking on words. He helped me get control of myself and I told him my story.

We went to the commander's office and the two of them spoke at length, then spread a map on the table.

"Can you read a map, Ishmael?"

"I think so."

"All right. Here is St. Peter's, the Great Mosque, the Turkish Clock Tower."

"Yes," I said, "I understand."

"The post office, the wide boulevard, and Immanuel's church."

I nodded that I followed him.

"Go another three hundred yards past the church along the Jaffa Road to this position." He pointed to a place on the map. "Over the road there is a narrow alleyway. A truck will be parked there. Do you have a watch?"

"No."

He unstrapped his own and gave it to me. "Wait here on your side of the road until eight-thirty. I will bring a patrol over and fetch you. I will call out the word 'Tabah' and you will answer by calling out 'Shemesh Kibbutz.'"

I repeated the instructions a half-dozen times.

"Do you have any questions, Ishmael?"

"Suppose there are Arab soldiers around?"

The Haganah commander broke in, speaking in Hebrew to Mr. Gideon Asch. I could pick up a few words here and there. He was apprehensive about giving out any further information. Mr. Gideon Asch told the officer that I could be trusted.

"Our information is that so many Arab militia have deserted that the lines are full of holes. If they shoot, they will shoot at our patrol. We will lay down enough fire to drive them off."

It took the rest of the day to gather my family and move them through the back ways to avoid the militias. When we crept to our position, my heart leaped with joy to see the truck over the road. The rest of it was easy.

The family huddled in the rear of the truck. I sat in front

between Mr. Gideon Asch and my father. I was tired again and each time I dozed I saw the vision of my mother, stepmother, and sister-in-law being raped. This time I had the comfort of my father's arm about me. Time and again he patted me and called me a brave soldier. I had won his honor. Between my dozings, I could hear him and Mr. Gideon Asch speak as the truck raced through Tel Aviv and continued north. I was so tired I could not even partake of the wonderment of the Jewish city.

"You'll cross near Tulkarm. A man named Said will be waiting."

"Once I get the family settled, I will walk through a thousand miles of molten lava to return to Farouk and get him."

"You can't go back to Tabah," Mr. Gideon Asch said.

"I do not care if it means my own death."

"Well, you have something to live for. Your dreams of revenge should keep you going for a long time, Haj Ibrahim. Tabah has little left. We moved Haganah in when you abandoned it. The same night the Jihad attacked and threw us out. When we returned, we had to blow up most of the houses. There is little left."

"My house?"

"Farouk moved into it."

The road came to an abrupt end at a roadblock that led into Arab territory. Mr. Gideon Asch took us to a small woods nearby and waited until dark. My father allowed me to go with him as he bid farewell to Mr. Gideon Asch. Money was pressed into my father's hand. He wished to refuse but was unable; we were nearly penniless.

"Too bad we didn't have a chance to solve our problems," my father mumbled, as if in a trance.

"I don't know," Mr. Gideon Asch said. "You warned me a long time ago that things would have been different if your hand had been on the water valve instead of ours."

"That is true," my father said. "You would have died of thirst." Mr. Gideon Asch laughed.

"Now that we go into different worlds, I want you to tell me who the informer was in Tabah."

"I had many. None better than your brother."

"He is not my brother," Haj Ibrahim said. "You are my brother."

The dark was suddenly pierced by the blinking of a flashlight.

Mr. Gideon Asch returned the signal and I gathered the family. After a brief introduction to Said, they moved out behind him.

"Well," Mr. Gideon Asch said, "keep your ear to the ground. In addition to Said, I have many contacts everywhere on the Arab side. They'll know how to reach me. Shalom."

"Shalom."

My father and I walked quickly to catch up to the family. Already we could see the distant lights of Tulkarm. I stopped suddenly. "I forgot to give Mr. Gideon Asch his wristwatch back."

"No, Ishmael," my father said. "He wanted you to have it."

A few days later, Jaffa fell to the Haganah and Irgun. Of the Arab population of seventy thousand, only three thousand remained when the final assault was made.

On May 14, 1948, David Ben-Gurion read the Declaration of Independence of the State of Israel. Within hours, the entire Arab world attacked.

END OF PART TWO

Part Three

Qumran

Chapter One

We walked briskly toward Tulkarm. Mr. Said was made nervous by our presence. He apologized that he was merely an impoverished apprentice pharmacist who lived in a single room with his wife and five children in the home of his father. He gave us directions to the center of town, told my father not to contact him unless there was a dire emergency, and disappeared.

We reached the market town in a matter of minutes to find a flash flood of humanity had inundated it with thousands of homeless families.

"We will find shelter in the mosque tonight," Ibrahim said, "and tomorrow we will see what there is to be seen."

He had spoken too soon.

So great was the crush of people, we could not get within a hundred yards of the mosque. A black wave of mourning women lay on the ground, trying to enfold their children. The men walked about in circles. We were part of a nameless and faceless lost human herd.

Ibrahim stood rudderless in the midst of this sea of agony. "Let us get out of here," he ordered, but it was the first time I ever saw him visibly denuded of some kind of command of a situation—or of himself.

We drifted away until the crowd thinned out and then we poked about the streets on the outskirts, looking for a covered shed, an abandoned building, anything with walls and a roof.

Then came the shocking realization that the houses of Tulkarm were padlocked against us. Chickens, goats, and livestock had been removed from the yards and corralled away against theft. Bony dogs stood hostile guard with teeth bared and hackles up as we passed. Behind every dimmed window one could sense a man with a gun watching our moves.

Beyond the town, where the farms began, many people were sleeping in the ditches along the road as the farmers prowled their fields to protect their crops. After a half mile or so, we came to a long stone wall encircling an olive grove. No one seemed to be on watch, so we climbed the wall and pressed against it, trying to disappear into it.

Ibrahim called out our names in the order we were to stand watch. He gave Omar his pistol and slumped down. At that instant, I caught his eye. They were glazed as though he had suddenly come face-to-face with a vision of hell. I stayed up and watched, for his behavior frightened me. He gave me a dull glimmer of recognition.

"Why do you stare, Ishmael?" my father's voice said softly.

"We have no cousins here," I answered.

"But we are still in our own land. There is confusion for the moment because the real war has begun, but we are among our own people."

"Father, they have locked us out."

"No no. They are frightened. The Jews are just across the road. You will see. In a day we will be provided with food and shelter. A camp of some sort will be made."

"Are you sure?"

"I have never turned a man away from Tabah. These are our brothers. Besides, it says in the Koran that we shall provide for one another."

"Are you certain it says that in the Koran?"

It was as though I had struck him a blow. My father's bewilderment was not only over the masses of fleeing people but the ugly reception we had received in Ramle and Jaffa and now in Tulkarm. The tradition of hospitality was ingrained in us and it was deeper in no man more than my father. We bragged of our hospitality endlessly. It was us, our culture, our humanity. Protection and providing for a guest were part of our very manhood.

"Go to sleep," he said.

"Yes, Father."

Neither of us slept, but we spoke no more. When his eyes finally did shut and he slid to the ground between his wives, I allowed myself to doze.

My sleep became hard and deep and filled with ugly scenes. Many times I knew I was lying on the ground in an olive orchard, but I was unable to move even a finger. Exhaustion had struck us half dead, yet it twisted my mind with nightmares. I knew that my father had suffered one of the most terrible moments of his life, in that our legend of hospitality might be a myth. This pene-

trated through my darkness, jumbled up with scenes of my
mother being raped. Other dreams were equally horrible . . .
the dream that Haj Ibrahim was no longer able to protect us and
make our decisions . . . oh night, night, night . . . END!

"Get off our land!"

We were hacked out of our sleep by a semi-circle of growling
dogs and their gun-bearing masters beckoning us to leave. My
father came to his feet first as the rest of us quivered up against
the wall. Haj Ibrahim surveyed them contemptuously.

"You are not Arabs," he spat out. "You are not even Jews. Your
assholes are so close to your mouths I can smell the shit on your
breath. Come, we leave."

Miraculously we found what seemed to be the last tree in
Tulkarm that didn't either shelter another family or stand on
hostile property. We gathered under it and waited until my father
came up with some sort of plan.

Every last belonging, except for Father's pistol and dagger, was
laid on a blanket, along with the money Gideon Asch had given
us and the few pounds that remained from Father's transaction
with Mr. Bassam. I was allowed to keep Gideon's watch. Ear-
rings, bracelets, the most sentimental and precious personal
trinkets went onto the blanket. Haj Ibrahim's silver buckle,
Kamal's ring, a few bits of gold my mother had hoarded and
hidden. My father reckoned we could live for a few weeks on
what we could sell and during that time he would devise a
scheme. Well enough, but he could not answer our questions and
did not allow them.

Hagar was sent into town to the market to round up a frugal
breakfast of figs, goat's cheese, and a cup of milk for Fatima's
baby, for her own milk had soured in the past week.

My father remained to protect the women and ordered my
brothers and me to search for a room to rent. In ordinary times,
we could find a room in a place like Tulkarm for a pound or two a
month. Now, even on the outskirts, the farmers were asking five
pounds for chicken coops and cow stalls and the price continued
to rise as we got closer to the central square.

Everyone was packed close to the mosque, where martial music
blared from the minaret's loudspeaker, interrupted every few moments by an announcement.

"THE ARAB LEGION HAS CROSSED THE JOR-
DAN!"
"THE IRAQIS ARE ALREADY IN NABLUS!"
"TEL AVIV HAS BEEN BOMBED BY THE EGYP-
TIAN AIR FORCE!"
"THE SYRIANS HAVE SWEPT DOWN FROM THE
GOLAN INTO NORTHERN GALILEE!"
"LEBANON REPORTS SUCCESS ALL ALONG ITS
SOUTHERN FRONTIER!"

Rumors of one victory after another deluged conversation. Every new report over the loudspeaker ended with a chilling declaration of what was going to happen to the Jews. On the one hand,
my brothers and I were swept up in the exuberance of the moment. On the other, we were shaken with hunger, our displace-
ment, and the total mystery of our situation. Within half an hour,
it was clear that any shelter to rent was beyond our means.

By the fourth day in Tulkarm, our quandary had deepened. We
had a tree that gave us shelter of sorts and enough money to stay a
half step ahead of starvation. Otherwise we did not know where
to go or what to do. No government officials or relief agencies had
made an appearance, nor did anyone know of a town that had
organized anything to help us. Haj Ibrahim seemed impotent in
the situation and this worsened our fears.

Rumors spilled out like a million leaves blown from a tree,
twisting and fluttering aimlessly. Things looked very good for
our armies. Even Father, who was always skeptical of exaggera-
tions, could not help but get caught up in the fever. He hinted
that perhaps the Arab leaders had been telling the truth when
they asked us to leave to make the way clear for their armies. Our
simple problem was to be able to hold out until we could return
to Tabah.

We had scavenged the area and had a makeshift tenting of skins,
canvas, wood, and tin. The women had set up a crude but work-
able stove. During this time, my brothers and I began to feel
closer. I even got along with Kamal.

We were in Samaria on the West Bank of the river. Three
towns—Tulkarm, Jenin, and Nablus—formed what was called
the "triangle." Within, it was all-Arab territory. Kaukji's Army of
Liberation began to move in, but we no longer feared them, for
we had no reason to believe they were still looking for Ibrahim.

Soon forward elements of the regular Iraqi Army linked up
with them. The military strategy was obvious. From where we
were in Tulkarm, it was only a distance of ten miles to the sea and
a Jewish city named Netanya. If Kaukji and the Iraqis could drive
to Netanya, the Jews would be cut in half.

Skirmishing was very close to us, but in a strange way it
helped. Every time a small battle erupted, the farmers would either run away or they would hide. My brothers and I took advantage of this to loot orchards, pull up what could be taken from the
fields, and run down stray livestock. With our stomachs filled, our
spirits soared.

The Arab victory march continued! As the Iraqis and Kaukji
poised to push to the sea, the Jews were on the defensive all over
Palestine. . . .

Egypt advanced in two columns. Gaza and Beersheba were
taken and the Kibbutz Yad Mordechai was captured!

Syria captured Kibbutz Mishmar Hayarden and spilled into
the central Galilee!

Moslem Brotherhood battalions under Egyptian command
raced up the Dead Sea toward Jerusalem!

The greatest victories of all went to the Jordanian Legion. The
four kibbutzim of the Etzion Bloc were captured, as was the Jewish Quarter of the Old City of Jerusalem. And West Jerusalem
was under attack! But most of all, the police fortress at Latrun
was in Legion hands! That meant the Legion was only two miles
from Tabah!

As suddenly as our mighty march had mounted, it seemed to
collapse. Kibbutzim which had previously been reported as having fallen were now reported as putting up stiff resistance. The
Iraqi breakthrough to Netanya never materialized. In fact, the
Jews were now attacking the "triangle."

When our forces agreed to a truce and freeze in place, it was
not in the manner of a victorious army.

On a grim night in the middle of June, Haj Ibrahim called us
all to the fire. "We leave tomorrow," he announced tersely.

"But, Father, why?"

"Because we have been lied to and betrayed. If we agreed to
this truce, it was because we did not succeed. Our attack to the
sea has been broken. It will only be a matter of days before the
Jews hit Tulkarm."

"But the Legion is on the walls of the Old City."

"They will never throw the Jews out of Jerusalem," Ibrahim answered. "Witness my words."

In the morning, we broke camp and took to the road again, this time moving deeper into Arab territory, into the mountains of Samaria, to Nablus. Again we were greeted by locked doors.

Chapter Two

Nablus, the major city of Samaria, nestled as a king of the hills amid the spine of low mountains that ran down half the length of Palestine. As the biblical city of Shechem, it had once held the Ark of the Covenant and had known Joshua, the Judges of Israel, and the conquerors from Rome. Nablus and its forty thousand people had a reputation for short tempers and the development of magnificent smuggling routes from Trans-Jordan.

Since the removal of the Ottomans, the city had become a fiefdom of the Bakshir tribe, a wily band of political survivors. The present mayor, Clovis Bakshir, appeared to be a mild sort, more clever than forceful. He had been a teacher who received the major part of his education at the American University of Beirut. Professional men were held in enormous esteem in the Arab society and the Bakshirs always had an heir apparent or two in college.

The predicament of the displaced persons was no better than it had been in Tulkarm. It was further inland and considered in safer Arab territory and there were more hillside nooks and crannies to afford a measure of shelter. But food, medicine, and other relief were not to be had. The welcome was icy.

The Nablus casbah, an ancient, dilapidated, scum-packed quarter, held the usual crush of people that inhabited a ghetto, but in any casbah one could always find space for one more or twenty more. Haj Ibrahim was able to rent a rooftop for the bloated sum of three pounds a month. A tent composed of various materials was pitched over the family's heads.

The Nablus area was enriched by sixteen natural springs and a well in the center of the casbah eliminated one of our most desperate needs, that of fresh water. Summer was coming on. The city's height of nearly three thousand feet would offer a smattering of relief, but when the wind blew hot over the Jordan it could melt steel. Casbah life on a rooftop was a treadmill of sounds, mostly sharp and vulgar; of odors, mostly foul; and sights, mostly threadbare.

There were a few extremely lowly jobs to be had. These were not pursued with zeal, for hard labor was repugnant. Obviously Haj Ibrahim could not be reduced to menial work, but he did have four able-bodied sons.

The displaced in Nablus and its surrounding hills died every day from starvation and disease. Some days there were one or two dead, some days a dozen. Nothing was done about it until the stench reached the homes of the wealthy. The municipality finally undertook the task of corpse removal. This created a number of jobs. Pits had to be dug, bodies collected and detoxified by a layer of lime. Omar and Jamil had the dubious distinction of keeping our family alive by burying others.

Although there were openings, collecting dead bodies was not for me. Neither was begging or selling chewing gum. Yet I was twelve years old and I had to carry my share. There were a number of Iraqi Army camps about, but the competition for jobs among boys of my age was fierce. Most simply begged for handouts. A few picked up a couple of pennies a day, running errands or doing work details that the soldiers had been assigned to do. Some lucky ones latched onto an officer and polished shoes and buckles and served tables. The higher officers, of course, had their own orderlies to take care of their every whim. Some of the more desperate and attractive boys sold their bodies to the soldiers.

Prostitution has always been the faithless companion of armies and Nablus was filled with hungry women. In addition to the old-time prostitutes of the casbah, there were hundreds of women now willing to take that final step. It had to be done with great care, so husbands and sons would not know. Widows, women one or two months pregnant, and spinsters were the safest. It meant instant death if one were discovered. The professional pimps could easily blackmail a woman and were avoided. Young boys from another clan proved to be the most skillful and reliable pimps. A clever boy working the camp gates for two or three women was able to feed his family without their knowledge of how he got his money.

The new arrivals came into competition with the established Nablus pimps and prostitutes and there were many killings each week. A young pimp always had his balls cut off when he was murdered. In other instances, fathers and brothers learned of a whoring mother or sister and death followed quickly. Along with the thieves and smugglers and dope fiends, the casbah was a frightening place.

Iraqi soldiers in the ranks were very poor and usually quite stupid. Yet they always managed to have something to trade for a woman: cigarettes, arms, a pair of shoes stolen from a comrade, food from the quartermaster. Low-ranking soldiers were not a bad deal because they got their business over with quickly—in the bushes. The women were always veiled so they could not be identified later and a smart one could service a platoon of men in an hour.

On the other hand, the Iraqi officers were demigods of abnormal power. These were serviced by the established prostitutes, who provided drink, oils, a softly lit room walled with carpets to cover the hideousness of the casbah, radio music, hashish, a well-pillowed bed in a dark corner.

Omar and Jamil were collecting corpses and we were still hungry all the time. I began to think about running a pair of girls. I had not lost my deeply ingrained morality about the honor of women, but honor and starvation have difficulty living side by side. Each time the thought came to me, so did the visions of the rape of the women of my family in Jaffa. Girls liked me very much and approached me many times to pimp for them.

But I always thought about Nada. I would rather see Nada die of starvation than submit. I had sworn to protect her from the moment we left Tabah. She was fourteen and had grown breasts and become alluring. I would not so much as let her walk through the casbah alone. I simply could not pimp for anyone's sister. I had a final consideration in the matter. If Haj Ibrahim ever knew I pimped, he would beat me to death.

We often finished our meals with our bellies still rumbling and I thought of joining Omar and Jamil on the corpse removal job but decided to try a few more days of hanging around the Iraqi camps.

If you keep your eyes on the street day and night looking for a penny, sooner or later one will show up. My good fortune fell on me from the sky one day. Many of the casbah refugee boys hung around the Iraqi quartermaster compound, waiting for convoys of trucks to be unloaded. The soldiers on the unloading detail would pay us an odd lira or two to do their job. One or two soldiers stayed to watch us so we would not steal and the rest of them either went to sleep under a tree or to the casbah to find a whore.

It never rained in Nablus this time of year, but a freak storm had driven everyone to cover so that there were only a few dozen boys around. By the Prophet's grace, a convoy of a dozen trucks suddenly showed up and we all had work. The soldiers assigned to the detail disappeared. The officer in charge of the convoy was of high rank—a captain—and he, too, headed into Nablus. Those detailed to keep an eye on us unloading were soon driven into the cabs of the trucks by the rain and within moments were asleep.

So here we were, emptying trucks into a warehouse with no one watching us. The only question was how much to leave for the Iraqi Army. One of the gang leaders rounded up four donkeys, loaded them to the breaking point, and fled.

I took the gamble of my life and stayed on. When the captain returned, I feigned mighty tears, then faced him with the fact that a dozen machine guns had been stolen. At first he went into a rage and tried to choke the names of the other boys out of me. I impressed upon him that even if I knew the names and we found the thieves, they could never be caught inside the casbah. Besides that, he was still responsible because his troops were supposed to have done the unloading. The captain was not very smart. His name was Umrum and he didn't know a mule's ass from a lemon.

Officers like Umrum usually were the sons of rich families who paid the Army for their rank. When enough wealthy families had enough sons with enough rank in the Army, their own comforts were well protected. Well, Captain Umrum had his balls twisted good. After his fury was spent, he began to weep about being ruined. At that time, I calmly showed him a way we could doctor the manifests to indicate that nothing was missing.

From then on, my family ate as well as anyone in the casbah. Because Kamal could read, write, and manipulate books, he also became employed by the Iraqi Army.

Haj Ibrahim never stopped seething over the situation of the displaced people. No family, however destitute, however poor a farmer and manager, however impoverished a widow, however gnarled a beggar, had ever missed a meal in Tabah. The institutionalized snubs of our brother Arabs all but devoured him with grief and rage.

To make matters worse, Omar and Jamil came home every night from their corpse burying job smelling so bad we could barely be under the same tent with them. They were often sick and vomited. Then they would go over the events of the day, imposing every gruesome detail of a rotted arm falling off or a family of five infants found dead in a cave or equally nauseating stories of maggots.

My father had the women patch up his robes and he made to the city hall for the purpose of an appointment with Mayor Clovis Bakshir. It was futile. The municipality was jammed from morning to night with hundreds of screaming displaced petitioners.

It is part of Sunna that it was the right of even the lowest man in the realm to be able to petition a king personally. This was also Bedouin tradition. The Bakshirs of Nablus and all the other powerful figures had long refined the Sunna. The petitioner was deftly moved to a minor official without authority who kept his job by magnificently, professionally lying. In Nablus no one had the chance of a two-legged camel. They wanted us out of their city, period.

Seeing my father's frustration waiver between fits of rage and fits of despair, I decided to take a hand in the matter. I took some official Iraqi Army stationery from the desk of Captain Umrum and wrote a letter to the mayor.

Most Honorable and Noble Mayor Bakshir, I and my troops have been poised for the conquest of West Jerusalem and will complete the mission the moment the truce is ended. Therefore, I have not had the honor of paying my compliments to you personally. I understand I and my troops will be stationed in Nablus until stability is returned. Until such time as we have the pleasure of a personal meeting and long friendship, I beseech you for a small favor.

My great personal friend, Haj Ibrahim al Soukori al Wahhabi, Muktar of Tabah and a powerful figure in his region, is a visitor in Nablus due to the unfortunate circumstances of the war.

As long as my troops will be stationed in your city for an indefinite period in the future, I feel such favors are in order. I would be personally and eternally grateful for you to meet with him. He is a distinguished man who has great interest in present and future events.

Haj Ibrahim can be contacted by his son Ishmael who awaits in your outer office.

Yours in victory.
Praise Allah!
Colonel I. J. Hakkar,
Adjutant, Nihawand Brigade,
Army of Iraq

I decorated the letter with seals and ribbons and set out for city hall. I had scribbled the "colonel's" name so it was unreadable. The Nihawand Brigade was named for the final Arab victory over the Persians in the seventh century. I knew they were in the Jerusalem area.

I pushed my way into the mob in the mayor's outer office and every time someone objected to me moving up the line, I held up the letter and they shrank back in respect. The mayor had four clerks at four desks screaming back at the waves of petitioners. I jammed the letter in one of their faces. He took a look at the envelope and disappeared into the mayor's office. In less than a moment, he returned and advised me that my father had an appointment at the home of Clovis Bakshir the next day.

Chapter Three

My father was chagrined at first that I had concocted such a clever scheme to get him an appointment with Mayor Clovis Bakshir. Of course, he had to agree to the existence of the fictitious letter writer, Colonel Hakkar. Then he thought again.

"A lie used in the proper time and place can be a piece of pure poetry," he assured me.

Since Kamal and I now worked regularly for the Iraqi quartermaster, that lazy and ignorant scum, Captain Umrum, we always had cigarettes to spirit home under our robes. The rich live on a gold standard. The Bedouin lives on a dung standard. In the casbah, we lived on a tobacco standard and it was better than money. Our cigarette sales put a few more pennies into the family pot. We insisted that Haj Ibrahim buy new robes for his meeting with the mayor so he would be spared the humiliation of his rags.

"No," my father said defiantly. "Let Clovis Bakshir see what we have been reduced to. Besides, as long as I have my dagger in my belt, I am well dressed. I am sorry you will not be with me, Ishmael." He patted my head and left alone.

For Ibrahim, the meeting was a renewal of an old alliance. The Haj had known the family briefly during the Mufti's revolt. From time to time, the Bakshirs had been hidden from the Mufti's troops in Tabah and later were taken down to the Wahhabis for safekeeping. Clovis Bakshir's welcome was sufficiently friendly and the fruit bowl well stocked but not overwhelming.

Clovis Bakshir was a small man, almost delicate, who spoke with outcroppings of his university education. He was a study in deliberate calm and smoothness. The only thing that gave away the churning in his innards was his chain-smoking and tobacco-varnished fingers.

"Obviously, it is not possible for me to know of everyone who is in Nablus in these times. Had I realized you were here . . ."

"Your predicament is completely understood," Ibrahim answered. "We only have so many eyes and ears."

They repaired to the cool of the veranda. One could not see the town, for the villa was in a rare wooded area. One of the underground streams surfaced nearby and continued on as a brook, with a petite waterfall just over the way. There was a café by the waterfall that was the central meeting place for the men of the Bakshir tribe. In more peaceful times, Clovis Bakshir held court by the stream.

Haj Ibrahim was puzzled and immediately suspicious to see a second man waiting on the veranda. He quickly noticed the man's ramrod posture, sun-baked face, and immaculately trimmed and plastered moustache. He wore a Western suit of superior material and a traditional Arab headdress.

"My good friend and confidant, Mr. Farid Zyyad. I was certain that your experiences and observations would be of great interest to him."

As coffee was served, Haj Ibrahim had already begun to maneuver to find out the meaning of this unexpected guest. Zyyad moved himself inconspicuously out of the line of conversation, off to a side. Highly polished shoes, something rarely seen in these parts, offered another tiny clue. Whoever he was, he was upper echelon.

Clovis Bakshir lit the first of many cigarettes, which were drawn on rapturously by long, thoughtful inhalations and exhaled in thin streams, like an extension of the man himself. The ashes were never flicked and never fell but only grew agonizingly longer. "Of course I will do what is possible to make your stay in Nablus more comfortable," the Mayor said.

Haj Ibrahim nodded an acknowledgment. "I am not the kind of man to lead you over the desert following camel turds," Ibrahim said. "I have serious things on my mind, other than my personal condition."

"Even so far away as Nablus, we have heard of Haj Ibrahim's notable candor," the mayor replied.

"I am bitterly pained by the behavior of the people. I never believed I would live to see our great tradition of hospitality suddenly fall from honor."

"Nor did I," Clovis Bakshir agreed.

"We are not foreigners. We are not Turks. We are not Jews," Ibrahim said pointedly.

"You must understand that this entire refugee situation crashed down on us like a sudden storm and has all but drowned us."

"Refugee? What do you mean, refugee?" Ibrahim said. "My village is less than two hours from here. I am a Palestinian in my own country among my own people. I am not a refugee!"

Clovis Bakshir remained professionally unflappable. "Victims of war," he corrected, "displaced on a temporary basis."

"I am a Palestinian and I am in Palestine," Ibrahim repeated.

"Yes yes."

"Be it known I was forced from my village—and not by Jewish gunfire. For months the entire Arab world spoke to us with one single voice. Get out. No one had a different opinion."

"What other opinion could there be with this Zionist monster growing right inside our bellies?" Clovis asked.

"We have chairs, we have tables, we have coffee, we have men. Men can come and sit in the chairs, drink coffee at the tables and discuss the possibilities of peace. I have lived half my life next to a Jewish settlement and only occasionally found them unreasonable. Let me say in my well-known candor that the Jews have never done to me and my people what has happened in the last two months at the hands of our own brothers."

"Fortunately your village was not Deir Yassin."

"Yes. I did not permit Tabah to be used indiscriminately to draw us into such a reprisal."

"Perhaps, in the beginning, there were different opinions," Clovis Bakshir said. "The voices of moderation and peace were too small and too weak. The obsession of destroying the Jews swept over every town and village in the Arab world down to the smallest peasant. It was a tidal wave."

A silence fell that was so great the sound of the small waterfall a distance away imposed itself onto the scene.

"Mayor Bakshir. The deepest hurt of my life has been the manner in which we have been treated. Not a crust of bread, not a blanket, not a cup of water has been offered us. And Nablus is not among the least innocent in this matter."

"I also am painfully aware of the matter, Haj Ibrahim. This is not the normal behavior of our people. One morning we suddenly awake to find our whole population fleeing. Even though we are here in safe Arab territory, we have been terrified by events. First Kaukji came and stripped our fields. Afterward the

Iraqi Army treated us very rudely. The Iraqis have fed and supplied their army largely from our crops and our shops without
payment. Are we patriotic Arabs or not? they ask. Our few police
cannot cope with armies. By the time the refugees . . . forgive
me . . . the displaced persons began pouring . . . flood-
ing . . . engulfing this part of Palestine, everyone here was in a
state of panic."

"I cannot accept these excuses," Ibrahim retorted. "The behavior of our troops has been a disgrace to Arab manhood. As for me,
for a quarter of a century I was the Muktar of Tabah and never
once in that time did we turn a stranger from our doors."

"But you never woke up one morning to discover fifty thousand people camped in your square. The catastrophe was simply
too great and came too quickly."

"What do you mean by suddenly? We have been planning this
war for ten years. It did not come suddenly. Months have passed
since the United Nations resolution. Month after month we have
been told that we are to abandon our villages to make way for our
armies. The leaders who insisted that we leave are damned well
responsible to see that we were welcomed, fed, and sheltered.
Every army has a staff to make preparations for war. Who prepared for us? Not a single tent city, not a single kitchen, no one
even on the roads to give us directions."

"Long-range planning has never been one of our stronger qualities," Clovis Bakshir answered. "And no one could have calculated the extent of the catastrophe." Clovis Bakshir put the cigarette butt into an ashtray gently, just as it was about to nip his
fingers. He lit another cigarette. "It is true. We were not ready."

"In the name of Allah, what are governments for, if not to care
for their very own people?"

"Haj Ibrahim, we have no Arab government in Palestine. The
entire Arab world is not a union of nations but a collection of
tribes. I have been the mayor of Nablus for ten years since my
beloved brother was murdered by the Mufti's gangsters. Look at
this neighborhood. It is very beautiful, no?"

"What are you getting at?"

"It is not a neighborhood," Clovis Bakshir said. "It is a collection of walled houses. My neighbors throw their garbage over the
wall, then come to me and complain that it hasn't been collected.
They say to me, Clovis Bakshir, why hasn't the government col-

lected the garbage? I tell them it costs money and if they will pay taxes, the garbage will be collected.

"Haj Ibrahim, did you collect taxes in Tabah to have paved streets or a school or a clinic or electricity? Did you ever try to form a committee to work for projects in Tabah? I fear that our people do not know how to participate in a community. Government to them is a mystical extension of Islam, something that falls out of the sky. They want rulers to take care of them, with no conception that they get only what kind of government they are willing to pay for."

"Why this lecture, Mayor Bakshir?"

"To remind you that the Palestinian people have never ruled themselves, nor ever attempted to rule themselves. We have been content for a thousand years to let people outside of Palestine make all the decisions for us. There was no possibility that any authority in Palestine could have prepared us for this war. Do you think the Mufti would have had food and shelter for war victims?"

"Haj Ibrahim," Farid Zyyad said, arising and stepping into the sunlight. "What do you make of the military situation?"

Well, this Zyyad person is here for a reason and the plot is about to unfold. I think he is a Jordanian. The Bakshirs fought the Mufti and have remained deadly enemies. Clovis Bakshir is certainly casting his fate with King Abdullah. Even though this front is manned by Kaukji and the Iraqis, contingents of the Jordanian Legion are filtering in. For what reason? Certainly to lay future claim to the West Bank. No doubt the Jordanians have a list of muktars, mayors, and other prominent Palestinians who had been enemies of the Mufti. My own name would have to be on such a list.

"What do I make of the war? I am not a military man," Ibrahim fenced. "Besides, I have been living on the run for almost two months."

"But you ruled a strategic village and most of the Ayalon Valley for a quarter of a century," Zyyad interjected. "Your modesty is not justified."

"Perhaps you would be in a better position to tell me what you think of the situation, Mr. Zyyad."

"Yes, of course," Zyyad said. "This is only my opinion," he said and went into a standard dissertation of the latest Arab line. "During the truce, the Arab armies were regrouping for their

final assaults. The Legion will eject the Jews from West Jerusalem
while the Iraqis and Kaukji will drive to the sea to cut the Jews in
half. It will be over in a month after the truce."

Why am I being tested like this? This man knows his story is out of
The Arabian Nights. *How shall I play the game?*

"We do not have the chance of a small fart in a large windstorm," Ibrahim said, sending the pair groping for cigarettes and
fishing in the fruit bowl. "If there is any truth to what you say, it
would not have been thrown out with the garbage."

"Garbage!"

"The truce is garbage. Winning armies do not agree to truces.
Our armies are spent. If we did not destroy the Jews with our
first blows, we will not destroy them. We had to overrun fifty or
sixty settlements. We had to take a major Jewish city. We have not
budged them, except in a few isolated places. Now Jewish artillery is starting to appear and if I am not mistaken they are attacking the triangle itself. The Jews have found old German war
planes. We no longer wave when we see a plane in the sky; we
run for a ditch. If the truce ends, the Jews are going onto the
offensive and may even reach Nablus."

"For a man who knows nothing of military matters, you ven-
ture some interesting opinions," Bakshir said.

"The Jews are not sleeping in the fields. We are. They are home
defending their settlements as we should have done. The Jews
will not run. The Jews will not surrender. They will fight to the
last man, not only over the radio and in the newspapers but on
the battlefield. You are a military man, Mr. Zyyad. How many
men will we be willing to lose trying to capture Tel Aviv, Haifa,
and Jerusalem? A million? Two? What combination of Arab armies will commit to such a sacrifice—and if they do, who will
have the stamina to carry it out?"

"What makes you think I am a military person?"

"Your straight back. Your accent is Trans-Jordan mixed with
English. You are British-trained. You are of Bedouin birth. You
have a tattoo on the back of your hand that tells me so. Put it all
together with your fancy shoes and that would make you an officer in the Arab Legion. Everyone in the casbah knows that
Mayor Bakshir and King Abdullah are in some sort of secret alliance. So . . . why all the mysteries?"

"You are taking all the joy out of this," Clovis Bakshir said.

If Zyyad owned a sense of humor, it was not apparent. "I am Colonel Farid Zyyad of the Arab Legion, as you surmise," he announced stiffly. "I am on a personal mission for His Majesty, King Abdullah. Your perception that the war may truly be over is an opinion that has merit and quite a few followers. Surely you realize that of all the Arab countries, Jordan alone will end up with Palestinian territory. We hold the police fort at Latrun. It is two miles from Tabah. One push to recapture Ramle and Lydda and you are back in your village."

Is that the shit I came here to listen to?

"Look at me, Colonel Zyyad. I am naked. A thousand thieves cannot strip a dead man. What you tell me is the cruelest hoax of them all. Your Legion is our best army, but your line is stretched so thin a feather could blow through it. You are not coming out of Latrun on the attack and you know it." Zyyad started to speak, but Ibrahim overrode him. "You know that the Jews have successfully built a road to Jerusalem through the mountains that bypasses Latrun. Now you are moving your last contingents here into the triangle to claim it for Abdullah and you are stretched even thinner. The Arab Legion could not raise another battalion of troops if half the recruits were camels. You want this war to end here and now."

The colonel and the mayor stared at one another, stunned.

"Now, my brothers, what is it you want of me?"

Zyyad nodded to Clovis Bakshir. "Haj Ibrahim," the Mayor said, "King Abdullah is not a fanatic on the subject of the Jews. I can tell you he was dragged into the war against his will."

"And I can guarantee you that the Arab states will never permit Abdullah to make peace with the Jews," Ibrahim retorted.

"Peace will come in good time," Bakshir continued. "The point is, we also believe the war will not go further. Palestine is up for grabs. We do not want to be pushed back across the river for continuing the war. What is important is that those parts of the country in Arab hands should stay in Arab hands. You challenged me about governing ourselves. We can't do it. Our only Palestinian choice is the Mufti and his people are already gathering in Gaza. With Egyptian backing, they may lay claim to the West Bank as the Palestinian state."

"By Allah's beard! That is already what the United Nations

offered us! Why in the hell are we fighting this war? Why are our people sleeping in the fields?"

"Nothing was going to be satisfied until our armies tried to crush this Jewish state. They came; they did not conquer. Now we are down to a choice between King Abdullah and the Mufti."

"The Palestine Mandate is a single piece of cloth," Colonel Zyyad said. "I considered myself a Palestinian all my life. Most of the people of Amman consider themselves Palestinians. When the British created Jordan, all they did was change the name of part of Palestine. We are the same people with the same history. King Abdullah's flag now flies over the Dome of the Rock in East Jerusalem and with the annexation of the West Bank we go from a small country to a great one."

It is also no secret, my dear brothers, that King Abdullah froths with ambition. He has fantasies of a Greater Palestine, a Greater Syria . . . Allah only knows, a Greater Arab Nation.

"It might not be very popular in Cairo," Haj Ibrahim said.

"We must also now accept that Jordan has always been part of Palestine," Clovis Bakshir interceded. "This will give us a traditional ruler and his army. Mainly, it gives us the means to stop the return of the Mufti."

"Let me match your candor, Haj Ibrahim," Colonel Zyyad spoke. "You are in a position to help us. King Abdullah is soon to declare that Jordan is open to all Palestinians displaced by the war. We will take the people from the fields and see to it they are fed. With your stature, you could convince thousands of displaced persons to end their suffering by crossing the Allenby Bridge and coming to Amman. It is not for general consumption, but there will also be a declaration that Jordan will grant automatic citizenship to any Palestinian who so desires."

How humanitarian, Ibrahim thought. The little king rules an impoverished Bedouin wasteland that cannot feed itself. If the British leave with their subsidy, it will be a beggar nation. It cannot survive without money from the Syrian and Egyptian and Saudi treasuries. Abdullah is now trying to artificially inflate his population and use us to lay claim to lands that do not belong to him. The king is farting higher than his ass. He will be dead within a year, assassinated by brother Arabs.

"We envision important roles for those Palestinians who cooperate with us now," Zyyad said. "If I were to submit your name as one of our supporters, no appointment is impossible, even up to Cabinet minister."

The man speaks nothing of returning us to our homes and fields. We are but pawns being used for Abdullah's ambitions. All he wants is collaborators.

"How does my personal friendship with Gideon Asch enter into your thinking?" the Haj asked bluntly.

Colonel Zyyad was once more jolted by Ibrahim's directness. "As I have stated, Abdullah is not losing sleep over the thought of a Jewish nation next to his. Obviously, we will not be able to recognize it publicly or make a peace treaty. However, we want to keep discreet contact with the Jews at all times. We can even envision peace with the Jews when enough time has passed."

"Surely, Colonel Zyyad, when this war is done, the Arabs will have suffered their greatest humiliation in all our history. Our society and our religion dictate that we must continue to fight the Jews forever."

"Why don't we concentrate our thoughts on what is the best course for our people here and now and let the future work itself out," Clovis Bakshir said. "We are being offered an opportunity to alleviate their suffering."

Haj Ibrahim listened, asked questions, and began to give indications that he was coming into the scheme. The meeting ended. Colonel Zyyad reckoned that it would take him two or three weeks to finish his work on the West Bank, return to Amman, and then come back with specific orders for Haj Ibrahim. He departed.

Clovis Bakshir slapped his forehead in sudden remembrance. "How stupid of me," he said. "I forgot. My brother has a small villa nearby. He left for Europe after the partition vote . . . to further his education. I offer it to you and your sons and the rest of your family."

Finally Clovis Bakshir wrote a letter on official stationery, permitting Haj Ibrahim to enter the Red Crescent warehouse and to help himself to food, blankets, clothing, medicine, whatever he needed.

"I am overwhelmed," Ibrahim said, "but I was led to believe there were no relief supplies in Nablus."

Clovis Bakshir held his hands open in a gesture of innocence. "In our situation, the military must be served first."

Chapter Four

One day onions, one day honey. Here we were, living in the wretched casbah of Nablus on Thursday, and on Friday we were moved to a villa. None of us, except Father, had ever been inside of a house so fine. The women clucked all day with joy as they went about their chores. Even Hagar, who had never smiled since Ramiza had come into our house, could not restrain her pleasure.

The owner of the home was Clovis Bakshir's younger brother, who had fled the country right after the United Nations partition vote. An engineer, he had a small office filled with books in Arabic and English, so I went very quickly from the first to the second paradise.

And then I discovered a third! There was a gymnasium—a school of higher education—in Nablus. I needed wait only till the right moment to bring it up with my father.

A week after we had moved in, Haj Ibrahim asked me out to the veranda in the evening to speak to him. Despite our change in fortune, my father did not seem very happy.

"I have many questions to ask you, Ishmael," he said.

It made me immediately proud that a man as great as my father would be seeking my advice. My ascension to the third paradise—enrolling in the gymnasium—was always in the back of my mind and perhaps this would be a good time to bring it up.

"Are you able to calculate how many tins of olive oil the family uses in a year?"

His question took me by surprise. "Mumkin," I answered automatically. "Perhaps."

"I don't want mumkin for an answer," Ibrahim said. "A billion times a day you hear mumkin. We live on too much mumkin. I want a direct yes or no."

"I am sure after I talk it over with Hagar . . ."

"Can you figure out other things like beans, rice, and other nonperishable staples?"

"For a year?" I asked.

"For a year."

"Everything we would need to eat in a year that would not spoil?"

"Yes."

"Mumkin," I said.

"Yes or no!" my father said, lifting his voice a notch.

Apprehension was creeping in. I could smell what he was getting at. I recalled the great jars and sacks of food at Tabah, along with the bins. "Yes," I answered unevenly.

"Can you calculate how many gallons of kerosene we would require for cooking, light, and heat?"

"I cannot be exactly, actually, and completely precise, but I can come close," I said, trying to create leverage for myself.

"Good, good. Now, Ishmael, tell me. Can you think of all the necessary requirements we would need, such as sleeping mats, cooking utensils, blankets, soap, matches . . . the various things in our home in Tabah? Items that cursed dog, Farouk—I spit at the mention of his name—had in the store at Tabah. Not things we would like to have, but things we need to have. Not cloth for new clothing, but needle and thread to patch up old clothing."

"Mumkin," I mumbled.

Ibrahim glared at me.

"These are truly difficult questions," I added.

"I will help you," he answered. "The main problem is whether all of this will fit into an Iraqi Army truck, along with the family."

It was as though I could feel the blood draining from my body. Why should we ever leave such a place? Had we not suffered enough? Yet one does not question the wisdom of one's father. "I cannot answer without many hours of calculation."

"It must be done before the next Sabbath," he said.

Four days! It was crazy! However, no one in our world likes to give a direct or disappointing answer, but there was no use trying to work around Haj Ibrahim. I nodded numbly.

"How long would it take Kamal to learn to drive such a truck?"

"We already can drive a little bit. Since the truce is about to end, there are many convoys of military supplies coming in from Baghdad. When they arrive, the soldiers driving the trucks either want to go off and sleep or go to the casbah. Often Kamal and I are left alone to organize a working party to unload. We hire the boys who hang around the gate and pay them in cigarettes. I and

Kamal can drive the trucks up to the loading docks and then park
them in the yard."

"And this Captain Umrum?"

"He is seldom around and when he leaves, the other soldiers in
his command usually slip away. He is crazy for women. Father, I
don't know what you are planning, but many of the items you
mention are not in our warehouse."

My father handed me a letter and told me to read it. It was on
the stationery of the mayor, Clovis Bakshir, an order by him to
give Haj Ibrahim anything he needed from the nearby Red Crescent warehouse. Between the two warehouses there was almost
everything we would need. With such a letter, we would have no
problem.

"Is that everything?"

"No," my father said. "We must have a machine gun, four rifles
and many thousand rounds of ammunition, and, most important,
Iraqi uniforms for Jamil, Omar, and Kamal."

"The uniforms, yes; the guns, no," I answered, daring to disap-
point him. "The warehouse with the guns are not in Captain
Umrum's section anymore and it is heavily guarded all the time."

"We may have to do without the machine gun," he mumbled.
"Getting the rifles will be no problem. The casbah is filled with
deserters of both Kaukji and the Iraqis. They are all selling their
weapons on the black market. We will need lots of cigarettes to
bargain with."

"Tobacco is possible," I said to mollify him at once. "Why must
we leave?" I blurted out. "Why can't we stay just as we are?"

"Tell me, Ishmael, why do you think we got this villa?"

"Because you are a great and respected muktar," I answered.

"The fields, the ravines, the hills all around here are filled with
great and respected muktars," he said. "You have read to me
many times about Abdullah. You know who he is."

"The Hashemite King of Jordan," I answered.

"And as an educated boy, you know who the Hashemites are."

"The Hashemites are of the same clan as Mohammed. They
come from Arabia, from the Hejaz. They were keepers of the
holy places of Mecca."

"That is right," my father concurred. "They are a clan of
mosque keepers. It is a bone they threw to these dogs because of
Mohammed. None of them were ever more than minor emirs and

these titles were honorary. We are sayyids. We are also related to Mohammed and direct descendants. Believe me, Ishmael, you have more right to be the King of Jordan than Abdullah. There was no Hashemite dynasty until three months ago, only a long line of mosque keepers. This king business was an invention of the British Foreign Office, just as the whole of Jordan is an invention. They are as much a royal family as a line of donkeys at a well."

He clasped his hands behind him, his worry beads in motion, and for a moment he recited many of the ninety-nine names for Allah, then became pensive. "We must leave because once we call Abdullah master, we are his dogs forever. In order to remain in Nablus, I must agree to lure our people from the fields and over the Allenby Bridge to Amman. Abdullah needs our bodies to fill his so-called kingdom. What do I lure our people to—a land of milk and honey? I am not Moses and Jordan is not our promised land. It is a kingdom of camel shit and sand, so impoverished it could not feed an extra mouth, even at the king's coronation. The Allenby is a one-way bridge. Once it is crossed, we will not return."

"I believe I understand," I said, almost breaking into tears.

"You must understand! If there is anything we have learned with salt in our eyes in the past months, it is that our penchant for brotherhood and hospitality is fine as long as our vines are full and there is peace. When there is fear among our people, they slam the doors of mercy in our faces. What fool believes it will be any better in that wasteland over the river? Abdullah is not my king and he is not your king. He has more enemies than any man in the Arab world and, believe me, I cannot count that high."

My father slumped and his face became an agony. The prayer beads in his hands were still. His voice groaned as he spoke. "Tabah," he said. "Tabah. We must return to what we know and love. We must reclaim our land, find our people, and bring them home. These idiots here will butcher each other for eternities trying to figure out who is the ruler of Palestine." My father then looked at me, his eyes filled with sorrow. "I would want to return to Tabah tomorrow, even if the Jews are in power."

It was the first time my father had confided in me in such an open and honest manner and I would never forget it. "I am already working on a plan," I said.

He put his hand on my shoulder. "I have come to depend on you. We spend far too much time conspiring and far too little time planning."

"I will not fail," I said. "Where are we going?"

"The final part of our escape requires the help of our fictitious friend, Colonel Hakkar. You must write an order on Iraqi stationery to pass us through all lines and roadblocks. With your brothers dressed as Iraqi soldiers, we can succeed."

"I begin to see."

"When I was a boy about your age, we had a terrible plague in Tabah. I was sent to live with the Wahhabis. It was at the same time that Farouk, may Allah strike him blind, was taken in by Christians and taught to read. Our clan always moved from the Beersheba area in the summer and traveled along the Dead Sea. There is an ancient Jewish fort midway down the sea called the Masada. North of the Masada to where the sea ends near Jericho is an area filled with hundreds, perhaps thousands of caves—great caves, little caves, hidden caves, caves halfway up the cliffs. These caves have been a haven for smugglers, for great religious men, for defeated armies since time began. They are cool in the summer. Some are as large as a house. Most of them are only a mile or so inland from the sea."

"Can we drive a truck close to them?"

"Only part of the way. We will carry everything in the rest of the way. We will need much rope to make slings and pulleys and to tie supplies to our backs. After we have emptied the truck, Kamal will drive me to East Jerusalem. It will not be difficult to get rid of a surplus army vehicle."

"What about fresh water?" I asked, knowing the Dead Sea was very salty.

"You are thinking," my father said. "There is a magnificent oasis and spring called En Gedi where our great King David hid from Saul. However, there is a kibbutz nearby and I am not certain if it is in Arab or Jewish hands."

"But don't others know of these caves?"

"Perhaps. However, no one goes back into that place without supplies and who else can do it? It is the Bedouin I am worried about. They will smell our first meal from a hundred miles away. That is why we must have arms."

"Father, I beg of you . . . so long as we will be living for many months in a cave . . . that . . . I be allowed to bring some books."

"Books! Will you never change? Well, the villa we are so kindly living in is the home of a learned man who fled. Help yourself, so long as there is room in the truck. And don't trick me by changing numbers. We need food more than books."

"I promise I will not trick you," I lied. "When do we tell Kamal, Omar, and Jamil of the plan?"

"Two minutes before we put it into motion," he answered.

Figuring the supplies was a head-breaking task. I slept in little snatches day and night. The beautiful part was that I got to work with my father all the time. My brothers were suspicious of our long, isolated talks.

When I had compiled what we needed, I located everything in either the Iraqi quartermaster warehouse or the Red Crescent warehouse. I drew a map with the location of food, fuel, ropes— everything on the list. When the time would come to leave, we would not be delayed by having to search the warehouses blindly.

I brought my father several dozen cartons of cigarettes and in a single day he found not only a machine gun but two rifles, two hand-held submachine guns, ammunition, grenades, and dynamite.

I kept the plan simple. The day we were to execute it, it would be necessary to get Captain Umrum out of the way. I knew of a boy who pimped for an especially beautiful woman and made a handsome deal with him. Afterward, I began telling Captain Umrum that I had seen this fantastic creature and knew she was available. Of course Umrum, the perfect idiot, took the bait and insisted I get her for him. I assured him that I would work diligently at obtaining her for an entire day, but she was very popular and it would be difficult. He drooled as I dangled the bait.

I made up requisition lists that would pass the test of any army, much less those stupid Iraqis. I also made up a letter from Colonel Hakkar to pass us through the lines.

However, one detail disturbed me greatly. I had located a recent military map and learned that once we left Jericho, we would be on a treacherous nonroad, a path used only for camel caravans. If we hit sudden sand or water, that could end the journey on the spot. The whole business of the mechanics of the truck was the weakness of the plan. I did not want to tell Haj Ibrahim because it was always easier to work around bad news than actually deliver it. The more I pondered, the more I realized we were in jeopardy. I waited to go to my father until I could wait no longer. When he informed me that the Jordanian Colonel Zyyad was returning to Nablus in two days, I had to confront Haj Ibrahim with my heart in my mouth. My eyes were red from work and my brain was fuzzy, but mostly I feared disappointing him.

"Father," I croaked, "I must be honest with you, very honest. Neither Kamal nor I are capable of driving to Jericho through these mountains, much less into the desert. Half the Iraqi motor vehicles are in repair half the time. They are poorly maintained and they all arrive in Nablus after traveling a great distance from Baghdad. Between that and bad roads, there is no possibility of getting to the caves without breaking down. Neither Kamal nor I have the slightest idea of what goes on underneath the hood of a truck."

I was grateful that my father took the news philosophically. He realized instantly that if we had a breakdown for any length of time at any point before we reached the caves, we were as good as dead. With all those supplies and with soldiers and desperate people everywhere, we would be massacred within an hour of a breakdown. He paled.

"I have thought of something," I said.

"By the Prophet's beard, tell me!"

"There is a boy who works in the garage in my compound. His name is Sabri Salama and he is sixteen years old. He is a wizard of a mechanic and knows how to repair trucks. He can take spare parts from a broken truck to repair other trucks with. He is a great driver as well. There was a battle at his town and during the fighting he got separated from his family. He was away when the Jews struck and he could not return. He is certain his family headed for Gaza. He wants desperately to get out of Nablus. I know he will come with us if we ask him to."

My father's face turned into a dictionary of suspicion. "He cannot get from Nablus to Gaza unless he has wings. As a mechanic, he can live the war out as a prince right where he is."

"Sabri confided in me that . . . that . . . that . . ."

"What!"

"An Iraqi lieutenant has taken him . . . made him . . . forces him . . . to be his . . . his girlfriend."

My father slapped my face. It would have hurt more, but I was prepared for the blow. "It is not his fault. He has been forced by painful torture."

Haj Ibrahim gained control of his temper. "How did he learn his profession? I mean, the profession of being a mechanic?"

"His father owned a garage and five trucks, which they used to pick up crops with and transport them to Jaffa from the villages around his town."

"What town?"

"Beit Ballas."

"Beit Ballas! A city of thieves! A den of Mufti cutthroats!"

At this point, I did not care if my father beat me to death. I could not doom my family by pretending this danger did not exist.

"Father," I said, "you are now slamming the door in the face of an innocent brother, just as doors have been slammed in our faces."

I was slapped again so hard I thought my head would roll off. I wanted to scream at him to drive the goddamned truck himself, but I merely stood at attention and waited for what seemed to be twenty minutes.

"Bring this Sabri to me. I will speak to him."

It was fortunate that my father used common sense over pride. Sabri Salama proved to be not only an excellent driver, but was the difference in our making it. We opted to leave early in the morning instead of night, for the night has eyes watching us that we cannot see. If there were to be a breakdown, it would be far better to make repairs by daylight.

We had our eyes on a newly repaired truck, but it was snatched from our hands at the last moment. We had to settle for a truck that had just made the grueling run from Baghdad. When the truck was loaded, we were packed in so tight that a belch could have been disastrous. We broke down four times between Nablus and Jericho, a distance of less than fifty miles through mountain roads. At each stop we nervously staked out a guard while Sabri dove under the hood or beneath the truck. Fortunately he seemed to have the answer and the spare part every time. His was an awesome display.

Directly below Jericho, we drove over bone-breaking ground along the Dead Sea. My father began to smell the place in remembrance.

"We are close. We are close. Keep an eye out for the ruins."

"There," Omar cried.

We had come to ancient Qumran, which was now no more than a pile of rubble. My father's eyes scanned the forbidding wall of cliffs and canyons inland from the sea. He chose the first wadi bed to enter because a dry gulch would offer us some kind of road. We inched in. Within a half mile, we were stopped quite close to a canyon entrance. The truck dropped dead and we, likewise, were almost as dead from being jarred around and choked by dust and the feverish heat.

It was quickly turning dark. We would have to await daylight before setting out to find a perfect hideaway. I was only twelve years old, but already I was an Arab general.

Chapter Five

We arose with the sun. Sabri went to work immediately, repairing the truck. He reckoned that the vehicle was very sick.

Jamil was left to guard the provisions, the women, and Sabri. The four remaining men—I call myself a man cautiously—started climbing a long steep slope toward the canyon opening in search of a proper cave. It was a great day for me: I got to carry a rifle for the first time.

Several hundred feet up, the wadi bed leveled off onto a higher plateau. We moved into the canyon with its great cliffs, many thousand feet in height, hovering over both sides of us. A quarter to a half-mile inland, we found an entrance to a second canyon and split the party into two sections. I stayed with my father, while Omar and Kamal took the fork.

I had the watch which Gideon Asch had given me and Kamal also had one, courtesy of the Iraqis. I suggested we co-ordinate a time to meet later, but Ibrahim did not trust timepieces. He pointed to the sun and indicated that when it reached the midday position in the sky, we retrace our steps to the fork and discuss our findings.

Within another half mile, my father and I began to run into caves, but nothing was suitable. Most of them were several hundred feet up the cliffs, making access extremely difficult or impossible. We came to another fork. My father opted to continue down the main wadi bed, while I would go into a mini-canyon that appeared to dead end. It was a serious mistake for us to split up. As I approached the apparent dead end, it suddenly opened up into another branch of the canyon and when I tried to retrace my steps I discovered I was in a labyrinth.

As the sun seared down, the canyon walls seemed to close in. I nipped at my canteen of water and told myself not to panic. After an hour I realized I was stumbling around in a circle, unable to get my bearings and unable to find the opening.

Perhaps I said I was a man too quickly because I felt like a little boy. Do not panic, I kept telling myself. The sun slipped into the afternoon sky. I began to shout and whistle, but my own voice mocked me in echoes bouncing off the walls.

The cliffs were so high that the sun became lost and as the heat lessened I knew late afternoon was coming on. Another series of frantic shouts brought no response but my echo. I slid down to the ground, put my face in my hands, and was about to cry when I looked up.

I thought I saw a cave opening that was only fifty or so feet up a cliff. I ran across the canyon floor to get a better angle. Yes! There was an extremely large cave above me! I wanted so badly to be the one to discover the cave that some of my fear passed.

The climb was sheer, but my hands and feet were like claws. I worked my way up like a spider. A familiar smell reached my nostrils. It was the stench of corpses. I hung there on the side of the cliff, trying to make up my mind whether to go up or down.

Come on, Ishmael, I admonished, get up there. I reached a small ledge by the opening. I was frightened again, really frightened. My hand shook almost uncontrollably as I flicked on my flashlight and advanced to the opening. The beam revealed an enormous cavern, many times the size of our house. My light probed the walls. There were a number of corridors off the main room. I dared go no further, for I was already lost in the canyon and didn't want to make it worse by getting lost inside the cave.

Suddenly I panicked. The flapping of wings, bloodcurdling screeches, and a mass of black birds storming toward me! I screamed as a half-dozen vultures poured out, almost knocking me off the ledge, then circling and coming at me angrily. I backed up against the wall and fired my rifle. I did not hit anything, but the shot drove them away.

I controlled my desire to flee and inched back to the cave opening and discovered the source of the smell. Four women, a number of small children and infants, and one single man. They were recently dead and had been stripped naked by the Bedouin. Billions of those awful little maggots were devouring them.

The sound of my own breathing and grunting was so loud that it startled me. I began to hear other eerie cave noises. Had the Bedouin been watching me all the time? I realized I had intruded on a domain belonging to foul little creatures and the elusive Bedouin. Yet the cavern was so great and so close to the ground I continued to probe. I made out bird droppings and assumed I would meet their owners shortly. Bats, no doubt.

I retreated back to the ledge. From here the entrance to the subcanyon was clearly visible and could be easily guarded. Above the ledge, the cliff went up straight for what seemed like a thousand feet or more. Not even a Bedouin could make his way down to us from the top without being discovered.

How to get back to the truck and find this cave again in the morning? Could we smell our way back in? If I threw the bodies out, could we locate the cave by watching the vultures? It was revolting, but I went back in, pulled all the bodies out and threw them over the ledge, and watched the vultures cautiously continue their banquet.

There! On the edge of the ledge! They had made a rope ladder! I tested it to see if it were rotted, but it seemed strong and I knew I must take the chance. I scampered down quickly.

It was turning dark. Do I stay here now and let Father and Omar and Kamal look for me in the morning? I fired another shot at the vultures, hoping it would catch my father's ears. I missed again, but it scattered them. It occurred to me to take a rock and make markings on the walls that could lead us back to the cave.

The night closed in on me terrifyingly. I could go no further. I tucked myself into a crevice, loaded the rifle, and tried to glare through the blackness.

All kinds of noises startled me—falling rocks, the jackal who cried out that he knew of my presence, the cackle of taunting birds sizing me up for a meal.

I kept awake until I could not hold my head up any longer, snapping up with each new eerie sound.

"ISHMAEL! Ishmael! ishmael! *Ishmael! ishmael!*"

I opened my eyes with thumping heart and dry mouth!

"ISHMAEL! Ishmael! ishmael! *Ishmael! ishmael!*"

Lights and shadows played off the canyon walls and ten trillion stars were above me. For a moment I did not know where I was and when I realized, majnun—the spirit that makes you crazy—began to consume me.

"ISHMAEL! Ishmael! ishmael! *Ishmael! ishmael!*" bounced through the canyon. It was Allah, calling out for me to come to him! No! No! It was my father's voice!

"FATHER! Father! father! *Father! father!*"

Oh God, please, please, please! I begged.

"Ishmael!"

"Father!"

"Ishmael!"

"Father!"

We could not find each other, even with the moonlight, but we managed to bring our voices closer and closer. "Can you understand me!" his voice called.

"Yes!"

"Stay where you are! Do not move! I will find you in the morning! We can call each other throughout the night!"

"Are you with Kamal and Omar!"

"No, but we hear each other faintly! Do not fear, my son, Allah will protect you!"

I wished I had my father with me instead of Allah at this moment, but suddenly I was no longer afraid. The moon passed directly over, making a great display of lighting the walls. Along with the stars, I was suddenly in paradise again. I was a Bedouin! Like a Bedouin, I slept sitting up, crouched over, with one eye and both ears open. Throughout the night my father comforted me with his calls.

At dawn I saw the sight of my father and brothers coming toward me. I had strange feelings. I wanted them to save me, but I had learned not to be afraid and I had seen the desert by night and wanted more if it. I went to them, trying to act nonchalant, but babbled with overwhelming excitement as I led them to the cave. It was simple to find, for the vultures were out in force.

We climbed up the rope ladder and into the cavern. My father surveyed the defensive possibilities.

"It is perfect! Let us hope the vultures do their work quickly and do not lead the Bedouin back to us!"

"Who do you think those people were?" Kamal asked.

"Only Allah knows. There seems to be only one man. The rest are women and children. The man was probably left to guard while the other men went looking for supplies. I'm sure they got lost trying to find their way back in and the women and children starved."

Ibrahim proved to be right, for in ensuing days we found the bodies of three men who had trapped themselves in a fool's opening. Nothing was left of their clothing or any supplies they might have been packing in. The Bedouin got them first and the vultures shortly thereafter.

We found the main wadi bed again and carefully marked the canyon walls to find our way back in. At twilight we reached the truck. Although the women could not embrace us in front of each other, they stood before us and wept, for they had been certain we were lost.

My heart sank as I saw the truck. Sabri had a hundred parts scattered about on blankets on the ground.

"Everything is clogged with dirt and sand. Each piece must be cleaned before I can put it back together."

"Will it run?"

"We have a problem. The radiator is broken. There is no water in it."

"If we don't get this truck out of here and sell it, we will be in a very dangerous situation," Ibrahim said. He was completely puzzled by what he saw spread before him and I knew he was thinking it would not be possible to put it back together again, much less run.

We made a plan to guard the truck in shifts. Sabri would stay and work, for we were now in a race against time. The rest of us would unload the provisions. A person could carry no more than twenty-five to fifty pounds of supplies and water on each trip, for there were stiff climbs and the heat was tormenting. We were concerned that the wall markings were not efficient. A false marking, made by nature, could easily lead us astray.

"When I was very young, before my father inherited the garage, I was a shepherd," Sabri said. "I would take the flock on winter pasture into the Bab el Wad. I marked my way back to my cave by piling a small pyramid of rocks every short distance."

The idea was perfect, but it annoyed me. Sabri had been in our life for only a few days, but already he had answers to most of our problems. What is more, he had lived for several winters in a cave. He would know even more answers. Since I had learned to read and write, I had beaten off Kamal and had brushed Jamil and Omar aside. I had had no challenges for the attention of my father and Sabri now represented a threat. I did not know how to contend with it, for we needed him.

We barely dented the supplies on our first trip and found the journey was even more grueling than suspected. Our initial chore was to burn the cave out by sprinkling kerosene around and igniting it. We not only killed the maggots but drove out the bats, which I had suspected were deeper in the cave. When the fire died and the smoke dissipated, we rigged up slings and pulleys to haul the provisions up. Father put us on rotating guard duty in the cave. Since the women could not stand guard, they were always in the supply caravan. Two round trips a day were all we could manage. In a few days our water supply, in five-gallon army cans, was diminishing severely.

We scavenged through the ruins of the Qumran settlement, knowing it had been picked over for centuries by the Bedouin, but hoping beyond hope of finding a source of water. The water works, which filled during the winter floods, were long since destroyed. All the cisterns were cracked, probably from the many earthquakes that ravaged the area down through time.

Ibrahim felt that we could build our own cistern or some method of damming and trapping water by winter, the only time it rained here. During an ordinary rain, water would stream down from the high cliffs and fill the narrow canyons. With no places to go into the rocky soil, the water would build up, then find its way to a wider wadi bed. When a half-dozen canyons emptied into a single wadi, the result was a flash flood which sent water gushing down into the Dead Sea. Ibrahim remembered almost getting trapped and drowned in a flood as a boy.

It was midsummer. There would be no rain for months and we only had a week or ten days' supply of water. Our caravan back and forth from the truck to the cave was slave business and it was all we could do to keep from devouring our water. It took a full week to unload the truck. During that time, Sabri had it almost put back together.

Sabri gave us the bad news that the radiator had many leaks and all the water was gone from the engine, the battery was cracked, and the spare not properly charged up. Even with new parts, he did not know for certain if the truck would start up again.

Meanwhile the cave was made livable by the women. Once up the fifty-foot ladder, they would seldom come down. It was cool inside and a refuge from the heat. We found a number of corridors off the main room to give everyone privacy, although pri-

vacy was tantamount to total darkness. We were allowed to flick
on our flashlights only to get back and forth to the main cavern. I
discovered a tunnel that led out to another opening and from
there I could climb to a ledge from where I could look down on
the entire north end of the Dead Sea. I claimed the place for Sabri
and me, much to the dismay of my brothers. If they wanted their
own ledges, they could find them as I had.

At the far end of the main room, we realized a slit of light was
penetrating. By picking away at the rocks, we were able to carve
out a chimney to the outside. It solved many problems. We could
build a permanent fire beneath the chimney that would also light
the main cavern and give us heat for cooking. In order to keep the
fire burning and not use up valuable fuel, a permanent daily
chore was to follow the wadis for wood. The winter flash floods
had made it possible for a variety of scrub brush and bushes to
survive. We gathered up wild raspberry, jujube, burnet, desert
tamarisk, and marjoram to feed the flame. When we stumbled
onto a fully grown terebinth tree, our fire problem was solved.

At first we tried to shoot the large desert hares that constantly
scooted across our path. We were all very bad shots and the rab-
bits were too quick. It was also dangerous, for Jamil got nipped
by a ricocheted bullet. Again Sabri had an answer. He knew how
to make rabbit snares and they could be easily lured with a handful of grain. We soon had ample rabbit meat to supplement our
diet.

We were down to four days' supply of water when Sabri had
the truck put back together.

"I must get to Jerusalem and get a new radiator. I need some
hoses, a battery, and a few parts," he reported.

That would entail a day's walk to Jericho and another day to
get a bus up to Jerusalem. Sabri said he knew the garage repair
area of East Jerusalem quite well, for he used it often when his
father owned five trucks.

It meant giving Sabri our last penny. What if he ran off with it?
Worse, we had many thousands of dollars' worth of food and
supplies. What if Sabri led a band of cutthroats back to massacre
us and take everything? We did not have the luxury of extended
suspicion. There was no choice but to give Sabri the money. As

we watched him disappear toward Jericho, we wondered if we would ever see him again.

On the third day after Sabri had left, I was on my turn guarding the truck. I read in the shade of the vehicle, but my eyes were lifting constantly to squint up the path along the sea. I prayed I would catch sight of Sabri returning. Every so often, I scanned in all directions through our binoculars for intruders.

Our situation at the cave was entirely desperate. We were out of water. There was a single five-gallon can in the truck, but we could not touch it, for we needed it to fill the radiator . . . if Sabri ever returned. Tomorrow Haj Ibrahim would have to come to a decision. We would have to abandon the cave and take our chances in Jericho. Our alternative was to cross the Allenby Bridge to Amman and become Jordanians.

As I scanned the horizon to the south for signs of life, I stopped on something that I had seen earlier. At the far reach of my binoculars, I thought I made out a minute green spot right at seaside. It was a mile or two south. Father had admonished us not to go south, for fear of running into Jewish troops or Bedouin. I concentrated on the green spot until my eyes blurred, then climbed to higher ground and looked again. There are cruel illusions in the desert, but I could swear the green line would not go away.

When the sun reached midday, Omar came to relieve me of my guard. "I am going along the sea to the south for a few miles," I told Omar.

"Has the heat made you crazy?"

"There is something down there."

"What?"

"I don't know. That's what I want to find out. If I have to go back to the cave and ask Father's permission, I won't be able to go there until tomorrow. Tomorrow will be too late if Sabri does not return and get this truck started."

"But you cannot disobey Father," Omar said.

"If we have to walk to Jericho, some of us may not make it in the sun. Mother cannot make it. Fatima's baby will surely die."

Omar, who never complained of working in the bazaar or waiting on tables at the café, was not about to get into a complicity with me. "You can go," he said, "but it is your decision and your responsibility."

I moved toward that green thing, remembering every surah of

the Koran to beseech Allah. Every night now I had been dreaming of waterfalls, rivers, rain. I dreamed I was standing naked in a
downpour, slopping water into my mouth.

Right on the sea, two miles below the truck, the green strip
became more and more visible. Then I heard it before I saw it! It
was the sound of water!

I told myself not to rush. Be cautious, Ishmael. Beware, Ishmael. I looked around for Jews and Bedouin. It was totally still. I
saw no movement. I prayed I was not being watched. Closer . . .
closer . . . then I saw what I had heard! Almost at the sea's edge,
water was gushing from a rock and filling two large pools. The
pools overflowed into the sea.

I crawled on hands and knees close to one of the pools, cringing
as I went, for I was certain a shot would ring out and kill me at
any instant. I sat alongside the pool for several moments to renew
my courage. I could stand it no longer. I dared dip my hand in
and brought it slowly to my lips.

Sweet water!

I stood up and began to cry out with joy, forgetting I might be
in someone's gunsights. I threw myself into the pool, screaming,
laughing, and crying all at the same time, and then I ran back to
the truck nonstop. The pains that hit my belly from drinking too
much too fast could not stop me.

"Water! Water! Water! Water!"

I must have acted mad, for Omar shook me. I tried to speak, but
my words stumbled over each other. Then things became really
crazy. Did I really see water? Drink it? Swim in it! Or was it all a
trick of the desert that one feels before one dies! Was I crazy or
did I really see a tiny spot on the horizon to the north?

I snatched the binoculars from Omar and stood glued as the
spot grew larger and larger. Yes, a person was walking down the
path from Jericho! I waited like a frozen deer until the vision
cleared. It was Sabri and he had a radiator strapped to his back
and he carried a package in either hand.

I ran back to the cave and babbled out the news! Kamal was left
to guard and one by one everyone made their way down the rope
ladder, even Mother. The water cans were lowered on the pulley
rig and we made for the truck.

Sabri had come in exhausted but went right to work on replacing the old radiator, hoses, battery, and belts. Our last full can of

water was poured into the radiator. As Sabri jumped up to the cab, my father cried, "Allah be merciful!"

We all closed our eyes and prayed in unison. He turned the key. Nothing! The women set up a wail as Sabri threw open the hood and played with the wiring, then back to the cab. Nothing!

"It's the ignition. I'll try to hot wire it."

Pop . . . pop . . . pop . . . pop . . . pop . . . pop/poop . . . pop/poop . . . rrrrrr . . . rrrrrr . . . rrrrumph! The greatest sound I'll ever hear! Rrumph, rrumph, rrrumph!

A spontaneous dance erupted around the truck. Madness! Men and women were dancing together and no one cared. Clucks of joy! War cries! Everyone except Father wept openly. The men all hugged and kissed Sabri. They remembered that I had found water and I was embraced too!

Ibrahim leaped to the cab. "I am off to sell this turd! We will return in two days with donkeys!"

"Wait, Father, wait!" I cried. "Let us go to the springs and fill our water cans first!"

He slapped his forehead. "Of course! Everyone in!"

I jumped into the cab alongside my father and Sabri. "Father, shouldn't you go first to Jericho and trade the rest of the cigarettes for grain for the donkeys while we still have a truck to haul it?"

He touched his forehead again. "Too much blessings from Allah at the same time. Yes, we go to Jericho first and get grain."

"Father, who will be in command while you are gone?"

He looked at me slyly. "You are too young and far too ambitious," he said. "On the other hand, you are the best suited. You will be in command. I will tell the others before I leave."

We reached the springs with my heart leaping with joy. Everyone drank until they were ready to burst, then we filled the cans. My father ordered the women into the back of the truck while the men stripped and plunged into the pool. It was our first bath in over two weeks. When we were done, we waited in the back of the truck while the women bathed.

"I must speak to you," I heard Hagar say to Ibrahim.

"Yes?"

"Instead of two donkeys, we will need only one, now that we have a spring."

"But two donkeys will bring twice as much water and we will only have to go half as many times."

"Why feed two donkeys when one can do the work?" my mother insisted.

"We can afford two donkeys. We can always use them. We can always sell them."

"If we needed the donkeys for the dung for the fire, I would agree," my mother insisted. "We have enough firewood, so we don't need their dung."

"Do I look like a man who would be satisfied with one donkey when I can afford two?"

"Two hours ago we could afford nothing. Are we not pushing Allah too far with getting two donkeys?"

"Suppose one donkey breaks his leg?"

"I have never seen a donkey break his leg."

"They will keep each other company."

"We have enough donkeys in our family to keep it company."

My father began to realize that Hagar had reasons. "So only one donkey," he said.

"One donkey and one milk goat," Hagar answered.

"Why do we need a goat? Fatima's milk is no good?"

"Fatima's milk is sour."

"It will get better now that we have found water."

"She is pregnant," Hagar said.

"But one pregnant woman doesn't need a goat."

"There are two pregnant women. Ramiza is also with child," Hagar said and climbed into the back of the truck.

Chapter Six

Jericho, one of man's oldest cities, had had an ancient glory second only to Jerusalem. At the eastern portal to the holy city, Jericho had known many kings, would-be kings, and their armies. Away from the eyes of Jerusalem, Jericho was a den of ancient conspiracies and murders and the first way station for defeated warriors in their flights to the desert.

Jericho, the lowest city in the world and one of the most torrid, melted into lethargy under the blare of the sun and evolved into a slow-motion hamlet of a few thousand souls.

These days it was more chaotic than Haj Ibrahim could have imagined. Everywhere one looked, people slept—in the streets and gutters, in the fields, all about the hills. There were thousands upon thousands of them in disarray and dismay. The nearby Allenby Bridge beckoned them to cross the river to Jordan. Some went, some stayed. The Allenby was a bridge of great uncertainty to the future, perhaps spanning a river of no return.

News of the war was equally distressing, but Ibrahim was not all that surprised. A second truce was in effect, but in reality the Arab armies had been stopped cold everywhere. The worst of it was that the Egyptians were in retreat in the Negev Desert.

Jordan's Arab Legion alone had had a measure of success. It held the Latrun Police Fort, East Jerusalem, and areas of major Arab settlement on the West Bank of the river. Otherwise, the military disaster was universal. While others in Jericho fed themselves on rumors and illusions, Haj Ibrahim knew that any hope for Arab victory had been burst. He realized that the Arab Legion would never leave the safety of the Latrun Fort for an attack. Abdullah would be more than content, for the moment, to hang onto his gains. After all, his quarrel with the Jews had been more of an exercise in Islamic nepotism than genuine hatred. He had been dragged into the war because of his British-trained Legion. Why shouldn't he sit tight in Latrun and claim the West Bank? But that meant that Tabah would be forever inside the new State of Israel.

After returning to the cave with a load of feed to sustain a donkey and a goat, Ibrahim and Sabri drove to East Jerusalem to sell the truck. They came up Jericho Road past the Garden of Gethsemane to where it ended at the Rockefeller Museum.

From here the Wadi el Joz road twisted and plunged into a gulley that eventually worked its way back uphill to the demilitarized zone on Mount Scopus. It was lined with catch-as-catch-can garages, a street notorious for black market dealing, prostitutes, and knives for hire. It had been on this very road that a convoy of Jewish doctors and nurses had been ambushed and slaughtered on their way up to Hadassah Hospital.

Haj Ibrahim was immediately wary of the street. It smelled dangerous. If he sold the truck and carried a large amount of money, he might never get out of the place alive. He ordered Sabri to turn around and retrace the route, then parked on a side road in the Valley of Kidron near the Tomb of Absalom.

"Walk back to the Wadi el Joz and bring the buyers here one at a time, but do not tell them where you are bringing them or else you might be followed by a dozen cousins," Ibrahim instructed.

Ibrahim knew that the first round of potential buyers was most likely in the game to soften him up for the eventual buyer. Their mission was to knock down the price by deprecating the vehicle. Sabri returned with a Syrian officer, a deserter who had built up a thriving business purchasing weapons from other deserters. A fair part of his arsenal had been smuggled to the Jews defending the opposite side of the city.

"This motor is like looking up a donkey's ass in a windstorm," he opined.

"So humble a conveyance is certainly unworthy of so noble a man," Ibrahim retorted.

Despite the foul condition of the truck, the Syrian made an insulting offer.

"I would give more to a prostitute, just for her smile."

When the Syrian huffed off, Ibrahim had Sabri move the vehicle to a new location near the Lions' Gate of the Old City wall. The second prospective customer was more promising, Ibrahim thought, because his insults came in torrents as he pointed out twenty real or imagined defects in the truck.

"This vehicle has been rolled in shit," he concluded. "It is worthless, except for spare parts."

Ibrahim merely had Sabri move to a third location near the Tomb of the Virgin. By now he knew that everyone along the Wadi el Joz had the word and they also knew Haj Ibrahim was a cool trader.

The fifth potential buyer, from a "fine old Palestinian family," expressed dismay that he was looking at a stolen truck. He was a self-proclaimed honest man who had a large family and would not risk imprisonment by dealing in hot goods. However . . . because of the unusual times. . . .

Ibrahim realized that he was the true buyer all the time, a man who had bought and sold dozens of vehicles belonging to any-man's army. He was also in business with the Bedouin who scoured the desert for abandoned vehicles and stripped them for spare parts.

A test drive was made. Sabri's repairs had held up famously. Now the man went into a plea of poverty and bargaining ensued for over an hour. They finally narrowed in on a respectable offer of close to three hundred British pounds after refusing to deal in Arab currency. Then came a series of hilarities to indicate a deal had been consummated. For Ibrahim it was a windfall. He could purchase a donkey and goat in Jericho and have enough money left over to keep the cave supplied for months.

After the buyer drove the truck off, Ibrahim made certain he was not being followed and walked with Sabri to the main street of Suleiman Road that ran alongside the wall to the bus terminal.

"You have done very well for me," Ibrahim said abruptly. He handed Sabri a five-pound note. "Have a night on the city. I will meet you tomorrow in Jericho at the market."

Sabri understood this to mean he was still not fully trusted. Ibrahim did not wish to walk around with all that money and Sabri at his side to possibly finger him for robbers. Ibrahim knew that all the "prospective" buyers had been paid off and he wondered if Sabri had also taken a kickback. Sabri covered the insult by smiling and feigning surprise at the five-pound gift and made off to have himself a party.

The Bab el Wad was still being hotly contested and closed to normal bus traffic. Ibrahim first traveled north to the city of

Ramallah and caught a bus that ran a parallel route inside Arab territory. The bus ended its run about a mile from the Latrun Fort at the outer encampment of the Arab Legion. Many local farmers and peddlers had set up a roadside bazaar to sell to the troops. A few hundred yards down the road toward the fort, a guard post ended passage for everyone except the soldiers. Ibrahim walked directly toward the guards.

"Halt! You can go no farther!"

He withdrew the magic forgery from Colonel Hakkar on Iraqi Army stationery and handed it to the guard with an air of authority. The guard could neither read nor write. Two other illiterate guards pondered the paper, one reading it upside down, then called for an officer. He was duly impressed.

A half hour later, Ibrahim had worked himself through the various rings of security to the very doors of the fort.

"What do you want?" the officer in charge demanded.

"I am Ibrahim al Soukori al Wahhabi, the Muktar of Tabah. I wish to go up on the roof so I can gaze upon my village."

"This is a zone of high military security. You have no business being here."

"I wish to go to the roof and see my village."

"It is not possible. Leave before I have you arrested."

"I will not leave until I see my village. I demand to speak with the commanding officer."

The argument broke into heated words, with only Ibrahim's audacity keeping him from serious trouble. As the words reverberated through the concrete halls, they drew the attention of the senior British officer, Lieutenant Colonel Chester Bagley.

"I say, what's the problem here?" Bagley asked.

"This man claims to be the muktar of the village down the road. He wants to see his village from the roof."

Bagley examined Ibrahim. Rags, these days, were worn by everyone and were not a true indication of a man's position. Ibrahim's stature and dignity spelled out that he had once been a man of authority. He perused Ibrahim's letter at length. "Come with me," he said and led Ibrahim to his office down the hall.

Ibrahim was offered a seat while Bagley continued to examine the letter and stuff his pipe. "Do you have any other papers?"

"Who has papers these days?"

"This letter is a forgery," Bagley said.

"Of course it is. Without it, I and my family would have been dead weeks ago."

Cheeky, Bagley thought. "We've had two bloody battles for this fort and we are apt to have more. How do I know you won't go up to the roof and study our emplacements."

"You mean I'm a spy?"

"Well, you don't really have very much to prove otherwise, do you?"

"Mister . . . Colonel. . . ."

"Bagley, Chester Bagley."

"Colonel Bagley, I would have to be the world's most stupid spy, wouldn't I?"

"Or the world's most clever spy."

"Aha, what you say has merit, great merit. There are a number of villages within a few minutes' drive from here. Any of them will verify Haj Ibrahim al Soukori al Wahhabi."

"My dear chap, we are in the middle of a war. . . ."

"Colonel Bagley, with all due respect. I know every trench and gun emplacement around Latrun, as well as the names of your units. I am sure I could tell you within five shells of what arsenal you have. The Jews know the same thing. This is not a case of numbers or secrets. You simply have a force here too great for the Jews to contend with. There is no mystery about Latrun."

For a moment, Chester Bagley was dumbfounded by the Arab's refreshing and unprecedented frankness. He lit his pipe as a stall.

"Colonel, I long to see Tabah with a longing that consumes me. Only Allah knows if I will ever have the chance again. I am not a man to beg, sir, so please do not make me beg."

"You're a little bit mad to come in here like this with this . . . ridiculous forgery. You could have easily gotten yourself hung or shot."

"Does that not testify to the depths of my longing?"

"You're mad," Bagley repeated. He handed the letter back to Ibrahim. "You'd better hang onto this thing, but for God's sake don't show it to anyone who can read. Come with me, Haj Ibrahim."

Bagley rapped on the adjoining door with the bowl of his pipe, then entered. Behind the commander's desk sat the Jordanian colonel, Jalud. Ibrahim spotted him immediately as of Bedouin stock, leathered beyond his years from the sun and soldiering so

one could hardly tell where his skin ended and the khaki of his
uniform began. He had not become a full colonel in the Arab
Legion through acts of grace. The arrogance and cruelty of the
man were apparent behind a pair of desert-slitted eyes. His po-
maded hair glistened and a great moustache served as a warrant
to his masculinity. In the scheme of things between the British
and the Legion, the Arab generally held the higher rank over his
British "adviser." In reality, the Englishman ran the show. The
fact that Latrun had held back two desperate and bloody Jewish
assaults seemed to confirm that Lieutenant Colonel Chester Bagley had designed and built the defenses and probably had commanded the actual battles.

Bagley was ever so soft-spoken as he presented Ibrahim's request.

"I cannot grant it," Jalud snapped. "This is not visitor's day at
the Dome of the Rock. Have this man locked up and bring to me
those idiots who allowed him into the fort."

"It will not augur well to alienate the local population while
this crisis is still at hand. Haj Ibrahim's identity and popularity
can easily be confirmed. The man has been the muktar for a quarter of a century. It would be a decent gesture."

"Decent gesture? He has penetrated a secret military installa-
tion. Get him out of here before he is in serious trouble."

"I will take the responsibility," Bagley pressed on firmly.

Ibrahim became enchanted by the exchange between the two.
It was apparent that Bagley, despite his lower rank, was indeed
the true commander of the fort. Colonel Jalud did not wish to
ruffle his feathers, much less take a risk of being left in charge of
the defenses himself. Jalud continued to argue along a slim borderline. As Bagley persisted, Colonel Jalud wove a spiderweb of
defenses for himself so he could be absolved of any future blame.

The exchange having run its course, Jalud gave Ibrahim a dis-
robing examination with his eyes. Men in rags often disguised
their true wealth. Ibrahim had prepared for the possibility of a
strip search. He hid his money in a field near the bus stop before
going to the fort. The only thing of value that showed was the
bejeweled dagger. Jalud's eyes stopped their wandering and became fixed on the weapon.

"It is a serious request," Jalud said. "I am taking a great risk.

Therefore it must be as important to me as it is to you. A gesture for a gesture."

I should have hidden the damned dagger as well, Ibrahim thought.

"I have nothing to make a gesture with," Ibrahim said. "Allah knows, you cannot strip the naked."

"Perhaps my eyes are playing tricks with me," Jalud answered, never taking his eyes from the dagger.

"It is my honor."

"Men with golden threads in their robes are the custodians of honor."

The insult was biting. "It is a price I cannot pay," Ibrahim said.

"Of course, I could take it from you and you would have no honor left at all. Where was your honor in defending your village? Get out of here while you still have your tongue and your fingernails."

"Colonel Jalud, I am going to insist that you allow this man to see his village."

Jalud leaned back in his chair and draped an arm over the back where he had slung his pistol and belt. "Oh well, this seems to be my day for shit. Let the dog go to the roof and bark at his village. He has five minutes." With a gesture of the wrist denoting "royal" dismissal, Jalud returned to the papers on his desk.

Ibrahim spat on the floor, the spittle running down the toe of the colonel's boot. As he made for the door, Jalud leaped to his feet. "Your mother's cunt is an oasis for camels!"

Ibrahim returned to Jalud's desk and put his fingers on the hilt of the dagger. It lashed from its scabbard so quickly that neither of the others could reach for his pistol. The point burrowed into the colonel's desk, striking so hard the wood split. Ibrahim's fingers rested on the edge of the desk, his eyes looking directly into Jalud's.

"Take it," Ibrahim challenged.

Jalud's eyes shot over to Chester Bagley, who wore a wispy smile. Bagley always hovered over him with his soft, sweet persistent "requests." They were not requests but orders! He seethed at the British having the authority over his troops. On the other hand, he did not wish to go through another defense of the fort without Bagley. Now the Englishman had the worst of all blackmails over his head. He, the great Colonel Jalud, had been cowed by a peasant. If Bagley wished, Jalud could be mortified and humiliated.

The colonel tried to summon the courage to reach for the implanted dagger, but the courage was not to be found. He slumped down in his chair.

"Come along," Bagley said, freeing the dagger and returning it to Ibrahim. "I will personally escort you to the roof and then back to your bus."

Colonel Jalud's hand reached for his phone threateningly, but the Englishman took it gently from his hand and replaced it in its cradle. As Ibrahim passed from the office, Bagley turned at the door and glared at Jalud, who remained in semi-shock.

"Why in the hell do you people have to make a bloody game out of everything!" he said and slammed the door behind him.

Chapter Seven

I am Ishmael,
You laugh and you say,
Who is this stupid little peasant boy?
But before your laughter consumes you . . . remember . . .
I have been to Eden
I have seen glory
That you in all your years
And in all your wisdom
Will never know

It is frightfully quiet
Nothing living moves
Except a drop of morning dew
And a snake slithering from its nest
To bask in the warming rays
Still, so still, so very still

But you are never alone

The night creatures, the bats and owls
Have bid us farewell
And overhead
The griffon vulture, the buzzard
The kite and the serpent eagle
Assume their circling patrols
Gliding on waves of rising simmering air
Then . . . careen . . . screech . . . snatch
The unsuspecting hare or skink

As the morning chill gives way
To a relentless legion of devouring heat
I go to our springs
That gush cold, clean sweet water
And I see the parade of little foxes
And wild asses and goats
And the haughty ibex
Devour the stuff joyously

We are always boxed in
By the jackal and hyena
Who cringe us with their bloodthirsty cackles
  and howls
I retreat
A gazelle flits by more quickly than a shooting
  star

Even in the blaze of noon
When everything must surely be dead
I am not alone
The gecko, the lizard and the chameleon
Have become my good friends
I speak to them by name
As they clean our cave of centipedes

I have seen the midday horizon beyond Jordan
Suddenly blacken
As a low and distant hum thickens to a roar
And a solid wall of locusts
Storm like avenging armies
Over the sea
And bash themselves on the mountain rock

You are never alone

At evening I climb very high from the cave
To a ledge that is my ledge
From here I can see Mount Nebo
Over the Dead Sea
That place where Moses gazed to the Promised Land
Then died. . . .
The dull sky brightens
The water turns an eerie azure
And purple flows in veins through the barren
  mountains
And they all fuse together
In a violence of sudden color
That is a hymn to the dying sun

It is darker than dark now
And every night
The clarity of ten trillion stars

Unfettered by human lights
Display themselves tauntingly
Asking questions that men can only speculate
Some nights I count a hundred comets
Hurling themselves from infinity to infinity
It is now that I am eternal as they
I am the desert
I am the Bedouin

Do you still think I am a stupid little
*   peasant boy?*
Well, you will never see my cave or my ledge
But remember
The greatest of ancient men knew of my cave
And sat on my ledge
And watched the shower of stars

What treasures did the Essenes hide deeply in
*   my cave?*
What defeated Hebrew rebels fleeing Rome came
*   upon it?*
I sit on the very throne that King David sat
When he fled from Saul
I sit where Jesus sat
When he went into the wilderness

I know of things you will never know
And when I am remanded to paradise
Surely Allah will allow me to return to this
*   cave and this ledge*
Forever . . .

We Arabs are an infinitely patient people. Add that to a natural lack of ambition and we had a combination of circumstances that made our living in a cave a rather pleasant experience. At least it was that way in the beginning. We had a stock of staples that would last for months and firewood, water, and small animals and birds to augment our diet.

There were certain routine chores of gathering wood, hunting, standing guard, and a daily trip to the springs. We built a series of descending dams of stones. When one would fill, it would overflow into a lower one and that into another lower one. The trapped water would eventually end up in a large cistern that was carved from solid rock and could hold water indefinitely.

For the most part, we were deliciously idle. We would all often retire to our individual ledges, perches, or private niches when the midday heat made work impossible and simply stare at the sea and the desert for hours.

I got to know my brothers better. Kamal would always harbor some hatred for me for having taken his natural place in the family order. But he was limited in both the resources and the courage to fight me. Kamal had gone as far as he could go with knowledge and was doomed to mediocrity. He was in his mid-twenties and without ambition, content to languish in the cave forever, if that be Allah's will. He was also less than the master of his own family. Fatima secretly ruled the roost. I liked Fatima very much. She made us laugh and was as capable as Hagar in running the home.

Three of our four women became virtual prisoners of the cave. The rope ladder up to the entrance was tricky to negotiate. My mother had to be hauled up and down by pulleys and once the rope broke and she fell from ten feet up. Fortunately, she landed on her well-padded rump. After Fatima and Ramiza became pregnant, they never left the cave. They didn't mind it, for Arab women, even in normal times, seldom left the perimeter of their houses and then only to go to the village water well and communal bakery. Beyond the village they could travel only in the company of a male member of the family. It was Sunna, our tradition.

My brothers were concerned by Ramiza's pregnancy, fearing that a male child might disrupt the family dynasty. I was not too bothered. We were living in a cave far from all humanity and what could a new half brother possibly take from us?

I was more concerned about Sabri. I loved Sabri personally. He was extremely clever and gave all kinds of excellent ideas, although I was glad he was not a real brother and I wished he weren't quite so smart.

There was so much spare time that Omar and Jamil often sought me out on my ledge and I taught them to read and write. Haj Ibrahim scoffed at the idea at first but, having no true reason to object, allowed their lessons to go on. That is when I got to know them better.

Omar was nearing twenty. He had been trained to be a merchant in our stall and to work in the café and store. He seemed
most content to be a servant. By running errands, standing extra
watches, and making extra trips to the springs, he won praise
from all of us and occasional attention from Father. It seemed to
be reward enough for him. He was simple, learned slowly, and
was destined to be plain all his life. He offered no threat to me in
the family scheme of things.

Jamil, who was between Omar and me in age, was another
story. He had always been the dark member of the family, an
enigma. He was the least talkative, the least friendly, and the
most alone. Jamil had been doomed by his age and position in the
family to be the shepherd—and later a farmer—because when it
became my time to be the shepherd, I had ducked it by going to
school in Ramle. I think Jamil secretly resented me for this. We
never fought, but he could be very surly and deep into himself.

He learned to read and write twice as fast as Omar. We did not
realize he was so smart. In fact, he was the smartest next to me.
He seethed inside and learning to read seemed to give him paths
to vent his frustrations. Jamil was the only restless one in the cave
and these days he often lashed out in anger over nothing. I did
not consider him a serious rival, although the more he learned,
the more he argued.

I felt most sorry for Nada. Three women were in the cave full-
time and didn't really need her. She was healthy and able to climb
up and down the ladder easily, so I took her with me as often as I
could when we set traps and worked on the cistern.

Her main job was going to the springs twice a week to wash
our clothes—or what was left of them. I manipulated matters so
that I was always the one to take her to the springs.

We named our donkey Absalom. I would ride him down the
long draw in the canyon with Nada walking behind me, as was
the custom. When we turned out of sight of our guard, I would
invite her up on Absalom behind me. She had to put her arms
about me for balance. I must admit I became excited to feel her
breasts pressing against my back. Maybe I should have been
ashamed, but I wasn't the first Arab boy whose prick got stiff by
touching his sister, however innocently.

It was a foolhardy thing to admit to myself, for I could never tell her or show it, but I loved Nada more than my brothers. When I came right down to it, I also loved Sabri better than Kamal, Omar, and Jamil. Sabri and I had much more in common. We spent a good part of our days together and slept in our own little room.

You can imagine my surprise when I realized that Sabri and Nada had started to give each other those looks and close passing brushes. There is that certain way an Arab girl gives a look that can only mean one thing.

At first I was surprisingly hurt at the notion that another boy could bring out that look in Nada. But why not? She was of an age when a woman can start being aroused and there was no one around but Sabri to arouse her. Still, it was painful. I wished she didn't like Sabri, just as I wished Sabri weren't so clever. Although I loved him, I didn't completely trust Sabri's intentions. He was an outsider and not truly bound to protect Nada's honor. I believed that he might have done something with her—kissed her, rolled around, or even worse. Fortunately, we lived in very close quarters and when they were out of the cave we saw to it that they did not go off together. One of my brothers or I were always on the watch. The women giggled about it and whispered behind our backs and didn't take it as seriously as we did.

Haj Ibrahim's favorite place was our guard post, a deep crevice in the cliffside set inside a beautifully shaded alcove. From here we had a perfect view down the canyon's only entrance, so that no one could enter or leave without passing directly under our machine gun.

Several times Jordanian patrols came within several hundred yards but did not enter the tricky labyrinth of canyons. It was the Bedouin we feared and it was night when we feared him most. We knew their unseen eyes were on us all the time. Once again Sabri had the answer. Each night we set some simple booby traps, using grenades. Anyone attempting to enter our subcanyon would have to trip one of a dozen wires that set off the explosive.

The Bedouin waited until there was no moon and had a sandstorm for cover. We sensed a raid and prepared for it. When a wire was tripped and the grenade exploded, the blast reverberated through the hollow passageways of rock, sounding like a battery of artillery. We lay down a tremendous fusilade of fire and they quickly melted back into the crevices of the mountains. By dawn there was no trace of them.

Our next fear was that they would try to catch us coming out of the canyon on our way to the springs or to Jericho, so we traveled in pairs, with one of us always carrying an automatic weapon.

Haj Ibrahim felt it was only a matter of time until they would set siege to us, hide in the rocks around us, and try to pick us off one at a time. He prepared for this eventuality by moving a second guard post closer to the sea, so we could observe all movement from miles away during the day. The eyes of the Bedouin became our first break in paradise.

The second break was my recurring nightmare. I was unable to erase the scene of my mother and the other women being raped in Jaffa. I was grateful to Allah that Nada had been spared and that she had no knowledge of it. More nights than not, I awakened close to tears or rage and always in a heart-pounding sweat. The eyes of those Iraqis never left my mind. I would meet one of them again. I had to.

Aside from the terror of the scene, the most frightening part of it was keeping a lifelong secret from my father. This gave me an awesome power over the three women and forced them into an alliance with me. I believe they trusted me, but when one holds such a secret above another, there certainly must be some suspicions.

My father and I also shared a secret that Sabri had had a homosexual affair with an Iraqi officer.

There was no doubt Sabri and Nada had some secrets between them. We couldn't watch them all the time, no matter how hard we tried. At times we would see her walking down a path alone and in ten minutes observe Sabri coming down the same path. Both of them gave themselves away through their telltale silence.

The women had secrets also. One could tell by how the level of conversation dropped when a man entered the cave.

And my brothers probably had secrets too, for they often spoke in little clumps, always speculating how they stood within the various alliances.

Everyone's secrets formed a tender balance of unspoken blackmail.

If there was a problem that could only be solved by Father, it was usually up to me to approach him as the spokesman on everyone's behalf. I would wait until I sensed Ibrahim was in a favorable mood and then slip alongside him at the machine gun post.

Sometimes we would sit for an hour before speaking, I always cautious not to break his meditation. By some gesture, he would recognize my presence.

"I smell the Bedouin," Ibrahim said, as though speaking aloud to himself. "It is wise that we have two men out in the forward position at night, with one of them constantly on patrol."

Our leisurely existence was being strained by such an arrangement. I waited for Father to ramble on.

"I will continue to remain here day and night," Ibrahim said. "In case they pick off our forward post, I must protect the women."

"It is an excellent idea, Father."

"It is not an excellent idea. In truth we have no protection, save Allah's will," he said.

It was a long time before I opened my mouth again. "I speak only after serious consideration."

"Consideration leads to thoughtful conclusions."

"We are very happy and content here," I said. "But after living here for several months, certain inconsistencies we did not foresee slowly become apparent."

"You speak words that hint of several possibilities," Ibrahim said.

"I speak of defense," I said, but hastily added, "We could find another subject to discuss."

"Yes, we could discuss something else," my father said, "and continue on until nightfall, but after that we would have no choice but to return to the first subject."

"It is not up to me to observe the qualities of our men when we have you as our leader," I said.

"But there may be several truths about the same situation," my father said, "depending on the circumstances."

"Our circumstances have created certain mathematical imbalances," I said.

"What could they possibly be?" my father said.

"So far, we have had a comfortable situation in rotating the tasks of the men—standing guard, going to Jericho and the springs, and setting traps and gathering firewood and working on the cistern. It has worked ingeniously . . . until now."

"You mention an imbalance?"

"Two extra guards at night, patrolling close to the sea. Forgive me, Father. When I am speaking, I often forget myself and honesty overcomes me. Kamal is useless as a night guard down there. Omar is questionable. That leaves Sabri, Jamil, and me."

"You, the youngest, are making judgments on your brothers?"

"I beg you not to be harsh on the honesty that overcame me. I know I am only repeating what you already know."

"Having stripped me of my prerogatives. . . ."

"Oh no, Father. We are naked without you. But sometimes even the Prophet needed a reminder."

"What you have observed offers various aspects I perhaps should be reminded of."

"Kamal will fare better at night in Fatima's loving arms," I said. "I have seen him run in the face of danger."

"Where?"

"In Jaffa. When he was left to defend the women, he fled. Fortunately, nothing happened to the women."

"I suspected Kamal. It is sad to hear."

"If he is down there by the sea at night, we might as well send Absalom or the goat. At least they will make a loud noise."

"And Omar?"

"Omar's failings are certainly not a lack of courage," I said quickly. "Just stupidity. He cannot maneuver in the dark alone. I have taken the guard with him twice down there and spent the night looking for him until dawn."

"Jamil, Sabri?"

"They are excellent."

"I did not know you thought so much of Jamil."

"He is my brother. I love him."

"But so are Kamal and Omar."

"I have come to appreciate Jamil's qualities. He is eager to fight."

"I will consider what you have said and perhaps leave it up to the three of you to stand the outer night guard."

"But that brings up the mathematical imbalance and that

brings up the honesty that has overcome me. We need two good sets of guards down by the sea."

"Surely you do not expect Haj Ibrahim to leave this most urgent command post."

"Such a thought never occurred to me," I added very quickly.

"Then there is no way to correct the imbalance."

"A vague possibility occurred to me," I said.

"Are you trying to reason with me or to persuade me?" Ibrahim said.

"Merely trying to correct an imbalance. We can increase Kamal's and Omar's daytime tasks to those things which they can handle. As you already know, Father, we can send neither of them to Jericho, for they have already bungled their tasks there. The information they return with is rarely sound and they may have even given away our location. They must do things like gather firewood and set traps and go to the springs. They cannot be given tasks in which a decision must be made."

"If what you say finds merit in my heart, then we will have to do it with three night guards."

"It will be a burden that we do not have to bear . . . mathematically," I said.

"Ishmael, do not try to enlighten me with your education. We have six men. I must remain at the command post and, according to you, two others are worthless. That leaves three men. Does that not make six?"

I closed my eyes, drew in that breath of fear that I had so often drawn in, and said, "We have a healthy, capable woman who has almost nothing to do."

"I do not grasp your meaning," Ibrahim said.

"Father," I said shakily, "I have taught Nada to shoot my rifle. I will put her up against anyone here . . . except you, of course."

"And you also allow her to ride behind you on Absalom and you are secretly teaching her to read and write," Ibrahim said.

OH! By the Prophet's holy name! I knew I would be thrown from the ledge fifty feet to the ground with a slap, a kick, a shove! I closed my eyes and waited for the collision. I had been so careful to keep it secret! So very careful!

"I am sure Sabri would like to stand night guard with Nada," Ibrahim said.

"Oh no!" I cried, jumping to my feet, exuding family honor. "I meant only myself and Jamil!"

"Sit down," my father said with an ominous softness. "What you are trying to do with Nada is not possible. It will only lead to a life of confusion for her."

"But our old life is gone, Father."

"Then we must spend years waiting for it to return and in the meanwhile we must not abandon what we know and who we are. What possible good will it be for Nada to read and write?"

"When we leave here . . . during the years it may take to get back to Tabah . . . Allah only knows. She may need a job."

"Never."

"But to read and write may . . . may bring her happiness."

"She will be happy with the man I marry her to."

"Father, things have changed!"

"Some things never change, Ishmael. Allow the woman to walk in the path in front of you and you will catch her wind for the rest of your life."

He was adamant and his orders for me to cease teaching and helping Nada were absolute. I had failed badly in my mission and I wanted to leave.

"Sit down," he said again. Looking out to the desert, he treated me as abstractly as he would a stone. "We must watch Sabri. He comes from a town of unscrupulous thieves. A family can have only so many male children, but only one son. You are learning your first lesson about forming close friendships. To be the son that follows the father, you must learn what is real about everyone around you . . . who will be your loyal slave . . . who will play both sides . . . and mainly who is dangerous. Few leaders outlive their assassins. If you have a hundred friends, throw out ninety-nine and beware of the other. If, indeed, he is your assassin, eat him for lunch before he eats you for dinner."

I must have seemed like an idiot. My mouth was too dry to respond.

"Well, my son, you have aspired to leadership from the time you could walk."

"I am stupid," I blurted.

"A combination of many stupidities can end up being a worthy man if he learns from his stupidities. The balance of man and

woman is like the balance of life in this desert . . . very fragile.
Don't play with it. As for Sabri. . . ."

"I am humiliated," I whispered.

"I knew of Sabri from the first minute," Ibrahim said. "Do you
really believe that he was forced to sleep with an Iraqi officer, to
live with him day and night?"

"He was starving!"

"A boy in Nablus with the skill of an auto mechanic starving?
Or perhaps, after looking over a situation of hardships, the comforts the Iraqi Army had to offer were too great."

"Why did he come with us?" I asked.

Ibrahim shrugged. "Maybe he was tiring of his Iraqi friend,
maybe his Iraqi was tiring of him. Perhaps they had a lover's
quarrel. Perhaps Sabri had helped himself to too many things
around the Iraqi warehouse and was about to be caught. Who
knows? He deals in opportunities. Perhaps he thought the opportunity to come with us was the best chance to escape some trouble or another in Nablus."

Was it all that baffling? How many times each day did Sabri
make me momentarily uncomfortable by an overextended embrace, a passing touch, a long squeeze of the hand, a woeful expression. How many nights did I awaken to find Sabri "acciden-
tally" askew in his sleep, with his body all up against mine so I
could get an instant feel of his hard prick, and him waiting cleverly for me to make the first advance?

What was going on between him and Nada!

I was ashamed of my stupidity. Of course Sabri was playing a
game. He could manipulate anyone with his charm and lull them
into believing he was their friend. At the same moment, he would
violate a friend's sister. I must get to know people better.

Haj Ibrahim continued to stare out at the desert. How wise he
was. How naïve and foolish I had been.

"We must watch him with extreme care. The best traitors are
the ones like Sabri who can gain your trust. If he lays a hand on
your sister, I shall condemn him to death. You, Ishmael, who
aspire to lead, shall have your first practical lesson. You will do
away with Sabri—in close—with a stroke of the dagger."

Chapter Eight

Something taunted me constantly above my ledge. Several hundred feet up was an opening to another cave. Of course, there were many caves around Qumran. Those that were easily accessible we explored from time to time. Others simply could not be reached, except by expert climbers with proper equipment.

This opening above was up a steep wall, but I had learned that there could be many routes to the same objective. One learns of little foot- and handholds, small leaps, the use of ropes.

For many hours and days, I watched the movements of the mountain goats through binoculars. It became the utmost challenge. Nothing of value had been found in any of the other caves, so I fantasized that this one was filled with treasure. It was becoming an obsession.

One morning I was sitting on my ledge with Nada, lolling the time away, when Sabri joined us. Despite my father's sharp words, I felt quite comfortable with them together there. Besides, we would be doing nothing wrong, only talking.

Soon the three of us were looking up to the high cave and speculating about the possibility of reaching it.

"I think I have figured out a way," I said.

"It would be no problem," Sabri concurred.

"Then let's do it!" Nada said excitedly.

Sabri shrugged. "I don't feel like it today. It is too hot."

Truthfully, I was glad he said it first because, well, it wasn't that I was scared . . . too much. . . . However, it was a sheer wall.

"Perhaps tomorrow," I said.

"Yes, perhaps tomorrow," Sabri agreed.

"Oh wait," I said, "I can't do it tomorrow. I must stand guard. How about the day after tomorrow?"

"I can't the day after tomorrow," Sabri said, "I have to go to the springs."

"And I am busy the day after that," I said.

"Next week."

"Yes, next week."

Nada jumped to her feet and laughed at us. "You're afraid!" she cried. "Both of you are afraid."

"No such thing!" we protested in unison.

"Then let's go!" With that she scampered up into the rocks like a mountain goat. "Come on," she called back tauntingly.

Naturally, neither Sabri nor I could tolerate such insolence from a female. We got to our feet shakily and puffed out our chests.

"I'll get some climbing gear," I said. I really hoped that by the time I returned she would have abandoned the idea. I made my way back to our cave painfully slowly. I rolled up a long line of rope and placed it across my shoulders, filled a canteen, grabbed a flashlight, and made my way back even slower.

Oh shit! Nada had not only not abandoned the climb, she was a good two hundred feet above, laughing and teasing Sabri, who was inching up, clutching at the rocks awkwardly. I begged my legs to stop shaking, said a prayer to Allah, and started up. Oh, the utmost horror of it! I glued my eyes to my hands as they seized protruding rocks. When my foot slipped, I made the mistake of looking down at it and the cliff plunged down at least a million feet . . . or even more. . . .

I was dying to scream out that I had had enough because it was occurring to me that we also had to climb down. Of course, I had to wait for someone else to quit first and I had an awful feeling that it wasn't going to be Nada. Every time I caught a glimpse of her black dress, I could see her scampering upward with an agility that showed no fear.

"Come on! Come on!" she kept shouting. "It is beautiful up here!"

Please Allah, there was a small flat spot where they had stopped to rest. I prayed that by the time I got to them they would have reconsidered the rest of the climb because I was about to pee in my pants. When I reached them, Nada was standing over Sabri, trying to comfort him. He had become frozen with fear, unable to move up, down, or sideways. He could not even speak.

"Phew," I uttered. I was deliriously happy that Sabri had quit first. "Well, no use going any higher," I said. "Don't worry now, Sabri. It is no shame. We will help you down with the ropes." I put my arm about his shoulder, reeking with sympathy and at the same time covering my own quaking. Sabri was fortunate to have such an understanding friend as me.

"Bad luck. We'll try again. Huh, Sabri?"

He emitted a little peep like a chick that had just broken out of its egg. When I looked up, Nada was gone again. Uh oh. I got to my feet very cautiously and flattened myself against the wall as far back from the edge as possible, but made the mistake of looking down again. Oh God!

"Nada!" I shouted, "you come back! This is a command!"

"Ishmael! Up here! Come! There is a large crack we can follow. It is much easier!"

I looked up. I looked down. I was dead either way.

"Sabri, let's finish it. Nada has found a way."

"I c-c-c-can't," he blurted.

No use trying to force him. He *was* paralyzed, locked from head to toe. "Then stay here and don't move. We will be back soon. All right?"

He managed to nod his head.

Things got easier because it was impossible for me to be more frightened than I was. Then I became downright bold as the cave opening loomed closer. Well, Nada wasn't afraid. She must have been crazy. I had never really depended on a girl before, but nothing ever felt so good as her hand pulling me up over the edge.

"Isn't this fun!" she panted.

"It was easy," I said.

We stood before the opening hand in hand. One always approaches the opening of a cave the same way . . . with caution. I flicked on the flashlight and prodded her to go in ahead of me. She tiptoed gingerly, waiting for bats to fly out, but there were none. I came up behind her and probed with the light around a huge room.

Nada shrieked and flung herself into my arms. *There!* In a corner! A pile of human bones.

"It's all right," I croaked. "They're dead."

Then we saw something sadder still. There was a huge jar which had broken to reveal the skeleton of a little baby with a small pitcher and some grain near its head.

"I wonder who it was," she said.

We poked around. There were more children's bones at a stone

altar of some kind which still had fire marks on it. We didn't
know what it all meant, but with each moment our courage became greater and we dared look deeper. We probed three halls
and each of them had evidence of former life. There were dozens
of small pots, most of them broken, a sandal, a braid of hair,
grain, bits of cloth and baskets, a kind of kitchen stove of stone,
utensils.

My flashlight dimmed, indicating that the batteries were wearing out. "There's nothing worth anything," I said, disappointed.
"We'd better get out."

"Wait! Back there," Nada said, pointing to an opening. It led to
a room so low that she had to get on her hands and knees to enter
it.

"Come on, Nada. If this light goes out, we'll be in trouble."

I was mad because she didn't listen to me, but I had no choice
but to crawl behind her. "It's too low," I complained. "No one
could live here."

"But they could certainly hide something."

We came to a dead end, all bunched up together, making it
difficult to get turned around again. I played my light around, but
all we could see was a pile of sticks.

"Nothing here," I insisted.

"Somebody must have brought these sticks in here," she said.

"So what?"

"Wait. Listen," she said.

"I don't hear anything."

"There, where you brushed up against the side, turning
around."

"Just some stones sliding," I said. "I'm not turning around
again."

"Ishmael! Point the light. What is that!"

All I could see was a small piece of basket that had slid out of a
crevice with some stones. Nada picked up one of the sticks and
dug at the spot. It was as though a trapdoor had suddenly opened.
Things started to fall out! There were many! Six or more! It was
so tight, we were almost on our bellies. We couldn't really examine what they were. I grunted my way into position, took a
stick, poked at the hole, and enlarged it so my hand could fit. I
reached in and pulled out three more metal things. My flashlight
dimmed again.

"Take what you can carry. I'll take the rest. Let's get out!"

We got back into the main hall just in time. As we reached the light of the cave opening, the flashlight went dead. We set the objects down and stared at them. They were beautiful things made of metal, copper I think, with all sorts of twists and turns and decorations on them. One was decorated with ibex heads and another, which looked like a crown, had a ring of carved birds on it. There were two other objects made of ivory that were curved and had many holes.

"What are they, Ishmael?"

"I don't know, but I think they are very important."

"We have nothing to carry them down in," she said. "Let's hide them and come back with baskets."

"No, they might be discovered and stolen," I said, pulling off my shirt. I was able to wrap half of them. What to do? Allah, help me think! "All right, Nada, your skirt," I said.

She took it off without hesitation and had only her ankle-length bloomers to protect her modesty. "I will try not to look," I said gallantly, "and if I do by mistake, I swear I will never mention it for the rest of my life."

"It does not matter. You are my brother. Besides, this is more important."

When we reached Sabri, he had gained a measure of control over himself. Our happiness would help make the trip down easier. When we were ready to leave, it occurred to me that we would have to explain all of this to Ibrahim. I realized we would have to make up a small lie and take an oath together. For the first time in my life, I was ashamed before a woman.

"Nada, we cannot tell Father you were climbing around with Sabri and me. I could say I was up there alone, but he would know I could not have brought everything down by myself. We will have to say it was Sabri and me."

Her big bright eyes were filled with hurt. Sabri lowered his own. He could not look at her, nor could I.

"You know Father," I mumbled. "He might beat me and Sabri to death. He might harm you."

We must have sat silently for a half hour. Nada took my hand and then daringly took Sabri's as well. "You are right, Ishmael. You and Sabri found these things. I was not there."

Chapter Nine

You can think of yourself as a Bedouin, believe you are one, and try to live like one. A few of that breed known as the desert rat manage to survive for a time, but if you're not born here, the desert will eventually suck you dry.

Paradise eroded a few months before my thirteenth birthday.

First it was the windstorms. The sky would blacken. At the start, we could not tell if it were locusts or sand. A reverse wind from the desert to the sea—called the khamsin, a wind with furnacelike heat—whipped over us. All you could do was find a place close to the ground and turn your back to the wind and lay there gasping, sometimes for hours. Billions of grains of sand bite at you with hurting velocity. You cannot move in it. You cannot open your eyes, for fear the sand will blind you. The sand rips into your clothing and sours your skin and strains your efforts to breathe.

No matter how we tried to seal off the cave, sand found its way into everything—our grain, our weapons, our fuel. Sand burrowed its way into our hair. We would spit it out for a week afterward, but sand was always in our teeth and noses and, no matter how we tried to clean the cave, there was always sand mixed in our food and pitted under our fingernails and embedded in our skin.

On the heels of the sandstorms came the little lice. They dug their way into our eyebrows and the hair of our bodies. We would douse each other with petrol, then go to the springs, but our soap was running low and, in order to destroy the lice, we had to live with petrol burns on our skin.

It always took days to strip our weapons and clean them after a storm and we were forced to use supplies faster than we wanted. Tallow, petrol, oil, soap, and some foods began to dwindle and it was impossible to replace them in Jericho. There was a shortage of everything there, a hundredfold increase in the population, and the inevitable, murderous black market. The hordes who had flocked to Jericho were soon out of money and jewelry. At the cave, we had reached a point of diminishing returns. We simply could not replace what we were using. In two months or less, we would be dry . . . depleted.

The worst part of the windstorms and our dwindling supplies was what it did to our minds. Ramiza and Fatima became miserable in their pregnancies, vomiting continuously and weeping hysterically. The rest of us became testy, quarreling over nothing. At times we flared so quickly we were tempted to blurt out our various secrets to stab home an argument and to inflict pain on the person we did not like at the moment. Of course, we did not give out our secrets but buried them deeper inside ourselves.

Then came the water. The first winter rain and flash flood wiped out our water-collecting dams and split the cistern, ruining a whole spring and summer's work. What little water we collected was dirty and silty, undrinkable and barely usable.

Fissures in the cliff allowed streamlets of water to sop into the cave. In a bad storm, we were ankle-deep in water. It was impossible to contain the leaks and the wet became permanent and mildew began to rot our grain.

The wet also brought vermin, which attacked our food and kept us awake with their sounds and by darting over our bodies.

Our shoes were worn through the soles. Our feet hardened in our climbs around the rocks, but they also tore and bled after jagged knifelike stabs. There was no medicine nor even village herbs to combat the continuous rounds of coughing, dysentery, and fevers. Our clothing was so dilapidated it offered us little protection from sun and heat.

We looked to Haj Ibrahim constantly for the word that we should quit and leave, for leaving became the lesser of the evils. Even with Father as our leader, our willpower had run extremely low. The confidence and family pride we had retained collapsed to universal fear, hopelessness, and suspicion.

What really broke Haj Ibrahim's back was the continuous bad news brought from Jericho. The second truce had ended. In rapid succession, the flagship of the Egyptian Navy was sunk, then the Jews captured Beersheba and were running the Egyptians out of the Negev and even crossing into the Sinai. What was left of Kaukji and the Army of Liberation was driven over the borders.

Syria was a dead issue—isolated in the Galilee—and Lebanon had never been a factor.

Even though in two more attempts the Jews could not capture Latrun, they had built a bypass road into Jerusalem and saved their part of the city.

With disaster imminent for the Arabs, the hour for tribal vengeance arrived.

Clovis Bakshir, the mayor of Nablus, was assassinated at his desk by a Mufti gunman for his support of Abdullah.

Abdullah retaliated by having the Legion's Special Squads eliminate a half-dozen pro-Mufti muktars and by rounding up dozens of sympathizers throughout the West Bank and jailing them in Amman.

As everyone's grand scheme to destroy the Jews collapsed, the sordid stories of one secret deal after another began to emerge in the backwash.

The first to come to light had been initiated by the Saudis, who had an enormous common border with Jordan. The Saudi family also had a long-standing blood feud with Abdullah. It had been the Saudis who had ejected Abdullah and his Hashemite family from Arabia. Such a thing would never be forgotten. The Saudis quaked at the thought of Abdullah growing powerful, for soon enough he would harbor thoughts of revenge.

Since it had always been paramount to an Arab victory to suck in Abdullah's Arab Legion, the Saudis paid off the Egyptians, Iraqis, and Syrians to lure Abdullah into the war. Their plot was to have the Legion grab up the West Bank, then assassinate Abdullah, dissolve his kingdom, and split it up among themselves. Abdullah craftily managed to stay clear of the assassin while his troops secured their West Bank gains.

A second plot was sponsored by the Egyptians, who had seized the Gaza Strip. They brought the Mufti to Gaza, where he and his followers set up an "All-Palestine Government." In truth, the Egyptians treated the Gaza Strip, not as Palestine, but as administrated military territory.

Now some of Abdullah's other deals began to emerge. Kaukji, it turned out, had been an agent of Abdullah all the time. Kaukji fingered many of the Mufti's men with whom he was supposed to be in a joint command. These men met the standard fate. In payment, Kaukji was to be proclaimed the first governor of the West Bank of Palestine and rule it in behalf of Abdullah.

Meanwhile, inside Egypt, Iraq, and Syria, the bloodletting, jailings, and killings between ministers and generals was under way over the loss of the war. Regimes tottered everywhere.

Our worst storm came right after the New Year of 1949. The flash flood was so violent that it leaped out of the wadi beds and found its way into our cave in a dozen places. We had come to within an inch of defeat. Kamal went berserk with fear one night, the pregnant women were a mess, Jamil and Omar got into a fistfight, and even Hagar, the woman of iron, was showing terrible strain.

I returned one day from a trip to Jericho and immediately found my father, who was entrenched, as always, by the machine gun. I saw him now bundled in rags, drenched.

"Father," I cried, "it is over. There is another cease-fire, but this time they speak of an armistice."

Ibrahim turned to me, his face dripping rain so I could not truly determine if there were tears coming from his eyes.

"Must we go with Abdullah now, Father?"

He laughed ironically, tragically. "No," he whispered. "None of them who forced us to leave will face this catastrophe. It will take them fifty years to come to the point. To admit the Jews have won? They cannot come to that point . . . never. We cannot wait, Ishmael. Let them hack at each other's flesh, let them break each other's bones. They will settle nothing. Curse them for what they have brought on us. We have only one mission. We are going to get back to Tabah. Think only of returning to Tabah. Think only of Tabah. . . ."

Chapter Ten

January 1949

Gideon Asch rather enjoyed his liaisons with Colonel Farid Zyyad of Jordanian Intelligence. As a product of the British military and a graduate of Sandhurst, Zyyad had chucked a number of the habits that plagued meetings between Arab and non-Arab. Zyyad was capable of getting to the point, of not trying to smother a weak idea in a rich sauce of words, and he kept slogans to a minimum.

The obscure village of Talal hosted their secret contacts. The village was near the battle lines around Ramallah where some of her fields spilled over into Jewish-held territory. Fighting was static on this front under a tacit understanding, a quasi-truce that allowed the peasants to cross back and forth to tend their crops.

Every so often, a Jordanian squad would sweep in and advise the villagers to clear their fields and stay inside their homes. Shortly afterward, a vehicle bearing Zyyad would whisper in and park near an abandoned observation post.

A few moments later, a lone figure would advance from the Jewish side and make contact by a signal lamp. With a return signal, Gideon crossed over and entered the post.

A bottle of Johnny Walker Black Label, which Gideon only saw these days at his meetings with Zyyad, sat on the desk awaiting his arrival. As Gideon entered, Zyyad filled the glasses.

"To our British mentors."

Gideon held up his glass in salute. "It has just been settled, Zyyad. The Island of Rhodes has been agreed upon for the armistice talks. Ralph Bunche himself has agreed to mediate. Abdullah will be informed within the hour in Amman."

"Then Jordan will be speaking with you first," Zyyad said eagerly.

"No, it's going to be the Egyptians," Gideon answered.

"You promised we would negotiate first."

"I promised I'd try. I tried. I couldn't swing it."

"It makes no sense. The Egyptian Army is completely routed. We hold territory. You must speak with us first."

"Unfortunately, the powers that be still consider Egypt to be the major Arab nation."

"They fought like women!"

Gideon shrugged.

"When does the conference begin?" Zyyad asked.

"In a week or ten days. I think January thirteenth was mentioned."

Colonel Zyyad twirled his glass, sipped, grunted. "How long can you stall a cease-fire with the Egyptians?"

"Not for very long," Gideon said, knowing he was to fly down to the Negev and give the order personally.

"The Egyptians are ready to collapse," Zyyad said. "Two days —three at most—and they will surrender the Gaza Strip to you with half of their army."

"We have no designs on the Gaza Strip," Gideon answered.

"Stop playing Arab games with me," Zyyad said with a trace of irritation. "Jordan must have the Gaza Strip and access to the sea through Israeli territory."

"I see that you gentlemen in Amman are already into future planning."

"The Kingdom has one outlet to the sea in Aqaba. Egypt can choke it off at will. We cannot remain at their mercy. We must have a port in Gaza."

"The British should have thought of that when they created the mess in Eastern Palestine, Zyyad. Besides, haven't you got it mixed up about who is your ally and who is your enemy?"

"You want me to say it? All right, I'll say it. Egypt is more our enemy than Israel. You know why we have to have Gaza. We also know what you want in return and we are prepared to deal."

"If you're going to ask us to capture and hold the Gaza Strip for you, then we are going to ask for a peace treaty in return. Not a truce, not an armistice, but a peace treaty. You know that Abdullah is not strong enough to make a treaty, even if he wants to."

Working with the new Jewish state through a territorial interdependence had great appeal to Abdullah. Economically, he stood to benefit by collaboration with the Jews. As "silent" partners, Israel and Jordan would cause Egypt, Iraq, and Syria to ponder heavily before trying another attack. After all, the Jews and Abdullah were artificially forced enemies.

A peace treaty? A thunderously bold idea. But it would be Abdullah's death warrant. Abdullah would be declared a non-Arab, a pariah, a leper. Even his own Legion might turn on him. No, such a bold move was not to be made.

Zyyad withdrew an envelope of royal stationery, but the back was not sealed. "Read it, please, then I'll seal it."

Honorable David Ben-Gurion,
Prime Minister, State of Israel

Most distinguished friend and adversary:

We have fought an arduous and bloody war, not always in our mutual interests and not always with great conviction. Unfortunately, there will be many unresolved questions. Since there may be several truths about the same situation and meanings are not constant from one state to another, quiet future co-operation between us is imperative.

As you may suspect, we are not always totally free to act independently, so we must be patient. Patience eventually will prevail. However, unspoken words and unwritten understandings can be as strong as a meaningless armistice paper. Such understandings could ensure us a long period of peace and growth.

I therefore implore you to complete your conquest of the Gaza Strip to eliminate a mutual enemy and think in terms of granting us future control. It would ensure my annexation of the West Bank and both of us the greatest chance for co-existence.

Give the Gaza Strip to the devil! But for God's sake, do not let the Egyptians have it.

With greatest sincerity and admiration,
I remain,
Abdullah

Gideon climbed aboard the waiting Piper Cub at the small, jerry-built airstrip near the Monastery of the Cross in West Jerusalem.

"Tel Aviv?" the pilot asked.

"No. Forward command post on the Southern Front."

"Where the hell is it?"

Gideon played with the map for several moments, then circled an unmarked grid in the Sinai a few miles from El Arish.

"There's a strip down there somewhere. Do you have a fre-
quency?"

"Yes, but the transmitter is pretty weak."

"Well, we'll give them a call and get the exact location when we
get close enough."

The plane circled three times to gain altitude out of Jerusalem
and flew down the corridor with its plunging ravines on either
side. As flat land showed below, they turned left toward the
Negev. The first inklings of a sandstorm began to bounce the
little craft around. Gideon, the boldest of men on a horse, turned
white-knuckled. The pilot laughed. He had parachuted many
rounds of ammunition and food to isolated kibbutzim in far
worse weather. "Hang onto your seat, Gideon. We're going to
have a ride."

The end of the war was bringing to a head a long-standing
philosophical split between Ben-Gurion and his generals. Although B.G. was a turn-of-the-century pioneer of Palestine's
swamplands and the leader of its great political struggles, some of
what he was had been carried out from the ghettos of Poland.

Ben-Gurion had a natural Jewish distrust of the military, for it
had always spelled repression. On the one side, he did not totally
trust Jewish fighting capability. On the other hand, he feared a
large Jewish military establishment. The new lads of the
Palmach, the Haganah, and now the Israel Defense Forces represented a generation gap.

Many in the new military felt that the Old Man had reached
his apex when he proclaimed Israel's Declaration of Independence. He had alienated himself early on with the Young Turks of
the Palmach and Haganah by putting more credence in political
settlement than in arms. He clung to an ancient theory that no
small country should go to war without the backing of a major
power. Since this was not possible, he opted to work things out
politically. He was usually at loggerheads with his officers, who
wanted larger battle formations and more money for arms. The
warriors had concluded that the new state would have to have a
tough Jewish army to secure its boundaries.

The rift was personified by Yigal Allon, who had been declared
the greatest Jewish general since Joshua and Joab in the Bible.
Like Gideon Asch, Allon had been born in the Galilee, was an

early kibbutznik, and as a young Palmach officer was dearly loved by his men. Allon had it all. He was the combination of mediator, planner, tough commander, educator, and, most of all, a completely honest and dedicated person. Like other leaders of the IDF, he knew his men better than most generals in most armies— anywhere. He had become the first commander of the Palmach, the first commander of division-sized formations, a father and builder of the new Army. He was only thirty years of age, but it was universally felt he was destined to become a future chief of staff, if not prime minister.

It was also felt that Yigal Allon should have continued to command the most vital Central Front, which included Tel Aviv and also Jerusalem. Perhaps his star was too bright because Ben-Gurion "exiled" him to command the Southern Front in the desert.

It was not that Allon represented a serious political rival but a new kind of Jew that B.G. was not totally familiar or comfortable with, despite his years in Palestine.

The airstrip was located by a weak radio signal that led them to ground panels. Gideon was whisked away as soon as the plane touched down at a tiny oasis within fieldglass sight of El Arish. Yigal Allon and Gideon greeted one another with bear hugs only sightly less forceful than clanging steel.

Allon was a portrait of frustration as he pointed out his army's position to Gideon. El Arish sat at the foot of the Gaza Strip where it crossed into the Sinai Desert. Time had recorded a hundred battles around El Arish from those of Philistine chariots to British tanks. A railroad line, hugging the sea, ran to the Suez Canal and on to Cairo.

"My Intelligence reports that a twenty-car train has arrived. The Egyptian officer corps is planning to flee tonight. I have broken up enough rail track so the train can't pull out until at least tomorrow. But, Gideon, we probed El Arish. They have nothing left. I can take it with two battalions and seal off the entire Gaza Strip."

Gideon was about to give his order to cease fire, but he did not.

"I've been pleading for a meeting with the Old Man for two days to get permission to attack. All I've gotten is silence. Can I bag them now?" Allon asked.

Gideon did not answer. Allon had the right to take his case to
B.G., the Cabinet, the chief of staff and the chief of operations.

"If you promise me you won't attack, I'll guarantee you a meeting with B.G. by morning," Gideon said.

"Suppose cease-fire orders come?"

"They didn't come on my plane," Gideon lied. "Yigal, stay
away from your headquarters for twelve hours. If you never personally received the order, you can't carry it out. Right? Now,
don't be a shmuck. Do as I tell you. I'll try to soften up the Old
Man for you. . . ."

David Ben-Gurion was a small man in build. His outsized bald
head was fringed with a horseshoe shock of snow-white hair, giving him the appearance of a cherub. He was at his petulant best
when Gideon arrived several hours later. He had spent a feverish
day trying to get the cease-fire implemented. It was all in place,
except for the Egyptians, where there were still reports of fighting and a hot young commander, Yigal Allon, demanding his say.
The sight of Gideon buoyed him for the moment.

"You saw Allon?" Gideon was greeted eagerly.

"I saw him about two hours ago."

"Then he has the cease-fire order, thank God."

"I didn't give it to him," Gideon said.

The Old Man's face blanched, then disbelief settled in.

"Yigal has been trying to reach you for two days. You have
deliberately ignored him. He is your southern commander. He is
entitled to speak to you and the Cabinet."

"Who the hell do you think you are, Gideon? Do you want to
be the first Jew executed for insubordination? Do you have any
idea how serious this has become?"

"Yigal is entitled to speak to you," Gideon repeated.

"For what! For permission to destroy the Egyptians? There are
also a quarter of a million refugees packed in the Gaza Strip. We
haven't got bread to feed our soldiers. What are we supposed to
do with theirs!"

Gideon lifted a pencil from the desk and snapped it in half. "We
have the Egyptians right here—trapped, finished."

"I'll see you shot! I'll see Yigal shot!"

"So shoot me. I resign!" Gideon barked and started out of the
office.

"Come back, come back. Sit down," Ben-Gurion said, lowering his tone to a rare conciliatory but ominous rumble. "At what time did you leave Yigal?"

"I flew out at three, just ahead of a sandstorm."

"So do you know who flew in with the sandstorm forty minutes later. No? Well, I'll tell you. The British are demonstrating very clearly that we are not to destroy the Egyptians. In addition to several battleships that have left Cyprus, they flew five Spitfires over our lines as a warning."

"British Spitfires? Against us?"

"British Spitfires. You better hear the rest. We shot them down in a dogfight. We're trying to find their pilots now. A half hour after that, the American ambassador called to advise me that if we don't go into an immediate cease-fire we will not get a single penny in aid. Do you have the faintest notion how bankrupt we are, Gideon?"

Gideon cracked his fist on the table. "Fuck them!" he screamed. "Why is everyone breaking their asses to save the Egyptians! Where the hell were they when Jerusalem was being starved out! Where! Well, I for one am glad we shot their fucking planes down —glad!"

The Old Man waited until Gideon calmed himself. "Nu," he said, "what do you think I should do?"

"Here is some petrol to put on the fire," Gideon said, sliding Abdullah's letter over the desk. Ben-Gurion read it and threw his arms apart in a gesture of futility. "This Abdullah is a real dog. Several hundred of our boys were killed trying to capture Latrun and now he tells us to take the Gaza Strip and hold it for him! The chutzpa!"

"Think of it, B.G. If we take Gaza, Abdullah will give us Latrun and the Jewish Quarter of the Old City in exchange. More than that . . . when we go into negotiations in Rhodes, it will be a powerful bargaining chip. The Egyptians will give us anything to allow their army to escape."

Ben-Gurion shook his great white-fringed head.

"Eventually, ten years, twenty years we must have to talk peace. Our first peace treaty has to be with Egypt. Unless it is, no other Arab state will follow. If we humiliate them further now, it will be fifty years before they will be ready to talk peace."

"Humiliation, my ass! They will only talk peace when they

have no other alternative. They will only keep a peace treaty as long as it suits their purposes. I'll tell you how grateful the Egyptians will be if we hand the Strip to them. They will turn it into a massive guerrilla base and launch a thousand attacks on us. We will pay for giving them Gaza in blood . . . in blood for the rest of our lives."

Ben-Gurion arose and walked to the window, seeing nothing as he stared blankly out to the greenery. "I will see Yigal immediately."

"You mean for a cease-fire."

"That's what I mean." He returned to his desk. "My comrade, we started this dream hoping beyond hope to create a tiny speck of a state. We now have much more than we believed possible. We have a viable state. Penniless, with terrible borders, but viable. If we play with a weak monarch like Abdullah, targeted for assassination, we will get sucked into one round after another of endless little wars."

"But you won't stop those wars by giving up the Gaza Strip. You'll only encourage the Egyptians. They are depending on our softness and they will take every advantage of it," Gideon argued.

"So I have been told. We can fight these wars only as long as we are right. That must be our gamble. Our energies must pour into other things. We have Jews to bring out of those wretched detention camps in Cyprus. We have to find the remnants of our brothers and sisters in Europe and bring them home. We have to get the Jewish communities out of the Arab countries before they are all slaughtered. We have to have a merchant marine, a national airline, we must remake the desert. The world must proclaim our scientists and artists and academicians. The Jewish state has too many priorities to play the Arab game."

"Remember, B.G., every time they raid us from the Gaza Strip in the future, that you have paid a fool's price to save the pride of a gang of decadent Egyptian butchers."

"Then find us new neighbors," Ben-Gurion said. "It may take a long, long time, but Israel has a special mission, unique in the world. We represent the interests of the Western democracies . . . yes, even the British, who threaten us with arms, and the Americans, who threaten us with economic blackmail. Eventually, they will become disgusted with the Arabs and come to realize that without Israel their own existence is in danger."

"How long, oh Lord, until your foolish dream comes true? How long before a Christian nation will place its fate in the hands of the Jews? I stand with Yigal," Gideon said and he left.

END OF PART THREE

Part Four

Jericho

Chapter One

Late Winter 1949

My father summoned me to his ledge one day after the third cease-fire. "We can stay here no longer. We must prepare to go into Jericho. It is Allah's will."

Allah had made the decision for us none too soon.

The cave had become a total disaster. Vermin and rain were rapidly diminishing our supplies. The main cavern leaked in a dozen places, so that dampness and chill were always in our bones and the smell of mildew in our nostrils. We had to keep a stronger fire burning to combat the mustiness, but at times water found its way down the chimney and would hit the fire and turn the cavern into a smokehouse. On several occasions, we were forced outside during the height of a storm to keep from choking to death.

Most of the small offshoot tunnels that led to our individual niches had low spots that had flooded, making passage impossible and forcing all of us to live and sleep in the single main room.

During one storm, Ramiza lost her footing, slipped, and plunged down through jagged rocks, battering herself up terribly and causing her to have a miscarriage. An infant would have been difficult to keep alive in our circumstances. Ramiza, next to Kamal, was the weakest of our lot and added to our burden. We made a required demonstrative show of anguish over the loss, but we did not mourn for long.

Other disasters mounted, but one dominant factor told us it was time to leave. We were becoming hungry. A major concern was what to do with our invaluable arms cache. Guns were always a prime item of trade and if we got into serious money problems we could sell off a rifle here, a pistol there. On the other hand, a man like Haj Ibrahim does not give up his weapons readily.

I was assigned the mission of finding a suitable dump for the arms someplace closer to Jericho. Tent cities were sprouting up all over the barren hillsides around the town. Inland from

Jericho, there rose a sudden string of steep cliffs much like the area of our cave.

Atop one of these cliffs, only a few miles removed from the town, stood a Greek Christian monastery called St. George. Nobody could hide from the world better than Greek monks. The main trail to the monastery came off the Jerusalem road and was scarcely negotiable by foot. From the Jericho side, the monastery was buried from view. I felt that if I could scale the cliffs under the monastery, I could find a foolproof hiding place.

It was impossible to dig a trench or hole to bury the cache, for most of the desert soil was so hard that in most cases the dead were not even buried but covered with stone cairns. If I attempted to dig in the earth, it could be detected immediately by the Bedouin.

It boiled down to finding a niche or small cave, hidden from all view, that our donkey Absalom could reach. I could not handle the task alone, so Father and I discussed who else would be the most trustworthy. I personally wanted Nada, but dared not bring up the subject. Sabri was the obvious choice, but we never fully trusted him. We settled on Jamil.

For the next several days, Jamil and I left Qumran in the middle of the night so we could pass through Jericho and the camps during the darkness and position ourselves up in the cliffs below St. George by daybreak.

I was disheartened to learn that the monastery was on a clifftop called Mount Temptation. This is where the Christians believed that Jesus spent forty days in the wilderness combating Satan. I was quite certain that our cave near Qumran was the true cave of Jesus and David. The Christians and Jews were wrong about many historic locations, particularly the tombs of saints and prophets. They did not really know where Moses and Samuel were buried until Mohammed received the word from Allah and revealed the true locations. So Christian pilgrims had been going to many wrong places for centuries.

We had to climb the cliffs carefully, for there were many observation points around the monastery. Our months at Qumran had taught us much about following wadi beds and tiny canyons. Jamil and I used that skill to slither about unseen like a pair of rock-colored lizards. On the fourth day, Jamil called me over to a crevice, an opening of perhaps two feet in height. It looked promising. No path or trail ran near it, it could not be seen from the monastery above, and we could coax our donkey Absalom up to it. We wiggled our way inside. The opening was too small to hold all our arms, but a fissure formed a narrow tunnel eighteen to twenty inches wide. It led us back to a second crevice, an opening of several square feet. We examined it for possible rain leaks but found none.

That night we loaded Absalom for the first of four trips it would take to move the arsenal. Again we worked our way into position before daylight, then struggled for many hours, crawling back and forth to the second crevice with only inches to spare.

When the cache was secured, we emptied the cave at Qumran of anything that still had value. Most of the supplies were carried on the backs of the men or wrapped in large bundles and balanced on the heads of the women. Even Fatima, who had a two-year-old baby in her arms and was six months pregnant, took a load.

Absalom was lightly loaded to make room for my father to ride. He did not appear quite so noble as he had aboard el-Buraq. The rest of us, trailing behind him, formed a threadbare, pathetic line of spiritually dehydrated human beings. Our shoe soles were stuffed with newspapers. Omar and Kamal had to wrap their feet in rags. After a mile, all our feet, except Father's, were bleeding. I marveled at Fatima, who was as strong as the men, despite her condition, and at Nada, who actually walked as tall and regal as a queen as we straggled toward Jericho. Actually, it was more of a crawl than a walk. Hagar had lost most of her plumpness to a sagging skin and was very weak. After the second time she fainted, my father mercifully allowed her to ride for short periods on Absalom.

There were two main tent cities forming about Jericho. At the northern tip of the town were the ruins of ancient Jericho and a spring called Ein es-Sultan, whose flow made the oasis that allowed Jericho to come into existence nearly ten thousand years earlier. The spring now supplied water for thousands of displaced persons. Two more camps were rising a bit farther north on the highway.

A second area south of Jericho, Aqbat Jabar, stepped up the

sloping barren hills toward the base of Mount Temptation. The camp forming here was much closer to our arms cache, so we settled for it.

No one was in charge and nothing was organized. Tens of thousands of people simply milled about aimlessly. There were no toilets, kitchens, or clinics. Red Crescent trucks arrived from Amman sporadically. Those in charge of distributing tents, food, blankets, and medicine had created an impossible bureaucracy that was already dominated by black marketeers. Food was flung at us as though we were a flock of chickens. Getting water meant standing in line most of the day awaiting a water truck that often never arrived and often ran dry with half the line still waiting. For the first fortnight, we slept on the ground and had to endure two heavy downpours.

At last a convoy filled with supplies arrived from Damascus. We were forced to line the streets and cheer as they drove through while a film crew recorded the arrival. Before anything was doled out, we had to listen to three hours of speeches about how the Zionists had brought us to this and how our Arab brothers were rushing to our rescue. Children were placed around the food trucks and when the cameraman signaled we all had to hold up our hands and scream like beggars.

We managed to get sleeping mats and two six-man army tents and discovered that none of the cargo came from an Arab country but were gifts from the world through the International Red Cross.

Now came our real problem. Most of the displaced were people who had fled together in a body—an entire village or tribe or clan. The most desirable ground at Aqbat Jabar was that closest to Jericho. Since there was no authority, a territorial argument raged. The larger groups with the most men had the strength to claim the best areas. We were a small family, cut off from our clans. Allah willing, they were someplace in Lebanon. There were other "stray" families similar to ours and Haj Ibrahim quickly went about locating them and banding them together under his leadership. My father's personal stature drew in several hundred families. They had known of him as the Muktar of Tabah and now his legend grew as our flight to the cave at Qumran became known. He staked a claim on behalf of his new followers.

Our area was called Tabah, just as the other tribes named their sections for their former villages.

At first we tried to build mud-brick dwellings, but the rains did not give the chance for them to dry out properly and each time it rained our hovels were melted. We went under canvas.

Haj Ibrahim slept in one tent with Hagar and Ramiza. The other six-man tent was divided into three parts by cloth curtains. Omar, Jamil, Sabri, and I had one section; Fatima, Kamal, and their daughter had the second; and Nada had a tiny space to herself. When all the mats were laid down at night, there was no room to walk, excpet over the top of one another.

The Bedouin tent is made of animal skins and furs and can withstand the fiercest weather. Our tents were from Italy and of thin canvas, unfit for their task. They leaked so badly we might as well have been in the middle of a running wadi bed. When the rains ceased, dust storms riddled them like shotgun pellets and, with summer, the sun rotted out what was left.

In that first year, no one escaped severe dysentery. Cholera and typhoid swathed through Aqbat Jabar like the ghost of death wielding his scythe. Many children went up to Allah, including Kamal and Fatima's little girl, who died of the cough. There was only one doctor from Jericho and one who had fled from Jaffa, along with a half-dozen nurses, to cope with the epidemics. They had to contend with over fifty thousand people in the five camps around the town. There was some vaccine but not nearly enough for all of us and it came down to the strongest clans and those offering the largest bribes who received inoculations.

When summer came, the heat dominated all other miseries. It was rarely under ninety degrees and often soared close to one hundred and thirty when the khamsin winds blew in from the desert. If one counted the flies in Aqbat Jabar, we had a population of billions. Open sores and open sewers were their meat of life, making a misery matched only by huge bloodthirsty mosquitoes. We constructed a mud-brick hovel that afforded us a bit more space than the tents, but no one had an iota of privacy. Not a tree grew at Aqbat Jabar and the only playgrounds were the wide paths of sewage that ran through the camp down to the Dead Sea.

Many visions of hell have been written about in the Koran. If they were all put together, surely hell would have resembled Aqbat Jabar.

What shattered me was the way most of the people reacted to this hell. We were told that, as good Moslems, we must accept our fate as Allah's will. The lack of desire to do anything about our own plight made Aqbat Jabar a camp of the living dead. My father had led, my father had fought, my father had pride. By Allah's holy name, most of us were simply dogs.

Oh, they complained all right. From morning to night, there was little spoken of except the injustice of the exile and a foggy notion of the return—and talk of the return was filled with childish fantasy. The war was done and we learned that conditions in the camps around Amman were no better than at Aqbat Jabar. Little help came to us from the outside and what did come rarely originated in Arab countries.

It was the realization of a nightmare. The most horrible aspect of that nightmare was that there were tens of dozens of camps all over the West Bank of Palestine. We were Palestinians in Palestine, but our own people didn't lift a finger on our behalf. Instead, they treated us like lepers.

Haj Ibrahim, with his constituency of several thousand "strays," had become one of the leaders in Aqbat Jabar. He and four or five of the other old muktars tried desperately to instill some semblance of dignity into our people.

We had artisans among us. We had woodworkers, copper workers, shoemakers, cloth weavers. We had a few teachers and merchants. Yet we did nothing. We did not plant a tree. We did not plant a flower. We did not open a school. We did not police ourselves. We did not seek land to farm. We made no attempt to create industry. We did not even collect and remove our own garbage.

We rotted and complained. We blamed the Jews. We became overpowered with self-pity. We waited for a guilty world, which we thought owed us everything, to come and save us, for we were incapable of saving ourselves.

My father sat in meeting after meeting most of the days and half of the nights. Every attempt he and his few allies made to organize the camp and govern it responsibly broke down into heated fights over tribal rights. The main argument was that if we did something for ourselves the Jews and the world outside would mistake it as believing that we accepted the exile. So long as we did nothing, we could continue to weep to the world and the Arab leaders could continue to harangue the Jewish state.

Ibrahim came into our hovel a hundred times, cursing and filled with despair over our lethargy and lack of dignity. When some camps were moved close to the border, he realized it had been done so the displaced could look over to their stolen land day and night and build a storehouse of hatred.

One evening after a particularly bitter meeting with the other sheiks and muktars, Father and I walked together near the foot of Mount Temptation, where we could look down on the crush of mud hovels.

"Ishmael," he whispered, "we are betrayed. We are prisoners in our own land. Deliberately created prisoners. Do you know who will eventually take over these camps? The strongest assassins. Allah only knows what kind of a breed we are creating here and Allah only knows what kind of disasters they are going to lead us to. Our hatred for the Jews will blind us to any attempt to become decent human beings again."

He put his hand on my shoulder. "Ishmael, you and I will go into Jericho every day. We will listen and we will look. Somewhere in that town, someone is in contact with the Jews and knows how to reach Gideon. Let us see if there is some way I can deal with the Jews and return to Tabah. Or else we will be left to die in this horrible place."

Chapter Two

Jericho, I have learned, is as old as any city in the world—nearly ten thousand years. The walled city itself dates back almost nine thousand years. Jericho was almost always an Arab city. In those ancient days, we were called Canaanites. The entire land of Canaan was stolen from us for the first time when Joshua conquered it over three thousand years ago.

I am grateful that Mohammed and the Koran corrected all the early misinformation the Jews gave about Jericho when they wrote their so-called Bible, a proven forgery. King David, whom the Jews turned on because they did not believe him, wrote his famous "Psalm 23" about the Wadi of Jericho, calling it "the valley of the shadow of death." David became a Moslem saint and prophet. With the gift of prophecy, he must have had visions of Aqbat Jabar and the other camps around Jericho and that's why he called it by such a name.

Mark Antony gave Jericho to Cleopatra as a present. Jesus knew the area well, for he wandered around in the nearby wilderness. He also walked in the very streets of Jericho, where he gave a blind beggar his sight back.

Herod, a pure Arab king who ruled the Jews, had a weekend palace and hot pools in Jericho where he drowned several relatives who threatened his throne.

It was a very famous town, but it didn't look very good these days.

We had to sell Absalom because we could no longer feed him. He had been a very good donkey and became my friend. We had many conversations when we went from the cave to our spring and into Jericho. Many peasants can be cruel to their donkeys, so I made certain that Absalom had a good master. Nada cried openly when he was sold. I hid my tears, naturally.

Haj Ibrahim and I walked from Aqbat Jabar into Jericho each day and listened anyplace where we could pick up clues of who might be doing business with the Jews across the armistice boundaries. We covered every café, souk, kiosk, and store and sniffed among the street peddlers. We fenced around with the beggars, who often were undercover traders in things like hashish. We listened around the bus station, the Red Crescent office, at the Allenby Bridge, the Jordanian military camps, even the mosques.

When we felt we had hit upon a likely agent of the Jews, we had to be extremely tender about how we approached him. In our world, it often took two men ten minutes to merely say hello to one another. If there were no point to the meeting, a half hour of fruitless parables and proverbs often drifted out of their mouths, followed by another ten-minute discourse to break off the meeting politely so that no one was left offended. It was painstaking work, but after a month's search we were left completely frustrated.

One evening I returned late from Jericho and reported to Father that I had found nothing new. He threw up his arms in despair and turned his back. I was enraged with frustration. Making contact with the Jews had become the obsession of my father's life. It cut me deeply not to be able to do this for him.

There were other reasons I had to succeed. Sabri had won a new place in my father's heart. With his great skill as an auto mechanic, he was the one in a thousand who could find work in Jericho. When he handed my father his pay each week, Ibrahim often patted his head and told him what a great lad he was.

Jamil was also coming more and more into view. He was hanging around all day with a gang of boys who talked nothing but vengeance. Their bravado was encouraged by the older men, who fed them on battles that never were, acts of courage that never happened. So far, Haj Ibrahim was not listening to the voices of revenge, but when one hears that talk day and night, Allah only knew when he would change his thinking.

As night crept into the valley, I would walk through the camp up to the base of Mount Temptation to get away from the mangle of people. I would climb up in the rocks so I would not have to look down on Aqbat Jabar. Once in a while, I had a reverie that I was back on my ledge in the cave before all the trouble began there.

The sky was never as clear at Mount Temptation because of the lights from the camps and the town. Yet there I could meditate, just as Ibrahim had done at the prophet's tomb in Tabah. One night I put all my might into thinking about our problem as I huddled in the rocks to sleep.

I awakened to the sound of music of a shepherd's flute. It was neither day nor night, but all around and about me was a strange, soft glow of light—blues and violets and yellows—that seemed to be illuminating and pulsating from the rocks. I walked toward the music and there, around the next boulder, sat a plump little man, bald on top, with a fringe of silver hair.

"Good evening," I said politely. "May God bless our meeting."

"He has, Ishmael," he said, setting his flute aside.

"How do you know my name?" I asked.

"Because I am a Moslem saint and prophet," he answered. Oh, now that scared me! "You have heard of revelation, haven't you?"

My mouth quivered out a yes of sorts. "Who . . . are you?" I croaked.

"I am Jesus," he said.

My impulse was to flee, but some strange power held me fast.

"Do not be frightened, my little friend." Whoever he was, he was a nice man and I began to feel I was not in danger.

"You look nothing like your pictures," I dared.

"Graven images," he snapped. "Do I look tall and red-haired and with a beard?"

"No."

"If I were, then I surely wouldn't be Jesus. I don't know how the rumors about my appearance got started. And I certainly don't know why a man with my aspect cannot be as holy as those graven images."

Just that quickly, he disappeared.

"Where are you?" I cried.

"Here!" bounced back crazily in echoes through the stone walls.

I chanced to look at myself. My rags were gone! I was dressed in a robe of fine black and white linen trimmed in gold with a breastplate of jewels.

"Here," the voice called . . . "here."

Suddenly I began to rise off the ground. I felt a rocking motion beneath me and looked down to see I was astride a magnificent huge beast and we were levitating over the cliff of Mount Temptation. The animal galloped in enormous strides, although there was nothing beneath his hooves, and he snorted blue lightning bolts from his nostrils, making no sound.

He turned his face to me and smiled. It was Absalom! But it was not Absalom. He was the color of flowing honey and wore a blanket of the same magnificent cloth of my own robes. I was sure it was Absalom, but his face reminded me of Nada and his great hooves were covered with diamonds. He wore no saddle, so I clung to his mane, which was braided into shiny black tails three feet long.

"Here . . . here . . . here," the voice called as we rose upward in leaps that covered a hundred miles.

I began to feel quite safe aboard Absalom as we plunged hell-bent into a belt of long-tailed comets. While they flashed past, I could see that each had the face of a Moslem saint but looked queerly like many of the old men who had died in Tabah. Once through the comets, we entered a rage of sheet lightning that boomed and distorted in the sky.

We had come to a sea as smooth as Nada's skin, and Absalom strode upon the sea with no trouble, then through great caves a thousand feet high, their salt icicles encrusted with silver dust. Beyond the caves, we rode on in total blackness. The wind was filled with the scent of myrrh.

"You may dismount now, Ishmael."

I obeyed without hesitation and there I was, standing in the middle of the universe. Absalom was gone, but I feared no evil. A path appeared before me, paved with large alabaster bricks that I followed into a forest of olive trees with trunks of ivory and leaves of twinkly rubies and fruit that appeared as cats' eyes.

The flute lured me off the path to a showering waterfall that fell into a pool of wine. There was a great open meadow past it, carpeted with deep rose petals of many colors and the softest grass I had ever felt. Jesus sat among the roses.

"Where are we?" I asked.

"The first paradise," Jesus answered. "I can go no farther."

"But certainly you can go anywhere in heaven!"

"Unfortunately, not until Allah makes a final disposition of my case. When I first arrived, Allah assured me that my followers and I had the exclusive use of heaven. It bothered me to have to evict everyone who had inhabited the earth and died before my birth. I was most troubled to throw the Jews out. I was once a Jewish rabbi, you know. However, an entire religion had been named for me and Allah had given them heaven, for they alone knew the truth out of all mankind. We could wander all the way up to the seventh paradise until he came."

"Who is he?"

"Mohammed."

"You know Mohammed!"

"Oh, indeed I do. Until he arrived, I was looked upon as the son of

Allah. Mohammed argued vehemently for centuries and I was finally demoted to being a Moslem saint and prophet."

"Well, what are you, Jesus? A Jew, a Christian, or a Moslem?"

"I am a true believer. Islam has the exclusive use of heaven now, you know."

"But why can't you go beyond the first paradise?"

"I still refuse to go along with Mohammed's contention that all nonbelievers must be burned alive. I have managed to convince Allah that the nonbelievers should be able to remain, at least in the first paradise. But I must say, Mohammed is persistent. He wants everyone else burned."

"Do the Christians know you are truly a Moslem?"

"They would refuse to believe it, at least until Allah renders his final decision on the matter. I don't want to trouble Allah because, after all, he has seven hundred and fifty-four billion trillion other planets to look after, to say nothing of all the suns and all those crazy comets."

"But if there is only one true heaven, where do the people go from all those other planets?"

"They all have their seventh heavens. One set per planet, that's the rule. But I came to help you with your problem, Ishmael," he said, changing the subject of heavenly politics abruptly. "You will soon see the golden ladder," Jesus said. "Climb it and you will find the answer."

"But that is an impossible riddle," I protested.

"Everything up here is a riddle. If we did not talk in riddles, no one would understand us."

Just beyond him, the mighty golden ladder appeared. I was now terrified. "O Jesus," I cried, "help me! What is the truth of heaven?"

"The truth is that Allah is one. He is all-good and also all-evil. He has planted an equal measure of both in all of you. You have been given a mind, in order to wage the war within yourself and to satisfy only yourself. Hang onto your own soul. Don't give it away. Find your own answer and you will be free."

"That is the most terrible riddle of all!"

"Someday you might understand it. Now climb, Ishmael. In order to answer your problem, you must climb to a level you have once climbed and you will find it."

"But . . . but . . ."

"No more questions. Use your mind. I must go. I still have a long journey and I have no horse."

At first, climbing the golden ladder was euphoria, a miracle. But as I kept going up, each new rung began to make my body heavier and my hands and feet less secure. I slipped! The ladder was gone! I was scaling a cliff—an impossible cliff—struggling and sweating and grabbing and grunting with fear. I fell exhausted on a ledge, bleeding and weeping.

There was a strange door before me. As I reached for it, it opened. I was in a room as great as a king's palace, but it was bare except for a tiny little ancient pot that bore an inscription: ASHES OF THE PAST.

At that instant, I began to plunge. I was falling and all the strange sights and scents and noises I had heard were jumbled together and mocking me. I could see the planet earth come into view. I fell faster and faster. The lights of Aqbat Jabar appeared as a distant spark that grew larger and larger. I would be smashed into a million pieces! Down . . . down . . . down. . . . O Allah, HELP ME!

A slit of sunlight pried my eyes open. I knew! I knew! I rushed down Mount Temptation to Aqbat Jabar, falling in my speed and skinning my hands and knees. I ran into our hovel breathlessly and grabbed Haj Ibrahim's hand and pulled him outside.

"Father," I whispered into his ear, "I know how to contact the Jews!"

Chapter Three

I could not tell Haj Ibrahim about my journey to the first paradise. The family would have believed me and would have been terribly envious that I had received a personal visit from Jesus.

When he had been the Muktar of Tabah, my father heard many strange stories at his table at the café. We do not scoff at something that appears to be fantasy. In fact, it is difficult for us to tell where fantasy ends and reality begins. My father alone usually doubted these stories, but never to the face of the storyteller, for that would have offended him.

I was certain my journey had taken place and had solved a baffling mystery. Yet I didn't want to take the chance of appearing foolish in Ibrahim's eyes. I decided to attack the problem with logic, for he was one of the few men who could respond to it.

"Look!" I cried, pointing to a sign below a second floor window across the street. The sign read: DR. NURI MUDHIL, PROFESSOR OF ARCHAEOLOGY.

"In the name of the Prophet, will you tell me what is going on?" Ibrahim demanded.

"Remember in Tabah, when the children hung around down by the highway? What did they do?"

"They begged," he answered.

"What else?"

"They sold drinks and produce."

"And what else?"

"The son is not supposed to give riddles to his father. It is the other way around."

"What else was sold?" I insisted.

"Arrowheads, potsherds."

"Who bought them?"

Ibrahim got caught up in my game. "Mostly the Jews bought them," he said.

"May Allah forgive me for bringing up my terrible indiscretion of entering the Shemesh Kibbutz against your will, but I must tell you what I saw. The Jews put up an entire museum of antiquities. All the children in Tabah knew that the Jews would buy anything from us that was an antiquity. I learned that many other kibbutzim had their own museums as well. The Jews are insane for museums."

My father's face began to light up. I pressed on excitedly. "Do you remember that once or twice a year someone would discover an unbroken vase or urn? We always took it to Jerusalem because the Old City dealers gave a better price. I have seen things we have sold to the Barakat family end up in the museum in Shemesh. Do you remember when I read to you from the Palestine *Post*, just before the war, that the Jews had paid tens of thousands of pounds for some scrolls found near Qumran."

"Aha," Father said.

"There are hundreds of caves all the way down the Dead Sea and there are many on the Jordan side. The desert is filled with tels covering ancient cities. Is it not logical that the Bedouin have scoured these sites? Is it not logical that he buys them?" I said, pointing to Dr. Nuri Mudhil's sign. "*And is it not logical that he sells them to the Jews?*"

I could see that my reasoning had struck its mark. "You may be right," he said.

My heart was pounding as I reached into my robes and withdrew one of the objects Nada and I had found in the cliffs above our cave. It was a metal stick about a foot long with twin ibex heads carved at the top. Ibrahim unwrapped the paper and wrapped it again.

"What about the other things?" he asked.

"It would be better if we held the rest back," I said.

"You are thinking, Ishmael."

"When you bargain, no matter what he offers, walk out," I instructed.

"You are telling *me* how to bargain!" he roared.

"Of course not. I am but a humble child. Only consider this. Listen to his offer and let him know that you have more similar objects."

"That was exactly my plan," Ibrahim said and crossed the street by himself, bidding me to wait.

Haj Ibrahim went up a staircase of crumbling plaster to the second floor hall. There were four offices, belonging to Jericho's

only doctor, only lawyer, and a freight forwarder of crops from
the West Bank to Jordan. The fourth office bore the name of Dr.
Nuri Mudhil. Ibrahim knocked and entered.

The room was large and haphazardly strewn with books and
papers. Long benches lined two walls, where objects were
brushed and cleaned. On one of the benches, several broken potsherds were in the process of being restored into a large bowl.
Another held drawings and measurements of several antiquities.
The walls were covered with certificates and documents and photographs depicting a warped little man at a dig site or at a banquet or at a university speech. Haj Ibrahim could not read the
documents, but he looked closely at the photographs. In nearly all
of them, Nuri Mudhil was among Westerners, many of whom
appeared to be Jews. How clever of Ishmael, he thought, to have
deduced that this man might possibly have an ongoing business
with the Jews.

The door of a small inner office opened. Dr. Nuri Mudhil had a
badly twisted leg, supported by a crutch under his left armpit.
His right arm was withered.

"Warm greetings on this blessed day," Dr. Mudhil said. "And
now, with the grace and beneficence of the merciful Allah, who is
indeed Almighty Jehovah, the one and only unseen God, and
truly the only God of the seven heavens above this, our own
swimming planet with all of its very own multitudinous and colorful fauna and flora within it, and all the other visibly heavenly
constellations above and around our earth."

"Allah is the greatest. All gratitude, thanks, and praise to Him.
I am blessed this day to have been guided to your office with its
infinite marvels," Haj Ibrahim responded.

"Is there anything about my humble workroom that entices the
eye of so noble a character as you?"

"All here shows a man gifted with great and unusual skills,
upon whom great blessings have been bestowed, so everything is
the same as anything."

"Your eye, I see, is keen and your tongue that of a man who has
learned many surahs of the Koran by memory," the archaeologist
went on.

"The Koran, its most holy words, and its glorified message,"
Ibrahim said. "This blessed book has never failed to move me to
tears and fear of the almighty Allah."

"Yes," Nuri Mudhil continued, "it is indeed a tremendous and mighty miracle for all righteous people living upon this planet."

At that moment, the coffee vendor, never far away, entered with a tray bearing a coffee finjan, cups, and a plate of sticky sweets.

"Your blessed name, sir?"

"I am Ibrahim, temporarily dwelling among the miserable at Aqbat Jabar."

"How may I be of service to you?"

"In my wanderings, since the exile, I have come upon a few items which may be of some interest."

"I am honored by your visit, Ibrahim," Nuri Mudhil said, ushering Ibrahim into his inner office, limping behind his desk, and bidding the guest to be seated. They sipped on their coffee and engaged in cigarettes. Ibrahim noticed that the packet was not a Palestinian brand and the tobacco was of excellent Syrian quality.

When all forms of greetings had exhausted themselves, Ibrahim unwrapped the object and placed it before the archaeologist. Nuri Mudhil's eyes narrowed and his face bore an expression of curiosity. He turned on a bright lamp on his desk and examined the piece with a magnifying glass and emitted a long "Hmmmmmm."

"It is necessary for me to make a few inquiries," Dr. Mudhil said.

"Then you are interested?"

"Yes, of course. Tell me, Ibrahim, did you buy this object or did you find it?"

Ibrahim weighed the question. It seemed innocent enough. "It was found," he answered.

"I will not question you about the exact location of your find, but eventually the location and your history of finding it will relate directly to its worth."

Aha, he is trapping me, Ibrahim thought. "It was discovered in this general area," Ibrahim said.

"Was this all that was found?"

"No, there were a number of pieces."

"A dozen?"

"Mumkin, mumkin."

Dr. Mudhil set the object and his magnifying glass down.

"Shall we take off our robes of politeness and save ourselves weeks of needless conversation and wrangling?"

"By all means," Ibrahim said. "Coming to the point is always first in my mind."

"You are Haj Ibrahim al Soukori al Wahhabi, are you not?"

"Your words have penetrated through many layers of caution. I am Haj Ibrahim. How did you know?"

"Your exploits at Qumran did not go unnoticed in certain circles, just as your entrance into Jericho did not go unnoticed. Am I to deduce that this was found in the caves behind Qumran?"

Ibrahim did not answer.

"Haj Ibrahim," Nuri Mudhil began with monumental patience in his voice, "you are a great man of many seasons, but in matters of antiquities you are a child. The dealers are notorious thieves. I will tell you straight off, without nonsense, you have something very unusual and perhaps quite valuable."

Ibrahim's defenses were shattered by the man's candor. Could it be that he is *not* trying to cheat me?

"I do not wish to boost myself higher than the king's camel, but I have a reputation as an honest man. I did not acquire the respect I have earned by cheating the Bedouin. Indeed, my eminent friend, your own uncle, the great Sheik Walid Azziz, Allah bless his name, has often sat in the very chair you occupy."

"May God forgive me for questioning the word of a man of your stature, but does not Walid Azziz, may Allah guide his way, use a dealer in Beersheba for the tribe's finds?"

"A dealer, yes. There are dealers in Beersheba, in Gaza, in East Jerusalem. But I am the only qualified Arab professor of archaeology in all of Palestine. Walid Azziz sells to his dealer in Beersheba the ordinary discoveries in clay. He knows as well as the next man the value of a pot or an oil lamp. However! When Walid Azziz finds that rare piece in ivory or metal or fine glass or an old piece of Bedouin jewelry, he comes to me. You see, I am qualified and so I can go directly to a number of buyers who trust me completely."

Mudhil opened his desk drawer, took out and unwrapped four small clay scarabs, and set them before Ibrahim. "From the Ta'amira Bedouin. Magnificent, aren't they? The same men tried to penetrate your fortress in the Qumran wadis and were almost killed by you for their efforts."

Haj Ibrahim picked up one of the scarabs and examined it. "What would this fetch?"

"A hundred, a hundred and fifty."

"So much? You are to be envied for the prominence of your clients," Ibrahim said.

The archaeologist wrapped three of the scarabs carefully. As Ibrahim handed him the last one, it crumpled to dust in his hands.

"Pity . . . pity," Mudhil said. "Do not worry. Such is the tender way of antiquities. Fortunately, the men who brought me these have seen objects blow to dust in their very hands. No one must weep."

Ibrahim gaped, tried to apologize, but Mudhil shrugged it off. "Do you feel you have a buyer for this?" Ibrahim said, pointing to his mysterious metal piece.

"I have buyers, provided it is what it appears to be."

"And just what does it appear to be?"

"We call it a standard. A decorative piece—probably a pole of wood was set into the hollow end. What is unusual is that it is not indigenous to this area. I do not recall that anything like this has ever been found in Palestine. This is generally likened to the area of Iran, maybe Iraq. In order to sell it, you must be willing to verify that it and the other objects you found were found around Qumran."

Haj Ibrahim realized that he was indeed a child in a cutthroat game. He seemed to have little choice but to go along with the professor.

"I must have this for a few weeks," Mudhil said.

"But . . . but why?"

"To authenticate it."

"But you are a professor. Surely you know what it is."

"I know what it seems to be. Archaeology deals us more mysteries than the Koran. We must test it to determine its exact age and origin."

"How is that possible?"

"What appears to be dead metal is, in fact, filled with all kinds of living organisms. They are road maps. We can tell its age within a few hundred years. If this is what it seems to be, it could be over six thousand years old. What puzzles me initially is, where did it come from? It is of copper, so we must determine the amount of arsenic and other properties. That will give us the clue of which mine the ore came from."

Ibrahim blinked in wonderment. More important than its worth was that it surely seemed that Nuri Mudhil's buyers were Jews. No Arab he had heard of would invest in antiquities. Ishmael had made a magnificent calculation.

"If I give you this for a week, then I am naked," Ibrahim said.

"You say you have a dozen more of these. It is an absolute guarantee that any buyer will surely want them all. Mohammed could not ask for greater protection."

Ibrahim's plan to outfox the archaeologist vanished. Plot and counterplot swirled through his mind. What if Mudhil told him the entire cache was forgeries and worthless? How could he know? Would it not be better to go directly to a dealer in East Jerusalem and take his chances? But wait! Mudhil had admitted it may be valuable.

"You may have it for a week, of course. No problem," Ibrahim said.

"You have made a prudent decision," Nuri Mudhil answered. He stood up, leaned on his crutch, and without the winding down of a long farewell, ushered Ibrahim to the door.

"I must rush off to Jerusalem," Mudhil said. "This is very exciting."

Chapter Four

Several weeks passed with no word from Nuri Mudhil. My father, who could recite endless parables regarding patience, saw his own become shredded. His fear of a conspiracy grew. He began to expect a raid by the Jordanians, who would find and steal the nine other artifacts from our hovel. I was instructed to take them out of the house and hide them with our arms cache. When Father finally received a note asking to see the archaeologist, he went into Jericho filled with apprehension.

"Ah, come in, Haj Ibrahim! May Allah bless this meeting!"

"May Allah, our divine light, bless all your days, Professor. Your sudden note caught me unawares. I did not expect to hear from you so soon."

The copper standard lay on Mudhil's desk as the two men hemmed and hawed through two cups of coffee, weaving toward the point. Haj Ibrahim was fine-tuned to Mudhil's every word to catch an inference, a hidden meaning, unspoken words between spoken words, unspoken lines between spoken lines. At the same time, he held his own qualms in check and showed nothing outwardly but patience and respect.

Mudhil lifted the twin-headed ibex artifact. "This has created a lot of excitement. However, it begs more questions than it answers."

"Questions that I am certain are not beyond the range of so eminent a personage as yourself and your colleagues, *whoever they may be.*"

"In order to answer the questions, we must have your full and unqualified co-operation," the archaeologist said. "The mysteries are deep enough as it is. We need all the supporting facts we can gather."

"Yes, of course," Ibrahim said. "Is there a potential buyer in the winds?"

"An excellent buyer."

"Aha, then Allah has blessed this day."

Mudhil held up a finger of caution. "Provided you are willing to allow such a buyer to examine the entire treasure trove."

"All the pieces?"

"Yes."

"I suppose you want me to turn them over to you."

"As you may have supposed, the buyer is not in Jericho and it would be difficult for him to come here. Even if he could come, the very tests for analysis could not be carried out in Jericho." While Ibrahim pondered, Mudhil held the standard up again. "We can assume now that this comes from a very, very early period. It is an enormously sophisticated piece of work, particularly for its time. Look at these twists in the handle, the hollow inside, the ibex heads . . . art for all ages. Would it not have to have been made by a very highly advanced people? We simply have little or next to no record of such people in Palestine during the Chalcolithic Age."

"Forgive me, I do not comprehend the time of which you speak."

"It was the age that followed the Neolithic or New Stone Age. Let us call it a copper age, an era of a thousand years between the stone and bronze ages. Curiously enough, we have dug up a number of objects of the stone ages, skulls, arrowheads, a rare agricultural settlement but nothing of the age which followed it. And look here what we are dealing with, exquisite artisanship, six to seven thousand years ago. Why, the copper mines at Timna weren't opened until three thousand years after this was made. Who were these people? How did they get to Palestine? Only through examination of the entire cache can we expect some kind of clues."

"And as to their value as well?"

Nuri Mudhil had the distressing habit of looking directly into the eyes of his listener when he spoke importantly. So intense were they, Haj Ibrahim had difficulty looking back squarely. "As a museum piece, this is priceless. It is also worthless."

"That is a riddle too difficult for me to follow."

"There are wealthy antiquities dealers. There is no such thing as a wealthy archaeologist, nor has any Bedouin been able to retire from selling artifacts. In the Arab world, we have placed very little value on preserving our past. From Egypt to Iraq, our ancient sites have been looted down through the ages, mostly by our own people. There is a department of antiquities in Jordan, but neither a university nor museum. The department exists mainly to interest foreigners in coming to Jordan to dig. They take almost everything out. London is where you will discover ancient Egypt, usually in an unlighted basement or a vault. You see, Haj Ibrahim, the archaeologist works only for the joy of his profession, to have his name on a book of his discoveries, for the thrill of having solved the puzzles of the past. He keeps nothing from the digs for himself, no matter what the value. It all goes to the sponsoring expedition. If a dig yields an enormous treasure trove, the archaeologist may be given a few pieces to grace his home. The rest of a surplus is sold off to dealers."

"Do I hear you correctly, Professor Mudhil, when you infer that I could make much better business by going directly to a dealer?"

"I would hate to see something of such importance end up on the black market or in the home of an unscrupulous private collector who robs an entire nation of its heritage."

"Are you truly telling me that no archaeologist pockets some of his finds?"

Mudhil laughed a wisdom. "It would be unheard of. Maybe that is why I am the only Arab archaeologist in Palestine. He would lose his standing in the academic world immediately. We do not want to lose this treasure trove. However, if the attempt to make a fortune is your object, I suggest you take your find to dealers in East Jerusalem. I will give you several names. Go play with them and may Allah protect you."

Haj Ibrahim's hand went up in a gesture to "halt." "Let me digest the wisdom of your words," he said. "Can you tell me what general area of compensation the buyers might have in mind?"

"How many pieces do you have altogether?"

"Nine more."

"Of the same quality?"

"From what I have seen."

Nuri Mudhil shrugged. "I am no expert on this, but I should think it would be worth several thousand dollars."

Ibrahim's heart pounding was well concealed beneath his robes. "But I am entitled to know who these buyers are, am I not? I would want to know that these go into the proper hands."

"Haj Ibrahim, one must come to a conclusion that your coming

to me was not entirely an accident. The story of how you fled
Nablus with half the Iraqi quartermaster's supplies is a local coffeehouse legend. The reason you fled to Qumran is also the subject of much gossip. One would be given to believe you are not
enormously enthralled with Abdullah and the Jordanians."

"Politics. What do I know of politics?"

"Your modesty is far too great," the archaeologist answered.
"Will you let me have the rest of the collection for examination or
not?"

Ibrahim wiped a sudden burst of perspiration off his face. "You
told me yourself that my protection was the fact that I was holding back the other nine pieces. Now you tell me to give them up.
Who will guarantee me a fair price then? How do I know—and
Allah forgive me for any doubts I might seem to have—but suppose everything is lost."

"Shall we get to the point?" Nuri Mudhil said.

"But of course. Directness is the greatest of virtues."

"Gideon Asch promises you a fair price."

Chapter Five

Professor Doctor Nuri Mudhil was the greatest Arab I had ever met—besides my father. Ibrahim had warned me to answer all his questions honestly. It was a frightening prospect.

I lifted the sack holding the nine other artifacts onto one of his long benches and untied it, then laid the pieces out side by side. Professor Doctor Mudhil limped up to the bench weighing heavily on his crutch and with a magnifying glass in his free hand. He labored onto a stool and bent over so his face was almost touching the objects.

"In Allah's name, this is remarkable," he repeated.

In addition to the twin-headed ibex standard that he had already seen, there were two simple standards and a third with an eagle on it. There were two ivory pieces, carved in an arc shape like a new moon. They had many holes cut or drilled out. Professor Doctor Mudhil reckoned offhand that they might be ceremonial scythes. The seventh object looked like a copper "horn of plenty" with a big bend in its stem. He described the eighth artifact as a mace head. It was the final object that brought him to the brink of tears, a large thick ring which looked like a crown and was adorned with many bird heads around the top rim. As he studied and made notes and measurements, I looked about his workroom filled with wonderments. From the photographs and certificates, he had lectured in many places of the highest importance outside of Palestine. His ordinary dress and modest ways were disarming for a man so renowned. After Professor Doctor Mudhil finished his initial examination, he invited us into his office.

"Ishmael is ready to answer everything truthfully," Haj Ibrahim said. "This boy is wiser than his thirteen years would indicate. He is my confidant and rarely lies. He knows everything, including my search for Gideon Asch. It was Ishmael who figured out that you, as an archaeologist, might have access to the Jewish side."

"You realize the importance of our secret, Ishmael?" he asked.

"Yes, sir," I said.

"You are right. The Jews are the most prodigious explorers of the past. They have an insatiable devotion to their roots."

He laid out aerial maps and photographs of the wadis and cliffs behind Qumran. "We must study these closely and see if we can locate both the cave you lived in and the one where you found the treasure."

I felt extremely important but deflated as I looked at the maps and photographs. I was completely puzzled. As Professor Doctor Mudhil explained their meaning, I became less confused.

"Here," I pointed tentatively.

My father looked but could not understand and nodded cautiously in agreement.

"So you saw an opening above your cave and were taunted into climbing up to it?"

"Yes, sir."

"You went up alone?"

"He went with a boy named Sabri, whom we took into our family at Nablus. Sabri is working in Jericho, but I can arrange a meeting with him," Ibrahim said.

"Well, answer the professor. You went up together," my father insisted.

"Sabri did not go all the way with me. He became frightened of the height and quit."

"You went the rest of the way alone?" Professor Mudhil asked.

"No, sir. I did not tell you, Father, because I was afraid you would be displeased, but I went up with Nada. It was Nada who found the objects." I tried to look at Haj Ibrahim and knew the only reason he did not beat me on the spot was because we were in Professor Doctor Mudhil's presence, but the rage in his eyes told me it would be very bad later. Of course I said nothing about Nada taking her skirt off.

"Then bring her here," the archaeologist said.

"It cannot be arranged," my father said sharply.

I should have lied. Sabri would have supported my story. I was crazy to tell Father about Nada.

Professor Doctor Mudhil looked from me to my father knowingly. "Well, let us go on," he said.

Under his questioning, I drew a crude map of the cave of the treasure showing its three rooms and the secret crevice of the discovery. He took notes of my every word.

"Were there skeletons?"

"Yes, they were the first things we saw. They frightened us." The fact that we found children's bones inside a large jar indicated to Professor Doctor Mudhil that the ones who had buried the child believed in a god or gods. The child was ensconced in the jar for a journey to heaven—of sorts. Other children's bones near a burned-out stone altar indicated that some had been sacrificed.

He asked me many questions about the cloth wrappings, grain, evidence of fire, and other objects.

"There were many pots, broken and unbroken. We did not take them because the trip down the cliff was very difficult and we feared they would be dropped and smashed."

Professor Doctor Mudhil mumbled that the Bedouin had probably looted the cave by now. He made a note to contact the sheik of the Ta'amira Bedouin who scavenged for antiquities in the area. They knew to bring evidence of weaving and potsherds. He explained to me about layers and strata.

"We have proof that the caves between here and the Masada were used by Bar Kochba, a Hebrew revolutionary after the time of Christ. His rebellion against Rome signaled the end of the Jews in Israel for the first time. No doubt some of the strata were from Bar Kochba and maybe even the Essenes, who were involved with Jesus and John the Baptist in that area."

The reason he explained strata to me was to try to establish that the Bar Kochba warriors and their families could have lived in the cave without being aware of the treasure trove.

"Yes, it is very possible," I reckoned. "The objects were extremely well hidden in a crevice deep into the smallest of the rooms. The room itself was not fit for people to live in because it was only three or four feet high. The only way the treasure could have been found was by digging for it. Nada found it because a wrapping had disintegrated and the rocks around it had slipped away."

He questioned me about wooden sticks in the vicinity. I remembered them. It indicated to Professor Doctor Mudhil that the treasure had been deliberately hidden from view by these unknown people. Sticks were used as digging tools in the prehistoric times. A wooden stick or grain, he explained, would often not disintegrate because of a lack of humidity in some of the deeper caves.

His questions went on for half the morning. At last he dropped his pencil and rubbed his eyes. "The mystery widens," he said. "Here, let me show you." He deftly whipped his crutch under his arm, limped into the workshop, and picked up the first artifact, the twin-headed ibex standard.

"Samples of the copper from this piece reveal to us an arsenic content to indicate it came from mines in Armenia. Armenia has tracings of civilization as old as those in Jericho and the Fertile Crescent. It was the very first Christian nation. Standards like this one have been found in nearby Iran, so Armenia can't be ruled out.

"However, look at this crown. The naked eye can see that the copper is much purer and similar to that from mines not far from Palestine." He lifted the two pieces—the crown and standard. "This and this did not come from the same mine or even the same region. Yet all eight of the copper pieces will undoubtedly prove to be from the Chalcolithic Period.

"And now the plot really thickens," he said, holding up the two curved ivory pieces with the holes in them. "These are hippopotamus ivory. The closest to Palestine one could find those animals would be in the Upper Nile Valley in mid-Africa. The people of that era did not travel great distances. They settled in fertile valleys and built small agricultural communities. They did not have ships. The camel was not domesticated, nor was the horse. How did three objects from distinctly different areas manage to converge on that cave six to seven thousand years ago?"

"I know! I know!" I cried. "Allah sent his angels down and flew everything to the cave!"

"That is about as good an explanation as we now have," Professor Doctor Mudhil said, "but it may not be accepted by the scientific community."

Oh, how I was eager to learn from this great man. "I will take you to the cave," I said.

"If I sell the treasure trove to the Jews, do you think Abdullah would let me take an expedition into Qumran? Besides, the King has no such priorities. But! The Jews still control half the cave area and they will certainly be spurred to explore them."

His gnarled arm reached out and he patted my head. "I see that you want to go out on a dig."

"Oh yes, sir!"

"I started as a boy on digs," he said. "Another little secret, Ishmael. I think I know of a Neolithic wall in the Jericho ruins. It may just be the oldest wall in civilized history. I have been in correspondence with Dr. Kathleen Kenyon, may Allah bless her ways. She is in London and has shown interest. Alas, it may take her two or three years to raise enough funds to organize an expedition."

"Kathleen? A Christian woman's name?" my father said sharply.

"Indeed, a woman," Nuri Mudhil answered looking hard at my father. "She is the greatest archaeologist of Palestine and the Bible who is not a Jew."

The awkward silence that followed left us very uneasy. My father was getting up his anger. Jews. Women. He wanted contact with the Jews on one hand. One the other hand, he disliked the reality that no Arab country would buy the treasure trove. And as for women archaeologists . . . well, that was never a part of Haj Ibrahim's beliefs.

"Where will these end up?" my father asked abruptly.

"At the Hebrew University, where they should be."

"Is there no Arab museum or Arab philanthropist who will buy them? These are Arab finds. What of the Rockefeller Museum of East Jerusalem?"

"Arab philanthropists, such as they are, make minor contributions to small orphanages and invest in large diamonds. The Islamic museums from Cairo to Baghdad are a shambles. I have seen priceless thousand-year-old Korans crumbling to dust from the bookworms in the Rockefeller Museum. The fact is that one of the finest collections of Islamic antiquities is in a Jewish museum in West Jerusalem."

"They are only trying to humiliate us," Haj Ibrahim answered.

"You do not like this whole business of dealing with the Jews," Professor Doctor Nuri Mudhil said. "And you like me even less because I co-operate with them."

The silence had gone from awkward to terrible as Haj Ibrahim wrestled with his guilt and fear of being branded a traitor.

"It is very difficult to deal with the Jews in this atmosphere of

perfect hatred we have created," Nuri Mudhil said. Then the
crippled man held his arms apart and stood as straight as his
wasted body was able. "Let me tell you about this creature before
you, Haj Ibrahim, so you will wonder no more."

"I did not mean to offend you," my father said coarsely.

"I was born as you see me," Nuri Mudhil said. "My mother
and father were first cousins and this is the result. It is a scourge
in the entire Arab world, this marriage between cousins. It has
given birth to a million other warped bodies like mine. Did you
have them in your village, Haj Ibrahim?"

We did indeed. My father's lips were tight.

"You came to me to seek out the Jews," Mudhil continued.
"Now you are being sanctimonious about it. Why did you come
to me? To seek out a better life for that boy because you know if
we follow our leaders you will die a wretched death after a
wretched life in that miserable camp. Or did you come because
you take issue with the Syrian prime minister, who said last week
that it would be better for all the Palestinian refugees to be exter-
minated than to agree to give up one inch of land. At least, he
said, by the death of a half-million Palestinians we will have created martyrs to keep our hatred boiling for a thousand years."

He turned and limped back into his office and crumpled behind
his desk, wheezing. My father and I followed cautiously. "Sit
down!" he ordered. "You too, Ishmael."

"I was the middle son of nine boys," he said in a voice that
spoke as though we were not in the room. "My father was a man
who traded in goats and sheep. At the age of four, he put me at
the Allenby Bridge as a beggar. Be proud, he told me. Begging is
an honorable profession and if you make yourself grotesque
enough, no Moslem can refuse to give you alms. Charity is a pillar
of Islam, he said. So, when the buses stopped for inspection at the
bridge, I and a dozen other beggars, all terrible cripples, poured
on the bus and screamed for baksheesh. My face was filled with
ugly sores, as well, so my earnings were substantial.

"When I was nine, I knew nothing but begging at the Allenby
Bridge. That was the year that the great Dr. Farber came to
Jericho to dig. I hung around trying to make myself useful to
him, but I was so ill that I needed hospitalization or faced certain
death. When my father learned that Dr. Farber had taken me to
the Hadassah Hospital, he dragged me from my ward and beat

me into unconsciousness and warned me never to leave the bridge again. It was then that Dr. Farber purchased me for a hundred pounds, money he had to borrow.

"He took me to his home and made me well and taught me to read and write. . . ." He stopped and fought off tears.

"I am very sorry to have offended you," my father repeated.

"No, hear the rest of it. When the dig closed for the season, I pleaded to stay and guard it. And I dug and dug. All summer I dug till my hands bled. I, Nuri, found a Neolithic skull, the wonder of the dig! Do you know what it meant when I handed this to Dr. Farber? You see that," he cried, pointing to the diploma over his desk. "That is from Hebrew University—and you can take your shit and peddle it among the thieves!"

My father nodded for me to leave and I did.

"What can I say?" Ibrahim said.

"We are a people living in hate, despair, and darkness," Mudhil said. "The Jews are our bridge out of darkness."

Ibrahim sunk into a chair, exhausted from further fight. "You can trust Ishmael," he mumbled. "He keeps a secret unlike anyone I have ever known. He keeps secrets from me. You will never be in danger because of him. Take the artifacts and get the best price you can."

"Only on the condition that Ishmael is not punished for taking his sister with him. She had the courage to keep climbing when another boy stopped out of fear. She has rendered a great service to humanity. You must swear on your father's honor."

Ibrahim heaved a number of sighs that diminished from determination to nothingness. "I will overlook my son's indiscretion this time," he said finally. "Now what do you hear from Gideon Asch?"

"There are going to be a number of conferences between Abdullah and the Palestinians. Your views on him are known. For the moment, he will not move against any Palestinians of stature, such as yourself. He wants to give every appearance that the Palestinians want him and not the other way around. It is a case, I believe, of a goldfish trying to swallow a shark. This is my advice. You should be a delegate to these conferences. There are other men who think as you do. You will find them."

Ibrahim listened and pondered for a time. "I want only one

thing of life. I want to return to Tabah and reunite my people there. They are somewhere in Lebanon. I will not return to Tabah alone or even at the head of my people. I will not be a traitor to the Arabs. Right or wrong, I cannot do that. I can only return to Tabah at the head of a line of many thousands of Palestinians as a vanguard to a full resettlement."

"I am about to reveal to you the most important secret of your life. You and you alone will go into these conferences knowing that Ben-Gurion and the Jews will agree to the immediate return of a hundred thousand Arabs, with the balance to be negotiated with a peace treaty."

"A hundred thousand," Ibrahim whispered in astonishment.

"A hundred thousand as a start," Nuri Mudhil said.

Chapter Six

It is Ishmael speaking to you again, honored reader. We were, in truth, prisoners of the Jordanians. It is necessary that you know of King Abdullah and his insane ambitions.

He came from the Hashem family of Mecca. Hashem was the great-grandfather of Mohammed, and the Hashemites were very important to the early rise of Islam. However, when Islam kept moving its center from Arabia to Damascus to Baghdad, the Hashemite family was gradually reduced to petty functionaries, keepers of the holy places in Mecca and Medina.

Centuries passed.

The head of the Hashemites, known as the Sharif of Mecca, cast his lot with the British in the First World War against the Ottoman Empire. He had hoped to end up as King of the Greater Arab Nation. Instead, he was tossed a few bones and was ultimately run out of Arabia by his archrivals, the Saudis, and lived the balance of his life in exile.

His son Abdullah was granted puppet status over Eastern Palestine, a beleaguered desert in the Trans-Jordan area. Its only purpose for "nationhood" was to serve as a British military base.

The Emirate of Trans-Jordan was a wretched wasteland largely inhabited by Bedouin tribes who lived off the camel, which provided the basic needs of food, shelter, and clothing. They drank the camel's milk and ate the camel's flesh. They lived beneath tents of camel's skin and wore clothing woven of camel's hair. Heat was provided by the camel's dung and transportation by the camel's back. This was an ill-tempered, ugly, smelly beast but one that knew how to survive in the desert, as did its Bedouin master. Life in Trans-Jordan was primitive and brutal, with endless tribal warfare. Abdullah was loathed by other Arab leaders, for he was under complete control of his British master.

A clever Englishman, John Bagot Glubb, transformed the Arab Legion and united the hostile tribes under a single banner loyal to Abdullah. He forged a fighting force blending modern weapons and tactics with gaudy uniforms and the pomp that appealed to the Bedouin. The Arab Legion became the only first-rate military force in the Arab world and provoked further jealousy against Abdullah.

Trans-Jordan, later to become the Kingdom of Jordan, continued to languish as a godforsaken, broiling, destitute land of fewer than a half million lethargic and dispirited inhabitants. It was a land of nothing: no cultural facilities, no literature, no university, no acceptable medical facility.

Abdullah proved as patient as he was ambitious. By placing the Legion at the disposal of the British in the Second World War, he was the only Arab leader to cast his lot with the Allies and used their victory as a springboard for his long-smoldering desires.

What were Abdullah's desires, you ask Ishmael? No more and no less than his father's and his brother Faisal's: to be the ruler of a Greater Arab Nation encompassing Syria, Iraq, Lebanon, Palestine, and Saudi Arabia. As you can see, his dreams were not small, nor particularly disguised.

My father, Haj Ibrahim, often said Abdullah was his own worst enemy, for he could not control his tongue. Abdullah openly boasted that there was no Jordan, and no Palestine, but only a Greater Syria, which the Hashemites were destined to lead.

Although the Arab League, our council of nations, seethed at the audacity of the little king in his ridiculous capital of Amman, it could not move against him, for he was well hidden behind the skirts of the British lion.

Everyone hated Abdullah. The Egyptians, who considered themselves the heart and elite of the Arab world. The Saudis, who quaked at the thought of the vengeance he would seek for the ejection of the Hashemites from Arabia. The Syrians, who were targeted by Abdullah to take over their country. The Mufti, who had considered Palestine his personal domain. And they all plotted his demise.

Abdullah came out of the war with the Jews alone among the Arab nations with victories, territory, and his flag planted over East Jerusalem and the Dome of the Rock.

Moreover, with the flight of the Palestinians, he ended up inheriting a population twice the size of his own kingdom, a half million West Bank Palestinians and a half million who crossed the river into Jordan.

Most were illiterate and destitute peasants. However, there were many thousands of educated Palestinians, all the right kind of people who had been missing from Jordan's society. These were to give the backward land a sudden infusion of education, trade, and finance that cracked open the curtain of the modern world.

Abdullah seized the opportunity by granting the refugees citizenship and freedom of movement. Many of the elite Palestinians were appointed to high positions in the Jordanian Government to legitimize his creeping annexation of the West Bank. He glued on a thin veneer of a constitutional government with half Palestinians in his Parliament. It was a fraud, for the king retained the right to appoint and dismiss anyone, veto any law, and dissolve the Parliament at his whim.

The Arab League, the formal association of all Arab nations, renounced the annexation attempt and vowed never to recognize it. This left Abdullah isolated in a sea of hostile neighbors.

Abdullah's long-time enemy, the Mufti of Jerusalem, had fled to Gaza, where he attempted to counter the king's claims. But the Mufti's glory days were over.

It surfaced that during World War II, when the Mufti was a Nazi agent, he had visited Poland to examine the extermination camps. Feeling that German conquest of Palestine was inevitable, he presented Hitler with a plan to set up gas chambers in the Dothan Valley north of Nablus. Here he would exterminate the Jews of any and all lands the Germans conquered in the Middle East.

Egypt alone recognized the Mufti's claim on Palestine but its support was weak and insincere. In truth, he had outlived value to the Arab cause. Haj Amin al Heusseini was to finish his life as a revered man in various Arab locales, but his political star was burned out.

Also in powerful opposition to Abdullah's annexation plans were many Palestinians themselves. The king was shocked to learn that all of Palestine wasn't flocking to the Hashemite flag. But his skin was not very thin. He went about securing his claim to the West Bank, careful not to antagonize important men in opposition. At the same time he made certain the refugees did not organize a countermovement.

Abdullah's agents and supporters infiltrated West Bank towns and refugee camps, coercing, bribing, and promising political payoffs to those who joined his cause.

The refugee camps on the Jordan side, spaced like satellites around Amman, easily fell under his control. He removed opposition from these camps by quiet imprisonments and assassinations.

On the West Bank he initiated numerous conferences and smaller meetings to fortify his position. At last he felt strong enough to unify Jordan with the West Bank and called for a great convention in Amman for the unstated purpose of offering him the crown of Greater Palestine, the first giant step on the way to Greater Syria.

My father watched these maneuverings carefully. He attended meetings, large and small, remaining low-key. He was in constant communication with Professor Doctor Nuri Mudhil. When the great Amman Conference was called, he knew he had to attend and put his beliefs on the line, even though it targeted him for imprisonment or death.

Chapter Seven

Early 1950

The Romans called it Philadelphia. Amman, capital of the biblical Am-monites, was that place where David the King sent his captain, Uriah, to certain death in battle in order to steal the man's wife, the magnificent Bathsheba. Like ancient Sodom, Amman had a reputation for unabashed hedonism and evil ways that made it incur the wrath of the prophets Amos and Jeremiah. Their forecasts of Amman's destruction were only partly fulfilled. Amman was never destroyed. It simply was never anything. It just lay there, stretched out on the proverbial seven hills, a forgotten way station along the King's Highway, the trading route between the Red Sea and Damascus. It stayed thus, weary under the sun, for nearly two thousand years, with little inkling of the world beyond.

Then came Abdullah and his ambitions and the British unifying of the Bedouin into the Arab Legion. Amman lifted its windy, dust-encrusted head and went from being the capital of nothing to a new center of Arab intrigue.

Can you imagine how thrilled and honored I was when my father told me that I was to accompany him to the Great Democratic Unity Conference in Amman! The Arab world seems to gallop from conference to conference, but I had never been to one, much less a democratic conference.

For weeks Aqbat Jabar and the four other camps around Jericho were ablaze with lively discussion. Jordanian agents inundated us with literature and persuasion. There were to be over a thousand delegates, half from the West Bank and half from among the Palestinians now living in Jordan.

If one could count, one could see that Abdullah had 50 percent of the conference locked up before he even began seeking out delegates in the West Bank. Those affluent Palestinians living in Amman and the others living in some fifty camps over the river were in Abdullah's pocket, and no one had any doubt about how they would vote.

Every day new delegates were announced from among the West Bank mayors, muktars, sheiks, clergy, and prominent Palestinians. These, too, were overwhelmingly Abdullah's people. A carefully screened, small, and controllable opposition was permitted, to "prove" to the world that the conference was to be democratic to the core.

Haj Ibrahim was among the opposition and set out to attend with a block of delegates from Aqbat Jabar and the other camps around Jericho. Although these compounds held over fifty thousand people, they were assigned a paltry twenty delegates.

Nonetheless, the scramble for seats was voracious. At first there was an attempt to hold elections, but no one knew how to conduct one or trusted that system. Selection of delegates came down to a traditional power struggle, with the strongest tribal leaders and those able to make the best alliances gaining the seats.

Despite Jordanian pressures, my father, the great Haj Ibrahim al Soukori al Wahhabi, emerged as the leader of the Jericho delegation.

With half the delegates pro-Abdullah from the outset, the Jordanian agents went to work on the other half. They were promised extra rations, cash, and future government jobs. When the agents had finished their "campaigning," Haj Ibrahim could count only a dozen men against the annexation of the West Bank. This number was further depleted when two of the most vocal anti-Abdullah delegates were assassinated and two others were taken off to Amman to face criminal charges for smuggling and black marketeering. The charges were transparent because these crimes were universally practiced, particularly among the Jordanian troops and their camp administrators.

When my father tried to replace his lost delegates, he was informed that the rolls were closed.

The prominence of the delegates was made apparent by their mode of transportation to Amman and the accommodations when they got there. The most important pro-Abdullah delegates were collected in private cars and assigned to villas and hotel suites and rooms. Others, like Father, all those living in the camps, were to be bused over the river and housed in a tent area of the Schneller Camp six miles beyond Amman. Although Schneller and Aqbat Jabar had the same populations, Schneller had a hundred delegates. It was a fact that some aspects of the conference would be less democratic than others.

Despite the deliberate humiliation of our being second-class

delegates, I was enthralled with the entire trip. The ride over the
Allenby Bridge through Salt, Suweilih, and into Amman at night
was like a floating dream.

My father and I shared a small tent. When we were settled and
fed, he called me close to him and told me to read him the agenda.
He ordered me to stand before him, then he reached up and
grabbed my ear between his fingers and shook it.

"You must keep this close to the ground," he said.

"I will, Father."

"First check the camp here," he said. "Abdullah's major selling
point among the exiles is that the camps in Jordan are much
better off than the camps on the West Bank. I must have the true
picture. He has also said that the exiles over here have access to
jobs and schooling. What is the truth of that?"

"I understand," I said.

"You must move about and smell out other opponents of annexation, like myself. Carefully, carefully, carefully. Do not make
contact with them, but let me know who they are."

"Yes, Father."

"And finally and most important, Ishmael: Keep on the alert
for foul play."

I awoke the next morning filled with anticipation of going into
Amman. Nothing has ever disillusioned me more. Amman was
pale stuff alongside Jerusalem. I could see my father's point about
who should be annexing whom.

At the center of the city, which was not much larger than
Ramle or Lydda, stood an unimpressive little fountain sand-
wiched in between the mosque on one side and the antiquity of
the Roman amphitheater on the other. Nearby, the Hotel Philadelphia headquartered the conference. A large banner straddled
the street reading: WELCOME TO THE GREAT DEMO-
CRATIC CONFERENCE OF UNITY—PALESTINE AND
JORDAN ARE ONE.

Other little trappings of welcome festooned the central area,
but what was most prevalent was the presence of the Arab Legion. Attired in their renowned red headdresses with white polka
dots, they were moustached mightily to a man and wore ankle-
length tan and red riding robes and very angry expressions.

Intermingled with the legionnaires were the king's other loyal

Bedouin. There must have been hundreds from the Beni Sakhr tribe with their pale blue and white robes trimmed in gold and bullet-filled bandoliers slung over their shoulders. The Beni Sakhr were known as the fiercest of all the Bedouin fighters, and their presence alongside the Legion bespoke the fact that, in Jordan, Abdullah was not to be taken lightly. It seemed there were ten armed Jordanians for every delegate.

My father and I made for the Hotel Philadelphia, where he was given credentials and assigned to a committee. Most of the committees were meaningless and had been invented to give many of the delegates something to do and a feeling of importance. My father's first act was to heatedly reject a place on the Committee for Islamic Values.

We were hustled off to a side room where a ferocious-looking Colonel Zyyad sat behind a desk.

"Ah, Haj Ibrahim, I see you found your way back from Qumran," he said in a voice filled with sarcasm.

My father did not blink.

I felt my knees were going to collapse in fear. I saw my end in a terrible Jordanian prison. Colonel Zyyad tapped away at the desk as though he were trying to reach a decision in code.

"You are a fool, a terrible fool," the colonel said.

I could see alternatives swirling through his mind and I suppose I must have prayed audibly, for Father shook my shoulder to be quiet.

"This is a democratic conference," Zyyad said. "I will reassign you to another committee." He shuffled through his papers, found a particular one, wrote in my father's name, and scribbled out an order. "You will attend the Committee on Refugees," he said.

"I object to the very use of the word 'refugees,'" my father retorted.

"Then take that up with your committee . . . and thank Allah that we are a democratic people."

My father had been saved by the fact that Abdullah wanted no chaos or disruptions at the conference, and at this point it was a small matter to pacify us. However, I was still shaking when we all assembled in the courtyard of the Great Mosque, where the Mufti of Amman, the country's Moslem leader, opened the conference.

After prayers the Mufti shouted down from the pulpit the words of Surah 57, which dealt with the punishment of the unbelievers.

"We have adorned the nearer heaven with lights,
and have made them projectiles for the satans;
and We have prepared them the punishment of
the Blaze.

"For those who have disbelieved in their Lord is
the punishment of Gehenna—a bad destination!
When they are cast into it, they hear from it
a roaring, for it boils,

"And almost bursts asunder for fury. Whenever a
crowd is thrown into it, its keeper shall ask
them: 'Did there not come to you a warner?'
They shall say: 'Yes! there came to us a
warner, but we counted him false and said:
'Allah hath not sent down anything.'

" 'Verily, ye are in great error.'
And they shall say: 'If we had heard or understood
we should not have been amongst the fellows
of the Blaze.'

"So they shall confess their sin: 'Away with the
fellows of the Blaze.' "

After a bloodcurdling sermon on the burning of the Jews, the Mufti of Amman beseeched Allah for blessings and divine guidance for the delegates.

When the prayers were done, we crossed over to the Roman amphitheater and listened to a three-hour welcoming speech by the Mayor of Hebron, a West Bank city. He was Abdullah's most ardent supporter in Palestine. His first hour was devoted to the coming vengeance against the Jews, while the last part of the speech proclaimed the glory of Islam and the beauty of Arab unity and brotherhood.

The Mayor of Hebron was followed by a half-dozen more welcoming speakers, each pounding home an aspect of the coming annexation. A single opposition speaker was democratically drowned out by the others after only a few moments. This enraged Haj Ibrahim and the handful of dissidents, who started to riot and scream anti-Abdullah slogans. We were subdued by a massive force of legionnaires, who had the amphitheater surrounded. No one was hurt and the meeting went on.

When the welcoming session was done, we were taken up to the Jabal al-Qal'ah, the dominant hill holding the ancient Roman citadel. The ruins of the Temple of Hercules stood in a great court where our afternoon meals were to be served by dozens of waiters. Abdullah knew how to entertain with British money, my father noted. From this splendid vista we could see the Hashemiiya Palace of the king, as well as the surrounding hills.

Now was a time for careful mingling. As we washed our hands in a fountain before a meal, I saw a delegate in traditional desert robes deliberately work his way alongside Father. I moved in close to listen.

"I am Sheik Ahmed Taji," the man said softly. "My people and I are in the Hebron Camp."

Picking up on his lowered voice, my father introduced himself quietly.

"I know who you are," Sheik Taji said. "I saw both of your performances today, at the Hotel Philadelphia and at the amphitheater. You are mad, truly mad."

The sheik slipped something to my father that appeared to be a talisman made of black rock. Father pocketed it quickly.

"We should meet after this conference," Sheik Taji whispered. "When I receive the talisman from you with a note, I shall come to you."

Father nodded, and as briefly as the two men had met, they went off in separate directions. I indicated to Father that I had gotten the man's name and drifted off to gather information on him.

That evening we were taken to the Hashemiiya Palace to meet the king. Never having been to a palace or seen a real king, I was genuinely impressed, even though it was Abdullah. Both Father and I were well dressed, having borrowed clothing from anyone who had anything decent left in our section of Aqbat Jabar. However, many of the delegates were in rags. The line inched into the throne room.

My knees rattled for the second time that day. Well, he cer-

tainly had a nice place. It was the only thing of beauty I had seen
besides the Roman amphitheater and the citadel. Although the
palace wasn't as magnificent as the things I had seen on my journey to paradise, it was suitable enough for Abdullah and Jordan.

And there I was before the very king! I think I was disappointed. His throne was only a large chair on a platform painted
gold. He had stepped down to receive the line of delegates; he was
encased by his Circassian guards. They were not real Arabs but
Russian Moslems who had come here centuries ago. They wore
fur hats with a silver replica of the king's crown and appeared
like pictures I had seen of Cossack horse riders. Advisers wearing
Western suits with Arab headdresses flanked the king and whispered in his ear as each delegate passed.

Abdullah was very short for a king and his robes were not
ornate, but he had the shiniest black shoes I had ever seen. He
was very jolly, and that surprised me because I had expected him
to look sinister like Colonel Zyyad, who was close at hand. The
colonel whispered to the king as we approached. Abdullah broke
into an abnormally great smile, embraced my father and kissed
both cheeks, then patted my head, even though I was almost as
tall as he was.

"Welcome, welcome, welcome to my humble kingdom, Haj
Ibrahim! May my land be as your home. We are blessed by your
presence. May Allah's wisdom guide you through the next days."

"Your Majesty, no words can adequately describe the ecstasy of
this moment," my father responded.

"Whatever you want, now or later, is all within your grasp,"
the king said, then turned to me. "Your name, my son?"

"I am Ishmael," I proclaimed majestically.

We were nudged slightly to keep the line moving, and ended up
outside in the greatest tent I had ever seen, one that held the
entire delegation. It was not difficult to ascertain who was a refugee and who was among the wealthy and affluent of the Palestinians as a show of rags and gold thread mingled in brotherhood.

The feast that followed was even greater than those my father
had given when he was Muktar of Tabah. Many of us had not
seen food like that for so long that we ate until we became bloated
and ill, then kept on eating. Music and dancers added to the atmo-

sphere of love and harmony. Hashish was slipped to us by the cadres of servants so our bliss would not wear off too quickly.

After the feast we witnessed camel races, demonstrations of horsemanship and falconry, and more music and dancing. We heard on the radio later that the king had slipped quietly from Amman because he did not wish to influence the conference by his presence or upset the democratic nature of the meeting.

Next day Father went in to his committee, which began and ended as a shouting match through his attempt to expand the agenda and not merely pass resolutions that had already been drawn up. He voiced objection to the use of the word "refugee" but was shouted down. I soon left to collect the information he told me to get.

That evening I gave Father my findings. Sheik Taji was the leader of a semi-nomadic tribe that had occupied an area north of the Gulf of Aqaba and the outpost of Eilat. In the beginning of the war with the Jews, the Egyptians ejected them from their homeland for military purposes and they fled to Hebron. The end of the war found the Jews conquering the Negev Desert and leaving Sheik Taji to wonder why he had left. Other Bedouin had remained and were left in peace by the Jews or co-operated with them by supplying trackers and intelligence.

While Sheik Taji regretted his mistake, he found himself in an impossible situation in the Hebron Camp. The mayor of the city was an Abdullah stalwart and had turned the camp into one of the king's strongholds on the West Bank.

My father showed me the little talisman Taji had passed to him, a black jasper pendant with an abstract carving. I recognized it as a common Bedouin talisman to ward off jinn.

"This will bring Sheik Taji to us later," my father said. "What did you learn about the camp here?"

I cleared my throat importantly. "Schneller and all the camps around Amman are much worse off than Aqbat Jabar," I said. "They live or die here by one rule. Abdullah has enlisted all the important old muktars and given them and their families all the Red Crescent jobs. If you are against the king, you do not eat and you do not protest. There have been many assassinations and imprisonments, so that all dissidents have been removed."

"It is as I thought," Father said.

"The same goes for the jobs in Amman. Only those co-operating with Abdullah can find work in the city. I am told that all the camps in Jordan are being similarly run."

On the third evening, I was able to report to Father that I had discovered another strong dissident, who, unlike Ibrahim, had kept quiet about his feelings.

"His name is Charles Maan. He was a teacher at the gymnasium in Haifa. He is very prominent in the Ramallah Committee."

"I have heard of him," Father answered. "The Ramallah group is strong. He can be trusted?"

"Yes, on all matters except one," I said.

"Aha, what is that?" he asked.

"He is a Christian, and you know how they lied about Jesus being their lord and savior."

"Is that the only thing?"

"Yes, sir."

"Nonsense," my father said, startling me. "The Christians and the Moslems have lived in Palestine for centuries without real trouble. Religious fighting around here is Lebanese madness. We even got along with the Jews until the Mufti." Haj Ibrahim's revelation confused me.

Charles Maan was also in the Schneller Camp, only a few streets away.

"Stay near his tent and observe without being observed," Father ordered. "When he is alone, approach him with great care and introduce yourself either by speaking to him or by giving him a note. Tell him I would like a quick, passing meeting."

"Where, Father?"

We both pondered for a moment. "At the latrine, where we do our business," he said.

I waited for over two hours near Charles Maan's tent, but delegates were coming and going endlessly. I decided to write a note. When there was a break in the line of visitors, I stepped in quickly and handed it to him.

He was a man older than Father, with bags of weariness under his eyes. He took the note in a hand with fingers yellow from tobacco stains.

I am Ishmael, son of Haj Ibrahim al Soukori al Wahhabi. My father would like to meet with you at the latrine at two o'clock in the morning.

He tore the note into shreds and nodded yes to me. The latrine was a long corrugated-tin shed built atop a running ditch that carried the open sewage to a series of collection pits. A few moments before two o'clock Father and I left our tent with great caution. It was extremely dark and quiet, and we hoped it would stay that way. We waited in the shadows until the tired, rumpled figure of Charles Maan, dressed in a worn Western suit, came down the path. He looked about and entered. Ibrahim followed him inside while I posted myself at the entrance to warn them if anyone came. He stood over the ditch, pretending to urinate.

"We must meet on the other side," Father said.

"I agree," Charles Maan answered.

"Do you know Sheik Taji in the Hebron Camp?"

"Yes, he is very dependable. A good man."

"I will bring him also," Father said.

"I agree."

"How do we make contact?" Father asked.

"When you and Taji are ready, send your son Ishmael up to Ramallah. I am in the Birah Camp. I have been able to open a small classroom. He will have no trouble finding me."

"Our meeting should be carefully concealed," Father said.

"I have a safe place in the Old City of Jerusalem. Do you know the Sisters of Zion Convent?"

"No," Father answered.

"Enter the Old City through the Lions' Gate. It is on the Via Dolorosa at the Ecco Homo Arch between the second and third Stations of the Cross. Ask for Sister Mary Amelia. She runs the school and will be aware of the exact time to expect you."

"I do not mean to offend you, but she is a woman. Is she entirely trustworthy?"

"She is my daughter," Charles Maan said.

"Someone is coming," I whispered.

My father arranged himself quickly as Mr. Maan buttoned up his trousers. "In a few weeks," Ibrahim said and left quickly with me.

The afternoon of the final day of the conference saw a parade of chairmen of the various committees present their resolutions for approval of all the delegates at the Roman amphitheater.

Resolutions rolled like heads being chopped off by an executioner.

Resolved. What was gained by blood will be regained by blood.

Resolved. Infidels corrupt Islamic values and are not fit to exist in Islamic lands.

Resolved. All Arab nations are one and never before so unified.

Resolved. Arabs who remained in the Zionist entity have committed enormous sin. Such Arabs, who carry passports of the Zionist entity, will not be permitted to enter Arab nations.

Resolved. Arabs who remained in the Zionist entity are leprous in nature and are forbidden to make the Haj to Mecca and Medina.

Resolved. Arabs who remained in the Zionist entity have been contaminated and are unfit to pray at the Al Aksa Mosque and the Dome of the Rock and will be forbidden entry.

Resolved. Arabs who remained in the Zionist entity are treacherous at heart and cannot reunite or otherwise visit members of their exiled families.

Thus the clergy and the committees on aspects of Islam had two dozen resolutions passed with only a smattering of opposition, soon subdued.

By evening over a hundred resolutions had been passed establishing the principle of eternal war against the Jews. When they were done, the final three major committees brought the conference to its predestined crescendo.

The Committee on Refugees, to which my father had been assigned, put forth a glowing report on how well things were being run in the Jordanian camps in contrast to the West Bank camps. The intent was to give the illusion that life would get much better for everyone under the national banner of Jordan. Father and I knew by now that Jordan had not delivered on the jobs, land, rehabilitation, or opportunities that had been promised. The only Palestinians who prospered were those who threw themselves to the Jordanians. Otherwise, one side of the river was as destitute as the other.

The vital Armistice Line Committee then gave its report. The end of the war had seen a zigzag truce line become a semi-permanent boundary, for the troops merely froze in place, making an impossible common border of three hundred miles. This put hundreds of thousands of dunams of former Arab fields on the Zionist side of the line. A Jordanian Border Commission had been established to try to retrieve as much land as possible.

The report of the Armistice Line Committee was that all claims had been resolved in favor of the refugees' being able to regain their lands. Individual claims as well as group or village claims would be honored as soon as the matter of West Bank and Jordanian unity was resolved.

"Abdullah lies in his beard," my father mumbled. "He has not regained an inch of that contested land."

As Father stood to protest the report, the men seated near him inched away and the Legion inched in. Once again my mouth went dry. Only the Arab tradition of protecting a guest could save us now! A miracle happened! By some fate Charles Maan was close to us and caught Father's eye. In that instant Ibrahim regained his temper and sat down quietly.

The final report from the Committee for Democratic Unity came as an anticlimax. It was announced that the Jordanian Parliament had passed a Bill of National Merger. A chorus of cheers arose from Abdullah's lackeys. This was followed by a democratic vote in which the conference approved the "Greater Palestine" by 970 votes to 20.

A closing announcement was made that a Conference on Refugee Claims and Rights had been called for Zurich, Switzerland. The refugees' case would be presented before an International Arbitration Commission of neutral nations. Jordan would send a delegation to protect all refugee interests. I grabbed my father's hand, which shook with rage. With all the strength I could muster, I half pulled him out of the amphitheater.

We left Amman with the taste of ashes in our mouths.

Chapter Eight

Running sewers and uncollected hills of rotting garbage breed voluminous flies and mosquitoes, and the stink from them is deafening. When you add that to total idleness and the constant prodding of bent and fanciful old men pretending to instill a pride and courage they never really owned, you have the birth of the Avenging Leopards.

My brother Jamil was a leader among them. They wore no uniforms because abject poverty was our heritage, so they identified themselves with headbands of bright orange cloth.

At the Ein es-Sultan Camp situated by Elisha's Spring, the gang was the Liberating Sharks. At the Bedouin Camp farther up the highway they were the Desert Wolves, and at the small Nuweimeh Camp farther north the Black May Gang was named for the awful date on which the Jews declared their independence. All of the gangs were prodded on by slothful, stagnating elders and by fanatical Egyptians of the Moslem Brotherhood.

A level of fear grew in Aqbat Jabar over the Avenging Leopards. They stalked about looking for boys like myself to recruit. Join or take a bad thrashing. I was able to stay clear because of Jamil. I think he didn't want me in because he suspected I might take over the leadership from him.

By night the gangs would climb up into Mount Temptation, where they conducted weird rituals on new recruits, including bloodletting. They had secret signs and swore an oath of revenge filled with ogreish promises of dismemberment and skull crushing and hot pokers in the eyes of the Jews.

"Blood, guts, entrails, balls, death!" we could hear them chant down the mountain on the leaden night air. They tested each other's courage with stick jousts, jumping from high ledges, running past a line of stone throwers, leaping over fires, biting off the heads of live chickens and snakes, and strangling cats barehanded. Their illusions of bravery and manhood, the ultimate Arab product, were perpetuated all day, every day, to alleviate their monotony.

Haj Ibrahim and the other old-time muktars and sheiks saw these gangs as a growing threat to their own rule, but they had to tread lightly in curbing them, for they offered no alternative. There were no schools or organized games, no movies, just a whining radio. The only lectures they heard were from the Brotherhood, glorifications of martyrdom and death.

"You are the great young soldiers of Allah preparing to become martyrs of the revenge!"

Revenge they heard in Jericho.

Revenge they heard in the sordid little cafés of the camp.

Revenge they heard in their homes.

And they grew ugly. None of them worked or tried to look for work, even during harvest-time when some field hands were needed. Their mothers and sisters did that labor. Instead, they began to hire themselves out to "protect" the farmers' fields.

If a man in the camp had a run-in with a Leopard, he could expect his hovel to be broken into and looted and his oldest son to be beaten up. Avenging Leopards were out in numbers down at the Allenby Bridge, where there was always a line of trucks awaiting inspection by Jordanian customs officials. If a driver dozed off or left his truck, the Leopards would quickly empty its contents.

They and the other gangs became a major factor in the raging black market. In order to do so, they worked out a tacit co-operation with the ineffectual and corrupt Jordanian-controlled camp police. With little curb on their activities, the Leopards prowled around Jericho and blackmailed merchants who had been fingered for them by the police. They routinely raided and robbed Red Crescent supply depots.

When things became outrageously bad, the Arab Legion would conduct a sweep and take a number of boys off to prison in Amman, but this always provoked a riot by protesting parents.

Things began to come to Jamil: a battery-operated radio, a wristwatch, new shoes, trinkets to give to the girls, hashish, and foods that were so sorely missing from our mushy diets. Father did not question him, but both of us became apprehensive about our arms cache. We feared Jamil might sell off our guns, or worse, give them to the Leopards.

As we accepted in silence the fact that Jamil had become a gangster and a thief, he grew more brazen. He had money in his pocket, gifts for his mother, tobacco for his father, food for the family table. He was quick to get around to thinking he was indispensable to the family, and perhaps he even harbored the notion he was the equal of Haj Ibrahim.

His boldness peaked when the Leopards broke into the house of a friend of Father's in our Tabah section of the camp. I did not realize when I met Jamil coming up our street at mealtime that Ibrahim had ordered everyone out of our home.

"Jamil, wait," I called, running up alongside him. "You had better take care. Father is very upset about the robbery at the home of Daoud al Hamdan."

"So, what about it?"

I had never heard words from sister, mother, or brothers that challenged Father's authority. I wondered if Jamil had gone crazy. I grabbed his arm to stop him but he jerked himself free.

"Father's day is over," Jamil lashed out. "He and all the other old men here are finished. There is a new order."

I blinked in disbelief, but then I suddenly realized that, at eighteen, Jamil was as tall as Father and very strongly built.

"Jamil, you speak crazy."

"Oh, do I? Well, Father brought us to this filthy life. Why did he not stay and fight for our land? Who is going to regain it? Him? My friends and I are the ones destined to return our honor and it is time I was respected for it."

I wanted to run to warn Father but only watched Jamil walk away. I followed him cautiously as he entered the house. Ibrahim was sitting in the one decent chair, fingering his worry beads, as Jamil entered. I observed from the doorway as Jamil committed the terrible sin of not kneeling and kissing Father's hand.

"Where is dinner!" Jamil demanded.

Ibrahim rose from his seat slowly and came face-to-face with Jamil. His fist lashed out so fast I could barely see it. Jamil was smashed to the dirt floor and lay there with a shocked expression and blood bubbling out of his mouth.

"Jamil, my son," Father said ever so softly, "you go outside and come back and show me that you have respect for your father."

Jamil groped to all fours, then looked up fiercely. "You don't own me anymore!" Jamil screamed.

Ibrahim kicked him in the ribs, splattering him against the wall, busting up a half-dozen mud bricks.

"Jamil, my son," Father repeated gently, "go outside and come in again and show me that you have respect for your father."

Jamil inched up, grasping the wall, until he stood, slightly doubled over, holding his ribs with one hand and his bloody mouth with the other. He charged at Father, shouting an oath, and struck him in the face! It was the most terrible thing I had ever seen! I rushed into the house to help Ibrahim, but his arm backhanded me and shoved me away.

"So, my little Avenging Leopard wishes to have some sport! Good! Good!" And with that, Father opened his arms, then brought the heels of his hands in a clap against Jamil's ears. Jamil shrieked, crumpled, and lay quivering.

"Jamil, my son," Father said again, not lifting his voice, "go outside and come in again and show me that you have respect for your father."

"Nooooo," Jamil rasped.

Ibrahim's foot caught him in the pit of the stomach. Jamil's body was disarrayed into a grotesque shape. Father planted his foot on Jamil's chest and once again repeated the instruction.

"Father, stop or you'll kill him!" I cried.

"No no," Father said, "I am only teaching him respect. Have you learned it, Jamil?"

"No more," he gasped.

"No more what?"

"I quit." He mustered his strength, crawled out on all fours, turned at the door and crawled to Father's feet, reached up and grasped his hand and kissed it.

"Now you hear me very well, my dear little Avenging Leopard. What I have just contributed to your education is but a tiny drop in the sea of what you will receive if any person in the Tabah section is ever set upon for any reason. Is that very clear?"

"Yes, Father," he whimpered.

"Now, Jamil, if you touch a single one of our weapons, for any reason, I am going to kill you the same way you brave martyrs of the revenge kill little chickens. I am going to tear your throat out with my teeth. You go to the home of Daoud al Hamdan and return what has been taken and humiliate yourself before him."

Father reached down, grabbed Jamil by the scruff of the neck, and hurled him outside.

Jamil was clever enough to realize that his great day of respect had not yet come and that the Avenging Leopards were not going to replace the old authority without spilling their own blood. He licked his wounds, then took another approach by becoming the "protector" of the Tabah section and endearing himself to the families as the fine son of Haj Ibrahim.

Within himself, though, Jamil had turned forever. From then on he wore an expression of the Blaze, with a rage in his eyes that revealed him to be saturated with hatred and always just a fraction away from an explosion of violence. He was a bit crazy now but not so crazy as to challenge Father's word. In fact, Jamil now delighted in groveling before Father to try to prove his worth.

A few weeks after the fight we received an announcement that King Abdullah had ordered a celebration of the West Bank merger with Jordan. This so-called festive occasion had been forced on the king by the powerful reaction of the Arab League, which had denounced the annexation in the saltiest of terms.

The king's ministers had waited for nations of the West to recognize the annexation. Abdullah continued to claim innocence. Allah forbid that he had coerced the Palestinians. After all, his ministers proclaimed, the unity conference had been a democratic expression of Palestinian desires.

The recognition Jordan sought came only from Britain and Pakistan. The British were still Abdullah's master and controlled the Arab Legion by subsidy and through its British officers. Although they were also leery of Abdullah's ambitions, they were forced by their marriage to the little king to go along with the charade.

The failure of the Arab world as well as the world at large to recognize his acquisition did not dissuade him. He felt that a holy endowed ruler such as himself was entitled to keep his divine marching order toward a Greater Syria. The foibles of mere mortals could not stop a king on a mission decreed by Allah. Deeper still, he believed that the Palestinian people would rally to his banner and make fools of the rest of the world, and he intended to demonstrate that his had been a popular move.

It was immediately suggested by his British colleagues that a plebiscite be held on the West Bank to confirm the decision of the unity conference. Abdullah did not like the idea of a vote that he

could not cancel by a personal veto. Surely, he felt, the Palestinians would vote overwhelmingly in favor. However, he did not
trust the vote. As a monarch, he had royal prerogatives to protect
the people from themselves, should they err.

Instead, Abdullah ordered parades in the major West Bank cities. He massed his supporters and lieutenants to make certain the
Palestinians erupted in a spontaneous show of support.

The Allenby Bridge rumbled and buckled under the hooves of
his Bedouin camel corps and horses of the desert police. The
Legion poured over the river in Land-Rovers and armored personnel carriers and tanks. Infantry and the bands were trucked
over. They dispersed in battalion strength to Hebron, Bethlehem,
Jericho, Nablus, and Ramallah.

East Jerusalem was avoided in fear of a Jewish military reaction. Abdullah had not kept the terms of the truce and continued
to refuse to allow the Jews access to the Western Wall, their holiest site. He did not wish to risk provoking the Jews into throwing
him out.

On the great day of the celebration, everyone had been rousted
from the camps and cities into the main streets, where banners,
flags, and garlands awaited our saviors, the almighty Jordanians.

Father fumed his way down to Jericho with me, as usual, at his
right-hand side, a step behind him. We went atop Professor Doctor Nuri Mudhil's building, where we would have a perfect view
over the procession.

The parade was led by the king's own elegant band, which had
played concerts for us when we were in Amman. The "Colonel
Bogey" March incongruously filled the air of ancient Jericho. Platoons of armored carriers bearing Legion warriors were followed
by batteries of artillery and a tank battalion that shook the buildings and drowned out the music with their mighty roars. Overhead airplanes in elements of threes zipped down at low level.

Now we could hear the honking of the camels ridden by the
desert police who patrolled Jordan's vast sandlands along its border with Saudi Arabia. The soldiers swayed arrogantly atop their
lofty perches. As fast as one could say "Allah is great," the street
in front of the camel corps was filled with dozens of youths wearing the orange headbands of the Avenging Leopards. In the following seconds, they unleashed a devastating barrage of stones at
the camels and their riders, then fled into the crowd.

One of the camels fell to its knees, dumping its rider, and several others bolted in confusion. They broke into an uncontrolled gallop and plunged into the crowd, grinding onlookers underfoot, scattering the rest, then smashing into peddlers' stalls. There was shrieking, and some shots. The crowd dispersed in panic while the Jordanians organized themselves furiously and bore down on the place of the ambush. Soldiers leaped out of their vehicles, bashing madly with their rifle butts at anyone near them. More shots. A woman fell in the street and was very still.

That night we huddled about the radio and dialed East Jerusalem and Amman, but there was not a word about the incident. We tried Radio Damascus and Cairo. All we were told was that there was a news blackout over the entire West Bank.

The next morning still brought no mention in the newspapers, but as the day wore on we learned that the Jordanian troops had also been stoned in Ramallah and Nablus and that six people had been killed.

The camp was ablaze with conversation as many of the ardent Abdullah supporters began to look around, thinking of new alliances. There was a constant pilgrimage to our hovel, with one sheik after another now pledging loyalty to Father. He accepted their homage with a well-disguised cynicism.

Jamil's eyes alone bore the tale that his generation was, in fact, the generation of liberation. All right, Father, his expression said, take glory in the victory but remember who struck the blow.

When the grovelers were gone Father took me aside, excitedly. "The time has come for us to take our destiny into our own hands," he said with a power I had not seen from him since the exile. "You will travel by bus tomorrow to Ramallah, to the Birah Camp, where you will find Charles Maan. When he fixes a date for us to meet secretly at the Convent of the Sisters of Zion, you will then travel to Hebron and find Sheik Taji."

Father handed me the black jasper pendant to identify myself. I repeated my instructions on how Sheik Taji was to find the convent and assured Father I would not fail.

Strange, what I remembered most about the day was not the sight in Jericho but the mockery in Jamil's eyes.

Chapter Nine

The Convent of the Sisters of Zion sat atop the ruins of the ancient Roman Antonia Fortress, which was brutally connected to the agony of Jesus. In a cellar room where traditionally Jesus was tortured and degraded by the soldiers of Rome, Sister Mary Amelia closed the door behind the three men who had slipped into the convent a few minutes apart.

They greeted each other nervously, then settled around a plank table. "There is no question about it, my brothers, Abdullah has failed," Haj Ibrahim said.

"The old Hashemite is wounded but he is not dead," Charles Maan said, lighting the first cigarette of a new chain.

"Then let us hammer the nail right through him," the gray-bearded sheik said, pointing to his forehead.

"We are in the right place when you speak of nailing up men," Maan noted.

"What do you think we should do?" Ibrahim asked.

"Assassinate him, of course," Taji answered.

"I have no objection to his assassination," Ibrahim said. "However, that will not help us achieve our goals. On the contrary, it will only whet the appetite of all the vultures from Baghdad to Morocco who are waiting to pounce on Palestine."

"Haj Ibrahim is right," Maan said. "To murder Abdullah will only bring us under more severe repression. We have already bloodied the Legion and they are impatient to strike us. You would be able to paint the city of Hebron red with our blood after an assassination of Abdullah."

"Maybe assassination is not such a good idea, after all," Taji recanted. "But Abdullah has been dealt a blow, his march has been stemmed. We must follow up with something. Why don't we simply declare our independence?"

"Independence? Now, that has some merit," Ibrahim agreed.

They turned to Charles Maan, who had sucked his cigarette dry and, when it was about to crisp the tips of his fingers, deftly used it to light another in a movement perfected by much prac-

tice. "We have already been offered independence and we refused."

"When were we offered independence?" the sheik challenged,
now flailing his hands.

"By the United Nations. Maybe we should have taken the offer
and run. However, all we did was run. Both the Mufti and
Abdullah have tried to take over Palestine, one with Egyptian
backing and one with British backing. Both failed. Who backs us?
Who are we? We are three poverty-stricken refugees sitting in a
cellar with the ghost of Jesus Christ. Our own brother Palestinians who are not refugees would fight against us. And do you
think the Arab Legion will drop dead with fear because we declare our independence?"

"Then we must enter an eternal struggle," Taji said impul-
sively.

"Struggle with what?" Charles Maan retorted with cynicism.
"We have no organization. Who do we represent? Who will sup-
port us? The Americans support the Jews. The British support
Abdullah. Who will recognize us? Madagascar? Albania? Outer
Mongolia?"

The old Bedouin was becoming frustrated with Charles Maan's
terse observations. He looked to Haj Ibrahim for support.

Ibrahim sized up his confederates. Maan was a logical and
learned man, the kind who would be sorely needed in the deftness required by Arab politics. Sheik Taji, if he could be controlled, had the fire in his stomach that was the salt of men.

"Who else has the right to declare independence if we do not
have it?" Ibrahim prodded.

"You see my point, then," the sheik put in hastily.

"Of course I see your point. But on the other hand, our eminent friend Charles also makes a point."

"What point?"

"That if we declare independence we will make the impact of a
whisper in the middle of a desert windstorm."

"Brothers, brothers, brothers," the schoolteacher soothed, "we
have a very bad history as far as believing we really have the
ability to rule ourselves. Since the time of the ancient Hebrews,
Palestine has been ruled by everyone but Palestinians." He held
up his hand and spread his fingers, then ticked off one finger after
another, counting as he spoke. "First it was Rome, then the By-

zantine Christians, then the Arabs from Arabia, the Crusaders, Saladin, the Mamelukes of Egypt, the Turks, the British, and the Jews again. The Jews always had a capital here either in reality or in their souls. All our decisions have been made from the outside, just like the decision that turned us into a people begging the world for pity. Independence is a dream that we never bothered to dream."

Sheik Ahmed Taji tugged at his beard while Ibrahim gnawed at his moustache with his fingertips. Charles Maan got to his feet to answer a knock on the door, spilling ashes as he went. He took a tray of coffee from his daughter and closed the door, then poured for the three.

"Why did a man of your wisdom flee Haifa?" Ibrahim asked Charles Maan.

"Do you think you Moslems cornered the market on Jew-hating? I was too arrogant to sit down with a Jew and negotiate. Again I ask you who will recognize us, our rights, our claims. Out of this whole catastrophe, only the Jews will sit down and talk to us. Why can't we bring ourselves to say that terrible word, *Israel?*"

They pecked at their coffee, then filled the chamber with tobacco smoke.

"I have spoken too much. I am afraid I have offended you, Ahmed Taji," Maan said.

"No, no, no, no," he answered. "It is difficult for us to eat this bitter fruit, then digest it."

"The biggest lie of all was that the Jews would murder everyone who did not flee. What has happened to our brothers who stayed . . . in . . . Israel? Were they thrown into the sea as we swore we would do to the Jews? Were they eaten? Were they sacrificed at the altar? Who were the fools, the ones who fled or the ones who stayed?"

"I fled because those mother-whore Egyptians forced me out to make way for their magnificent army. And you, Haj?"

"My older brother rules my village. I was tricked into leaving, and not by the Jews. So, we are three fools who admit to being fools. But we are among a half-million fools who will not admit it."

Sheik Taji began to breathe heavily and unevenly. He closed his eyes and his voice quivered with emotion. "I do not want to die in that camp," he whispered. "What is it we must do, Charles Maan?"

"We must go at it one step at a time. First we must form a high committee to establish that the refugees have a voice of their own."

"Ha!" Taji cried. "When will you get a committee of Arabs to agree on anything?"

"Let Charles speak," Ibrahim prodded.

"We are the higher committee, the three of us," Maan answered.

"That begins to make sense," the sheik said.

"And we call for a democratic convention of the West Bank refugees," Maan continued.

"Democratic convention. We have just been to one in Amman," Ibrahim said sarcastically.

"Let Charles speak," Sheik Taji said.

"So, speak, Charles," Ibrahim said.

Charles Maan lit a new smoke, more thoughtfully than he had lit the others. "Do we agree among the three of us that life in the Jewish state is preferable and that we can take the humiliation of living in there without being swept up in this madness for revenge?"

"I agree that things can be no worse," Ibrahim said.

"I do not want to die in that camp," Taji repeated.

"Do either of you brothers have reason to believe the Jews will negotiate or that they won't negotiate?" Maan asked.

Ibrahim and the sheik went silent. Ibrahim had the secret knowledge that the Jews were willing to take back a hundred thousand refugees at once. He wondered if Charles Maan had the same information and who Taji was in contact with. And they wondered about each other, as well.

"Do you have any such information?" Ibrahim fenced with Maan.

"Yes, I have reason to believe we will get a better deal from the Jews than from the Egyptians and Syrians, to say nothing of Abdullah," Maan answered.

"How sound is your information?" Ibrahim asked suspiciously.

"I have contacts in Haifa among my own relatives," he said. "They have spoken to certain Jewish officials. The door is definitely open."

"Do you have numbers?" Ibrahim probed.

"No," Maan answered with enough directness to convince Ibrahim. Maan apparently did not know about the hundred thousand figure.

"And you, Ahmed Taji?" Ibrahim asked.

"I have heard from your own uncle, the great Sheik Walid Azziz, who now roams the Negev Desert freely. He has gotten information to me that the Jews would not object if I and my tribe return to our lands, provided we do not make trouble."

"What of you, Haj?" Maan asked.

"Well, let me say we have all the same information. My belief is that they will negotiate."

"We realize that if we accept this undertaking we will have to do so in the face of Arab outrage. We will be denounced as traitors," Maan said.

"That is not enough to blackmail me into dying in that cursed camp," Taji said.

"Nor me," Ibrahim added.

"Then here is what we must do. We must hold a convention of West Bank refugees. I repeat, refugees only. Not the wealthy who fled. Not those who sold their asses to Abdullah. We must pass a resolution to negotiate a return with the Jews and, most important, we must send a delegation to the International Arbitration Commission in Zurich."

"Now it is you who is the dreamer," Taji declared. "How do we get five hundred refugees to agree to such resolutions?"

"By inviting only the right people," Charles Maan retorted. "I can control who is in the delegation from every camp north of Ramallah."

Taji's white beard took a number of keen strokes and he narrowed his eyes. He rolled his hand with a maybe yes, maybe no gesture. "If I had some funds to pass around, it would be no problem."

"What you must do, Sheik Taji, is give each delegate the promise that he and his family will be the first to return. Believe me, they will run back even faster than they fled."

"It has possibilities," Taji answered, already going over his alliances in his mind.

"Haj?"

"Jericho has strange camps. We have collected all the leftovers, the broken tribes, the broken villages. There is less than no unity. My best approach is to simply announce a list of delegates and see to it that no opposition forms."

"How?"

"We have a lot of young boys running loose in gangs terrorizing everyone. I can put them to proper use."

"Good enough," Maan said. "Keep the date a secret so the Jordanians do not get wind of it. We will announce the convention one or two days before it takes place. The main trick is to have all the resolutions passed in a single day and adjourn before the Jordanians know what hit them."

"Yes, that is good," Haj Ibrahim concurred.

"We will convene the conference in Hebron," Taji said.

"Hebron would be a mistake," Charles Maan said quickly. "Your camp is isolated in the south in the middle of Abdullah's greatest West Bank stronghold. Why go into a lion's den?"

"Charles is right," Ibrahim said. "Hebron would be a trap waiting to spring. As for me, Jericho is just too damned close to the Allenby Bridge. Your people in Ramallah are the best-organized refugee group. What of Ramallah?"

"Ramallah! It is scarcely in Palestine," Taji roared.

"Brothers," Charles Maan said in a soft manner, to indicate he had already thought the problem over. "I propose Bethlehem."

"Bethlehem?"

"Bethlehem?"

"Bethlehem."

The sheik covered his heart with his hand in a flourish to denote sincerity. "Bethlehem is a city of divine holiness for you, my brother Charles. However, except for its one day of purity a year, it has always had a reputation for the worst prostitutes in Palestine."

"What a terrible thing to say!" Ibrahim snapped.

"But he speaks the truth," Maan said. "The whores of Bethlehem are a known fact. Fortunately it is only known in Palestine. To the outside world, to whom we must appeal, the name of Bethlehem has a sacred ring and an immediate identity. I assure you that it will arouse the curiosity of the foreign press."

Taji tugged on his beard and deliberated with himself. He looked over to Ibrahim, who nodded in approval. "So it is! One

month from now in Bethlehem. Let us go back and select our
delegates with great care, then hold a democratic convention."

Charles Maan's nicotine-stained hand shot out to be taken in a
deal. Sheik Taji grasped it, then Haj Ibrahim added his hand. All
three put their free hands atop the other three and shook six
hands in rhythm, and for the first time in months, they broke into
laughter.

Chapter Ten

Haj Ibrahim and his co-conspirators went about their task of delegate selection as subtly as a desert mirage. No one was assigned a specific number of delegates. The object was to select only those who would swear to an oath that they would vote for the convention's "resolution of the return."

My father summoned Jamil and gave him a chance to redeem himself. The Avenging Leopards were assigned to see to it that no opposition was allowed to form after Father's delegate list was announced. Jamil was thirsting for action and received the idea like a blood transfusion. Indeed, there were a number of vocal complaints, and each of the complainers got a "kiss" from the Leopards in the form of a not too subtle warning: a dead animal, a cat, dog, rat, snake, nailed to the doorpost.

With nearly seven hundred presworn delegates in place, Charles Maan called a news conference in East Jerusalem, where the Western and Arab press had bureaus. He made a short announcement that a West Bank Refugee Convention, with seven hundred democratically selected delegates, would convene in two days in Bethlehem. Maan then declined to name the delegates publicly.

The Jordanians had been caught off guard. They were still reeling from the rioting that had greeted their parades. That, plus their failure to get world recognition of the annexation, had driven them into temporary timidity. When the press questioned Jordanian ministers in Amman, they had no choice but to declare they had no objection to a refugee meeting.

Despite every precaution, a number of Abdullah's people had infiltrated the delegate lists.

Father gave Jamil the task of having the Leopards and their counterparts from other camps act as stewards inside the hall. Outside, they would ring Manger Square and provide security. The air had an ominous scent to it as we departed for Bethlehem.

As we approached the town, we could see Arab Legion soldiers just off a highway that twisted through precipitous terraced ter-

rain. Delegates were arriving in every kind of broken-down conveyance available on the West Bank. We reached Manger Square
to see it flooded with Avenging Leopards and other gangs. However, the rooftops were filled with Arab Legion and they were
highly visible.

A meager encampment had been set up in Shepherds' Field.
The refugees came with their prayer rugs and some sort of tenting gear and carried their own bread and drink. It was truly a
convocation of the destitute.

Bethlehem, like Jericho, had seen greater glory. Everything
centered around the Church of the Nativity and the Grotto of
Jesus' birth. The square was bordered by shops that catered to the
busloads of pilgrims: counters filled with olive-wood carvings of
crucifixes, Christian symbols, and works of Bethlehem lace and
embroidery. In the square a battalion of peddlers, beggars, and
hustlers mixed with pilgrims and Avenging Leopards under the
watchful eyes of the Arab Legion.

At the far side of the square stood a battered and defunct old
movie house, the Eastern Star, which was the location of the convention. Father felt the theater should be safe from possible
Jordanian attack because so many foreign reporters were present.
Although the building was made of stone, its interior was highly
flammable, and he was certain that the notion of burning us alive
had passed through the minds of more than one Jordanian official.
As they entered, all the delegates had to unroll their prayer rugs
and the security gangs searched for bombs, incendiaries, submachine guns, and other lethal paraphernalia.

The theater filled as technicians struggled with the faulty
sound system. When it finally connected, it blared off the stone
walls with an intensity that forced me to cover my ears. The
theater was peeling and had bad smells that somehow befitted a
meeting of refugees. Just as the leaders took their places behind a
long table on the stage, Father took me aside.

"Find a place in the theater where you will be very small.
There may be trouble. If there is, don't try to reach me but get
back to Aqbat Jabar to defend the women."

I found a narrow stone stair behind a door and groped my way
upstairs to a hallway and a small room. I had been in a movie
house a few times in Ramle and knew from its size and shape that
this was once the projection room. Through the little openings I

could look down on the entire hall. There was also a window to the outside overlooking Manger Square. From here I could see Jamil and his "troops." I knew the new seeds of hatred that had been planted in the camps were in Bethlehem in the form of these gangs. It was not hard to tell what the future would be like if Father did not succeed.

"Hear, O brothers," Sheik Ahmed Taji began, appearing potent in new borrowed flowing robes, "we are gathered here in democratic brotherhood because we know full well that the lone man belongs to the wolf and that one hand cannot applaud. Revenge is sacred and hatred is noble. Yet what we long for must be delayed by certain realities. We will not return to our land just because the Jews are willing to take us back. No, that will not lure us. We will not return because they will give us schools and hospitals. We will never submit to such obvious crude briberies. We will only return so we can work silently for the moment of vengeance. We shall lure the enemy until our strength has grown to insurmountable proportions, then we shall prod him with a hot poker."

Sheik Ahmed Taji was in rare form. He spoke not to reason but to persuade, and the value of his words could be measured only by their quantity.

"Patience dries up oceans and erodes mountains. Allah is with the patient. Patience is the key to salvation. We, the victims, must modify our great lust until we are again planted on our sacred soil. Then and only then shall we begin appropriate actions. So let us return and dwell among the jackals until we are ready."

His tongue rolled off words without meaning and he spoke now only to incite the senses. . . .

"We have been the victims of bad luck, and when bad luck humiliates a man, everyone steps on his feet and the ways of the wrongdoers grow like mountains. We roll in the dust. Our stomachs are empty. With each small meal there is a great quarrel. With each bite there is a worry. Poverty makes us ill-tempered.

"Show your teeth, O my brothers, and everyone will fear you. They are chewing us but they cannot swallow us. We know what each other feels, for we are like one single brother and nothing knows the trunk of the tree better than its bark. What fate has befallen you has also befallen me. None of us are immune and protected from the fate of bad luck. If the time comes for us to weep, we will see that there are less fortunate brothers who have been blinded. If the time comes for us to run, others have no legs.

"We who have tasted the sweetness of life must also taste its bitterness. But joy always follows sorrow, as the bird follows the wind. Sadness is only separated from joy by time. And the time has come to turn the page. But remember, my brothers, if we had not tasted bitterness, how would we appreciate sweetness?"

It was becoming extremely difficult to follow Sheik Taji's trail of words without ideas or substance as they wove, tickled fancies, raised and lowered emotions. Nevertheless, his speech was received with enthusiasm.

Charles Maan came to the rostrum, a complete contrast to the first orator. His suit of Western cut was rumpled, as was his small, thin body. He hefted a report of many pages, opened it with browned fingers, and read without passion but as cuttingly as a man with a razor blade for a tongue. His report was a dispassionate analysis of the reasons we had become refugees. It was a moment of great truth for this gathering, because no such words had ever been displayed before an Arab audience. Charles Maan had the extra stature of being a Christian schoolteacher, and his composure at this moment began to glue restless men to their seats and hold their mouths agape in silence.

"The leaders of the Arab world must bear the main responsibility for our problem," he said. "They, the wealthy Palestinians who fled before a shot was fired, and the Mufti who tried to rule us through terror and assassination are the unholy trinity. They told us, 'Brothers, we are working for your interests and victory is close at hand.' This was the first of many lies that undermined our existence."

Murmurs of agreement floated up to the projection room. I believe that, to a delegate, everyone was awed by the courage of Charles Maan.

"The Deir Yassin massacre was deliberately blown out of all proportion, as well as false reports of Jewish atrocities. What man here will secretly whisper in my ear that his wife was really desecrated and his child was thrown into a well and drowned? These were lies that flitted from false tongues to false ears.

". . . It was the outright refusal of anyone to step forward and speak the ways of peace with the Jews. It is a peace now enjoyed by a hundred and fifty thousand of our brothers who remained in

Israel. Does not their existence, your cousins and my cousins in the Jewish state, put to rest the perfidious propaganda of the Arab leaders who stated that anyone who remained would be murdered by the Jews?"

Chucking their fear, a number of men began to rise.

"Charles Maan speaks the truth!"

"We have been betrayed!"

"Death to the liars in Damascus!"

The little teacher held up his hands for silence. "We were put upon, sent into a war for which we were not prepared and which we did not need. It ruined agriculture, created unemployment, the black market, and famine, and forced us to leave. Once our noble armies breached Israel's borders and her settlements were attacked for plunder, the Jews were not under any obligation to protect a hostile Arab population. Do any of you believe we would not have annihilated the Jews if we were winning the war?"

The murmur in the audience grew to a rumble.

"What have the Jews done to us to compare to what the Arabs have done to us? The Syrian refugee camps have no sanitation, no allotments of clothing, and the only food is from international charity. No Palestinian in Syria can travel beyond the camp in which he dwells. Hundreds of our people have been thrown into Syrian jails without charges and without trials. Their attempts to organize have been brutally crushed.

"The Lebanese took in our wealthiest citizens, who bought respectability with dollars and sterling. But their camps are no better than these dismal rat-breeders we live in. Do you know where you can get Red Crescent supplies? They are sold openly in the streets of Beirut. The Lebanese are very generous. They allow our people to work. You will find our children sweeping the streets, cleaning the toilets, peddling, washing dishes in cafés. But you will not find them in schools, for it is forbidden to educate a Palestinian child. Aha, the generous Lebanese allow our people to leave the camps and rent homes where the rates are double what is charged their own citizens. The drinking water is foul in many Lebanese camps, and the sale of water often robs our people of their last penny. Hear this, O brothers, the Lebanese Refugee Committee has issued this statement," he said, holding it aloft. "They blame the Mufti of Jerusalem and the leaders of the Arab nations for their plight! Not the Jews but the Arabs! Read it, my brothers. Read it and weep. Do I have to speak about Jordan, my brothers? Do we not know the bitterness of that tale?"

"Death to Abdullah!"

"Death to the Arab Legion!"

"Be careful," Charles Maan said, "be careful. Abdullah has ears among us. Ears that should be sliced off and pickled in a jar." He turned the page of his report and looked down from the stage, and spoke in hammer blows. "Now I come to our own Palestinian brothers on the West Bank. They, more than anyone else, have forced us into these camps. All available housing rents have been raised by 500 percent. We cannot even bury our dead without paying a grave tax. Despite the fact that the Red Crescent alone supports these camps, we must pay municipal taxes to adjoining cities. There is no employment or education, and what isn't done to us by our own people is finished by the Jordanians."

"Death to our brothers!"

"I am not through, because we still must speak about the worst of the lot. We live in paradise by comparison to the camps in the Gaza Strip under the control of the almighty Egyptians. Do you know what it is like for a refugee to get a travel permit from Gaza to Egypt? First you must bribe a half-dozen officials for papers. Then, at the border, you must pay exorbitant customs duties or leave all your belongings to the Egyptians. Our boys have been pulled out of the camps in the middle of the night and forced to serve in the Egyptian Army, trained in abominable conditions and thrown into battle totally unprepared. We cannot even imagine the number of our people who have been pushed into prisons and tortured to death. Each day there are over a hundred new deaths from tuberculosis and dysentery and typhoid and cholera. When we tried to organize in Gaza, what happened? The Mufti of Jerusalem, under Egyptian orders, sent in his assassins. When a man is jailed, his wife and daughters and sisters and his mother can expect a visit from Egyptian soldiers who will rape and desecrate them!"

"Charles Maan lies!"

"Death to Charles Maan!"

The seats, barely bolted in place, were being ripped up and hurled toward the stage. "Aha! Here come Abdullah's dogs, right on cue!"

The Avenging Leopards closed in with homemade batons coming from under their clothing, but pandemonium had been created and there was the start of a mass charge for the exits.

At that moment, my father, the immortal Haj Ibrahim al Soukori al Wahhabi, pulled Charles Maan away from the rostrum, stepped up to it, took out a huge pistol, and fired into the air right before the microphone. It sounded like no fewer than a dozen cannons erupting, and the echoes off the stone walls all but shattered our ears. Everyone dived for cover, cowering.

"Kindly remove the traitors and we shall go on," he said in a calming voice. His orders were not carried out until he fired several more times. "Please, my brothers, we are not finished with our work. This is a democratic convention. You will return to your seats." The final pistol shot sent everyone scurrying back to his place and order was restored.

"We have sinned!" my father cried. "After fourteen centuries of hatred we finally deliberately and with calculation and arrogance picked a war we thought we could not lose. We did not defend our land!

". . . None of us have been exactly blinded by the bright sunlight of hospitality from the Arab leaders, and that goes double for our own Palestinian brothers on the West Bank.

"*Kaif,*" my father said, changing this tone to softness. "It is a word of profound significance to us. It means do nothing, say nothing, think nothing. We deceive ourselves by saying that kaif is the perfect form of patience, but in truth kaif is a philosophy of deliberate idleness, of being half-awake without leaving the world of private fantasy. We go into kaif, a state of semi-consciousness, to alleviate the reality of our suffering. We are men locked in boxes inside our own minds. Here the keys are being placed before you. We failed in our other test in the war—but dare we fail again? It has been said that it is not necessary to instruct our children, for life will teach them. Can you see what life is teaching our children?"

Haj Ibrahim had captured silence and held it in his hands. I had never heard him speak like this. It must have come from many hundreds of hours of meditation, and the audience looked up to the stage as though they were listening to a prophet.

"In our dream world we would like to think that we are so lofty that a thousand ladders could not reach as high as our heads.

We consider ourselves noble men who would rather die from starvation than ask for help . . . that our left hand does not need our right hand . . . that it is better to die with honor than to live with humiliation. We would like to think that the head that has no pride deserves to be severed. If we believe these things, then why do we accept life as slovenly dogs in these wretched camps?

"Our time for kaif is over, my brothers. We must ford a boisterous river. We can no longer trust our fate to thieves who have abandoned and pilfered from us. We can no longer be lulled to sleep by the false music of revenge. We must have the character to admit to a terrible mistake. Only such an admission will unlock us from our boxes and allow us to step onto the path that will lead us back to our homes and our land. Otherwise our diet will become decades of false promises and our beards will grow white with age and our stomachs and minds become so rancid that even the vultures will not wish to pick our bones. . . .

"As for the Jews, they did not run away in 1948 and they will not run away in the future. The sweet dream of a new Arab invasion is a cruel hoax because it will be impossible to throw a desperate people into the sea without destroying ourselves in the process. The price for armed victory over the Jews will only be spent in words, not in blood. We must face the Jews with our genuine desire for peace and the world will be in our corner. We no longer have the luxury of having our greatest joy in life come from killing a Jew. We must appear reasonable at every turn. We must establish trust, and I believe the Jews can be dealt with. The real war we have to win is to enter an honest dialogue with the Jews, and the only conquest we have to make is of the minds of the West."

There was scarcely a smattering of applause at the end of my father's speech. As the severity of Father's words and his challenge sank in, I knew he was trying to swim upstream against many centuries of calcified hatred. I became filled with fear that some hothead would take his life. And then my fear gave way to a swelling pride. Oh, Haj Ibrahim, so utterly magnificent, so courageous. What other man from the desert to the sea would stand before his brothers and dare speak such words?

"We have the resolution of this convention to be voted upon," Charles Maan said. "I will read it to you. 'Be it resolved that this convention has been attended by delegates who truly represent the refugees of the West Bank, the principal sufferers of the war. We hereby express our conviction that we should have an equal voice in our own fate. We hereby demand to negotiate to return to our homes and have our assets unfrozen, no matter who rules Palestine politically. We express our willingness to sit down and speak with representatives of the State of Israel for the purpose of ending our exile. We hereby elect a delegation to represent us and our aspirations at the International Arbitration Commission that is convening in Zurich later this summer. This delegation shall consist of Haj Ibrahim al Soukori al Wahhabi, Mr. Charles Maan, and Sheik Ahmed Taji.' "

The vote came as anticlimax. What was important was that the leaders had kept the convention together, spoken harsh words, opened minds, and ended with a favorable resolution all in a single day. The delegates paraded up to the table on the stage and picked up their ballots: white for approval and black for disapproval. The preconvention pledges held firm.

As they voted, the delegates also put a contribution into a large box for the expenses of the meeting and of sending the delegation to Zurich. I waited in the projection room while the money was counted as the delegates drifted from the hall. I could hear the disappointment. They did not meet expenses, much less have the money to travel on.

"Does anyone know how much this will cost?" I heard over the microphone, which had not been turned off.

"It all depends on how long the Zurich meeting lasts. Many thousands of dollars, anyhow," my father said.

"My air ticket will be paid for by some Catholic charities who will also house me in Zurich," Charles Maan said. "But I cannot go alone."

"We are truly done for," Sheik Taji moaned. "We are all in debt up to our throats."

"Somehow Allah will provide," Father said.

"I think that Allah may not hear us," Taji answered.

"Perhaps I can help Allah help us," Father said. "I know of some secret funds, so do not despair."

I was about to leave the projection room when the air was abruptly filled with the sound of whistles, the shouting of military commands, and the clumping of boots running fast over the stone square. I ran to the window! The Arab Legion had converged from all four sides, grabbing, clubbing, and dragging off the Avenging Leopards and other gangs who had conveniently identified themselves with special armbands. I saw my brother Jamil being carried off by four Jordanian soldiers and thrown into one of a dozen army trucks parked before the Church of the Nativity. Father, Sheik Taji, and Charles Maan rushed out of the theater. A half-dozen Legion soldiers leveled their weapons at them and led them away.

Chapter Eleven

The operation had gone smoothly. The sweep of Manger Square had netted Colonel Farid Zyyad fifty-two of the so-called Avenging Leopards and their counterparts from ten separate refugee camps. A clean wedge had been driven between the refugees and their plans to create trouble in Zurich. A soldier entered the office and announced that Haj Ibrahim had arrived at the police fort.

Farid Zyyad buttoned on a tunic replete with the ribbons and decorations of a proper Legion colonel. He inspected himself in the mirror, moistening his white teeth with a brush of his tongue, and retired behind his desk.

"Send him in."

As Haj Ibrahim entered, Colonel Zyyad made the unusual gesture of arising, offering his adversary a chair, and ordering coffee. Ibrahim knew at once that it was to be a stick and carrot situation.

"Where are Sheik Taji and Charles Maan?" Ibrahim demanded.

"They have been released, with apologies."

"My son, Jamil?"

"He is in safekeeping for the moment, along with the other boys." Farid Zyyad glanced at a paper on his desk. "Fifty-two of them."

"It is a deliberate provocation. Are you looking for an uprising in the refugee camps?"

"I doubt that one will take place unless you incite it, and I doubt that you will incite it so long as these boys are in custody."

"For safekeeping?"

"For safekeeping."

"You are aware that the foreign press may not be very kind to His Majesty over this incident."

"While I applaud the clever way you three have manipulated this meeting and the press, two can play that game. We have given a release explaining the situation." He handed Ibrahim a sheet of paper.

"I do not read English."

"I shall read it for you, then. 'Today's roundup is the culmination of months of investigations into a situation that has disturbed King Abdullah and the Jordanian authorities. Gangs of youths have gone on a rampage of terror in the refugee camps, encouraged by older gangster elements. Among the charges against these gangs are black marketeering, grand larceny, blackmail, extortion, et cetera, et cetera, et cetera.' "

"Does the foreign press know that any of those charges could be made against almost any Jordanian official on the West Bank and that your splendid Arab Legion has collaborated with and encouraged these activities?"

Zyyad went back to his desk and held up his hand. "That is what I wanted to speak about to you, Haj Ibrahim. I recall our first meeting in Nablus in the home of the late Clovis Bakshir, may Allah retrieve his noble spirit. I found you to be an extremely intelligent man. You have tweaked my nose now on three occasions, yet I bear you no grudge. However, you have made your position extremely clear. It is no longer tolerable."

"So the boys are being held hostage to curb our tongues and blunt our aspirations."

"That is an extreme choice of words. Yes, they will remain in custody. We will continue to interrogate them about their activities. In due course there may be a trial or there may not be a trial," Zyyad said, shrugging with newborn innocence.

"Depending on the outcome in Zurich," Ibrahim said.

"Such is life. Even now, within hours, some of them are volunteering information . . . on the reasonable provision that they will inform on the others if we drop the charges against them."

Zyyad's maneuver was clear. What to do? Bellow and roar? Make it clear there would be massive uprisings? Or calm down and listen? Zyyad wanted something. He would find out.

"You have my absolute attention," Ibrahim said.

"Good," Zyyad responded with the slightest glimmer of a smile. He zipped open a pack of cigarettes, offered Ibrahim one, and lit both of them.

"You recall our conversation in Nablus, Haj?"

"In detail."

"Then you recall that I confided in you at that time that His Majesty Abdullah is not your typical Islamic fanatic on the mat-

ter of the Jews. He entered the war, largely against his will, for
the sake of Arab unity. All of his recent utterances against the
Jews are mostly for public consumption and to let the world
know that the Arab leaders have a solid front. Can you go along
with me on this point?"

"Let us say that for the moment I accept your statement."

"Good. So we can understand each other's situation. We find no
great pleasure in having you remain in the camps. We have done
more than any other Arab state. We offered immediate citizenship, freedom of movement, jobs, government offices."

"And suppression," Ibrahim said.

"Yes, of course suppression," Zyyad agreed. "We cannot entertain the anarchy of upward of a half-million people running loose
like an unchecked flash flood."

"We have rights," Ibrahim said.

"Certainly you do. Whatever the king grants you."

"You are not happy that we did not fall on our knees and look
upon Abdullah as our savior," Ibrahim shot back.

"Frankly, we don't care at this stage. Nor do we care for your
rights. We have gotten what we want from the Palestinians. The
rest of you will come along when faced with the realities. Let me
speak to you with the candor for which you are famous. In our
analysis we feel that the Palestinians do not have the fire of rebellion in their guts. You and your brothers are amazingly easy to
control and you have never amounted to a damn as fighters. We
do not think you are going to change more than thirteen centuries of history."

Ibrahim held his temper. "We have never been locked up like
this. What you see happening with these young boys, the Leopards and the Sharks, is only a forewarning that this next generation of Palestinians may be of a different ilk. After all, Colonel
Zyyad, we all once believed that the Jews were a passive lot, easy
to trample upon. Generations do change. I think it is a lesson you
had better heed."

"We don't intend to let these boys run wild. We will put nice
uniforms on them and channel their misplaced energies into hatred of the Jews and convert it into disciplined guerrilla action
against the Jews. It will supply further proof to our Arab brothers that we are in the fight with them, no? As for the vast majority of Palestinians, I believe they are disposed to sit in these

camps and rot forever. They have no spirit and less dignity. They are weepers and beggars."

Ibrahim rose from his seat and leaned forward on Zyyad's desk, coiled to strike, but words did not come. He blinked and slowly sank back down. It was horrible to hear such truths. That was why they were never spoken.

"Good," Zyyad said. "We recognize a chronic condition."

"I hear your words," Ibrahim rasped.

"Why must we continue as enemies? When we narrow our goals down, you will see there are ways to resolve our differences. No, I am not going to try to bribe you. I learned in Nablus that does not work. You are a man of principle. So rare. I have a reasonable offer."

"I have reasonable ears," Ibrahim said.

"Good, Allah is blessing this meeting." Zyyad opened his bottom drawer and produced his omnipresent bottle of Scotch and offered Ibrahim a drink.

"No thank you, whiskey would burn my insides out," he said in an automatic refusal, then reconsidered. "Perhaps a little, very little."

"The point in question is that nothing is going to stop King Abdullah's march to a Greater Syria—nothing. Not harsh words from the Arab leaders, not the refugees, not the Jews. It is destiny, divine destiny. The point is, we both have use for the Jews, so let us use them."

"If the king is to fulfill his destiny," Ibrahim said, trying not to make a mockery, "does he think he will destroy the Jewish state?"

"Incorporate it."

"Incorporate it?"

"Yes, as a province of Greater Syria."

"Do the Jews know about this?"

"They will learn in good time. Give them a decade of isolation along with the realization that as a loyal province under Abdullah their own future is secured."

"In the Prophet's name, they will never agree to such a thing. Jews and Arabs as allies?"

"Not as allies, as subjects. But what is so farfetched? In ancient times we in Jordan were Gibeonites and Gibeon was a province of Israel. King David's court itself had Moabites, Hittites, and a castle guard of Philistines. Solomon had Celts and Rhinelanders!"

Farid Zyyad's voice had suddenly risen and become shrill and his eyes rolled wildly. Haj Ibrahim stared at the man in disbelief. Then it became terribly clear. He, Colonel Farid Zyyad, who had been a Bedouin under the British, now saw himself as a general in command of the Jewish province! In that instant Ibrahim recognized all the insanity of Arab politics rolling from the tongue of one man.

"I am to assume," Zyyad continued, "that since you left your cave you have made contact with Gideon Asch. Before you deny it, let me observe that you would not have spoken as you did in Bethlehem today if you didn't have something in your pocket, some kind of understanding."

"I don't confirm, I don't deny."

"Fair enough."

"Please go on, I am filled with fascination," Ibrahim said.

"What is it that you refugees want? To return to your homes? So make your deal with the Jews in Zurich. Take a thousand, fifty thousand, two hundred thousand back with you. We don't want the burden of these camps. The Jews will house you and feed you and educate you. That is their weakness. And when the time is ripe for the Greater Syria, we will have many more thousands of our brothers in place to force a peaceful takeover of Israel. However, whatever deal you make, you must make it quietly. The world is not to know. Break down your camps slowly and steal out of them silently.

"In public, Jordan must continue to denounce everything," Zyyad continued. "We will denounce your delegation in Zurich, for we must keep up the show of Arab unity."

"What do you want in exchange?" Ibrahim asked.

"Stop your activities against King Abdullah, do not let Charles Maan go bleating to the foreign press, and above all, your deal with the Jews is to be secret. Now, isn't that reasonable?"

"I must think about it. I must talk it over with my friends. What about the boys you have under arrest?"

"Are we still dazed by the perfume of candor?" Zyyad asked. "Speak openly."

"If you make any noise in Zurich, some of those boys will not live long enough to grow moustaches."

"I wish to see my son," Ibrahim whispered.

"Certainly, please use this office. I will have him brought to you."

As Farid Zyyad stepped outside he had made the judgment: Haj Ibrahim was probably willing to take the loss of the boy Jamil. It was another son, the little Ishmael, he would move mountains to save. As soon as Haj Ibrahim left for Zurich, Ishmael would be taken into custody, as well . . . for insurance.

Jamil seemed to have found some kind of greater glory in his arrest and in being singled out as a leader.

"I am going to Zurich in a short time, Jamil," his father said. "The Jordanians will continue to hold you as a hostage. Bear in mind that they do not have British law as we had it in Palestine. The law is what the king wants, and they can charge you with anything they care to. You have no chance in a Jordanian military court. I urge you to keep your boys quiet. The Jordanians boil fingers. Do you understand?"

Jamil's eyes looked very weird. "Do not worry about me, Father. You do what you have to do in Zurich, no matter what becomes of me."

"I think you enjoy this whole business," Ibrahim said.

"Enjoy it? I don't know. I think it makes no difference if I live or die."

"Come now, no one wants to die."

"I and all my friends will have to die sooner or later for the struggle you have imposed on us. What else is there for us to do except die? We can go no place; we can do nothing; we are told to think of nothing except the vengeance and the return."

"I am trying to make a better life for you."

Jamil erupted with a maddened laugh, tossing his head back and spitting futility. "It makes no difference to you if I die, my father. It would even help you if I became a martyr."

"Shut up!"

"So, beat me up again."

"Jamil, you are my son. I am trying to get you out of this."

"For what? Don't bother. I am not your son. You have only one son. Ishmael. Isn't that right, Father?"

Ibrahim slapped his face. Jamil got to his feet. "I hit you once, Father, and I still feel the ecstasy from it. Jailer! Jailer! Take me back to my cell!"

A few days after Father returned to Aqbat Jabar, he took me into Jericho, to the office of Professor Doctor Nuri Mudhil.

"I received eight thousand dollars for your treasures," the archaeologist said. "Here are the air tickets for yourself and Sheik Taji. We thought it best for you not to go to Amman again, so you will take a small plane from East Jerusalem to Cyprus and then continue on to Zurich. I have had to fly many antiquities out of East Jerusalem and I know the people at the airport well. The air tickets and special attention to certain officials have eaten up over twenty-eight hundred dollars. These here are your travel papers. The visas are attached."

"But they are not passports," Father said.

Mudhil shook his head. "There is no nation of Palestine. There is only Jordan, and Jordan will not give you passports. You must travel on these."

Father scanned one of the documents and handed it to me. "What does it say?"

"It says you are a stateless person and this is a visa to Switzerland and back, good for thirty days," I said.

"Unfortunately, I had to pass off a thousand dollars for each of these documents," Nuri Mudhil said, running his fingertips against the tip of his thumb. "Baksheesh, the standard bribe. We could have given you Israeli passports at no cost, but you would never have received credentials for your delegation in Zurich. The Arabs would have blocked any recognition."

"How much does that leave?" Ibrahim asked me.

"Thirty-two hundred dollars," I said.

"Less another five hundred. It is illegal to carry cash. I had to transfer your money through the church charities. It was necessary to pay one of the priests in the archbishop's office five hundred dollars. So, with new clothing for yourself and Sheik Taji, that should leave you about a thousand dollars each for room and food."

"But this forces me to leave my family penniless except for Sabri's salary. If they have to depend on Red Crescent rations alone, they might starve. And what if I run out of money in Switzerland?"

Nuri Mudhil opened the drawer of his desk and took out a packet of Jordanian currency. "I am making you a personal loan for the expenses of your family. You do not have to worry about paying it back. As for yourself in Zurich, Gideon Asch will keep you floating if you run out of funds."

"Beggars, we are beggars," Father said, taking the money, tickets, and cash.

"I am very sorry, Haj. It was the best I could do."

"No, no, my friend. You have done too much already." Father then turned to me, strangely. "Ishmael, you will wait in Dr. Mudhil's workroom. I wish to have private words with him."

They spoke for a time. I don't know how long because I always ascended to heaven when I could walk around Professor Doctor Nuri Mudhil's studio, filled as it was with wonderments. At his bench was a complex drawing of a Byzantine mosaic he had uncovered that was once a church floor. I studied it. At last the office door opened and I was summoned to return and told to sit down.

"You are leaving with Dr. Mudhil," my father said tersely. "Right now."

"I do not understand."

"While I am away it would be better for you not to be in Aqbat Jabar."

"But, Father, why?"

"Because your life is in danger!" he barked.

"It would be cowardly of me to go!"

"Not cowardly, only wise."

"Who will defend the women?"

"There is Sabri, there is Omar, and there is Kamal. The women will be safe."

"Sabri must work and Kamal is worthless. Omar cannot do the job by himself."

"He will have to," my father said.

"But where do I go?"

"You will cross the Jordan River," Nuri Mudhil said. "Then deep into the desert to the border of Iraq, where you will stay among my very good friends the al Sirhan Bedouin. And you may take many of my books with you."

I began to weep, then felt a strange and most wonderful thing. My father stood over me and placed his hands on my shoulders with great affection.

"What of Jamil?" I finally blubbered.

"I will not be blackmailed by those dogs in Amman. Jamil's fate is in Allah's hands. Allah has told me to make a terrible decision which of my sons must survive." I looked at him.

"I have made that decision, Ishmael."

Chapter Twelve

Fawzi Effendi Kabir reclined on an elevated Romanesque couch in a remodeled boathouse downlake in Zurich's sumptuous suburb of Zollikon. There were four steps down from this "emperor's throne" to the mats of a circular room, mirrored all around and lit for debauchery.

Several control panels were at the emperor's fingertips. He could touch off a range of music from the atonalities of Hindemith and Bartók or to shrill Stravinsky, or lofty Beethoven, or muted Mozart, or the sweaty driving thumping of the *Bolero*, or Wagner's wings to Valhalla, or *le hot* or *le cool* jazz, or sentimental French love songs, or the familiar and deliciously discordant wails of the Orient.

The large control board next to it activated a limitless selection of lighting effects, some two hundred thousand combinations from swirling maddening little octagonal dots to sudden bolts of lightning.

Yet another set of buttons could release a plethora of special effects down on the revelers on the mats: tropical mists tauntingly perfumed, slithering oils, fog, live snakes, rose petals, doves, and occasionally, when everything was working, he could lower trapezes from the ceiling or ropes for dwarfs to slide down.

The final panel rotated the emperor's couch so he might observe every part of the room below and raise and lower his couch on a hydraulic lift much as one sends one's automobile aloft for repairs.

There were other rooms: a generously stocked bar and buffet; a hot pool with a waterfall; a dressing room filled with costumes from Greek togas to leathers, to animal skins and all sorts of toys, the full assortment of whips, chains, masks, dildos, torture and debasement devices. The selection of drugs was also complete: basic Lebanon number one hashish, heroin, pure cocaine, slow-down dream substances, speed-up pills.

The boathouse had been re-created by a team of the best motion picture technicians and interior decorators on the Continent at a cost of slightly over two million dollars.

Fawzi Kabir rarely got down on the mats, and when he was visited at throne level his participation was abstract, for he was bloated, generally drugged, and without potency. Nonetheless his perverse imagination was bottomless and the games to be played and performances to be performed were endless. His lust for inflicting pain and debasement provided him with unique wild bursts of orgasmic joy.

The whores of Zurich were as bland as the country and limited in number. The Effendi preferred German men and women. When it came to an orgy, they were peerless. Ursula traveled to the fleshpots of Munich, which she knew intimately and where she obtained the players.

It took about a dozen couples to fill the mattresses and their mirrored images ran to infinity. At times a live string quartet performed along with a poetry reader. Muscled, cocoa-buttered men and sultry girls with panther movements performed individual and collective feats of wonderment. Party themes varied according to the limitations of Ursula's imagination and often lasted for a hundred hours, ending usually with a superman or superwoman contest. The winner! A diamond bracelet, a gold watch, a car.

The whores of Munich were drawn magnetically to the Arabs. Not only did Islam's high and mighty potentates require servicing, but the Arabs generally traveled with enormous entourages, so there was enough business to filter down to the most lowly servant. Cash up front, no bargaining. The whores and their pimps earned their fees, for they were often treated crudely and always with an undertone of savagery.

Ursula convinced Kabir that if he was to partake of such sights, it was the one place he could not guard his pocketbook. Couples, food, transportation, lodging, drink, costumes, drugs, repair of the room, individual performers, gifts could run a party to upward of a hundred thousand dollars.

On this night the players were heading into a third straight dawn and the Effendi had reached the point of collapse. Before he spun into a gasping glob, he had gone on a binge, pelting faces and bodies with bunches of juicy purple grapes, urinating down from the throne, overturning gallon cans of body paint until he collapsed with a ripsaw battle between sleeping pills and cocaine raging in his body and head.

Ursula climbed up to his couch, where he now lay moaning incoherently, and broke a capsule under his nose. He twitched and blabbered to some sort of consciousness, lifted himself to all fours, his belly nearly touching the floor . . . and vomited.

"Wake up, Fawzi!" she demanded over thunder bursts of storm music and dizzying flashes of light.

He mumbled an unintelligible complaint and vomited again. She put another ammonia capsule under his nose, then doused him with icy water.

He looked up at her, dripping perspiration, his eyes rolled like ball bearings on polished floor, and he tipped flat on his face. She whacked his buttocks hard. "Wake up!"

A few of the revelers, in Mardi Gras masks, howled in delight at the foot of the steps.

"You dirty bitch, leave me alone!"

Kabir groped for the emperor's couch, but he slipped on the oil and wetness beneath his body and skidded down to the mat and lay on his back bleating to be left alone. The revelers pelted him with a tattoo of grapes, ripe plums, and kirschwasser until Ursula beat them off.

He breathed in short gasps.

"Prince Ali Rahman has phoned," she said. "I put him off for a half hour."

"The prince! Oh God!" Kabir groaned. He tried to swim to his feet but skidded down again. "I can't . . . I can't . . . oh God . . . what . . . what . . . time is it?"

"It is four in the morning."

"Oh God! The prince. *No!* No more to sniff. My head is splitting."

"Throw up again," she commanded, signaling a pair of servants to bring cold water and sponges and to clean him up. As he was attended, Ursula dimmed the music to a soothing, drifting theme and set the lights at a pleasant shade of pastel. The partygoers then either collapsed and slept entwined in twos, threes, and fours, or crawled off to clean up.

He was set upright but toppled over again and lay still. Ursula reached across his blubbery back.

"It was a good party," he said.

"Yes, Fawzi, a wonderful party." She stroked him with the tips of her meticulously sharpened and painted claws. "A wonderful party."

"Get the doctor. I am sick. I need a shot."

"He is on his way from the main house."

Within the hour the Effendi was sobered enough to return Prince Ali Rahman's call. The voice on the other end of Kabir's line screamed a string of Saudi obscenities, commonplace when Ali Rahman was angry, which was a good part of the time. Kabir waited patiently for the royal wrath to wane with a calming repetition of "Yes, my prince," and "No, my prince."

"Have you *seen* the morning papers!" Rahman demanded.

"No, my prince. I do not usually get out of bed and read the papers at five in the morning."

The prince shrieked out a front-page story that a three-man delegation of West Bank refugees had arrived in Zurich and demanded credentials to the arbitration convention. They had said in a news conference that King Abdullah was holding fifty-two refugee boys as hostages in an Amman prison.

"Who are these intruders, Your Highness? What are their names?"

"There is a Bedouin, a Sheik Ahmed Taji. There is Charles Maan, the nonbeliever of whom we have already heard, and there is a Haj Ibrahim al Soukori al Wahhabi."

"I know them," Kabir answered.

"I want them assassinated!" the prince screamed.

"No, that will do us no good in Switzerland. Look, give me an hour and I will be at your villa."

Prince Ali Rahman was attired in a silken morning gown. His long thin face held an indelible stamp, the beak of the Saudi family resembling that of a desert hawk, which he truly was. Although far down the line of succession, Prince Rahman had emerged into the top circle of power in a royal court stocked with hundreds of princes and princelings.

Ali Rahman was of the proud old breed. He had ridden alongside his grandfather, the great Ibn Saud, who went to war for control of the Arabian peninsula at the turn of the century. Ibn Saud had rid the place of the Turks, outlived a British protectorate and had driven their archrivals, the Hashemites, out of the Hejaz. Ibn Saud declared a nation, which without the burden of modesty he named after his family. In the early 1930s he had initiated oil explorations with the Americans, a move that was now beginning to cause billions of dollars to gush into a dry treasury.

Ali Rahman was given the task of investing the new fortunes. He was not a sophisticated man in matters of international finance but he had native shrewdness.

Fawzi Kabir had long had an operational base in Switzerland and during the war had shown great finesse in the intricate business of arms dealing and transforming or hiding funds. When one of the ranking princes dropped nearly a half-million dollars in IOUs at the Monte Carlo gaming tables in a twelve-hour streak and could not make his markers good, he became a candidate for imprisonment. Fawzi Kabir cleverly bailed out the wayward prince, a move that caught Rahman's eye.

Kabir could offer a full range of financial services, interesting investments, floating of high-interest loans, stashing untraceable millions. He made enormous sums for the Saudis and enormous commissions for himself, so much so that Kabir moved into Zurich, a crown city of hidden accounts. The Effendi had only to sit behind the desk of his mansion in Zollikon and appraise the endless petitioners from banks, arms merchants, drug runners, floundering little nations with mineral deposits.

The royal family was just getting around to placing its young heirs in American and British universities. There were fifty of them on the Continent now, with their entourages. Kabir controlled their funds, covered their gambling debts, their fifty-thousand-dollar hotel bills, their purchases of jewelry and cars, their pursuit of European flesh. He kept their excesses out of the papers and saved the royal family from numerous potential humiliations.

When the United Nations called for an arbitration conference to present all outstanding Arab claims from the war, Kabir engineered its location, had it held in Zurich, and had himself named as head of one of the Palestinian delegations. Prince Rahman leased an enormous villa in the wooded Zürichberg district and the two conspired to manipulate the conference. A new chapter in Saudi political thinking had opened: the use of vast oil revenues combined with blackmail and the outright purchasing of allies. The prince knew that if he could control the avaricious mind of Fawzi Kabir, he might well control the Arab world, or, at least, manipulate it to Saudi whims.

Kabir's first move was to get a signed agreement from all the Arab states and delegations that none could negotiate with or sign an agreement with the Jews on their own. The Saudis had not fought in the war, except for a token unit, nor did they involve themselves with the refugees. Their main purposes were to avenge Moslem and Arab honor for the insult the Jews had inflicted on their manhood, and to claim leadership of the Arab world. This solid Arab front that they had helped create was now being broken by the arrival of three ragtag delegates representing the West Bank refugees.

"Why can't we assassinate these refugee dogs?" Ali Rahman demanded.

Fawzi Kabir rested his belly on his legs on the edge of his seat and politely refused the fruit bowl, a sight that gave him more than usual discomfort this morning.

"Let us put it this way. We are guests of the Swiss. We are under their tent, in a manner of speaking. They have made a career of not getting involved in other people's wars in order to service other people's money. They will not permit foreigners to shoot each other in their streets. They are adamant about such details."

"Then we take our money elsewhere!"

"If it were only that simple, Your Highness. They have built a great reputation for caring for money with great tenderness. Nowhere else is money so safe. We can sleep at night. This is the Swiss culture, the Swiss innovation. If we start shooting in Zurich it won't even be a question of them throwing us out. They will. Besides that, my prince, the assassination of the refugees would create a bad image for us in the press."

"I do not understand what kind of idiotic press it is that is not operated by a royal family or the government."

"It is a terrible system, I agree, but the press is very strong in the West. They can make something out of nothing and in the end it will do our noble cause no good."

"A royal personage has no rights," Rahman grumbled.

"Yes, Western behavior is very strange," Kabir agreed.

"Well, if we cannot get rid of these refugee dogs in the time-honored manner, then let us purchase their loyalty. At least they won't be as expensive as the other delegations."

"Again, a bizarre situation, my prince. Neither Charles Maan nor Haj Ibrahim is open to the bribe."

"What? I cannot believe that!"

"I know, but they are very sick, obsessed men. We can probably reach Sheik Taji. A good idea to splinter him off from the other two. It would weaken their delegation tremendously. A brilliant idea, my prince."

"You will deal with him, then, Kabir."

"At once, Your Highness. However, Taji might well ask that his tribe be allowed to resettle, maybe even in Saudi Arabia."

"That angers me, and my grandfather will never permit it. Our golden principle is that there is to be no refugee resettlement."

"Yes, my prince, exactly, no resettlement. I must be free, then, to make Taji a handsome offer. Let us, say, make him a special adviser to His Majesty Ibn Saud on refugee affairs."

"How much?"

"How important is it that we break them up?"

"A hundred thousand?" Ali Rahman ventured on the low side. "Dollars," he added quickly.

"A hundred thousand . . . sterling," Kabir returned.

The prince wondered to himself how much of it Fawzi Kabir would pocket. But no matter, if the investment held, it was a pittance. He nodded for Kabir to proceed.

"Now as for the other two," Kabir continued, "let us give them credentials."

"Are you mad!"

"Please let me finish. The rules of the convention are like this. Small committees made up from all the delegations will have to agree on what demands and what agenda we will present to the International Arbitration Commission. Charles Maan and Haj Ibrahim will be drowned out in these committees. Let them argue for eternity how many hairs there are on the camel's neck."

"That could be dangerous. They might start conspiring with each other."

"Your Highness, you are the grandson of the great Ibn Saud, who is rarely out of my prayers, may Allah bless his immortal

name. What are our principles? No peace with the Jews. No negotiations with the Jews. No recognition of the Jews. No return
of the refugees to the Zionist entity. No resettlement of the refugees in Arab lands. Every other delegate agrees to this. We are
solid. These little intruders will not change that. So we put them
on a treadmill. We talk. One week, one month, six months. Soon
they will collapse."

Ali Rahman struck a statuesque pose and pondered with
princely might. Kabir knew the strange ways of the West, a world
in which he was still a stranger. The calculated creation of chaos
in the committees would indeed preserve the five principles, and
this was what his grandfather had told him to do at all costs.

"What are we spreading around to the other delegations?"

"A few thousand here, a few thousand there," Kabir answered.
"Key generals and ministers, a bit more. Enough to ensure that
our wishes are carried out."

"What about the nigger slave?" Ali Rahman asked.

Kabir cleared his throat. "Please do not use that expression in
public, my prince. Dr. Ralph Bunche is a very respected man,
despite the misfortune of his birth."

"Can we get to him?" Ali Rahman said, rubbing his fingers
together.

"We explored this carefully. He does not take gifts. However,
he is naïve to our ways. We will swamp him." Kabir licked his
lips nervously and spoke tentatively. "Certainly your immortal
grandfather, all praise to him, has given you the instructions I
have requested. . . ."

"Concerning what?"

"Our long-range plans to lock in Syria and Egypt after the
conference."

Ali Rahman cracked his long fingers, stroked his goatee, and
nodded. "Tell the Egyptians and Syrians they will receive one
million dollars a day from the Saudi treasury for arms."

"That is what they are waiting to hear, my prince," Kabir said,
scarcely able to control the rush of excitement within him. "And
the other matter . . ."

"What other matter?"

"As I have explained, the Western press is very strong. The
West is buying our oil. I speak of making a gesture to sway them,

the donation for the refugees' relief. It will sit very well with them."

"No!" Ali Rahman interrupted. "We will not get involved in relief. The refugees made this situation for themselves."

"But it was the United Nations who created this Zionist monstrosity," Kabir persisted.

"Exactly! The United Nations is therefore responsible for the refugees. It is a world matter, not an Arab matter. The point is that if life is made too comfortable for the refugees, they will be content to sit and rot in the camps. They must be kept thirsty for vengeance."

"I believe I have an idea," Kabir said, feigning the inspiration of sudden discovery. "Do not jump out of your seat, my prince, but suppose we were to announce to the Western press a series of plans to resettle the refugees in Arab lands."

"What!"

"I implore you, let me finish. Do not underestimate the importance of winning the sympathy of the West. Let us say Egypt announces a plan to take the refugees now in the Gaza Strip and move them permanently into the Sinai. Libya will go along with taking others. Suppose, now, Syria announces a resettlement of the refugees from Syria and Lebanon to the Euphrates Valley."

"Your tongue is preparing itself for amputation, Kabir!"

"No, no, no, my prince. Please, hear me. After these announcements, the great royal house of Saud declares it will donate a million dollars a day to implement the resettlements."

Rahman's face reddened, but he also began to smell the deftness of Kabir's thinking.

"All these proclamations are only for consumption in the West. We prove we are not intransigent. We prove we are humane. Time passes. This conference is over. More time passes. The resettlement plans fade over the horizon like a desert sunset. The million a day has never been spent but is shifted now into arms purchases. It will give us a great propaganda victory here in Zurich."

The sense of outrage diminished and the silken deliciousness of the scheme became apparent. Prince Ali Rahman's desert cunning was now producing juices of intrigue.

"I will speak of it with my grandfather and the crown prince. As men of the desert, they could see the merit of the scheme."

"Meanwhile, I will keep all the delegations under control, believe me. And let us deal the Lebanese in," Kabir said.

"For what? They are nothing but a land of cheap merchants filled with nonbelievers."

"Ah, but they are only second to the great house of Saud when it comes to progressive thinking. Even now, the princes of Kuwait and Oman are discovering the . . . the . . . the magnificent alternatives to Switzerland. Beirut is becoming Paris, Mecca, the seven paradises all rolled into one. And despite the presence of a great number of Christians, they are truly our own people. A gesture to the Lebanese."

"Keep it tidy, Kabir."

"A pittance."

"Very well, but before I present this to my grandfather, I must have the foreign ministers of Egypt, Syria . . . and Lebanon here, in this room, together to make certain that our understandings are complete."

Fawzi Kabir sucked in a fast deep breath, bit his lip, and shook his head. "You ask the impossible, my prince."

"We pay the bills! They will appear here!"

"I beseech you, Your Most Noble Highness, let me speak to them privately."

"Why can't I speak to them together?"

"Have I not always treated you with honesty?" Kabir asked.

"I demand to see them together, this day, this hour, this minute!"

Kabir sighed sincerely. "I beg you to hear my point. No delegation here is ready to make a commitment in front of any other delegation. The Syrians do not trust the Egyptians. The Lebanese only trust money. No one trusts Jordan. The various Palestinian delegations are under the control of their host countries. They argue furiously in closed committees, which is what we want. However, when they appear in public before the arbitration commission, they all close their mouths, for one fears the other. Everyone is suspicious of everyone, and even now each is maneuvering against the other. May Allah help us, but some of them are even trying to make side deals with the Jews. We cannot put them together in the same room, my prince. Trust me. You see, the only real unity we have is hatred of the Jews."

Strangely, Prince Ali Rahman understood the twists in Kabir's mind and thinking. A splendid, delicate job had been accomplished till now. The conference had to end on a note of war against the Jews. However, was he manipulating Kabir or was Kabir manipulating him? If every Arab delegation had the same goal, why were the Saudis spending millions in payoff money? Well, he knew the answer to that. It was because the Saudis had the money to spend. Do not throw camel shit into the machinery, Ali Rahman told himself. Do not make a failure before Ibn Saud.

The prince looked about the room suspiciously, even though it was empty, then leaned forward in his seat. "What have you done about Abdullah's assassination?" he asked.

Fawzi Kabir plucked a single grape from the bowl. "Very tricky. Abdullah has been in the survival business for three decades. His palace is encased by an outer guard of the Arab Legion. Abdullah spreads around British pounds like candy to ensure their loyalty. The palace is very tight. On the inside he has a personal guard of fanatical Circassians."

"Not even Moslems," Ali Rahman scoffed. "They are Russians."

Kabir clasped his hands together in a washing motion. "Let me say, we do not yet have the man with his hand on the hilt of the dagger. However, we have made progress. I have made contact with a key Jordanian minister here in Zurich who knows the king's movements in advance. He will play. He will cost but he will play. When he returns to Amman, he can report to us where and when Abdullah will appear outside of the palace. We will have the finger on him. Once we know a week in advance that Abdullah will be in Hebron or Nablus or East Jerusalem, we can then import a member of the Moslem Brotherhood from Egypt or one of the Mufti's assassins. We have a list of such men who are available on short notice. No one can get too close to Abdullah, so it cannot be with a knife. Even a sniper from a distance cannot hope to escape alive. That, of course, is why we need a fanatic willing to make a martyr of himself. A machine pistol from a crowd at close range. However, we must be patient, my prince."

They continued with a range of trivial financial discussions. Prince Ali Rahman's own favorite grandson had bribed his way into the Sorbonne and had purchased a forty-room villa on the outskirts of Paris. Ali Rahman cursed and fumed but agreed to pay the bill. The boy was an integral part of his own ambitions within the royal court and, after all, he had to be educated. Ibn Saud was generous in these matters, but fifty princelings on the Continent were eating up even more than the million dollars a day that was being promised to the Egyptians and Syrians.

Fawzi Kabir's inoculation was wearing off and his head became sweaty. He prayed to be dismissed.

"One more matter, Kabir."

"Yes, my prince."

"What if this Maan or Haj Ibrahim decides to sit down and talk to the Jews on his own?"

"The Jews are making all sorts of offers to the arbitration commission. That, of course, is why we must also appear reasonable. However, Maan and Haj Ibrahim cannot legally consummate a treaty without the approval of all the Arab delegations. We shall launch the most tremendous campaign possible in the Arab press and over the Arab radio. We shall paint these two so vividly as traitors that they will be drowned in the spit of their own people."

Chapter Thirteen

Early Autumn 1950

Tick, tock, tick, tock, bong, bong, bong, bong, bong, intoned the mammoth clock in the tower of the Lady Cathedral.

Bong, bong, bong, bong, bong, retorted St. Peter's, only a quarter of a bong behind.

Haj Ibrahim stepped out of the dimly lit Congress Hall into a blare of late-afternoon light. The air was chilled as autumn announced itself. Charles Maan had gotten Ibrahim a secondhand coat to go along with his single secondhand suit. The new coldness made him feel even more isolated from Palestine. Some of the strangeness of Zurich had worn off. He looked forward to his evening ritual, a walk from the conference to his room in a boardinghouse across the river near the university.

"Do you think you will be going home soon?" the landlord had asked with delicacy. After all, the university had begun its fall classes and students needed lodging. If Ibrahim left in the middle of the semester they might not be able to rent his room until spring.

At first there had been chocolates on his pillow at night and Frau Müller had found an old pair of bedroom slippers and a used bathrobe. She had set the slippers out each night at the foot of his bed on a small clean white towel. The chill of autumn was in the landlord and his wife as well, and their uneasiness was reflected in Ibrahim's growing weariness.

"Palestine is an Arab problem that can only be settled by the Greater Arab Nation. We do not understand why this so-called delegation of West Bank refugees is even here. Our refugee brothers are more than represented by the legitimate Arab powers," spoke one minister after another, belittling the Haj's role.

Tick, tock, tick, tock, tick, tock.

How Ibrahim had come to hate the ridiculously high ceilings and the polished paneling of the committee rooms. Forty sessions. Forty wasted days. Words bolted out over the grand mahogany table with the speed and violence of summer lightning. Their meanings dissipated as quickly as lightning. Slogans regurgitated patented propaganda with the regularity of the Swiss clocks bonging from their Swiss steeples.

Bong. Egypt demands the southern Negev Desert for security reasons. Jordan objects.

Bong, bong. Syria demands the western Galilee as an integral part of its Ottoman history. Lebanon objects.

Bong, bong, bong. Jordan demands that its annexation of the West Bank be ratified. Everyone objects.

Bong, bong, bong, bong. Lebanon demands the annexation of the eastern Galilee. Syria objects.

Bong, bong, bong, bong, bong . . . democratic dialogue . . . parliamentary procedures . . . point of order . . . instructions from my government . . . brotherhood . . . unity . . . protocol . . . viable considerations . . . the subcommittee of the subcommittee requires further study . . .

Words hiss out like dueling rapiers, swish, clang. Moods of rage and disgust bounce off the lofty heights of the committee rooms and the intellect becomes dull and insulted. There are rational conclusions to be drawn, but they disappear into echo chambers. The Egyptian hears things one way. The Syrian hears the same words another way. The Iraqis do not hear.

It is not that they are vicious liars, Ibrahim thought as the hours ground away. It is that they are natural liars, honest liars. Ideas that emerge from torrents of words are as vacant as a desert without an oasis.

It changes now, for we are out of committee and in the open before the International Arbitration Commission and the mouths have suddenly become dumbstruck.

"Has your committee reached any conclusions about what the boundaries of the Palestinian state should be?" Dr. Bunche asked.

"We still have a few disagreements to iron out."

"I have asked you a thousand times to come before this commission, one at a time, and put forward your individual ideas."

"But we cannot do that. We have signed a pact of unity."

"Has your committee reached a unified position on the status of Jerusalem?"

"We are working on it."

"Dr. Bunche, we are bogged down in a swampland of words!" Ibrahim cried out in disgust.

"We are not in a jungle," the Egyptian delegate answered. "We must follow the rules of orderly debate. Do not force us to reexamine your credentials, Haj Ibrahim."

"So you have no position on these matters?" Dr. Bunche pressed.

"We are working on it in committee."

"The International Arbitration Commission is called to order," Dr. Bunche said. "I have asked that you comment on the various proposals put forth by the State of Israel; namely, it has expressed a willingness to negotiate the repatriation of separated families and has agreed to an initial number of a hundred thousand persons. The State of Israel has no quarrel about paying compensation for abandoned Arab lands that were cultivated before the outbreak of war and it has agreed to release frozen accounts as well as securities and precious possessions being held in Israeli banks. Now, what position has your committee reached on these various proposals?"

"To clarify the matter, Dr. Bunche: We do not recognize the existence of the Zionist entity. Therefore we cannot speak to someone whose existence we do not recognize."

Ah, but they are talking to the Jews, one at a time, in secret places all over Zurich!

"How are the issues going to be resolved without face-to-face negotiations?"

"We cannot speak to someone who has no face. Either the Zionist entity will accept our demands or there will be eternal war."

"But what are your demands?"

Silence.

Tick, tock, tick, tock, bong, bong, bong.

"I wish to negotiate a return!" Ibrahim answered.

"I consider that a step forward," Dr. Bunche answered.

All the delegates were on their feet. "This is an insult to the legitimate Arab governments! You are giving these intruders unjust rights. We demand their credentials be removed."

"But I did not sign your fucking unity pact."

"That is just the point! You are illegal!"

"We have already agreed to the credentials of every delegation here," Dr. Bunche said, "and none will be revoked. The West Bank refugees have every right to be at this conference."

"You see! He takes the side of Zionists and traitors!"

Haj Ibrahim clasped his hands behind him and strolled to the first bridge where the Limmat River flowed grandly out of the jewel-like Lake of Zurich. Once a Roman customs station stood on the site. Once Lenin and Einstein and Jung and James Joyce and Goethe and Richard Wagner walked the same path.

One would think this was a city of great thinkers and patriots, but mostly such men were only passing through from some place to some place else. It was no Paris, only a convenient refuge for the dispossessed, a passing sanctuary for the disenchanted.

The heaping plates of food had warmed his hungry belly at first. Even in a student's boardinghouse there were great mounds of potatoes and beef. Ibrahim beseeched Allah to forgive him, but he could not refrain from partaking of the thick slices of Swiss ham, a conscious profanation of his religion. Bowls of dumplings, strudel, cutlets and bratwurst, and many-layered cakes. . . .

The afternoon band concert on the quay floated out the notes of a Strauss waltz to the ears of older strollers and listeners whose faces were uniformly fixed in concrete. Laughter and lovers seldom came.

The double trams moved as though they were on cushions of air and the people moved around the traffic with exquisite precision. No horns blared, for everyone was patient. No aromas of cardamom and spices, no arguments between buyer and seller. The price was the price. Everything else was in order as well. The potted geraniums, the clipped trees, the gleaming benches, the gleaming awnings of the cafés, the gleaming trash cans and five-story flat-fronted buildings neatly lined both sides of the river. Water taxis glided silently with not much more than the flutter of the Swiss flag to be heard. Even the ducks paddled along in formation.

Everything was completed here. No slums, no castles. Every blade of grass was in order. The country was done, immaculately finished.

Ibrahim reached the Münster Bridge, second in a line of fifteen that stitched the two sides of the river together. On either side of the bridge the steeples of the two cathedrals pierced a low skyline. Lady Cathedral and her mighty clock bordered the Old Town, the ancient walled city. Just across the way from Ibrahim stood the twin phallic towers of the Grossmünster. The cathedrals appeared like rival fortresses ready to disgorge regiments of mace, pike, and halberd bearers to clash in the center of the bridge for its possession.

Ibrahim took a familiar table at a familiar café and ordered his daily coffee from a sympathetic waiter who adopted him for this hour each day. Sheik Taji, who had no committee meetings today, was not there again. This made three days in a row he had not shown up. Nor had the sheik come home at night to their rooming house. From the beginning, Ahmed Taji had made a bit of a sensation in Zurich in his desert gowns and with his rippling wisdoms. He had found his home away from home in the Old Town, the Niederdorf, a well-run tenderloin neatly set aside for sinning.

That was where Fawzi Kabir had found him. It was only a short Rolls-Royce ride from the genteel poverty of the Universitätstrasse rooming houses to the manor in Zollikon.

This son of the desert who had built many of his philosophies on parables dedicated to patience had lost his own by the end of the fifteenth meeting of his committee. And who could blame him? Ibrahim saw him begin to tilt but could not stop him. For Ibrahim, Palestine was a sudden pang, a hurt, a hunger. For Sheik Taji, Palestine became veiled in a mist and grew more vague as fantasies were whispered into an ear that became willing.

One day Taji sported a new gold watch. He and Ibrahim argued, drew daggers, wept, cursed, and were almost evicted. Then talk between them became strained. The next week a tailored suit, and one night he spent several hundred dollars.

When they left the Congress Hall each day, lines of limousines awaited the other delegates. Ibrahim, on a suspicion, followed the sheik around the corner and up Beethovenstrasse to a waiting Rolls. It was now only a question of when their fragile coalition would be splintered. Taji's defection would be a brutal blow. Ibrahim begged Allah for the wisdom to make one grand appeal, and that time was at hand.

The Haj looked about mournfully as his waiter and new friend, Franz, set down the contents of his tray. Franz set out four different slices of sumptuous cake, which were not ordered but always spirited out of the day-old counter. Ibrahim smiled in gratitude and Franz fluttered his eyes bashfully, the decent Christian, the pious man with leftovers. They spoke pedantically in pidgin Arabic and pidgin German.

He waited and nibbled. Tick, tock, tick, tock, bong, bong, bong, bong, bong, bong. Six o'clock. Charles Maan was due.

Ibrahim looked about at the women with their stiff layered hats on their stiff layered hairdos. And the men in their stiff collars and homburgs, always black, and generally with a walking stick tapping the street in a mechanical cadence.

Can people be so contented that their manner becomes placid and they can acquiesce to a norm that is without anger or protest? Even the underlife in the Niederdorf was uninspired and by the numbers. Could he stay in such a place forever? What could he do? Perhaps he could obtain some robes and become a colorful doorman. No, not even that was possible. It took a lifetime of work, an unpleasant notion, to be promoted to a Swiss doorman. Even so, an Arab's robes would be too gaudy. Why didn't somebody *yell* at somebody sometimes?

The budget was broken, but he allowed himself the luxury of a second cup of coffee. Swiss coffee was good, even a tiny bit passionate, but it certainly did not create the sensations and emotions of Arab coffee. He did the plates clean. No Charles Maan.

Charles had been a true ally and friend. With him there were no tricks, no dirty business. What value had they served? Without them the conference would have been a total farce. They had forced the major Arab delegations into all sorts of evasive maneuvers, public promises, and occasional embarrassment. In turn, they were loathed.

As the conference and its futilities wore on, Charles had drifted more and more toward discussions with the Christian institutions. The Christians were beyond the reach of the Arabs, and they could neither prevent, coerce, nor circumvent them. There was no accurate census of the refugees, but one supposed Christians made up around 10 percent of the camp inhabitants and were within grasp of being saved. With Ibrahim's blessing, Charles pursued the Christian option to the fullest.

A Vatican observer, Monsignor Grenelli, had been in Zurich since the second week and confided to Charles that he had sent off a favorable report to the powers that be.

It is apparent to this observer that all the Arab delegations, save the one of the West Bank refugees, have adopted a deliberate plan to keep the refugees locked up in their camps for the purpose of infecting them with hatred of the Jews. They have disregarded any humane solutions in favor of perpetuating the conflict with Israel. . . .

Israel, on the other hand, has shown a sincere willingness to discuss all aspects of the situation, but the Arab states refuse to meet the Jews face to face, although secret meetings are known to be taking place on numerous occasions. . . . Any Arab leader who shows a willingness to deal publicly with Israel faces certain destruction by the others.

. . . fully recommend that we intervene through a variety of relief and charitable organizations to salvage our Christian brothers and sisters in these camps. . . .

The report had been in Rome for a month when Monsignor Grenelli was suddenly recalled for consultations. Charles did not know what was being discussed or when the monsignor would return. An occasional note or secondhand message indicated that something might be brewing in the Vatican.

At half past six Franz looked to Ibrahim and shrugged knowingly. Well, no faithful ally tonight. It was getting quite chilly. He left the café, bundling his coat about him, passed the Grossmünster, padded up the quaint narrow Kirchgasse, and climbed the steps to the steep knoll where the university offered yet another staggering view of smashing mountains, a smashing lake, and a tidy urban arrangement below.

He did not want to go to the rooming house. He had become a pleasant oddity to the students and he liked most of them, but on this night he could not face another repeat of meat and potatoes and the boisterous rattlings of a language that he only grasped occasionally. Nor did he want to go through the agonies of pidgin German in the parlor and then the stark loneliness of his attic room.

The thought of phoning Emma Dorfmann occurred to him. Emma was a plump widow lady who owned a small variety store near the university that sold stationery, school supplies, magazines, and tobacco. She and her late husband had lived for several years in Cairo, where he had been a foreman of a Swiss firm installing factory machinery. Ibrahim was obviously attracted by her bits and pieces of Arabic, and the rest fell naturally into place.

She had a neat little flat above her store, immaculately doilied and needlepointed. Emma had little to attract steady male callers. She generally contented herself with a few jokes a day with the students, her church activities, and her widowed mother and widowed sisters. Ibrahim was looked upon as an unexpected windfall, fitting into the scene occasionally and comfortably.

Emma fussed over him during his one or two visits a week, filled his constantly empty stomach a bit less blandly than he got fed at the boardinghouse, and proved a warm and pleasant bedmate. She had those great slappable and bitable buttocks that could drive Ibrahim into fits of primitive passion, and her outsized breasts proved to be a lullaby. In fact, she was not all that dull for a fat Swiss widow, and it kept him from the prostitutes for whom he had no budget at all.

The most important part of the friendship was that she wanted Ibrahim's favors quite a lot more than he wanted hers, so he had a controllable margin to work with.

Ibrahim hovered at the corner of Schmelzbergstrasse and Sternwartstrasse and peered down the lane to Frau Müller's dormitory. On an impulse he wheeled around and walked back to the neo-Baroque, neo-castle-like giganticness of the university building, to a line of pay phones near the entrance.

"Hello, Frau Dorfmann speaking."

"Emma, this is Ibrahim."

"Oh, I am excited to hear from you. You are fine?"

Ibrahim allowed the longest sigh of his life to whisper out of him. "I would like to come over."

"My goodness, Ibrahim, why you didn't call me earlier? Because you were here last night, I surely did not expect you to call again so soon. I am afraid my mother and sister have come all the way from Sellenbüren. You will come tomorrow?"

"Perhaps."

"Ibrahim, you are all right?"

"I am fine."

"I am so sorry, Ibrahim."

He squeezed his eyes together, clenched his teeth, and almost let out a tear. "I am very lonely," he said, not able to stop himself. "I need you."

She had never heard such words from him, for he had never

spoken them to her, or anyone else. "Ibrahim, give me an hour to send them off, then please, hurry over."

"Thank you, Emma."

Ibrahim allowed himself to be cuddled, and this made Emma feel very happy. He just pressed next to her and sighed repeatedly, and she soothed him without questions. At last he fell into a deep snoring sleep, but this was broken by the ring of the telephone.

"It is for you," Emma said.

"Forgive me for not meeting you today and forgive the hour. Have you seen tonight's newspapers or heard the radio?" Charles Maan asked.

"No."

"Taji has defected."

Ibrahim flung the covers back and sat up fuzzy-brained.

"Where is that motherwhore?"

"He's already out of the country. He showed up with Fawzi Kabir and Prince Rahman at the airport. He told the press that he had accepted an appointment as the adviser to the Saudi royal family on refugee affairs. He's leaving behind his tribe, his family, everyone. He mentions you and me as having brought a corrupt influence to the conference, and so forth. He flew off on Rahman's private plane."

"What does this mean to us, Charles?"

"It means you had better start thinking about yourself."

"I'm staying," Ibrahim cried. "I'm staying until they throw me out or kill me!"

Chapter Fourteen

The Haj roared. For a month that followed Ahmed Taji's defection he pounded his fist on any and all committee room tables. He demanded answers to embarrassing questions. He spoke to sympathetic reporters and questioned the honesty of numerous delegates. He gave a lecture at the university to an overflow crowd of students and teachers, denouncing the Arab delegations' deliberate torpedoing of the conference, and he used the forbidden word "Israel." He went before the International Arbitration Commission alone and demanded permission to negotiate directly for the return of the first hundred thousand and the unfreezing of their assets.

As Ibrahim launched his one-man crusade, the Arab delegations united in a furious counterassault by questioning not only the man's politics but his character as well. Was Ibrahim on the Zionist payroll? Did Ibrahim indulge in weird sexual practices? Was Ibrahim mentally sound?

It became colder and colder in Zurich's autumn.

The rain pelted a slanting garret skylight. Ibrahim rose from his prayer rug on the floor, glowered down on the glistening empty street below, then stretched out on his back on the bed and grunted. A knock.

"Yes, enter."

Charles Maan came in and emptied the contents of a paper bag on the little square table. The usual pauper's fare emerged of salami, bread, cheese, a few sweet cakes, some cheap wine. "Look, two oranges. Jaffa oranges, no less."

"Then we are rich," Ibrahim said, sitting up.

They peeled and ate. Ibrahim noticed that Charles was in one of his somber moods, for his face sagged more than usual.

"Well, Charles?"

"Is it so obvious?" Maan asked.

"You would make a very bad camel trader."

"Monsignor Grenelli returned from Rome last night."

Ibrahim covered that swift gush of fear which swept through

him. He fiddled with the cork on the wine bottle, told himself to gain control.

"He brought good news?" Ibrahim asked.

Charles Maan nodded. "I've been asked to come to the Vatican by invitation of the Pope."

"The Pope. Whew! That is impressive. And you know what the Pope wants?"

"Yes."

"So, tell me, Charles."

"I am to make a plan for the removal, relocation, and rehabilitation of all Christian Arabs in the camps."

"But that is magnificent!" Ibrahim said, quickly involving himself in removing the cork from the wine bottle. It popped. He poured and managed to cover up the trembling in his hand. "That will be good for me as well. I can hold this up before the International Arbitration Commission and demand the same from Egypt and Syria. You see, all they have done is vaguely promise to relocate our people. This will force them to agree before the International Arbitration Commission. Like a treaty."

"Come on, Ibrahim," Charles retorted. "You know any treaty will only last as long as it is convenient. No Arab nation truly considers itself bound by a treaty."

"But it is a weapon. It forces them into the open for the first time," Ibrahim replied.

Charles reached out and took Ibrahim's hand and lowered his wineglass. "The Pope has attached a condition. He will not get involved if it means an open fight with the Arab world. Everything must be done under the table."

"That's the fucking Vatican for you! Everything a secret!"

Charles offered him a cigarette, which he refused. "Isn't it enough that they are humanitarian enough to get involved? You know damned well that no Pope can openly defy Islam. What do you want, Haj, another hundred years of warfare like the Crusades?"

"Of course not. It makes perfect sense," Ibrahim said, calming down. "Are the Jews involved in this deal?"

"They quietly agree to unfreeze some assets."

"Are they letting any Christians back into Israel?"

"Not without recognition or a formal treaty."

"I see," Ibrahim said. "Which of the Arab countries have agreed to take the Christians?"

"None," Charles Maan answered.

"Then how can it work?"

"We will look elsewhere around the world. That will be part of my job, to find a place to move them. America will always take some. I know that, in Central America, Honduras needs shopkeepers. Who knows? I don't know. Thirty, forty thousand . . . we will find them homes."

"You will begin your work when the conference is over?"

"The conference is over, Haj. In truth, it never began. It was never anything more than an exercise, a game."

"When are you leaving, Charles?"

"When you give your blessing."

"That is all you really ever came here for, to get the Christians out! So leave!"

"Ibrahim, I want your blessing."

"Take my blessing and choke on it!"

"Ibrahim, I want your blessing."

The Haj slumped into the creaky little wooden chair and wrung his hands, then, tremblingly, sipped at the wineglass and asked for a cigarette. "In my lifetime I have buried two sons and also two daughters. Jamil now sits in a Jordanian prison and there is a chance he will die for what I have done. Yet I have not wept. Of course I am happy for you, Charles."

"Ibrahim, I strongly suggest you make your own plans to leave. There is no longer a purpose for you to remain in Zurich."

"I will stay. I will not give up. Someone will listen to me, sometime."

"It's over, go back."

"To what! To Aqbat Jabar?"

"To Israel," Charles Maan said.

"I have thought of that many nights, Charles. I have prayed for the strength to do so. Yet it is not possible, somehow. It is every day for the rest of my life I worry about. Haj Ibrahim, the traitor."

"Traitor to what?"

"Myself."

"Your Arab brothers have imprisoned you for life. Those camps will be turned into madhouses. Ibrahim, you know and I know that the Jews are easier to deal with and eminently more fair, but if you are waiting for them to disappear from the region because we insult them or try to humiliate them, then you are mistaken. The trees will grow tall in Israel, but they will never grow in Aqbat Jabar."

"Charles, you asked for my blessing," Ibrahim said unevenly. "You have it. I am honest about this. I give you leave to go. You have been more than a brother. Now please leave. Do not stay and look upon me weeping."

"You have refused to see Gideon Asch," Maan pressed. "I beg you to think about it. Here is the name of a Swiss factory owner. He is only twenty minutes by train from Zurich. He is a Jew but an honorable man. He has arranged most of the clandestine meetings between Asch and the various Arab delegations." Charles scribbled out a name and phone number and placed it carefully under the wine bottle. He patted Ibrahim's back and left.

The Haj put his face in his hands and wept.

Chapter Fifteen

Goethe ate here at the Golden Head. One might say that that was the beginning and the end of Bülach's history. The major crime of the past several months had been when someone was caught tossing a cigarette butt onto the sidewalk. Bülach, so insignificant it rarely made the Swiss guidebooks, had a second distinction. It was between Zurich and the airport and acted as a landmark for incoming aircraft.

Ibrahim had whizzed on precision Swiss rails through twenty minutes of immaculate rolling countryside to the Bülach Bahnhof. He detrained, looked about, and was recognized immediately.

"Haj Ibrahim?"

"Yes."

"Herr Schlosberg," his contact said, offering a hand while guiding Ibrahim into a waiting automobile. Schlosberg, one of Bülach's two Jews, owned a small but exquisite factory for cutting and polishing those perfect little jewels that went into Swiss watches.

He drove through the flawlessly preserved Old Town, a six-by-six-block circular configuration that had once been encompassed by the wall required to preserve the feudal order that was honed over the centuries into an immaculate Swiss sense of neutrality.

"Goethe ate here," Schlosberg said as they passed the Golden Head Hotel and Restaurant. Ibrahim nodded. Schlosberg pulled up before his modestly affluent home in a wooded area called the Brüder Knoll and led Ibrahim to the library and closed the door behind him.

Gideon Asch sat behind Schlosberg's desk. "You rotten son of a bitch," he said angrily. "Why haven't you contacted me before this?" He shot out of the chair, turned his back, and glared out to the rolling vista.

Ibrahim came up behind him and they stared together. At last they turned toward each other and embraced hard and wordlessly. Out came the whiskey.

"Only a drop," Ibrahim admonished.

"What the hell were you thinking of?" Gideon asked. "Three months ago I might have been able to work some kind of deal, a trade-off, something. Anyhow, you're really fucked now."

"So is Israel," Ibrahim retorted.

"I'd rather be in Tel Aviv than Aqbat Jabar."

"I would too, if I were a Jew."

Gideon's age showed suddenly as he emptied his glass and drew another drink from the bottle.

"We were fools, of course," Ibrahim said, "but we had a great deal of hope when we arrived in Zurich. After all, we were not in Amman but in a true Western nation, a democracy. Here, with the eyes of the world staring at us, surely our delegations would act in a civilized and rational manner. Surely sympathy for my people would emerge from the press. I was a naïve child. Who cares? Well, maybe the Jews care. You know what we say. The Jews are liberal. Take advantage of them."

"They also believe they can humiliate us out of existence," Gideon said. "It won't happen. We've been humiliated before by perverse societies."

Ibrahim blanched for a moment at the remark. What was the use of fighting with Gideon? "If I had come to you in the beginning the result would have been the same as it is now. Humanity was the last thing on the minds of the Syrians and Egyptians. Perpetuation of hatred was the first thing, and in that they have succeeded."

"Yes, they have," Gideon agreed. "They will continue this charade until the dead horse has been flogged a thousand times over. And then another conference, and another and another. Then a war, and another. And, my brother, you'll still be in Aqbat Jabar."

"What is there left for us to do, Gideon?"

"Rebel. However, no revolution has ever come from the Arab people, only coups, holy wars, and assassinations. Why, in the name of God, is it that you can only exist under a military boot and fanatical holy men?"

Ibrahim downed his whiskey hard, ignoring Gideon's anger, flushed and coughed and asked for another. "Have you heard any word of my son Ishmael?" he asked at last.

"No. It is just about impossible for Nuri Mudhil to contact me

in Switzerland. Too many messengers can spoil the message and
they could also put Mudhil in danger."

"I understand."

"I should think that Ishmael is safe. I'm afraid I can't say the
same for Jamil. I do have contact with Colonel Zyyad. He's spoil-
ing to settle his score with you."

"I do not fear Zyyad. I can handle him."

"Sure, as long as you had stature and importance the Jordanians weren't going to play around with you, but don't underestimate Farid Zyyad's brutality. He can show a civilized face to the
outside world, British training and all that, but don't go to him
expecting mercy. You won't be the strong leader you were when
you left. That's what he is waiting for. I fear for Jamil."

"I knew that when I left Palestine," Ibrahim said.

"I still have a few things the Jordanians want from me,"
Gideon said. "Let me try to make a deal for you and your family.
I'll think of something."

"I will not dishonor my son's courage."

"Courage for what, Ibrahim? To grow up to be a terrorist?
Suppose it were Ishmael in that prison? Would you make a deal
for him?"

"I would let Ishmael die first," Ibrahim answered without hesitation.

Gideon's face suddenly reddened with anger. His fist pounded
on the desk; he was unable to speak.

"I did not come to argue with you, Gideon. It has always been
you who has said that the Arab lives in fantasy. Well, are you not
living out the greatest fantasy of them all? Do you believe you
will overcome the entire Arab world?"

Gideon was rocky and weary from months of frustration. He
went to the bottle again.

"I'll tell you what your Ben-Gurion fears," Ibrahim pressed.
"He fears Israel will end up as a Levantine nation doing things
just as we do them."

"Oh no," Gideon snarled, "it won't happen, because peace is a
value to us. Love is a value to us." He bolted out of the chair and
paced, almost like a caged man. "I came here to Zurich believing
that one iota of truth, of reason, might penetrate those locked
vaults you carry around in your heads." He leaned over the desk
close to Ibrahim's face. "What kind of perverse society, religion,

culture . . . what kind of human being . . . is it that can generate such volcanic hatred . . . that knows only hatred, that breeds only hatred, that exists for hatred? So, let your son die. Be proud, Haj Ibrahim!"

They stood shaking, two gladiators on the brink. "Go on," Gideon dared, "pull your dagger. That's all you know."

Ibrahim turned away. "I don't know if we will ever see each other again. I did not want this to happen." Then he walked to Gideon and threw up his arms. "Can't you see, I am beaten!" he cried in anguish. "If I cross the border into Israel, my heart will be dead."

"I know . . . I know, Ibrahim," Gideon whispered.

"Gideon, my brother, I am beaten." He wept.

Gideon held him tightly, then fell into the desk chair and hid his face in his arms on the desk.

"If it had been up to you and me, Gideon, we would have made peace, wouldn't we?"

Gideon shook his head no. "Only if you didn't have your hands on our water valve."

There was a desperate silence.

"Only Allah can give me peace now," Ibrahim grunted.

Gideon heard the library door close. The Haj was gone forever.

Chapter Sixteen

Those outdoor umbrellaed tables, so colorfully arrayed along the quays of the Limmat River, broke camp under the steady march of increasing cold. Although Ibrahim could no longer afford his daily respite of coffee, he remained welcome at the café. Franz still greeted him as a respected guest, found him a quiet corner table, and supplied him with coffee, sweets, and an occasional bowl of soup when the weather outside was particularly foul.

"Haj Ibrahim."

"Yes, Franz."

"There is a telephone call for you in the manager's office."

"For me?"

"It is a lady. She asked to speak to me and she said, are you the gentleman who serves an Arab gentleman every day? She said she was an old friend whom you met in Damascus."

"Where do I take the call?"

Franz ushered him into a speck of an office and left discreetly.

"Hello?"

"Hello. Is this Haj Ibrahim?"

"Yes."

"Do you know who this is?" Ursula's voice inquired.

"It is a warm voice in a very cold place," he replied.

"I am sorry I had to reach you in such a mysterious manner. I'm sure you understand."

"Yes."

"There is something extremely important I have to discuss with you. Can you meet me?"

Ibrahim became cautious. "Perhaps."

"Do you know the Bahnhofstrasse?"

"Only to look into store windows at things I cannot afford."

"That's the street. Near the Baur au Lac Hotel you will find a shop called Madame Hildegard's, which sells beaded and tapestry purses. I am calling from there. Can you come soon and make certain you are not being followed?"

Ibrahim did not answer.

"I know what you must be thinking. I can assure you that you will be safe. I have kept many rendezvous here over the years. Hildegard is a close personal friend. We have done each other many favors . . . without questions."

"All right, I will be there shortly," Ibrahim said after another pause.

"Use the trade entrance. Hildegard has a small showroom in the back for special clients. She will be alerted for your ring."

The Bahnhofstrasse, one of the world's pricier shopping avenues, wore an elegant uniform of nearly matched, almost perfect nineteenth-century buildings. The shops therein contained a king's hoard of treasured merchandise.

Ibrahim found Madame Hildegard's and after a final hedging of suspicion pushed his finger on the doorbell. The door opened. He imagined the woman before him to be close to fifty years, but she was scented, beautifully bloused, elegantly coiffured, and obviously well traveled in the top echelons.

"Ursula is waiting," she said and led him to the private showroom door. He entered and looked about. A small sitting room for the elite. Ursula stood in shadows wearing a hat with a veil.

"This is where Hildegard shows the bags with the jeweled clasps."

"Is that you, Ursula?"

"Forgive me for not greeting you more warmly. You will realize in a moment that I have been ill." She stepped forward and slipped into a brocaded easy chair but was still shadowed. Ibrahim approached and took the chair opposite her. Through the veil he could distinguish a face gone pasty. "I have been on drugs," she said, startling him with her candor. "I am not the Ursula you knew in Damascus."

"But I would still like to make love to you," Ibrahim said.

She pecked out a laugh. "You are gallant."

"It is not a lie," Ibrahim said.

"Can we speak now?"

"Yes, please tell me why you called."

"Fawzi Kabir plans to have you murdered."

"I cannot say that comes as news, but tell me more."

"Prince Ali Rahman, the Saudi, owns Kabir, you know."

"So I have heard."

"When the conference first opened, they discussed the possibility of assassinating the three of you. Anyhow, Kabir talked the prince out of it. It was considered too dangerous here in Switzerland. With Sheik Taji and Charles Maan now gone, they have taken a second look. You are extremely annoying to them. They are certain they can get away with it now."

"How do they intend to do me in?"

"They have been following your moves. At both your rooming house and at your lady friend Frau Dorfmann's, you must turn into and walk down very narrow lanes. It has been observed that on numerous occasions you leave Frau Dorfmann in the middle of the night. They plan to jump you in one of these lanes—"

"Knife?"

"No, they are wary about making a mess in the streets. The Swiss hold too much of their money. Kabir has one particular bodyguard who does the dirty jobs. He's an Iranian by the name of Sultan. They call him the Persian. He's a former heavyweight wrestler close to three hundred pounds, very mean, very well conditioned. He will jump you, put a choke hold on while a second bodyguard knocks you unconscious with a club. They will carry you off in a waiting car to Kabir's boathouse at his villa. There they will finish you off, take you to the middle of the lake, and dump you. It is planned as an unexplained disappearance."

Ibrahim grunted and patted his moustache, then laughed heartily. "It is not often that a man hears of his murder in such vivid detail. I am armed with a good pistol. I take it the Persian's skin does not stop bullets."

"Believe me, Kabir and Rahman have far too many resources for you to cope with. They'll get you, one way or the other."

"The one way they will never get me is by my running out of Zurich. I thank you most deeply for your warning. Now I must think."

Ursula's hand reached out beyond the shadows and grasped his. "If you want vengeance, so do I," she said.

"Tell me why, Ursula."

"Oh God, it's a long story. Of course, you have a right to know. Look, Ibrahim, I got myself involved with Kabir knowingly, but I was very young. Despite my profession after the war, I was also quite naïve. I overlooked one hideous thing after another until . . . I did nothing really to stop it . . . the money, the gifts seemed too easy. Well, let us say, too easy for a whore to give up.

Anyhow, I learned that I still have a line I cannot cross. There are still things in this world that disgust me."

"That is good to be able to hold such beliefs."

"Kabir is the devil's father. The grossness of his perversions has become more and more detestable. What can I say? Male prostitutes, female prostitutes, he pays them enough for them to allow themselves to be debased. Even what he makes them do with animals, including pigs, dogs, horses . . . all right, weird is weird but . . ." She stopped for a moment, terribly uncomfortable, then began again with trembling voice. "When we are back in Damascus . . . It's the children! I've seen virgin boys and girls, nine and ten years old, all but butchered. You want to see what he has done, I show you!"

She lifted her veil and put her face into the light. It was a ghastly chalk color. Her eyes were numbed. There was a deep purple blotch on one cheek. "Take a good look, my Haj, that is a cigarette burn. There are scars on my body as well. But the real scars are on the inside. He began to fear I would leave him. After all, I arrange most of his fun. I was physically forced to receive shots of heroin. As you can see, I have become an addict."

"My God, I didn't know I could still be shocked," Ibrahim said softly.

"I have a chance of getting well if I can get away from him. There are clinics. I am not too far gone. Well, Ibrahim, do you want your revenge or not?"

"Do you have a plan, Ursula?"

"I do."

"Then you also have a partner."

The Persian hulk flicked on the lights inside the boathouse and made a check through. It was clear. He took his master from Ursula and helped him stagger in. Kabir was spongy-brained from earlier drugs. He was taken to the emperor's couch while Ursula fiddled with the light panels and started some music.

"When are they coming?" Kabir slurred. "Look at this damned couch. I paid ten thousand dollars for those Swiss dogs to repair it. Look, it does not either go up or down or turn," he said, banging on a console of buttons.

"They still have some work to do on the cables," she said.

"They are all thieves."

"Do not fret, my dear. You won't need the couch for this exhibition."

"What do they do? You promised me something crazy unique."

"They will be along soon and you will see for yourself. It is like nothing that has ever taken place here. This couple is original beyond description." Ursula nodded to the Persian that she had things in hand and for him to take up his guard post.

When Sultan hesitated, she felt a pang of queasy fear. "Well?" she demanded.

"I am hungry," the Persian said on cue. Ursula had depended on the Persian's appetite. He did not fail and she was relieved.

"It will only be a two-person show tonight," she said. "I did not assign a chef."

"But I am starving," the Persian insisted.

"Why don't I fix you up a plate from the kitchen? I will bring it to your station."

Sultan broke into a great grin, revealing a mouth patched with gold. He moved his massive frame down a short corridor to where the big speedboat and a half-dozen sailboats were docked under a roof. The guardroom was small but contained the latest security innovation. Cameras covered all the rooms of the boathouse. Their pictures could be viewed on a half-dozen screens. Sultan was able to observe his dozing master as well as Ursula in the kitchen.

She prepared a tray of four heaping plates to fill his bottomless stomach. It was very spicy food, spicy enough to completely disguise the sprinkling of cyanide she managed with her back blocking the camera's view. She set the tray before him. "This should hold you for a while."

"Ursula," the Persian whispered, seeking a confidence, "what do you have going tonight?"

"It's like nothing you have ever witnessed," she assured him. "Keep your eye on the screen."

He chomped down a baby lamb chop, and another. "You won't leave me out of it," Sultan asked with a wink.

"If the Effendi passes out, as he usually does, it will be no problem to include you in some sport. Leave it to me, Sultan. Don't I always see to it you are taken care of?"

"Ursula, you are a true friend."

She smiled and left and walked to the main mirrored room and

quickly turned up the music just in time to drown out a horrendous shriek from the guard post. She dared look into the corridor
to see a wide-eyed, murderously angry Sultan lurch toward her.
He screamed, grasped his throat, sank to his knees, crawled,
reached out . . . fell flat. She approached him with terrified caution. A half minute agonizingly ticked off. He twitched, then remained still.

Ursula quietly closed the door.

"What was that noise?" Kabir grumbled from the couch.

"I did not hear anything, darling."

"I thought it might be our act."

"They will be along soon. Why don't we have some H together.
Something to set us dreaming, and when your eyes open again,
everything will be ready."

"You are good to me, Ursula, so good."

She opened a leather kit with a velvet lining holding "his" and
"hers" needles. His had been filled earlier with Dilaudid, enough
to keep him under until Ibrahim arrived. She expertly plunged
the needle into his arm and sleep followed quickly.

The "funeral march" from Beethoven's Seventh Symphony inundated the boathouse. Lights had been set to twirl in a billion
sparklets. Ursula broke an ammonia capsule under Fawzi Kabir's
nose. He groaned to consciousness, then clamped his eyes closed
against the lights of whirling luminescence. He tried to cover his
ears to shut out the music but he could not move his hands. They
were handcuffed behind his back.

"Ursula!" he screamed.

"I am here," she said from the foot of the couch. "Are you all
awake now, dear?"

"My hands are cuffed!"

"That is part of the game. Trust me."

He tried to wiggle but to no avail, for his feet were also bound.
"I do not like this! Turn me loose!"

"But you will ruin everything. The players are here now.
There are three altogether. You are one and I am one. Surprised?"

Kabir panted and broke into an instant sweat as sound and
light continued to blare at him. He felt a hand on his naked back.
"And I am the other," a voice said.

Kabir twisted his thick neck in order to see, but he was too obese to turn himself around.

"Guess," the voice said.

"I don't like this business!" he cried.

"But, darling, we went to so much trouble," Ursula soothed.

He was rolled over onto his back. A man stood over him with a devil's-head mask from the costume room. He removed it slowly. The Effendi's eyes bulged. His fat body glistened with wet fear perspiration.

"Sultan! Sultan!" he screamed.

"Ah, but he cannot hear you, my darling," Ursula said. "He is quite dead and awaits in your speedboat for you to join him." She turned the music up several notches. Ibrahim straddled him and his dagger came from its sheath with a zing.

"Talk! Let's talk," Kabir begged.

"Yes, please do speak," Ibrahim said.

"Money. All the gold you can swim in. Millions! Millions!"

Ibrahim sat on the edge of the couch and placed the point of the dagger against the jugular vein and pressed it slightly. "How many millions do you have in mind?" Ibrahim asked.

"Millions, millions. Five, ten . . . more. . . ."

"But if I take your money it would lead the police to me."

"No, no, no. I get you money. Cash. I call and have it brought here right now."

"Do you hear that, Ursula? He wants to give me money."

"He is a liar. He has code words with his banker."

"I do not lie! I do not make tricks! I am honest!"

Ibrahim backhanded him hard over the face, then grabbed him by the short ringlets of hair on the back of his neck and jerked his face up and looked into his terrorized eyes. Kabir wept and babbled incoherently. A smattering of a smile crossed the Haj's lips. He was sorely tempted to prolong the Effendi's agony. What to do? Beat him with hoses and whips? Ibrahim felt himself tremble with a sudden rush of perverse sensations. The music thundered and the lights spat out wild flashes. Oh Allah I am enjoying this, Ibrahim thought.

He signaled for her to turn down the sound. "Good. Now we will be able to hear his very last heartbeats." An awesome silence fell. No noise but the exaggerated breathing of the three and Kabir's interspersed whimpers.

"When I lived among the Bedouin I watched my uncle, the great Walid Azziz, take revenge on a boy who had fucked one of his favorite daughters. If this is done properly, he will drown by choking on his own blood without any mess and we should actually hear the air leave his body."

"Partner . . . you are full partner in everything . . . take it all . . . I want nothing . . . nothing . . . millions . . ."

The point of the dagger slid down Kabir's Adam's apple to a place at the base of his neck where the collarbones joined and the windpipe bulged ever so slightly. Ibrahim jabbed the point into Kabir's throat, moving in a downward motion.

"I confess to everything . . . mercy . . ."

"But each time you open your mouth the blade goes in a little deeper, like this."

A circle of blood oozed out. Ibrahim held the knife in this position for several moments, luxuriating in Kabir's agony. Ursula came into view and spat on him. The blade probed a fraction deeper. . . .

"You are enjoying this too much, Ibrahim."

"Yes, I am."

"I don't want to be a beast like him. Finish him."

"Soon . . . soon. . . ."

A light hissing sound was heard as air leaped toward his punctured throat, then mixed with the growing pool of blood and the hiss turned to a gurgle. Ibrahim pressed the blade in just so and held it motionless again. Now the blood came out in spurts.

"You are starting to make a mess," she said. "Finish it."

"Just a little longer. See, the life is beginning to leave him." Kabir tried to speak but blood gorged out of his mouth.

"You are making a mess!" Ursula screamed.

"YAHHHHH! YAHHHHH! YAHHHHH!" the Haj yelled as he pulled out the knife, then plunged it into the Effendi's heart up to the hilt. "YAHHHHH! YAHHHH! YAHHHHHHH!"

He withdrew the dagger and stood panting in joy. Ursula leaned against him and closed her eyes.

"We make love now, Ursula!"

"Are you crazy!"

"Yes, I am crazy! Take off your clothes and we make love!"

He kicked Kabir's body off the couch and it skidded down the steps. He flung her on the couch and leaped on her. It was like a thousand insanities of pain and happiness in a thousand paradises and hells. It was, she was, entirely magnificent.

Ibrahim wrapped Kabir in sheets of plastic as Ursula cleaned up the traces. They dragged the corpse out to the dock and dumped it unceremoniously into the speedboat alongside the poisoned Persian. As he tied an anchor around the legs of Kabir, she placed Sultan's dishes in a sack to be dumped with their quarry. In a moment they sped out to the middle of the lake.

Both Ursula and Haj Ibrahim remained in Zurich as though nothing had happened. The Effendi Kabir had been known to disappear for days and even weeks without explanation. For two weeks he wasn't even missed and everyone thought surely he had rushed off to Saudi Arabia. When it became apparent that he had vanished, it was impossible to establish foul play. There was no body, no witnesses, no apparent crime. Some routine inquiries were made, but the final police report said that the Effendi and his bodyguard had simply disappeared without feasible explanation. So far as the Swiss were concerned, that was the end of that.

When the first snows of winter fell, the arbitration conference broke up in disarray. On a bitter cold December day, Frau Emma Dorfmann and Franz took Haj Ibrahim to the airport for the long flight back.

Ursula remained in Zurich for several more weeks, then quietly slipped out of the country to rejoin the fortune she had skimmed off Kabir over the years.

Chapter Seventeen

While the conference went on in Zurich, Colonel Farid Zyyad had obtained confessions from almost all of the Avenging Leopards who had been arrested in Manger Square. The co-operative ones were permitted to exchange their prison sentences for "volunteer" service in a special unit of fedayeen, or freedom fighters, and were put into training for future guerrilla raids against Israel.

The few who did not co-operate after weeks of interrogation and torture were given long prison terms. Aside from knocking their teeth out and other crude beatings, Farid Zyyad had perfected favorite forms of inflicting pain. Both were creations of the desert and the desert's heat.

The victim was tied on a table and covered with a wet cloth. He was then pressed by a hot iron from foot to chest. By controlling the temperature of the iron, they could ensure that the resulting burns and infections increased only slightly with each pressing.

Zyyad's second favorite form of torture was saved for the most persistent of the rebels. They were simply wrapped each in a heavy blanket, tied up, and laid out in the midday sun. When one passed out from heat prostration, he would be revived long enough to gain sufficient strength to be wrapped up once more.

Jamil had gotten it all. His teeth were gone, he was a mass of bruises. He had been pressed a dozen times until his body became bloated with pus. He had been wrapped in the blanket on another dozen occasions.

About the same time Haj Ibrahim changed planes in Athens, Jamil was dragged between two guards before Zyyad. The boy was in blistering agony but conscious enough to still feel every bit of pain.

"Well, you dirty rotten little animal, I don't have to play with you anymore. Do you know what I am going to do with you, Jamil? I am going to give you to your father as a present."

Jamil was taken to a secret enclosed and dreaded little yard in a far corner of the prison where one of the guards tended several dozen cats. Jamil was placed into a large burlap bag, six cats were thrown in with him, and the bag was sewn shut.

When Farid Zyyad beat on the bag with a stick, the cats went berserk. He beat and beat until Jamil's screams were no longer heard.

The cats had eventually clawed through to the bone. Face, eyes, sexual parts had been ripped away. All that was left was a blood-soaked mass of flesh so torn it was unrecognizable. The coffin was sealed, and the next day a story was released that Jamil had been serving on a secret mission against the Jews. He stepped on a land mine, the story continued, so his body was too disfigured to allow for an open coffin. The coffin was presented to Haj Ibrahim as he landed in Amman in a formal military ceremony reserved for heroes.

For the moment Aqbat Jabar forgot that Haj Ibrahim had been branded as a traitor, a spy of the Jews, and a man who had apparently sold out for several dunams of orange groves.

Jamil's funeral became a crush of screaming and weeping refugees, fifty thousand of them, who jammed the highway to Jericho's mosque, passing his coffin overhead. Hagar wept with suitable hysteria and collapsed a half-dozen times among the mourners. From that day on she would be called Umm Jamil, the mother of Jamil, a title of respect earned by his death.

Hundreds of placards bearing Jamil's photograph were waved aloft along with other placards holding slogans of the fledgling "revolution." As Jamil was laid to rest in a place of honor in the mosque courtyard, the former Leopards, now redeemed freedom fighters, shot volleys over his grave and the priest swore vengeance on the Zionists who had killed the boy.

The first martyrdom of the Palestinians had come to pass.

END OF PART FOUR

Part Five

Nada

Chapter One

While my father was in Zurich, I passed my time among the al Sirhan Bedouin. The eastern desert of Jordan that bordered on Iraq and Saudi Arabia was so remote that there was no sign of civilization for a hundred miles in any direction. Because of Professor Doctor Nuri Mudhil's stature, I had been taken in by Sheik al Baqi, the head of a large clan, and was treated as though I were one of his sons.

Sheik al Baqi and his sons taught me horsemanship, falconry, tracking, and, mainly, how to read the desert. Each day began with the sound of coffee being crushed, setting off another cycle of survival, the struggle that dominated our lives.

Until I came to the al Sirhan, I had always been a dreamer. No matter what the fates had imposed—Jaffa, Qumran, Aqbat Jabar —I felt that things would get better, that someday I would end up in a lovely villa back in Tabah or even go beyond to a great university in Cairo or Damascus. The desert and the Bedouin taught me that certain things are final in life.

In the brutal heat and poverty, it became easier to cope by finding some shade, seeing mirages, and allowing fantasy to enter and take over my mind. Through the Bedouin I came to know why the Arab adopted a passive acceptance of the unmercifulness of life. Everything was predestined by fate, and there was little one could do but accept the bitterness of earth and look forward to the relief of the trip to paradise.

The al Sirhan made no pretense of an equal society. One was born, lived, and died locked into a rigid caste system, staying in place from birth to death without protest. Within this ironclad conformity few marriages were arranged between families of different stations.

Sheik al Baqi's face and body bore a road map of scars to testify to his manhood and leadership. He kept a half-dozen slave boys. Although slavery was outlawed, the al Sirhans were so remote they were beyond the reach and rules of ordinary society. Three of his slaves tended his sheep and another was his personal servant. The other two had been castrated, made into eunuchs to guard his wives and his harem of concubines. Two had been purchased from families within the clan and the others were captured in raids.

I arrived at a time when Sheik al Baqi was making peace with a rival tribe after eight bloody years of tribal warfare. It had started when a frustrated lover had kidnapped a girl from the al Sirhan and fled to a tribe over the border in Saudi Arabia. Peace had come only after the woman was sacrificed by murder to avenge al Sirhan honor. There was a great feast of brotherhood between former foes.

Everyone out here seemed preoccupied with sex, but one could do little about it. The women were more totally enslaved than in Tabah. They worked harder and did everything of a menial nature. Although very old women were allowed to sit by the fire with the men and were treated with respect, the others had no means of joy. They were quick to become hysterical, for weeping was generally their only means of relief from frustration. I noticed that Bedouin women were extremely affectionate with one another, and I was certain that this was a secret way they found pleasure.

The law out here did not always come from the Koran, but from the harsh order of life.

Men can kill but they must do so face to face.

Men can steal but not from their own.

Rape is no crime against a woman from an enemy tribe.

Lying and cheating are quite permissible so long as they are done to someone from another tribe.

There were strict laws requiring vengeance. Punishments often meant amputation of a limb. Life was dire. The law of survival begets cruelty.

The desert is a wicked master, but it is in the sole possession of the Bedouin and when you enter the desert you are at his mercy. Mercy is not for those who break his rules.

I learned my lessons well, stayed out of trouble, and won a measure of respect because I was the only one in the clan who was literate.

The true pleasure in life came around the fire at night, drinking coffee, retelling the story of a raid or an epic of personal heroism. The dervish family in the clan would join us and, in their capacity as witch doctors, dance away evil spirits. They whirled themselves into a trance, then walked through the hot embers of the fire barefooted and became weak. They had proved their magical powers once again.

Everything happened with deliberate slowness. The continual reconstruction of the past gave us a place to disappear and helped us cope with the reality of daily existence.

The awesome sunrises often found me alone with Sheik al Baqi as the last around the fire.

"Wealth and property are something Allah passed out unjustly," he told me. "We have many deaths, but it is no tragedy in the desert. Mainly, Ishmael, we are free. The peasant is a slave to his land. The city man is a slave to money and machinery. They are evil societies. The Bedouin does not need them."

Perhaps.

A large part of the tribe's income came from its being the "protector" of a section of the trans-Arabian oil pipeline that ran through its territory. When a new arrangement was offered by the Saudis, for less money, it was time to give them a reminder. I was about to go on my first raid, to sever a section of the line, when word came that I was to return to Aqbat Jabar.

I cannot say I left with sorrow, for I longed to see the Haj and Nada again. Yet I was wiser, for I knew now how the Arab and fatalism were eternally linked together.

Chapter Two

I returned to Aqbat Jabar to learn that Jamil had won a victory from me in death that he could never have accomplished in life. He had become a martyr. This caused me a great deal of displeasure. I had worked diligently all my life to become my father's favorite. I was known as the most clever, the bravest, the one who would succeed Haj Ibrahim. I had overcome my oldest brother, Kamal, and brushed aside Omar. I was the light of my father's life. Now some of that had changed. There were large pictures of Jamil in the cafés in Aqbat Jabar right alongside the photographs of the great Arab leaders.

The Jordanians were recruiting and coercing Avenging Leopards and other gang members into guerrilla units to cross the border and raid the Jews. They had blamed Jamil's murder on the Zionists and named a battalion of fedayeen in his honor.

My parents, who had scarcely paid attention to him all his life, plunged into mourning. Jamil's photograph was the centerpiece of our hovel. Flowers, which had never graced our home in Tabah, were placed in little vases alongside his picture and votive candles burned before it.

Hagar now took pride in being called Umm Jamil, the mother of Jamil. Strangest of all was the behavior of my father. Guilt, an emotion Ibrahim had never been burdened with, had slipped into his soul. He had beaten Jamil. He had contributed to Jamil's murder. Now he grieved. I got an inkling that he wanted to make himself believe it was really the Jews who had killed his son.

Suddenly I was Jamil's younger brother. My head was patted by everyone. Wasn't I proud?

You are saying that Ishmael was cruel. Had he no compassion for his slain brother? Don't fool yourself about me any longer. I might have been a boy in everyone's eyes, but I was very smart and very strong and you would not want to play around with me. I had come to learn that life is not as important as martyrdom.

I had to regain my position.

If truth be known, it was Nada whom I missed and longed for the most when I was with the al Sirhan Bedouin. We are obsessed with defending the woman's virtue. We do not do it for the woman but for the man's pride and honor. I loved Nada differently. I loved her for herself. It was not a sexual love. It was because she was good and she always delighted me.

I loved Nada's eyes, filled with curiosity. When we were alone together I loved to see those eyes turn to mischief. I loved to watch her wash by the springs and braid her long thick brown hair. I loved the sway of her hips when she walked. I loved her white teeth when she threw her head back and laughed.

I wanted to marry a girl like Nada someday. Until I did, the protection of her virtue was my most important mission in life. So I loved my sister and I did not grieve for my brother. At least I am not a hypocrite like my parents. Hagar I could understand. I could not understand Haj Ibrahim and prayed for his guilt to go away.

Because of my overpowering concern for Nada I was very quick to detect that something had surely been going on between her and Sabri in my absence. Usually Ibrahim would have smelled out something like this, but he had not been the same since he returned from Zurich. A fire inside him had dimmed. Something terrible must have happened to him over there. There was also this thing with Jamil that added to his misery.

Hagar, Ramiza, and Fatima possibly knew about Nada and Sabri. The women keep many secrets among themselves. In Aqbat Jabar, as in Tabah, the women of the clans fought among themselves constantly, and their mouths could be as foul as garbage. Yet there was a line that women did not cross when dealing with one another. Because their own fidelity meant their lives, they rarely gossiped to the men about women's business.

Sabri Salama's coming into our life had been a mixed blessing. We might well all have been dead if it hadn't been for Sabri's skill and ingenuity.

Father had spent all our money from the sale of the antiquities by going to Europe. True, we still had our cache of guns to fall back on, but we really depended on Sabri's salary and his side deals for our existence. He never complained about turning everything over to Father.

At first I felt threatened. Sabri would win too much favor with

Ibrahim. But that passed. Sabri had his own family in Gaza and spoke constantly of his desire to join them. Fortunately, Ibrahim's early suspicions always kept him out of our intimate circle.

There had been this business about his sleeping with the Iraqi officer and perhaps other men. At times he had made me physically uneasy. Yet there was really nothing in his behavior that gave us cause to worry.

Nevertheless, I was concerned about him and Nada. Because Ibrahim seemed oblivious of the situation, I decided to look into matters more closely.

Sabri worked in a large garage in Jericho. The building had once been a warehouse from which West Bank crops were shipped into Jordan and Saudi Arabia. The place was abandoned during the war, then taken over as a garage for the steady stream of vehicles crossing the Allenby Bridge to and from Amman.

Wherever there are trucks and goods being moved, there are deals to be made. Sabri did very well by us. There was a small room in the rear of the place where he and another mechanic slept and alternated as night watchman. No one could blame him for not wanting to come back to our crammed place in Aqbat Jabar. The camp was filthy and families fought and yelled every night and all night.

I noticed that Nada generally slipped out of the house before sunset on the days Sabri stayed over in Jericho. It did not take one of the prophets to figure out why.

One evening I waited for fifteen minutes after she had left, then headed into town. The garage was closed for the night. I went around to the back and tried the door. It was locked. I tried a number of windows, but they were all sealed shut by years of grime.

After examining the building for footholds, I found what I was looking for and shinnied up to the roof. Two trapdoors were padlocked. With a stick I was able to pry off the rusted hinges.

I hung by my hands and dropped into the back of a truck, smarted for a few seconds from the fall, then made my way toward Sabri's room cautiously.

I could hear sounds through his door. Sabri and Nada were making all kinds of lovers' noises. I tried the knob slowly. It gave. Then I flung the door open.

They were lying side by side on his mat on the floor. PRAISE

ALLAH, THEIR CLOTHING WAS ON! Their arms were wrapped around each other and their private parts, through their underclothing, were pressing and moving in rhythm. He had freed a hand to hold her breast while her hands clutched at his back. They were groaning and panting like they were really doing it.

Nada saw me first and screamed as I pounced down on Sabri. "I'll kill you!" I cried.

I was smaller than Sabri but hardened from the desert and knew no fear. I was all over him, wildly driving my fists into his face.

Sabri had been taken by surprise and could only cover up and try to defend himself. My onslaught had him dazed. I bashed out at him again and again, cursing him as I did. His lip and nose spurted blood. I wrapped my hands around his neck and squeezed.

Something horrendous crashed into my head. Everything spun and became dark. The next I remembered I was looking up from the floor and seeing Nada standing over me, in a blur. She had a wrench in her hand.

"Stop it!" she screamed.

I lay there quivering from the smashing blow, reached, and felt blood coming from the back of my scalp. I was weak and gasping and groveled about, trying to brace myself for an attack. My eyes focused. Sabri was bunched up in a corner with his face in his hands and he was crying.

"Ibrahim will kill me!" he wept over and over.

I propped myself up on an elbow. Nada poked the wrench in my face, threatening to hit me again. "No," I pleaded, "no . . . no."

Her hand holding the wrench went limp. The weapon fell to the floor and she sank to her knees over me. "I'm sorry," she sobbed.

Nada's face was distorted with anguish and she erupted into uncontrolled weeping. She threw herself on the floor, clawed at it, and nearly choked on her tears.

"Ohhhhh shit," I moaned.

We all cried in our places. At last she got to her feet, wobbled from the room, and returned with a pail of water and some rags. She wiped the blood from my head, then put her arms about me and rocked me as though I were her doll. After a time she crawled over to Sabri and cleaned his face as well. We fell into a silence that seemed to last forever. Nada looked at me with a pleading in her eyes. In truth, she was begging for her life.

"I don't know what to do," I said.

"Please don't have us killed," she said. "We couldn't hold it in any longer. We really didn't do it. We were only playing. Don't have us killed."

"Allah, help me," I muttered.

"Ishmael." Sabri spoke. "You must believe I would not have gone all the way. I honor Nada. I love Nada. What can we do? We were going crazy. We have spoken about going to Ibrahim and getting permission to marry. We are destitute. I have no money. You know he would never agree . . . you know that."

Nada came to me again. "When I knew we weren't going to be able to control ourselves, I wanted Sabri to leave here and find his parents in Gaza."

"I wanted to go so I would not dishonor your family," Sabri said. "How can I leave? I have no money and no papers."

I could see how desperate they were.

"Will you spare us, Ishmael?" she begged, grasping my hands and kissing them.

I made the mistake of looking into her eyes again. "I won't tell. But Sabri must leave."

Both of them flung themselves into my arms and I held them. And we all cried again. Then we sat as we had done on the ledge of the cliff when we had found the treasure. We held hands in a circle and made our vow. But the vow did not solve Sabri's problem.

"I want to stay because of Nada, but I realize that I am bringing shame to her," he said. "I have given your father every penny I have earned. I've kept nothing for myself. It will take over a thousand dollars to bribe the right official for travel papers. To find my parents, I must cross into Jordan, go up through Syria, and catch a ship from Lebanon to Gaza. My passage will cost as much as my papers. I'm going crazy!"

I prayed. As I felt Nada's hand grasping mine, I remembered the time she reached down, took my hand, and pulled me up over the ledge to the treasure cave. I knew what I had to do.

"I know where I can get you the money," I said unevenly.

"Two thousand dollars?"

"Yes. You certainly remember our guns. Jamil and I hid them up in Mount Temptation. I will sell them."

"But when Father finds them missing he will beat you to death."

I was fully in control now. "Sabri must write a letter to Ibrahim. The letter must say that before Jamil died he bragged about the guns and told you where they were hidden. Ibrahim will believe that, because he was always suspicious that Jamil would reveal the location. If I get the guns tomorrow, can you find a buyer?"

"Yes," Sabri whispered.

"It's dangerous for you, Ishmael," Nada protested.

"We all have secrets," I said. "We must keep this one, too."

"But, Ishmael—" Sabri began to argue.

I cut him off. "That is what we will do. Write me the letter tonight."

I stumbled to my feet, left the room, and waited in the garage. I did not look back. They had many things to say to each other.

At last they came out. Sabri embraced me once more and tried to speak, but was too choked up. He spun out of my arms and returned to his room, closing the door after him.

Nada poked around the lump on my head. "It has stopped bleeding."

"Don't worry, it's not too bad."

We washed our wounds and our sorrows and were soon on the road to Aqbat Jabar. When we saw the camp, we stood with each other in the darkness, hand in hand, and stared from the highway at that awful array of mud-bricked misery. Then we climbed to Mount Temptation and watched the stars.

"Don't ask me how I know," she said, after a time, "but I know what happened to Mother and Fatima and Ramiza in Jaffa."

"But—"

"It is too much for you to hold such a terrible secret by yourself. I want to share it with you. I've wanted to for a long time. I knew that by your silence you would become a wonderful man."

A great burden had been lifted from me.

"I love you, Ishmael," Nada said. "I love you more than Sabri, in a different way."

"You don't have to say that."

"You are a better man than Father because you can love more than you can hate."

"I worship Father. I have always wanted to be like him."

"You are different from Father and from all of them, even Sabri." She smiled at me in the moonlight, her white teeth like stars. "I love you because you cannot kill what you love."

Chapter Three

The murder of Charles Maan came as a blow from which my father never really recovered.

The plans to resettle the Christians had soon reached the hostile ears of the Arab leaders. In order to prove a unity of hatred, the Christians had to be kept in the camps along with their Moslem brothers. Charles Maan's death went out as a clear-cut message.

He had been kidnapped in East Jerusalem after leaving a meeting. His body was found in a garbage dump near Ramallah a few days later. The assassins had shoved a three-inch pipe far up his rectum, placed several small diseased rats into the pipe, and forced them up into Maan's intestines. His legs were tightly bound so the rats could not be disgorged.

I had never seen my father so distraught at the news of a death. When I took him to Maan's funeral I literally had to hold him upright. Maan was buried in a crypt in Bethany, outside Jerusalem on the road to Jericho. It was the place where Jesus had resurrected Lazarus from the dead. Charles Maan would not be, on earth, the recipient of any such miracle.

The one glimmer of hope that came from his death was when his daughter, Sister Mary Amelia, told us that a number of Christian Arab priests had vowed to take up his work and get their people out of the camps.

It was a brutally hot day. A debilitating freak reverse khamsin wind was blowing off the desert. During the funeral services my father almost fainted. He seemed too dazed to be able to return to Aqbat Jabar. Sister Mary Amelia suggested we be put up at a hostel. It was a blessing. After a night of agony, Ibrahim seemed to have gained control of himself.

It was the Moslem Sabbath. Father felt that as long as we were in East Jerusalem we should go to the Al Aksa Mosque and pray for the soul of Charles Maan. The city was divided these days by a no-man's-land running alongside the Jaffa Gate like a gash. Each side could look at the other, sometimes almost within touching distance.

Despite the sorrow it would bring him, my father could not resist climbing the steps up the wall at the Citadel. From here we could look over the no-man's-land to Jewish Jerusalem, to the landmarks of the King David Hotel and the YMCA tower . . . to where the Bab el Wad began just beyond Jewish Jerusalem. Tabah was only a half hour away.

"Come on, Father," I pleaded. "This is no good."

He let me take him by the hand and lead him down the steps. In a moment we were swept up by masses of worshipers in their white Sabbath dress pouring into the Old City through the Jaffa and Damascus gates. The narrow streets bulged with a surge of foot traffic toward the Haram esh Sharif.

Soon the golden Dome of the Rock soared above us as we ascended to the immense plaza amid thousands of the faithful. We had to wait to get to the ablution fountain for the foot-washing ritual, then inched toward Al Aksa, the mosque built in honor of the termination of Mohammed's mythical journey from Mecca.

Thousands of pairs of shoes were neatly laid out near the entrance. We pressed for the door, now able to hear the Koran reader inside. At that moment a commotion erupted throughout the plaza. King Abdullah and his grandson, Husain, had entered the Haram esh Sharif and were making their way to the mosque!

We were in a perfect position to see them pass before us. I became entranced by the sight of his grandson, who was about my age. A vision of the Hashemiiya Palace in Amman flashed through my mind. Did the young Husain even know we were alive? What did his grandfather tell him about us? What a wonderment life must be for him.

The king's guard forced a narrow lane through the crowd, but the people closed in, trying to see and touch him. Abdullah, who gloried in the adulation, kept shouting for his guard not to imprison him, so he could talk to his subjects. As he moved freely, chatting and shaking hands, it occurred to me that his security was badly diminished. Soon Abdullah and Husain were virtually alone in the sea of excited worshipers.

My heart thumped as they passed directly in front of Father and me. They were almost within touching distance. As they reached the door, the king turned and waved to the throng. At that instant a man stepped out of the shadow of the mosque's interior, raised a pistol an inch from the king's head, and fired.

I saw the bullet enter the back of his head and come out of his eye as he fell and hit the ground and his turban rolled off.

Chaos!

"Our lord has been shot!"

The errant guard smashed forward, shooting. The Koran reader inside the mosque had not heard the shots and his voice continued to fill the inside of the building over the loudspeakers. The assassin kept firing wildly, with his bullets ricocheting off the marble floor just inside. Father and I shrank back as the king's guard brought the killer down, almost at our feet.

"The king is dead!"

I saw young Husain felled and dazed, but still alive. My impulse was to reach out for him. Ibrahim grabbed me, jerked me to him, and whispered in my ear. "Drift back very, very slow," he ordered. "Do not get involved. Do not break and run. We will just melt away."

Abdullah's death had been at the hands of a Palestinian, a Mufti gunman, and that shot triggered vicious reaction from his Bedouin subjects. He had united them and ruled them for three decades, and they remained fanatically loyal to him. Tribesmen bore in from their desert lairs in a rage of retaliation against the refugees on the Jordanian side of the river. A dozen Palestinians were seized and hanged before the gates of various refugee camps.

The next day the bodies were cut down, carried into Amman, and dragged behind galloping horses. Arms and legs were severed and tossed to a wild crowd. The torsos of the corpses were kicked, spat upon, and stabbed.

When this had been done, the lust was still not satisfied. The Bedouin formed up to storm into the camps. At last the Jordanian prime minister, a Palestinian, convinced the Legion that it had to prevent a monumental massacre. Much against their will, they surrounded the major camps and the cities of Amman, Salt, Suweilih, and Madaba to protect the Palestinians.

When the king was laid to rest on a hillside outside Amman, a Cairo journalist at the funeral noted that in the past six years the Arab world in its fledgling experiences with self-government had eradicated a number of the men who had been charged to rule them. In addition to Abdullah, there was . . .

Imam Yahya, the ruler of Yemen, who was murdered, as well as . . .

President Husni az Ziam of Syria, and . . .

Prime Minister Ahmed Maher Pasha of Egypt, who was followed in office and death by . . .

Prime Minister Nokrashy Pasha of Egypt, and also . . .

Prime Minister Muhsen el-Barazi of Syria, and . . .

A prime minister of Lebanon, who had been followed in Jordan where he was visiting and riddled by bullets from a passing car, and also . . .

The Commander in chief of the Syrian Army, Sami el Hennawi, and . . .

Shaikh Hasan al-Banna, the leader of the Moslem Brotherhood of Egypt, as well as . . .

Minister Amin Osman of Egypt, and . . .

An assortment of ministers, judges, police chiefs, and military commanders.

To say nothing of the dozens of unsuccessful attempts.

Iraq had four coups.

Jordan changed prime ministers on what seemed a monthly basis.

And a degenerate, corrupt, and disgusting Egyptian king was removed by an officers' revolt, after which he fled to a life of perversions on the Riviera.

Abdullah's son the Emir Talal ascended to the Jordanian throne. For two decades he had whiled away his life in boredom and a bitter relationship with his autocratic father. When he was crowned, the other Arab leaders praised him as an enemy of his late father and a patriot who would end British domination in that country.

Alas, King Talal was insane. He had spent half his youth in private European sanatoriums, and was returned to Jordan from a mental hospital in Switzerland to claim the throne. Talal's tenure was short. The mad king, propped up in place by the British and the Legion, was obviously unfit to rule.

By secret agreement between the military and the Parliament, Talal was deftly removed and spirited from the country. He was

to spend the rest of his life in exile, first in Egypt and then in a
forlorn villa in Turkey.

Talal's oldest son, Husain, was named king under a regency.
Young Husain had escaped death at Al Aksa when one of the
assassin's bullets, meant for him, glanced off the medals on his
fifteen-year-old chest.

Chapter Four

If there was a time ripe for rebellion, it was at the moment of Abdullah's death. As a reaction to Jordanian repression, riots flared throughout the West Bank camps. They were ugly and often bloody, but there was no real objective except for the relief that seemed to come from rioting.

A voice was desperately needed to rally us. I had fully expected Haj Ibrahim to step forward and unite us and provide us with leadership and direction. Instead, he lay low and slipped through the Jordanian backlash unscathed and unnoticed. My brave and noble father, the object of my worship, had been silenced. The fire in his belly had dimmed to nothingness. This came as a terrible blow and disenchantment to me.

While the Arab Legion clamped down crushing dissent, the Haj and what was left of the old leadership fended for themselves, saved their own skins. I began to hate them for their incessant whining about the exile and the return. Whatever pride and dignity they might have had was gone. They were the wronged, entitled to pity, content to live on handouts in stagnation for the injustices inflicted on them.

Now came the United Nations to take over the camps, administrators with blue eyes and golden hair. They would make our decisions for us.

The Jordanians were no longer after my father, for he had demonstrated that he had been pacified. Ibrahim still had stature from his past and recent glory from Jamil's martyrdom, which he used to wangle a United Nations position to head a committee that was to create industry and promote agriculture in the Jericho region. He quickly got Kamal a job at the UNRWA medical supply depot. It was perfectly tailored for Kamal. He had little to do except doze in a cubbyhole most of the day with an assistant to fetch him coffee and handle any real work. Kamal, never tall in my eyes, had grown completely slovenly.

Once spirited and amusing, Fatima had become drained by Aqbat Jabar. The two of them scarcely bothered to beat the flies off anymore. Kamal would grow old, follow Father's generation into the café, play backgammon, suck on a water pipe, fantasize about the huge villa in which he had lived in Tabah, and send his children into the fedayeen to regain his freedom from the Zionist dogs.

Omar came as a surprise. He stayed most of the time in Jericho and pestered shop owners until a merchant in a small grocery store finally gave him a job. Omar enhanced the job by brewing coffee and peddling sweets to the waiting lines of vehicles at the Allenby Bridge. He ran errands for the truck drivers and finally created a job for himself at the post office.

Mail to a refugee camp was a confusing piece of business. There was no delivery. If someone was expecting a letter, he would send a child to the post office to spend long hours waiting in line for a letter that most often was not there. Omar made up a delivery route, charging a halfpenny to deliver a letter and a penny for a package. This was difficult, because the hovels were not numbered and he had to learn the vicinity of every family, clan, and tribe by heart.

Haj Ibrahim's position with the UNRWA gave the family an inside track on rations and other benefits. With Kamal and Omar both working, our fortunes lifted. It managed to take the sting out of "Sabri selling our guns and running off with the money." Keeping the truth of that vow had become a matter of life and death between Nada and me.

For me, what was there to do? I hated the idleness. I secretly continued to give Nada lessons up on Mount Temptation. I helped Omar with his mail delivery. I hung around Professor Doctor Nuri Mudhil, but he had very little work to do these days except prepare papers that were too difficult for me to work on.

I prayed to Allah mightily for something to come along—and Allah heard me! Can you imagine how elated, how ecstatic, how overjoyed I was to learn that a boys' school was being opened in Aqbat Jabar? There were places for only three hundred students. Although there were thousands of boys of school age, I knew I would be accepted. Indeed, the students were picked from the sons of former muktars, sheiks, and now UNRWA officials.

Every Arab nation kept pet Palestinians on its payrolls, ostensibly to help its refugee brothers. In reality, they worked for the interests of the host nation. Dr. Mohammed K. Mohammed was a well-known physician who fled from Jaffa before the war during the exodus of the elite. Because there were so few learned men of consequence, we tended to venerate people such as doctors, dentists, lawyers, and teachers. The homage paid them was out of proportion to what they had really accomplished.

Dr. Mohammed K. Mohammed was an astute politician. Using his medical reputation as a springboard, he established the Palestinian Refugee Aid Society in Cairo. He smelled out the coup that changed the country's rulers and offered his organization and himself to the new order. The ruling officers saw future benefits from him and pushed him to the forefront of the political wars, proclaiming him as the true leader of the exiles.

Despite the disasters in their war against the Jews, Egypt remained the most powerful of the Arab nations. Its main area of influence among the Palestinians was in the Gaza Strip, a finger of land it controlled that contained over a hundred thousand refugees. However, Egypt, along with Syria and Iraq, was always on the prowl to penetrate the late King Abdullah's territory on the West Bank.

When an American philanthropist was moved to establish the school for refugee boys in Jericho, Dr. Mohammed K. Mohammed was at the head of the line to receive his moneys. He had cleverly made his aid society an associate of UNRWA, to siphon off funds. Here was a chance for Egypt to gain a foothold.

A two-story building was erected near the highway midway between our camp and the camp at Ein es-Sultan, a bit to the north. The school was called the Wadi Bakkah, after a monumental Arab victory over the Visigoths in the year 711.

It was an open secret that Dr. Mohammed was bisexual. He had a wife and a large family tucked away in a villa in Alexandria but was generally in the company of male companions.

My people do not speak of men making love to men. It is permissible for men to be affectionate with one another in public, to kiss and to walk holding hands, but we pretend that nothing of an intimate nature goes on. Any hints of homosexuality must be suppressed. Why? There are Mohammed K. Mohammeds everywhere.

Dr. Mohammed K. Mohammed was an impressive man with a stern face, the required moustache, and a fine suit of Western clothing. He was around fifty years of age, of ordinary build, was enthusiastic, and spoke with flower in his language. The Wadi Bakkah School was a personal victory for him and he opened it with great fanfare.

There was a shortage of qualified teachers, but the doctor had already considered that possibility. Members of the Egyptian Moslem Brotherhood, thinly disguised as Palestinian refugees, had infiltrated the West Bank camps. Most had some experience as religious teachers; they were literate and knew their Koran, which was the basic element in our education.

I was made an upperclassman in a group of ten boys who were also used as part-time instructors. Dr. Mohammed came and left with only a slight tinge of gossip in his wake. The curriculum was something else.

Although the Koran spoke for itself on matters concerning the Jews, the Moslem Brotherhood teachers made my old schoolmaster, Mr. Salmi in Ramle, seem like mild stuff by comparison.

Our history and geography lessons had no maps showing Israel. The only mention of the word "Israel" always carried a slander with it. We were taught that Canaan was an Arab land before Joshua stole it from the Arab people. For four thousand years Palestine had been stolen land.

After Islam arose to remove the Crusaders, the Turkish Ottomans perverted and weakened Islam, robbing the Arab people of their true role as leaders of the world. In recent times the British conspired to install the Jews in Palestine as advance agents of imperialism. The Jews went on to destroy Palestine as part of their wanton pact with the devil.

At no time were the Arabs responsible for the series of calamities that had befallen them. When we Arabs lost a battle, it was merely Allah's way of reminding us we had not been perfect Moslems.

In the math class the younger grades were taught addition and subtraction: "If you had ten dead Zionists and killed six more, how many dead Zionists would you have altogether?" Multiplying and dividing dead Zionists became more intricate as the grade level increased.

Every classroom had a piece of art by every student pinned to

the walls. They overwhelmingly depicted bloodthirsty hook-
nosed Jews maiming and killing Arab children, Zionist airplanes
attacking helpless refugee camps, glorious fedayeen goring Jews
with bayonets, glorious fedayeen stomping on Jews whose pockets bulged with blood money, glorious fedayeen chasing fleeing
Jewish cowards, glorious fedayeen standing atop a mound of Jewish skulls in Tel Aviv, glorious fedayeen reading sweet poems to
Arab children.

There was the occasional picture of flowers, tents, water wells,
trees, birds, and animals, but such pictures were discouraged and
never won a prize.

Each month there was a poetry contest. The theme never varied.

> *The Zionist is the assassin of the world,*
> *Children and trees and birds die before his*
> *   bullets,*
> *All the poor people cry,*
> *For their homes have been destroyed,*
> *And the world will pay.*

As the grades grew higher, the words grew hotter.

> *Whip me!*
> *Bring more whips!*
> *More executioners!*
> *By the thousands!*
> *Beat my skin to shoe soles!*
> *Rub salt into every wound!*
> *Old wounds and new wounds.*
> *With my blood I shall write*
> *A million songs of protest.*

We had a variety of textbooks from many different lands. In the
upper grades we read from the *Egyptian High School Reader:*

> *O MOTHER OF ISRAEL*
> *O mother of Israel! Dry your tears, your*
> *children's blood which is being spilled in the*
> *desert will produce naught but thorn and wormwood.*
> *Wipe off your blood, O mother of Israel, have*
> *mercy and spare the desert your filthy blood, O*

> *mother of Israel. Remove your slain, for their*
> *flesh has caused the ravens bellyache and their*
> *stink causes vomit. Cry, O mother of Israel,*
> *and wail. Let every house be the Wailing Wall*
> *of the Jews.*

Slogans wrapped around the walls of every classroom, vowing death and destruction. Jokes were told in the schoolyard.

"How many Jews fit in a Volkswagen?"

"Thirty. Four in the seats and twenty-six in the ashtrays."

Our physical education was actually a program of military training. We hiked out of the school grounds for "nature study," to comply with UNRWA rules. We marched to secret fedayeen training sites. Our courses consisted of learning to live in the field, tracking, hand and knife fighting, crawling under barbed wire, leaping through fires, grenade throwing, and strangling live animals to prove courage. We worked very hard for the privilege of being allowed to fire live ammunition. Shooting a machine gun filled us with a tremendous feeling of power and exultation. A nine-year-old was our best marksman.

The ten upperclassmen, which included myself, were honored to have a ranking holy man from the Brotherhood to teach us. Our course was on the publication of the Conference of the Academy of Islamic Research in Cairo, a gathering of fifty of the world's leading Moslem scholars and holy men from all over Islam. In addition to delegates from the Arab nations, there had been some from such diverse places as Togoland, Russia, Indonesia, India, Yugoslavia, China, and Japan. These were the Muftis, the professors, the ministers of religion. There had been dozens of speeches, lectures, scholarly papers, forums, and resolutions. All dealt with the "Five Great Themes":

1. The Jews are the enemies of God and humanity.

2. Jews have been evil throughout history. Their Bible is filled with scandals and debauchery that reveal the true nature of their religion. It is a counterfeit work falsifying God's message.

3. Jews are scum and do not constitute a legitimate nation.

4. The State of Israel must be destroyed, for it is the culmination of the historical and cultural depravity of the Jews. Their state is a total contradiction to Allah's "abode of Islam."

5. Islam is superior. Its grandeur guarantees its ultimate triumph over all religions and peoples. Arab defeats throughout
history were designed by Allah to teach the Moslems a lesson to
renew their purity and purpose.

We were out of sight of those administrators with blue eyes and
blond hair who buried themselves behind walled villas in Amman. All teaching was left to the Arabs. When UNRWA personnel did come to inspect us, we were always forewarned. A select
few of us knew the school's great secret. Guns and ammunition
were being stored in our basement.

Dr. Mohammed K. Mohammed returned before our first anni-
versary. We were assembled in the broiling sun in the school
yard, where a number of speakers praised our progress and dedication to the revolution. As future fedayeen, we had come a long
way in our spiritual development. Our Arab brothers, solidly
united, were just over the border and girding for the war of extermination. Many of us would be heroes.

We were wilting by the time Dr. Mohammed K. Mohammed
stepped forward to speak.

"Today is the second of November by the Christian calendar,"
he bellowed into the microphone with his fist rising. "Do any of
you know what this means?"

"No," we replied in unison.

"It is one of the blackest days in all of Arab history."

"Oh," we mumbled.

"It is the day the British imperialist dogs sold our birthright to
the Jews by giving them false claims to our sacred lands in Palestine."

"Oh."

"It is the day they issued the infamous Balfour Declaration.
Down with the Balfour!"

Our teachers, on a small raised platform behind the doctor,
stood in unison. "Down with the Balfour!" they cried.

We, the upperclassmen, sprang to our feet. "Down with the
Balfour!"

Dr. Mohammed K. Mohammed came down, formed us up, and
led us out of the school yard chanting in unison.

"Down with the Balfour!"

We swarmed outside to a small line of kiosks and a café that held a fill of older loafers. As we passed them, they got up and joined us.

"Down with the Balfour!" they cried.

We were out on the highway. Over the road several hundred women and girls were lined up awaiting the water tanker. They broke ranks excitedly. "Down with the Balfour!" They marched behind us as we headed toward the camp at Ein es-Sultan. More hundreds of people swarmed down from Aqbat Jabar. The highway was soon flooded with humanity.

"Down with the Balfour!"

We came to a small two-story isolated house belonging to a shoemaker, an Armenian named Tomasian, who had lived in Jericho all his life.

"What is going on?" he shouted down from his balcony.

"Down with the balcony!" someone cried up to him.

"Down with the balcony!" became the new chant.

"Down with the one upstairs!"

A peddler with a donkey cart was shooed off the highway as we surrounded him.

"Down with the donkey cart!"

"Down with Abdullah's corpse!"

"Down with the United Nations!"

"Down with the American criminals!"

The mob was now being orchestrated by the Moslem Brotherhood. People broke off and tore into the Armenian's house, plundered it, and cried in rhythm that Tomasian was a traitor.

"Jihad!"

"Holy war!"

"Down with the Armenians!"

Obviously, someone had co-ordinated our growing riot, for a Brotherhood teacher came toward us from Ein es-Sultan with a hundred boys running at full steam behind him. As they joined us, we could see that they were exhausted from the heat, sweaty and shaky. As they merged with us, one of the boys began to throw up, then another and another. In a moment mass vomiting broke out.

"The Zionists have poisoned the springs!"

"Down with the Zionists!"

People began dropping to their knees in dozens, gagging and vomiting all over the highway.

"We have been poisoned!"

Hundreds of people collapsed on the ground, writhing and screaming. Some began to see Mohammed. Others saw Allah!

The few Red Crescent ambulances up from Jericho were inadequate to handle what had become a universal outburst of hysteria. Women fainted. Men ran in circles frothing.

Automobiles and trucks that had been blocked sounded their horns angrily. The vehicles were stormed, turned over, and burned. The air was soon filled with stone missiles flung aimlessly. Blood joined the vomit.

"DOWN WITH THE BALCONY!"
"DOWN WITH THE BALCONY!"

Chapter Five

From the moment Per Olsen entered our hovel, we could tell that he was different from the usual breed of bureaucrat. Our new UNRWA administrator was Danish, about fifty, but had neither blue eyes nor blond hair. He was an infectiously decent man with that good humor that quickly overcomes the feeling of formality one has with most foreigners.

Per Olsen had earned his credentials in the backwash of one of the bloodiest civil wars in history, one between the Moslems and Hindus in India. In the exchange of populations following the creation of Pakistan some twenty million refugees came into being almost overnight. Olsen won high acclaim for humanitarian work among them. For him to come to Jericho spelled something more than an ordinary rotation of positions.

My father had been impressed with Per Olsen from the beginning, when the Dane called in his Arab associates for a series of meetings.

"This is an excellent man," Ibrahim told me. "I am certain he has special business here."

I had turned seventeen and had become proficient in English. In addition to a regular teaching position at the Wadi Bakkah School, I acted as the translator for my father. Thus, I was part of the friendship between him and Per Olsen from the beginning.

After getting his feet on the ground and sorting out the capabilities of his Arab staff, Olsen called on us at our home.

"I want to be able to depend on you as a personal adviser, Haj Ibrahim."

"I am but a humble employee of the United Nations. My services are always at your wish and command."

"We are going to have an interesting time here," Olsen said, whipping out a long, thin Schimmelpenninck cigar from a packet in his shirt pocket. My father tried one.

"Hummm, different," Father said. "Quite nice."

"Now that we have billowed smoke in your home for the required forty seconds, let me speak to you, not quite as a brother, but as a man I must have on my side."

Father smiled.

"What do you want to know about me?" Per Olsen continued.

"Your title and prestige have preceded you," Father said.

"I have seen the worst of it on the borders between India and Pakistan. Do you need the details to know that I know what I am doing?"

"Only time will tell if India can be translated into Palestine."

"I have witnessed too much of man's depravity to be lulled into any sense of false security. To be brief," Per Olsen said, "I am from neither wealth nor poverty. I am not interested in Jewish and Arab politics. My first wife was a Jewess, killed by the Nazis in Dachau. No children, thank God. My wife now is a Moslem, a nurse who worked with me in India. We have three children. So you see, I am totally mixed up."

"Excellent cigar," Father said, luxuriating in it.

The two men engaged in a long silence that tried to cut through time, space, cultures, suspicions.

"What is it you want?" Father asked.

"I agreed to come to the Jericho area because I could go forward with a special mission. As you know, idleness and despair are the twin curses of the refugee. Hunger and disease can be coped with. All of it together breeds the crime, the terror, the madness. If I have a God, it is the principle of self-help. I am in a position to help you start helping yourselves. I want to do something in Aqbat Jabar that will startle others in the refugee situation from their lethargy."

"What do you know of the Arabs?"

"I am not a fool, Haj Ibrahim. That is why I have come to you. I first learned of you from Monsignor Grenelli, the Vatican observer on refugees. He told me at great length of your one-man war in Zurich. I made it a point to learn as much about your background as possible. Well, what do you say? I have funds and I have plans."

"My first advice, Per Olsen, is to move slowly. Very slowly."

My father seemed to undergo a spiritual resurgence as Olsen and UNRWA triggered a rash of activities. The sound of building was heard in the Jericho Valley.

Six schools were erected, two of them for girls.

A variety of sorely needed medical facilities were built, clinics, a malaria control unit, a chlorination plant, a rehydration building, supplemental feeding centers concentrating on infants and the young who had undergone a terrible mortality rate.

Mosques, a ritual slaughterhouse, stores, a police station, food warehouses, distribution centers, and transportation yards sprang up along the highway.

The activity amounted to nudging us from our deep-seated lethargy, signs that life was replacing death. With Per Olsen using Father as a liaison to the sheiks and muktars, things began smoothly.

One evening, six months after Olsen had arrived, Father and I were in his office, the three of us smoking away on Schimmelpennincks, when he opened his desk drawer with a twinkle in his eye.

"Here it is," Olsen said. "The authorization to create a development plan. Factories, mines, industry, agriculture. A pilot scheme that can pave the way for similar plans all over the West Bank."

"But won't that be very costly?" Father asked.

"It is primed to pay for itself in five years."

"Five years?"

"You said yourself to go slowly."

"Yes, go slowly because life here at the bottom of the world is slow. Slowly, because we cannot absorb too much from the outside that is different. But you say it will take five years to pay off something permanent. Acceptance of permanency here crosses a political boundary. We are not looking to stay in Jericho forever."

"However long you stay, you must find self-esteem," Per Olsen said. "If life is decent, some will remain. If the facility is here, others will come here to work when you leave."

Ibrahim was disturbed. "It might be difficult to sell, Per."

"Do you reject the idea yourself?"

"I lived side by side with the Jews for many years. We could not comprehend what they were doing. We must remain simple and stay with things we know. Oh, perhaps the Saudis believe they can purchase a modern society. . . . I don't know, Per, I don't know."

"Stay with me, Haj Ibrahim. If we succeed, we can make things better for a lot of people in many places in the world."

The Jericho Project was announced with great bravado. A number of world experts made their way to Aqbat Jabar to develop the scheme. Father suddenly found himself a wise man constantly being consulted by scientists, doctors, engineers, teachers. His native wisdom and practical knowledge of the way our world worked made him invaluable.

For the moment he forgot past defeats. Perhaps he also forgot reality. It was a magnificent time for me, reading papers for him, translating in important meetings, being the first son of the great Haj Ibrahim.

"We are going too fast, Per."

"It won't wait."

The plan? Oh, by the Prophet's beard, what a plan!

There were large tracts of barren acreage along the Jordan rift and Dead Sea that had never been farmed because of the lack of rain and below-marginal soil conditions. A huge parcel of land was staked out and destined to become an experimental farm to be irrigated directly from the river. Studies would be undertaken to determine what kinds of crops might succeed and what existing crops might be improved.

Grasslands of tough, proven desert seeds would be sown for sheep and cattle. Orchards would be planted with the hardiest varieties of olives, oranges, bananas, dates, and fields of cotton, peanuts, and strains of desert wheat that had fared well in arid soil.

Glasshouses covering many acres would concentrate on vegetables, while an experimental farm would constantly seek out and introduce crops from low-yield soils.

The agricultural part of the Jericho Project would consist of twenty thousand dunams and employ a thousand people and twice that number during the harvests.

Now to exploit the Dead Sea, known to be rich in potash and other minerals. The Jordan River had flowed into the sea for millennia; but the sea had no outlet and acted as a natural catch basin. The Jews were already working their side of the sea in the south. Blueprints were drawn up to build a mining operation in the vicinity of Qumran that would initially employ three hundred workers.

The third phase of the plan dealt with industry and called for an ambitious factory complex. Food from the farm would be processed, packaged, and canned. Dead Sea minerals would be refined and shipped through Jordan's single port in Aqaba. That meant the building of a major new road as well as other support roads.

Light industry within the capabilities of the refugees would be installed, and a training school for boys would be built to develop needed skills. Small factories would make rugs, building tools, cloth and clothing, utensils, building materials. A stone quarry would make blocks, and the sand and gravel pits would provide the materials for a glass factory.

As the experts began closing out their thick booklets of data and projections, it fell to Haj Ibrahim to sell the Jericho Project to our people. I went with him to meeting after meeting, watching him extol the scheme.

"We will beat the Jews at their own game!" he bragged. "We will turn Aqbat Jabar from a place of despair into a proud, self-sustaining city. Our families will work and earn salaries. This is our great opportunity to take off our rags and build decent homes. We have lived too long in uniforms of striped pajamas."

Do not think the Haj a fool. Even as he sold hard, I knew that rivers of doubts were overrunning their banks within him. Had our people gone too long without work or hope? Had they become content to continue on as the world's charity wards? Would they respond?

Oh Allah, the bitterness of the disenchanted!

It started when UNRWA sent out a call for several hundred construction jobs. Only a third of them were filled by Aqbat Jabar residents.

Despite my father's prodding and threatening and downright pleading we finally had to go to outside contractors and labor had to be shipped in. The same happened when road building and farm jobs became open.

School enrollment scarcely filled half the classroom seats, and most of those who attended did so on an irregular basis.

Tribal avarice moved in and the grandiose scheme died aborning. Every man of some kind of clan authority staked out a claim for a supervisory or executive position, and along with him brought an entourage of employees from his own people. The fight for positions was truly a fight for authority. Endless haggling led to endless haggling. Fists flew and guns were pulled at planning meetings. The losers sulked. The winners extended their power on the principle that a one-man job could be better handled by five members of the same family.

When building materials began to arrive, pilfering became rampant. Construction went on at a nearly motionless pace. There was a lack of labor, a lack of competent supervision, a lack of planning. Confusion and lethargy surrounded the scheme.

In our world, when five men do the work of one, four justify themselves through obstruction. Cruel games were played by an army of rubber stamp wielders. Permits and inspections were held up endlessly. People with no expertise made a farce of trying to figure out complicated installations. It could take a week to requisition a bag of nails.

In came the fedayeen gangs, who organized the theft of materials, then set up a security service to prevent further thefts. The fedayeen also demanded of Father and the other Arab leaders that they set up a clandestine factory to make arms and munitions.

The imams from the mosques got into it. Priests demanded large outright bribes, threatening to impede work by delivering sermons against the plan from their pulpits.

Chaos begat chaos.

What was pounded into the minds of our people was that UNRWA was their new government, a mystical father to care for them. Yet they wanted no responsibility toward it or for bettering the lives of their families. UNRWA would provide. Did they not deserve that for the loss of their lands?

Although the heartbeats of life were provided by UNRWA, it was deeply resented. Should not the United Nations be dedicated to the struggle of returning them to their villages? Should not the world throw the Jews out of Palestine? Was not UNRWA really just another of those invasions of foreigners making decisions over their lives?

I watched the Haj become despondent as his meetings grew uglier in tone.

"No, Ibrahim," his sheiks cried, "we will not draw a drop of water from the Jordan River, for that means making an agreement with the Jews. We will die of thirst before we share it with them."

"Listen, Haj. If we build factories in Jericho, will the Jews not get a message that we have accepted our exile?"

When UNRWA's beautification plan to plant trees and gardens, build playgrounds, and install streetlights was under way, they were all ripped up by angry mobs.

"Death to UNRWA!"

"Death to the agents of imperialism!"

THE RATION CARD, THE ALMIGHTY PRECIOUS RATION CARD!

Cheating UNRWA became a way of life. When a child was born, the mother registered the infant for a ration card. The next day another female from the same family would register the same baby and was issued a second card. Babies in a given clan were often registered under a half-dozen names.

No one with income reported it. Deaths were never reported, in order to keep the ration card valid. Any family able to leave Aqbat Jabar kept an address in the camp and the ration cards that went with it. Bedouin who drifted home to their borderless world kept their addresses and drifted back to collect rations every month.

Some had hit it rich through racketeering and now lived in East Jerusalem and Nablus. They came to the camp, often in new automobiles, to collect their rations.

Impoverished peasants in Jordan and on the West Bank squeezed into the camps and claimed to be refugees. A raging black market came into existence for surplus ration cards.

When building materials were offered to improve our hovels, few bothered to claim them. "We don't want to let the Jews think we are building permanent homes."

Conversely, the new wealthy among the black marketeers erected small villas right in the middle of Aqbat Jabar's squalor.

The refugee numbers game exploded. In the beginning of the war it was established that a half-million Arabs had fled their homes. Their numbers had been inflated to over a million and were still growing. An accurate census became impossible as Arab administrators in the UNRWA turned a blind eye to the abuses.

I do not know the exact moment or what triggered the most violent wave of demonstrations, but what does it matter. We were always a short spark away from a riot. Most of the riots were initiated in the schools. The teachers had become more important than our parents and completely controlled the children's minds. The target was usually the UNRWA headquarters, and once a demonstration got under way there was no telling how it might end.

The "plight" and the "day of the disaster" and the "exile" were always suitable reasons to demonstrate. The rest of it was fear, fear of ration cuts, fear of epidemic, fear when the water tankers were late. If a clinic shortened its hours because of a lack of personnel, a demonstration soon followed.

On the night the rioters set fire to a clinic, Haj Ibrahim was denounced as a tool of the Zionists. The clinic had been burned because an emergency shipment of vaccine had been accepted from Israel to stem an outbreak of cholera.

The next day we went to Per Olsen, who was barricaded, and under the protection of the Arab Legion. His letter of resignation sat on his desk.

"It is over, Haj. The Jericho Project is officially dead," he said.

"If you want the riots to stop," my father said, "just start pulling ration cards. It will stop."

"I cannot keep track of all the games being played here," Olsen said shakily and angrily. "It is beyond human reason or any man's ability to bear. I am leaving."

"I am sorry for what you must think of us, Per. You will condemn us, won't you?"

"No, my friend, that is not the way the system works. UNRWA does not want any wrenches thrown into its machinery. Too many bureaucrats would have to look for honest work. It will be smoothed over. Don't you know, it will end up being blamed on the Jews. The United Nations is becoming quite good at that. You tried, Haj Ibrahim, but you knew all along what was going to happen."

"I am afraid so," my father whispered.

"So, I leave you a legacy. Four cases of Schimmelpennincks. That should hold you for a while."

We walked home from UNRWA headquarters filled with pain. At that very moment I saw the Haj begin to grow old. He stopped and looked around. A few stakes in a rocky field denoted the outlines of the great experimental farm that never yielded a crop. A few decaying concrete foundations with poking fingers of steel rods were what was left of factories that never produced a single bolt of cloth.

"Why, Father?"

"It required teamwork. Teamwork requires trust. There is no trust among us. We pride ourselves on our potency. In truth, we are impotent.

"There are impounded building materials," Father said bitterly. "We shall take them and build a decent home closer to the highway. One that befits an UNRWA bureaucrat."

Chapter Six

1954

My eighteenth birthday was entirely memorable, for what young man can ever forget his passage into manhood!

Widow ladies without the protection of an extended family or clan were quite vulnerable to sexual annoyance or assault. But not those under the protection of Haj Ibrahim. We had several in our section of camp and they were entirely safe from harm. Only one man dared challenge my father, and he lost his tongue for his efforts.

Hilwa was an older woman, perhaps as old as twenty-six. Her husband had been dead for over a year. He was killed when a bus to Jerusalem he was riding on overturned, and she was left with four young children. Hilwa was one of those who had become separated from her people during the war and settled in the Tabah section of Aqbat Jabar. When her husband died, she appealed to the Haj for protection, which he readily afforded. As I have stated, my father's word was law in our part of the camp, and Hilwa was never in further danger.

As part of my neighborliness I would look in on Hilwa to see if she and her children were getting enough rations, and I personally saw to it they got proper medical attention when they were ill. We became good friends.

In our world, where almost everything about sex is dangerous, forbidden, and secret, most young men have their first worldly experience with a widow or a divorced woman. What I did not realize was that the widows were just as eager to have sex as the men. This mutual need came as a revelation!

All the time I believed I was seducing Hilwa, she was seducing me. When she told me she had a special present for my eighteenth birthday, I thought surely it was a little gift, perhaps a cap or something she had embroidered.

The first taste of the pomegranate was not what I had dreamed it would be. Although Hilwa had four children she was naïve, almost innocent, about making love. She was filled with the usual fears and taboos from childhood. These fears got into the bed with us. Between guilty weeping and strange outbursts of giggling, it was a disjointed and embarrassing experience.

Fortunately, our relationship overcame that first night. Hilwa would discreetly nod to me in passing when it was a safe time for her. The visits became frequent and things got extremely pleasant.

I felt deep down that something was wrong with the way we were going at it. The spirits told me we should not be in such a hurry. We needed discipline, like fasting during Ramadan. When I discussed the matter, Hilwa would blush and look away. We tried. We were rewarded.

Then Allah bestowed upon me the greatest of all honors. One night she confessed that I was a much better lover than her late husband. She complimented me many times about my gentleness and she became less afraid to talk things over and to explore hidden places.

It became very comfortable, too comfortable.

We lived in packed quarters, so my comings and goings began to be noticed. Several times I could not attend to her when she wanted me and she became upset and demanding. I began to squirm. Now that the novelty was gone, I feared her growing possessiveness.

Frankly, I was relieved the night she broke down and wept that we would have to stop seeing each other, for she had a legitimate and serious suitor. I feigned terrible sadness, I beat my chest, I even pretended to be jealous. But when I left, I could have screamed out for relief.

Having thus added this new dimension to my character, I continued to pursue the matter. As a teacher in the Wadi Bakkah School, I knew that a number of my students had widowed mothers and sisters. I made it a point to call on each of them to discuss their sons' scholastics.

Amazing how quickly a prowling wolf is given the scent. It was purely astonishing to learn how many women wanted to do it and even more astonishing to see how much I became in demand.

I do not wish to boast like other men, but I was assured by almost all of my widow friends that I was among the greatest lovers in the world. I'm certain that the patience and tenderness made me different.

Although it was difficult, I kept it to myself. I did not wish to dishonor these women, nor did I wish to share them. I accepted my manhood modestly.

After the departure of Per Olsen my father seemed content to go along with the bureaucracy. Until the collapse of the Jericho Project, he never allowed us to take advantage of our position. Now our family of nine, including Fatima and Kamal's new infant, acquired fourteen ration cards. Ibrahim requisitioned building materials and had a nice home constructed for us closer to the highway.

Per Olsen's replacement was a tiny man from Burma named Ne Swe. Father did not underestimate the man's capabilities because of his size. Ne Swe was also shrewd enough to realize that life would be simpler and smoother with Haj Ibrahim on his side. He had come from a land where exchanging favors was as much a way of life as it was to us. They got along famously from the beginning.

Until now Ibrahim scarcely ever mentioned the old villagers of Tabah or tried to contact them. Oh yes, he would often speak of his longing to return, but rarely spoke of people by name. For some strange reason, I think he bore guilt over having to split from them, although, Allah knows, it was not his fault.

"No shepherd loses his flock for whatever reason," was all he managed to say on the subject.

Our fine new home meant that Ibrahim was settling down and coming to terms with the exile. But Tabah would not go away, and the more settled he became, the more he wondered about his old friends. He finally asked me to find out.

Because of his position, he could send letters of inquiry on their whereabouts through UNRWA. In addition, Ibrahim also had two married daughters, my sisters, who had fled with their families. We had been out of contact for years. I wrote letters asking after them as well.

Several months passed before we received answers. Our villagers were still more or less intact and living in a camp outside Beirut called Shatilla. My sisters were also in Lebanon, in a camp near Shatilla called Tel Zatar.

After receiving their letters we plunged into a spell of nostalgia. The women asked me to read the letters over two or three times a day, and they wept each time. We learned who had married, who had children, where people worked, who was the temporary muktar looking after them. They complained. Although the Lebanese treated them with contempt and cruelty, there were jobs and Beirut was certainly better than Jericho.

In the next exchange of correspondence they appealed for Father to join them and lead them again. Ne Swe did not want to lose Father, but realistically felt there was a possibility of transferring him to Beirut.

I was elated and soared to paradise! In Beirut there was the famous American University but none in Jordan or on the West Bank. The thought of becoming a university student was a dream I had never dared to dream.

When we spoke about moving, at first our voices were firm and our spirits were high. We would see family and old friends! We would be a people again!

I came down faster than I went up. Each day Father's will became less passionate, less resolute. To move all of us to Beirut would be a monumental task. Ibrahim was now at peace with the Jordanians. He was in a position that required little work and carried much influence and privilege, and our living conditions were decent.

Why move to the unknown? In Shatilla he would have to fight long and hard to establish himself and acquire the same status he now had. In truth, Father was weary. The flight to Jaffa, to Qumran, to Zurich, Jamil, Charles Maan, the Jericho Project had all taken pieces of his spirit.

This powerful man who had only played around the fringes of fantasy now dipped into it. Oh, I pressed hard for Beirut, but he became dotty about it, irregular in his reasoning.

I continued to write letters to individual villagers and to my sisters, but it was strange: I couldn't remember their faces too well. Even Father was unable to keep straight the relationships between the clans and families of Tabah.

At the end of a few months, Beirut was a mirage.

On the days Father had his private meetings with Ne Swe, I translated for him to make certain there were no misunderstandings. Father would wait for me at a café across the road from the school. When classes were over, we would stroll to UNRWA headquarters. On these walks I began to notice the changes in him. He had become very diplomatic and pragmatic, avoiding trouble, keenly playing the tribal game. Shrewdness had replaced anger.

I was surprised to see him in the doorway of my classroom one day. He was visibly distressed, an emotion he never displayed in public. He nodded. I quickly received permission to leave and followed him from the school.

Out on the road he stopped and gripped me. I believe I actually detected fear in his eyes.

"I have received secret information from Amman. In two weeks the Jordanians are going to order all boys of military age to register for a draft into the Arab Legion."

"Oh my God," I said shakily.

"You are safe," Father said, "but they will take Omar."

I am ashamed to admit I was more relieved for myself than sorry for Omar. After the murder of Abdullah, and the exile of Talal, the regency rule around his grandson, young King Husain, had taken firm hold. Once again the Jordanians pressed forward with their obsession to annex the West Bank. Putting Palestinian boys in Jordanian uniform was a cleverly thought out trick. It would give the impression that the Palestinians were loyal to the king. Furthermore, if there were riots and troubles, Palestinians in the Arab Legion would be used to do the dirty work. We would have the blood of our own people on our hands while Jordan would be clean.

Father was badly shaken. Why? He was no longer a political threat. He was at peace with the Jordanians. Surely he would know how to get Omar exempted. I could not comprehend his reaction.

Ne Swe greeted us in a manner that reflected Father's urgency. I explained to him that Father had been tipped off by a Jordanian minister.

"Father says we must arrange immediate travel papers for Omar to get into Lebanon."

Ne Swe blinked a bit, realizing the quagmire of bureaucracy and bribes he had to wade through and the pressure of time. He thought hard. "The quickest way is to hire Omar for an UNRWA job in Beirut."

"Can that be done in time?"

"It is possible."

There was a large United Nations complex in Jerusalem on the Hill of Evil Council. There Ne Swe could make direct radio contact with UNRWA in Beirut. The world of favors and the system was already at work. Father seemed much calmed as we made for home.

The instant we entered our house I realized why Father had been on the brink of panic. I saw Jamil's photograph with the little vase of flowers and the burning candles. Jamil's hand had reached out from the grave.

Colonel Farid Zyyad was a patient man with a long memory. Ibrahim feared that Zyyad's thirst for vengeance had not been fully appeased by Jamil's death. Once Omar was taken into the Legion, Allah only knew what could happen to him. It would be too much for Haj Ibrahim to lose two sons in such a manner.

The necessary papers were in our possession within the week. We had quietly traded to get a new suit of clothing and shoes, obtained enough American dollars, and plotted the safest route to Beirut. Once there our clansmen would take him in at the Shatilla Camp.

In the blink of an eye, Omar was off to Lebanon.

Omar's tale was much the same as Jamil's. He had been scarcely noticed by the family all of his life. Of us all, he had been the most taken for granted, a sweet, simple, hardworking boy with no special attributes. Yet the weeping and wailing that followed his departure made one believe we were losing the son of Mohammed. Before he left, our photographer friend, Waddie, took his picture. After he was gone it was placed alongside Jamil's.

It wasn't the loss of Omar that really devastated Father. It was the loss of his ability to protect his family. Even more, it was the growing loss of his family.

We had changed from simple farmers living out a cycle of planting and reaping into a destitute people in our own land. Now we were beginning to change again. The sons were leaving the camps as soon as they were able. We were starting to become the wanderers of the world.

Omar's departure hit hard on Ibrahim. It was foremost for a man like the Haj to control his own destiny. Most of the time he had succeeded, even under great adversity. But my father had also taken losses a proud man could scarcely bear. He had lost his village and his clan. Now he was taking the most devastating defeats of all: the loss of one son after another. And the losses were out of his hands, beyond his powers.

For me, it was to be one of the most crushing moments of my life. I realized I was all that was really left for my father. He depended on me, leaned on me more and more. He treated me as a man and, at times, almost as an equal.

Every time I thought of my own departure it ended with a terrible depression. It would be unthinkable for me to leave so long as my father and family remained. How could I live knowing I was a traitor to my father?

Ibrahim repeated over and over that the seed of the Soukori clan would have to survive through me. I was his chosen. That was what I had wanted and fought for. Now, I would never be able to go with his blessing. All dreams, no matter how vague and unreal, suddenly shuddered to a halt.

Haj Ibrahim slowly began to shift his views. For the first time he took up the theme that the Zionists were the cause of all our troubles. No longer able to combat or cope with the evils of our society and leaders, he made convenient rationalizations about the enemy over the border.

There had been an officers' rebellion in Egypt that disposed of a decadent monarch. An Egyptian republic had been declared. The driving force behind the coup was a commander named Gamal Abdel Nasser. He had been a soldier in the war against the Jews and had been humiliated by capture. His hatred of Israel was the most potent in the Arab world, and that was saying a great deal. He fanned the flames of Arab nationalism. He would rally us all under his banner.

The Arab radio was always in competition for the minds of the West Bank refugees. Nasser stormed into their imaginations. He would liberate them. He would return them to their homes.

Bit by bit the words of Nasser penetrated my father's mind and started to cloud his once great ability to reason.

Chapter Seven

We received a message through the UNRWA radio in Jerusalem that Omar had made it safely to Beirut, had joined our clan, and had been given the promised job. Like all the sons who had left, he would send his salary home.

In the end we were to realize that perhaps Omar need not have left. The Jordanians ordered the military registration and made up all-Palestinian units of the Arab Legion. Although under the command of British officers, these battalions were soon noted for their lack of discipline, massive desertions, and general trouble-making. They refused to quell refugee disturbances and showed no loyalty whatsoever to the Jordanian king. The British soon considered their combat value as nil.

The Palestinian battalions were broken up and their troops were mixed with Jordanian regulars. Fighting between the two factions went on nonstop. Within several months the scheme collapsed and no more Palestinians were drafted.

The emphasis was now on creating a large fedayeen force and stepping up the terror raids over the Israeli border. In the Wadi Bakkah School, boys began their training at the age of nine.

Although our fathers retained their traditional powers and respect, the teachers truly controlled the children's minds. Our fathers did not protest so long as we knelt when we entered our homes, kissed their hands, and paid lip service to their wisdom.

Students were organized into cells by age and anointed with revolutionary names. They all became the "sons" of something.

There was Ibn Nimer, "son of the tiger." There were sons of the lion, the jackal, the eagle.

There were sons of storm, fire, and lightning.

There were sons of Mohammed or of a recent martyr who had not returned from a raid on Israel. There were no less than a dozen Ibn Jamils named after my brother.

There were sons of the brave, the noble, the trustworthy, the fierce.

They distributed the daily barrage of leaflets, plastered the walls with posters, painted the slogans. Mainly, they were the backbone of the demonstrators who would riot on any pretext at a moment's notice.

I never got over the horror of watching their graduation ceremonies, performed before their parents. After a demonstration of "military prowess" and personal courage the ceremony ended with their biting off the heads of snakes. As the blood dripped down their chins, they roasted the dead animals for a victory feast. Other schools had the children strangle puppies and drink their blood.

I had been in such despair over Omar's departure and my own imprisonment that I did not give much thought to Nada's plight. She was twenty years old now, beyond the age when most girls married. For Hagar this loomed as a disaster, for the unmarried and childless daughter was considered a family shame.

Nada was very beautiful and many boys her age and many older widowers desired her, but Ibrahim rebuffed them all. He responded to their ardor by stating that Nada would be properly married to a man of station only after we had all returned to Tabah. I wondered if he really believed that. At any rate, his reluctance to let her go became very apparent.

Nada began to drift toward the fedayeen, who were encouraging girls to join. This was an enormous break with tradition, one bound to bring fathers and daughters into conflict. Nada had always been my first responsibility of the heart, and I decided I had better start taking care of her more diligently.

I went up with her into Mount Temptation for respite as we had done many times. It was sad that Father did not permit her to go to one of the schools for girls. She would have been very smart, even smarter than some boys. It was terribly unfair because she had so much idle time.

Nada became more and more active in the fedayeen. She joined other girls between the ages of sixteen and twenty who were stepping outside the authority of their fathers. They were listening to secret lectures from teachers, the Brotherhood, and those crazy outcasts the Communists.

I planned to admonish her severely, but the more I thought

about it, the more it seemed I should reason with her. When I began, she said:

"Don't bother, Ishmael. I have already taken an oath," she said, stunning me. "I am a daughter of the revolution now. My group is called the Little Birds. I am the nightingale. Do you know why? They are the only ones who have ever heard me sing except you."

"There are dangers in getting too deeply involved."

"I don't care," she said tersely.

"Well, Father cares."

"Father? Cares about me?"

"Yes, he does."

"There were many nice boys who tried to court me. He drove them all away."

"Only because of our situation."

"Father cares about my preserving his honor and that's all," Nada said. "Anyhow, I don't care whether Father cares."

"What do you mean, you don't care whether Father cares!"

"That's what I said."

Of course I knew that Nada had spice but was rarely able to show it. Maybe I was the only one who knew of the fires in her. Well, perhaps Sabri knew a little of it. When she was home, even among the women, she scarcely said a word and always did her tasks without complaint.

"We must have a serious discussion," I said at my manly best. "You're going to get into bad trouble with this crowd."

"I'll always listen to you, Ishmael, but I have made up my mind about certain things."

"Such as?"

"Maybe we're never getting out of this place."

We became quiet.

"It is a distressing situation," I said at last. "But don't be crazy."

"I know what you think of the fedayeen, but they are the first people who have treated me as an equal human being—as a person with pride and dignity. So I am their nightingale and Hala is their dove and Sana is their bluebird. We were never told anything like that before. We all sing together. We tell stories. We laugh. The boys learn they are not dogs and they soon become men."

"Oh, I've seen how manly they are," I said snidely. "They ride around in open trucks before going out on a raid and shoot up all their ammunition into the air to prop up their courage. By the time they get to the Israeli border they throw down their guns and flee to another camp."

"Time will show how brave they will become. Who do you think is going to get us out of Aqbat Jabar? Father? He is turning old before our eyes. No, Ishmael, only the fedayeen will liberate us. They will return us to our true place."

"What true place? Who do you think we are?"

"The Palestinians are the most educated, the most intelligent in the Arab world—"

"Shit! Any educated Palestinian with two dollars abandoned us long ago and fled. Look down there, Nada, what do you see? A proud and dignified people?"

"That is exactly why we must turn to the fedayeen."

I clamped my hands over my ears. Nada was excited and glared into my eyes. I calmed myself and shook her shoulders slightly.

"Nada, you said you would listen to me. Please listen. I hear these slogans at school every day, all day. Because of our terrible misery it is easy for us to believe words without meaning. Who are these fedayeen who are trying to lead us? What do they know of government? What do they know of freedom? What do they know of reason, of truth? They steal from widows and cripples. They run the black market. They deal in hashish. So they wrap up their gangsterism in a flag of revolution, and this is supposed to make them noble?"

It was her turn to clamp her hands over her ears. I pulled them down.

"They are sending boys my age over into Israel in suicide squads. They go without maps, without knowing their targets, without proper training. Find a stray Jew, an old Jew, a child, a woman, and murder them. Do you believe that will get us back to Tabah?"

"The Zionist dogs stole our homeland!"

"Now you shut up and hear me good, Nada. You know Waddie, the photographer? Well, do you know him?"

"Of course I know him!"

"So do I. He works for the fedayeen. A boy goes into the suicide squads because his family sells him for a hundred dollars or he is forced because he is pressured and his manhood is questioned. When he enters training his photograph is taken. Why? Because even as he trains for a mission, they are printing posters of him to put up on the walls so that the instant he is killed in Israel, he is a new martyr."

"I don't believe it!"

"Oh, there's much more, Nada. The last three weeks before his mission he is sent to Nablus or Bethlehem to live with a whore and is kept in a stupor on hashish. He is thrown over the border like a piece of dog meat because the fedayeen don't want him back. They want martyrs. Is that your revolution?

"And your noble fedayeen commanders. Do you see them leading any raids? Hell no. They are cynics sending dumb peasant boys to their deaths to keep up the hatred and cover up their racketeering. Oh, come to us, dear little nightingale, sing for us, write poems of the great struggle. We will give you your first true home away from home. We will let you run down to the highway and demonstrate with the boys. Isn't that nice? You're being used, Nada!"

"Stop it, Ishmael!"

"I am telling the truth!"

"I know," she cried. "Can't you see! I must get out of the house! I choke in there! At least I have some friends—"

"But, Nada, these are the same kind of men who got us into this mess. They are leading us into an eternity of bloodshed and horror. They will win us nothing. The only thing they will save is their bank accounts. All these raids are meant to do is perpetuate hatred, no matter how many boys they butcher. And they love it when the Jews strike back and some of our children are killed. They love it!"

"You don't have to shout," she said, standing and walking away from me. She turned into a path so that we were really forced to look on the sprawl of Aqbat Jabar. "Tell me if there is another way. Father tried another way and they destroyed him for it. How long can we go on living down there? What is going to happen to your own life, Ishmael?"

Then I found myself rocking back and forth, hitting the heel of my hand into my forehead. An uncontrollable pain shot up from my stomach to my throat. "I am trapped!" I shrieked. "Trapped!"

"We were always trapped, Ishmael! From the day we were born."

"I am trapped!" I screamed over and over until my own echo frightened me. I was soon numbed.

"It is true," Nada said, "I don't believe all that much in the revolution. But you had better listen to me now, my brother."

I feared her words.

"Come, let us go higher and sit where we don't have to look down on that place," she said.

I let her take me by the hand. She was always so agile climbing among the rocks, even barefooted. My outburst had tired me strangely. I hung my head and chewed on my lip.

Nada was extremely sure of herself. "You who weep for yourself, now weep for me. I have never been allowed to draw a free breath in my entire life. My mind, my voice, my desires have always been locked inside a prison cell. I cannot walk into the gathering room of our house and speak. I can never, in my entire life, eat a meal there. I cannot walk any farther than the water well alone. I will never be able to read a real book. I am not permitted to sing or laugh when a male is near, not even my own brothers. I cannot touch a boy, even slightly. I am not permitted to argue. I cannot disobey, even when I am right. I must not be allowed to learn. I can only do and say what other people allow me.

"I remember once in Tabah I saw a little Jewish girl waiting for the bus on the highway with her parents. She carried a doll and she showed it to me. It was very pretty, but it could do nothing but open and shut its eyes and cry when it was hit on the back. *I am that doll.*

"Obey . . . work . . . what is joy, Ishmael? Oh, my beloved brother, I have seen the wonderful bounce to your step as you ran off through our fields in Tabah to find the stream or steal a sip of wine. I see you now walk into a room and speak out, even to Father. I see you read. How wonderful to be able to read and not be afraid of being slapped for it. I watched you go to Ramle to school every day by yourself . . . get on a bus . . . ride away . . . and not come back until dark! I remember the times you and your brothers went into the movie house in Lydda and I curled myself into a corner and cried. I remember you riding off on el-

Buraq, sitting behind Father, holding on to him, and galloping to the winds. I remember . . . I remember. . . .

"I have been molded into a lump that is not supposed to have feelings. My emotions have been controlled and enslaved from the time I was a little girl—shame . . . slap . . . forbidden . . . slap . . . shame, shame, shame. Even my body is not my own. My body exists to defend Father's honor. It is not mine! I cannot use it for any pleasure. And when I am sold into marriage my body will belong to my husband to do as he wishes whenever he wishes. I have no say in the matter. So you think you are trapped, Ishmael?"

"I think I am going to be ashamed," I managed to say.

"Oh, my brother, there is more, much more, to being a woman in our world. You feel the pain of it until you become like Mother and can feel no pain anymore. So now I can talk with boys and girls and sing and demonstrate. What do I care about what the demonstrations mean? I am their nightingale. I look at boys and smile. I brush past them. I flirt. Sabri showed me that there may be something tremendously wild and beautiful in life. Why shouldn't I find out?"

"I cannot approve of such . . . talk. . . ."

"Have you ever had a girl?" she asked.

"I am not going to answer that."

"Well, have you done it?"

"Only with widow ladies."

"Was it wonderful?"

"Nada!"

"Was it?"

"Well, once you get over the fear, and if you have an understanding widow, well, there is incredible wonderment."

"You did it. You felt it. Everything has been denied me, but you have felt it. And you will do it again when you have a chance."

"This talk is getting dangerous," I said.

Nada did not hear me. She was in a trance. She swayed back and forth with her eyes closed. "I see myself and a boy. I don't know who he is, but we have gone to the springs alone. We throw off our clothes and stare at each other. I look at his sacred part. It is magnificent."

She opened her eyes and smiled. "I used to look at your sacred part all the time when you were a baby. All the girls like to change diapers on their baby brothers so they can look and even play with the sacred part. I want to feel everything about a man. I want to touch everything. To kiss everything. I want a boy to look at me with wonderment because I am a wonderment! Oh God, it must be incredible!"

"Nada, please be careful. Please, please, please be careful."

"I will not die like Hagar and Ramiza and Fatima, as receptacles. I will not be kept in a cage."

"Please," I said to her again, as in prayer: "Be careful, please be careful."

With Omar and Jamil gone, Father began to sense shifts in the family winds. When Nada was missing from the house, it was noticed. These days she was gone a great deal, and it did not take much to figure out where. The little birds of the fedayeen were a flock in constant flight. The Haj did not like it. There was bound to be a clash.

One morning after the meal, Father summoned us together. It was unusual to do so at this hour of the day. We entered, one by one, knelt, and kissed his hand. Kamal and I took our seats on either side of him and the women on stools along the wall.

"Nada," Ibrahim said, "stand up."

She did as she was told.

"I have been extremely fortunate to find a position for you in Amman in the home of a United Nations official. He is a great and honorable Syrian, Mr. Hamdi Othman. Although he is an Alawite by religion, he is still a man highly beloved in the ranks of UNRWA. He has three small children. You are to attend them. I have made an arrangement whereby you will be able to come and see us every second month. In many ways this is so fortunate for you. The Othmans are very kind people. They have traveled in the West. It is so crowded here. Now you will have a room of your own, which you will only have to share with two other girls. I know this must please you greatly." There was silence. "Well, Nada, it does please you."

"Yes, Father."

"Good, then I am pleased that you are pleased. I know the honor of the Soukori clan will be foremost in your mind and heart. Before you leave, to ensure modesty, your mother will cut off your hair, and you will henceforth veil yourself in public. Let us move it along. Mr. Othman and his wife will be here to fetch you shortly."

Haj Ibrahim got up and left.

Instantaneous weeping, an oft-occurring matter, broke out among the women, except for Nada. I have never witnessed such fury in anyone's eyes. She remained motionless as Hagar ran the scissors through her lovely thick brown hair and let it fall around Nada's ankles. When her head was shaved smooth, Mother tied a kerchief about it, then fled to gather her belongings.

I had to be alone. I did not even want to speak to Dr. Mudhil. I went up into Mount Temptation. May the prophet have mercy on me, but I believe I had begun to hate Haj Ibrahim. There would be no photograph of Nada to go alongside Jamil and Omar. Just an ignoble dismissal.

My head spun a million plots to escape. I would go to Amman, kidnap Nada, and escape with her. We would plunge into the desert and take refuge among the al Sirhan Bedouin. Oh, curse it. What would surely happen then? Nada would be taken in marriage to the old sheik.

Beirut. Money would be difficult to obtain for travel papers. I could steal it. That would take time and planning. If we could get to Lebanon, we could not go among our own people. Ibrahim would find out and come after us.

Cairo. It was impossible for a boy to travel with a woman that far. We could not enter Egypt anyhow.

How about fleeing to another refugee camp? The idea revolted me.

Damascus. With great courage we could walk to Damascus. But we would be illegal. Some from our camp had tried it and were thrown into prison and tortured. Nada would be raped.

Where is there to go! We are trapped! We are prisoners!

Baghdad . . . oh, that's really crazy.

Oh God! Oh God!

"You have not spoken to me since Nada went to Amman," Father said.

"I am sorry, Father."

"You think I was cruel to Nada."

"No, you were very kind and loving, Father."

He slapped me hard, but I did not even feel it.

"What do you want for your sister? A life in Aqbat Jabar?"

"I don't know."

"Oh, come now, Ishmael, you always have all the answers. What do you want for her? Why do you think they are letting girls into the fedayeen? For the noble revolution?"

"I don't know."

"You have two sisters in Beirut. I made arrangements for their marriages to fine men. They are now together with their husbands and children and their families. I did well for them. What can I do here for Nada? She is my last daughter. What kind of life can I arrange for her in this place? Don't you think I want to make a nice marriage for her?"

"Let me take Nada to Beirut," I begged. "Omar has a job. I will find one. We will take care of Nada. We will see to it she is protected and we will find a suitable man."

"Without me! Let my last daughter go! You speak like a fedayeen. Go, break up a family! Let it die! They are luring these girls, making lovely little birds out of them so they will be their prostitutes. They are destroying our families."

"Yes Father, no Father, yes Father, no Father."

"Come back here!"

"Yes, Father."

"You will learn in good time that I have done the only possible thing for Nada to keep our honor."

"Yes, Father."

"And you must get over this. You must remain with me always, Ishmael."

"Yes, Father."

I could not even attempt to speak to Haj Ibrahim about letting Nada be free to find a man she loved and love him and take on life together, even in Aqbat Jabar. That was why she was driven into the fedayeen . . . into the company of cutthroats.

He would never understand and I was not all that certain his motives were honest. Did he really fear that some boy might take Nada away? Was he really not secretly glad that he did not have to marry her off so long as he had the excuse of Aqbat Jabar? He had made up a lie to himself in order to hold on to Nada. I think he loved her in a secret way that was not entirely healthy.

Chapter Eight

Greetings, Ishmael!

It is your old comrade Sabri Salama who writes to you at last. I have been writing this letter in parts for many months but have been unable to send it until I found someone trustworthy to place it directly into your hands. As you will read, it contains many confidences and secrets.

Greetings to your beloved, noble, and compassionate father, Haj Ibrahim.

Greetings to your generous and loving brothers, Kamal and Omar.

On this glorious occasion I want your father to know I am not a thief. I have every intention of paying back the money I borrowed from the sale of your weapons. I cannot pay it right away, but the day is coming soon.

My adventures, since I left you over two years ago, have not been unlike those of Sinbad the Sailor.

After I sold the guns to an unscrupulous dealer, I crossed over to Amman and let it be known I was a valuable truck mechanic. Because trucks are always breaking down in the desert along the King's Highway to Damascus, it was easy for me to arrange a ride in exchange for repairs.

I started the journey with two great fears. Firstly, that my papers would only get me into Syria, and once there, I could go no farther, but only to a refugee camp. Secondly, that I was carrying a great deal of money. Even though I dressed poorly, I knew I would be searched. I figured out a way that served me well. I put the money into bills of large denominations of American currency, wrapped them tightly inside a plastic bag, and swallowed it. Each day after I shit, I cleaned the bag and swallowed it again. I was searched many times, but the money was never found. You must remember that if you travel.

My first moment of terror was when our truck crossed the border into Syria at Deraa. I was automatically taken to the border fort, put into jail, and questioned for several days. There was no reason for the questioning except that it is dull duty at the fort, and when the Syrians have a chance to play with you, they are very dirty about it. All I could think of was not to get caught passing and swallowing my money.

At any rate, I became friends with the Syrian captain in command of the border post and stayed for another week out of friendship when he kindly allowed me to continue to Damascus with a personal letter guaranteeing me safe passage. All praise to this kind man, who also gave me a letter of introduction to his cousin, who was a wealthy merchant and lived alone with his servants. This was fortunate, for otherwise I would have had to report to a refugee camp and be interned. The Syrians keep a very close watch on the Palestinians, and if you are caught without papers it can mean three years in prison.

At first I believed that Allah had blessed me. The merchant had just lost his chauffeur and personal servant. It was risky for him to keep me, but he showed great compassion in the beginning. Unfortunately, it took many weeks to figure out how to escape his hospitality. The threat of being turned in was used against me. You see, I was such a good mechanic he didn't want to lose me.

My other problem was how to get into Lebanon. It is very difficult and dangerous for a Palestinian, since the Lebanese are viciously on the lookout for us crossing into their country. If I were caught, it would mean an even longer prison sentence.

How could I solve this mighty dilemma? One night I was driving the merchant home from a party. He was very drunk and unconscious. At that moment Allah sent a message to me. I carried a pistol, for I also acted as his bodyguard. I shot him and buried his body in a very hidden place, then stole the papers of another servant and drove to the Lebanese border. I had my chauffeur's uniform, papers, and an American Cadillac.

At the border I could tell the Lebanese wanted to play games with me. I told them I was going to Beirut to get my master and warned them it would go very hard on them if I did not show up on time. When they started shuffling me around from official to official, I boldly demanded to telephone my master. They fell for the bluff and let me through. Oh, Ishmael, it broke my heart to have to ditch such a magnificent automobile, but I was certain that if I kept it, it would have led to my capture. Anyhow, I did strip it of all the valuable parts I could carry and sell, and I made my way into Beirut.

Once in Beirut, it was easier to hide at first, for there are many refugee camps around the city and Palestinians are allowed to come and go freely. The reason for that is we do all the filthy work for the wealthy Lebanese.

They are a very cruel people, particularly the Christians, and they deride us unmercifully about our misfortune.

A Lebanese joke: Question: Who has a pair of pants? Answer: Four Palestinians.

The Lebanese are only interested in making money. One day we will have to get our vengeance on them as well as the Syrians.

But even the refugee camps are not truly safe. The camps are all divided by clans. Strangers are quickly noted and looked upon with suspicion, for many destitute Lebanese Moslems slip in, pretend to be refugees, and try to get ration cards. I also learned that one must be very careful, even among brother Palestinians, because people like me without papers can be blackmailed.

Gangs of boys roam the camps and have everyone intimidated. The cowardly Lebanese do not let them form into fedayeen units, and they do not permit raids from their territory over the border into the Zionist entity. Believe me, Ishmael, in the Prophet's good time the Lebanese will become involved in our struggle.

I realized I had to make a courageous move. I had to go down and "play" the waterfront. There is a street called the Avenue des Français that has many nightclubs to lure sailors. Between that street and the central police station is where most of the prostitution takes place. In addition to sailors and tourists, many rich Saudis and Kuwaitis roam that area in search of sport. You know how it is in places like this which deal in special services. The pimps will kill you if you are not careful, and everyone is on the watch for strangers.

I bribed a police detective to take me around with him to the clubs and let everyone know that I was okay and under police protection. Then I spent some of my money on some girls. They are mostly European girls trying to act as belly dancers and not very good, but everyone, and the Saudis in particular, likes blondes. So after a time I became friends with the owner of the Miami Club and made myself valuable by fixing his automobile so he could run hashish in it safely.

From my base at the Miami Club and a nearby hotel I was able to know all the ship movements. It took patience, but I finally found a Portuguese tramp steamer that was destined for Gaza. How did I find out? Some Portuguese sailors came into the club one night and were soon off with the girls for a party in my hotel. One of them became very drunk and passed out and was left there. I knew the girl and talked her out of rolling him and personally took him back to his ship. The captain of the ship was grateful. We talked over my situation and he offered to stow me aboard and take me to Gaza. It would take all the money I had left.

What could I do, my brother? Once we were on his ship and out of the harbor, he could have fed me to the sharks. I had to pay him in advance. The ship was old and the engine room in bad condition. Here I showed my skill, and it impressed him. Then a true friendship developed and he was honorable to his word and delivered me in Gaza.

After a week of search I finally found my family in the Rafah Camp on the border of Egypt and the Sinai. It was the day of my great bereavement. Oh, my dear brother Ishmael, I still weep at the thought and sight of it. My beloved father, may Allah comfort him personally, had died of tuberculosis. He, who was the greatest living garage mechanic in all of Palestine, to die in such a place! While he lived, the family had managed. Now they were beyond destitution. Sixteen members of my clan were living in two rooms of a corrugated tin shack. Three of the children had died along with my father, and half of the rest were ill. The Rafah Camp is larger and far worse than Aqbat Jabar.

How can I make such a statement, you ask? Well, at least the Jordanians allowed us to travel freely. The Gaza Strip is jammed with humanity from one end to another and is kept like one large prison by the Egyptians. We were locked in like beasts. Before the UNRWA came, our people were so devastated by the Egyptian brutality that they did not have the will to protest. Fortunately, I gathered up enough extra ration cards to keep us alive.

The intimidation here to join the fedayeen was also much stronger than in Aqbat Jabar. The fedayeen were the only ones with jobs and were being paid five hundred percent more than ordinary wages. They were constantly making raids, but only a fool could not see there were too many losses and no successes.

What to do in such a place? I learned there was a special unit of the Egyptian Army made up of Palestinian commandos in training for the holy war against the Zionist intruders. It was an elite unit. The Egyptians promised that anyone who served in it would be given travel papers to Egypt. I did not trust the Egyptians, but there was no other way. My blessed mother sold the last piece of her jewelry of what had once been a great collection. With the money I was able to bribe the officer in command of the unit to enlist me as a sergeant and put me in charge of the vehicles.

It saved my life and the life of my family. Had I gone in as an ordinary commando, I probably would not be writing to you. People with the rank of sergeant and above did not have to make raids, only the privates and corporals. Those who did not get killed by Zionist bullets were so badly treated by the officers that most of them deserted. But that was their problem. Once I took over the garage the money came in. I was able to buy more ration cards on the black market and much more for my beloved family.

At last the gods of good fortune rained down on us when General Naguib, Colonel Nasser, and the Free Officers threw out the corrupt Egyptian king. With officers in control of the government, many raids were launched on British military posts along the Suez Canal. Although the attacks did not quite meet with the success we had hoped for, the new government and a friendly press played up the actions. They were very popular with the Egyptian people. After one raid in which we suffered great casualties, General Naguib brought us back to Cairo for a parade and personally gave the Palestinian unit a citation for courage. I again was able to bribe the commanding officer to discharge me from the unit to allow me to enroll in Cairo University.

Let me tell you, Ishmael, the university was not all that magnificent. There were fifty of us boys in a single dormitory room with our beds separated only by small nightstands. It smelled very bad, for it had not been cleaned in years. On the very first night my clothing and all my money was stolen, and I had to attend classes in my pajamas. We found out that none of the courses were free and the teachers were corrupt. Good grades went to the sons of the wealthy. Do I have to explain why? As destitute Palestinians we were the scum of the place, terribly maligned by the Egyptian people. They hated us and wanted to keep us locked up in Gaza. The Arab League paid our tuition and gave us four Egyptian pounds a month for food. When they stopped our subsidy, we were evicted from the barracks.

There is a cemetery on the outskirts of the city that is five miles in length, holds thousands of large sepulchers, and is called the City of the Dead. Almost a million people live there. Many of them have never known another home. I and four of my comrades were able to rent a large tomb for six Egyptian pounds a month. We were utterly destitute and on the brink of starvation and so began to demonstrate before the Arab League offices. We came back again and again until they restored our scholarships and allowances.

Many times our money was cut off, and when we demonstrated, more Palestinian students joined us. I and all of my comrades spent much time in jail. I was arrested on six different occasions. Yet we would not be dissuaded. Other Palestinians at Faud University and elsewhere were as desperate as we were, and in time we formed the Union of Palestinian Students. The Moslem Brotherhood was trying to bring down the new government, so we joined them. We got several martyrs, but the union was in business.

Just over a year ago the Brotherhood attempted to assassinate Colonel Nasser. Nasser dismissed General Naguib, claiming he was behind the attempt and then Nasser took complete charge of the democratic government. I and three brothers who were leaders of the student union were in jail for sixty-four days. During that time our brothers rioted constantly.

One day Dr. Mohammed K. Mohammed visited us. He was in charge of the Palestinian Refugee Aid Society. He had been our enemy because we felt he was a tool of the government. How wrong we had been! He is the true and noble leader of the Palestinian people. He told us that he had convinced Colonel Nasser that we students were truly the spearhead of the revolution and should be allies in the holy war to rid Palestine of the Jews. Can you believe that the four of us were released and invited to visit Colonel Nasser himself!

If there is Allah on earth, it is Colonel Gamal Abdel Nasser. I, Sabri Salama, was there before this mighty man. He made total and complete peace with us. He revealed many secrets. Fedayeen would now be able to travel freely to and from Gaza, and large bonuses would be paid them. As fast as units could be formed and trained, they were put into the conflict. He told us the greatest of secrets, that large shipments of arms were arriving from Czechoslovakia. He had already cut off the Zionists' shipping lanes in the Straits of Tiran, and soon he would take the Suez Canal from the British.

Very soon, Ishmael, we shall be united. All Arabs shall be under Nasser. I am now starting to travel with Dr. Mohammed K. Mohammed to convince various Arab governments to support our movement and contribute generously to the fedayeen. Soon we will no longer be dogs, rootless, frenzied, and anguished. Some unscrupulous nations such as the Syrians and Iraqis think they are fooling us because they plan to use the Palestinians for their own purposes. In the end we will trick them because we will unite and take over our own destiny.

If you ever hear the name Abu Rommel, you will know it is me. It is the revolutionary name I took in honor of the German general who nearly liberated Egypt during the world war. I urge you to get very active in the fedayeen. There is much money to be made in arming our boys. Tell your father I will pay him back soon. When you see me the next time, I will be in my own car and I will be wearing a gold watch.

I depart now, my beloved comrade Ishmael. I greet you once again in the name of the glorious revolution. All praise to our noble Dr. Mohammed K. Mohammed. All praise to Colonel Gamal Abdel Nasser, the greatest Arab leader since the Prophet, who will take the Arab people to their righteous destiny.

I weep for your martyred brother Jamil, who was slain by the Zionist pigs. We will live to see Tel Aviv in ashes and the Mediterranean Sea run red with the blood of fleeing Jews! Victory is ours!

My sincere greetings to the rest of your family.

Abu Rommel

Chapter Nine

Nada knew that the abruptness of her departure had the women in shock. She refused to join them in their tears as Hamdi Othman's white, chauffeur-driven United Nations car stopped before the house. She stood before Hamdi and Madame Othman, eyes lowered, as she was introduced and scrutinized. Mutual assurances were made. Nada's qualities were extolled by her father for the first time in her life. In turn, Hamdi Othman promised that the girl would be well looked after.

The chauffeur took the single bundle of Nada's belongings, and she and Madame Othman went outside as the men exchanged final pleasantries.

Nada looked about for a moment in desperation. Ishmael was gone! At that instant she felt as if she might break down, but instead she bore the pang in silence.

Nada had ridden in the back of two trucks but never inside an automobile. This and the elegant difference of Madame Othman shifted her mood from sorrow to curiosity.

Cars inside the camp always attracted a crowd of urchins. Othman's chauffeur was adept at driving them off like unwanted flies. The faces of Hagar, Fatima, and Ramiza filled the windows, sobbing their farewells. Haj Ibrahim remained inside as the car whisked away.

She knew three sets of curious eyes were on her. Strange, despite the intended humiliation of her baldness, Nada knew she was beautiful. She knotted her kerchief and tilted her chin up.

As they passed through Jericho, a sense of relief filled her. She caught Hamdi Othman's eye. His look was one of studied boredom. Obviously so high a personage would not have come over for her personally except for her father's stature. He ordered the chauffeur to bypass the waiting line of vehicles at the roadblock before the Allenby Bridge with the authority of a head of state.

"Stop the car!" Nada cried suddenly.

"What!"

"Please, it is my brother, Ishmael."

Othman made a magnanimous gesture as Nada flung the door open and threw herself into her brother's arms.

"Oh, I thought you were not going to say good-bye."

"I could not bear to be around the others," Ishmael said.

"I love you, Ishmael."

"Oh God, your hair . . ."

"What is the difference if I lost my hair, so long as I still have my head. Don't be sad, my brother. I am not sad. Do you understand? I am not sad."

Nada watched Ishmael grow smaller while the car drove noisily over the flapping timbers of the bridge. As they made for Amman she felt no sorrow. In fact, she was filled with anticipation and the sudden sense of freedom. A terrible burden was gone.

"Charming" was the word heard most about Hamdi Othman. A Syrian, Othman had developed his charm when the French governed his country and educated him. Charm was a paramount requisite for an aspiring diplomat.

When the United Nations unleashed its new bureaucracy, an army of middling functionaries swarmed to the bonanza. Each nation claimed its share of the lucrative posts, where quota, not quality, was the criterion. Hamdi Othman was one of Syria's questionable gifts to the new world order.

As a professional United Nations official, he crafted his way quickly through a mediocre corps, wiggling into a top-echelon position. Othman, as one of the UNRWA heads in Jordan and on the West Bank, wielded power and controlled large funds in a small kingdom of scores of refugee camps.

Personal involvement in the scenes and smells of privation in the camps belonged to the middle- and lower-rank UNRWA officials. Hamdi Othman's self-imposed status dictated an expansive villa on one of the bleak hills that crowned Amman.

Although the city was the capital of an Islamic state, its long British legacy had eroded the Moslem ban on alcohol. Life was boorish in this forsaken outpost, and the smattering of embassies, the United Nations agencies, and other foreign entities clung together desperately and isolated themselves from the hot dusty unpleasantness of Amman. Their modus operandi was the endless cocktail party.

There were cocktail parties to welcome or say farewell to am-
bassadors, first and second secretaries, consul generals, consuls,
military attachés, and United Nations officials. There were cocktail parties celebrating Bastille Day, the Fourth of July, and the
liberation, freedom, and independence days of every nation in
Jordan with diplomatic representation. Managing directors of
foreign corporations, visiting dignitaries, the airlines and tourist
industry, leading Jordanian businessmen, all had a place in the
pecking order of cocktail parties.

It was the same old troupe of wandering drinkers whose faces
wore dull-eyed masks. The conversation was either equally dull
or made up of slashing gossip, for the news of who was whoing
whom was the only real excitement except for an occasional royal
falcon hunt. The hand-kissing and the stifled yawns and the cast
of players seldom varied.

Hamdi Othman was a product of the cocktail party. Even in
Amman he thrived on it. His was one of the more "interesting"
invitations. His villa was sumptuous; his larder bulged with tax-
free, duty-free liquors and French delicacies. The mounds of
gourmet food were prepared by his French chef and a battery of
kitchen workers. All of this befitted the head of a relief organization.

Amman was still an Arab capital and Hamdi Othman was still
an Arab, and despite all that charm the sexes separated themselves, with the women herding together in one room and the
men in another.

Madame Othman represented the liberated Arab woman, educated in France, dressed in an elegant French wardrobe, and striking to behold. Still, if one peeled back the layer of Western veneer, Madame Othman was an Arab woman with an Arab
husband. Although she did not have to work, she was not allowed
to participate in much beyond social functions. Her life centered
on endless prattle at the city's one wretched country club. She
was never permitted outside their stifling world of kept, painted
birds, partying in lavish birdhouses that were really cages by another name. When the automatic handshake and smile were not
required, she was a sad, dull lady, locked into a life of uselessness.

Hamdi Othman prided himself that all of his household staff
were refugees, all fourteen of them. Hamdi Othman was neither
kind nor generous. Wages were a trifle, and what was not pro-

vided for in his expense allowances could be easily manipulated through his control of the UNRWA budget and the almighty ration card. His servants were barracked, and conditions and hours were severe.

His chauffeur, gardeners, bodyguards, butler, and houseboys occupied one cubicled dormitory. The six female employees lived as cloistered as nuns, in a barracks with curtained partitions. Four were kitchen help. There was Madame Othman's personal maid and there was Nada.

Nada was nursemaid to the Othmans' two daughters, ages three and four, and their five-year-old son. When she subsided from her initial anxiety and culture shock, Nada assumed her position firmly and rather joyously. Much to the relief of Madame Othman, Nada finally took the children off her hands, releasing her for more hours at the country club and before the dressing room mirror.

The Othmans' affection-starved children were soon tendered more love in a single day than their parents had ever afforded them. Nada was the perfect nanny. She sang many songs, read what she was able to read, laughed with them, told mystical and magical tales, hugged, kissed. She was quite stern when she had to be but never with a slap. She controlled them with a mere raising of her voice. There were never too many questions they could ask or games they could play. Nada did not complain. Nada worked any and all hours. What a little gem!

Aside from the madame's personal maid, Nada was the only female servant permitted in the main part of the villa. This was when she attended the children at play and meals and for the nightly parade before their father for their pat on the head or to show them off before company.

Although she had a curtained-off space with the other female servants, she slept on a mat on the floor of the girls' nursery.

"Nada!"

"Nada!"

"Nada!" they would cry, racing to get to her first in the morning.

"Well, let's see if I can hold three ugly bears all at once!" And she did.

Life burst open for her. Three beautiful and helpless little crea-

tures needed her, and she did not have to raise them in Aqbat
Jabar.

"Why don't you have hair, Nada?"

"To make you laugh."

The Othman villa, formerly belonging to a ranking British official, contained over twenty rooms, with a separate office compound where Othman worked with his UNRWA staff. Most
prominent of these was his personal secretary, a young French
diplomat named Bernard Joxe. Bernard aped his master's charm
and kowtowed to his master's will. A bachelor, his own quarters
were on the second floor of the main villa. He was an elegant
escort for Madame Othman when her husband traveled. He was a
great asset at cocktail parties, the target of many flirtations, although one had to be extremely careful in an Arab country.

The women servants had a walled-off yard containing a washing shed and an outdoor shower. Nada had been cautioned by her
fellow workers that the yard was not completely secluded. From
his apartment, Bernard Joxe was able to peer down and see a
small corner of the yard, so one had to take extra precautions for
modesty.

The house livened considerably with Nada's presence. Bernard
Joxe suddenly displayed a newborn passion for small children,
tweaking little noses, tossing screaming little bodies up into the
air and catching them, playing the horse in search of wee riders.

Conversation between Nada and Joxe was trivial and jovial.
She let her eyes do most of the talking. Perhaps Bernard Joxe did
not realize the risk of stalking a young Arab Moslem virgin girl.
Perhaps he did. He had a lovely boyish grin and winning man-
nerisms, and he wore his passionate nature close to the surface.
The game was on.

Nada's dreams became sweeter by the night.

A whole world centered around the accidental meeting, and
touch began to dominate her thoughts. Both of them put a great
deal of planning into where, when, and how to just happen to run
into each other. Her eyes made him shiver. The flush at suddenly
coming around a corner into one another, the brushing past, his
eyes riveted on her backside as she swayed by, his bashful stutter-
ing as he tried to speak . . .

Nada lay on her mat at night and felt her body and pantomimed holding him. Then: You are a foolish girl. Bernard Joxe is a selfish, ambitious young man who slobbers fearfully over his boss. He comes from a world that is utterly strange. He must have loved many girls and will love many more. I can be no more than a passing fancy.

Well, what do you want, Nada? Eternal love in a hovel in Aqbat Jabar? Can you even have that? You will take what Haj Ibrahim gives you. How lovely will that be?

What do you crave, Nada? You know it. You are away from Ibrahim's eyes. You have the place, the time, the young man drooling. Shall I? Shall I not? Shall I . . . her heart banged in her chest . . . shall I?

I will not do it fearfully. I'll do it either freely and wildly or not at all. I am not bringing shame in with me.

Shall I?

Nada had more freedom than the other women servants. She began to take her showers at a time when the yard was empty and when she knew Bernard Joxe was in his apartment. A bit of maneuvering and she could expose a wet arm or leg in that part of the yard that was not hidden. She knew instinctively when he was watching, and she grew bolder.

One day she stepped from the shower naked and dried herself, luxuriating in the sun in full view of the upper apartment. She stared up at it and held her eyes on it for a long time.

"You are driving me crazy," Bernard Joxe whined.

"Well?" Nada answered.

"It is very dangerous, you know that," he said.

"Well?" she repeated.

"For God's sake, what do you want me to do?"

"What do you *want* to do?"

He emitted a horrendous sigh, flopped his arms, and hung his head. She did not take her eyes from him. He swallowed. Nada touched his cheek and pressed her body against his shirt so he could feel the softness of her large lovely breasts. He wrapped his arms about her, closed his eyes, and groaned with happiness. The kiss was sweet.

"I like that," she said excitedly.

"I want it to stop right here. I must be honorable. You are not letting me be honorable," he muttered.

"Tell me, Bernard, have you made love with many women?"

"It is a ridiculous question."

"It is not. I want a man to take me who knows what he is doing and who is tender."

"Nada, do you really understand how complex this is?"

"Yes."

"I . . . I . . . there can be no question of . . . well . . . hurting you. We cannot fall in love. I have my career, my parents to think of. A scandal would be disastrous."

"Don't you want to do it with me?"

"Of course I do, but . . ."

"Bernard, I want absolutely nothing from you but your tenderness and a little time together. I want to have a beautiful time. If you will be patient, I will learn very quickly. You do not have to worry that you will break my heart or that I will make problems for you."

"Why, Nada, why?"

"It is a long story, Bernard, but I must know love and I will not be a little girl about it."

He twitched about nervously.

"You are kind and concerned and I like that," Nada said. "Let us be lovers and I will flit away when it is time."

"Don't look at me, Nada. You destroy me when you look at me. Don't press against me that way. . . ."

She spun away from him. "I think I'll take a shower," she said, walking off.

"Nada!"

"Yes?"

"The Othmans have a formal dinner tonight at the Indian Embassy. They will not be in until very late."

"I know," she answered. "I have played very hard with the children today. They will sleep through without a sound."

"Take your shower. The door to my apartment will be open."

He could not stop kissing her body.

"You are lovely," Nada said. "It was not so painful as I thought. How crazy my life has been to stifle something so lovely. Bernard, you sweet man. You are very thoughtful."

"It is you, Nada. How did you become so free, so, so uncomplicated."

"I will be freer now. And you will try everything, teach me everything. I want to do it all. Let me know what parts excite you and how to excite you. I want it all. I want to eat you alive."

"Oh yes, Nada . . . yes, yes, yes."

"Come in, Nada, sit down," Hamdi Othman said.

"Yes, sir."

"You have seemed fairly glowing this past month," he said, opening the cigar humidor and going through the ritual of clipping, wetting, spinning, lighting.

"I am very happy with the children," she said.

"Only the children?"

She looked into his thin debonair face, his eyes sparkling, a bit cruel, a bit tense.

"Life is much kinder here than in Aqbat Jabar. I hope my work has been worthy."

"The children adore you, you know that. Would you take the kerchief off your head, Nada?"

"I do not have much hair."

"Does that bother you?"

"Oh no, but when people look at me, they seem to feel uneasy."

"Well, will you take it off?"

She slipped it from her head. A growth of a few inches had returned. Somehow it made her look more poignant, even stunning.

"See, it doesn't offend me," Hamdi Othman offered. "In fact, you are an extraordinarily beautiful girl. Your father cut your hair, for modesty, didn't he?"

"Yes, sir."

"Well, you haven't been too modest, have you?"

"No," Nada answered without wavering or showing alarm.

He placed a tape recorder on his desk. "Have you ever seen one of these? Do you know what it is?"

"No."

"It makes a recording of people's voices. Would you like to hear yours?"

"Of me making love with Bernard," she said bluntly.

Hamdi Othman almost bit through his cigar. Her reaction took him completely off guard. "Well, do you think your father would like to hear it?" he said with a touch of menace.

Nada glowered, then shrugged. Othman studied the girl for a long time. She was apparently quite unafraid of him and completely in control of herself.

"There is an opening for a high UNRWA position in Syria. I am recommending Bernard for the job."

"As punishment?"

"It is an advancement."

"Does he know?"

"Yes. He is quite willing to leave Amman at once."

"Very well, Mr. Othman."

"You don't seem too upset, Nada."

"I will miss him very much, but we made no promises. I have no desire to hold him. We always knew it would only be for a short time."

"Now you tell me, Nada, what should I do with you?"

"I would like to remain in Amman in your home. I love the children. I don't know when I will have children of my own or if I'll ever have Allah's blessing. They give me much happiness."

"This business with you and Bernard is very serious. Fortunately, no one other than I knows about it. Shall we keep it that way?"

"Do as you wish, Mr. Othman. If you want to hear me plead with you, you are wasting your time."

His expression was that of a man who had been struck. The girl was becoming more interesting by the moment.

"Tell me, Nada, how would you like your own room?"

"I have never had my own room or even dreamed of such a thing."

"It could be arranged. Of course, with this secret we share . . . I realize I am not a young man like Bernard. . . . On the other hand . . . I am, shall we say, rather mature. As you know, Madame has a very full schedule, particularly on Thursdays. She spends the afternoon at the hair salon, after which there is her bridge club. What I am suggesting . . ."

"You want to make love with me."

He laughed. "You are a very cool piece of business, young lady."

"I think you are a very attractive man, Mr. Othman, and I do not mind making love in your wife's home. You do it with many women. However, I will not do it out of fear of your secret."

"Of course not, Allah forbid."

A small Mona Lisa smile crossed her lips. "If I am to stay, I would like the Sabbath and one other day each week when I do not have to work. Zeinah in the kitchen is quite capable of taking my place on those days. The children like her very much."

"Just what do you intend to do in Amman by yourself?"

"I want to join the fedayeen."

"You must tell me honestly, Nada, you must. Am I as good as Bernard Joxe?"

Nada rolled over on her back, stretched, and sighed happily as he kissed her nipples.

"Well, tell me, you damned little wench, tell me."

"You are magnificent, Hamdi."

"I am as good as Bernard Joxe. Say it."

"Am I as good as Madame Othman?"

"You are a bitch, a bitch, a little bitch. How does a peasant girl like you know how to make love this way?"

Hamdi Othman was indeed a lover with some finesse. But he was selfishly in love with himself. He demanded. He let himself go when he was ready. Then Nada simmered him down and demanded to be delighted by his many tricks.

She knew she would have to leave soon. The atmosphere was growing thick. Madame Othman had soured on her. It had happened with the woman many times before.

Hamdi Othman could never reveal the affair without bringing the walls crashing down on himself, for Nada was not to be intimidated. Moreover, she had gotten beneath his skin and he was now babbling out little cravings for her, showing little jealousies.

Nada had been careful to do it only during the safe times, and nothing had happened to get her with child. Making love with him, selfish as he was, had had different and wild moments. She now realized the new power of being able to drive a man slightly mad. It was a wonderment.

The moment Nada's eyes fell upon Joul, she knew that this could be the deep and meaningful love she craved. The fedayeen commander who exuded bravado and wore a revolutionary name proudly: Abu Azim, Father of the Leader. Joul was known for his bravery and cunning, having survived three raids over the border.

Nada saw through the outward mannerisms. He had Ishmael's penetrating eyes and wit. Joul had the sensitivity of her beloved brother. This love would be pure.

He was flattered by her attraction to him. Many other girls pursued him, but they were not Nada. Joul became uneasy about her forwardness at first, but he was hopelessly trapped in the web of her beauty. They spoke long and passionately about their plight and growing feelings. He was bound to a traditional family, but one of low station. Nada knew Haj Ibrahim would reject him out of hand.

There came that day and moment of complete aloneness with him, away from the mad atmosphere of the camp and the stilted air of Amman. Joul poured out his love. Nada spoke of making love. He was perplexed by a lifetime of conditioning. He did not know what to do. But he was going wild with wanting her.

"I want you, Joul, and I am not afraid of afterward. Let's have each other and let tomorrow take care of itself. You don't have to promise anything."

"I love you so much. I think of nothing but you, Nada. I am going out of my mind."

"Let us feel each other without clothing."

"Yes," he whispered.

Nada took his hand. "Before we do it, you must know that my virtue has been taken."

Joul registered astonishment.

"It happened in Jaffa after we had fled our village. One day I was walking alone through narrow alleys from the market. Iraqi soldiers seized me and raped me. Three of them."

He could not look into her sad eyes. Tears ran down his cheeks.

"Does it matter?" she asked a bit apprehensively.

"No."

Nada unbuttoned her dress and lowered it down her shoulders until she had revealed her breasts. She took his head and pressed it against her. "They're yours. . . . Softly . . . sweetly . . . Oh yes, I knew you would be so gentle."

Slowly and beautifully Nada opened the gates of paradise to him. It was a free and unashamed love that did not dim or tire.

Hamdi Othman was furious when she locked her door on him.

His threats fell flat. Her counterthreats warning him about the fedayeen scared him into sobering. He had been discarded and he had to live with it.

Nada and Joul remained lovers for several months. All of their bottomless frustrations and anger exploded into lovemaking. There were tears this time, deep, bitter tears. There was the quandary of their prison.

When the time came for her to visit Aqbat Jabar she sent a note that she was ill and could not come until her next time off. The lovers devoured one another, clawed desperately to get deeper inside and shut out that ugly world around them.

Pressures built. Gossip surfaced. They were discovered by one of his friends. Secrets of such a nature were impossible to keep in this tight little watching world. Joul was beyond dirt poor and he was swallowed up by the desperation of their situation.

His manliness turned to confusion. He could not bring himself to rise and take on a fight for her. As the moment of truth awaited, Joul cowered and fled.

Chapter Ten

Shortly after Omar and Nada left, my own spirits were unexpectedly lifted. I hung around Dr. Nuri Mudhil to make myself useful. He could only shoo me away so many times until he gave up.

For several years a British archaeological expedition had been uncovering ancient Jericho. Dr. Mudhil was an associate, their Arab connection. At first Ibrahim forbade me to get involved. This only whetted my appetite. After Nada was exiled, Father knew well of my bitterness. Rather than invite the risk that would cause me to run away, he relented. It was a relief to get out of the Wadi Bakkah School, which had turned into a hate factory, where all values of peace and love had been totally lost.

The Jericho dig set off a rash of secondary activity in the region. A Bedouin discovery across the river created a new flurry of excitement. Some ancient Hebrew artifacts had been discovered at a site near the base of Mount Nebo, the place from which Moses saw the promised land and died, after commissioning Joshua to take the tribes across the Jordan River into Canaan.

Dr. Mudhil was granted funds to mount a small exploratory dig in search of a possible ancient Hebrew settlement. If our clues proved out, it could turn into a major discovery. My work at Jericho had been so good that he went to Ibrahim to get permission for me to run the Arab crew.

Father agreed reluctantly. He realized if permission were denied, it might cause a permanent rift between us. His objections soon faded when he understood that the best way to curb my wanderlust was to keep me digging around Jericho.

The Mount Nebo exploration had an archaeologist, ten student volunteers from Europe, and a dozen workers. I organized their camp, was foreman of the Arab laborers, got the permits, made the payroll, kept the supplies, water, and medicine current, and set up security against Bedouin infiltration.

I was excellent at the job. I now had my own Jeep and was able to slip into Amman every fortnight to see Nada. Although I knew how she craved love, she did not tell me her secrets at first. She feared I would revert to our most sacred canon and demand vengeance.

She had blossomed into a magnificent flower. Her eyes were keen, her way was sure, her entire personality had soared. Despite the dangerous road she was traveling, I knew that she was experiencing what might become the only richness and fulfillment she might ever know. As for me . . . if you love someone, as I loved her, then her happiness became more important to me than killing the man or the men who were making her happy. Does that make sense? Was I betraying my own sense of honor? Somehow it did not matter. Only Nada mattered. I did not want to meet those men face to face, for that might have triggered false pride.

When it came down to it, out of all our family, Nada and I were the only two who truly trusted one another.

What I did not like was the tension between her and Father. He sensed her growing independence, her maturing as an individual. Although she was completely obedient on her visits to Aqbat Jabar, Ibrahim was reading between the lines.

Meanwhile, I was engaged in an affair of the heart myself. One of the European volunteers was a nice-looking English girl of twenty named Sybil. I had heard that English women were cold in matters of sex. I laugh my socks off when I think of it now.

Sybil came to Jordan filled with girlish notions of being swept off her feet by a romantic Arab sheik. Well, I filled the role and more than adequately, I must admit. My Jeep had to serve as the noble Arabian stallion that whisked her off to our desert lair. We both lied to each other with extreme sincerity about the eternal nature of our love. I confess that, even with my vast experience with widow ladies, Sybil taught me numerous wonderments.

When the digging season ended before the summer's heat of 1956, I became glum. Sybil and the others packed off to Europe. I was left with hundreds of pieces of a broken heart as well as broken pottery to fit together.

Although we were finished digging until next year, I still had a great deal to do at Mount Nebo. We had come tantalizingly close to uncovering an important site, perhaps a wall, and there were indications we might hit a graveyard and an altar. One can only endure a dig in the desert if one dreams that tomorrow or the day after or the day after we will uncover a monumental find.

Since anything built by the ancient Hebrews would have a great deal of mud brick, it could easily be washed away. So in addition to setting up a full-time guard, I had to cover the site against rain.

My ultimate reward was to be able to work side by side with Dr. Mudhil as we went through the painstaking business of recording, restoring, measuring, and drawing what had been unearthed.

I was working one day with a puzzle of two hundred potsherds hoping for a unique restoration. My mood obviously spilled into the workroom.

"You are getting very sloppy with that pot," he said, peering down the bench from where he was making drawings.

I muttered a nothing.

"It is always a sad time when the dig closes for the season. But . . . another year, another Sybil will come. You would not think upon observing this bent creature that I have been invited into the tents of many lady archaeologists and volunteers. Ah, I see you are in no mood for small talk. What is it, Ishmael?"

"Jamil is dead, Omar is gone, and Kamal is worthless. It is just that when everyone leaves, I remember again that I am still here." I found a piece I was looking for. It seemed to fit on the pot I was building. But even these illusive and taunting little potsherds were easier to put together than one's life.

I was afraid to bring up the subject because I dreaded his answer, but I knew I must. "I heard a rumor that this is your last season."

"It is not a rumor."

I shut my eyes for an instant to bear the jolt, then toyed with the little bit of broken clay in my hand. "Where are you going?"

"I have been invited to London to work on the publication of our findings. In truth, when one is as crippled as I, one is not a candidate for long life. I am seriously in need of medical attention."

"I am ashamed," I said. "I have been so filled with my own problems, I should have seen that you have been in pain." I wanted to cry for his pain and for me, losing him. I fumbled about for words. "What about your contact with the Jews?"

"Someone else will be found."

"I have always marveled that you were never caught."

"Oh, but I was. I was never a real spy. Long ago both sides saw a use for me to deliver messages. The contact between Jordan and Israel must always be kept open."

I was afraid he was going to ask me to take the job. I quickly changed the subject. "Father believes in Nasser. He says, How much longer must we Arabs bear Western guilt for the holocaust and how long will the Jews collect interest on it? Father says the Zionists are bringing in hundreds of thousands of Jews from Arab lands to replace us in Palestine. But they live in squalor, just like Aqbat Jabar. . . . He says—"

"However," Dr. Mudhil interrupted, "the Jews are not bleating to the world to make charity cases of their brothers. They are dismantling their refugee camps as quickly as they can build towns. They are moving thousands into decent homes and giving them useful work. They are clearing land to be farmed. The lives of those Jews who fled Arab countries destitute will be different than yours. Do you realize, Ishmael, that over twenty million refugees are in the world today from India to Africa? Of them all, the Arabs alone have the resources to dissolve their refugee problem, if they wanted to. We have vast oil moneys, more jobs in the Gulf states than can be filled by all the Palestinians put together. We have rich lands in the Euphrates Valley and the vast emptiness of Libya. The only thing we lack is the one thing the Jews have in abundance."

"What is that?"

"Love. Yes, the Jews love one another. They will not tolerate fellow Jews living in such pestholes as Aqbat Jabar."

"Deep in Father's heart, he knows that. He cannot admit it to himself anymore. After all, Father did try to do things differently."

"Yes, he did."

"But now . . . sometimes I don't know him. He says that with the Russians as Nasser's ally, Nasser will be able to unite the Arab world like no one since Mohammed."

"Nonsense. Islam is unable to live at peace with anyone. We Arabs are the worst. We can't live with the world, and even more terrible, we can't live with each other. In the end it will not be Arab against Jew but Arab against Arab. One day our oil will be

gone, along with our ability to blackmail. We have contributed
nothing to human betterment in centuries, unless you consider
the assassin and the terrorist as human gifts. The world will tell
us to go to hell. We, who tried to humiliate the Jews, will find
ourselves humiliated as the scum of the earth. Oh, put down that
silly potsherd and let us have some coffee."

In a moment we were seated on either side of his desk, my
favorite place. It was the best place to be until I saw him wince
with pain.

"As you know, Ishmael, I never had children. I feared something warped like me might be born. Have you considered the
possibility of going to London with me?"

"Oh, Dr. Mudhil, I have dreamed of hearing your words. But I
know that if I leave, I will never be able to face myself. I cannot
be a traitor."

"To what? A social system that will never grant you freedom or
the beauty of unique thought?"

"I will not leave Nada until she is safe. And, as for Father . . ."

"Don't you understand? You and Nada are pawns in his mind
about a world he will never see. Ishmael is a vague dream of Haj
Ibrahim's future. Nada is a vague memory of Tabah and his past,
the euphoria of selling her to a great sheik or into wealth. Do you
want to live out your days for an old man's fantasy?"

"Please, stop. You yourself told me a hundred times that no one
can break the bonds of Arab society. Will you be free, even when
you are in London?"

"No, I will never be free, but I will end my days without frustration and rancor. All you can have is half a loaf. Try for it,
Ishmael. Take your sister and escape."

"Don't you think I haven't spent a thousand and one nights
plotting an escape?"

"Then go, boy, go!"

"Where to, Dr. Mudhil, the seven paradises?"

I stepped into the streets of Jericho and filled my lungs with
hot stale air. As I passed the line of cafés and stores, everyone
nodded in greeting out of respect to my father.

A truck filled with fedayeen roared down the street, stirring up
a cloud of dust. They fired their rifles into the air.

"Itbakh al Yahud!" they chanted. "Death to the Jews!"

Cairo radio crackled over a loudspeaker. President Nasser decried American and Zionist treachery.

War fever was swelling. Everyone was pumping himself up for the coming fight against Israel.

Street urchins played in a sewer.

I stopped before a beggar of grotesque proportions and gave him a coin. Dr. Mudhil had once been a beggar. He had been saved. No such luck for this fellow.

What was it that Dr. Mudhil had read to me by T. E. Lawrence, that great English hero of the Arabs? He said . . . let me think . . . yes, I remember: The Arabs have no halftones in their register of vision. . . . They exclude compromise and pursue the logic of their ideas to its absurd ends, without seeing the incongruity of their opposed conclusions. Their convictions are by instinct, their activities intuitional. . . .

Clever man, that Lawrence of Arabia, clever man.

Chapter Eleven

WAR!

From the moment Colonel Gamal Abdel Nasser had seized control of the Egyptian Government two years earlier, he had marched down an irreversible path. His goal was the oft-stated obsession to destroy Israel.

Father and I watched events unfold with opposing reactions. I did not see any purpose for a war insofar as the Palestinian refugees were concerned. Despite Sabri's exuberance, Nasser would really do nothing to better our conditions. If he won and we returned to our homes, we would only be exchanging Jordanian tyranny for Egyptian tyranny. He was only using us.

On the other hand, Haj Ibrahim had been completely swept up by Nasser fever. He could think now just in terms of a war against the Jews. He was unable to foresee what would happen beyond the day we returned to Tabah.

I do not give you the various episodes in their order of occurrence, for they often overlapped and intertwined. However, what Nasser and the other Arab governments did was important.

Nasser undermined Jordan by promoting refugee riots in the West Bank, then forced Jordan into a military alliance under his command. He was heavily bankrolled by the Saudis, who were the mortal enemies of the Hashemites and who were as interested in Jordan's demise as they were in the defeat of the Zionists.

Nasser encouraged Syria to attempt to cut off Israel's source of water at the Jordan River headwaters.

Nasser stopped all ships destined for Israel from using the Suez Canal.

Nasser closed the Strait of Tiran to all Israeli shipping, to and from Eilat, thus denying Israel a route to the Orient. These closures of international waterways were, in themselves, acts of war.

The United States was committed to funding the building of a high dam on the Nile at Aswan. When Nasser arbitrarily seized the Suez Canal and nationalized it, Americans withdrew their support for the dam.

Russia had a centuries-old dream of a warm-water port and was eager to get a foothold in the Middle East. The Soviet Union rushed in to fill the vacuum created by America's withdrawal from Egypt. Billions of rubles were pledged to complete the dam. Along with it came a massive influx of Russian weapons.

After seizure of the Suez Canal, Nasser refused to attend an international maritime conference to discuss the waterway's future, thus putting the Western economies in peril and suddenly giving Russia a frightening position in the region.

Nasser had at his beck and call the armies of Syria, Yemen, and Saudi Arabia and received assurances of full co-operation from Iraq and the balance of the Arab world.

During this period Egypt armed and trained the Palestinian fedayeen. Nasser was responsible for launching three thousand fedayeen raids into Israel on missions of murder and terror.

Flaunting international law and promising daily to exterminate the Jews, Nasser moved his legions, bulging with Soviet weaponry, through the demilitarized zones of the Sinai.

On October 29, Israel struck first.

I remember well the smell of war in the air and a tension so awesome it crackled like electricity. The sky seemed dark at noon. It was like our last days in Tabah and the battle for Jaffa all over again.

We were to learn later that Israel had gone into a secret alliance with the British and French, who were still enraged over the seizure of the Canal. The plan was a two-pronged strike. Israel would hit first, crossing the Sinai. Britain and France would then take the Canal.

The British and French lost their nerve under American and Russian pressure and quit in mid-battle. Israel had to go it alone.

On the first day Radio Cairo announced one smashing victory after another. Demonstrations proclaiming Nasser as the new Messiah erupted like wildfire among the West Bank refugees. With each new bulletin, a new madness was unleashed. People were going absolutely berserk with joy. We would be returning home within the week!

The first night was long and sleepless as we gleaned the airwaves for any kind of news. Everyone was exhausted but euphoric on that second morning. Then, a faint taste of ashes, a first bewilderment. Cairo began to modify its victory announcements. The French and British were bombing hospitals and schools. Those advances into Israel claimed on the first day were now being reported as "fierce" battles in which Egypt was "defending" positions it had previously reported as having captured.

The craziness around us screeched to a halt. Where was Syria? Where was Jordan? Why had they not joined the battle?

By the end of the third day the truth could no longer be contained. Minute by minute, hour by hour, stories and rumors flooded in.

Israel had routed the Egyptian Army!

The Jews had swept over the Sinai and in less than ninety hours crushed Nasser's legions and sat on the eastern bank of the Canal.

Nasser screamed foul!

On the fourth night of the war all illusions were shattered. I had returned to the dig at Mount Nebo and was awakened by a radio call from Dr. Mudhil.

"Ishmael, you must return to Jericho at once. A panic is starting to sweep through the camps. Ibrahim cannot be found. Find him and bring him to my office. It is urgent!"

It was no small task to pick up the desert track in the darkness and link up with the main highway. Although distances were short, it took me several hours to return. The Allenby Bridge was alive with Legion soldiers. Fortunately, my documents were from a high minister and my comings and goings to and from Mount Nebo were known by the guard, and I crossed over with only minimal problems. Yet it was past midnight when I reached Aqbat Jabar.

Rumors that the Jews were on the way to conduct a massacre wailed from mouth to mouth. A state of near-hysteria had seized the camp. People were running about confused while others were packing. Oh Lord, it was the recurrence of a nightmare!

There was a place on Mount Temptation where I knew that Ibrahim meditated. I had shared it with him on many occasions. I ran through the camp and fought my way up into the hills with my flashlight darting off the stone walls.

"Father!" I called frantically.

The only response was my own echo.

"Father! Father! Father!" I screamed.

My light hit him. He sat stilled, obviously numbed by events. Oh, his eyes were beyond weary. For the first time I realized that his beard had gone almost completely white. He stared up at me, but not seeing. Tears fell down his cheeks.

"Father . . ." I panted.

"Is it over?"

"Yes."

"Allah!" he moaned. "This is the most horrible moment of them all. I let myself be taken in. I listened like any other poor dumb fellah. I allowed my brain to be twisted. Ibrahim! You are the worst of fools! Nasser!" he cried and spat on the ground.

"Please, Father, you have no time to berate yourself now. The people are overcome with fear. They are running around in circles screaming that the Jews are going to slaughter them. Families are packing up to flee. Dr. Mudhil has received messages. You must come with me at once to his office."

"Run! Why? There are three thousand fedayeen here to protect them."

"The fedayeen have fled."

By the time we arrived at Dr. Mudhil's office, Ibrahim had gained control of himself. It was past four in the morning. Clans were already forming up in Jericho to bolt at daybreak. We entered through the workroom. A small light beckoned us from his office. Nuri Mudhil's twisted body was at the window. He stared down at the growing fright in the streets. On the other side of the room a man leaned against a bookcase.

"Colonel Zyyad!"

"Yes, it is I, Haj Ibrahim."

Oh, how Father wanted to kill him! With anxiety, I watched his hands open and close. I stepped between them.

"Your boy is clever," Zyyad said. "All right, here it is. The Egyptian Army is defeated. King Hussein wisely declined to get involved in Nasser's folly. Instead, we struck a deal with the Jews. The Legion will not move against Israel, and Israel will not move against East Jerusalem and the West Bank."

"There is no cause for panic down there," Dr. Mudhil said.

"When they are frenzied like this, nothing can stop them," Father said.

Dr. Mudhil pulled back from the window and limped over to us. "Colonel Zyyad has two battalions of Legion at the bridge. He has orders to shoot to kill if anyone attempts to cross."

"In Allah's name, what for? If you open fire, they will swarm over in a hundred places. What will you accomplish by killing two, three, four thousand terrified people with their wives and children?"

"The more Palestinians there are in Jordan, the more our kingdom is in danger. We have had our fill, Haj Ibrahim. If it were up to me . . ."

"Shut up, Zyyad," Nuri Mudhil demanded. "We know what you would do. After all, what is one massacre more or less in our history." Dr. Mudhil grabbed my father's robes. "Fortunately, the king has issued an order to allow us to try to make a peaceful attempt to stop them from crossing the bridge. You, Ibrahim, are the only man who can turn these people back."

The smallness, creakiness, and dilapidation of the Allenby Bridge gave no hint of its tremendous importance.

"Move your men out of sight, beyond the first ridge," Ibrahim said to Colonel Zyyad. "And bring me a loudspeaker."

"Remember, if they push past you and cross the bridge, we shall return and open fire."

"Yes, I know, Colonel Zyyad. You are hoping I will fail, aren't you?"

Dawn.
I took my place alongside my father before the bridge. We were by ourselves, naked in the gunsights of a thousand rifles. The mass coming toward us from Jericho took form and shape like locusts sweeping in from the desert. At that moment my father had regained my heart. Alone and noble, he faced the frantic crowd. His great presence shocked everyone to halt, and in that flickering of a second he grabbed command of the situation.

"Stop!" he roared through the bullhorn.
"Do not try, Haj Ibrahim! We are crossing!"
"The Jews are attacking up the Dead Sea!"
"They will be in Jericho within the hour!"
"Their bombers are already on the way!"
"Thousands have been slaughtered in East Jerusalem!"

"Rashid!" my father commanded of an aged sheik at their head. "Step forward!"

Rashid turned to the mob, held his hands up to quiet them, and walked alone toward Father and me.

"It is no use, Ibrahim," Rashid said.

"We have fled our homes once without making a stand and look how we have suffered for it! You cannot flee again!"

"We will be murdered!"

"Ibrahim, stand aside," Rashid warned.

The crowd pressed forward.

"I have been to Mount Temptation!" Ibrahim called out like a Moses. "I have spoken to Mohammed!"

The mob was shocked into stillness.

"Mohammed came to me last night! He told me that Allah has placed a curse upon this bridge and this river! The first man who tries to cross will not reach the other side alive! Allah will strike him blind! Allah will open up his stomach and let the vultures feed on it before he reaches Jordan!"

"Ibrahim lies!" Rashid cried.

My father stepped aside and left a clear path over the bridge.

"I invite Sheik Rashid to cross first!" Father called through the loudspeaker. "If you reach the other side alive, may Allah strike me dead!"

The raging fire within them had been stopped as though by a miracle. Sheik Rashid chose not to step onto the bridge. He backed up.

"Who will save us from the Jews?"

"I, Haj Ibrahim al Soukori al Wahhabi, give you the sacred word of Mohammed that you will not be harmed! Now return to your homes!"

"Haj Ibrahim is great!"

"Allah will save us!"

Little clumps of men and women splintered off and started to drift back toward Jericho . . . and others . . . and others. Then Rashid made his own way back.

After a time Father and I were alone again. He looked at me and patted me on the shoulder. "You are a brave young man, Ishmael," he said. "Come, take me home. I am tired."

"I love you, Father," I cried. "I love you."

Chapter Twelve

A week after the war I returned to Mount Nebo. Although universal grief and bewilderment overcame the refugees, a strange and different thing happened to Father and me. Instead of despair, Haj Ibrahim seemed to have come through a long, dark tunnel. He had snapped back to realism. He would follow Colonel Nasser no further. Indeed, he gave off a hint or two that life might have more in store for us than Aqbat Jabar. He did not speak directly of returning to Tabah or of making a deal with the Jews. He did, however, call on Dr. Mudhil a number of times. I felt he was fishing about to find an honorable way to end our exile.

Being out there in the desert, perhaps I had lulled myself with the stars and the stillness, but a surge of hope ran through my veins. Father listened to me. Given time and very careful planning, I might convince him it would not be the end if I went off to study. Surely, within a few years we could all be reunited and resettled in a decent place. Maybe even away from Palestine or the Arab countries.

Or was I crazy? What of Nada? Father must never know of her loss of virtue. That would be fatal to any plan. My first order of business was to try to make peace between them. At times they seemed to care for each other, but always their visits ended with acid.

Something was under their skins close to the surface and ready to flare. Nada had decried her life, but she never really spoke out directly against Ibrahim. Sometimes I felt she hated him. True, he would never come to terms with an independent woman, but they were both so great there had to be a way for them to find mutual respect.

Why did he always seem to pick an argument?

Yes, my first task would be to bring them into a friendly relationship. Then we could dream about a move.

I studied the sky. It didn't look good. Nada was coming home tomorrow for three days, but I still had a section of corrugated roof to finish ahead of the weather.

I called Dr. Mudhil on the radio.

"Yes, Ishmael."

"I think I'd better stay tomorrow and finish the roof," I said. "I don't want to leave this section open for three days."

"Good man."

"Would you get a message home to Nada that I will be late?"

"Yes, of course, I'll take care of it. Everything else all right out there?"

"Fine, just wonderful. I am happy here."

Ibrahim had to admit to himself that he was actually looking forward to Nada's visit the next day. Why not admit it? He had missed her. When Dr. Mudhil came with a message that Ishmael would be late in returning, a lovely new thought passed through his mind. Maybe, during this visit, with Ishmael late in returning, he would take Nada on a stroll and speak to her, person to person. He had never done that. She seemed to be learning much in Amman.

He had judged his children. Of the eleven who had been born, died, survived, married, he had to admit to himself that Nada was his favorite after Ishmael. On this visit he was determined that he would bite his tongue before he spoke harsh words to her. If he cared for her so, why did he always have to try to hurt and offend her? he wondered.

The women cackled over Nada as though they were in a chicken yard. How beautiful she looked! She had become even more so in just the few months since her last visit. There was something wonderful about Nada's ways. She carried an air of surety that few women had.

Nada rekindled her auntship to Fatima's children. She brought gifts, little nothings that the Othman children had discarded. In a place where toys did not exist, these were like jewels.

"Come, Nada, your father is waiting for you," Hagar said. She felt her mother's hands nervously edge her out of the kitchen. "Please try not to fight this time. I believe Ibrahim has really wanted to see you." Nada entered the gathering room. The women followed her in and went quickly to their stools.

Ibrahim postured in his new deep seat as his daughter stepped before him and bowed. She smiled, but it was not a smile of sweetness. There was bitter brew beneath it. Ibrahim drank her in for a long time but squelched any ideas of commenting about her loveliness. He motioned for her to bring a stool up closer to him.

"How was your journey?"

"The ride does not change between the bus station in Amman and the bus station in Jericho."

"I would have sent Ishmael to escort you, but he is racing the weather at Mount Nebo. I know it is not proper to allow you to travel alone, but as long as it is a direct route I felt it was all right this one time. It will not happen again."

"There is no need to worry, Father."

"Ah, but no woman in my family travels alone."

"Of course, Father."

"And how is the honorable Hamdi Othman?"

Nada merely nodded.

"And your position?"

She nodded again.

He was becoming annoyed by her closed behavior. Her eyes bore down on him in such a manner that he began to feel slightly ill at ease. Ibrahim had occasionally seen a woman act out a protest. It is time that Nada did so. She thinks she is worldly. Well, I will put that in order. Ask her for that stroll? No, not in her sour mood. I shall be patient, he thought.

"You must have a great many tales to tell," he said.

"There is nothing all that exciting about taking care of three small children. Fatima can vouch for that."

Fatima giggled at the recognition.

"Surely it must be exciting to be in such a grand villa with all those important officials coming and going."

"I am scarcely part of that, Father. I only go into the living areas on occasion, generally to show the children before their bedtime."

"Madame Othman is kind to you?"

"As kind as she can be under the circumstances."

"What circumstances, Nada?"

"I am a servant. They have many servants."

"But you are special."

"I don't feel very special."

"Certainly you are. You are the daughter of Haj Ibrahim al Soukori al Wahhabi!" Ibrahim scratched the back of his hand uncomfortably under her continued hard stare. "We must have a talk together during this visit. Yes?"

"As you wish, Father."

He flushed a bit at her cold terseness. It was what he was beginning to suspect. Being in a villa like that in a city, she was mingling with girls who did not respect tradition. It might have been a mistake to send her there in the first place. Well, a little rebellion. He certainly did not want to make a fight but he was not going to let her get away with treating him this way.

"I have a surprise for you, Nada. Since your last visit I have suddenly become aware that you have flown past the usual age when I should have found you a husband. Because of the cruel circumstances of our life here, I was determined not to be too hasty in this matter. Our fortunes have changed for the better. Omar will soon be going to Kuwait, where he will have a job as a clerk in a fine hotel. Ishmael has had good earnings with Dr. Mudhil, and I have reached a position of comfort. It is time to reconsider the matter of your marriage. I have been approached by a number of fathers desirous of entering into an arrangement. I wanted to make certain you have as fine a husband as your sisters have. Seeing how you have matured, your value as a wife has increased greatly. I have waited until offers of substance were made. We need wait no longer."

The women opened their arms in joy and emitted long "ahs."

"I am not in a hurry. I am very happy in Amman."

Aha, Ibrahim thought, now my dear daughter does not act so arrogantly! She knows who her father is again. Of course I am not going to marry her off so soon, but I shall play a bit. I shall keep her guessing . . . in her place.

"We will speak of your marriage possibilities at length while you are here," Ibrahim pressed. "Since you are my last daughter, I am even going to allow you to be part of the decision . . . but depend on me to select exactly the right man. I am very good at that."

Nada arose from the stool and walked toward him. "I will not marry until I am ready," she said, firmly speaking the first words of defiance to him in her life. The women shrank back.

Ibrahim's eyes narrowed. "It is as I suspected. I believe you are cavorting with indecent girls who do not have the proper respect for their fathers. You will never speak to me in that tone again and you will marry where, when, and whom I tell you." He clapped his hands for his wives and Fatima to leave.

"Wait!" Nada commanded them. They froze in astonishment. "I will not marry until I am ready," she repeated, "and I will marry whom I wish."

Ibrahim arose authoritatively. He slapped her face. "Have you veiled yourself in public as I ordered?"

"No."

He slapped her again and jerked the scarf from her head. "You have grown back too much hair. I find it offensive. Hagar, get the scissors."

"No, Father, you will not cut my hair."

"Hagar! Bring the scissors at once. Let me tell you, Nada, that the honor and virtue of this family are going to be kept!"

"You need not worry about your honor and my virtue any longer," she said.

"Be quiet, Nada!" her mother cried.

Ibrahim glowered in disbelief. "What do you mean by that?"

"I am no longer a virgin."

Wails arose from the women. Ramiza swooned and fainted. Ibrahim's eyes widened crazily.

"You are lying!" he screamed grotesquely. He waved his hands about in a quandary. "Is it true what you say!"

"Yes."

"You were raped, forced against your will. Is that not what happened!"

"No, Father, I was willing."

"You . . . you are with child!"

"Perhaps, perhaps not. What does it matter?"

"Who is he!"

"They, Father."

"You have done this to deliberately humiliate me!"

"Yes, I did, Father."

"Deliberately . . . to humiliate me . . . to destroy my honor. . . . You did it . . ."

"I have heard you ask many times, Who will tell the lion his breath smells bad? You are a savage, Father. If you feel pain now, feel it deep and hard because it is the pain you have made me bear every day of my life. I do not fear for my life because it never really began. It never really happened. I never lived for me, only for you. So do your noble duty."

"Nada, come back here!"

"Go to hell, Father."

"Nada!"

"Ishmael once read to me about the whore of Jericho who hid the spies of Joshua. So avenge the shame your daughter, the whore, has brought upon you. I will be walking in the alleys of Jericho. You will find me."

As she left, Ibrahim stormed into his bedroom and returned strapping his belt and dagger on. He tore for the entrance. Hagar blocked the way, fell on her knees, and threw her arms about him.

"No, Ibrahim! Send her away. We will never speak her name!"

Ramiza flung herself at him and clutched him. He threw them off violently, then kicked them back. They writhed on the floor rending their hair as he staggered out.

Nada's body was found the next morning in a gutter of Jericho. Her neck had been broken and her throat slashed. Her hair had been crudely hacked off.

Chapter Thirteen

The moment I saw Dr. Mudhil at the Allenby Bridge and the agony on his face, I knew what had happened without being told.

"Nada," he said and nothing more.

How strange. I did not cry. Dr. Mudhil begged me not to go to my father's house. He begged me to come with him to London.

"No, I am going home now."

Strange . . . I could not cry . . . and I was not frightened. . . .

I could feel the terrified eyes of my mother riveted to me as I pushed past a fearful knot of neighbors. I entered the gathering room.

Haj Ibrahim sat in his great chair awaiting me. His eyes bulged twice the size of normal and red veins flooded through them. His face echoed weird shadows from the flickering light before the photographs of Omar and Jamil. I stared at him, probably for an hour. Nothing could be heard but our grunting breathing.

"Speak! Speak! I command you to speak!" he said in a voice foreign to me.

Another hour passed. His eyes rolled back in his head. He fought his way out of his seat and walked unevenly to the table. He opened his robes, took out his dagger, still with Nada's blood on it, and sank it into the tabletop.

"You . . . you were once my hope . . .," he rasped. "But you do not have the courage of a woman." He came to me and bared his throat. "Go on, Ishmael, do it!"

"Oh yes, yes. I am going to kill you, Father, but I'll do it my own way. I don't need your dagger. I'm just going to talk. I'm going to talk you to death. So open your ears, Father, and listen very carefully." He stared at me. I began. "In Jaffa, I witnessed both of your wives and Fatima being raped by Iraqi soldiers!"

"You are a liar," he snarled.

"No, Father, I do not lie. There were eight or ten of them, and one after the other they came at the women and I saw their big wet slimy pricks coming inside them!"

"Liar!"

"They jerked off on the naked bodies of your wives. They laughed and slapped their asses! They had a wonderful time!"

"Liar!"

"Go on, Father! Pull your dagger out of the table and kill me. Kill us all!"

Ibrahim suddenly grasped his chest and screamed as an awful pain hit him. He gasped for air: "My heart . . . my heart . . ." He reeled about the room, bumping into everything. He fell. I stood above him.

"Can't you get your knife out of the table, Father? No? Too bad. I watched Mother being fucked on the floor by a half-dozen of them! Fucked on the floor!"

"YAHHHHHHH!"

He was on his hands and knees, crawling and wheezing and gagging, with slobber coming from his nose and eyes and mouth.

"YAHHHHHHH!"

He reached the table and tried to pull himself up. He put his hand around the hilt of the dagger and tugged. It would not come out. The table toppled over. He lay and gurgled, screamed, and then was very still.

Chapter Fourteen

The family crept back into the house, chilled with terror. I expected them to rant and rage at the sight of Ibrahim's dead body at my feet. Oddly, they did not. They stared at me, then shrank back in fear. It suddenly occurred to me that in that instant they completely accepted me as their new master. I remained impassive, almost removed. And then, a flush of elation. I had avenged my beloved sister and I had done so by bringing down the most powerful and awesome man I had ever known. I could have screamed for joy at the way I killed him. He died in pain with a thousand ants eating his armpits.

But God . . . I still loved him . . . can you understand that? *I loved him.*

As whispers quickly rampaged into excited news, the cafés and hovels emptied and a huge gathering took place before our home. I went out to the veranda, unafraid, and glowered at them. There were hundreds and more were coming. Yet no words were shouted against me. There was no contesting what had happened. Of course it all followed, didn't it? If there was one thing these people knew it was that I, Ishmael, had done in the Haj in our time-honored tradition and that I, Ishmael, was now the power to be reckoned with.

"Haj Ibrahim has left us," I announced almost blandly. "He died of the heart."

The most glorious moment in the story of Haj Ibrahim came after his death. The outpouring of humanity and their display of grief at his funeral was of a nature usually reserved for high holy men or great heads of state. They came from every camp in the West Bank and Jordan, hundreds of thousands of them. In the end the Arabs venerated, adored, worshiped him, but they never really knew why. All they knew at this moment was that Haj Ibrahim was gone and they were naked without him.

A tomb and a small mosque were already being built in the foothills of Mount Temptation overlooking Aqbat Jabar. It was here that he was set down and vengeance was sworn against the Jews, although I don't understand why. I kept my composure, my aloof silence, throughout the ordeal. Although many foul things were whispered behind my back, no one dared speak out in accusation to my face. They understood who their new leader was when they confronted him. They knew of my power. They groveled before me, expressing their grief. They kissed my cheeks and the slovenly among them kissed my hand.

Future generations would come to consider his tomb as a holy place and with the passage of time the Haj would become a saint.

When the funeral was done and they departed, going back to their hellholes, a horrible nausea overcame me. I had to be away. I went to the one place and to the one man who gave me warmth and comfort. I could see that Nuri Mudhil was frightened for me. I mumbled over and over that I still loved Ibrahim. He seemed to know that I was due to break. You see, I had not spoken of Nada since her murder. I had forced myself not to think of her. And then I mentioned her name and collapsed in his arms.

"Tell me where she is, Dr. Mudhil. I must take her to where she can be in peace."

"No," he said, "you cannot."

"But I must."

"You cannot," he repeated firmly.

"What are you trying to tell me?"

"Not now, Ishmael, later . . ."

"Tell me. I demand that you tell me!"

"There is nothing left of her. She is strewn about in a hundred places in that awful disposal pit near the river. Please, ask nothing further. . . ."

I screamed, "I will avenge!"

He sighed painfully. "Yes," he whispered, "of course you will avenge . . . of course you will avenge . . ."

I stormed about the room, longing to burst. I stood before him and shook. . . . "Why can I not weep. . . . I want to weep. . . . Why can I not weep!" I fell to my knees and clutched at him. "What have we done!" I shrieked. "Why! Why! Why! Why!"

He held my head in his lap and stroked me and I sobbed until nothing was left. A wild burst of dying sunlight flooded the room and we remained in darkness.

"Why?" I whispered, "why?"

"You were three beautiful people who loved each other fiercely. But you were born into a culture which has no place for such love to express itself. We are accursed among all living creatures."

"What is to become of us all?" I said, as much a groan as a question.

He was silent for ever so long. I watched the outline of his shadow swaying, moaning.

"You must tell me, Dr. Mudhil."

"I shall tell you," he said softly, in agony. "We do not have leave to love one another and we have long ago lost the ability. It was so written twelve hundred years earlier. Hate is our over-powering legacy and we have regenerated ourselves by hatred from decade to decade, generation to generation, century to cen-tury. The return of the Jews has unleashed that hatred, exploding wildly, aimlessly, into a massive force of self-destruction. In ten, twenty, thirty years the world of Islam will begin to consume itself in madness. We cannot live with ourselves . . . we never have. We cannot live with or accommodate the outside world . . . we never have. We are incapable of change. The devil who makes us crazy is now devouring us. We cannot stop ourselves. And if we are not stopped we will march, with the rest of the world, to the Day of the Burning. What we are now witnessing, Ishmael, now, is the beginning of Armageddon."

. . . I do not know the exact moment the blackness overcame me . . .

I was packing my suitcase to leave when suddenly my hands could not hold things . . . my mind became a haze . . .

. . . I fought hard to regain clarity, but it only came through in snatches . . .

Each day the blackness won out more and more until I ex-hausted my powers to prevent it . . .

. . . and so, I succumbed . . .

Everyone says I am insane because I have stopped speak-ing . . .

. . . many times when Dr. Mudhil came and pleaded with me . . . I wanted to speak back to him, but I was unable . . . his words were so hard for me to comprehend anymore . . .

. . . One night I went berserk about Nada and smashed up the photographs of Jamil and Omar and Ibrahim . . .

. . . after that I was chained to the wall on my cot . . .

. . . every time I thought of Nada, the terrible pain swept over me and I seemed to lose control . . . again and again . . .

. . . All day long children peek into my door and point at me and taunt me . . . I do not care . . .

. . . So I am chained . . . every day Hagar stands over me and spits on me and kicks me. I hear Kamal and Mother plot to sell me to a suicide squad in the fedayeen . . . they pay three hundred American dollars now and they need the money . . . I am not mad . . .

. . . But they are desperate . . . Kamal has no work . . . Omar's salary cannot keep them alive . . .

. . . oh yes, I hear them plot . . . what they do not know is that I have found happiness, for now I can speak to Nada . . . I see her every night . . . she comes to me . . . she keeps telling me to run away . . .

. . . stupid Kamal has never done anything right . . . he does not know I have worked the bolts in the wall loose and that I can rip them out whenever I choose . . .

. . . yes, Nada, I will escape . . .

I will follow you . . .

. . . the wadi leads back into the caves . . .

. . . the sun is so bright . . .

. . . I should have brought water and worn shoes . . . but I had to follow Nada immediately, for fear she would disappear again . . .

. . . I have come very far into the canyons . . . my feet are starting to bleed and burn . . . I will rest . . . damn these chains on my wrists . . .

. . . Wait, there is Nada climbing up in the rocks . . .

. . . "Nada! . . . wait . . . I will climb to you, my beloved sister . . . oh, Nada, stop teasing me . . ."

. . . climb . . . climb . . . get up there to her . . . do not slip . . . do not fear . . . "Nada, take my hand and help me, my chains are so heavy . . ." Hot . . . in the Prophet's name it is so hot . . . oh, Ishmael, you were foolish to come back here without water . . . But I had to run or they would have taken me away to the fedayeen . . .

. . . oh God, I think I followed the wrong canyon in . . .

I am lost . . .

. . . There is Nada again . . . she climbs like an ibex . . . so graceful . . . so lovely . . . suddenly she sits on the edge of the ledge, taunting me and laughing . . .

. . . "Nada, I am coming to you . . . and from your ledge we can fly to the seven paradises . . ."

. . . look how high I have climbed . . . from here I can see the vastness of the desert . . . the Dead Sea . . . all the way across the river to Mount Nebo . . .

. . . In Allah's name, do I hear locusts? No, there is a thickness moving toward me, but they are not locusts . . . they are . . .

People . . . yes, I see clearly, the desert is filling up with millions and millions of people! *They see me!* They are calling me.

"Ishmael, save us!"

"Go back, all of you, go back! Do not come any further into this wilderness! Go back! I command you!"

. . . Why don't they listen! They keep coming, millions and millions . . .

"Ishmael, save us!"

"Fools! Fools! Turn back. Turn back or the Day of the Burning will be upon us. In Allah's name, turn back! This is Armageddon!"

. . . Oh my God, they do not listen . . . they just keep coming . . .

. . . I will speak to them again . . . but the climb has made me tired and the chains have worn me out . . .

. . . First I must rest . . . I must lie down for just a little while . . . my face feels too hot pressing on the rock . . . I'd better stand . . . I cannot get to my feet . . . No, I think I will sleep for a while . . . the sun is hot . . .

. . . I am so tired . . . so very tired . . .

THE END

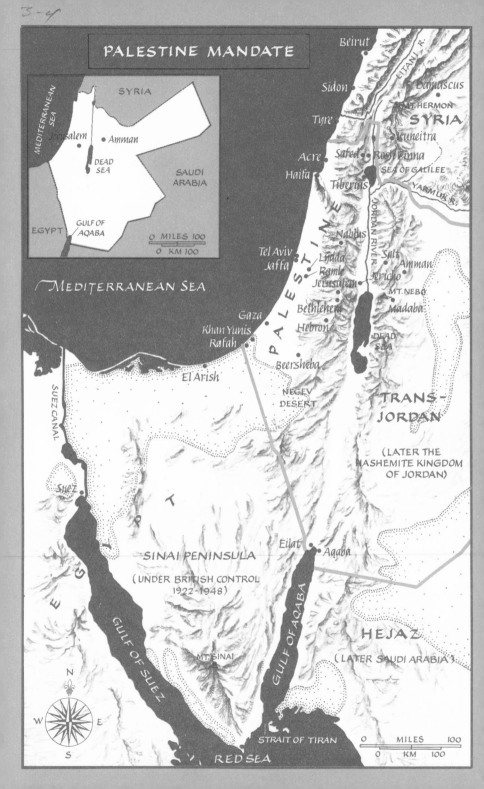